ASBURY PARK

ASBURY PARK

Rob Scott

The right of Rob Scott to be identified as the author of
this work has been asserted by him in accordance with the
Copyright, Designs and Patents Act 1988.

First published in Great Britain in 2012 by
Gollancz
An imprint of the Orion Publishing Group
Orion House, 5 Upper St Martin's Lane, London WC2H 9EA
An Hachette UK Company

This edition published in Great Britain in 2012 by Gollancz

1 3 5 7 9 10 8 6 4 2

A CIP catalogue record for this book
is available from the British Library

ISBN 978 0 575 09391 1

Typeset by Deltatype Ltd, Birkenhead, Merseyside

Printed in Great Britain by Clays Ltd, St Ives plc

The Orion Publishing Group's policy is to use papers that are natural,
renewable and recyclable products and made from wood grown in sustainable
forests. The logging and manufacturing processes are expected to conform
to the environmental regulations of the country of origin.

www.sailordoyle.com
www.orionbooks.co.uk

For Kage

The screen door slams ...

The kerosene . . . you never quite wash it all off.

GUY MONTAG

How I wish, how I wish you were here.
We're just two lost souls swimming in a fish bowl,
Year after year.
Running over the same old ground,
What have we found?
The same old fears.
Wish you were here.

PINK FLOYD

East Side, West Side, all around the town
The tots sang 'ring-around-rosie', 'London Bridge is falling down'
Boys and girls together, me and Mamie O'Rourke
Tripped the light fantastic on the sidewalks of New York.

JAMES W. BLAKE

INTRODUCTION

Masked Monsters

There's a barber shop on the corner of Steiner Avenue and Cameron Drive, near a back gate where middle-school kids jaywalk in the few minutes before the morning bell. A rail-thin teacher, spooky-thin, with wiry arms and a polyester blouse, stands distracted at the gate, separating the street riff-raff from the adolescents. I peg her for a maths teacher, sixth grade. She's got *least common denominator* written all over her.

The barber shop has one of those candy cane poles outside, spinning for ever, bloody bandages hung out to dry. I know it's just an optical illusion, but it's a good one. The kid in the hooded sweatshirt passes beneath it before crossing Cameron. His clothes are threadbare, but he carries a hundred-dollar hockey bag. Who's playing hockey in Neptune, New Jersey, in September?

I wonder where they've built a rink.

He smokes a cigarette, the dumbass. He's maybe thirteen and I want to stop him, grab him by the throat and squeeze until he promises never to buy another pack. Then I'll steal his smokes. Why not?

It's humid, in a recipe that only New Jersey and maybe Mexico City can cook up: thick, sliceable air, infused with an amalgam of grimy pollutants, each taking its daily bite out of the ozone layer. It sticks to my skin, makes me want to shower, but I don't care: I'm a couple of of miles from home and working up a good sweat. The air clings like warm paste and finds its way into every wrinkle, every cranny in the cracked sidewalk. There's no place to hide from it.

The ocean is behind me, too far away to hear. I worry that it might not be there when I get home.

My desire for Dan's Doughnuts has brought me here this morning, away from the ocean and the predictable security of my morning walk along the beach. Neptune is another planet, literally and figuratively. I regret not bringing a gun. Gotta have those doughnuts, though. What the hell; I'm a trooper. Troopers are supposed to eat doughnuts. Especially Dan's, without question the greatest doughnuts in Neptune; in fact I'm confident they'd be the greatest doughnuts *on* Neptune. They're well worth the walk along Cameron and across Steiner. Ben wants a Boston cream. Anna wants sour cream glazed – not that she said as much, but I can read her mind. *Sour cream glazed* ... sounds nasty, but they're magic.

Jenny wasn't talking to me this morning. I'll get her a cruller.

Crullers are outstanding peace offerings, any cop will tell you that.

The smoking hockey player is wearing a hooded sweatshirt. Why? Is it going to rain later? Feels like it. Maybe the rink's cold – that's probably why. Or he checked the weather; he's some gifted freak watching Channel 12 over his Rice Krispies.

Greasepaint tattoos would wipe off: greasepaint, like the old theatre actors used to wear, some fatass opera star got up in black-face to play *Othello*. That's the kind of tattoo to have, one you can change later if you decide you'd made a mistake, or maybe the dove or the heart or the Asian character didn't quite capture the desultory nature of your mood. That's the kind of tattoo I'd have: greasepaint – but not on my face. I don't have biceps to speak of, so my biceps would be out of the question. Maybe on my shoulder or my leg.

Gang tattoos, prison tattoos: those don't wipe off. The shit thugs will carve into their skin makes me want to puke. And prison tattoos never look like they do in the movies; Christ, Hollywood couldn't have it more wrong. Up close, prison tattoos are a nightmare, poorly drawn, sloppily inked, blurry – and painful as hell. And some of those lunatics get them on their face, because nothing quite says *I'm rehabilitated and ready for a desk job in polite society* than permanent teardrops and a six-inch KA-BAR knife inked across your forehead by Vincent van Six-to-Ten from Cell Block B.

Tattoos on your face are like a mask – no, not like: they *are* a mask.

And who wears masks? Fat-ass opera stars playing *Othello* and kids out trick-or-treating for Mars Bars. The two assholes I deal with this morning wear masks, one greasepaint, one tattoo. I'm wearing a sling and Jenny's old Rutgers University sweatshirt, but no tattoos, not even a shamrock or a Claddagh.

The teacher, the thin one in polyester, she has a tattoo on her ankle. I don't get a good look at it from where I end up sprawled on the basketball court but it looks like a unicorn, or maybe a puppy. The gang thug has shit scribbled on his face that could eat her tattoo on a cracker. It almost makes me laugh, but my shoulder hurts too much.

Cameron Drive has cars parked on both sides, and what remains of the road is almost too narrow for drivers to pass each other. Massive elms, planted forty feet apart, easily embrace above my head, over the faded yellow line. Smoking hoodie boy crosses in front of me, head down, hiding his cigarette, probably from the skeletal-thin maths teacher on gate duty.

An older guy with a tubby belly, bandy arms and flyaway hair leans down to talk to someone in the passenger seat of a beat-to-hell Ford parked at the corner, beneath the streetlights that look too much like hanged men in a Clint Eastwood movie as they dangle twenty feet above the intersection. Tubby forgot to put a shirt on this morning; he shows off his beer-belly for a gaggle of giggling schoolgirls hustling inside the gate and across the cracked basketball court behind the school. Tubby's wearing an old pair of knee-length shorts with a Hawaiian pattern, like exploding pineapples. His feet are bare. He pockets something and hurries north on Steiner Avenue.

The Ford idles. Drug dealers.

Lovely.

They're not fifty feet from an oblivious teacher ushering her charges in for another day of borrowing from the hundreds. I wonder what gangs have this street, elm-lined Cameron Drive in Neptune, and silently promise myself I'll walk on the boardwalk again tomorrow, out where there's a breeze.

Hoodie hockey player leans against one of the elms that's even more oblivious than polyester maths teacher. He's hiding his face, though he's not got a cigarette now, but still he won't look up.

Something glints above the intersection: the hanged-man street-light, flashing yellow. A Monmouth County school bus roars north, beating the red, making a break for freedom.

Polyester pulls the gate shut, but she doesn't lock it. She shouts, 'First period; don't be late!' to a group of older kids shooting baskets, wearing hand-me-down clothes, cheap jeans and torn canvas sneakers. They're bigger, probably eighth graders. They groan and beg and mutter what I figure are pretty disparaging things under their breath. After a barrage of failed three-pointers, they head inside, chins high, clearly on their own terms.

The teacher checks the pockets in her skirt. She's looking for something. I'm betting it's the key to the gate. She ought to check the pockets in the hockey player's hooded sweatshirt – but that's just me.

Hoodie smoker kid turns away, facing north across Cameron. I figure he's ditching class in a whole body legerdemain. The elm, not giving a shit either way, grants him a hiding place behind its back.

The hanged man flashes green; everything clicks into place.

No doughnuts today.

I run as fast as I can with my gimpy shot-to-shit leg and my cane. I swing it like a bat, low, and it breaks. 'Lock down the building! Lock down the motherfucking building!' I scream.

Polyester stares. She cries out and runs inside.

Then I'm grabbing, pulling, wrestling, shoving, tearing, and eventually falling – hard – on my shoulder. *God, curse that shoulder!* One-armed, I roll to my right, throw as much weight on my outstretched legs as I can, and scream.

For one thudding heartbeat I am face to face with death, but it's painted on, like cadaverous make-up on a hanged man in a Clint Eastwood movie. I hope I've broken his leg and wonder if leg is stronger than cane. Walking cane – candy cane, like a barber pole, just bloody bandages hung out to dry—

Greasepaint tattoos wipe off, some wipes off on my shoulder, a miniature tattoo I might save for Hallowe'en.

Hoodie smoker kid has two arms to my one. One reaches for a cord, a fuse, a string, some goddamned thing he's got wrapped around his waist, beneath the sweatshirt. I don't know what it is, but I know he can't be allowed to reach it. I grab both his wrists in my hand, then one and we roll, me grabbing for his other wrist. We're two idiots shaking hands in Hell.

Then green, blue and red tattoos – ugly face tattoos. And gunshots: two pops that hang in the thick morning, then waft out near half-court, redolent of cordite, and dissipate for ever. I scream again, this time just *No!*

My chest hurts, and my shoulder. I am curled up somewhere between the free throw line and the top of the key on a basketball court old enough to have happy yellow dandelions growing in tenacious clumps between its cracks, cracks where polluted humidity goes to rest at the end of the day.

The barber pole climbs to Heaven.

The hanged men flash red.

The beat-to-hell Ford screams north on Steiner Avenue.

I hang on, fighting a one-sided battle I can win with one arm.

And the world slows long enough for monsters to alight along the Jersey coast, monsters in masks ...

SATURDAY

Down the Shore

Bradley Beach to Asbury Park and back: 2.7 Miles

Lust and regret.

At 9:30 on a Saturday morning in September I hadn't smoked a cigarette since 10:00 the previous night. Compensating with as much caffeine as my body could absorb seemed like the only way I would be able to make it through the day without either getting a divorce or committing murder. Two hours earlier, my head had cracked open and spilled my brains onto the linoleum floor in my mother's kitchen. I refused to look in the mirror for fear of seeing inside my own skull, like one of Jason Voorhees' teenage victims. If I could make it to 10:00 a.m. without firing up I'd smoke one an hour until 8:00 p.m. Then I'd eat a huge bowl of fudge-a-licious chocolate-chunk ice cream, chase it with three or four Nytol and with any luck pass out before the nicotine cravings came looking for me again.

I'd been off prescription pain medication since Labor Day – doctor's orders – but I hit the Advil and Aleve as if they'd been invented last month. Advil were my favourites – the cinnamon coating made them taste more like candy than the others – but they didn't actually work. Nytol remained the big boy on the over-the-counter block. Since I wasn't allowed alcohol to wash them down I'd sneak an extra couple in the interests of sleeping through the night, or most of the night, at least. Jenny hadn't started keeping track of how many were left in the bottle. Not yet.

But she would.

I could see it in her face as she climbed into bed beside me. *No, I don't trust you, Sailor, you prick* was just about scribbled across her furrowed forehead. The fact that I was off the OxyContin – for now – off the booze – for now – and trying to cut back on the smokes – for motherfucking now – made Jenny about as happy as one enraged wife could be. There was no question she would hold my hand as tightly as I needed through the puking, the shakes and the unbearable cravings that had me chewing pencil erasers and gnawing on aluminium foil. But she was also first in line to barbecue me for Sarah Danvers and the six months of naked Olympics I'd enjoyed in her apartment on West Grace Street in Richmond. I didn't know how long it was going to take for Jenny to get past that one. Maybe never.

They'd taken the cast off my leg about a week earlier, revealing pallid, shrivelled skin. For the few seconds before I touched it, actually felt the creased, itchy flesh, I wasn't entirely certain it was mine. It looked more like a mannequin's leg that someone had sneaked into my cast while I was flying over Stafford County on Demerol. But it was mine, and the unpleasant smell confirmed that it was badly in need of a scrubbing.

I also had my first gunshot scars – not that I was bent on starting a collection. The one on my shoulder had healed nicely into a pink pucker the size of a half-dollar, but it hurt when I raised my arm above my head, and the physiotherapy left me in tears most days. The Amazonian assigned to bend, stretch and Pilates me into shape suggested I learn to see sweat as pain leaving my body. I don't know where people like her learn such inane platitudes but I duly tried it. Most days it failed to ease my suffering one little bit. Instead, I thought of Marie, my sister the cross-country runner, who had learned to master pain before she'd finished middle school. I'd wince, and recall her lithe form gliding by in a blur of Freehold Catholic green and gold while I stood on the sidelines simultaneously cheering and craving a cigarette. That sometimes helped.

The shot through my thigh looked like a hickey from a boa constrictor. When I looked at it I'd have to fight down whatever I'd eaten, and then concentrate on the flesh around the stitches – I'd have given a year off my life for five minutes of unbridled scratch time. Jenny and I had read about dissolving surgical stitches – the shit they can do these days is amazing – but what the articles all left out is that the thread – *rope* – tends to irritate as it dissolves, especially when it's also encased in fibreglass for two months.

But a couple of weeks later I was pretty well mobile – shaky and stumbly, but mobile. I could get around with the help of a cane, but when I played with Ben and Anna I put it to one side; something about being on Dad Duty made me want to manage without a crutch. That was a feeling I hadn't experienced before, one of several I'd been grappling with in the weeks since Doc Lefkowitz had discharged me from MCV Hospital.

I'd had only a few sessions with Amanda the Amazon before Jenny and I decided to head home to New Jersey for a month – but those appointments were plenty for me to learn a veritable cordon bleu menu of painful exercises, most of which could be exacerbated by the inclusion of a coloured resistance band: yellow for *Okay, I can almost do this*, green for *Hey, that hurts*, blue for *Jesus Christ, are you trying to kill me?* and red for *Just harpoon me and finish me off, why don't you!*

Before I left for Jersey, Amanda the Amazon very kindly printed off a six-page exercise regimen, bagged up my own personal set of coloured bands, and encouraged me to 'swim as much as you can, Detective Doyle, and remember to walk every day'.

Swim. That's what she'd said: *swim*, in the waters off Belmar, New Jersey, swim with my gimpy shoulder and my pallid mannequin leg. *That's great, Amanda, you crazy bitch: in that surf, I'll be dead in twenty minutes, but at least then I won't have to endure any more of your medieval torture.*

I didn't say that, though. Instead, I lay on the purple floor mat and gasped, 'Swim, okay. And walk. Got it.'

'Stick with the Aleve.'

'Okay.'

'And do your resistance exercises every other day – all the way through – until you come back.'

'I will,' I panted. She could have suggested that I sack Troy on a stolen moped and I would have agreed; right then, swimming in the washing-machine waters off Belmar was the least of my worries.

Getting up off the floor, *that* was the first order of business on my agenda. After all the pulling and pushing and twisting and bending my leg – the agony cleverly enhanced by her Amazonian death bands – I wasn't certain I'd be able to drive myself home, let alone go walking in sand or swimming through heavy surf.

Then we were off, away from Virginia and the confused memories of the past year. Thoughts of my father, my sister, of Sarah Danvers and Huck, of OxyContin, coral snakes and copperheads, all flurried through my mind like wind-blown leaves. I needed a break, a clean separation from the things that made me Sailor Doyle. I didn't know if I wanted to be a state trooper, a homicide investigator, a doctor, a lawyer, even an opera singer in greasepaint tattoos. I needed time away, time to cut the threads that bound me to who I had become; I couldn't achieve that on the all-too-familiar streets of Fredericksburg.

One of the nice things about Nytol, especially my sleight-of-hand double doses, was that I didn't dream, not the full-on Technicolor nightmares I used to have, of bridges, icy rivers, and shitty Saturn sedans tumbling ass-over-handlebars into the water. Clubbing my brain senseless with over-the-counter medication while my wife changed Anna's last diaper of the day resulted in nights of misty black-and-grey images of things abominable: plague victims tattooed with purplish buboes, dismembered housecats, their fur in tatters, and knuckled knobs of hastily sewn flesh on the scarred end of Carl Bruckner's severed knee. But none of it made sense; none of these dreams had a plot. There were no paths leading from my nightmares to the cathartic bars of Shockoe Bottom.

So I held fast: no pills and no booze. I'd smoke ten cigarettes a day, I'd take my handful of drugstore happiness, and I'd wait for the hazy images to leave on their own. I'd give it a month. I'd swim. Walk. And wait.

I had one month to erase the board.

I'd been suspended pending the outcome of a hush-hush investigation into my drug abuse: the Virginia State Police needed to know if I was high on OxyCodone when I shot Burgess Aiken. It didn't appear to matter that he had injected me without my consent, stolen my gun and attacked me with dozens of dangerous snakes. No, the question VASP desperately needed to know was whether or not I had taken illegal prescription drugs when I defended myself by shooting him in the shoulder. Jesus Christ. No one seemed to care that I had stolen drugs from crime scenes – from sealed evidence bags, no less – or that I'd beaten a few handfuls of Percocet out of teenage street thugs. Nope; the Brass suspended me while they determined if I had been shitfaced when I shot a lunatic Bible thumper with a snake fetish.

Jenny's boss gave her a month off. Hell, I was a national hero, after all: President Baird had said so on CNN, and that had to count for something. Jenny's co-workers encouraged her to take all the time she needed to help get me back in the saddle. Between us, we figured a month away from home, a month at the beach, would either reconnect us for ever, or show us that we were doomed.

I couldn't recall ever wanting to work so hard at anything in my life, and that I counted as one stumbly step in the right direction. I wasn't embarrassed by the suspension – VASP had kept it quiet because the national news media was busy heralding me as the Saviour of the mid-Atlantic states and the last thing Captain Fezzamo needed was for the world to find out that I had been three sheets to the wind on hillbilly heroin when I found Molly Bruckner. The captain pulled a cover over the whole works. My best friend Huck Greeley hung around Division Headquarters with his ear to the ground, and I trundled off to the Jersey coast with my family and a month's worth of diapers and plastic beach toys jammed in the back of Jenny's minivan.

After two days at my mother's place, we started for Belmar and the old beach house. I survived two miles of Route 9 traffic before I needed a third cup of coffee and a cigarette.

The 7-Eleven at the corner of Manalapan Road and Route 9 has one of those automatic push-button café machines that vomits out foamy mochaccino/cappuccino/vodkaccino drinks on demand. Huck had tried a few of them as we hit the 7-Elevens and Quick Marts around Richmond. He's actually not much of a frothy-milk guy; he drank the muddy-water concoctions more for the novelty than anything else. To me they all tasted like ersatz Kahlua-and-Krispy-Kreme. I guess they were about perfect for the suburbs, where, thanks to the Starbucks baristas working every other street corner, we had essentially forgotten the taste of real coffee.

The woman speaking too loudly into her Bluetooth while she queued up a twenty-four-ounce coffee frappé this morning smelled good, like wildflowers that don't grow in New Jersey. I caught a whiff of her when she rudely elbowed past me to grab the biggest of the Styrofoam cups 7-Eleven had stacked on the counter. She had cut me off on Manalapan Road, too, pulling her behemoth Yukon in a hard right across my lane and nearly tearing the front bumper off the minivan. She had been towing a trailer loaded with four matching Jet Skis – Kawasakis, nice ones – and a colourful selection of custom surfboards. No one else had been in the SUV, though, which looked as though it could comfortably accommodate the Brady Bunch, with a couple of extra seats for Lori and Keith Partridge.

I selected a twenty-ounce cup of my own and poured it full of generic high-test as I watched her multitask in front of the colourful plastic display. She wore an expensive-looking sheer wrap over a skirty bathing suit, one of those mini-loincloth deals designed to camouflage Mom Hips in a forty-three-year-old desperately clinging to the hazy recollection of her twenty-seven-year-old body. Above the waterline, she had hoisted her ample – if fraudulent – boobs in a string bikini that screamed: *These babies were expensive, so go ahead and look.*

It was excessive for 7-Eleven on a Saturday morning, but like every other guy in the place, I couldn't help but stare. Her make-up had been tastefully done, no blue eye shadow or flashy pink rouge. Big pearl studs in her ears complemented the string around her neck, and I was genuinely surprised that she could lift her hand for the size of the stone in her wedding ring. Hubby must be a New York lawyer or some corporate raider screwing the Third World for a handsome holiday bonus. Boobs' hair was dirty-blonde, highlighted with sunny happiness and looking as though it had taken an hour to primp for a day in the sand. Even her flip-flops – sandals, I suppose – were crisscrossed with tiny rows of glittery yellow stones, plastic tourmalines or something.

Fortune 500 beachwear. Obviously.

Apart from smelling nice and retaining a talented cosmetic surgeon, however, I couldn't find much else about Boobs Manalapan to admire. It was impossible not to eavesdrop on her conversation, since she was near as dammit shouting into her Bluetooth, just another self-important, gated-community pussy wanting the world to know she had expensive plans for the weekend.

She prattled on in a faux, finishing-school accent, '—have the Jet Skis and the surfboards on the trailer outside … uh huh … hmm? … Oh, that's funny … did he—? … Right, we'll meet the guys there … Jim has the kids in the Beemer; they like riding with the top down—'

The Froth Master gurgled and spat her mocha, dribbling the last drops off its plastic chin with a mechanical cough. '—I don't care what it costs, we've just got to have one … have you seen it? Me too … Oh, I don't even want to talk about that idiot maths teacher he's got this year … I'll call the principal and have him moved to a new class next week … I mean, the man's a bleeding idiot; I swear. Jim says they're spending too much time in cooperative groups … right, not really teaching them anything. Who hires these fools?'

Christ, I can't imagine being her kid's algebra teacher.

She sidled towards the registers, cutting me off a third time. I didn't care, because I was too busy gazing longingly at the ranks of cigarette boxes lined up inside their emergency-access, quick-draw dispensers behind the counter.

I checked the pack in my shirt: nine left. Apparently I'd smoked eleven yesterday, one over my limit.

Shit, that'll only get me to 7:00 tonight.

I wasn't supposed to buy a new pack until tomorrow … I tried to comfort myself with the notion that tomorrow actually started at midnight. I might sneak one past the goalie – Jenny – on a technicality and run out for a pack at 12:01.

Boobs Manalapan made her impatient way to the cash register where a Sikh with sandpaper complexion sporting a neatly wrapped turban scanned items, punched keys and counted change with the alacrity of an Atlantic City pit boss.

Boobs said, too loudly, '—just have to come with us to Saint Bart's next month ... pull the kids out of school ... I just love the chef at the Imperial; the man's a genius ... Wait, hold on, Harriet. I'm almost at the register ... 7-Eleven – no, just for coffee and gum, I have to deal with, you know ... right, always working. I guess it gets them into Valhalla or Nirvana or wherever they go for their twenty-nine virgins.'

Turban behind the counter heard that bit. He didn't look pleased.

Boobs Manalapan didn't care; she placed her twenty-four-ounce coffee beside the register, grabbed two packs of minty gum, a yellow bag of peanut M&Ms and a *Glamour* magazine from the rack, then she mined around in her handbag for cash.

'You shouldn't say such things,' Turban whispered, just loudly enough for her to hear.

'Right, sorry, whatever.' Boobs waved a nonchalant, exquisitely manicured hand. 'I don't know anything about – whatever, Islam or the Taliban—'

Sweat beaded on my forehead: I wanted a pack of cigarettes badly enough to kill a close relative. I sipped my coffee, tucked two Louis L'Amour novels under my arm – New Jersey 7-Elevens carry the greatest selection of Louis L'Amour outside the Library of Congress – and reached for a pack of Swedish Fish for Ben. He could eat his own weight in Swedish Fish.

'I am a Sikh,' Turban said, 'not Islam.' He had one of those Indian-Oxford British accents that always reminded me of that skinny guy who played Ghandi, whatshisname.

'Right.' Boobs sighed rudely. 'Right, whatever, Al-Qaeda, what*ever.*'

'Al-Qaeda? *Al-Qaeda!*' Turban was pissed off now. He puffed up, clearly ready for a fight.

Ah, shit. Here we go. I wished I had my gun and could shoot both of them, or myself. A cracking good headache came thundering in, and my leg started to throb like a satanic metronome. I should have brought my cane. It wasn't the walking as much as the standing in line behind Boobs that was getting to me. I started shifting my weight back and forth. I needed exercise, but I dreaded the thought of uncoiling Amanda the Amazon's coloured bands. I closed my eyes and waited for it to end.

But of course it didn't. Instead, Boobs Manalapan turned indignantly, as if to rally me into some kind of suburbanite alliance, and her handbag, another costly accoutrement, toppled her big-ass mocha, spilling it over a stack of *New York Times*, a rack of Hershey bars and a cardboard container filled with cigarette lighters just waiting for some desperate smoker to grab one in a hurried run-by.

'Ah, shit, lady,' I murmured, 'not today—'

'Al-Qaeda!' Turban shouted. 'How *dare* you, you ignorant woman! Stupid, *ignorant* woman!'

'Listen, Osama, or whatever, I'm going to need to see the manager. Your boss.' Boobs glanced at the mess, but she made no move to clean it up. She was smart enough to know she had fucked up, but bitch enough not to give a shit.

'I *am* the manager!' Turban poked himself in the chest with a hairy finger. 'I am—'

'You couldn't possibly—'

'And why not?' Turban's beard glistened here and there with flecks of spittle. If he'd had a flamethrower, he'd have fried her, then and there. 'Why can I not *possibly be the manager*? This is my store – my store! And you: you are going to pay for this ... all of this you've ruined.' He gestured at the wreckage across the counter.

Cigarettes – cigarettes. Just give me some motherhumping cigarettes.

'Then bring me the owner,' Boobs interrupted him. 'Who's the owner? I need to talk with him. Get him here, or get him on the phone – I can wait. You have been rude and insulting, and that's not how—'

'Shut up!' Turban screamed. 'Shut up your mouth right now! *I* am the owner. *I* am the manager. This is my store, and you're—'

Behind me in line, a grease monkey mechanic, a high school kid and a guy dressed to coach Little League all gave up simultaneously. With a shared groan, they either politely returned their items to the racks or simply abandoned packs of gum, newspapers, Pepsi bottles and cups of coffee on the back counter. As one, they walked out; the grease monkey mechanic mumbled something off-colour.

I pulled a twenty from my wallet and placed it on the counter, outside the steaming puddle of mud-brown mocha. 'Keep the change,' I said, and limped for the door.

14

Neither Turban nor Boobs Manalapan appeared to notice me. Boobs pressed speed dial numbers on her Droid while Turban shouted towards a back office, looking for reinforcements, or someone to call the police.

I took a last look at the wall of cigarettes and pushed through the glass door into the parking lot. I'd left Jenny's minivan in a space behind the gas pumps on Manalapan Drive and had to shuffle past Boobs' Yukon to get there. She had filled it with eight-hundred gallons of Premium before coming inside to push me out of the way of the coffee machine. I hesitated for a moment, admiring the brightly polished Jet Skis and the Technicolour surfboards.

It's just not goddamned fair.

I set my coffee and my Louis L'Amour novels on the concrete island, lifted the Premium gas pump and hooked the metal handle over the raised locking device on the Yukon's trailer hitch. As furious as Boobs was, there wasn't much chance she'd notice it when she either left in an indignant huff, or fled the scene in her tourmaline flip-flops.

This is not good, Sailor, not good. What would Dr Krandall say?

'She'd say, *screw this arrogant bitch*,' I murmured and looped the gas hose around the back bumper, making certain the carnage would be memorable. Mr Jim Corporate Executive Hubby would have to break out his platinum card to pay for this one.

In the minivan, Jenny said, 'What took so long?'

'Nothing.' I handed her the paperbacks. 'I hate coming here.'

She frowned at my choice of reading material. 'Louis L'Amour? Really, Sailor? Never going to grow up?'

'Not today,' I said, 'and besides, those are great stories. Where else can you read about guys named Buck and Harley who roll their own cigarettes one-handed while riding hard through the chaparral?'

'Whatever,' she mumbled. I don't know how long we'd been married before I'd been able to infer *I'm pissed off with you, shithead* in that one word.

'Hey, let's not fight today. Huh? C'mon, we're going to the beach, and my leg really hurts.'

'You should have taken your cane.'

'I don't want to fight.'

'I don't want to fight, either,' Jenny said out of her window. I heard her, though; she knew it.

Jenny wore a pair of army surplus cargo shorts with the threadbare Rutgers University sweatshirt she'd been wearing the first weekend we spent together in New Brunswick ten years earlier. We'd screwed each other's brains out that weekend; half the time at least one of us had been in that sweatshirt. Today, it didn't matter that the temperature might top eighty-five humid degrees along the Jersey coast: Jenny'd known for two weeks that she was going to wear that thing over whatever new bathing suit she'd bought to celebrate the last of Anna's baby weight falling off her hips. She'd peel that old sweatshirt off right in front of me, too, and I'd be reminded for the ten thousandth time in the past two months how monumentally I'd buggered things up.

Jenny Doyle: subtle, but brutal.

My wife's beach attire was less flashy than Boobs Manalapan, but infinitely more sexy, at least to my horny-and-deprived husband's taste. She hadn't been willing to have sex with me since I'd been released from MCV Hospital near the end of July and I was about ready to blow a gasket. I'd had to go back to periodic visits with the women of Victoria's Secret.

Thank Christ they send that catalogue every two weeks.

I didn't push Jenny on the issue, or try too hard to get her to give in: she was furious with me. We'd been fighting about every day since she stopped worrying that I might die of plague.

Worry first; get angry later.

I knew she still loved me, and I also knew I was going to be on a short leash for a good long while.

I turned down Route 9 towards the beach, wanting to be well away from the 7-Eleven before Boobs tore the gas pump out by its roots. My mind pinged from one inane topic to another, trying to come up with something to say, anything to get Jenny talking normally. We were going to be spending four weeks together in my parents' beach house – I just couldn't sit around Fredericksburg for a month waiting to hear if I'd lost my job – and I needed to reconnect with my wife.

From the back seat, Ben saved me. 'Daddy?'

'Yes, Muzifar Quazilbash?'

'Daddy, why does Luke Skywalker fly an X-wing fighter and Princess Leia fly a Y-wing fighter?'

'Well, that's chromosome envy.'

'Daddy?'

'Yes, Geronimo O'Toole?'

'Daddy, what's chromes— what you said just then?'

I glanced at Jenny; she wouldn't smile, not yet.

I said, 'I think it means you're a monkey-face.'

He laughed, a noisy splutter. 'Well, you're a turkey-face!'

'A turkey-face? Do I have a turkey's face?'

'Daddy?'

'Yes, Filibuster Fartknocker?'

'Daddy, why does Luke Skywalker fly an X-wing fighter and Princess Leia fly a Y-wing fighter?'

I tried to make eye contact with him in the rear-view mirror, but he was staring out of the window, watching trees pass in a green smear. 'I think they have different planes—'

'Fighters, Daddy.'

'Sorry, *fighters*, because they come from all over the galaxy, and they work together to make the Rebel Alliance.'

'Daddy, what's a Rebel Elias?'

'They're the guys who fight Darth Vader.'

'Daddy?'

Now Jenny did smirk, just a hint, and she tried to hide it with a turn of her head, but I saw it. We would be all right. I'd take a beating for the next month, but we'd make it. That tiny smirk said it all: I could have hope.

'Daddy?'

'Yes, Simon Bar Syphilis?'

'Daddy, why does the Rebel Elias fight Darth Vader?'

'Because he has ADHD.'

'What's that, Daddy? ADHD?'

'ADHD is suburban parents' excuse to give dangerous medications to their children, because they don't want to deal with their kids' bad behaviour.'

'Daddy?' Ben turned to look at me in the mirror.

'Sweetie,' Jenny interrupted, 'Darth Vader doesn't have ADHD.'

'Why not?'

I jumped in. 'Because he's from the inner city, and his parents can't afford medication; so his history grades are really bad.'

Jenny smacked me hard on the shoulder; Ben fell into another fit of sputtery giggles.

'What?' I said.

'Don't teach him those things.' Any hint of her endearing little smirk was gone.

'He's five.' I shrugged stupidly. 'What's he going to do, slip up on MSNBC?'

'He could make some bonehead comment in the grocery store or at preschool and I'll look like an idiot mother raising a foul-mouthed five-year-old.'

'All right, all right.' I let go the wheel to raise my hands. 'Sorry.'

'Mommy,' Ben said, 'are you mad at Daddy?'

'No, sweetie,' and she turned to tickle his dimpled knee with her fingernails. 'It's just that Daddy's ... a turkey-face.'

Ben laughed again. Jenny shot me a look I couldn't read, then started fiddling with the GPS on the dashboard. The six-inch LCD screen mapped our way to a beach house I had visited about seven hundred times; I was pretty confident I knew the way without it. Between Jenny's BlackBerry and the GPS, we could have driven to Argentina and back without getting lost even once. Belmar, New Jersey, was a cinch.

When she settled back in her seat Jenny allowed her left hand to linger a minute or two on the gear-shift near my leg. I didn't want to read too much into anything, but that felt hopeful to me, like the smirk. Mind you, for a guy who'd spent the last ten weeks face down in the muddy flats of Rock Bottom, Virginia, I could find hope almost anywhere. Jenny hiked up the sleeve of her old RU sweatshirt, revealing the Ironman athletic watch she'd bought when she started exercising again. She'd taken off the 'RML' anklet – *Reclaim My Life* – and strapped on the workout watch shortly after she'd learned that I was going to live, ideally live with her.

She bought me one, too. Knowing how I felt about exercise,

running especially, buying me a running watch was a gesture that spoke volumes: *Save your own life, Sailor. You need an addiction? Here you go.*

I was clean and sober for the first time since my seventeenth birthday party and my wife had asked me to keep it up. Route 9 gave way to Route 18; I wondered how long I would go before falling. It was coming for me. I knew it; I suppose Jenny knew it, too.

I was in grade school when my parents and my grandparents on my mother's side went in together on the house in Belmar, one of hundreds of pastel clones lining D Street, between Shark River and Spring Lake. The place was close enough to the beach to be convenient, but far enough out to be affordable. While Belmar had some nice homes – places along the river could run to over a million dollars – ours was all-at-once something special and not-so special, a simple cottage with a wraparound porch, a postage-stamp yard, nice neighbours (because they were seasonal neighbours) and two parking spaces, one in the garage and one in the driveway.

Throughout my school years, even into college, Belmar was my weekend Mecca. Packed to the gills with Catholic girls, beachfront bars – where essentially any ID would get you keg beer – and the best food deep fat could fry, Belmar represented more than any of us ever imagined we could want out of life. We were young, in shape, plenty horny, plenty drunk, and convinced that the future consisted of the next weekend, when fifty or sixty thousand of our closest friends and enemies would hit the sand again. We bragged about fighting more than we fought, talked about sex more than we ever got laid, and walked up and down the boardwalk a hundred million times looking for adventure, buried treasure, dead drug dealers, easy women, just about anything to get us through the next five days in geometry class.

Coming back now with a wife, two kids and a faggoty minivan, the thought of hanging out on the beach made me simultaneously nostalgic and a little sick. The high-schoolers were all still there, the guys lean and shirtless, the girls in cut-off jean shorts and bikini tops, their teenage breasts magically defying gravity in a way that no seventeen-year-old boy can really appreciate until he's pushing thirty-five. Jocks and drunks, tattooed skaters and post-modern punks – New Jersey still had punks, not goths – lingered on the same boardwalk, stretched out on the same sand and ate the same artery-hardening cholesta-burgers my friends and I had devoured a hundred years earlier. From the side or behind, they all looked familiar, ageless and immortal.

Only I'd got older.

We parked a couple of blocks off the beach, loaded Anna's stroller down with two blankets, four towels, three toy dinosaurs, a bright yellow bucket and matching shovel, four swimmy diapers and a tub of diaper wipes. I grabbed a half-gallon of SPF 8,000 suntan lotion for Ben, who wouldn't wear more than shorts until it was almost time to rake leaves.

Jenny carried Anna so I could smoke without destroying her little lungs. She shifted Anna a bit higher on her hip. 'You hungry?'

I inhaled a lungful of sweet North Carolina contentment. 'Not any more.'

'Smoking lunch?'

'I figure I've got to die of something.' I smiled at her and blew twin plumes out my nose. 'I've quit just about every other vice I've got.' My leg twinged as I stepped off the curb. I leaned a bit heavier on my cane, but couldn't hide the grimace.

'You want me to push that?' Jenny reached for the stroller.

'No,' I said, 'I've got it.'

'You take anything this morning?'

'Couple of Aleve with breakfast.' I was thrilled we were talking, banal though the conversation was.

'Well, you can lie down all day if you like. Or maybe swim some – the doctor said you should swim, right?'

I took another drag. 'If I can get beyond the breakers without my leg folding up beneath me, I might just swim – I'll see how chilly it is.' She knew I'd always been a pussy about cold ocean water.

'All right – but we can take the minivan to the beach and back all week if you need to,' she said. 'It's a bit of a hike from your parents' house to the sand.'

'It's four blocks.' I held up my wrist, reminding her that she'd bought me the damned watch. 'I'm going to walk. What the hell, I'll even time myself, out and back. I mean, I've got a hundred-lap timer. Maybe after a month I can get some strength back, lose the cane. Who knows? I might run the Boston Marathon next April.'

'Not smoking *those* things, you won't.'

I tossed the stub into the gutter. 'They're Ultra Lights, practically good for me.' I leaned over to nuzzle Anna's chubby neck, and blew a raspberry onto her shoulder. 'Aren't they, Smurfette?'

Anna gurgled and blew a spit bubble. She wore a baggy terrycloth shirt with the VASP crest and *My daddy is a policeman!* in a colourful scribble.

Was a policeman, I thought, *until about two weeks ago.*

Jenny said, 'I think that's a great idea, Sailor. The sand might not be the best place, though – maybe up on the boardwalk. You can push your daughter in that fancy new jogging stroller your mother bought.'

'Okay,' I said, 'I'll start today.' Anything to keep her in this mood. 'We'll see how far we can get, won't we, Smurfette? You want to walk with Daddy on his shot-up gimpy leg? Huh? C'mon; say yes: it'll be fun!' I kissed her miniature nose. 'I'll take you up to Asbury Park and show you where I found that dead lady a hundred years ago. I remember right where it was.'

'Don't be gross, Sailor,' Jenny chided.

'I'm not sure the baby understands, Jenny.' I kissed Anna again. 'But I promise we'll talk about nicer stuff. Okay, Smurfette?'

Anna gurgled again.

Jenny said, 'See? She's excited about it.'

I checked the digital readout on my watch: 11:08, fifty-two minutes until my next cigarette. I wanted another already.

At the corner of Third and Ocean, the first gusts of ocean breeze hit me in the face and a hundred thousand memories rose to greet me through the humidity. New Jersey needed a thunderstorm to scrub the skies.

*

21

Two hours later I'd smoked three cigarettes and limped the two miles between Bradley Beach and Asbury Park, skirting the lake inlet at Beach Avenue, pushing Anna's stroller while she jabbered away incoherently. We spent most of our time trying to remember the list of presents my true love sent to me during the twelve days of Christmas, and agreeing we didn't really know what we'd do with eight lactating maids or eleven lisping lords, we suggested a few alternatives – eight runway models, seven roasted chickens, six mashed potatoes …

When we finally got back to Jenny and Ben, I was sweating and my leg throbbed with deep tissue pain, but it felt good to have done something rigorous. I was dying for a beer – hell, a case – but contented myself with a couple of slugs from Jenny's Diet Coke. It tasted like laundry water, but I drank it anyway, trying to ignore the hollow tremors now roiling in my gut – that was the OxyContin calling. I hadn't had a craving in a couple of days, and I could already tell this one was going to be bad.

Ben stood in a waist-deep hole he'd dug in the sand, headed for China, Jenny rested next to him on a gargantuan towel, her eyes hidden behind Audrey Hepburn sunglasses. She looked positively edible in her white one-piece bathing suit. I half-sat, half-collapsed into the sand beside her, but she didn't acknowledge me. While I'd been working out my leg, she'd been thinking, and the more she thought, generally, the angrier she got. We might have been getting along relatively well all morning, but during the two hours of alone-time on a perfectly pleasant beach she'd obviously been stewing on all the reasons why she was so pissed off with me.

'You awake?' I tried.

'Uh huh,' she mumbled. She was using that old Rutgers sweatshirt as a pillow.

'We're back,' I announced unnecessarily.

'How's your daughter?'

'She fell asleep about twenty minutes ago. She's in the shade.'

'I've got to feed her. My boobs are going to blow.' Without looking at me, Jenny adjusted her suit.

I peeled off my damp T-shirt, got a glimpse of myself and groaned in disgust. I'd lost some weight as well – hospitals'll do that to you. But

I badly needed to get back into shape, build some muscle, tighten up my midsection.

Jenny's pre-baby figure had returned, complete with engorged breasts that were driving me insane – and she knew it; *that* was embarrassing: my own wife knowing full well I'd be resorting to the *Victoria's Secret* catalogue again. Jenny knew she looked good; she knew I regretted every single move I'd made in the past year, and she knew how badly I wanted to reconnect with her this month. It was only a matter of time until she made her decision: either she'd throw me out or take me back. In the meantime, though, I was in Hell.

I'd fucked up royally, wandering off the reservation when my pregnant wife got tubby. Was I really that shallow? I suppose so. And now I was the tubby one, with my paunchy waist and my injured leg, while Jenny looked like she had when I first met her, a twenty-two year-old with a taut ass and narrow hips. My wife, the love of my life. I needed to get my act together, scrub my own skies.

'We walked pretty far,' I tried again. 'It hurt a bit, but I'm all right. I'll try some more later tonight.'

'No need to push it.' She might have been talking to a stranger. 'Take it easy. We've got all month.' She still didn't open her eyes.

'You want me to get you some lunch?'

'No.'

'Ice cream?'

'No.'

'Should I leave?'

'Whatever, Sailor.'

'What? What'd I do?' I said, stupidly. 'I thought we were having an okay morning—'

Now she did look at me. Pulling her glasses down her nose just far enough to peer over them, she said, 'Did you ever fuck that Danvers woman and then come home to fuck me? Tell me the truth, Sailor: did you fuck her and then fuck your pregnant wife?'

Christ, here we go. 'Um …'

'Just say it, Sailor.' She ground her jaws together.

'Yeah … yeah, I did,' I said. Vertigo sneaked up on me and my vision tunnelled, just for a second.

23

'No condom, nothing, right? No thought for the baby, your *daughter*, growing inside me?' She rested a hand over her abdomen, splayed fingers tan against the stark white of her bathing suit. *I* wanted to touch her there. 'Right, Sailor? Never bothered to wear a rubber with your little girlfriend?'

'Right,' I said, 'she was on the Pill – I wasn't … Jenny, I wasn't all together, in my head – you know—'

'Don't give me that bullshit, Sailor; go peddle that self-denying crap to your therapist, Dr Cranberry, or whoever she is.'

'Krandall,' I said, regretting it as I corrected her, 'sorry – I am, Jenny. I'm so sorry.'

'I know it.' She propped herself up on her elbows, long enough to glare at me. 'You are sorry, Sailor.'

'I—'

'Don't.' Jenny fell back onto the sweatshirt, conversation finished. She had a vicious slash-and-retreat fighting style. Our spats were generally over before I had managed to put together three coherent sentences, leaving me bleeding and broken before I even knew what I wanted to say.

I sat up, sucked in my gut and pulled the waistband of my bathing trunks over the flabby roll beneath my belly button, just in case anyone was looking at the ugly guy with the sexy wife. I picked up one of the Louis L'Amour novels and tried to get into the story while my leg throbbed in time with every thudding beat of my heart. The ghosts of OxyContin past tied my guts into knots. I breathed deep, sucking in as much damp New Jersey summertime as I could, then blew my lungs empty.

A car passed along Ocean Avenue; through its open window Bob Marley tried to convince me that everything was going to be all right.

Sure. This from the guy who got shot before *dying of cancer.*

Ben dug steadily, hauling sand away in his plastic bucket. 'You find any treasure in there, monkey-man?' I asked.

'Not yet, Daddy,' he said, without interrupting his work.

'You want some help?'

'You wouldn't fit in here, Daddy.'

'That's true,' I said. 'Maybe when you get it a bit deeper, or when you get tired, I can take over for a while, okay?'

'Okay,' he said, and dragged another load over to the hillock he'd created while Anna and I were out walking.

I stole Jenny's newspaper, the *Asbury Park Press*. A Warren County farmer wanted reimbursement for his pig, a prize-winning three-hundred-pound sow named Auntie Carla. Apparently Auntie Carla had been killed in an overnight attack at the Monmouth County Fairgrounds, hacked to death by some lunatic with an axe, or maybe a cleaver. Pieces of Auntie Carla had gone missing, but enough was left behind for fair officials to determine that she had been alive while whole sections of her back and hindquarter were torn off.

Slash and retreat.

'Hmm,' I said to no one, 'you'd think a three-hundred-pound pig would put up more of a fight.'

Jenny answered, without opening her eyes, 'You only weigh a hundred and eighty, Sailor.'

Now I ignored her. 'Must have been noisy … surprising no one heard anything.' The paper had run a photo of Auntie Carla's empty pen on a facing page. Even in black and white it was clear to see she'd lost quarts of blood. The pen slats had been stained in wild Pollockian splashes, the straw was drenched in the stuff and the concrete floor looked black in the photo where Auntie Carla had bled out, probably bellowing in agony.

'Jesus!' I held the paper closer to read the caption. 'What kind of demented cafeteria lady pulls something like this?' I reread the story. 'Teach him to come all the way out here to show off his pig, I guess. Should've stuck to the Warren County Fair, maybe.'

'What are you saying?' Jenny murmured, half-asleep or feigning it like a world champion.

'Nothing.' I used my cane to pull myself to my feet. 'I'm going to sit in the water for a while, try and get the swelling down in my leg.'

'Fine,' she said. 'Watch for Ben if he comes down that way.'

'All right. You've got Anna. She'll probably sleep another half-hour.'

Jenny didn't answer.

25

I left my cane and limped down the beach, stumbling once intention-ally, in the hope of garnering a bit of sympathy from Jenny later. In the shallow foam above the breakers I stumbled again, unintentionally this time, staggering a couple of steps before sitting down hard.

'God-freaking-rat-turds!' I curbed my initial string of vicious profanity, suddenly conscious of the children playing nearby. Two suburban moms, watching their kids run back and forth through the foam, glanced over disapprovingly. *God-freaking-rat-turds* apparently wasn't in their lexicon of acceptable beach chatter.

The water retreated around me, tugging my trunks down at the back, and as I shifted to pull them back up another breaker splashed between my legs, filling my crotch with shockingly cold water and gritty sand. I couldn't stop myself yelping. But my leg felt better almost immediately and I silently promised to sit in the ocean every day.

I avoided eye contact with the moms and awaited the next wave. The chill water stung like a hard slap, but after a moment of pins and needles, my muscles relaxed and I imagined I could feel the swelling ease in my scarred muscle tissue. To passers-by I must have looked like a crippled, overweight buffoon sitting in the frothy shallows while a hundred sun-baked children played ball and searched for shells.

Screw them. I felt good, and I used my palms to shift myself into deeper water. The sand between my toes felt like a journey through time. I was far enough into the water to appreciate the gentle beating I received, yet far enough up the beach that the waves didn't crash over my head or knock me about too mercilessly.

Somewhere behind me, I heard Ben's giggle; he shouted, 'Mommy! Look at Daddy! He looks *funny!*'

I didn't hear Jenny's reply over the wind and the waves, but she probably agreed that I looked absurd. Whatever. As I sat there, minutes blurred together in the familiar seam between warm sun, hot sand and frigid water. I smelled French fries and boardwalk pizza. Two kids nearby tossed a bright orange football; another threw popcorn to a riotous flock of seagulls that looked ravenous enough to carry him off somewhere and pick his bones clean. Ben said something, then laughed again; I heard him as if from across a field.

My eyes closed and the predictable rhythm of the waves pushed me gently towards sleep. I breathed in sync with the ebb and flow of the waves, finding perfect timing, like a marathon runner. On the breeze, I caught the distant sounds of a calliope, a breathy, out-of-tune melody I knew but didn't care to place: four notes, descending intervals. There were lyrics to it, but they escaped me. The calliope faded.

Where's a calliope around here, anyway? It's got to be a hundred ye—

The breaker crashed over my head. I hadn't heard the mothers ushering their little charges a safe distance away, hadn't heard Ben shout, 'Uh oh, Daddy!' as he watched the wall of water rolling inexorably towards me. I felt like I'd been hit with a garbage truck as water slammed into my face, flooding my sinuses with searing brine and sharp-edged bits of sandy grit. I swallowed what felt like a gallon of the North Atlantic, choked, tried to cough my lungs clear and realised I was still under water, rolling first up and then down the beach. One of my feet broke the surface, and I imagined it jutting out crazily, like the sinking mast of a pale, fleshy barge headed for the depths.

I managed to get an elbow underneath me and to dig in with my good foot as I choked and sucked in a desperate gasp before the next wave, a miniature clone of the garbage truck, crashed into my chest and sent me tumbling backwards towards Ohio.

'Sailor!' I heard Jenny scream through the hollow roar of the water. She grabbed my arm and heaved me up the beach.

Incandescent, crippling agony exploded in my shoulder as the healthy tissue, new-grown in the past ten weeks, came apart. This was so much more painful than being shot; I screamed, swallowed more seawater and choked until my wife, looking sexy as hell in her new bathing costume, finally hauled me out of the surf.

I lay in the sand wheezing, coughing my lungs clear. My arm hung limply as my heart beat, a wild scherzo now, echoed in the torn ligaments and muscles above my knee. I silently prayed that *those* repairs had held together.

Jenny knelt beside me. 'You all right?' With the flat of one palm, she struck the centre of my back, hard enough to hurt. 'C'mon Sailor, cough it up.'

'Everything all right, ma'am?' Though blurry, the lifeguard standing with his hand on my wife's shoulder was younger, thinner, and more attractive than I'd ever been.

I tried to nod.

'He's fine.' Jenny reached down to tug up my sagging trunks. *Lovely. I'm sure that frightened the children.*

'Lemme help you get him up.' Blurry Lifeguard moved behind me. His abdominal muscles might have been carved by Michelangelo.

'No,' I wheezed, 'shoulder – Jenny— My shoulder.'

'Oh, Jesus Christ,' she whispered, then to Blurry Lifeguard said, 'I've got him, thanks. He'll be fine. I'll just let him rest here a second.'

'Do you have an injury in your shoulder, sir?' Blurry Lifeguard nearly shouted, just in case the breakers had rendered me stone-deaf.

'He's all right.' Jenny sidled between us, nudging David Hasselhoff out of the way with her hip. 'I've got him.'

This time, I managed a nod.

'All right, ma'am. I'll be on the tower if you need me.'

Jenny smiled at him, her grin more genuine than I'd seen in months. 'Thanks again—?'

'Curt.'

'Thanks, Curt.'

Blurry Lifeguard – *Curt* – disappeared from view, making room for Ben, who plopped down on both knees and said, 'Are you okay, Daddy? Mommy, is Daddy okay?'

Get up, shithead. Get up. I used my good arm to press my shoulders a few inches off the sand. Reading my mind, Jenny helped lift my head far enough for me to sit up on my own. 'Easy, easy, Sailor,' she said.

I closed my eyes and memorised the tiny places where her fingers, so gentle, touched the back of my head. 'I'm okay, monkey-man,' I said, then coughed until my lungs burned. 'Daddy's fine, just got a lungful of water, that's all. Where's Anna?'

'She's fine,' Jenny said. 'Still sleeping.'

'You can go,' I said. 'Don't leave her up there by herself.'

'You sure?' Jenny stood. I wanted badly to reach over and brush the gritty bits of sand from her knees. Or maybe just nibble on them for a few minutes.

I do love one-piece bathing costumes. Forget those bikini-wearing swizzle-sticks.

'Yeah, thanks. We'll be right there. I just need a chance to catch my breath.'

'Your shoulder okay? Sorry – I wasn't thinking about which arm I grabbed.' She sounded like she meant it, and that was good.

'Yeah,' I wheezed. 'I'm fine. Ben'll stick with me, won't you, buddy?'

'Sure, Daddy,' he said. 'I'll get my bucket.' He took off up the beach.

Jenny leaned over. I felt her breath on my cheek. 'Your leg all right? You want your cane?'

'No,' I said dejectedly, 'I can walk.'

She trailed a finger over my shoulder.

Ben was back at a full sprint, his yellow bucket half-full of sand and shells. 'Daddy?'

'Yes, Alfredo Sauce?'

'Daddy,' he whispered conspiratorially, 'I saw your heiny when Mommy pulled you out of the water.' He leaned in to tell me this, as if he understood how tragically wrong it was.

'That's okay, man-cub. I don't have much of a heiny, anyway. And as long as no one took pictures, I don't mind.' Not entirely true: I really could have done without baring my ass for Curt the Blurry Lifeguard and the suburban mothers. I rotated my shoulder as far as I could a couple of times. Yep, it hurt every bit as much as I'd expected.

'Can we get ice cream now?'

'That's a great idea, monkey-man.' I dragged myself to my feet, Ben helping by taking my elbow and lifting with all his might.

'You and me,' I said.

'Me and you, Daddy.'

'What kind of ice cream do you want?' I didn't hear what he said; a gust off the water carried that same throaty calliope tune I'd heard right before the ocean came after me: four notes in descending intervals, this time followed by a jaunty five-note response before it faded.

'What is that?' I asked no one.

'What's what, Daddy?' Ben's swimming trunks hung low on his non-existent hips, and the hems reached all the way to his always-grazed

29

knees. He yanked the waistband up, but they promptly slipped down again. He needed a belt.

'Nothing, buddy.' I took a gimpy step and from his tower, square-jawed Curt the Blurry Lifeguard shot me an idiotic thumbs-up. *Yeah, sure, asswipe. Stop checking out my wife.* I forced myself to wave thanks. 'C'mon Monster Mash.' I took Ben's hand. 'Let's go.'

At our beach blanket, I stopped long enough to drape a towel over my shoulders; there was no way I was getting a shirt on yet. I grabbed my cane and a few dollars from Jenny's purse.

'You okay?' She looked up at me as she knotted Anna's used diaper into a plastic bag.

'I love you, Jenny,' I blurted. 'I want to stay married. I need you to forgive me, some day.'

She held out the bag. 'Get rid of this.'

'Some day,' I said.

'Some day.' She buttoned Anna's onesie.

Ben tickled Anna under her chin. 'Mommy, do you want ice cream?'

'Coffee.' She made a face at him. 'But maybe I should take you, buddy. Daddy needs to sit down.'

'I've got it,' I said.

'Okay, then.' She didn't look at me; to Ben, she said, 'Coffee. A double scoop.'

'Can Annie have some, too?'

'Not yet, buddy. Maybe next summer.' Jenny held Ben down long enough to spray him with a second coat of SPF 8,000. 'You're a good little man, thinking of your sister like that.'

Their exchange took less than ten seconds, and I'd come so close to missing it – *all* of it. With each throb, more regrets stacked up in my mind, but still I couldn't escape the lingering images of Sarah Danvers: Sarah in a lace thong; Sarah wrapped in an old blanket; Sarah making breakfast naked: lust and regret. Lust and regret. I craved a cigarette, a half gallon of Scotch and an excruciatingly slow blow job. Lust and regret. *Jesus, Sailor! Get your head on straight.*

'I want to stay married,' I said again, sounding as dopey as a lonely fat kid at the senior prom.

'Well, your son wants ice cream, and so do I.' Jenny gestured towards the boardwalk. 'I've got Anna.'

Ben dragged on my good arm; I grabbed my cane and started up the beach. The sand might as well have been molten lava. At first, Ben wasn't bothered by it; I used it as an effective means of distracting myself from the vicious pain in my shoulder.

Fucking Secret Service. Fucking Robert Lake.

Finally Ben let go and sprinted for the safety of the elevated planks. 'Come on, Daddy! It's too hot on my feet!'

'I'm coming.' I snorted my sinuses clear and discreetly spat snot, sand and salt water towards the dunes. The calliope melody danced around in my head; I hummed until I was able to piece it together – a song I remembered from the midway carousel in Seaside Heights or Asbury Park, back when I was Ben's age and my parents brought Marie and me down for the day. I didn't know the words, but the melody played in my memory, as out of tune now as back then.

Beyond the dune, another car, a convertible, cruised along Ocean Avenue, and I could hear David Gilmour as he sang how much he and the other members of Pink Floyd *wished you were here*. As I limped through the molten sand I sang along, the calliope music fading with each wobbly step.

'Are your feet on fire, Daddy?' Ben danced on the top stair, clearly relieved to be off the coals.

'They sure are, monkey-man.' I tossed Anna's diaper into a nearby trash can. Something tickled the hairs on the back of my neck; I turned to see Jenny, holding Anna and watching me. I raised my cane, feeling stupid for having stumbled on purpose, right before nearly drowning in two feet of water.

Jenny waved.

I climbed the weathered wooden stairs to the boardwalk and let Ben lead me to the ice cream shop. It never crossed my mind to wonder how one wave, out of an infinite number rolling up the sand at Bradley Beach, had managed to grow so impossibly large.

*

After dinner, I stretched out on the sofa my grandparents had bought when they moved to Freehold back in the forties. It weighed nearly a quarter of a ton and had been reupholstered more times than I could remember. Fifty-year-old eight-millimetre movie reels in my mother's basement revealed the vomit-orange flowers it had sported in the mid-sixties, before my parents were married. One photo, on the mantel in my grandmother's house, showed my nineteen-year-old mother in her wedding dress. With perfect porcelain skin and a strand of fake pearls, she was all at once young, pretty, anxious, hopeful, and just a bit ter-rified. I didn't know who'd taken that picture – my grandfather, most likely – but with one click of the shutter whoever it was had captured a transcendent view of my mother. The only thing that ruined that photo was the beached whale of a sofa in the background, covered with massive sunflowers.

Tonight it wore an indestructible coat of sky-blue polyester, the upholsterer's answer to Teflon, the colour matching the beachfront blue of several of the houses along D Street. I propped my head up on one of the cushions and Jenny slid a bag of frozen peas beneath my shoulder and pressed a bag of frozen carrots over my collarbone. Gingerly, she wrapped the whole works – neck, shoulder, chest, peas and carrots – in Ben's Spider-Man blanket.

'Thanks,' I said.

'No problem.' She tucked the blanket under my pillow, holding everything in place. 'You want something for the pain?'

'Two Aleve and two Nytol.'

She dug around in her ten-gallon beach bag until she found them. 'You need water?'

'Any chance it's been fermented into beer?'

'Nope, there's not a beer within fifteen miles of this place.'

Fifteen miles. Naturally.

'What're you drinking?' She'd deftly tried to hide her wine glass.

'Something your mother left in the wine rack, *Cuveé du Château Cat Piss*, I think.'

'Please don't mention cat piss.'

'Sorry, I forgot.'

'Anyway, it sounds yummy.' I cocked an eyebrow at her. 'How about a swig with my meds?'

'Nope. Sorry,' she said, then, reconsidering, 'actually, I'm not sorry.'

'C'mon, Jenny. My mother chose it: there's probably more alcohol in Anna's formula.'

She gave up. 'Fine – just a sip.' She found one of Ben's curly-Q straws in the sink, dropped the handful of pills into my mouth and brought the straw close enough for me to suck in a mouthful. I lifted my head far enough to catch a glimpse of Doctor Octopus, looking furious, on my chest. Jenny was right: the wine tasted just like that antiseptic shit dentists used to scrub off coffee stains.

'Whew, that's *bad*.' I let my head fall onto the pillow.

'I'm just having this one,' she said. 'I don't want to be too knocked out if your daughter wakes up later.'

'Sorry I won't be much help,' I said.

'I'm used to it, Sailor.'

She hadn't been trying to sting me, but it still hurt. I didn't retaliate; I deserved it. 'I'm going to close my eyes for a while. I'll be up and around tomorrow, no worries.'

'You need anything else?'

'How about a cigarette? I think I have one left for today.'

'Not in the house.'

'My father smoked a thousand acres of tobacco sitting on this very couch, Jenny.'

'Well then, you'd better roll over and inhale whatever memories might be trapped in the cushions. But be careful – who knows what else he did on that couch?' She chuckled to herself.

'Gross, honey, really.'

Ignoring me, Jenny stacked plastic plates and cups inside a cabinet above the dishwasher. Watching her in those tattered cargo shorts and her old Rutgers sweatshirt, I imagined her crossing the scrubbed linoleum floor to stand on the rug in the living room, between my mother's old Zenith television and the sky-blue sofa. She'd listen intently for a second or two, ensuring that the children were asleep, then she'd slip out of her clothes – no strip-tease or sensual peepshow antics, just the economic undressing she might do before changing clothes or stepping into the shower. With a quick tug on my sweat-pants, she'd straddle me, right there on my grandparents' sofa, and we'd rock quietly together, connecting again. Finding what we'd lost when I fell.

Instead, Jenny caught me, slipping a hand inside my sweats – I hadn't meant for her to see. My face flushed, and I was glad to be half-shrouded in frozen vegetables. She crossed the room in three hurried steps; for a moment my hopes rose as she bent in close, her lips brushing lightly against my cheek. Working her hand inside my boxers, she stroked me gently, her fingers like fire along my shaft. 'What are you doing?' she whispered.

'Hoping,' I said.

'Really?' She played her fingers up and down.

'Christ, that feels good ...' I closed my eyes.

Jenny stroked a bit faster. 'You like that, Sailor? Feel good?'

'Yeah,' I moaned.

The sexy, husky tone in her voice evaporated in a heartbeat. 'You thinking of her, Sailor? *Sarah Danvers?*' Jenny pulled her hand free, leaving me with a boner that could mine bauxite. 'How does she look in your imagination, love of my life? Does she look pretty good? Nice tits? Tight ass?'

'Jenny, I—'

'No,' she snapped, 'you *nothing*!' She searched around inside the beach bag again and pulled out a dog-eared copy of *Vogue*. 'Here.' She tossed it onto Doctor Octopus; it landed with a flutter. 'That should help. But try not to get any on your mother's couch.'

Slash and retreat.

She flipped off the kitchen light, gathered up her briefcase and laptop and disappeared into the master bedroom down the hall. Before the door closed, I heard her mutter, '—head full of wet cement—'

The chill from the peas and carrots seeped deep into my swollen shoulder, a harbinger of the frosty season ahead. After a few minutes groping for some self-righteous excuse, I gave up and slid my hand back inside my pants.

Sarah in a lace thong. Jenny in a white bathing costume. Jenny un-dressing for a shower. Sarah making breakfast naked. Lust and regret.

Sarah in her red holiday dress. Sarah wrapped in a flannel blanket.

Lust ...

I let go with a groan.

... and regret.

If I'd had my gun, I might have shot myself.

'I want to stay married, Jenny. I *do*,' I said to the darkness, then closed my eyes and waited for the Nytol to take me.

An ancient calliope played four falling notes, followed by a jaunty five-note echo. *I know that song. I remember.* But I didn't, not right then. Pink Floyd followed; David Gilmour *wished you were here* and plucked a few sorrowful notes on his guitar. Four falling notes blew in through the open window, carried on the ocean breeze. Pink Floyd and the old carousel tried for a moment to find a common rhythm, a tonal centre, and failed.

The wind lifted the curtains and I gave in for the night.

SUNDAY

The Ballplayer

Belmar to Spring Lake: 2.4 Miles

Yellow: *Okay, I can almost do this.*

There were a few things that could wake me from a Nytol coma: global thermonuclear war, a grizzly bear attack, being dipped in a vat of boiling oil were all high on that list – but nothing was as effective as an OxyContin craving. Who knew you could have cravings while you slept? That's appallingly fucked-up. I'd never been a full-on, head-over-asshole junkie – I didn't think so, anyway. Granted, I'd taken pills, lots, sometimes eight or ten in a day, but I'd only sucked off the time-release coating and snorted my way out of trouble on a few desperate occasions.

That didn't stop the cravings from hunting me down, and holy shit, but I wanted a blast of indestructible teenage glory right now, at 3:07 a.m. by the neon-blue light of my new watch. The defrosted vegetables were gone from my shoulder and I'd been draped in a blanket, so I figured Jenny must have been up with Anna already though I hadn't heard a thing.

The cravings always began the same way: as a white-hot ball of discomfort in the pit of my stomach, rife with clenching gravity and threatening to suck my extremities in like SpongeBob Squarepants. When the discomfort spread, it didn't blow outwards, like a hand grenade; rather, it sent nefarious tentacles, coiling fingers of desire that threaded their way through my muscles and bones, polarising every cell in my body towards one magnetic truth: *Get fixed, shithead. Do it* now.

36

I sat up and tested my shoulder, and was pleased to find that despite being stiff, it moved surprisingly well when I reached for my cigarettes—

Cigarette, dopey: singular. You never bought a pack yesterday.

Rather than piss Jenny off any further, I decided to go outside for a smoke. A slight breeze fluttered the pages of *Vogue*, now on the armrest near the window. I couldn't hear the sea four blocks away, so it was likely low tide.

'Maybe a walk,' I whispered to no one. 'Take a walk, get some cigarettes, sweat out this craving – what do you think, Sailor?'

I think I'd rather just wait here to die.

'Nope, not an option. Get up, get moving: you gotta fight this.' I didn't know why that was so important, but it was true: something about this particular craving was demanding action. I'd pop a couple of aspirin, grab the biggest coffee from the first place I could find and smoke myself stupid as I walked until my leg gave way beneath me. I *had* to beat this one down.

I found my lighter and my cane and took my shoulder sling down from a hook behind the kitchen door. After a minute of awkward fiddling with Velcro straps and plastic eyelets, my arm was trussed up against my chest. I picked up the spare key dangling from the chipped ear of the ceramic Mickey Mouse next to the telephone before helping myself to a long swig from Jenny's god-awful wine, then I mentally slapped myself. *I bet she checked how much was left. I bet she did, god-damnit.*

The 7-Eleven at the corner of Twentieth and Ocean, three-quarters of a mile away, stayed open all night. I'd head there, then see how I felt.

Twenty-five minutes later I was sitting on a park bench, my leg propped up on the concrete barrier between the dunes and the board-walk as I smoked two cigarettes and sipped a boiling hot (but tasteless) black coffee. Nothing moved on the beach. Incandescent light from the store windows brightened the street and the raised boardwalk, casting ranks of low dunes in shadow. A quarter of a mile away timid waves splashed softly on the sand.

My craving had quieted, just a bit, but it wasn't gone yet. If I went back home now I'd be writhing and dry-heaving on the linoleum in an hour or two, so I decided instead to keep walking it off. My hands shook, and I knew things might yet get horribly embarrassing when my body gave up on me.

'To hell with it,' I muttered, grabbing my cane, 'if it gets bad, I'll shit in the dunes. It's dark enough.' I picked up the pace, wanting to raise my heart rate. Though it was late September, the humidity was still high – maybe not the wet blanket that wrapped New Jersey all summer but still enough that moisture trickled down my back.

That's good, Sailor, keep going: sweat it out.

Million-dollar and multi-million-dollar homes lined the perfectly manicured streets of Spring Lake, the richest jewel on the old Irish Riviera. The fascist zoning laws ensured no beachfront bars, restaurants, ice cream parlours or junk shops, nothing that even remotely resembled the *Down the Shore* idiom so perfectly captured by towns like Belmar or Point Pleasant. There was no aroma of fried food, beer, or even suntan lotion within *these* town limits.

I knew I'd have no chance of finding a public bathroom down here, not at four o'clock in the morning. So either I kept exercising until my OxyContin fireball blinked itself out, or I headed for the beach and let my body shake itself senseless.

I tried to walk it off, hustling south with a rhythmic step: *limp, cane, step, limp, cane, step, limp, cane.* Nicotine helped. Breathing hard helped. Feeling my blood pumping helped – everything helped, but I was only half a mile into Spring Lake before I gave up. This was going to be a bad one.

I stumbled down the concrete steps to the sand, and as I tried to mop my face on my shirtsleeve my aching leg muscles gave way on the uneven ground and I fell hard onto a patch of resilient dune grass, thankfully landing on my good side.

'Fuck,' I panted, dragging myself back up. Hazy circles of yellow splashed intermittently along Ocean Avenue, cast by overhead sodium lights. I headed for the darkness waiting patiently between the dunes. My stomach was clenching hard as I dragged myself a few yards further in. The sand helped tug my sweatpants down to my knees, before I cried out, '*Jesus!* Jesus Christ, *help* me,' and rolled onto my side, puking violently as my bowels loosened and I shook like an epileptic, the muscles in my bowels, stomach and throat continuing to constrict and release until my body had painfully voided itself of everything I'd ever eaten.

The spell passed.

Breathing through my mouth, trying to ignore the stench of my own waste, I tuned my ears and listened to my heart – *still beating, not dead yet, motherfuckers* – as it slowed from 160 to 120 and finally down to somewhere around 108, if I was counting right.

I laughed, surprising myself, and blew out a tiny spray of snot and sand. 'Good morning, Sailor, out for a walk, are we?' I laughed harder now, almost maniacally, as I murmured, 'How ever are we going to get up, my friend? We're two miles from home, and most likely about to roll into our own aromatic by-products. Lovely.'

If only my son could see me now . . .

It took me ten minutes to get up and clear of my own foul mess. I tore up handfuls of rough cordgrass to clean myself off, and once I'd managed to bury the evidence in the dune I rubbed my hand clean in the sand. Then I limped gingerly back to the Spring Lake boardwalk, lit a cigarette and contemplated the absurdity of my predicament. I was too far from home to make it back on foot, and there was no chance of any passing Med Evac helicopters spotting my outstretched thumb. I had my cell phone, but it was only 4:15 a.m., way too early to call Jenny.

I breathed slowly, savouring the cool, salty air. I felt as though I'd been struck by lightning just seconds after being run down by a combine harvester. *Never again, Sailor.* Sarah Danvers had said it: *never again in my presence.*

Who knew that snorting hillbilly heroin would lead to shitting and puking your guts up in the dunes? *The FDA ought to put that warning on the label . . .*

Spring Lake's beach glowed eerily alongside the cold darkness of the ocean. I watched the waves as I considered my options. A little over half a mile to the north was the 7-Eleven; south was a massive oceanfront hotel, the Warren & Monmouth, one of those ornate turn-of-the-century places where rich Irish families from New York

City used to spend summers sipping champagne on the beach, casually dressed in bespoke three-piece suits and ankle-length dresses with matching parasols.

The hotel looked to be about ten feet closer than the 7-Eleven, but it was still a good half-mile away. Soaked with sweat as I was, with my underwear full of sand, I didn't for a moment imagine I'd be welcome in such a place – but I decided to head south regardless. It was closer, and right now every step counted.

Step, limp, cane, step, limp, cane, step, limp, cane . . .

A breeze freshened off the water, cooling my skin, and I felt a bit better. The Warren & Monmouth sat alongside Ocean Avenue like a cruise ship that had docked above the dunes. The historic edifice towered over even the grandest of Spring Lake's mansions, sporting a golden cupola, half a dozen widow's walks over a slate roof interrupted at regular intervals by double-window dormers, each with its own spotlight, its own flag and its own heavily planted windowbox. From this far out, it was impossible to tell how many floors there were in the old place; I guessed six, but it might have been seven or even eight from basement to attic. The grand old hotel was a full block long and half a block deep, and had soaked up a million Jersey shore legends and memories. Even in the aftermath of my collapse I felt oddly excited to be walking that way, and anxious to see inside the lobby.

Though I'd been coming to Belmar for thirty years, I had visited Spring Lake no more than half a dozen times. The town had its own way of suggesting visitors keep the hell away, with its narrow sidewalks and impenetrable hedges, no public toilets, nor much in the way of beachfront amusements. And though my sister Marie and I used to jog along the beach, I couldn't ever recall going inside the Warren & Monmouth, not even for a drink. I had no clue how the place kept running – with so many beaches and golf resorts within easy reach of the New York airports; I couldn't think why any Park Avenue millionaire would want to come to Spring Lake, especially in the off-season.

Powerful lights artfully hidden in shrubs or secreted between rocks cast brilliant light in conical swaths, illuminating the old edifice as if it were midday. Why the place needed to be so bright at 4:30 in the morning was a mystery to me; with the Sea Girt lighthouse rotating tirelessly only half a mile further south, the Warren & Monmouth's façade looked more like a prison, complete with sweeping searchlight, than a proud monument to a bygone era of grace and gentility.

As I limped closer I could see the grounds were as carefully maintained as any in Spring Lake. A glass atrium jutted like a massive bug's eye from the rear courtyard, while a wraparound deck, whitewashed to match the building, offered ample oceanfront seating for all those hungover millionaires sipping their mimosas and Bloody Marys.

I crossed Ocean Avenue, staring at the wide Rhett Butler staircase that opened into the lobby and trying to count the wrought-iron verandahs that covered the front of the building. Most of the rooms were dark, though I could see many had left verandah doors open, allowing the sea breeze and the surf to comfort them through the middle watch; only a few insomniacs or early risers had the lights on.

I was buoyed by having beaten down another craving and encouraged that my leg, however wobbly, remained upright beneath me. I remembered days at the Virginia State Police Academy when we'd exercise, study, shoot, lift weights and box for twelve straight hours and still manage to polish buttons, clean bathrooms and kiss the sergeant's German ass, feeling strangely good at the end of the day, as if we could go straight on and eat nails or wrestle felons. I recaptured a thimbleful of that feeling now, ten years, fifteen pounds and a great sackload of regrets later: I felt unexpectedly strong climbing those whitewashed stairs into that old hotel.

My footsteps were silent on the gargantuan Persian carpet the Warren & Monmouth used for a welcome mat. They had one of those brass doorknockers that looked strangely like a girl I had dated in high school, her gilded mouth open in a perpetual howl. My hand shook and I clenched my fingers to relax them. The bellhop must have been catching a nap or watching *The Late, Late, Late Show*; either way, I was left to heave open the twelve-foot-high door myself.

I'd got three steps across the Persian rug-covered marble tiles when a concierge appeared from behind a cherrywood desk. There wasn't a wrinkle to be seen in his spiffy forest-green uniform, nor a spot of dust on his highly polished shoes, and his tie, a double Windsor three

41

decades out of style, was cinched all the way up beneath his cleanly shaven chin.

'May I help you, sir?' He didn't need to add, *Who the hell is this vagrant?* He got that over by the way he stood: all pomp and circumstance and holier-than-thou.

'Um, yeah—' I pulled myself up as straight as possible. 'I was hoping to camp out here in the lobby, just for an hour or two, until my wife can come and get me. I've got a bit of a leg injury and I've walked further than I should this morning—'

The foppish concierge didn't flinch, or let me finish. 'I'm sorry, sir, but that will not be possible. I would be happy to call you a cab, if you'd like to wait outside.'

I glanced down at my sandy sweat pants. I couldn't see any puke stains, or smell anything, nothing too egregious, anyway, but I had sweated through my T-shirt and I did look like I'd slept on the beach. 'Listen, I'll buy coffee, breakfast, whatever,' I started. 'I'm a cop – I was shot a couple of months ago, and I'm trying to get back on my feet ...' I went for the pity vote, or at least a chance to sit down with a coffee and a bagel.

It didn't work.

'I'm sorry, sir,' he repeated, clearly not in the least upset, and gestured towards the door almost as if leading me onto a dance floor. *Do-si-do and out you go, stinky!*

'Are you kidd—?' I started, then stopped myself. Punching him out was last thing I needed this morning.

'Sir, we have a discriminating clientele here at the Warren & Monmouth; they don't appreciate non-guests *camping out* in the lobby before dawn.'

'Yeah, all right.' I raised my hands in surrender. 'I hear you. I'm going.'

'Can I call you a cab, sir?'

I watched a formally dressed waiter, an Italian-looking kid, pushing a trolley with a shining silver tea service and a plate of fresh fruit and muffins down the hallway behind the concierge desk. 'No. Thanks.' I kept my voice down, but I longed to belt him, just for grins.

'Very well, sir.' He pushed the door open effortlessly. 'Good morning, sir.'

'Yeah, whatever.' I stopped on the shallow end of the Persian doormat. I wanted to ask if he and his family had avoided the plague this summer, if anyone he knew had got sick – and if he even cared that it was me they had to thank that they were all still alive. I'd saved his stuck-up ass, I'd taken the infection upon myself, the Gentamicin, the broken bones, the fucking bullets, all so he could play lord of the manor in a pretentious *empty* hotel at 4:30 in the morning.

But I didn't.

He hesitated a moment, as if expecting me to tell him off, then, nodding curtly, let the door swing shut.

'Cocksucker,' I murmured.

To my right, somewhere along the porch, someone answered with a laugh, 'Oh, you've got *his* number.'

'Sorry.' I raised my cane in apology. 'I didn't know anyone was there.' Whoever it was had chosen a table outside the brilliant spotlights secreted around the grounds. His silhouette moved from the shadows beneath the striped canvas awning. The Sea Girt lighthouse beam circled overhead, illuminating the second and third floors in a rotating stripe. 'Sorry,' I said. 'I can't really see—'

There was a strike of a match, then a candle flickered and a big man, older but healthy-looking, with a decent head of hair, came into focus behind the flame.

'It's my fault. I shouldn't sneak up on people,' he said, 'especially in the dark.'

'It'll be light soon,' I said. 'No blood, no foul.'

He covered the candle with a hurricane glass and the flame settled, revealing a breakfast table draped with immaculate linen, set for one. A paperback kept the *Asbury Park Press* from blowing away.

'Care to join me for a cup of coffee?' He waved a hand towards an empty chair. 'You look like you could use a cup.'

'Thanks,' I said, hastily brushing sand from my clothes and hair. 'Sorry. I'm not really dressed for this place.'

'Nonsense.' He frowned in the half-light. 'Dress codes, starched shirts – it's all nonsense. Have you ever worn a starched shirt, Mr—?'

'Doyle.' I extended my hand. 'Sam Doyle. My friends call me Sailor.'

'Sailor it is.' His hand was meaty, with long, powerful fingers. 'I'm Mark Stillman. My friends have always called me Moses.'

'That's a curious nickname.' I slid my cane beneath the table. 'Where'd you pick it up?'

'Ever played minor-league baseball, Sailor?'

'Can't say that I have.'

'Everyone has a nickname. "Moses" is about the kindest of the litany I was saddled with during my years in the game, so if one of them had to stick, I'm glad it was that one.'

'How long did you play?'

'Nine seasons.' He shifted the book on the paper, then shifted it back. 'It was exactly nine seasons too many, and about nine seasons too few; you know what I mean?'

I nodded. 'Actually, you'd be shocked at how thoroughly I can empathise with you, Moses.'

'And the name Sailor – where'd you pick that up?'

I pointed over the water. 'About three miles that way. My sister christened me one bitch of a windy morning.'

'So are you an actual sailor, Sailor?'

'Good lord, no,' I said. 'It's— well, it's a long story.'

A door opened further along the porch, spilling harsh white light onto the planks. The waiter I had seen in the lobby came out and turned towards our table.

Moses Stillman called, '*Buongiorno, Antonio. Un altro caffe, per lui.*' He looked to me. 'You drink espresso?'

'Please,' I said, 'a double, if they can swing it at this hour.'

'*Una doppia espresso ... due doppia espressi—* Actually, what is that, *due caffe lunghi?*'

In the candlelight, Antonio grinned and in perfect English he said, 'You know, Mr Stillman, I'm from Bergen County, not Calabria.'

'Ah, Tony' – Moses frowned – 'how am I going to remember anything if I don't practise? You've at least got to humour me. Christ, I'll be dead in a couple of years; you think I want to die having forgotten all my Italian?'

'When you die, Mr Stillman, I don't think anyone will care if you've forgotten how to speak Italian.' Antonio – *Tony from Bergen County* – set out muffins, yoghurt and fresh fruit. He attempted to pour a cup of coffee from the fancy silver decanter, but Moses waved him off.

'Not this morning, Tony. I have a guest and we're having espresso, *doppia espressi*.'

Tony wasn't sure what to do with the decanter. 'Really, sir? Should I leave this pot, though? It's fresh.'

The Sea Girt light rotated overhead and Moses caught me gazing at the pot. 'Yes, please pour out for Mr Doyle – he needs a blast right away.'

Tony filled my porcelain cup. He was a carbon copy of the football players I'd known in high school: his black hair slicked back, olive skin darkened by the summer, his body toned and muscular from hours lifting in the gym and swimming in the sea – but the boy was cursed; unless he started to cut way, way back on the lasagne, Tony from Bergen County would go from sexy Italian muscle-man to jowly Uncle Vito. He sported the obligatory gold crucifix around his neck and I'd have bet a week's salary that somewhere in his uniform he'd stashed a pack of Winstons.

Moses slid me a spoon and a small sugar bowl and I thanked him again, and added, 'You're right, by the way: I'll probably drink the entire pot.'

As Tony left us Moses unfolded his napkin and handed it to me, then passed over the basket of muffins; I took one from the top of the pile. 'Thanks—' I started, but he laughed.

'Do stop thanking me, Sailor,' he said. 'You're the only company out here at 4:37 in the morning.'

I surreptitiously poked the LIGHT button on my running watch. 4:58. The first hint of dawn's glow inched its way above the horizon somewhere out near Portugal.

Moses sliced a muffin in half and slathered it with butter. 'I'm no sleeper.' He spoke with his mouth full. 'Never have been, not since my Katherine died anyway, back in '94. I never seem to make it past 4:15, so I'm generally dressed and down here by 4:37. I pay extra to have Tony here at the crack of goddamned dawn to fetch me my muffins.' He considered what remained of the one in his hand, then added,

'Probably the most expensive frigging muffins in America when you think about it.' He laughed. 'So I don't!'

'All right, Mr Stillman, I'll stop thanking you, but you don't know how much you've helped me this morning.' I took a slug of coffee. I wasn't ready to test my stomach with a blueberry muffin, not just yet. 'I'm actually a cop from Virginia, a state trooper – I managed to get myself shot full of holes a couple of months ago, and I'm up here trying to get back into shape. Last night – tonight, today, whatever the hell it is right now – I couldn't sleep either, so I took my newly healed leg out for a walk, got all the way down here, and realised I wasn't sure I could make it back.'

'Back to—?' he interrupted.

'Belmar.' I pointed north. 'Twelfth and D.'

'Good Irish neighbourhood,' he said. 'I can run you back if you don't want to wake your wife – or is she an early riser as well?' He leaned over the table and I had a chance to get a better look at him in the candlelight. Moses Stillman wore an extra sixty pounds like a retired athlete, distributed well enough over his frame that even at seventy-or-so years old he exuded good health. I had a hard time determining if the candlelight was enhancing his leathery complexion, or if I was romanticising it, imagining him playing in the outfield at some North Carolina stadium summer after sweltering summer. He was freshly shaven and dressed better, at 5:00 on a Sunday morning, than I had ever been, in neatly pressed linen pants and a cotton dress shirt. I flushed at the thought of me breakfasting in my underwear, watching ESPN highlights while wolfing down a bowl of oatmeal. Perhaps the grass truly was greener in a place like Spring Lake; I didn't stand a chance of ever getting there.

'What do you think?' he asked. 'Need a ride home?'

I flexed my leg a couple of times, careful not to kick him under the table. 'You know, if you don't mind me sitting here for a few minutes more, I might risk it and see how far I can get on my own.' I had no idea where that came from. Less than an hour ago I'd been shitting myself in the sand; now, one cup of Antonio's coffee later, I was seriously considering hoofing it all the way back to Belmar.

'Well, if you want some company,' Moses said, 'I may come along, part of the way.'

As I raised my cup in salute, our double espressos arrived. 'I look forward to it.'

Tony made a show of dropping off the tray and a place setting for me. *'Due caffe lunghi – doppia espressi,* if you prefer.'

'Grazie, Antonio.' Moses stirred sugar into his, toasted me in return, then gulped it down with a flourish. 'So, Sailor, how did you get shot? Was that in line of duty? Or did you phone your wife too early for a ride home one morning?'

I sighed through my nose. 'Did you happen to follow that business down in Richmond this summer?'

Moses slapped the table hard enough to send two strawberries and a grape fleeing across the linen. 'That was you! Great leaping Christ, you're that detective – I saw you on *Good Morning America*! You're the one who tracked down that poor woman—' He scowled at the great oaken doors of the Warren & Monmouth Hotel. 'And that limp-wrister in there threw you out, didn't he?'

I ran a hand through my hair, brushing away yet more sand. 'What the hell, I don't look all that presentable this morning, and I suppose I stink, just a bit. He's doing his job.'

'And glad I am he did.' Moses handed me another muffin. 'I am mighty pleased to meet you, Sailor Doyle – no, excuse me, *Detective* Doyle. I'm not sure I'd have been able to do what you did, no sir. That was heroic. Truly.'

'I was terrified pretty much the whole time,' I admitted, and we talked for a while about my antics ten weeks before, Moses sitting almost motionless, staggered at what I had accomplished in thirty-six hours over the July fourth weekend. I left out the part about being stoned within an inch of my life and so failing to actually notice the onset of plague symptoms because I had ingested so much OxyContin – no one really wanted to hear that part, except my darling Jenny, of course, who homed in on *that* detail every time we had any sort of discussion about my first solo investigation. Strangers all wanted to hear about saving the world (which I never actually did). I guess most people like to imagine themselves as heroes, fighting terrorists or carrying wounded soldiers out of harm's way, and so few of us ever truly find ourselves in situations that demand heroic measures that it's easy to lock on to someone else's actions, call it *heroism* and plaster the name across the marquee for fifteen minutes of glory.

But I'd lived it and I knew it was all bullshit. I'd just got fabulously lucky finding Molly Bruckner. Doc Lefkowitz and Grace Wentworth were the genuine heroes; without them, I'd never have left that old farm and Molly would have made it to Ashland, infected a handful of motorists headed onto I-95 and spread what Burgess Aiken called *the plague upon the land* and *the wrath of God* up and down the east coast. Doc said it best: we'd have been *leaves in the wind.*

Moses interrupted my reverie. 'We don't have to talk about this if you don't want to, Detective, but I do hope the Virginia State Police have given you all the time and convalescence you require to get back on your feet. To me you were – *are* – a national hero.'

'Thank you, Moses,' I said. 'If it's all right with you, I'd just as soon not discuss it any more. My wife and I are trying to put that weekend behind us – though it doesn't want to go away.' I finished my coffee and stirred a couple of sugars into the espresso, a little porcelain cup of steaming midnight.

'I can't imagine it will.' Moses leaned back, knitting his fingers behind his head. 'I don't know you at all, but I'd bet it's probably the defining moment of your adult life. I can't see much coming close – certainly nothing in *my* life.'

'Dunno about that,' I said. 'I've never played pro ball.'

'Pah!' He dismissed the notion with a wave, leaned back and hummed a snippet of some song, four descending notes.

'Hey!' I stopped, the espresso poised at my lips. 'What's that you're humming? I've been hearing it all—'

The canvas awning ripped, the fabric shrieking, and a body crashed head first through Moses Stillman's linen-covered breakfast table, shattering crockery and sending the silver cutlery flying. Yoghurt, fruit and muffins splattered as if we'd been hit by a cannonball.

'Fucking Christ!' I cried as I tumbled backwards, scalding my chest with the espresso. I hit my head on the porch planks and rolled instinctively to my left, protecting my bad wing.

When I looked up Moses was lying on his side, one foot trapped under the collapsed table. 'What the hell?' he cried. 'What the hell was that?'

I sat up. 'Holy shit! Holy shit!'

'What?' He lay still, panting. 'What happened?'

I sucked in a deep breath, trying to stabilise myself, 'Goddamn, it looks like a suicide.'

'A what? I don't understand.' Still he wouldn't look over.

The Sea Girt light circled above us as dawn painted the horizon warm orange. I pulled myself up using the porch rail, then knelt. 'Lie still for a second, Moses; let me get this off you.'

'I can't—' he started, 'I can't move that foot—'

'Don't try,' I said, too sharply, 'just— Just rest there a second.'

'All right ...' His voice trailed off.

His loafers reminded me of Doc Lefkowitz: soft Italian leather. 'Can you move your toes?' I asked, trying to sound matter-of-fact. 'Bend your toes.'

He tried, grimacing. After a moment he said, 'Yes, yes, I can, I can move them just fine. Fine.'

'Good,' I said, 'stay down a second, okay?'

'Sure, Sailor.' Now he did look, briefly, then turned his eyes away, content to watch sunlight creep up the beach.

The jumper, an elderly man, had come to rest with his shoulders caught in the curved metal braces that had supported the tabletop. His head hung suspended about six inches above the whitewashed plank floor of the porch. Both shoulders had been dislocated; one was bleeding from a deep gash where the table strut had nearly chopped off his arm. He was wearing only pyjama bottoms, bunched up at the knees, and his pink-and-blue striped legs jutted angrily through a pool of strawberry yoghurt. His hairless calves twitched like broken hands on a gruesome clock. His forehead and cheek had been sliced open to the bone and blood was running down his bald head in tiny streams, then dripping onto the porch. Gravity kept it running for a few minutes, long enough for the fresh morning light to turn the black puddle crimson before it seeped through cracks in the deck to stain the sand below.

His mouth hung open and his bulging eyes stared at the Persian carpet.

Tony from Bergen County and the limp-wristed concierge pushed through the double doors; both pulled up short at the sight of the carnage. The fop gave a yelp and pressed both hands to his open mouth. Even from where I was I could see his fingers quaking.

Tony quickly overcame his shock and hustled to help. 'Mr Stillman! Are you all right, sir?'

Moses stammered, 'I— I'm stuck here—'

'He's fine,' I said reassuringly. 'Call 911, will you?' I lifted the table edge far enough for Moses to free his foot. 'Actually, no' – I pointed at the concierge, still frozen on the woven doormat – 'you, Reginald—'

'Thomas,' he managed.

'Thomas. Call 911. Tell them we need an ambulance and the police. Tony, you get anyone else on duty this morning – waiters, cooks, cleaning staff, security, everybody. I want the lobby and this porch closed to guests and anyone off the street. We need to figure out who this guy is – *was* – and what room he was in, and keep everyone out. No one goes in that room until the detectives get here, understand? *No one*. If the door is open, leave it open; if it's locked, leave it locked. Change *nothing*, but keep everyone out – don't even touch the doorknob. Either of you know this guy?'

Thomas the Fop stammered, 'I— Uh—'

'Never mind, call 911. Go!' To Tony I said, 'Where's your security office? Is there an overnight guy?' I reached under the table, used two fingers to check the body for a pulse. Nothing. 'Shit.'

'Just Mitch,' Tony said, 'he doubles as the night guy on the front desk. He and Thomas were the only ones on last night. I come in at four o'clock to serve breakfast for the early risers. Cleaning crew and the sous crew arrive between five and six.'

'Where's Mitch now?' I tried again, lifting the head and pressing hard on the carotid artery, to no avail. I'd never get him out of there without a frigging crane, and I couldn't do CPR with one arm. 'Huh? Where's Mitch?'

Tony scratched his chin. 'I dunno – the desk? Patrolling? Maybe the back parking lot?' He swallowed hard. 'He goes every couple of hours with a flashlight. It gives him a chance to sneak a cigarette, you know, check the place out, call his girlfriend, whatever.'

'He have a radio?'

'Yeah.' Tony helped me get Moses into a wicker chair near the railing. 'And a cell.'

'Good. Get me the radio, and on your way, tell Mitch to get his ass out back ASAP. Watch the exits, as many as he can monitor from that parking lot – it's probably no use now, but the police will want to know if anyone left. We need model, make and tag number of any car that leaves – Mitch should stop them if he can.'

'Got it.' Tony hurried towards the lobby doors.

'One thing,' I added, 'do you know CPR?'

His face fell. 'No. Sorry.'

'It's all right. Bring me that radio!'

Thomas the Fop returned, and braced himself to leave the safety of the Persian rug. 'Can I—?'

'Don't touch anything.' I gestured at the rip in the awning. 'Can you figure out what rooms are above here? Are they numbered 101, 201, 301, in a column? You know what I mean?' I gestured up an imagined staircase.

Nonplussed, he stared, then understood. 'Uh, yes, yes. That's 1103, 2103, 3103—'

'Good,' I said. 'This guy was probably up pretty high, judging from the way he hit the table like a frigging bomb. How high do the numbers go? 5103? 6103?'

'6103.' Sunlight finally washed the porch and I could see blood trickling from the jumper's head slowing to a leaky-faucet drip: death with the coming day.

'Do you know who was in that room?'

Thomas took a wary step closer. 'Shouldn't we—? Should we try to—?' As he reached out a delicate hand the jumper's right leg twitched unnervingly. Thomas recoiled with a cry.

'Help him?' I asked. 'He's dead.'

'How do you—?' His voice cracked. 'How do you know? Are you a doctor? I thought you said you were a police officer.'

'He's not breathing, his heart isn't beating, and he isn't bleeding.'

51

'What's that then?' He aimed the toe of his polished wing-tip towards the puddle accumulating beneath the table. He wasn't about to touch the body himself.

'That's gravity, Thomas,' I said. 'Look at his shoulder; his frigging arm is damned near torn off. No blood pumping. He's dead. He might even have been dead before he came off the balcony. That's why we need Mitch on the radio.'

'I don't understand,' Moses finally spoke. 'Already dead? How did he jump?'

'He might not have jumped, Moses.'

'Oh my heavens.'

Tony burst through the servers' entrance, adjacent to the kitchen, as a siren, still distant, welcomed the sunrise. He brandished a radio. 'Mitch is out back. No one's left yet, not that he's seen, anyway. And Chef Sam is upstairs in the 6100 hallway.' He jogged over to join us.

'You tell him what to do?'

'*Her* – Chef Samantha. And yes.'

'All right,' I pressed the CALL button. 'Mitch, this is Detective Sam Doyle. I'm with the Virginia State Police. I just happened to be here this morning.'

Static. Then Mitch's voice came through. He sounded about seventeen. 'Yes, sir, I'm in the back lot, sir. I can hear sirens coming down Sussex.'

'Yeah, we hear them, too. Thanks, Mitch. You sit tight. Try to keep anyone from leaving, but don't be a hero. If you can't stop them, get the tag number. Got it?'

Static again, then, 'Yes sir.'

'Spring Lake PD will be there shortly.' I leaned against the porch rail, resting my leg. It didn't hurt, neither did my shoulder, testament to adrenalin's usefulness as a painkiller. Wind off the water picked up and I heard the breakers as Tony sidled up to Thomas and they exchanged harsh whispers.

'Don't worry, guys. He can't hear you.' I dug in my sling for a cigarette and lit one with steady fingers. Moses looked expectantly at me; I tossed him the beaten-up pack.

'You know him?' I asked. 'He's a regular?'

Tony from Bergen County nodded. 'I think so – now that the light's better … it's funny how different he looks, but I'm pretty sure that's Mr Hanley.'

Thomas the Fop, more composed now, lit Moses' cigarette with a silver lighter, then stole one for himself. 'Harold Hanley,' he said quietly.

'He a regular or something?' I asked.

'Comes down on weekends in September only,' Tony said. 'He's a teacher from New Brunswick or something, says he needs this place to get through the opening month of school. He's been doing it for decades.'

I choked on a mouthful of smoke, just as the first Spring Lake cruiser screeched around the corner, red lights ablaze, followed seconds later by a howling ambulance. 'Say that again—'

'Weekends.' Tony took the cigarettes from Thomas the Fop, considered the pack, then flipped them back to me. 'He's a teacher, says he needs the therapeutic whatever of this place, just in September, though. It gives him the strength to get through another year, I guess.'

I knelt by the puddle of Harold Hardass Hanley's blood. 'Sonofabitch.' I shook my head. 'He was my US History and Government teacher at Freehold Catholic High School – it must have been, what – eighteen years ago, maybe 1993 or '94.'

'That's it! Freehold,' Thomas said. 'Up Route 18.'

Marie in my memory: *Can you imagine that? Me and old Hardass Hanley sharing a classroom or hanging out in the teachers' lounge swilling coffee?*

A linen napkin that hadn't been splattered with yoghurt or blood lay crumpled beneath Moses' overturned chair; I pulled it out and draped it over Harold Hanley's shattered face.

Four paramedics and two Spring Lake PD officers hurried up the stairs. I found my cane and limped to a nearby table. Moses Stillman joined me. They'd want us to stick around for questions.

One of the cops, a skinny kid with red hair and a cheese-grater complexion, stopped on the Persian rug. 'Mother of God! Ed, we've got to pull him out of there!' He didn't come any closer, though.

53

Harold Hanley's body was probably the worse thing they'd seen in Spring Lake in the past century.

Kyle's partner, a stout cop with a flat-top and a blurry tattoo on his forearm, took one look at Hanley and sighed. 'No hurry on this one, Kyle.' To one of the paramedics, he said, 'You want to call the coroner, Dave?'

'Yeah, sure, Ed,' Dave replied. Of the four paramedics, he was the only one with his name stitched above the pocket of his shirt. I figured this must give him rank above the others. He flipped open a metal clipboard. 'But I think Jerry's at his cousin's wedding this weekend, up on the Hudson somewhere.'

'Jane Tyler, the ME at Centra State?'

'She's off Sundays.'

'Not today she isn't,' Ed said, scratching something in a spiral-bound notebook.

Thomas the Fop, now every bit as hospitable as the management of the venerable Warren & Monmouth would expect of him, hastily ground out his cigarette and welcomed the officers and medics to the hotel.

Ed, the only seasoned-looking one in the bunch, walked three laps around Moses Stillman's ruined breakfast table, taking in the scene, while the paramedics debated whether there was any reason to move Harold Hanley before the medical examiner pronounced him dead. To me, Ed looked like a town cop, no more than two or three years to retirement, without a clue what to do next. How an old dude like him had pulled the eleven-to-seven shift escaped me. Finally he clicked on his shoulder mic and said, 'Spring Lake dispatch, this is 318 out at the Warren & Monmouth.'

Another voice from behind a static curtain: 'Go ahead 318. 5:14.'

He turned to look at Moses and me. Into his shoulder mic, he said, 'Be advised, we need Hodges and a coroner to this location.'

'Copy that 318. Be advised, Spring Lake coroner is unavailable before Monday.'

Jesus, just say that Jerry's at a wedding upstate.

'Ten-four, dispatch. How about the ME over at Centra State on 527?'

'Copy that 318. I will call. Five minutes. 5:15.'

'Ten-four.'

I doubted Spring Lake cops referred to New Jersey State Police detectives quite so informally so I figured Hodges was either the town detective, if Spring Lake had one, or the on-duty detective for Monmouth County. Either way, I'd be here for a while.

Surprising everyone, the paramedics included, Ed knelt beside the broken table. He grunted with the effort of lowering himself, and cursed when his knee cracked a shard of glass. He removed the linen napkin from Harold Hanley's face and checked the body for a pulse.

'He's plenty dead,' Dave offered.

'We need to pull him out of there?'

'I don't think so, not until the ME pronounces him.'

'You guys gonna catch hell for it, leaving him there?'

Dave thought this over. 'Yeah, maybe. Probably. But shit, Ed, that guy's dead. No sense pissing off Detective Hodges.'

'All right ... Let's get him out of there.' Ed stood with a grunt, then dug around in his shirt pocket. Facing the beach, he lit up, ignoring the rest of us, and hummed a tune to himself. I avoided straining to make out the melody. If it was Pink Floyd's *Wish You Were Here*, I didn't want to know.

Since we were waiting for the Ocean County detective, Hodges Whomever, I lit another cigarette, then offered the pack to Moses. 'One more?'

'No thanks.' He crushed what remained of his first and flicked the butt towards the bristly evergreens alongside the porch. 'One's enough. Those things'll kill you.'

'Gotta die of something.' I glanced at the bushes. 'But from the trajectory of that butt, my friend, I'll wager you've smoked your share.'

'Before you were born, Sailor.' Like Tony, all the healthy colour had left Moses' face. He made and held unnerving eye contact with me, afraid to look at Hanley's body, but needing something to distract him from the depressed skydiver who had so dramatically interrupted his morning coffee. I figured a bit of chitchat wouldn't kill either of us. 'So where'd you play?'

'What?' His eyes wandered right.

'Don't,' I said. 'Don't look at him.'

'I—'

'Where'd you play ball?'

He didn't answer and I gestured to Tony. 'Can you get Mr Stillman some water, please?'

Tony, glad to have something to do, checked with the cops and paramedics, then announced, 'That's fine. Waters all around.'

'Thanks,' Moses murmured, twirling his wedding band around and around his finger, hoping perhaps to disappear like Frodo Baggins.

'Where'd you play those nine years?' I tried again, hoping to get him to relax. 'With just one team? Or did you move around?'

Moses obviously felt desperately uncomfortable chatting with a still-warm corpse a few feet away, but he managed a half-smile. 'I pitched middle relief, before they even called it middle relief. Double-A farm, Sailor – I'm not sure there's a team in the western hemisphere I didn't pitch for or against at least once. But it didn't matter; every game was exactly like every other. It wasn't like it is now, with family nights, kids' games between innings, adverts on the outfield walls – back then, playing in the minors was a prison sentence. I remember fields in Ohio where we'd have to chase the cows off before we could have batting practice. The goddamned place was a minefield of stinking cow shit. As a pitcher, I made nine grand a season, with a four-dollar-a-day allowance for food on the road; that was a couple of thousand more than a starting infielder. My roommates and I, we spent every penny on beer, pizza, bags of pot that got you baked after only eighteen or nineteen tokes, and whatever fleabag apartments we could find where the landlord didn't mind five guys crashing on the floor.'

'Sounds *great*,' I said.

Now he did grin. 'It was, for a while. Most of us, the ones who didn't have a chance of playing in the majors, evolved through four phases: hopeful to get called up, injured but still hopeful, injured and jaded, then poor, drunk and numb. I managed to hit all four before my thirtieth birthday. The few who did get called up, they were like gods among us. Invariably they promised to stay in touch, meet up on the road, buy the drinks when we got together – you know the song. But they never did.'

'Like anything, I guess.'

'The best times were when some hotshot big leaguer would get hurt and they'd bust him down to play with us for fifteen days. Granted, some of them were assholes, grade-A self-indulgent pricks only looking to score expensive drugs and booze, but every now and then they'd send us a good guy, some beer-swilling Okie who loved the game and didn't care that he was making money by the barrel.'

'Anyone I'd know?'

'Almost certainly.' Moses accepted a water bottle from Tony. '*Grazie*, Antonio.' He couldn't help but notice the paramedics extracting Harold Hanley from the wrought-iron spiderweb beneath the table. Dave and Ed, wearing gloves, were trying to tug free the support strut that was jammed several inches deep into Hanley's shoulder. It had clearly snapped his clavicle and shattered his scapula. They worked gingerly, with the measure of decorum befitting a dead body in Spring Lake. Moses looked ready to hurl his breakfast, so I decided against regaling him with any of the strategies Huck and I had used to get dead dealers and crack junkies out of car trunks, bathtubs and Shockoe Bottom dumpsters.

I checked my watch: 5:43, still too early to call Jenny.

Staring now, Moses said, 'It isn't like the movies.'

'No,' I said. 'It never is.'

'I hadn't expected the sounds. Corpses don't make sounds in the movies.'

'Or the smells.' I shuddered at the memory of Carl and Claire Bruckner's farm; my stomach still clenched every time I recalled that amalgam of death and cat shit.

'I can't smell anything.'

'Be glad.'

'And why is he twitching like that? Shouldn't they be trying to revive him if he's still twitching?'

I sighed. 'You've been watching too much TV, Moses. He'll twitch for a while; you just need to ignore it. My friend Doc Lefkowitz, the

57

Deputy ME for the Commonwealth back home, he'll tell you stories that'd chill your blood: bodies rolling off the gurney, opening their eyes, exhaling, farting hours after death. There's probably a General Order in Monmouth County that police and paramedics employ all means in their power, *blah, blah*, to maintain the integrity of this poor mother's life, but Moses, *that* is one dead old man, trust me; I've seen my share. I think that cop, the big guy, Ed, he has, too.' I nudged him back into our conversation. 'Anyway, you were saying—'

'What?'

'Where you played?'

'Oh, right, yes. I guess the best years were spent in Ottawa, the Ottawa Pioneers.'

I took a swig of water. 'Bullshit, *Canada*? In the '60s?'

'And '70s,' he corrected. 'I'm not that old, Sailor!'

'Minor league baseball in Canada in the 1970s? Wasn't that like the Ladies' Auxiliary? I thought they were all hockey players that far north – you mean to tell me there were some who couldn't skate?'

'Many,' Moses laughed, 'and they made damned good ballplayers, too.'

'Nine years in Ottawa. *Jesus*. What'd you do on weekends? Ice-fish?'

'Not the entire nine years,' Moses said, 'just the best years.'

'I figured your best seasons would have been in Florida or South Carolina.'

'Arizona,' he corrected. 'I spent a few Winter League seasons pitching for the Yuma Rattlers, and I can say without hesitation that was the worst experience of my significantly-less-than-Hall-of-Fame career.'

'Pitching in Ottawa was better than pitching in Arizona?'

'You have no idea.' Moses stood to test his ankle. 'There was this Italian place, not far from our apartment. The owner was a big Pioneers fan, so he'd have the bus boys box up whatever they had left in the kitchen after closing. We'd finish night games by eleven and pick up dinner on our way home. It was always a surprise: some nights, spaghetti and meatballs; other nights, fettuccini Alfredo – at a buck a bag we didn't care. We could eat as much as we could carry. Beer was $1.30 a six-pack back then, and that skunky Canadian brew really grows on you after eight or ten bottles. I was a twenty-three-year-old with an eighty-eight-mile-an-hour fastball. I didn't know life could get any better.'

'Five guys in an apartment, eating cold Italian food at midnight,' I said.

'Don't forget horny for Canadian women.'

'Yikes.'

'*Go Ugly Early*; that was our mantra.'

It was such an incongruous thing to hear from someone like Moses Stillman, all spruce and neatly appointed, that I sprayed a mouthful of water across the porch, snorting embarrassingly. Kyle shot me a disapproving glare, his cheese-grater brow furrowed. 'Sorry. I'm sorry.' I held up my hands, half-expecting him to put me in cuffs for disrespect.

'What can I say?' Moses added. 'It was Ottawa, not Oslo.'

It was close enough to six for another cigarette, although I'd need to get back on my hourly regimen before too long. 'How's your ankle?' I asked.

'All right, I think.' He took a few steps, then spun on the ball of his foot, checking his flexibility. 'Bruised a bit, that's all. Your shoulder okay? You fell pretty hard.'

'It'll hurt like an unchained nightmare in a couple of hours.' I adjusted the Velcro strap around my neck. 'But right now there's enough adrenalin pumping that I can't feel a thing.'

'You got shot, right?'

'Thanks to the US Secret Service,' I said. 'Your tax dollars at work.'

'I'm retired,' Moses said. 'I don't pay that much in taxes any more.'

I joined him at the porch railing and we watched as a Mercedes convertible and a nondescript Taurus parked near Ed and Kyle's cruiser. A white van with *Monmouth County Coroner* stencilled in boring letters on the door followed about two minutes later.

'Cavalry's here,' I said. 'Come on; they'll want to talk to us.'

I peered up through the torn canvas, trying to get a decent look at the uniform balconies jutting like teeth over the wraparound deck. Beside Hanley's balcony, assuming the old man had been staying in room 6103, a grim-faced gargoyle stared back at me, its concrete mouth snarling down, looking as pissed-off as any sculpture I'd ever seen. I wondered what it'd witnessed. The creature's countenance brightened as the sunlight hit it, but its disapproving glare didn't change.

Two hours passed in a bureaucratic blur. Tony from Bergen County found a vast reservoir of generosity that Thomas the Fop clearly couldn't stomach, and after a non-verbal battle of wills that Tony won breakfast arrived by the wheelbarrow. Paramedics, Spring Lake police officers, county deputies, even Marta Hodges, the on-duty detective from the Prosecutor's Office, ate well: fresh fruit, New York bagels, Technicolor pastries imported from some chichi little bakery on the Lower East Side, and made-to-order omelettes compliments of Chef Sam. I was a long way from digging around in landfills with Uncle Hucker.

After his interview with Detective Hodges, Thomas the Fop excused himself and left in a huff, ostensibly to lock the other porch doors and see to the hotel's inquisitive guests. Hodges impressed me, despite her unorthodox approach to breakfast with a dead body under the table. A fit black woman about forty years old, Hodges looked like she'd just come from a fundraiser golf tournament, dressed in ironed khakis and a *Monmouth County PD* polo shirt. I guessed Sunday mornings were business-casual for crime scenes at the beach. Hodges had arrived with the county's ME and her assistant, a hungry but otherwise bored-looking older guy in a frumpy brown suit. His sole responsibility appeared to be to wait around for the ME to pronounce Hanley dead, which took about fifteen seconds, and then to haul the body to the morgue.

Jane Tyler, the ME, stuck around for all of twenty minutes herself. She confirmed the exact time of Hanley's unexpected arrival at break-fast and busied herself snapping pictures. She bagged his feet, hands and head in different-sized Ziplocs – I wondered why, as it seemed a bit excessive for a skydiver, especially one with a history of visiting this hotel to manage work-related stress. Maybe all suicides required an autopsy in New Jersey? That made sense to me, and I left her alone, content to wait with Moses on the sidelines.

After noting Hanley's core temperature – 95.8 degrees; I overheard her tell Ed and Hodges – Dr Tyler checked his arms for needle marks, peered up his nose and down his throat and scraped out the traces under his nails and on the balls of his feet. With that cursory inspection behind her, Tyler agreed to call Marta Hodges with Hanley's bloodwork as soon as it came back from the lab and promptly left in the green Mercedes.

Wham, bam, thank you, ma'am; no chin-scratching deductions, no brilliant connecting the death to an international conspiracy; just, you're dead, dummy. Now, what's on ESPN?

Detective Hodges had been on the porch for about two minutes before taking over completely. She was irritated with Kyle and Ed for allowing the body to be moved – Hanley was clearly dead; he could've waited where he'd fallen. I wondered how all homicide detectives managed to speak the same language, despite background, geography and cultural differences. Huck would have been proud of her.

'Anyone get photos before you moved him?' Hodges asked, already knowing the answer. She talked down her nose to the Spring Lake cops. *That* bugged me: cops were cops, even here in Spring Lake, which was like being on duty at a country club. We didn't talk down to one another – screamed and swore, yes, but berated and belittled, not so much.

Still, Hodges impressed me. She quickly identified what she needed, what evidence she wanted collected, what she was willing to overlook and who she expected to drop everything and take care of the to-do list for her. Even the guests, a few of the snootier customers who tried to make a case for breakfast on the porch – it *was* a sunny morning, after all – learned quickly that Marta Hodges was in charge. Thomas the Fop hadn't been seen since she dismissed him.

Hodges shuffled papers, signed city and county forms, documented everything in a laptop she'd plugged into a wall outlet, and scribbled ceaselessly in a notebook tucked in the back pocket of her khakis. From a utility bag she withdrew a county-issue digital camera. Tossing it to Kyle, she said, 'Get everything: the awning, the table, all the bloodstains. Put your pen beside them for scale. Then get the victim, any injuries, anything under his fingernails, in his mouth, the works. Be thorough.'

To Ed, she said, 'Master Chief, I need you to interview that chef, the one who went upstairs. Let's find out what she saw, if anything. Please do not go into Mr Hanley's room without me.'

'Yes, ma'am.' Ed deferred immediately; he must have worked with Hodges before. He was not at all interested in a fight, not after screwing up with Hanley's body.

'Then talk to that security staffer, whatshisname.'

He checked his notes. 'Um, Mitch.'

'Mitch. Get his statement, find out what he saw out back. Anyone coming or going? Lights on, then off? Windows open, then closed? Anything. Then have him copy all the security tapes in this place, everything from midnight on, every camera. Send Kyle to Radio Shack in Belmar if you need extra discs. Keep the receipt.'

Ed nodded. 'Sure thing – but Detective, don't you think this is a simple suicide?'

Without looking up from her notes, Hodges said, 'Nothing's ever simple, Chief. There isn't much blood here. That's not a good sign. You've been around long enough to know that.'

'I have.'

'And thanks to whomever sent Mitch out back and that chef upstairs, we've got to punch a few extra tickets this morning. Appease the curious masses. Know what I mean?'

'That'd be him, Doyle, a trooper from Virginia out for a jog, a walk, something.'

Without looking at me, Hodges bent to check beneath Moses' breakfast table. 'I don't know how much blood seeped through the planks. We'll need to get under there, Chief. If we're lucky it'll be concrete and we can tell how much this guy actually bled after his almost-perfect one-point landing. If there's an eight-foot puddle, then I'm willing to look at this as a suicide, but if there's just a bit of blood, we've got a problem.' She decanted a cup of coffee from a silver urn, foregoing sugar or cream. 'His core temp was below ninety-six degrees. That bothers me, too. He could have died up to three hours ago.'

'Why?' Ed asked. 'You know that's a give-or-take figure. It was almost seventy-five degrees out here all night. With the air-conditioning in this place, his room might have been in the low sixties, high fifties – and that's not to mention what medications he might have been taking. Hell, he could have had hypoglycaemia. Ninety-six shouldn't bother you.'

'It bothers me, Chief, because it bothers Dr Tyler. We'll wait for toxicology, see what he was taking. And you're right: maybe he had low blood sugar or diabetes, but until we know for sure, we don't cut corners.'

Ed clearly didn't give a shit either way. 'Fine, Detective. It's your weekend.'

Hodges turned her attention to Moses and me. 'Good morning, gentlemen.'

'Good morning,' Moses said. 'Care to sit down?'

'Thanks.' She introduced herself again for our benefit and pulled up a chair.

'He didn't kill himself,' I said, embarrassed at sounding like a know-it-all. I eased up a bit. 'I'm sorry – I should say, it doesn't look like he bled enough to have killed himself. Both Mr Stillman and I were here when he – um, interrupted us. He didn't speak, didn't appear to breathe, didn't bleed much, and there were only a few post-mortem movements, spasms, whatever.'

Marta Hodges considered my outfit with obvious disdain. 'And who are you? Paramedic Joggers R Us?'

'My name is—'

Moses interjected, 'This is Detective Samuel Doyle of the Virginia State Police, Mrs Hodges—'

'Detective,' she corrected.

'*Detective* Hodges,' Moses pressed on. 'He's the young man who chased down that woman, Molly Bruckner, this summer, the one with the septicaemic plague. You remember seeing that; I'm sure.'

Hodges' countenance didn't change. Still looking me over contemptuously, she said, 'And you just happened to be jogging by, *Detective* Doyle?'

Not interested in a fight, I tried to explain. 'I was just out for a walk this morning. My parents have a place up in Belmar. I'm staying for a few weeks, trying to rebuild some strength in my leg.'

'Well, well, well.' Hodges sipped her coffee. 'Aren't we lucky you were here?'

Hey, back off, sister.

'You have a problem with that, ma'am?' I asked.

'No.' She scratched another quick note. 'It's just I don't often have out-of-town witnesses – *cop witnesses* – at crime scenes taking over investigations and offering opinions.'

'Well, what a tidy life you must lead.' Screw her if polite wasn't working. I said, 'I find that just about everyone at my crime scenes has thoughts on what happened, and rarely do any of them, the innocent ones anyway, struggle to tell me what they're thinking.'

'Why'd you send Mitch out back to the parking lot and Samantha Whatshername upstairs to Hanley's room?'

'Seemed like the prudent thing to do in case Hanley'd been tossed over the railing. I'm not getting around too quickly these days; so having help from the hotel staff made sense—'

She cut me off again. 'You didn't think that maybe you were getting everyone all fired up?'

'Sure, nothing wrong with fired up, Detective. I was alone here.'

'Uh huh.'

'You'd have handled things differently?' Hot blood flared in my cheeks.

'Uh huh,' she said, 'you've got the employees thinking there's been a murder upstairs—'

Now *I* interrupted, 'How do you know there hasn't been?'

Hodges ignored me. 'A tired old man takes a header at five in the morning—'

'And didn't bleed at all.' I half-stood. 'You said so yourself, *Detective*.'

She didn't like that. '*Detective?* You need to sit yourself back—'

'Oh, go to Hell, *Detective* Hodges. You mentioned it not ten minutes ago—'

'I *said*' – she stood and pointed at me. Her nails had been neatly filed, polished – 'I *said* that I wanted to get beneath this deck to see how much Hanley bled out. So anytime you like, Doyle, you can keep your editorial comments to yourself.'

'Yeah, right, whatever,' I said, pissed off, craving a cigarette and

64

an OxyContin and a Scotch and a fucking howitzer to ram down this snooty cow's throat. I was sweating again, and I looked like I'd just come in from a run around the block. With my own badge and my own gun I'd not have taken an ounce of shit from her, but without my badge, without my gun and sitting here in sweaty running clothes, I'd lost something. My usual bullshit swagger had abandoned me, left me here with my gimpy leg to get yelled at by some skirt with a chip on her shoulder. I pretended not to care. 'Look, Detective Hodges, I'm just trying to help you. And Officer – Ed—'

'Hess.'

'Officer Hess there is probably right; there are a few reasons why Hanley's core temp was a bit low. So why don't we—?'

Again, she ignored me. 'You see anyone else out here this morning, Doyle? Anyone along the beach, on the lawn, or passing by?'

'Nope,' I bristled, 'just Mr Stillman here, and the concierge, Reginald, whatever his name is. Tony, the waiter, he brought out some coffee and breakfast, but other than that, I don't recall seeing anyone until Mr Hanley tore through the awning.'

'Uh huh.' Hodges scribbled in her pad. 'Mr Stillman? Anyone?'

'Just Detective Doyle, that's all.' Moses caught my eye. He looked unsettled that cops would disagree in public, or show obvious dislike for one another. 'Thomas and Tony are always around when I wake up. Chef Sam comes in early some mornings, depending on what she has planned for the breakfast buffet. Sunday brunch is a big deal, so she gets here early on Sundays.'

'Uh huh.' Hodges turned to a clean page, kept writing. 'You two eat breakfast together often?' She asked this with just enough saccharine sweetness to get away with calling us fags. Huck would've have made some lesbian cop joke. I couldn't think of one; I wasn't that quick.

Moses missed the insult entirely. 'Um, no. Actually, today's the first time we met.'

Staring at me, but speaking to Moses, Detective Hodges asked, 'Are you in the habit of inviting strange joggers to breakfast, Mr Stillman?'

Moses beamed. 'I am when they're national heroes, yes, ma'am. I was thrilled when Detective Doyle stopped by this morning. *Thrilled.*'

Under her breath, Hodges muttered, 'Hero. *Right.*'

Jenny called before I could tell Hodges to go spank herself. I raised a rude finger, begging a moment and said, 'Hey, honey. You guys awake?'

'Where'd you go?' Jenny didn't sound irritated. I was happy to take that as a good sign; my day might improve significantly.

'I couldn't sleep,' I said, 'I went for a walk.'

'Where are you?'

'Can you come and get me?'

'Where are you, Sailor?'

'Spring Lake, about two miles down Ocean Ave, at the big hotel. I don't know if I can make it back on my own.'

'We're coming,' she said.

I tried to read her mood, but it was tough through the cell phone and an onshore breeze. 'I'll be on the deck, near the main entrance.'

'What have you been doing all this time? Did it take you three hours to walk two miles? What's going on?'

'I'll tell you when you get here.'

'We're leaving now.' I heard her shout for Ben, then the line clicked off. She didn't say goodbye. I saw them in my mind's eye: Anna preparing for Round 73 in her interminable wrestling match with a stuffed Eeyore big enough to eat Tokyo. Ben, barefoot and dragging a plastic dinosaur around the breakfast table, his bathing trunks barely clinging to his narrow frame. And Jenny, checking her watch as she washed the dirty dishes, pulling a T-shirt over Ben's head with one hand while shaking a bottle of formula with the other. She'd throw bottles, pacifiers, diapers, wipes, sunscreen, assorted toys and mismatched flip-flops into our Rhode Island-sized beach bag, jam three towels under her arm, lift Anna and Eeyore – still battling – with the other, use one foot to guide Ben towards the screen door, turn out the lights with her shoulder and close the house up tight with her hip as she ploughed the entire family apparatus down the steps and into the driveway. She'd have strapped Anna and Ben into the minivan and be rolling towards the beach before I'd managed to smoke half my cigarette.

And *I* was the one exhausted and selfish enough to have an affair.

Nice, Sailor. Top of your game.

Ten minutes later, Marta Hodges went to the sixth floor with Kyle Cheese-Grater to finish up in Hanley's room. Moses and I heard, through Ed's radio, that room 6103 had been locked from the inside. When I saw Jenny's minivan I said, 'I'll have to take a rain check on our walk.'

'You're leaving?' he asked. 'You can just leave?'

'Yeah,' I said, 'screw Hodges. I don't work for her. I'll catch up with you another time. I'm interested in hearing more about your years on the road.'

He stood with the confident grace of Gary Cooper. 'Very well, then, Detective Doyle. I hope you'll find your way back down here in the next few weeks.'

'Count on it.' I shook his hand. 'And please, call me Sailor.'

'Moses.' He winked at me like my grandfather might have thirty years ago. 'I'm almost always down here for breakfast, like I said – about 4:37 or so.'

Strange.

'Got it.' I stacked my cutlery on my dirty plate and pushed it towards the centre of the table, signifying to Tony that I was done gorging myself on his excellent free breakfast. The plate nudged Moses' copy of the *Asbury Park Press* and it flopped open, revealing a Louis L'Amour novel. 'Huh. You read westerns?'

'Just when I'm at the beach,' he said, trying to mask a guilty look. He obviously believed his was the only copy of Louis L'Amour in all of Spring Lake.

'Me too,' I said. 'I can't resist them. My wife doesn't get it, but I don't care.'

Moses checked his watch. 'I'll see you again, Sailor.'

'I look forward to it.' I limped to where Ed Hess sat, talking on his phone, I guessed, with his lieutenant.

I borrowed a pen, scrawled my address and phone number in the margin of a surprisingly good sketch Ed had made of the porch, the table, the awning, even Harold Hanley's injuries. *I'm going home.* I mimed.

'Hold on, please, sir.' He covered the phone with one muscular paw. 'How long you in town, Mr Doyle?'

'Another month,' I said. 'I'll be on Belmar beach, near Twelfth Avenue, if you need me.'

'Thanks. See you.' He went back to his call. I hovered a moment, pretending to look closer at his sketch, but instead I was checking out the tattoo on his forearm. It was cheap work and had blurred years ago, but I could still read *USCG*.

From the sidewalk, Jenny called tentatively, 'Sailor? You okay, sweetie?' She wore green Army Surplus shorts over her white, one-piece bathing costume.

Sweetie. Yup, my day's improving; no doubt about it.

Ben came up the sidewalk at a sprint. 'Daddy! Look at how big this house is!'

I grabbed the whitewashed railing and hurried down Rhett Butler's staircase, not wanting Ben anywhere near the broken table or the bloodstained planks. 'It's a hotel, monkey-man.'

He dived into my arms. 'It blocks out the whole sky!'

'Sure does.' I carried him to the minivan, and tried for eye contact with Jenny, but she was wearing sunglasses so I couldn't tell if she was looking at me, or taking in the incongruity of the sunny morning, the manicured grounds, and the grab-bag of police and emergency vehicles parked along the sidewalk.

'What's going on?' she asked eventually.

'You drive,' I said, 'and I'll tell you on the way.'

Halfway through my story I noticed two Belmar cruisers, their lights like rolling gumdrops, parked near the corner of Seventeenth and Ocean. 'What's this?' I asked.

Jenny slowed down. 'Dunno. They weren't here ten minutes ago.'

'Isn't that Seibert's?'

'Yeah.' She rolled down her window. 'Look! The lobster tank!'

Seibert's Seafood was a Belmar mainstay, serving decent fish family-style, which kept the place hopping from well before Memorial Day until long after Labor Day, when the cold northeasterlies finally closed down the Jersey shore for another winter. My parents had loved the place, thinking it classy because you didn't have to unwrap the butter or rip open the sugar. Low expectations. I always liked the haddock sandwiches. I was invariably up for Seibert's, even if it meant a shower and a clean shirt.

The restaurant had one of those massive Plexiglas tanks out front so hungry diners could get to know their own personal lobster five minutes before it was murdered in a vat of boiling water. Two cops were standing there, one taking pictures while the other talked to a squat, elderly woman in a stained apron, maybe Mrs Seibert herself. As we passed we could see a ragged grapefruit-sized hole had been punched in the side. Apart from a couple of claws lying on the sidewalk there wasn't a lobster in sight.

'Jesus!' Jenny shook her head, unbelieving. 'Who steals thirty-five lobsters?'

'Fraternity brothers,' I said.

'What's that scratching on the glass, next to the hole?' She slowed even more. 'Are those *claw marks*?'

'Don't let your imagination run away with you,' I said. 'It looks like a gang-tag. It's odd, though, they normally use paint or marker pens. I wonder why they hung around long enough to scratch it into the glass like that?'

'Some kind of initiation?'

'Maybe,' I said. 'If so, he's one stupid thug. All these Belmar boys will have to do is squeeze some dumbass street kid and they'll have a name.'

'They all look the same to me,' she said, 'the tags, I mean. Are they all scribble-scrabbled like that?'

'Yup,' I said. 'You've got to be able to read *Illiterate Dyslexia* to make heads or tails of most of it. Huck's fluent.'

'Figures,' she said. 'I don't like street gangs. They scare me.'

'That's their goal,' I said. 'If I was investigating this one I'd check the local colleges. School's in session, it's football season, and someone somewhere is having a kegger for the game this afternoon. Clever frat boys might drive around town, copy a gang-tag or two and then make damned certain the local beat cops find it at the scene. No thug I've ever met hangs around long enough to carve his initials into a crime scene – they might paint the stop sign, something to outline their turf, but signing their tag to a felony? Something's rotten.'

Jenny sped up. 'I hope you're right. I don't like thinking there are gang members this close to the house.'

I didn't have the heart to tell her that they were just about everywhere. MS-13 had grown as strong in Northern Virginia, a few miles from our house in Fredericksburg, as they had almost anywhere in the country. Instead, I tossed her a handful of comfort. 'Yeah, no worries. I'm sure it's frat brothers: they've probably got a bunch of horny sorority sisters coming over to watch the Giants this afternoon and they want to make an impression.'

'Thirty-five lobsters-worth?'

'That'd do it,' I said. 'I'm betting they've got table-linen, white wine, the works; all they needed was a main course to get those sorority babes in the mood.'

Jenny pretended to mark reminders off a list. 'And the girls are thinking, *Bring beer. Check. Show up naked. Check.* Would that make an impression?' She put her hand on my thigh and finally looked me in the face.

'Sounds like a recipe for a successful afternoon to me.'

'You okay?' She tightened her grip.

'Yeah; what's a dead body falling out of the sky? No big deal, even if I did have him for US History – twice.'

'That's not what I meant.'

'I know,' I said. 'I'm fine. Are you all right?'

'Let's talk later.'

'All right.'

She took her hand away to make a turn, but I left my leg where it was, not wanting to move an inch, just in case she decided to reach over again. She didn't.

'Too bad about Seibert's,' Jenny said. Back to small-talk.

'Yeah,' I said. *I guess we'll talk later.*

My parents' place had a dead-end hallway, a few feet of unused space beyond the door to the master bedroom. The hallway floor creaked – my father could never get home and into bed, drunk, without waking everyone in the house. Now, as I creaked my way towards a hot shower and a change of clothes, I noticed two suitcases in that cul-de-sac. My dad had bought them to take my mother to Ireland back in the early seventies, before Marie and I were born, and over the years the vinyl had been scratched to hell in train stations, car trunks and airports all over.

'What're these?' I asked without turning around. My stomach rolled. I was glad I had already been through the explosive diarrhoea part of the morning, because I could feel the wheels were about to come off the wagon.

'Can we talk later?' she asked without a hint of animosity in her voice.

'What's wrong with now?' I creaked another step closer to the master bedroom, thinking maybe I'd find sanctuary there.

Jenny waited an interminable moment, then took a deep breath; I swear I felt it empty the hallway of oxygen. She said, 'I found them downstairs. They're for the kids and me – I want to have a plan. I *need* to have a plan, just something to get me through the next thirty days. I don't *want* to use them, Sailor, I swear it, but I've got to have something ready, something so I feel as though I'm working with a net beneath me, you know? That's all. I can't be here waiting for you to screw up and not have a plan of my own.'

'Where will you go?' I felt strange talking to the authentic-imitation oak panelling and the pinstripe wallpaper, but I was too terrified to turn around.

'Hopefully, nowhere.' She creaked a couple of steps up behind me. 'But I've got to have a plan, just in case this doesn't work. Just in case …'

Smouldering rage warmed me from within and I clenched my teeth, held my breath until it passed. *I will not get angry at you, Jenny. I won't do it.* Exhaling deeply, I said, 'Okay. I understand. But I'm not going to screw up, Jenny. I'm *not*.'

'You might, Sailor.'

Creak.

'You gotta have a little faith in me, baby.'

Creak.

'No, I don't: I have to have a plan for Ben and Anna and maybe for

71

me, for my own sanity. That's what I have to do.' She was behind me now; her breath warmed the back of my neck.

'Okay.'

'Let's drive up to Bradley Beach or Ocean Grove today,' she said. 'You've walked enough.'

'Okay.'

In the car, Pink Floyd's *Wish You Were Here* came on the radio and I hit SEEK. I'd listen to anything else – whale songs, didgeridoo for toddlers – but the next station, a New York jazz channel, had Art Tatum wailing like a coked-up madman, his scorching piano hot enough to melt my face. I listened for a minute, then pushed OFF.

'What's the matter?' Jenny said.

'Nothing. Radio's broken.'

She laughed through her nose, then sang ruefully, to herself, '*How I wish, how I wish you were here. We're just two lost souls swimming in a fishbowl, year after year ...*'

Jenny and Ben played in the surf, too close to Curt the Blurry Lifeguard for my tastes. *Jesus, but that kid was in shape. Does he eat nothing?* I couldn't get my body into that condition if my life depended on it. Embarrassed, I kept my T-shirt on all day. I would have welcomed the chance to beat the shit out of Curt just for looking that good – *and* for ogling my wife all afternoon, as if there wasn't a platoon of nineteen-year-old clones in string bikinis circling the lifeguard stand all afternoon, vying for his attention. Silently I prayed that some octogenarian would swim out a bit too far, maybe even get attacked by a shark – not a great white or anything scary, just something large enough and nasty enough to distract Curt, maybe have him earn his keep today, pulling someone – *but not me* – from the breakers.

Then I figured he must be gay, and just interested in the cut of my wife's bathing costume as something he might wear to a nightclub, and Anna agreed with me wholeheartedly as she sucked on Eeyore's ear. 'Doncha think so, Smurfette?' I adjusted the mini-umbrella casting shade down on Anna's blanket. 'He must be gay, right?'

I rooted around in the diaper bag. 'Do you want your bottle?' I propped Eeyore behind her head, made certain every last inch of her was in the shade, then popped the formula bottle into her mouth. She was just old enough to hold it on her own, right up until she dropped it. Just in case, I brushed every errant grain of sand from her blanket, trying to avoid her getting the nipple coated as thickly as a deep-fried cutlet.

'Then Daddy will be in trouble again, Smurfette,' I said, 'and we don't want Daddy in trouble again today, do we? When you're done, we'll take a walk.' I watched Ben splash in the surf, chasing a miniature Giants football Jenny threw for him. He squealed and leaped, and Jenny laughed and clapped for him, not once checking out Curt who was watching them, hawk-like, from his overhead perch. To Anna, I said, 'We'll walk every day; I've got to keep walking—'

Something in the bag caught my eye and I dug through of the piles of baby stuff until I extracted the formula-stained copy of yesterday's *Asbury Park Press*. I brushed off the sand and ducked beneath Anna's frilly umbrella to shade the image I'd only glanced at the day before.

'What the hell?' The photo, taken inside Auntie Carla's pigpen at the Monmouth County Fairgrounds, showed the bloodstained aftermath of the vicious attack on the prize-winning sow. What I hadn't noticed before were the scribbled scratches in one of the weathered slats of the pen. I squinted and brought the page closer to my face, turned the paper ninety degrees and said, 'Sonofabitch.' Anna, thankfully, ignored me.

After dinner I washed dishes while Jenny and Ben read about a bear that learns to ride a bicycle, one of Ben's favourites. I sort-of listened while I sort-of washed dishes and sort-of thought about that photo of Auntie Carla's pigpen. I wondered if those scratches really were a match for the gang-tags on the Seibert's lobster tank.

With the story finished, Ben gave me a kiss and a headbutt and trundled off to bed. Jenny helped him get his PJs on and his teeth brushed. 'Good night, Daddy!' he called.

'Good night, monkey-face.'

'You and me.'

'Me and you.' I didn't know quite what I'd do with myself the first night he forgot our little ritual.

Jenny disappeared into our bedroom and I heard her moving around in there for a few minutes. Then the door closed and the light switched off.

The digital clock on the microwave read 8:23 p.m. – too early for bed. I had two cigarettes left in the pack, so I grabbed my mother's old Bible off the bookshelf, went onto the porch and sat dangling my feet in the snapdragons. I was halfway through my last cigarette of the day and pretending to read from the Gospel According to Mark when Jenny joined me. Even in the dim glow of the porch light I could see the flush in her face. She sat on the top step, too far for me to reach her.

'Really?' I blew smoke towards Pennsylvania.

'What?' She fussed with her hair, then gave up. 'Don't make fun of me, Sailor. I have needs.' She smiled and looked away, embarrassed at using such a pedestrian phrase.

'You know, every time you tickle that thing, an angel loses its wings.'

'*Gains* its wings, stupid,' she joked. 'Why do you think they call it *ringing the bell?*'

I laughed and coughed, too shocked at Jenny's confession to be angry with her for doing it without me. 'Nope,' I said, 'you're wrong. Every time you masturbate, an angel plummets from Heaven, very nasty. It's in the Bible; you can look it up.' I tossed the book to her; it landed with a leathery thunk and slid against her lovely thigh.

'Oh, really?'

'Yup. Joe, chapter sixty-nine, verse sixty-nine.'

'Joe? Or *Job?*'

'Joe.' I got a leg under myself and tried to stand without groaning or farting. I remembered having sex appeal once or twice, about five years earlier. Of course, I'd been whole back then, no rusting parts or gunshot wounds. 'I'd be happy to help you with your *needs*, Jenny; I know what buttons to push. It hasn't been that long.'

'Please, Sailor – let's not joke about *length*.' She took up the Bible and opened the door for me.

'I can get it.' I limped inside.

'Don't make fun of me.' Jenny shelved the book, strode unhurriedly down the hall and disappeared back into our room. My parents' old suitcases waited in the hallway. They were scratched enough to look like a bear had dragged them behind a bicycle.

'I wasn't making fun,' I said. Then, trying to coax her back out, I added, 'You want Dan's Doughnuts tomorrow morning? It's the Doughnut El Dorado, just a few miles from here.'

Nothing.

'*I* want Dan's Doughnuts tomorrow morning.'

Still nothing.

'Shit.' I sat at the dining table, a stained-glass-fruit chandelier the only light in the room. I figured I'd give Jenny some time alone before I trundled down the hallway and into my PJs. My leg felt good; I had the walking to thank for that. And while my shoulder had swelled up after falling into the waves, I decided to forego my usual pharmaceutical clubbing and try to wrangle an honest night's sleep out of whatever peace of mind I'd earned helping the Spring Lake PD at the Warren & Monmouth Hotel that morning. Feeling oddly rejuvenated, I reread the story about Auntie Carla's bloody death at the Monmouth Fairgrounds. I wanted another look at that lobster tank, up close this time. I hoped it would still be there tomorrow.

'After Dan's Doughnuts, though.'

My mother's Bible fell over with a hollow thunk and I crossed to the bookcase and stood it up again. At eight zillion onionskin pages it dwarfed every other book there. I braced it with a Mason jar half-filled with sand labelled *Smathers Beach* and shifted a couple of pictures on the bookcase: Ben in diapers on the boardwalk, my mother holding Anna in the hospital, Jenny and me in snorkel gear off Smathers Beach. About a thousand years before Ben arrived and changed the universe, Jenny looked like any of the scores of pretty college grads I'd known in my early twenties: lean, athletic, tanned, with small, firm tits and trim legs. Even I looked good, also tanned, and wiry, no puppy fat, wearing my early twenties like the promise of a long, happy marriage. Shame everything lied: *Stay thin and healthy? Shit, no. Stay hopelessly in love? Trying. Stay loyal, dependable, steady? Yeah, right.*

And what had Jenny done during these ten years? Not much – just managed a law degree, passed the bar exam, had two kids and balanced wifing, mothering and working without a complaint. She'd stayed fit, lost the baby weight, kept the house presentable for the Fredericksburg Mothers' Mafia, and continued to love me as I worked up a healthy reliance on pills and booze and put on twenty pounds of belly flab – although, granted, that was down to about nine pounds these days.

And now, in her early thirties, Jenny had most of the Suburban Woman's Package all sewn up: solid education, good job, nice kids, tidy house and great prospects. All that was missing was an impregnable marriage to a trim, gainfully employed professional.

I wondered what Jenny had thought when she first realised I was the wrong guy. Did all that pressure build up at once? I didn't remember any frustrated explosions, no white-trash frying-pan-throwing outbursts, no screaming matches; rather, Jenny had asked, nicely: *Please, Sailor, no pills tonight. I don't want to worry.*

And what pressure was on me? Go to work, bring home a pay cheque, keep my dick in my pants, be a decent dad and a bearable husband. It was easy-peasy – and I'd fucked it royally.

MONDAY

Gabriel Lebow

Belmar to Neptune: 1.6 Miles

My plan to sleep through the night came apart by 4:15 a.m. I went to the bathroom, read a few pages of Louis L'Amour by the light of my cell phone and finally gave up. By 4:40 I was dressed in cut-off sweatpants, Jenny's Rutgers sweatshirt and my Nikes. I tugged the straps of my shoulder sling tight, stole a twenty from Jenny's purse, tucked Louis L'Amour into my waistband and headed out. It was only a couple of miles to Dan's Doughnuts so I planned to park myself at the nearby Starbucks and read for a couple of hours, then hit Dan's at seven. I'd be home forty-five minutes later, in time for breakfast, with doughnuts and five miles under my belt.

I'd only gone a couple of blocks when I remembered Moses Stillman. I wondered if he might be up too, working through another pre-dawn breakfast at the Warren & Monmouth. He had left me with an open invitation, providing I was awake and moving by 4:37 – *odd time, whatever* – but I shrugged him off this morning, figuring I'd catch him later in the week for fruit and yoghurt. It'd be a rare day in Hell when fruit and yoghurt could beat down Dan's Doughnuts, which were epically good.

I brought along my cane, but I tried not to use it, and I got all the way to Starbucks without bracing myself once. I ordered a giant coffee, nothing frappéd, lattéd, drizzled, skinnied or non-whipped, just a coffee, then ruined my manly impression by slipping one of those hot-finger thingies onto the cup. The two construction workers in line behind me chuckled and elbowed one another; they were both huge, so I didn't make any off-colour comments or try to pick a fight. Fuck them, anyway; in four hours, I'd be relaxing on the beach with my kids while they'd be sweating over tarpaper on a roof somewhere.

I checked out the Plague Risk chart on the front page of the *Newark Star Ledger*. Associated Press were responsible for the daily chart, which was similar to the Department of Homeland Security's Threat Advisory levels. A few zealots around Richmond still wore surgical masks in public, as if that would make a difference, but most of us ignored the threat level, figuring it for political posturing before the coming election. The mid-Atlantic states had spent five weeks at Plague Risk Level 2: Moderate, and the past five weeks at Level 1: Low. Captain Fezzamo mentioned it the day he suspended me; he thought it would probably run for five months, until the first cold snap froze everything north of Jacksonville. Apparently plague bacteria didn't do well when covered in ice.

I considered buying the paper, then decided to go with Louis L'Amour instead. After hitting the lobby of the Oceanside Hotel across the road for a pack of smokes, I settled in at one of the sidewalk tables. The sun was just colouring the horizon, my leg felt strong and my shoulder was comparatively numb, all fuelling my unexpected but welcome optimism. I propped my ankle on a wrought-iron chair and dived into the American West, where Buck and Harley smoked non-filtered roll-your-owns while driving cattle through Sioux country.

By 6:45, Louis L'Amour had me by the throat. Buck and Harley were in deep shit, driving an ever-waning herd across the prairie. They hadn't found water to bed down by the previous night and now they were desperate to find a stream or a spring. The sun baked the backs of their necks to impermeable leather while they squinted into the distance, hoping to avoid the bands of homicidal Sioux patrolling for wayward cowpokes. Somehow they'd picked up a silent, dangerous-looking cowboy named Otis, who was helping to drive the herd. Clearly, Otis was the story's *deus ex machina*; I couldn't wait to learn whether he really was a shithead deep down.

I turned pages as fast as I could one-handed to see whether Buck, the leader, would take Otis' advice and turn southwest – a mistake in my opinion, *deus* or no *deus* – or listen to his own best counsel and continue on their current trail. There might not have been any bicycle-riding bears but it was a wicked-good story all the same, albeit a pinch politically incorrect, notably with regard to the Native American characters. But I didn't care; it was all I could do to stop reading, dog-ear the page, tuck the book into my sweats and start walking again.

I didn't glance ahead, though I badly wanted to – there was no doubt in my mind there'd be a shoot-out in the next chapter. I thought of Otis and his twin nickel-plated Colts, and if I could take him down with my slip-and-glide .45 It'd probably scare the shit out of him, my futuristic laser pistol bringing death with unimaginable speed. Otis would probably take one look at a Glock 21 and piss right down his leg.

Cameron Drive was a microcosmic socio-economic map of the area from the beach to the old Monmouth County neighbourhoods along Routes 71 and 35. A narrow no-man's-land had emerged between the Garden State Parkway and the beachfront towns, where million-dollar homes on the sand quickly gave way to middle-class single-family places like my parents' house in Belmar; a few blocks west you'd find broken-down cottages and dilapidated split-level shitholes behind storefronts and businesses erected in the 1960s and '70s, a time when nobody cared about zoning laws as long as the local crime bosses were greased twice a month.

Neptune City was doomed to spend eternity in the shadow of the Parkway. It hadn't attracted the same urban-renewal investors in the post-industrial wave that had brought the coffee shops, bookstores and boutiques to the abandoned brick warehouses along the Jersey coast; instead the street gangs moved in – why not; the rent was cheap. Drug use, violent crime and prostitution rose as average incomes fell. Small businesses failed and foreclosures outnumbered the derelict cars along Route 71, where the front lawns grew thick with weeds and the sidewalks buckled in the summer sun and winter cold.

I wasn't old enough to remember the heyday of the Jersey shore; the damage had been done before I was born. When I was a kid, my mother wouldn't allow us on the boardwalk in Asbury Park or Seaside Heights after dark, where stoners and drunks passed out on park benches or ran wildly up and down the boardwalk, babbling incoherently on coke imported from southeast Asia via some street corner north of Central Park.

President Clinton's good times changed things. Some of the seaside towns hired more cops, who ran the gangs west, into the intestinal loops of Monmouth County's highways. The real estate agents returned to those towns which had rebounded nicely. Sadly, Asbury Park and Neptune City had not.

So given the neighbourhood, I wasn't surprised to see the old Ford idling on the corner, just up the block from Robert Morris Middle School. I assumed at once they were dealers, though it bothered me that the Neptune PD would allow them to peddle junk so near a school. For a moment I hoped that maybe they were legit, just some parents dropping their kids off for another day in class.

Then Tubby approached from Steiner Avenue and I swallowed dryly. I knew I'd been right the first time. He was shirtless and shoeless, with hair that might have been washed last *during* the Clinton administration; clearly a crack junkie, maybe a PCP loser out for his Monday morning commute to the corner and back. Strenuous work.

I bet he gives cigarettes to trick-or-treaters every year.

Tubby leaned into the Ford's window while the streetlights overhead flashed from red to green, and before they'd turned yellow again, he was hurrying back across Cameron, barely noticing the kid with the hockey bag.

He surprised me. Most of the students filing through the gate, across the macadam basketball court and into the school were black or Hispanic, but the kid with the hockey bag was white, and apparently trying to hide it. With the hood of his sweatshirt pulled up over his head, he sneaked across Cameron, ducked between a van and an old Chevy and huddled behind a scarred elm big enough to star in a Tarzan movie. I couldn't figure what he was doing until he dug in his sweatshirt pocket for a pack of smokes and lit up.

'Nice,' I grimaced. 'If only you knew, dummy.' For a heartbeat, I thought about crossing over to him, slapping the cigarette out of his mouth and making him call his mother from my cell phone – but it was already after seven o'clock and it was still three blocks to Dan's Doughnuts. If I shifted it, I could get to Dan's and be back by eight, still in time for breakfast with the kids.

A bandy-legged teacher stood gate-duty on the north side of the basketball court, near Cameron. I could see why. With thugs dealing coke and whatever less than a hundred feet away, I'm sure her principal wished she could be out here with a grenade launcher. Instead, she gripped her cell phone nervously as she checked Cameron and Steiner for stragglers: *get 'em in the gate and they'll be safe for at least seven hours. Hey, it's something.*

She hadn't noticed the hooded smoker behind Tarzan's elm.

'Ditching first period?' I asked, but he didn't hear me. 'I invented that one, by the way. Just check the fine print at the bottom; it says: Samuel Doyle, copyright 1991. That's okay, though. You can ditch. I haven't seen a royalty cheque on that for the last decade.'

The kid, Hoodie, didn't look up, just worked that cigarette like a chain-smoker. He must have been hot in that sweatshirt. I had sweated right through Jenny's in the muggy morning air. There wasn't a whiff of sea breeze this morning; the leaves on his elm hadn't budged since I started up the block. The scars in the ancient bark looked like claw marks left by some subterranean beast.

'Maybe he's playing hockey later; it's gotta be cold at the rink, right? His mom probably made him wear it.' I left Hoodie there, thirteen years old, taking his first steps towards lung cancer.

The guard-duty teacher closed the gate, looping a length of chain through the rails. It looked convincing enough. She searched her pockets for something, then called to a group of boys shooting baskets, 'First period; don't be late!'

The hoopsters grumbled under their breath and fired up another round of three-pointers.

I crossed Cameron, not wanting to come up behind a carload of thugs dealing hundred-dollar happiness out their window. They'd not appreciate that, and they might even choose to let me know it in a particularly noisy, painful manner. A step or two from the opposite sidewalk, I noticed the streetlights again. An instant before they flashed yellow, a Monmouth County school bus roared through the intersection, beating the red in the northbound lane. I watched until the lights above Cameron blinked green again, then turned to watch the skinny teacher.

Beneath the elms, colour had faded from the world. The trees, the kid in the hoodie, the hockey bag, the teacher's emaciated cheeks, everything turned the bluish-brown of a week-old bruise. Only the streetlights remained, unfettered colour suspended overhead.

'Something's wrong.' I took a wary step towards the schoolyard. Skinny teacher searched her pockets, looked around on the ground, then went through her pockets again. She checked the gate, checked the sidewalk, considered her phone, then gave up and started towards the building.

7:05 a.m.

Halfway across Cameron, I saw Hoodie push through the gate, jump down the five concrete steps to the basketball court and start towards the rear entrance at a quick jog, unzipping the hockey bag awkwardly with one hand as he ran, like a commuter hurrying to catch a train.

'*Fuck!*' I ran, and it hurt.

He'd left the gate open – thank Christ for that. If he'd heard me come crashing through he'd have turned and shot me before I'd even got down the steps, but luckily, he was watching the skinny teacher, waiting for her to turn; hoping she wouldn't. The fate of the world, as much of the world as I could see, anyway, hinged on that teacher's movements in the next ten seconds.

I wanted to shout, but I wasn't close enough. I needed another four or five steps, needed to be close enough to surprise him. Skinny teacher reached for the double doors.

Turn around, lady. Turn around. *Check once more for stragglers, just once more*, please, *one more time!*

She didn't, and my leg barking in protest, I lunged the last few feet, swinging my cane like an axe. It splintered against the outside of Hoodie's knee.

Skinny teacher was halfway through the door when I screamed,

'Lock down the building! Lock down the motherfucking building!'

Hoodie's leg buckled and he dropped the sawn-off 12-gauge he'd pulled from his hockey bag. He dropped to his knees and yelped like an injured animal.

I was on him a second later, driving his face into the macadam while trying to immobilise his hands. I heard the teacher shout for help.

That's good – hurry!

Hoodie rolled to his left, snarling up at me, and I fell off him, landing on my damaged shoulder. This time I screamed. He kicked out at me wildly and I threw my legs over his, hoping to tangle his up, tie them in such knots that neither of us would get up for a month. Hoodie used his free hand to try and escape, and that was a mistake; I brought my fist down hard on his elbow, hopefully breaking his arm, but probably just dropping him down on the side of his head.

I groped, wrestled, and clawed – *like some subterranean beast* – trying to capture both his hands, or at least his wrists, in mine. I managed it for a second before his hood fell off and my blood froze.

He'd painted his face with greasepaint, the oily stage make-up white opera stars wear to play *Othello* – only this kid hadn't gone from white to black; he'd gone from Caucasian pinky-beige to death-mask white, his face a bleached-skull white, with ebony hollows around his eyes, nostrils, and mouth.

'Jesus fucking Christ!' I slammed my bad shoulder into his lower jaw, again hoping to hear bones break, or to get him to bite off his own tongue.

Hoodie tugged viciously at my hand and snapped at my face, his jaws clicking together – *like one of Molly Bruckner's cats, God help us all!* His sweatshirt rode up at the waist and now my fingers brushed over something bulky and irregular, something he'd wrapped in duct tape and strapped to his stomach.

Holy Mother of Christ – this kid's going to explode – Jesus! Help me, someone help me!

He broke a hand free, elbowed me hard in the ribs and scrabbled around for a string, a pullcord or fuse, some fucking thing. I didn't know what it was, but I wasn't about to let him yank on it. I forced all my weight over my hips, rolling up on him.

'There, motherfucker!' I snarled. 'Now stay down.' I headbutted him as hard as I could on his ear, then again on his temple, and I saw stars. It was the most vicious thing I'd ever done, a hundred miles from the endearing forehead bonk Ben had given me before bed last night.

Hoodie was out of his mind now, possessed by something almost inhuman. He extended his right leg, found a toehold in a crack in the macadam, and with an incoherent cry, he shoved, rolling me onto my back.

I could do nothing but hold onto his wrists. My hand throbbed, ready to cramp, and I cried out, 'No, please – *no*. Someone—' I waited to hear sirens, security guards, Neptune cops, anyone coming to help, but the roar in my ears drowned out the ambient sound.

I'm gonna lose. This kid's gonna kill me. At least they locked the doors. At least the school's locked down. Sorry, Jenny.

Then there was red, blue and green paint – sloppy paint – and a knife. Teardrops. Letters, brown skin and overcast grey sky, blotted out in an all-of-a-sudden eclipse of Heaven. Dark sunglasses, and a phrase, mumbled: 'Not today, mothafucka.' And two loud pops.

Hoodie squealed. It had to be the sound Auntie Carla, the award-winning pig, had made when midnight attackers sliced her to ribbons. He twitched, sort of bounced twice, farted like a rusty muffler, then went still.

I didn't let go.

Sound and sunlight rushed back to New Jersey, bringing colour and catastrophe with them. The world was impossibly loud, rife with shrill screams, barking horns, and bleating fire alarms. And behind it all, unmistakably, as if resonating on another wavelength, one chosen for me by God, was the screech and roar of an old Ford, racing north on Steiner Ave towards Asbury Park.

A teacher, some kid in khakis and a golf shirt, leaned over me. His lips moved; I had no idea what he had said.

Another, an older woman in a polyester print dress, knelt beside me and screamed, her fingers splayed over her mouth and cheeks.

The skinny teacher moved as well; I had no idea where she was going. *Back to that fence, shithead: she forgot the key to the fence, or*

Hoodie stole it Friday before catching the bus home. Another tattoo, this one bobbing up and down on her ankle, grinned at me: a Florida Gator, smiling at the prospect of Seminole Indian for breakfast.

A man in a tie – the principal, maybe – put his hand on the older woman's arm and shouted into a walkie-talkie. He dialled a cell phone, pointed at the building and shouted again.

Other adults came running, some from the school, some from Cameron Drive. I heard everything and nothing, I saw everything and nothing, but I knew where I had to go.

The principal, the one in the tie, held fast to my upper arm, my good arm. I didn't care. Staggering up, I searched for my cane, saw that it was broken like a leg bone, so I left it there. Propping myself up on his shoulder, I dragged the confused principal through the gate and towards Cameron Drive.

He was talking into the radio the entire time; I could make out a little of it: '—don't know yet! ... Cameron Drive ... just the one ... like a jogger, his arm's hurt—'

Just a few more steps, just down here.

His tie fluttered; I didn't know how that was possible – there wasn't any wind, hadn't been even a breath of breeze all morning. Yet his tie waved back and forth, the printed pattern of little Mickey Mouses – *Mickey Mice?* – swinging golf clubs. Around his neck was a New York Islanders lanyard sporting an ID badge; grinning up at me was a younger version of himself, letting me know that his name was C. Porter, Assistant Principal.

'Over here.' It was all I could manage to say. My legs gave way; C. Porter held me up.

'Sir, I really need you to remain on campus with me – sir, the police are on their way. I need you to—'

'Shut up!' I finally broke. 'Shut—' I fell to my knees where the sidewalk cracked to make room for the massive elm that had so deftly hidden the death-mask shooter, Hoodie, while I made jokes about cigarettes and skipping school.

'What's here, sir?' C. Porter tried to understand. 'Was there someone else?' A voice crackled over the radio and he answered, 'I'm not sure, ma'am. He's taken me out to Cameron Drive, and I'm afraid there might be someone else, another student, another gunman – I'll call again in a minute.'

Crackle, crackle.

'Yes, I'll bring him back, or better yet, send the police out here.'

Crackle.

'Not Tompkins, he's got to lead the search.'

Crackle.

'As fast as you can, yes.'

I ignored him, wiped my eyes on my wrist and blinked the gargantuan trunk into focus, then started running my hand over the elm's centuries-old bark. It was there: the same pattern of fissures, an illegible gang-tag carved half an inch deep into the bark. I lost my grip and tumbled into the gutter beside a rusted Dodge with a broken headlight, like a black eye. With the side of my face resting on the macadam and tiny tar-coated pebbles sticking to my cheek, I shouted for Jenny, but she didn't hear me.

A barber shop on the corner of Cameron and Steiner had one of those striped poles hanging outside and I watched, transfixed, as bloody bandages spun towards Heaven for eternity.

C. Porter helped me up. I had pissed myself, like Otis, Louis L'Amour's *deus ex machina*, but I didn't care; there was no *deus* here. 'Is there someone else?' C. Porter tugged urgently at my sleeve. 'Another shooter—? Another kid?'

'What?' The barber pole, that's where I'd first seen Hoodie. He'd come down Steiner from somewhere north of here and crossed Cameron at the corner, behind the drug dealers' Ford POS idling beneath the streetlights.

'Another gunman?' On his tie, Mickey Mice tee'd up multi-coloured golf balls and swung for the fences.

'He came from there, alone.' I pointed towards Steiner. 'That way, north, across the street. Where's your SRO?'

'Officer Tompkins.' C. Porter glanced towards the building. 'He was in training over at the high school; He should be here – I dunno, maybe thirty seconds. He'll take the first two Neptune officers that arrive; they'll go room to room.'

'Good. Keep the building locked down until he clears the place,' I said. 'Who were all those people outside just now?'

'Teachers,' he said, 'first-period planning in the library. No kids.'

'You've got to get them— Ah, damn it. It doesn't matter.' Huck and I had been to a two-day training programme on how to handle school shooting incidents. Having all the off-duty teachers running around the crime scene hadn't been one of the PowerPoint slides. I wiped sweat and tar from my face on Jenny's sweatshirt.

C. Porter's radio crackled again and this time, I heard whoever was on the other end, just a snippet: '—need help getting him back here?'

'No,' he answered, then to me said, 'Sir, we really need to go back to the school. The police are on their way.'

On cue, sirens howled in the distance, lots of them. In about thirty seconds, the whole block would look like it had been plugged in for Christmas. I ran damp fingers over the scars in the elm trunk, discolouring the tree's already two-tone skin.

'Sir?' He had my sleeve again. 'Please, this way.'

We started up Cameron towards the back gate, both of us hesitant. I ignored the trickle of aromatic piss cooling on my thigh and instead focused on getting my thoughts together. Hoodie was dead, either dead, or shot up pretty badly. He'd gone limp, twitched a bit, but he had basically been a wet dishrag before the first teacher had shown up. Some thug – *just a passer-by with a gun?* – had shot him.

'No,' I stopped, 'that's not right.'

'Sir?'

'Wait – just a second. I've got to get my head straight. Wait.' Fear and shock, both as inflexible as oak planks on my chest, began to soften at their edges; my limbs loosened a bit in their sockets. A breath or two, that's what I needed. Brief embarrassment at having pissed my pants flooded over me, then it was gone. Toss it all, anyway. Nobody else cared.

'Sir, are you—?'

'It wasn't a passer-by: it was one of those assholes in the Ford, up at the corner, the dealers. Do you know who they are? Are there security cameras out here? Maybe one in that barber shop? There was no one on Cameron except me and that kid, your student, with the hockey bag. The one who shot him, he came from that piece-of-shit Ford – I think it was an old Fairmont. It was right up there.' I pointed towards the end of the street. 'They were dealing; I saw it. There was a fat guy, shirtless, shoeless, with scribbled hair. He can't have gone far.'

We were at the chain-link gate now and the Assistant Principal was putting the pieces together in his own head. 'Oh my God, sir! Are you saying—?'

I pulled my arm free and pressed my palms hard into my eyes, trying to see it in my memory. 'Yes.'

'But sir—?'

'Yes.' I pressed harder. 'He came from that car.'

'An African-American?'

'Yeah, black guy, early twenties – some gang asshole. A drug dealer. He had tattoos on his face, serious shit, something he probably picked up in prison.'

'He's a *hero*. He may have saved hundreds of people – kids and teachers.'

'He's a thug who just shot a fucked-up adolescent.'

Four Neptune Police cruisers, an unmarked sedan, probably Monmouth County PD, three ambulances, a paramedics' van, and two fire trucks converged on Cameron Drive and Steiner Avenue, effectively closing down traffic in all directions. Pedestrians and locals lined up along the fence; a few tried to get past us onto the basketball court, but C. Porter, thinking quickly, pulled me inside and closed the fence behind us. He locked the gate with a key from a ring affixed to his belt.

'They'll be going room to room now?' I asked.

'Yeah, they'll determine if others were involved—'

'I didn't see anyone.'

'Then we'll clear the kids out, send them home and search the lockers, as well as any book-bags or backpacks they left behind.'

'The teacher who was out here,' I started.

'Ms Martin, Hannah Martin,' he interrupted. 'Is she okay? I didn't see her.'

'She's fine,' I said. 'She was inside before I caught up with Hoodie. But she didn't have the key. She looked around for a while, thinking

88

she had dropped it, then she looped the chain through the gate back there, she didn't lock it in the end.'

'I'll— I'm not sure what—'

'It doesn't matter,' I cut him off. 'I bet they find it in Hoodie's sweatshirt.'

'Who?'

'The kid – the shooter.'

'Gabe. His name's Gabriel Lebow. He's an eighth-grader.'

'Troubled kid?'

'Actually,' C. Porter paused, then said slowly, 'no, not that I'd ever noticed.'

Now I took *his* sleeve. Mickey Mice jumped unnervingly. 'Don't tell *anyone* that, okay? Not a word. Don't talk to anyone but the police, and don't let anyone else in – *anyone*. Not parents, the superintendent – no one gets inside this school until the Neptune Police open the doors. Understand?'

'Yes— Um, yeah, okay.'

'You have no idea what this shithead kid might have rigged inside, in his locker, in the teachers' lounge, wherever. He's got something strapped to his waist already, probably a bomb, so no one should go near it but the bomb squad. Did you call them?'

'I have no idea, sir. I was out here with you.'

'Call them now.'

C. Porter relayed my request to whomever was on the other walkie-talkie, but I didn't know if anyone heard him; I could hear voices charged with emotion shouting, begging and interrupting one another over the radio. Robert Morris Middle School had too many walkie-talkies for their own good; clogged radio traffic made real communication impossible.

'Try your cell phone,' I said. 'Get someone at Neptune Township PD, not your SRO, Tompkins; he won't answer, he's too busy. Tell them we need the bomb squad; we've got at least one device strapped to the shooter's body, and we're keeping everyone clear except medical personnel.'

As if reading my mind a woman, the school nurse maybe, was busily compressing young Gabriel's chest, kneeling in his blood and weeping openly but never breaking her rhythm. I watched for a few seconds, waiting to see if she'd put her lips over his and blow air into his lungs. I wasn't sure I'd've been able to do it, not with his face made up to look like a ghastly Hallowe'en decoration. I hoped she'd be smart enough to avoid the ripcord around his waist.

C. Porter looked down at my hand, still wrapped tightly around his biceps. 'Who are you?'

'I'm no one,' I said. 'I'm a cop, but I'm not from around here.'

He blinked and I let him go. 'Okay,' he said. 'We should get back.'

I dug in my sling for my cigarettes. My hands were shaking badly and I fumbled the lighter. I finally offered one to him.

He shook his head. 'Thanks, but no. Against Board policy.'

On the basketball court, Gabriel Lebow's body lay like a bas-relief sculpture atop a tomb. Onlookers gathered along the chain-link fence where it ran the length of the sidewalk on Steiner and, behind me, down Cameron beneath the elms. Peering into the sunken court, they stood uniformly silent, watching the nurse with her bloody knees valiantly try to save this boy's life. Inquisitive rubberneckers gripped the chain-links with whitening knuckles and silently urged the nurse on, just as they might have willed a running back towards a touchdown. Others held cell phone cameras between the links, hoping to capture a tragedy or a miracle for friends and friends-of-friends-of-friends (a.k.a. frigging strangers) on Facebook.

Only the nurse's cries and the incoherent babbling of the few teachers who weren't locked inside classrooms interrupted the stillness; whatever breeze had lifted the Mickey Mouses tie beneath the scarred elm had disappeared. C. Porter and I watched from the concrete steps beneath the back gate.

The macabre theatre in the round went on until a team of Neptune paramedics took over. The older teacher, the one who'd screamed down at me in the first few seconds after Hoodie'd been shot, escorted the bloodied nurse back inside the building. They looked as defeated as soldiers retreating from a hopeless front. The paramedics moved satchels, a portable crash-cart and a gurney into place, blocking the view from the sidewalks.

With Assistant Principal C. Porter in tow, I hurried across the half-court line and warned the paramedics not to shock Lebow. 'Keep it hidden,' I said, 'but check beneath his sweatshirt. He's wearing something. I didn't get a good look at it, but it's got a fuse, like a pullcord.'

Nodding, one of the paramedics, a beefy kid with a crew-cut, lifted the bloodstained shirt, just far enough to see the duct tape wrapped like mummy bandages. 'Holy shit, Joan! Look at this. We gotta get some help out here.'

Joan, whoever she was, decided to continue chest compressions. Lebow hadn't detonated while the wailing nurse had leaned on him; hopefully he'd flunked bomb making for dummies. Before the EMTs began, however, they made everyone else clear off.

A few of the better-informed onlookers shouted, angry that the medics hadn't powered up their portable defibrillator. Crew-cut loaded a needle with clear liquid, showed it to Joan twice, then injected it into Lebow's arm. When that didn't help he tried again: new needle, different clear fluid, a second double-take for Joan, who was still pressing and counting aloud.

Like the dozens of curious passers-by, C. Porter and I watched Joan push rhythmically on Gabriel Lebow's chest, all the while talking with Crew-cut, who barked requests and directions into a handheld radio. Sirens sounded from everywhere at once. With each compression I winced, waiting for whatever was strapped around Lebow's waist to explode.

The EMTs kept it up, pausing just long enough for a second team to heft Gabriel onto a gurney and load him into an ambulance that had cut through a parking lot and over the soccer field.

I watched and smoked. Maybe ten or twelve minutes had passed since he'd been shot. Gabriel died in a hurry. He'd been ready to; that much was clear.

Police teamed up to disperse the crowd, some in uniform and others in street clothes. Their efforts did little good. Other jurisdictions arrived in short order: Belmar, Avon, Bradley Beach and Asbury Park cops moved in to assist with crowd control, some using their cruisers to divert traffic or close off sidewalks.

I thought I caught sight of Ed Hess and Kyle Cheese-grater, the

Spring Lake cops who'd eaten omelettes with me the previous morning while Harold Hanley hung upside down in the table struts. They pulled their cruiser across Cameron Drive near Tarzan's elm, cutting off westbound traffic from Belmar and Avon. I didn't need to be a sociologist to read the writing on the wall of this one: a white kid, presumably a *Jewish* white kid, armed with a nightmarish assortment of guns, knives and bombs, was tackled by an out-of-state cop, a *suspended* cop, and held down long enough for a black gang member and drug dealer to shoot him dead on the grounds of the local middle school, where, coincidentally, the dealer did much of his business.

Magnificent.

So who's the hero and who's the villain? That's the game we'll all be playing for the next few days, my friends, and me stinking of Starbucks-flavoured piss. What am I doing here?

Right: going for doughnuts: one Boston cream, one sour cream glazed and a cruller for Jenny.

Marta Hodges emerged from double doors at the back of the school. Crossing to where Neptune officers had rounded up witnesses, she peeked inside Gabriel's hockey bag, spoke into a radio and began shouting out orders. An official-looking cop in uniform, probably a Neptune Township sergeant, accompanied her.

'She's the one you need to talk to,' I said to C. Porter. 'That's the Monmouth County detective. Tell her about the Ford, the dealers on the corner. I didn't see them go, but somebody did. And I'd bet you a beer they went north, towards Asbury. She ought to check every security camera along Steiner, anyone who might have captured a partial on the tags or a decent image of the thugs.' I turned slowly, taking in the sheer number of people who had shown up in hope of witnessing a miracle or a tragedy. I looked for Tubby, but didn't find him. He was probably halfway to Valhalla on smack by now. 'Jesus, half these people probably know the two shitheads in that car. Who knows how many of them are customers?'

C. Porter grimaced. He'd probably grown up three blocks away, loved Neptune and wanted to raise his children and grandchildren here. 'That's some nasty cynicism you're pushing, Officer—?'

'Doyle,' I said, 'and one man's cynicism is a Vice cop's Old

Testament truth. You don't like it, fire me. My question to half these people is this: why aren't they at work at seven-fifteen on a Monday morning?'

'Why aren't you, Officer Doyle?' he fired back at me, mistaking my negativity for racism or classism, or some politically-incorrect-ism. I didn't give a shit.

I blew him off. 'Marta Hodges – Detective Hodges. Tell her what you know.'

'Won't she want to talk to you as well? Get some kind of description of the guy with the gun, the killer? I won't know how to say it right.'

'Yup, but I've got to call my wife first. I'll be there in two minutes.'

Marta Hodges spoke with C. Porter for about six seconds before they both turned to stare at me. A look of slack-jawed confusion passed over Marta's face, but she tamed it and tucked it away before anyone noticed.

I waved, *give me one second*, with my cigarette and willed Jenny to pick up her cell phone.

'Doyle!' Marta yelled. 'What the hell are you doing here?'

I didn't answer. *C'mon, Jenny, don't leave me out here in wet pants! Come and get me – rescue me, whatever. I'm scared and I want to go home.*

'Officer Doyle.' Marta made her way across the basketball court, assigning uniformed cops to different posts along the fence. One, a wiry kid with a downy moustache and stringy muscles in his neck, pushed past me to stand beside the back gate, where he watched Cameron Drive and monitored the crowd. He looked about ready to piss in his pants.

No worries, youngster; pretty soon we'll all be doing it.

No one wanted a race riot before lunch, certainly not a twenty-two-year-old standing alone behind a rusty gate he hoped would hold back the entire township.

Jenny's voicemail answered for her.

Marta was three steps away and coming up fast.

I turned my back and whispered quickly, 'Jenny, please come and get me. There's been an accident. I'm at the corner of Steiner Avenue and Cameron Drive in Neptune, just west of 71. And, honey, please, bring me a change of clothes. I love you.'

'Doyle!' Marta grabbed my elbow.

'Good morning, Detective Hodges.' I flipped my cell phone off.

'You mind telling me what you're doing out here this morning? And what the hell's going on? This is a grade-A cluster-fuck, Doyle, and I need to hear something convincing, *Detective*, or you might just leave this schoolyard in handcuffs. You ever go out for a morning jog when someone *doesn't* end up dead?'

'Hey!' I shouted, leaning into it. If our foreheads butted, I didn't care. I'd already headbutted Gabriel Lebow halfway to the Elysian Fields. 'Back off me, Hodges. I just saved you, Neptune Township Schools, Monmouth County and the frigging Garden State from global embarrassment at your inability to control your streets, your kids, even the lock on that piece-of-shit fence. I don't know what that kid had on him, but I bet you his plans were to shoot *everyone* and then blow himself to Hell on an express bus.' I tossed my cigarette towards the foul line. 'You need help? I'll help you. Get everyone you've got north of here looking for a beat-to-hell Ford Fairmont, the colour of primer and dog shit. That's your boy. He's black, and he's got gang tattoos all over his face; he won't be hard to find. They left here about fifteen minutes ago, in a raging hurry, towards Asbury Park or somewhere north of there – Long Branch, the Parkway? Ask the road guys from Neptune Township; they'll know. Shit, half the retards lining this fence are probably his second cousins. Or check with the barber in that place on the corner. He's got to know Tubby—'

'Tubby?' She waved a hold-it-right-there finger in my face. Her nails had been painted soft pink, nothing flashy.

'Some loser, smack junkie, probably. He's black, forty years old and maybe two-thirty. Six feet tall, hairy, shirtless, shoeless, and wearing those shorts – the ones everyone wore back in the eighties, they look like Jimmy Buffett threw up on them—'

'Jams?'

'Right! That's them; jams,' I said. 'You can't miss him.'

Marta softened, just a bit. 'What are you doing out here? This isn't your neck of the woods, Doyle.'

I kept it polite. 'I was just going for doughnuts, Detective. Now, if you plan to arrest me, that's fine, but if you do, you'll not get a pinch of squirrel shit out of me until Captain Arthur Fezzamo and Lieutenant Edward Harper arrive from the CID Office in Richmond. I am a Virginia State Trooper and a material witness to a shooting. I'm not here for you to slap around.'

'Mm hmm.' She pressed her lips together. 'Yeah, I looked into your situation last night, *Officer* Doyle. Just here on convalescence, are you? Or you got something you want to tell me?'

'Fuck off.' I held my wrists out to her. 'We're not having this conversation. You want help, I'll help you. Otherwise, arrest me, and I'll clam up tighter than your grandmother's sphincter.'

'You take any pills this morning, Doyle?' This she whispered; I appreciated that.

I offered my wrists again. 'Captain Arthur P. Fezzamo, Criminal Investigation Division, Virginia State Police. I figure he can be here in two days, give or take.'

'He doesn't want to hear from me, Doyle.'

'Well, as much fun as this little pissing contest is—'

She grimaced.

Damn, that was stupid, Sailor. Why not announce it to the entire neighbourhood?

I went on as if nothing had happened, 'I'm not answering anything until he's here, holding my hand.'

'You're a thorn in his side.'

'Bullshit. You saw the news in July. I'm a goddamned intergalactic hero.'

'Yawn.'

'Yeah, whatever.' I dismissed her with a smirk. 'Either way, we don't go down that road until he's here.'

'You saw the shooter?'

'Looked him dead in the face.'

'Got a tag on the car?'

'Nope.'

'A partial?'

'I told you; I was going for doughnuts, not working.'

She frowned again and I wondered what colour exercise band I'd equate to slapping the attitude out of Detective Marta Hodges. Red: *Just harpoon me and finish me off, why don't you!* That'd be therapeutic.

We stared each other down for ten seconds. I knew what she was going through – I'd been through it all myself, sweating through my new shit-brown suit on the aromatic front porch of Carl and Claire Bruckner's farm not three months earlier. Marta Hodges was in charge, despite the sergeants and shift officers and even the lieutenants crawling all over this place like fleas on a dog. She had an SRO, Tompkins somebody, doing a room-to-room search that might end up with more shots fired and another assailant killed. The entire solar system was in disarray, and in about eight seconds, a television crew would show up and start filming.

I'd watch it later with Ben and a bowl of popcorn. First: footage of angry, mostly black and Hispanic citizens pressing against the school yard fence, shouting for justice. Next, police from local jurisdictions, most of them white boys, show up, using their cars to establish a perimeter, a nasty show of force, with lights ablaze and sirens shouting. Ten minutes later, there'll be footage of a sawn-off Remington 1100 12-gauge shotgun, loaded with Double-0 buckshot for maximum damage. It's resting halfway between the free throw line and the baseline of the Robert Morris Middle School basketball court. But the talking heads won't call it a *basketball court*; nope, they'll call it a *school playground*. Lovely. Then there'll be a close-up shot of a hockey bag loaded with an assortment of guns, bombs, shit, maybe even a flame-thrower. That'd be the best of the lot: news speculation that Gabriel Lebow had an incendiary device on a timer, and no one bothered to check inside the bag. And finally, footage of Monmouth County Detective Marta Hodges as she sucks her thumb and cries for her mother to get her the hell out of here.

Yup, Marta was about to have a shitty day and I didn't envy her. While we read each other's minds, we both realised that I had far less to lose than she did in *our little pissing contest*.

She cracked. Into the radio, she said, 'Monmouth County dispatch, this is Hodges out at Morris Middle. I need you to contact shift officers at Asbury Park and Long Branch PD. We need all available units to search from the beaches to Route 18, north of Cameron Drive in Neptune. We're looking for a Ford Fairmont, greyish in colour, rusted, from—?' She raised a narrow eyebrow at me.

'1985, maybe '86,' I said. 'Jersey registration. No idea on the tag.'

Into the radio, Marta added, 'Mid-eighties. Jersey reg. No partial on the tag.'

A dispatcher replied, 'Copy that, Monmouth. 7:27.'

'Two—' Again she paused and looked to me.

I nodded.

Into the radio: 'Two black males, late teens, early twenties. Consider them armed. At least one has multiple tattoos on his face—'

'And neck,' I said. 'And dark sunglasses.'

'And wearing sunglasses.'

'Copy that, Monmouth. 7:29.'

'Be advised: they're suspects in the shooting here at Robert Morris Middle School. They fled north in the grey Fairmont on Steiner, from Cameron Drive at approximately—'

'Seven-ten.'

'—seven-ten a.m.' Marta stared at a point halfway up the chain-link fence. Sighing, she pressed the CALL button on her radio again. 'Monmouth dispatch, this is Hodges.'

'Go ahead, Monmouth.'

'Contact State Police dispatch at Holmdel Station. Pass along that information and have them monitor traffic on Route 18 and the Parkway. Give them my contact information should they locate that vehicle.'

'Copy that, Monmouth. 7:30.'

Two minutes later, I heard the APB through the open window of an Asbury Park cruiser on the sidewalk. Its engine running and the service radio cranked up to *Led Zeppelin* level, just about everyone in Neptune Township heard it. Our thugs wouldn't get far.

Marta tucked the radio into her belt and pulled a pair of rubber gloves out of a tasteful bag she wore over one shoulder. The tawny leather matched her belt and shoes and complimented the light ochre

97

fabric in her suit. Compared with Sunday morning's polo shirt and khakis, she was dressed for serious police work. I figured she had a court appearance or a meeting with the county prosecutor today, probably a follow-up on the investigation out at the Warren & Monmouth. She tugged on the gloves then waved over to the Neptune cop who'd arrived with her. 'Sergeant Collins!'

'Yeah?' Collins, also wearing examination gloves, was kneeling beside the hockey bag and snapping photos, documenting whatever weapons Gabriel had brought to school. As he typed his notes straight into an iPad, Collins carefully avoided bringing anything into view, where they might be seen, or worse, videotaped for the nightly news or the Internet. 'What do you need, Detective?'

'You hear that APB?'

'Yes, ma'am.'

'Get your LT on the phone, whoever's on duty this morning. We need all the officers you can spare.'

'Got it.' Collins set his iPad on the ground and punched a number on his phone. Waiting for someone to pick up at the station, he said, 'Detective, if you have a business card with your email address, I can forwards these photos and notes to your phone from here.'

Marta crossed half court to hand him one. 'Thanks.'

'Don't mention it,' he said, without standing. 'I'll update you after I talk to the lieutenant.' He frowned down at his phone as if it had insulted him, then pushed another series of buttons.

'*And* when you hear from Tompkins and the troops inside. I expect the school superintendent to be here any second. She's all yours. Work it out with her and Tompkins, however they want to get these kids out of here. Tell the superintendent we'd appreciate it if only one of theirs and one of ours speaks with the media.' She started back towards me. 'I'll be over here with *Detective* Doyle.'

'No school tomorrow?' Collins asked.

'Not likely,' Marta said.

'You'll be a local hero for that one.' He laughed.

Looking at me, Marta said, 'Whaddya know, there's heroes all over this place.'

Irritated, I blew a lungful of smoke at her neatly tailored suit, hoping to stink it up for her meeting with the prosecutor. 'You know something, lady—'

Her radio crackled; she raised a hand to shut me up.

Really, bitch? How about I leave now and you can subpoena me like some asshole informant? I'll be on the beach with my kids if you need me. I turned to leave, asked the cop standing fence duty, 'They give you a key to that thing?'

He didn't answer, but Marta did. 'Doyle' – she waggled her radio in one hand, as if I gave a shit who called – 'one second, please.'

Through the tinny speaker, I heard, 'Detective Hodges, this is Monmouth County. 7:33.'

'Go ahead, Monmouth,' Marta answered, watching me over the radio dials.

'Hodges,' the voice crackled, 'go to two.'

Marta flipped her radio to Channel Two and a quick glance around the schoolyard confirmed that nine or ten other cops did the same. Some things never change.

Marta said, 'Go ahead, Monmouth.'

'Be advised that your victim arrived 10-105, DOA at Jersey Shore medical, Detective.'

She closed her eyes, just for a second or two.

That's right, sister. Your day just got a little bit worse. Still want to boss me around, put me in cuffs? Or do you have bigger fish to wrangle now?

Marta pressed CALL and said, 'Roger that. Thank you.'

'You're welcome, Monmouth. 7:34.'

She pinched the bridge of her nose and pressed her eyes tightly shut. I hadn't noticed how flawless her skin was until that moment, like porcelain. Marta Hodges was beautiful. Of course, that didn't stop her from being an unbridled pain in my ass.

'I need a statement.' Her tone had ratcheted down significantly. She wasn't whipped, not by a long shot, but she was through arguing with me.

'I'll write you one,' I offered.

She shook her head. 'I've got to question you.'

'That's fine,' I said, 'I'll write it up – I'll even use a Monmouth County form, save you a step, and when I'm done, you can come by the house and we can talk all you like. Or I'll come to you. Either way, let's not make this any more difficult than it needs to be.'

She turned a slow circle, assessing the breadth and depth of the shit waiting for her. 'Two hours.'

'I'll have it done, printed and signed.'

'Where you going?'

'My parents' beach place. Twelfth and D in Belmar. Northeast corner.'

'I'll be there' – she checked her watch – 'say nine-thirty, maybe ten.' She motioned for the frightened-looking kid to let me through the gate.

'Yes, ma'am,' he said.

'Actually—' Hodges stopped. 'Why don't you drive Detective Doyle home?'

'Will do, ma'am.' Moustache-cop gestured towards the parking lot, thrilled to leave his post before the riot broke out.

'Please, no,' I said. 'My wife's on the way. She'll be here any second.'

'She won't be able to get past Memorial Drive.'

'I'll walk, really.'

To Moustache, she said, 'Walk Detective Doyle to the end of the block. I want to be sure he gets through this crowd without incident.'

'I'll be fine,' I said, but she was right. While the onlookers had thinned along Cameron Drive – there wasn't much to see now – having someone escort me down the street made sense.

'It's no problem, sir.' Moustache unlocked the gate and held it open for me, but apart from a question or two shouted from the crowd no one harassed us. From the basketball court, Sergeant Collins shouted, 'Hey! Hey, wait! Detective Hodges, I need to sign him in.'

Hodges waved him back. 'I've got it, Sergeant.'

'He keeping the book?' I asked through the chain-link.

She nodded.

'Prosecutor's Office will call me?'

She sniffed. 'Maybe a couple of days. They'll have a goddamned battalion of lawyers assigned to this mess. I wouldn't worry.'

My cell buzzed before I reached the cross street. 'Hey, honey.' I nodded silent thanks to Moustache-cop, who lifted a hand and turned back to the crime scene.

'Daddy, the policeman won't let us through!' Ben sounded fired up, as if someone had put an extra quarter in him this morning. It had to be all the emergency lights. He'd be clawing at the back windows like a caged animal.

'Good morning, monkey-man!' I tried to sound cheery. 'Is Mommy there?'

'Uh huh. She's talking to the policeman out the window.' He moved the phone, and I heard him say, *Mommy, Daddy's on the phone.*

Tell him we can't get there.

I did.

Can he walk?

'Can you walk, Daddy?'

'Sure can, buddy. I don't even have my cane.' *Could* I walk? I had been for the past half-hour, but that had been on some pretty high-grade adrenalin.

To Jenny, Ben said, *Daddy can walk. He doesn't even have his cane.*

Tell him we're at Cameron and 71. That's as close as we can get. Jenny sounded nervous. This was two days in a row she had had to pick me up at a crime scene.

'Daddy—'

'I heard her, monkey-man,' I said. 'Tell Mommy I'll be there in five minutes.

'Okay,' Ben said, 'Daddy, why are all these police and firemen here? Was there a fire?'

'Something like that,' I said. 'I'll tell you when I get there.'

'Okay.' He said something; I couldn't make it out. Then, to me, he said, 'I wish you were here.'

'What?' I played deaf, lying to myself. *He didn't just say that.*

'I wish you were here, Daddy.'

The only breeze I'd felt all morning kicked up, blowing salty air along Cameron Drive like a summer memory. My leg and shoulder suddenly throbbed, as if the sea breeze had been infused with shards of broken glass.

'Daddy?'

101

'I'm coming, monkey-man,' I said, worried that I might collapse with my next step. 'See you in a minute.'

'Bye, Daddy.'

'Bye, buddy.' I inhaled deeply, content to let the ocean air wash over me for a moment and dry the sweat on my face and the piss in my shorts. Another gust freshened the stale streets of Neptune, and a tropical scent, like orchids, found me. I waited. I could see it coming as clearly as that pattern of fissures clawed into the elm tree. 'Come on,' I said to no one. 'I'm standing right here.'

But nothing happened and I limped across Memorial Drive and on to Main Street where Jenny's minivan waited beside a Bradley Beach cruiser with its lights rolling. When she saw me Jenny opened the automatic side door and Ben burst through like a parolee, shirtless, in sagging shorts and mismatched flip-flops. He sprinted down the sidewalk.

'Hey, monkey-man!' I hefted him onto my hip with one arm. 'Did you eat breakfast?'

'Not yet. We thought you were getting doughnuts.'

'I tried.'

His brow wrinkled into furrows. 'Daddy, you smell funny, like pee-pee.'

'Yeah, well, I'm sweaty. Sorry.'

'Can we get doughnuts now?'

'I don't see why not.'

'I want a Boston cream.'

'I know.' I loaded him back into the minivan and strapped him down with a peanut-butter-stained seatbelt.

Anna gurgled from her car seat and I reached in to touch the tip of her nose. She shook a Winnie the Pooh rattle hard enough to knock the silly old bear's IQ down a dozen points. I pulled the minivan door closed and made quick eye contact with Jenny through the window. She'd perfected that look over the past three months: anxious, but doing her best not to look anxious.

As I started for the passenger side a Bradley Beach cop in achingly cool mirror-lens sunglasses watched me go. He leaned against his cruiser, apparently content to spend his entire shift here, cutting off access to Neptune City and the nightmare unfolding at Robert Morris Middle School. He wrinkled his nose and hummed tunelessly to himself. I knew that tune with its four descending notes, sounding like breathless calliope tones, followed by the upbeat five-note response.

There it is. I should've known.

Two hours later, Marta Hodges arrived with bad news.

Ben insisted; so Jenny and I took him to Dunkin' Donuts in Belmar. Thank Christ they had a drive-through window, because I was just about done parading around in my filthy shorts. Ben got his Boston cream and Jenny ordered a cruller – I nearly tore a rotator cuff patting myself on the back for having guessed right.

Would have been better if you'd brought it back for her, shithead. And Dunkin' Donuts can't hold a candle to Dan's; no comparison.

Riding home, I told Jenny about the attempted massacre. I left out the gory details, but I was straight with her about pissing my pants and thinking I was going to die.

She cried; I don't know why. Maybe it was because she thought she might end up alone after all, alone on someone else's terms, some lost, confused kid with a hockey bag full of suffering and death. She hadn't been afraid to be on her own; getting out my parents' old suitcases was evidence enough that she was ready to light the fuse on that idea. But I figured Jenny cried because something horrible had crawled from the muck right at our doorstep: this was a school shooting; every parent's unspeakable nightmare had stalked across Cameron Drive and onto the Robert Morris Middle School basketball court.

Playground. Kids' playground.

At the house, I took a shower, threw my cut-off sweats in the trash and brewed a pot of coffee. I half-expected a white-hot need for OxyContin to take my legs out from under me, but I tried not to think about it. Like a kid counting the hours until his birthday, I figured everything would be all right if I could just keep my mind occupied with something else – Marta Hodges' witness statement would do nicely. I took a handful of Naproxen and poured the coffee.

Jenny loaned me her laptop and I lost myself in a disturbingly clear recollection of the morning's events, leaving nothing out, but avoiding speculation or opinion. Granted, I was a state cop, so my opinions would count more than the average schmuck walking around – I knew I would have to justify my decision to pursue Gabriel Lebow through the back gate, but I didn't want to start speculating on what he might have been planning. Victims' parents almost never appreciate a cop's best guess when it's their teenager on the autopsy table.

Lamb of God, who taketh away the sins of the world, have mercy upon us.

I described Gabriel's hockey bag, his movements behind the elm tree, his (or *his father's?*) 12-gauge shotgun, and the device, whatever it was, strapped around his waist in concise detail, whether to justify my actions or to keep myself out of civil court, I didn't know. Marta could address those sticking points when she officially interrogated me later.

After three pages, I filled in all the bits and pieces that felt thin or unsupported, details I had forgotten first time around.

After four pages, I added the words *In my opinion* wherever I had written something a defence attorney might use against me.

After five pages, I quit. It was enough. Marta could read it, ask me anything she liked, edit the text on Jenny's laptop and have my signature on the bottom line. For the address, I listed our home in Fredericksburg. If I got lucky, the defence counsel would figure I was a late-season vacationer out for a jog.

With Anna in her lap, Jenny read my statement and cried again. Halfway through page two, she reached over and took my hand, squeezing it hard.

When she finished, Jenny wiped her face, indecorously, on one of Anna's burp towels. *There's a move you never see in a singles bar!* I grinned; with a gun to my head I couldn't have helped it.

Jenny simultaneously sobbed and giggled at herself. She sniffed and pushed her hair behind her ears. 'Sailor, what could his parents have done? What made a middle school kid turn into such a – a monster?'

'Dunno, honey; neglect, maybe – both parents working fourteen-hour days? Bullies at school? Drugs – bullies in the street, on the boardwalk. It might have been a combination of things. The assistant principal over there – Porter – he said Gabriel wasn't really troubled, but I don't know what he meant – by the time Huck and I meet these kids, they're generally so far gone on pills or booze they can barely remember their own names.'

She dabbed at her eyes again, this time with a napkin from the table. 'But why kill your classmates? Your friends and teachers?'

'Oh, I bet Gabriel didn't have too many friends at that school. That might end up being the biggest piece of this whole shitstorm. Who knows how many times this kid cried out to his parents and teachers? Shit, Jenny, we may find his parents dead at their house this afternoon. He may have offed them after breakfast this morning, just painted his face up and let fly over a bowl of cornflakes.'

She wrestled with that special torment that came with knowing it had happened so close to us, the street where we spent so much time playing with Ben and Anna. 'Sailor,' she said, finally, 'sweetie, please tell me that we'll never, never miss something so—' She cried again. 'Please tell me we'll never miss something so obvious, so much pain in one of our kids, in Ben. Promise me that, Sailor: I want to hear you say it. This is the most important thing you or I will ever do, and I need—' I took Anna as Jenny broke down. Her chest heaved as she buried her face in her hands and sobbed. This had been a long time coming; things would be better afterwards.

A few minutes later, I held her hand and for the first time she didn't fight me. Pulling her close, I said, 'Jenny, we will never be that distracted, that full of ourselves, that selfish—'

Again. Never again, you mean to say, right, Sailor?

'—it'll never happen to us. I promise.' It felt like a madman's promise, something to save myself from the gallows, but it worked. Jenny went to the bathroom, washed her face and returned to the old Formica dining table just in time to meet Marta Hodges.

The doorbell rang before Jenny could say anything more and Ben came galloping from the playroom shouting, 'I'll get it, Mommy! I'll get it!'

'Benjamin.' Jenny's voice didn't go up a decibel, but Ben slammed on the brakes regardless. She had perfected a don't-make-Mommy-clobber-you tone that made even me sit up and take my elbows off the table. Jenny prompted him: 'What's the rule, monkey-face?'

He stood, Parochial-school straight, and parroted, 'Never open the door unless you or Daddy are there.'

'Right. Are we there?'

'Almost.'

'Could a bad guy get in with us over here?'

'Yup.' He looked at his feet, then bravely made eye contact with her. *Good man!*

'So?'

'So I have to wait for you to come over.'

'All the way over.'

Could a bad guy get in? I didn't know how long Jenny had enforced this rule, but it was a good one. I flashed back to her face, the worry-lines across her forehead when she'd spotted that gang-tag scratched into the Plexiglas lobster tank at Seibert's. I hadn't summoned the courage yet to tell her about Auntie Carla's pigpen or the elm tree. 'It's for me, anyway. Go ahead, buddy; then put a shirt on! What is this, the beach?'

Ben pursed his lips in an endearing imitation of his mother. 'Um – it *is* the beach, Daddy.' He pulled the door open with both hands.

Marta Hodges smiled. She had immaculate white teeth, straight save for one crooked incisor. She said, 'Yes, Detective Doyle, it's the beach.' She crouched down in her skirt, a move they must teach in third grade because all classy women can pull it off with the same demure style. She wore a wedding ring and a delicate gold cross; I hadn't noticed either before – some detective I was.

She extended a hand to Ben. 'Hello there. I'm Marta Hodges.'

Ben beamed. 'Hello Mrs Hodges.' He shook her hand enthusiastically. 'I'm Ben Doyle.'

'Nice to meet you, Ben.' Marta stood and shook hands with Jenny.

I made the introductions awkwardly, with Anna on my chest; Jenny invited Marta in while Ben took off down the hallway as if he were on fire.

'I can't really stay,' she said.

'Don't you need to question Sailor – sorry, Sam?' Jenny asked, handing her my statement.

Marta looked it over, flipping through the pages. She replied without looking up, 'Actually, no, not yet.' She dug inside her suit jacket and came out with a yellow highlighter. Colouring a line or two, she finally looked at me. 'Lebow never fired a shot.' It wasn't a question.

'No,' I said, 'the teacher, Martin – something Martin?'

'Hannah Martin.' Marta filled in the blank. 'You're right: she saw everything.' Checking my notes as if to confirm, she went on, 'She was almost inside, she heard you yell for them to lock down the building. Fearing the worst, she pulled the back door closed and screamed to one of the security staff on duty, someone with a radio. He called the office, and an announcement was made to lock down the classrooms. Everyone did. The librarian and her assistant herded a few kids into the media centre – the library, I guess – and made everyone sit on the floor between the stacks. Doors were locked; lights were off, and no one moved until SRO—' She paged back to the beginning of my notes.

'Tompkins,' I offered.

'Yes, SRO Tompkins led a room-to-room search, which Neptune Township is wrapping up now.'

'So Lebow acted alone?'

Marta coloured another sentence banana yellow. 'I believe so. I haven't had a chance to speak with Officer Tompkins yet. He's leading a county SWAT team in a locker search while our dogs work the entire building, checking any backpacks the kids left behind.'

'The building's empty?' I asked. 'The kids have gone home?'

She placed my pages on the dining table. 'There's a Monmouth County DOT garage across Steiner. The principal, assistant principal and superintendent escorted the teachers and kids, room by room, across to the big warehouse, you know, where they store all the sand and salt for the roads in the winter. Parents can pick kids up there, or they'll cycle the buses through later. I can't imagine we'll release the building by tomorrow so the kids will have a day off. Superintendent Mihalko's been all right, not in my hair too much. We'll see how the afternoon goes.'

'That's good,' I said. 'Sounds like you're letting her do her job and she's letting you do yours.'

'So far,' she said.

Jenny interrupted, 'Can I get you some coffee? Water? Anything?'

'No thanks.' Marta glanced around at my mother's décor, politely ignoring the toys scattered like autumn leaves. She was holding something back. I'd been lied to since my career began; I could read a liar from across a grocery store parking lot. Jenny didn't have an ounce of my experience, but I could tell from her expression that she knew Marta Hodges was full of shit. The other shoe was about to fall.

'You sure, Detective?' Jenny tried again. 'Sailor's got a pot on.'

'I'm fine.' Another bullshit smile. 'I've had my gallon today.'

I decided to press her a bit. 'So you don't need me now?'

Marta took a deep breath and held it. She said, 'Maybe later. Right now I've got to run over to County Psych at the Jersey Shore Med Center and pick up a family therapist, one of their social workers. We're headed out to Lebow's house to talk with the parents.'

'Ah, I see.' I didn't envy her that duty. 'They don't know yet?'

'There's no answer at the house or on the parents' cell phones. The AP said Lebow's mother works out of the house. I'm hoping to catch her before she gets the news third- or fourth-hand.'

That's why she doesn't want to talk to you now. So what's she doing here?

'Okay,' Jenny said. 'Should we stay around the house today? I mean, we don't have too many plans, just a beach day with the kids.'

'Where you going?' Marta asked. 'Right here?' She pointed towards the Belmar boardwalk.

'Sure.' I shifted Anna, propping her up on my sling arm. 'We'll be there all day.'

Marta paused. Neither Jenny nor I had any idea what to say or do next. We both waited.

Finally, Marta said, 'I just felt as though I should stop by to let you know that your story matched what Hannah Martin saw from the back door, after yelling for help.'

'Well, that's good, right?' Jenny said.

'There's a bit more,' Marta said.

Here it comes.

'What?' I asked. 'The hockey bag? What did he have strapped around his waist?'

As she pulled her spiral-bound notebook out of her jacket I noticed a soft leather holster clipped to her waistband, with what looked like a Glock 27: small enough to wear comfortably, but powerful enough to drop a three-hundred-pound cokehead in a bar. She read, 'Lebow had a Remington 1100 12-gauge with the barrel and stock sawn down, an old .38 revolver, a Smith & Wesson six-shooter with duct tape where the grips had cracked. He brought along a bundle of road flares, six of them, taped together with a cheap plastic alarm clock. It looked enough like a bomb, I suppose—'

Wait a minute. Oh, shit, wait a minute, don't say it—

'—and he had an Italian 9 mm, another old one, like whatshisname, the AIDS guy, might have used in *A Farewell to Arms*.'

'Rock Hudson,' Jenny said, not sure where this was going.

'Yeah, him.'

'And?' I prompted.

She turned a page. 'And a pack of cigarettes, a few books of matches, a small flashlight, a three-inch Swiss Army knife, a copy of the *Torah* and a white index card with some Hebrew written on it. One of the Bradley Beach cops thinks it's a prayer, something called the *Sh'ma*. I guess Jews say it—'

'—right before they die,' Jenny added. 'It's a prayer all Jewish kids learn in their first twenty minutes of Hebrew school. They're supposed to say it in the moment before death to ensure the soul's ascendancy, or something like that. It goes *Sh'ma Yis'ra'eil Adonai Eloheinu Adonai Ehad*. There might be more after that. I can't remember.'

Marta looked confused. 'You're not Jewish, are you, Doyle?'

'Look at me, Detective: I'm not two steps off the ancestral potato farm,' I said. 'I married one of the smart ones at Rutgers; I just aimed high and got lucky.'

Jenny blushed.

'So what did he have strapped around his waist?' I asked again.

At last she looked at me. 'It was a water pouch, one of those form-fitting backpacks cyclists and marathon runners wear. Lebow had filled it with gasoline, sealing it except for one small opening. He had stuffed a handkerchief into it, just far enough to get soaked on his walk to school, to seep up enough gas—'

'—to act as a fuse,' I said. 'How'd he plan to ignite it? What was that pullcord, ripcord, whatever it was he kept trying to yank?'

'Exactly that,' Marta said. 'He had rigged the striker on a road flare with some duct tape; one decent yank and he'd have had a spark.'

'That wouldn't explode, though,' Jenny said, 'would it?'

Oh, Mother of God – no, don't let her say it. Don't say it, Hodges.

'No,' Marta said, 'it would have ignited, but not exploded.'

The air rushed from the room and I took an unsteady step back, overcorrected and nearly stumbled into the table. Jenny caught my arm and quickly took the baby. My face broke out in a cold sweat and I swallowed and turned to Jenny. 'Will you open a window, please?'

Jenny's face was ashen. She held my arm a moment longer, then said, 'Sure. Of course.'

Marta pressed her lips together again. *This is why she decided to be nicer to you.*

I breathed through my mouth, fighting to stay upright. 'So, Detective Hodges, you didn't mention his ammunition.'

'No, I didn't.'

Jenny gasped; it said: *We're not ready for this, Sailor.*

Dear Christ, I headbutted him, tried to break his arm, his leg, drove his face into the tarmac, a kid seven years older than Ben. God, forgive me. Jesus Christ, forgive me.

I said, 'How many know?'

'You, me, Sergeant Collins from Neptune Township, and the CSI guy from the Prosecutor's Office, an investigator named Harmon.'

'That's it?'

'That's it.

'Where's the media?'

'On the scene in force right now, but they'll be heading this way once they figure out who you are. Hell, Doyle, it'll make national – that's why I felt I needed to stop by. There's not much I can do about it now, talk to them myself, maybe, give them enough that they leave you alone.'

'But—' My stomach roiled. I needed to empty my guts, puke or shit or something, right away. 'I can't have – we can't have that. Jenny and I can't – I'm not— I'm here getting myself together after an unholy nightmare this past summer, and now I—' The tears came; I didn't try to stop them. 'And now I beat and fight and headbutt, and fucking break my cane over a thirteen-year-old kid who was trying to commit suicide? Who had no intention of hurting anyone?'

'He forced your hand,' she said. 'You had no choice.'

'Oh, yeah, Jesus Christ, I'm sure that'll ease his mother's pain: suspended Virginia cop holds suicidal teenager down so crack dealer can shoot him in the chest. That's just what every grief-stricken mother wants to hear.' I was about two seconds from losing it completely.

Marta ignored my sarcasm; she'd been a cop for long enough. 'I figure he planned to go after the SRO, Tompkins, or maybe hole up in a room full of kids and make someone shoot him – Tompkins, a sniper – but no, he didn't have a round of ammo, nothing. He couldn't have killed a squirrel with a brain tumour.'

I picked up the same cloth Jenny had used to wipe her eyes. Folding it over, I ran it across my forehead and down the length of my face. It smelled of diaper ointment and spit-up. I took a minute, grateful that neither Jenny nor Marta said anything. 'You find the Ford?'

'Nothing yet. Asbury Park and Long Branch are on it, along with the state troops on 18 and the Parkway.'

'Okay.' I crossed to an air-conditioning unit crammed awkwardly into the window that looked like a big-assed burglar trying to escape. I turned the TEMP button to HIGH COLD and let the frigid air hit me in the chest like a winter wind. 'We're going to the beach today. I'll try to avoid the media. We can go up north, to Avon or Bradley, someplace maybe where they can't find me. I'll call my boss. I'll let him know what happened—'

'I can call him if you like,' Marta interrupted, opening her notebook again and groping in her jacket for a pen.

'Thanks.' I gave her the number at CID. 'The last thing I need is more press coverage. We came up here for a quiet month to get me back into shape. I'll give you anything you need for the investigation, Detective Hodges. I'll even go with you to ID the shooter; I'll put the cuffs on myself, if you like. But I need to stay out of the spotlight on this one. I don't have enough fight left in me.'

'I can't control what Gabriel's parents say. I can encourage them to understand your position, your need to protect the kids at the school, but I don't know them and I don't know how they're going to respond. They might—'

'—lash out,' Jenny broke in. 'Of course they will. They'll want the world to know that their unarmed son was attacked by an off-duty officer, badly injured in a struggle and then shot. Isn't that right, Detective?'

Hodges half-nodded. 'Yes, I suppose that'd be the worst of it. They'll say that Detective Doyle had no idea what their son was struggling with emotionally, *cognitively*, whatever baloney armchair psych name they've got for crazy kids these days. And rather than calling for help, Detective Doyle attacked Gabriel after it was too late.'

'But that's not fair,' Jenny argued, 'how was he supposed to know this kid was unstable or suicidal?'

'She's right, Jenny,' I said. 'The media will eat me for breakfast. Half of them will say I'm a hero who *restrained* a felon; the other half will credit me with getting this kid killed after *assaulting* him. It's going to be a Shakespearean fucking tragedy.'

'We can go back home.' Jenny latched suddenly on to that idea. 'Yes, we can pack up and get out of here today, right now.'

'I'm afraid not.' Marta slid a chair back from the table. 'May I?'

'Sure. Sorry,' I said, and sat down myself. 'We can't leave, Jenny. I'm graduating from witness to *possible* suspect and almost certainly to defendant in a huge civil suit.'

'Shit!' Jenny started pacing. 'I don't want to do this, Sailor. I don't—'

'We'll talk about it on the beach, Jenny.' I stared down at the chipped Formica. 'Right now Detective Hodges has important things to do. We've got to let her get on with her morning.'

'I do,' Marta said. She took a few minutes to read my statement through. After a couple of follow-up questions and a bit more high-lighting, she handed me her pen. 'Sketch me the shooter's artwork, please.'

'The tattoos?'

'You said he had multiple tattoos on his face. Can you draw them? Are they anything you've seen before? Gang symbols you're familiar with?'

'Tear drops, far enough down his cheek to see below his sunglasses; so maybe six or seven of those. He had a knife on his forehead. I'm not sure if it had anything written on the blade, you know. And some scrawly design, like letters linked together. I couldn't make out numbers or letters, but if I had to guess, I'd say letters, maybe two, overlapped, like the New York Mets logo. He had shit up and down his neck as well, but I can't recall it. And the sonofabitch wore sunglasses. Those hid half his face.' I drew the shooter's tattoos as well as I could on the back of my statement. 'I can ID him, no problem. If you find him, call me. I'll go out with you.'

Jenny's brow furrowed. She didn't like that idea; it didn't align with our plan to get things right. My chasing bad guys had dragged our marriage through hell. Things weren't supposed to unfold this way, at least not for the next month.

Marta didn't notice. 'All right: I'll ask if one of the gang guys can stop by to talk to you. They've got a laptop full of recent photos; if he's there, you'll find him.' She leafed through the statement again then folded it and tucked it inside her jacket. 'It's good, Doyle. Thank you.'

'No problem. We'll be at Avon today if you need me.' I gave her my cell number and walked her to the door.

'I'm sorry,' she said as I saw her out. 'If I can, I'll keep all that business from the summer under wraps.'

'I'd appreciate that.'

'Thank you, Mrs Doyle.' She stepped onto the porch, her heels thunking on the old planks.

I leaned out as she moved down the sidewalk. 'Any luck on the Hanley suicide?'

'Nothing yet,' she called back, 'though I admit I haven't thought about it all morning.'

I have, Detective Hodges; I'm thinking about it right now: two suicides in two days?

*

113

I locked the door and moved slowly past Jenny, down the hall into the master bedroom. I peeled of my T-shirt and climbed into bed.

'Sailor?' Jenny followed me in. 'You all right, sweetie?'

'I just need to think for a minute.' I pulled the covers under my chin. The sheets felt wrong, the wool of my parents' old blankets too itchy. I struggled to sleep in my own bed at my own house; I was über-sensitive to irritants – hotels, guest rooms, relatives' pull-out sofas: I hated them all.

'You want some water? Your coffee?' She hadn't been this tentative with me since she first showed up at MCV Hospital in July, when she had sneaked into my room on tiptoe, no idea if I was alive, disfigured or covered in buboes.

'Jenny? How old are eighth-graders?' I couldn't quite get my head around the maths.

'Um, thirteen, I guess, but, sweetie, you can't think about that. You can't beat yourself up on this. From any point of view, that kid was deeply troubled and looking to end his life. God, where were his parents?'

'I know,' I whispered. 'It's just that— Jenny, you should've seen him. He was out of his mind – he fought like an adult, like we used to get on domestic calls from forty-year-old men, not thirteen-year-old boys.'

'He was probably on something.'

'We use that excuse too often.' Something crashed in the guest room: Ben playing King Kong in a building-block Manhattan.

Jenny slipped into bed beside me, slid an arm around my waist and another beneath my neck. Pulling me close, she ran her leg over mine, as if she were trying to swallow me up, bodily. 'I know,' she whispered, 'but you can't think of him as a kid, Sailor. He was—'

'A beast,' I found one of her hands and squeezed. 'He tried to bite my face, like one of those cats. I could hear his jaws snapping together. God almighty, it was as loud as the traffic on Steiner.'

'We can stay here all day.' She pulled me closer. 'Just pull the shades, let Ben watch *SpongeBob*—'

'It never ends.'

'It never does.' She cupped the side of my face and pulled my head into the nape of her neck. She smelled tropical, like the orchids from earlier, suntan lotion, or maybe some soap my mother'd left in the bathroom.

'Let's do that,' she said. 'We'll order pizza and stay in.'

'Hide, you mean.'

'Whatever. We'll read and eat and watch TV with Ben and – I dunno, plan our overthrow of Canada.'

'We do have a minivan,' I joked. 'Chances are we could whip most of the Canadian Army in that thing.'

'See?' She hugged me as tightly as she had on our wedding night – tighter, even. 'It's coming together already.'

'I need to get a look in Hanley's room,' I said, without knowing why, 'down at the Warren & Monmouth.'

'What are you talking about?'

'Nothing, really.' I tried to explain. 'It's just some cop thing: my mind is trying to make connections between completely unrelated events. I think I need to go down there and bribe the desk clerk to get a quick look in that room. I keep thinking there's something I'll find, but part of me knows I won't.'

'You're not making sense, Officer Doyle.' Jenny ran her thigh up and down mine, then used it to pull my legs closer to hers. 'What do you think you might find there that you're convinced you won't?'

I couldn't help but laugh. Hearing my own lunacy repeated back to me made me loosen up. I exhaled, and let myself be swallowed up by my wife. I said, 'Since you put it that way, I guess nothing.'

But you're going down there, aren't you, shithead? Yup, probably about 4:37 tomorrow morning. Just another walk down the beach.

Jenny said, 'So, back to my stay-in-all-day idea.' Her thigh moved again, perhaps of its own volition. I didn't care; I wasn't about to argue with skin on skin. *She's coming back to you, Sailor; all it took was another brush with death. I wonder if all married folks are like this.*

'I admit: it has its merits,' I said, thinking, *Don't even bring up the Pink Floyd lyrics, or that calliope music. Let it go, Sailor.*

Ben burst in. 'Daddy! Look what I coloured – look at my picture.' He waved a piece of construction paper in my face. 'I made it for you.'

'Benjamin.' Jenny hit him with that tone again.

'What, Mommy?' He stared down at his drawing, knowing he'd screwed up.

'How do you come into our room?'

'Knock first.' He shifted from one foot to the other, clearly exacerbating his embarrassment with a severe need to take a leak.

'Knock first,' Jenny confirmed. 'You want to try again, buddy?'

'Why don't you go to the bathroom first, kemosabe,' I said. 'I'll wait to look at the picture until you get back.'

'All right, Daddy. Sorry, Mommy.' He left, head bowed, his tail between his legs. Ten seconds later, we heard him in the bathroom, singing about the animals on Mr Mullen's farm.

I shifted a bit. 'It *was* a good idea while it lasted, but maybe we should hit the beach. I don't know that the two of us are strong enough to contain him today.'

Jenny relaxed her protective grip. I hoped we'd sleep a little closer that night, maybe even travel back in time together. With a hand flat on my chest, she sighed. 'Okay. The beach. I need time to get all the lunch and other shit together.'

'Nope! No, you won't.' I sat up. 'I'll do it. Anna's napping. That's good. You read, or work on your computer if you like. Ben and I will get everything together.'

'Sailor—'

'It's fine, Jenny.' I let go her hand, but sneaked another breath of tropical orchids from that miraculous place between her hair and her neck. 'I need something to distract me for a few minutes. Then I'll call Fezzamo.'

She sat up. 'I thought Detective Hodges was calling him.'

'She is.' I found my T-shirt and pulled it back on. With Ben's picture in hand I started for the hallway. 'He'll want to hear from her, you know, that I was sober, not cooked up on pills or sneaking hits from a flask of Scotch. As soon as she confirms that, he'll want to hear from me. This is a potential PR nightmare for him too, so I need him, and Harper, I guess, to hear that I'm laying as low as possible and avoiding the media.'

Ben knocked.

'Who is it?' Jenny said sweetly.

116

'C'mon, Mommy, *you* know.'

'Come in.' She might have been talking to a Bible salesman going door to door.

Ben threw the door open. 'Did you see my picture, Daddy?'

I sat on the edge of the bed. 'No, man-cub. I was waiting for you.'

He held up the construction paper as if for a presentation in art class. The drawing was from the Left-Handed Smudgy Crayon period: light blue sky over dark blue water and sandy brown beach, with the sun, a perfect yellow circle, which had been given a pair of dark sunglasses and a shit-eating grin, normally invisible to the naked eye. To the strand, Ben also added myriad colourful umbrellas, beach blankets, towels, and even a few ergonomically appalling lounge chairs.

I pointed to the lone swimmer, paddling left to right across the idyllic scene. 'Who's that, buddy?'

'That's the bad guy who might try to come in our house if I'm not careful about the door.'

I hugged him close, and coughed to hide the next dip on my emotional rollercoaster. 'You're a good boy, monkey-face. You keep following Mommy's rules and I'll worry about the bad guys, okay?' I wiped my eyes before letting him go.

'Okay, Daddy' – he wriggled free – 'but look: the bad guy doesn't see it.' He pointed to a smudge of darker blue, also moving left to right through the water.

'I didn't see that either.' I ran a fingertip over the shadow. 'What is that?'

'That's the shark, coming to get the bad guy.'

'Ah.' I held the masterpiece up for Jenny. 'Look, Mommy, the shark has arms.'

Disgruntled, Ben frowned up at me. 'Some sharks have arms, Daddy.'

'They do?'

'Yup, round here they do. I saw one outside my window the other night. It was scary.'

'A shark? Really? On land?'

'With arms, uh huh.' He was so endearingly adamant that I hugged him again. 'It had a face like a person, but with a shark's mouth, and arms like a shark's.'

'Sharks don't have arms.' Jenny propped a second pillow behind her head.

'Not *shark* arms, Mommy, but person arms, made out of sharkskin, all grey and drippy.'

'Oh,' I said, 'well, that makes sense.'

'I *saw* it.'

'I think you're done watching *Animal Planet* before bed.'

'Okay.' Ben couldn't have cared less. He took the picture from me and ran for the hallway, hell-bent on the next adventure of the morning.

I looked at Jenny. 'I love you,' I said, 'I do, and I'm sorry. You've got to believe me.'

'I do. I do believe that you're sorry, Sailor; you don't have to convince me of that.'

'I was truly scared this morning,' I whispered now, afraid that God or someone might hear. 'I thought I was done.'

She crossed the bed on her hands and knees; her hair fell down, framing her face. She moved in close.

I held my breath. 'Jenny, I—'

She kissed me, gently at first, then harder, ardently enough for me to know: she was ready for another step forward. I might not yet be forgiven, but Jenny understood how I felt. I tried to fall back onto the bed, to let her take me right there, but she stopped me. 'Not today, Navy boy. You're on beach duty. Your son's waiting for you.'

'Got it.' Lanced clean through by a blast of warm hope, I stood, my leg strong beneath me. 'Beach duty. We'll be packed and ready in twenty minutes.'

'Then you've got to call Captain Fezzamo.'

'Right. Fezzamo.'

The beach stretched from the town of Asbury Park, passing through Ocean Grove, Bradley Beach, Avon by the Sea, Belmar and Spring Lake, to the town of Sea Girt, a seven-mile unbroken ribbon of camel-beige sand. Rich New Yorkers started migrating to the Jersey coast in the 1890s, buying up cheap beachfront real estate they could develop into clean-air, clean-water, alcohol-free, Jew-free settlements for like-minded Christians to spend sober summers reading the New Testament. Ocean Grove, an expensive pseudonym for Neptune Township, had been founded by teetotal Methodists who spent summers in tent compounds just off the dunes; today a few diehards still erected white canvas tents. Back then, seasonal residents kept to themselves, with their own zoning laws, their own mayors and their own taxes. Town lines blurred a bit, but even now, seven Monmouth County towns had seven school boards, seven mayor's offices, and seven police chiefs, on a stretch of beach that could probably be managed by one dedicated supervisor with a kickass assistant and a laptop.

Marta Hodges, the detective who'd drawn the short straw this weekend, had a jurisdictional nightmare on her hands. The shithead who shot Gabriel Lebow could be anywhere. Granted, he probably hadn't run to Spring Lake, but that Ford Fairmont might be spotted in Belmar and pursued through four or five towns before being collared on the Circuit in Asbury Park.

Standing waist-deep in the relatively calm waters off Avon, I scanned the beach, from the dilapidated Casino on the Asbury Park boardwalk down to the gilded cupola atop the big-boned Warren & Monmouth Hotel five miles south. A cool northeasterly breeze reminded me that autumn would soon be whipping down the coast, blowing all the Parkway pollution south and leaving the shore towns freshly scrubbed and smelling clean. As I listened for distant sirens, I thought of Marta Hodges again and said to no one, 'I'm glad I'm not on point for this one. She'll be pouring bourbon down her throat before she's through.'

I'd waded into the water when the chitchat got irritating: *I heard it was a black kid, probably one of those gang members from Asbury Park High School. I bet they never go to class. None of them graduate. It's in* The Press *practically every week.*

Martin's sister sent me a text that she heard from her neighbour's kid that some stranger interrupted a shooting, before the boy was killed.

A shooting?

What stranger?

Just some guy off the street, a jogger.

119

So he was shot?

I don't know. I think it was just the one boy. They haven't released his name yet, not until the families are contacted.

This whole area has gone to shit.

Tell me about it – not like when we were kids. Remember?

Well, it wasn't – you know – like this back then, was it?

Quite the rainbow.

Have they caught the killer?

Dunno. But I bet it was drug-related.

In middle school?

Oh, you have no idea; there're drugs all over that school. The principal should be fired for not cleaning that place up.

I blame the parents.

Oh, you said it.

Jenny, who'd mastered the fine art of ignoring the Bitch Squad back home, simply Zenned out the bullshit while she played with Anna and Ben in the sand. I couldn't stomach it and sought refuge in the water, feeling the sand between my toes and waiting for the first of the TV news vans to drive up. I'd seen half the major networks passing back and forth along Ocean Avenue; they obviously didn't have a goddamned clue where they were going, or what they were looking for. Two thugs in a rusty slate-grey Ford – how hard could they be to find? Unless they were long gone, up the Parkway and headed for Manhattan. I quietly prayed that none of the news jockeys connected the incident with me.

They will, though. Hodges' report will get released to the media. It's just a matter of time.

I don't know how she'd done it, but Marta'd kept my name off the radio all morning. She didn't owe me anything, but I appreciated it, nevertheless, especially after behaving like a jackass at the Warren & Monmouth yesterday.

Sunlight coloured the ocean, brilliantly illuminating the quiet pool of intertidal water between Bradley Beach and Asbury Park. It flickered and danced like diamonds strung on an invisible strand of filament, and I wanted to walk up there and touch them, maybe lift a few precious gemstones off the surface for Jenny. A lone surfer paddled idly on his board, waiting for the wind to pick up or the tide to turn.

Not a bad way to spend the afternoon.

Beyond the jewelled waves was Asbury Park, once a grand old lady of the Jersey shore, now a ghost town rife with abandoned buildings, street gangs and the tangy aroma of raw sewage on the breeze. Hopeful entrepreneurs had recently been buying up derelict land, and some new businesses and restaurants had opened on the boardwalk between Madame Marie's and the Casino ruins, but who knew whether this was just wishful thinking or harbingers of a bright new future for the town.

I thought about all those summers I'd spent here as a kid, all those early morning jogs with Marie, and I felt bad for Asbury Park. Generally I didn't give a shit about that kind of thing; I figured it was because of my sister and her damned running loops: a five-mile sprint from the Casino to the drawbridge and back, the ten-miler from Convention Hall around Lake Como and back, but you had to touch the white street marker at Seventh and E-Street in Belmar or the miles didn't count, and finally the twenty-miler, a ball-busting out-and-back from the Berkeley-Carteret Hotel to the Sea Girt lighthouse – and you had to run a whole lap around the lighthouse, not just get within shouting distance of the frigging thing. I'd never managed that one; why would I? Jesus, twenty miles: who runs twenty miles unless they're being chased by the Frankenstein monster? I always gave up at the lighthouse. I'd collapse, shout encouragement to Marie as she turned north and then lie on the warm stone jetty craving a cigarette until Marie picked me up in Dad's old Dodge. Looking spry as a fifth-grader, she'd lean out the window and shout to wake me up.

We'd been running in Asbury Park the day I came upon the dead body. I'd jogged up the boardwalk while Marie ran hard for Shark River. I felt pretty good that day and decided to hit the beach for another mile or so – running in sand always made me feel as though I had done something out of the ordinary, something *rigorous yet simple*.

The sand hadn't changed since the last century, when sober Bible-thumpers had walked up and down the beach in their three-piece suits or sturdy corsets, badmouthing the Flappers, with their rolled stockings and bare arms. But the corpse, some housewife who'd been depressed enough to try and swim to Reykjavik, was a stark reminder that hard times had fallen on Asbury Park. She was the first dead body I'd ever seen, and though I'd been around hundreds since, she lingered in my memory. I couldn't look at that abandoned boardwalk without thinking of her, her body bloated, all greyish-green, except where she'd been nibbled away by bluefish and stripers.

Jenny shouted and waved my cell phone over her head; it had to be Fezzamo. I started back, my leg feeling stiff but strong in the cool water. I credited all the exercise I'd managed in the past few days, that and the lingering tendrils of Naproxen.

Jenny said something into my phone, held a hand up at me as if to say *wait a minute*, then tucked it inside her beach bag.

I mimed *What?*

Jenny cupped her hands around her mouth and yelled, 'He's sending Huck!'

Huck? Why? When?

I hurried in, as fast as I could. 'Huck?' I gasped, throwing myself onto the blanket.

'Right.' She adjusted the towel over Anna's bassinette. 'He's coming up tomorrow.'

'Why?' I shouted, too loud now, and lowered my voice. 'What for, did he say?'

'You need to call him back.' She opened a small bag of popcorn and handed it to Ben, who ate a few kernels, then tore down the beach, tossing handfuls to a flock of untrustworthy seagulls who looked determined to get him back to their lair for questioning.

'Not too far, buddy!' I watched him run, then sat on a towel. 'Where is he?'

'CID, I guess. He didn't say.'

'I wonder why he's sending Huck – I mean, I'm fine, I don't need Huck.'

Jenny sprayed suntan lotion on my back. For a woman who loved the beach, she had cultivated an unnatural fear of skin cancer. 'He said something about wanting one of the other CID guys, just to help you.'

I didn't want anyone here, but if I had to have one of the CID troops, I was glad it was going to be Huck; Fezzamo had never struck me as stupid; he knew that as well. 'Okay— I mean, what can I do? I just want to lay low, keep my name out of the news, you know?'

'I do.' She rubbed the lotion in, her fingers more therapeutic than loving. I must have been turning pink back there. 'Your shoulder okay?'

I rolled it, testing it out. 'Not too bad. Leg's feeling better. It'll be good to see Huck.'

'Sure – Ben'll be excited. You know, you ought to work out with those bands tonight, just your arm.'

Marriage: God bless whoever came up with the idea that two people would be around each other long enough to sustain three conversations at once.

'I can. I will. I will, Jenny. And when Huck shows up, I'll have him connect with that forensics guy from Neptune Township, whatever his name was—?'

'Collins. And the guy from the Prosecutor's Office was Harmon. They're the only ones besides you and Detective Hodges who know that boy wasn't carrying any bullets, ammunition, whatever.' She found a clean towel in the bag and draped it over my back. 'You're going to burn. You're the only guy in the western hemisphere who can burn in September, Officer Doyle.'

I pulled the corners of the towel tight, like a cape. Huck: the idea grew on me. 'Huck can come, he'll check on me, see that I'm happy and healthy and still married and still sober—'

'And he can report back that you're keeping your eye on the ball.'

'Sure,' I said. 'And he can fill us in on the case.'

Jenny's hand slipped from my shoulder. 'I guess.'

'It's okay.' I turned to look at her.

'You think?' Worry lines tugged her forehead.

Man, she's going to be beautiful when she's fifty. I've got to hang in there; get my ass in shape.

'I love that bathing suit.' I leaned back to kiss her.

She gave me a quick peck on the temple, something she'd give Ben before bed. 'It's white, a fashion atrocity. I still can't believe I bought it.'

'You look good – no, great: every guy on this beach is wondering how it's even possible that you have two kids.'

'Stop it, Sailor.' She shoved me playfully away.

Yup, nothing like a brush with death to take the edge off.

'What?' I said. 'I'm not kidding.'

'I've got two hundred pounds of Day-Glo baby loot that I lug around wherever I go—'

'So maybe you're the babysitter, or the really-involved Aunt Jenny who's hot enough to be a stripper.'

'Yeah, uh huh.' She pouted, deepening her worry lines. 'You tell yourself that, Navy boy.'

Ben squealed as fifteen cackling herring gulls dive-bombed him. He sprinted towards us, crying, 'I don't have any more! I don't have any popcorn!' He threw the bag over his head and two birds caught it in mid-air, tugged a moment, then let it fall to the sand. 'Daddy!'

'Come under here, monkey-man!' I held up one side of my towel and Ben dived into my lap, nearly knocking me over. 'Stay down, buddy,' I whispered, 'I don't think they see you.'

'Daddy, my *legs* are sticking out – they can see my legs.' Panting, he hugged me tightly around my waist, his head and shoulders crammed beneath my arm.

'Hold still,' I warned.

'Okay.' Heat radiated off Ben's body. After a minute, he asked, 'Are they gone?'

A pair of gulls landed nearby. I eyed them, and they ignored me. 'They've left a couple of sentries, but the rest of them have gone down the beach after that lady in the striped bathing suit. I think she had a cranberry muffin.'

Ben squirmed to his feet. Apparently, two-on-one were odds he was willing to risk. Brushing his sandy hair back, he said, 'Do you think seagulls like cranberries?'

'I know they do,' I said.

'Go and get that popcorn bag,' Jenny said. 'You don't want to be a litterbug.'

Ben dashed to retrieve it, carefully skirting the two gulls left to spy on him. He crumpled it up and tossed it to me. 'Here you go, Daddy.'

'You hungry, monkey-face?'

'No. Yes. I guess so. Sure. Can we have chicken fingers, Mommy?'

'Do chickens have fingers?' I asked. 'Maybe to write letters to their grandmothers? Or to count money at the dog track? Whaddya think?'

Ben frowned at me in a stark imitation of his mother.

Jenny said, 'I have to feed Annie, then we can go eat.' She pushed back the umbrella hood on the bassinette and lifted Anna out. I covered Jenny with my towel, ensuring her a thimbleful of privacy.

Ben said, 'C'mon, Daddy.' He grabbed my wrist and leaned back with all his weight. 'I – can't – get – you – up.'

'And guess what, buddy: Uncle Hucker's coming tomorrow for a visit.'

He tumbled gleefully in the sand. 'Uncle Hucker! Woo hoo!'

I found my feet, pulled on a T-shirt, and picked him up. 'You're covered in sand, beach boy. C'mon, we need to clean you off.' I carried him down towards the water.

'Don't throw me in, Daddy.' He gripped my forearms with white knuckles.

'I'm not going to throw you, Obiwan. I'm just going to dunk you to get the sand off, so we don't get kicked out of the restaurant for bringing in a sand monster.'

'All right, but check for sharks first.'

I cupped a few handfuls of water and washed the sand from Ben's legs, back and arms. As I glanced north towards Asbury Park, I noticed that the surfer was gone.

Ben whined when I turned off *SpongeBob Squarepants* for the evening news, 'C'mon, Daddy. I was watching that!'

Jenny was fresh from the shower, wrapped in a fetching Twister towel, complete with coloured circles. As she leaned over, drying her hair with a second towel, she said, 'Buddy, even from the bathroom I can hear it, and I have seen that episode at least three times – and that means you have seen it *thirty*-three times. Turn it off, please.' She ducked back into the bedroom.

'Sorry, monkey-man.' I sat on the old couch with Anna in my lap, gurgling and drooling on Eeyore's head.

Ben whispered, 'C'mon, Daddy, *pleeeese?*'

'Not tonight, guys.' I surfed the channels, heading for New Jersey News on Channel 12. As glad as I was to have moved to Virginia, I still felt a gentle wellspring of pride at having come from a place with enough bullshit going on to merit its own news channel. As ever, New Jersey didn't disappoint. The lead story was a break in a case involving a North Jersey politician, a city council member, who had been using public accounts to launder money received for organs harvested from recently deceased patients at nursing homes and public hospitals. Working with doctors, funeral parlour directors and community leaders, the councilman had used illegal funds to reimburse schools, temples, churches, even the county medical centre for legitimate expenses, then funnelled the same amount of taxpayer dollars into a county slush fund which was used to purchase property in Aspen, Palm Beach and Sedona, as well as entertainments in the form of drugs, cars and scantily clad young ladies.

Martin Scorsese had this place down cold.

The square-jawed reporter who looked like a young Mel Gibson explained the investigation was ongoing but would certainly impact North Jersey communities at their very core in the coming months.

'That's a lot of missing organs,' I mused. 'Did no one notice Aunt Martha looked thinner in her coffin? I can hear them now: *She looks good, so slim. Death agrees with her.*'

Ben climbed onto the couch beside me. 'Did no one notice what, Daddy?' He sipped from a water bottle.

'Nothing, kemosabe, just bad guys doing bad things.'

'Are they around here?' He looked worried.

'North of here, nothing to worry about.'

From the bedroom, Jenny shouted, 'Is it on yet?'

'Nope,' I called back, 'just our trusted community leaders selling organs stolen from dead bodies. God bless us, every one!'

'Tell me when it comes on.'

Ben and I watched a commercial for a pizza place in Long Branch that made me want to drive straight up there and dive into their Meat

Lover's Super-Supreme, a heart surgeon's wet dream if ever I saw one. That was followed by a public service advert for a fund-raising golf tournament at a country club out west, with a well-fed businessman in vomit-coloured slacks teeing off in front of the Jenny Jump Mountains. Finally a thirty-year-old commercial, which had probably been filmed before I went to kindergarten, encouraged New Jersey to attend the world-renowned Monmouth County Fair. Colourful images of farm animals, exciting – if rusty – rides, and popcorn, ice cream and cotton candy vendors, all enticed *children of all ages* to enjoy the fun of the fair. I had seen this very same commercial hundreds – *thousands* – of times over the years; only the dates and hours of operation changed over the decades.

Ben was nearly breathless with excitement. 'Daddy, can we go there?'

'We'll see, monkey-man.'

'I want to ride that spinny octopus thing!'

'Buddy, every ride on that thing was a life-and-death gamble twenty-five years ago. I'm sure that *octopus* has taken dozens of lives since Aunt Marie and I went there as kids.'

He giggled. 'That's not true!'

I thought it over a second. 'Actually, it might be.'

'Can we go?'

'Let me talk to Mommy about it, okay?'

It was all the encouragement he needed. In a flash, Ben was bounding down the hallway. 'You'd better knock first,' I warned.

Jenny met him in the hallway, heaved him into the air, then carried him into the living room. She tossed him onto my father's old chair and wriggled in beside him. 'Is it on yet?'

Ben interrupted, 'Mommy, can we go to the fair? There's an octopus ride and cows—'

Young Mel Gibson was back, frowning at us. 'A terrifying tragedy was averted today at Robert Morris Middle School in Neptune Township—'

'Mommy!' Ben tried again.

'Benjamin Owen: shush! *Now.*' 'Benjamin Owen' meant business. He quieted immediately, looking disgruntled.

Young Mel spoke over video footage taken shortly after Assistant Principal C. Porter and I had met Marta Hodges on the basketball court. 'The community is reeling tonight from news that an eighth-grade student armed with multiple weapons, including this modified shotgun, attempted to enter a back door to the school facility. The community could have been facing a Columbine-style massacre.'

Jenny said, 'I hate that *Columbine-style* has become a perfectly acceptable adjective these days. I absolutely *hate* that.'

Young Mel said, 'The student, whose name is being withheld by the police until his family can be notified, apparently entered school grounds through this gate, near the intersection of Cameron Drive and Steiner Avenue. We understand that the gate had been left unlocked by the on-duty teacher. Monmouth County detectives are investigating whether or not the gunman—'

There it was: call him a gunman.

'—had stolen the key before leaving school last Friday afternoon. Sources in the Monmouth County Prosecutor's Office have confirmed to Channel 12 News that the assailant was interrupted by a passer-by, apparently a jogger. The unknown man tackled the armed student on the school's playground—'

And number two: call it a playground.

'—wrestling him to the ground, where, he was apparently shot by a third man, who entered the playground through the same unlocked gate, according to police reports.'

'Ken, as I understand it, the Robert Morris student was killed, but *not* by the Samaritan who just happened to be jogging by. Is that accurate?' A second talking head, a blonde in pearls and a tasteful blue suit, chimed in with her pretend interruption, a technique popular in local broadcasts, designed to make viewers feel as if they were right there, sitting around the news desk, chatting with their community reporters. Tonight's 'interruption' provided a careful segue from a story about a ghastly tragedy averted to one about a child killed by fugitive drug dealers.

'That's right, Barbara,' Mel-Ken went on, 'Monmouth County Detective Marta Hodges reports that the boy—'

Look at that: now he's a 'boy'.

'—was shot twice in the chest and pronounced dead on arrival at Jersey Shore Medical Center.'

Jenny shook her head in disgust. 'Do you see what they did just there?'

'Ssh—' I held up my hand and immediately regretted it. 'Sorry, one second, please.'

Ben whispered, 'What happened, Mommy?'

Jenny whispered back, 'Nothing, buddy.'

Tastefully Suited Barbara added, 'Tonight, state and local police are searching for two African-American men, both in their early to mid-twenties. They were last seen fleeing the school playground in a mid-eighties Ford Fairmont, greyish in colour, with New Jersey plates. At least one of the fugitives was wearing dark sunglasses and was heavily tattooed on his face and neck.' A sketch-artist's rendition of my tattoo drawings appeared on the screen. It wasn't a dead-on match, but still the drawing pulled my skin into gooseflesh.

Mel-Ken wrapped up, 'Anyone with information on the where-abouts of these men should contact the Channel 12 News hotline. Monmouth County detectives consider these fugitives armed and dangerous.' The hotline number appeared as Mel-Ken sat back in his chair and shuffled a few pages – they might have been menus from a local restaurant for all I knew – and then turned to Tastefully Suited Barbara. 'A terrible tragedy averted there at Robert Morris Middle School today.'

Tasteful Suit: 'And no idea on the identity of the good Samaritan who broke it up?'

Mel-Ken: 'Not yet, but we're promised a more detailed statement tomorrow from the courthouse.'

Tasteful Suit: 'And Robert Morris Middle School is closed at this time?'

Mel-Ken: (uncertain glance down at the menus), 'That's right, Superintendent Mihalko has closed Morris Middle until further notice. We'll carry full details of that story at six-thirty.'

Tasteful Suit: 'I understand some Neptune residents are calling the fugitive killer a hero.'

That's good. Mention it in passing, not in your report. Nice way to stir the pot, Blondie.

Mel-Ken: 'That's true, but we have to remember that the Samaritan apparently had the boy subdued when the shooting took place.'

Also nice: give the network deniability. Well done.

Tasteful Suit: (sympathetic sigh, compassionate headshake), 'Hmm. He might have saved the lives of dozens of students and teachers. It's a tough story.'

Mel-Ken: (practised grimace), 'It sure is.'

Jenny snarled to the screen, 'Oh, shut up, you two.' I tossed her the remote. 'Sorry, Ben: I know Mommy shouldn't say *shut up*. It's not very nice to tell people to shut up.'

Ben didn't care. 'That's all right, Mommy, those people can't hear you. Anna does it all the time but Eeyore never answers her.'

'Does she?' I asked. 'Do you, Smurfette?'

Jenny covered Ben's face with kisses. 'Never answers?' She tickled him until he squealed. 'How dare that donkey ignore your sister!'

Ben squirmed away, howling with laughter. 'Daddy! Help me!'

'All right, let's turn this silliness off,' Jenny said. 'No one mentioned Daddy's name, and it's time for reading anyway.'

'Then dessert!' Ben shouted.

'Then dessert.' Jenny caved without a fight. She raised the remote to shut down Mel-Ken and Tasteful Suit's absurd banter when Mel-Ken moved to the Ocean Grove boardwalk.

'Hold on, what's this?'

Ben and Jenny were still talking, so I leaned in to turn the TV up by hand. A windblown correspondent, nowhere near as handsome as Mel-Ken, spoke into a microphone over a red and white graphic saying MISSING SURFER: '—was last seen surfing here, off the beach at Ocean Grove. Witnesses saw Landon paddling in the waves, but no one saw him come ashore, or swim away. No one reported anyone in trouble on the water. Landon's surfboard was recovered on the Asbury Park beach about an hour ago. The board itself had been badly scratched, as if Landon might have struck a rock—'

There was no wind out there today, not enough for surfing, let alone enough to kill yourself on a rock.

'—or was perhaps struck by a passing boat.'

Mel-Ken appeared in a split-screen image. 'Chris, does anyone know if Jeremy Landon was with friends? Was he surfing with anyone?'

'Ken, at this time details are still coming in, but from what I understand the Ocean Grove beach had only a few visitors today, and no one remembers seeing other surfers. As you can see, the wind has picked up a bit with the incoming tide, but conditions were quite mild this afternoon.'

'Thanks, Chris.' Mel-Ken furrowed his brow for the camera.

'Sure thing, Ken. We'll have a follow-up report on the search for Jeremy Landon tonight at eleven. Until then, this is Chris Sommers, reporting live from Ocean Grove.'

Jenny flicked the OFF button; Channel 12 News went black.

Petrified, Ben stared at the screen. 'Mommy?'

Jenny knelt beside him. 'What's the matter, buddy?'

'Did the shark get that surfer? Did he get *eaten*?'

Jenny hugged him. 'No, oh no, monkey-face. That boy might have hit his head, or got too tired to swim in to shore. Maybe his surfboard got away and he tried to swim after it.'

'Is he okay?'

I jumped in. 'I'm sure he is, buddy. He's probably at a pizza shop with his friends. I bet it's that one we just saw, with the giant pizza with all that meat and cheese on it.'

Jenny took my lead. 'I bet Daddy's right. His surfboard probably got away, and he *didn't* swim after it, because that would be dangerous. He probably came to shore and is waiting for his board to float up on the beach.'

'What about the police? They said it was all scratched up.'

Jenny hugged him again. 'You're such a smart little man; did you know that?'

'What were the scratches, Daddy?'

I deliberately downplayed the whole business. 'The board washed around out there for a while – it might have scraped a rock. It's no big deal.'

'You sure, Daddy?'

'I'm a policeman – we see this kind of stuff all the time.'

'C'mon,' Jenny distracted him, 'it's reading time, anyway.'
'Then dessert.' It wasn't a question this time.
'Then dessert.' Jenny heaved him onto her lap.

TUESDAY

Wish You Were Here

Belmar to Spring Lake and back: 5.3 Miles

Green: *Hey, that hurts.*

Ben woke twice that night, complaining of nightmares about sharks outside his window. Jenny went in first, about one-thirty. A gentle yellow glow from his nightlight brightened the hallway between our rooms. Jenny whispered to him for a few minutes, then all was silent.

Ten minutes later the light went out and Jenny padded quietly back to bed.

'He okay?'

'He's fine.' She pushed her pillow a few inches closer to mine.

Hope rose in my chest, but I dampened it down. *Not yet, shithead. Don't get your hopes up too high. You're still in the dog house.*

Jenny lay on her side, facing me, the blankets pulled up to her chin, but she snaked a hand between the sheets and let it rest, splayed open, on my bare chest. Her fingertips left indelible marks; I knew I'd find five tiny blisters there tomorrow morning. I thought about sliding her hand slowly down my chest and across my stomach. What the hell, if she wasn't up for it, I'd know in a hurry. She might not say anything, but she'd sure as shit roll over. I shook the thought away and tried to ignore my hard-on. *It's okay. One step forward. This is okay.*

'Good night, sweetie,' she said.

'Good night, hon.' I slipped a hand her way, leaving it gently on her thigh, near her knee.

133

Jenny didn't pull away.

Two steps. Good.

Ben screamed.

I sat bolt upright and pressed the faint light on my watch: 3:49.

'I'll go,' Jenny groaned.

'No, no.' I pressed her down gently. 'I've got him.'

Ben's bed looked as though his blankets had erupted. He was sitting up, hugging his knees to his chest.

'Hey, monkey-face.' I peeled the wool blanket back. 'You okay?'

He moaned, 'I had a bad dream, Daddy.'

'The shark monster again?'

'He's outside the window.' He pointed.

I clicked on the bedside lamp. 'No, he isn't, buddy, because there are no shark monsters walking around Belmar at four o'clock in the morning.' I untangled his sheets. 'You can trust me on that.'

Ben wasn't buying it. 'He's out there now, Daddy.'

'I'll look, okay?' I pulled back the linen curtain, probably hung there by my grandmother. Two trees grew in the narrow side yard between my parents' house and the O'Meara place next door. A tall elm – at least I think it was an elm – near the house blocked much of the view outside. Behind it, near the street, grew a scraggly pear tree my father and I had planted one summer a lifetime ago, maybe during one of my mother's naturalist phases when she'd insisted on canning her own preserves or making her own jelly. To my knowledge, the tree never yielded a single piece of edible fruit, but it did attract a colourful, if destructive, family of bluejays every autumn.

'Is he there?' Ben squeaked in terror.

'Nope' – I stepped back, holding the curtain open – 'see?'

He ducked beneath the sheet. 'I don't wanna look.'

'Okay, well, trust me, man-cub, there's nothing out there.' I dropped the curtain, then quickly lifted it again. 'What the hell?'

'What, Daddy?'

'What—? Nothing, buddy – it's nothing.'

'Did you see something?'

'Nope, not a thing,' I lied as a wrist-thick branch metronomed up and down.

There's been no breeze today, certainly not enough to do that.

I squinted, trying to see through the darkness. The elm leaves were quiet, not a rustle.

Raccoon?

'Is it gone?' Ben asked, his voice muffled by the pile of bedding over him.

'It was never there.' I tucked the sheet beneath him and pulled the wool blanket up, but Ben pushed it away.

'Not that one – that one's too hot.'

'They are pretty warm, aren't they? I don't know why Grandma has these heavy blankets on the beds in the summertime.'

'I get sweaty.' He yawned and rolled onto his side. 'Good night, Daddy. I love you.'

'I love you, too, monkey-man.' I kissed his temple. 'Sleep tight, okay? I'm going for a walk.'

Ben, curled into a ball, didn't answer.

Lieutenant Harper had commandeered my Glock 21 the morning he placed me on administrative leave. *With pay, without gun.*

I didn't much care for the Glock anyway; I preferred my Uncle Paul's old Smith & Wesson .357, a nickel-plated revolver that could have brought down the *Hindenburg*. Uncle Paul had given me the cannon for my thirtieth birthday – no papers; no permit. I carried it from time to time as a back-up when working plain clothes with Huck in Richmond. It would fire both .38 and .357 cartridges, but I preferred the heavier loads – if I was going to carry the Lone Ranger's personal howitzer, there was no sense playing with candy-ass rounds. My Glock, a .45, packed a more powerful punch, but those silver bullets always made me feel like I was hunting werewolves.

I pulled on a T-shirt and dug in my gym bag for the Smith & Wesson. Jenny didn't like the idea of me carrying a gun in New Jersey, and I worried a bit now, too: it wouldn't look good, me shooting a prowler with an illegal handgun while on suspension.

Administrative leave.

'Screw it,' I whispered to myself, and clipped the leather holster to the waistband of my sweats, which immediately slipped to my hips. I yanked them up and pulled the drawstring tight.

'Where you going?' Jenny murmured.

'I think I'll take a walk,' I said. 'My leg feels pretty good.'

'No dead bodies today, okay, Sailor?' She didn't roll over, or lift her head.

'Very funny.' I pulled my T-shirt over the gun in case she sat up. 'I won't be long.'

'Ben okay?'

'Fine. Go back to sleep.' I leaned over and kissed her cheek, then pulled on my Nikes, flipped off the porch light and cracked the door an inch or two. I listened. Somewhere, a bullfrog thrummed like an out-of-tune cello, and from the beach, an irritated gull screamed a shrill warning down Ocean Avenue.

Eyes closed, I tuned my ears to the night and waited, counting to one hundred.

Nothing.

Gun drawn, I took two tiptoed laps around the house, checking every shadow and listening to the myriad sounds of Belmar, New Jersey, just before dawn. Finding no one to shoot, I went back inside, returned the gun to my gym bag – Jenny didn't move – grabbed my Louis L'Amour novel and started south towards Spring Lake.

I was halfway up the Warren & Monmouth's flagstone path when Moses Stillman hailed me from his breakfast nook. He sat where he'd been when I met him two days ago, outside the hotel's floodlights and beneath the roving eye of the Sea Girt lighthouse. The striped awning through which Harold Hardass Hanley had plunged was gone, rolled up so as not to call attention to the missing bit.

Moses, lit only by his hurricane candle, stood and called, 'Detective Doyle! A pleasure to see you. Please, join me.'

I waved from the flagstones. 'I'm out for some exercise, not really dressed for this place again today,' I lied; I was here with the specific intention of hooking up, not just for a first-rate breakfast, but to get inside Hanley's room for a quick search.

'Would you stop with all that rot and get up here?' He gestured towards an empty chair. 'I was hoping you'd come by – and really, at this hour, who's going to see you?'

'Good point.' I took Rhett Butler's stairs one at a time, but my leg felt good and I didn't need the handrail. Behind me, the ocean kicked up and dark clouds slogged over the horizon, heralding rain. Maybe we'd take the kids to the library later, or a movie.

'How's your leg feeling?' Moses pulled a chair back for me. 'You make it down here all right this morning? Any cramps or pain?'

'Not bad actually.' I sat. 'And your ankle? Any problems after the other day?'

He hoisted a linen trouser leg and rotated an Italian loafer for my inspection. 'Doing fine, Detective. No squeaks or creaks, just a bit of a bruise.'

'Sailor.'

'Sailor.' Moses opened a napkin in his lap. 'You hungry?'

'Now that you mention it, I am.'

'Excellent.' He slapped a palm on the table, his signature move. 'I've yet to order this morning, but I expect Antonio will be here shortly.

'Thanks,' I said. 'I figured you had a standing order for breakfast.'

'I do,' he admitted, 'but today we'll queue up something different. It isn't every morning I get to host a genuine hero.'

My face reddened. 'Moses, I appreciate the breakfast, but really, we can back away from all the hero stuff. I'm trying to—'

'Yes, yes, yes, I know.' He held up his hands. 'Sorry. I know: you and your wife are trying to put that weekend behind you. My fault. Sorry.'

He wore a light sweater over a golf shirt, while I could have stripped naked and still been sweating from every pore. I'd welcome the rain on my walk home. He handed me a napkin and a laminated menu card with the day's breakfast fare noted in frilly script. 'See what catches your eye.'

'What are you having?' I asked, like a high school girl not wanting to outdistance her date's wallet.

'I dunno – steak and eggs, I suppose.'

'Works for me.' I wedged the card beneath his candle as the wind freshened off the water.

'Your wife know you're down here?'

'She was racking pretty well when I left,' I said. 'I'll call her if my leg cramps up, but I'm hoping to make it back under my own steam today. It'll be my longest trek to date – granted, I'm no threat in this year's New York Marathon, but I'd like to be up to six or seven miles a day before we head back to Virginia. I've been working out with resistance bands as well.'

'It's good to have goals when you're coming back from an injury.' He sounded almost like Amanda the Amazonian physiotherapist. 'Trust me, I've bent, broken, fractured or torn just about every moving part possible, and I can tell you from an abundance of first-hand experience, if you don't have recovery goals, it's all that much easier to hit the hammock.'

'I know what you mean,' I said. 'And this month's particularly important for me, because I'm not just coming back from a broken leg and gunshot wounds.'

'Really?' He leaned forwards, his elbows on the table. 'So what's doing?' Then, 'Sorry, I don't mean to pry—'

'Nah, it'll feel good to tell someone about it.'

Tony appeared through a side door, carrying a tray laden with a porcelain tea set that matched the one Hanley had shattered on Sunday morning. He saw me and said, 'Good morning, Detective Doyle. Nice to see you.'

'Hey, Tony.'

'Will you be joining Mr Stillman for breakfast?'

'Please.'

'Is Chef Sam here this morning?' Moses asked.

'Just arrived, sir. She's got the sous crew loading fresh bread, biscuits and rolls into the ovens now.'

'Very good.' Moses switched to Italian. '*Due doppia espressi, Antonio, per favore. E due bistecca e uova.*'

'Bullshit!' Tony frowned. 'Sorry, sir – it's just that I'm surprised.'

138

Moses said, 'No bullshit, Antonio. We'd like steak and eggs this morning, on my tab. Rare for me, and—'

'Well done.'

He grimaced. '*Medium* well for my guest.' He turned back to me. 'Philistine! What sort of carnivore are you, Sailor?'

'You've never met my wife,' I said. 'Most everything we eat has been burned to within an inch of pure carbon: steak, chicken, breakfast cereal, you name it.'

Moses laughed. 'Rare and medium well, *per favore*, Antonio.'

'Very good, sir.' Tony left, taking the yoghurt and fruit with him.

'You were saying?' He poured two cups of coffee, despite our espresso order.

I sighed. 'I'm bouncing back from a pretty nasty OxyContin habit. I dunno if I was a full-on addict, but I hit the pills pretty hard, especially in the end, around July fourth and all that nonsense at the Bruckner farm. On the one hand, I guess I was badly screwed up, high on painkillers with unnerving regularity, but on the other hand, I have to thank the OxyContin for getting me across those fifteen miles of Virginia hell.'

'I remember reading that,' Moses said. 'You were on foot, right?'

'Dehydrated, hungover, stoned, infected with plague and wearing dress shoes.' I spooned sugar into my cup. 'If I hadn't been deep into the pills that day, I'd never have made it to Ashland. I have to credit the dope for keeping me numb enough to walk, jog, crawl, whatever I did, despite the fever and the aching body – hell, I didn't even know I had a fever until about eight miles out.'

'Nasty bit of business,' he said. 'And no one knows?'

'My wife, my boss, my old partner, the Deputy Medical Examiner for the Commonwealth, and my former mistress—'

'Ouch.'

'You have no idea.'

'So you and your wife—?'

'Right: trying to tie off all the loose threads this month.'

'I see.' He sipped his coffee. 'Well, Sailor, if it's any consolation, we've all been there.'

'Really? Because I have to say, Moses, you don't strike me as the kind of guy who'd get wrecked on illegal meds and fool around on your wife.'

He cleared his throat and adjusted his chair a few inches closer to the table. Candlelight found the crags in his leathery face, ageing him. 'Oh son, you have *no* idea. Remember, I played minor league baseball in the 1970s. We practically invented recreational drug use, free sex and self-absorbed behaviour. I'm just fortunate I married a forgiving woman. If I hadn't, I'd probably be dead by now, or worse.'

'Worse?'

He arched one eyebrow. 'Worse. I'd be living in Ottawa and working as an assistant manager in a grocery store. My Kate was the reason I got out of baseball, found my way back here to New Jersey and got involved in the bond business, which turned out to be fairly lucrative when the smoke cleared on the 1980s.'

'How'd she die? Sorry – if you don't mind me asking?'

'She drowned.' He pointed east towards the whitening horizon. Lightning flickered over the water. 'How did you put it? *About three miles out there.* Kate and our daughter, Lauren, were boating, just an old catboat I'd bought from a friend up in Long Branch. It started as a perfectly pleasant day, but you know how things can change quickly on the water. A furious squall came up, and the waves broke over the boat …' He pondered this a moment, then let it go.

I didn't press him for details. 'Jesus Christ, I'm sorry.'

Moses wiped his face with a napkin. 'Long time ago, Sailor.'

'Yeah, well, I'm sorry anyway.'

Tony returned with our espressos; I changed the subject. 'Have the police been back on the Hanley suicide?'

Tony said, 'They spent most of the day here Sunday, until I left at one-thirty. But I didn't see anyone here yesterday. That detective, whatshername—'

'Hodges,' I said.

'Yeah, her,' Tony said. 'I didn't see her at all yesterday.'

'She had her hands full,' I said.

'That business over in Neptune?' Moses rebounded, pleased with the change of topic.

'Yup,' I said, keeping quiet on my own involvement. 'If she was the on-duty detective, you won't see her out here for days – actually, they'll probably hand the Hanley investigation over to someone else. That shooting at Morris Middle School will tie her up for weeks.'

Tony nodded. He was a good-looking kid, maybe twenty-two, with muscular, southern-European good looks and a thick head of wind-blown hair. He said, 'I dunno if they found anything. They were in Mr Hanley's room and that hallway for a long time. Rumour is the old guy just got frustrated and took a header off the balcony. The door was locked, and no one else was inside the room – no overnight guests, girlfriends, boyfriends, whatever. You know.'

Moses said, 'Ah, the old locked-door mystery.'

'The what?' Tony slipped his tray beneath one arm, but he didn't sit down. Things were relaxed at five in the morning, but certain protocols reigned regardless of the hour.

'Locked-door mystery,' Moses said. 'A favourite of Arthur Conan Doyle, the gentleman who wrote the Sherlock Holmes mysteries. He published several stories about bodies, obviously murdered, but discovered in a room that had been locked from the inside.'

'Ah, I get it,' Tony said.

I said, 'My favourite had a snake as the killer, damned creative way to die.'

'But not in this case,' Moses added.

'Probably not.' I chugged my espresso, relishing the bittersweet sting. 'When a body falls from the balcony and the door's locked, there's a good chance it's a suicide.'

'Looks like a duck, quacks like a duck.' Tony picked up my dirty spoon.

'Exactly,' I said. 'The only troublesome part about Hanley's death was how little blood there was when he landed. Suicide victims' hearts are generally thudding about a hundred and eighty times a minute, unless they're checking out on sleeping pills. Jumpers tend to bleed a lot. So blood moving, vicious trauma and, in Hanley's case, gravity should all work together to make a very messy crime scene.' I peeked at the deck beneath the table; not a stain remained. 'Hanley barely bled.'

Moses leaned forward again. 'So you think Mr Hanley was dead before he tumbled over the rail? That he died on the balcony and then happened to fall head-first through our yoghurt?'

I looked up as the Sea Girt light warned shipping off the shoals. The balcony outside room 6103 jutted like a promontory. 'I've seen stranger cases.'

Tony shivered. 'Ugh, creepy.'

'Sure is,' Moses confirmed.

'I'll get your food.' Tony excused himself.

The ugly gargoyle I'd seen Sunday morning peered down at us with that same slack-jawed frown. Through the shadows, it looked hungry.

Steak and eggs at the Warren & Monmouth Hotel ranked among the most delicious breakfasts I'd eaten in my lifetime; I silently promised I'd never eat anything but Chef Sam's cooking from now on. Naturally, I'd have to convince Jenny to move into a suite at the hotel, something I'm sure we could afford handily with our combined income, providing we sold both our children to an Arabian oil baron or a South African diamond miner. What the hell, Ben loved digging in dirt.

Moses and I ate in silence as lightning flashed along the burgeoning squall line, illuminating the distant cloudbank, although there was no thunder, not yet. My steak was soft enough to cut with a fork.

'They don't sell meat like this where we shop,' I said through a mouthful.

'Oh, I bet they do.' Moses skewered a bloody morsel. 'It's the price tag that gets us – I mean, who wants to pay eleven dollars a pound for choice beef when they're going to slather it with steak sauce and burn it to char on the barbecue?'

'I suppose,' I said, then, 'So tell me a bit more about playing ball. Impress me with a war story or two.'

'War story?' he murmured, gazing over the railing towards the beach. 'I tell you what: let's finish breakfast; I'll square up with Tony, and we'll walk a bit north towards your place.'

'Deal,' I said. 'So: how long are you staying at the hotel?'

Moses focused on his eggs. In a noncommittal murmur, he said, 'Not sure. I like it here.'

'We'd have to skip groceries for a week just to stay here for the night.'

He grunted again, still considering his food. 'I'm old, Sailor. I get settled and it takes a crane to get me moving again.'

'Nonsense: you look healthy enough to me.' I decided not to press him on his plans, though. I didn't care if he stayed until Christmas; I was just hoping to have him around for the next month. 'Anyway,' I started.

Now he did look up. 'What's on your mind?'

'Nothing.' I skewered a bit of beef. 'It's just nice to chat with someone who isn't pissed off at me or expecting me to watch cartoons all afternoon.'

He teased, 'Damn. And I had a nice Winnie the Pooh video picked out for us.'

'Don't mess with the bear,' I warned him. 'I've got a doctorate in Hundred Acre Wood lore.'

Moses sat back and sighed. 'I remember those days – the best years of my life, really. Most parents don't realise it, but the best years we get are when they're first born to about four or five, before they discover friends down the street.'

'The hero years.'

'You said it.'

'You and—'

'Kate.'

'—Kate, you had just the one daughter?'

He nodded. In the candlelight, it was hard to tell if he was nostalgic or sad. 'Lauren. I could do no wrong. Of all the women I've known in the past four hundred years, she was the only one who truly loved me, and forgave me unconditionally. You know that? Marital love is laden with all manner of contracts, clauses and nasty weight-bearing semi-colons. Motherly love? I don't know if my mother had it in her, but I've read that it can be something special. So again, for my money, give me a daughter's love any day.'

'She was on the boat with your wife?'

He looked down at his plate. 'Both of them were excellent swimmers, too. And they had life preservers – you know how it is: the

143

goddamned Coast Guard won't let you out of the slip without life jackets, flare guns, whale harpoons and a signed copy of *The Rime of the Ancient Mariner.*'

'They weren't wearing them?'

'Tanning.' He said this word as if it alone could extinguish the sun. 'Can you believe it?'

Odd that they didn't notice a storm coming. The sun's usually the first thing to go.

'I'm sorry,' I said.

He waved the entire conversation off like a mosquito. 'It was a long time ago.'

And yet still you sit here and stare at the ocean every day.

I tried to divert us to safer ground. 'Were you vacationing down here?'

'We lived here.'

'I thought—?'

'Kate was from Ottawa, just outside the city, but I grew up north of Asbury, back when you could still walk around up there.' He tilted his head towards all of North Jersey. 'My grandparents settled there, had a farm in what is now Long Branch. Can you believe it? They moved down from Hoboken a hundred years ago or more, shortly after James Bradley built this whole area up. My mother played piano, it'd melt your heart to hear her. She was some kind of prodigy; these days she'd be swept off to Julliard or the Paris Conservatory, but back then, you know what she did to practise?'

I arched an eyebrow. 'No idea.'

'She played for the silent movies, down in Asbury Park. It was all the rage back in the twenties, before theatres could afford to wire up for the talkies. She was pretty modest about it. She and my grandmother would walk down Kingsley on Saturday mornings to the Ocean Theater – they renamed it the Baronet until they knocked it down. Then the great Walter Reade built the St James Theater, down by the lake, complete with a pipe organ, to draw patrons away from my mother's playing.' Moses frowned. 'I don't know about you, but for me, silent films need piano accompaniment – organs take themselves too seriously, all those Bach fugues and Buxtehude hymns. Spare me.'

He'd lost me, but I nodded to give the impression that I was still with him.

'Anyway,' Moses sighed, 'where was I?'

'Walter Reade—'

'Right!' He slapped the table again. 'So my mother stayed on at the Ocean until the late twenties, when talking pictures arrived and killed the silent era. I wish I could have heard her – imagine the chops a fourteen-year-old kid would have to develop. She'd walk all the way into town and preview the films, plinking out a few improvisations, and then sit down and play all afternoon for live audiences.'

I couldn't really think of anything to say. 'It must have been something – I've never been that talented at anything.'

'Me either,' Moses said.

'Did she teach you to play?'

He laughed, remembering something embarrassing. 'She tried, right up to the moment when my father bought me my first baseball. I was probably six years old at the time. The war had ended. The Marshall Plan was rebuilding western Europe in the most boring architectural style you could imagine, and the Giants–Dodgers rivalry was the most exciting thing to happen to organised sports, on earth, ever, anywhere. The greatest division in American culture since the Civil War.'

'So what brought you back?'

'From Ottawa? We moved after Lauren was born, when it was clear I didn't have a hope of signing with a big league team. That was a tough decision.'

'Those hopes hang on pretty tenaciously?'

'You have no idea, my friend.' Moses dabbed at his mouth with a napkin, then tossed it to one side of his plate. 'I'd been injured a few times, but nothing so devastating as to smother my hopes overnight. I knew a guy, a catcher, big kid who hit the ball so hard you swear you'd hear it cry for its mother every time it sailed over the infield. Anyway, he was going up; the contract was in the mail. We all knew it, the whole International League. So what'd he do?'

I guessed, 'Celebrated with a skydiving trip?'

'Close,' Moses said. 'The dumb sonofabitch bought a motorcycle. Can you believe it? A *motorcycle*! Half the city of Ottawa called or sent him letters telling him what a fool he was. But he was twenty-three and indestructible; at least he thought so.'

'Crashed?'

'Two days later.' Moses laughed wryly. 'He shattered his wrist, ended his career overnight.'

'Not the case with you?'

Moses pushed a crust around his plate. 'No. My career ended like most minor leaguers: I held on, stayed in shape and counted the seasons while I recovered from irritating but minor sprains and strains.'

'Why'd you finally quit?'

'I had a wife and daughter, and I couldn't stand being away from them seven months out of the year – I suppose it wasn't too bad when it was just Kate and me, but once Lauren was born, I never played well on the road again. I'd be calling every couple of hours just to check on her – I swear I wasted half my salary those years plugging quarters into payphones. Those were the days before cell phones, instant messaging, all that instant gratification they're pushing now.'

'So you left pro ball to be a better dad? There's no shame in that, Moses.' I tried to sound like a wizened sage but just came off haughty.

'That's the way history recalls it, anyway,' he said.

'Really?'

He laughed through his nose, 'What the hell, right? It's five o'clock in the morning: a perfect time to tell the truth.'

'We barely know each other; that makes it easy.' I polished off my coffee and poured out for both of us.

'I hurt my elbow for the second time back in '78, not too badly, but it was a sign from the gods to quit. Man, I tried to come back from that one, ice and heat and counting pitches before more ice and more heat and more counting. Our manager talked about moving me down in the rotation, maybe making me a closer – I did have a vicious fastball – but I could read the writing on the plaster cast. It was time to go.'

'I'm sure it made Kate happy,' I said.

'She was thrilled,' he said, 'and over time ... well, you know how stories get once you tell them a certain way enough times: it was a case of conscientious parenting rather than a career-ending injury—' He considered this, then corrected himself: '—career-*dimming* injury. It

146

wasn't a career-ender, not like a fiery motorcycle crash, but it was just enough to turn the dimmer switch down, you know, blow out a few of the candles on the mantelpiece. Full recovery for me would have been improbable – don't you hate that word? *Improbable*. Give me *impossible* and I can handle it. Clear as a church bell: *impossible*. But *improbable* is a nasty bedfellow; it's all wrapped up in hope and desire and disappointment. I mean, heck, I was going to strike out Pete Rose on three pitches.'

'Never faced him?'

'Never even *encountered* him.'

I thought back to Jenny and all her hopes for a new life after I'd transferred to Homicide from Vice/Narcotics. Five hundred hits of OxyContin, fifty poisonous snakes, a case of plague and an administrative suspension later it certainly hadn't turned out the way we'd planned.

Moses looked at the darkening seas. More lightning flashed, and this time, far off, we heard thunder. 'Kate loved the ocean and I had had about enough of Ottawa's nightlife so we packed everything we owned into my old Caprice Classic and drove down here to start over.'

'You miss it?'

'Baseball? Or Canada?'

I laughed. 'Either.'

Moses pushed his plate out of the way and propped an elbow on the table; I didn't know if it was the one that had ended his pitching career. 'You know what I miss, Sailor? In a twisted old man's voyeuristic way, I miss the seventies.'

'The 1970s?' I looked askance at him. 'The decade?'

'I do.' He toyed with his leather watchband while he spoke. 'It was just about the most embarrassing time to be an American. Gasoline was scarce – people queued for miles, and you could only buy gas on odd or even days based on the numbers in your licence plate. I remember brawls, Christ, full-on riots, breaking out at the gas pumps. What a travesty. The Ford administration was willing to buy oil, as much as OPEC would sell, but after the Yom Kippur War in – what was it, '73? – the embargo eventually led Carter to fix gas prices, so there was only so much money oil importers could make on a gallon of gas. The futures market took a cornholing – what a shitstorm! – and the government's answer was for everyone to drive at fifty-five miles an hour. The double-nickels campaign: what a crock of deep-fried excrement.

'And to top that off, the whole country – the whole hemisphere – was stoned. Marijuana was one of the basic food groups; my roommates and I used to grow it in our apartment. Stupid bastards: we might as well have been smoking lawn clippings.' Moses laughed out loud at this memory. 'And cocaine was *good* for you. No bullshit, we actually believed it would expand our minds, speed us up a bit and bring the whole world into sharper focus. I suppose we all knew that heroin was dangerous, but that was really more of a black drug, inner-city stuff, you know, it never made the front page like it does today. No one gave a shit about inner-city blacks. Heroin was bad for us, so we stayed away, for the most part. Cocaine was good, and pot was as normal as cold beer. Imagine that: professional athletes all coked up, hitting the bong and cruising York Street for easy women. God bless and keep the nineteen seventies.'

I admitted, 'My father was as buttoned-down hospital-cornered as any teamster could be. He'd buy two six-packs of Pabst Blue Ribbon on his way home from work on Friday; by Sunday night, the beer would be gone and he'd be back in his boots and Dickies for another week pushing the rock up the hill. The idea that he and my mother would ever light a spliff was about as foreign as red meat on Fridays. The worst Dad ever managed was a couple of swills of Jameson's on St Patrick's Day – and that was only because my Uncle Paul always brought a bottle in exchange for my mother's corned beef and cabbage.'

Tony emerged from the staff entrance and asked, 'Gentlemen, can I get you anything else this morning?'

'*Grazie*, no, Antonio,' Moses said. '*Questo è stupendo.* Please pass my compliments on to Chef Sam.'

'Of course, sir.' Tony collected our plates. 'Anything for you, Detective Doyle?'

'Actually, yes, Tony, I wonder if I can ask you a favour.'

He stood straight, our dirty plates balanced in one hand. 'Certainly, sir.'

'Tony, I'd like to get a quick look inside Mr Hanley's room. Do you think we could swing that, just for a couple of minutes?'

Tony stammered, 'Uh – well, sir, I don't know if I'm supposed to—'

Moses interrupted, 'C'mon, Antonio, you can sneak us in there, can't you?'

The young waiter stared down at Moses Stillman, obviously communicating telepathically: *Are you crazy, sir? You know what Thomas will do if he catches me in there.*

Moses set his jaw. 'Come on, Antonio: it'll be an adventure.' He looked at me. 'You don't need much time, Detective?'

I winked thanks at him. 'Nope, should take less than five minutes, actually.'

To Tony, Moses said, 'If you're uncomfortable with this, perhaps you could just slip me a master key later today and I could—'

'No, sir,' Tony cut him off, then sighed. 'All right, but we'll have to wait until I'm off-duty.'

'That's fine,' I said. 'I can come back later tonight.'

Moses raised his coffee mug. '*Eccellente!* This will be the best night we've had around here in a long while.'

In the flickering light, Tony from Bergen County looked distinctly queasy. 'Okay, then, tonight.' He shuffled back towards the kitchen.

Moses asked, 'You don't think Harold Hanley committed suicide?'

'He probably did. I'm just a curious cop who can't rest until I see for myself that all the points line up.'

He glanced over the bill. 'And if they don't?'

'Then I need to light a fire under Detective Hodges.'

Moses signed our tab with the silver fountain pen he had tucked in his shirt. 'Whatever you say, Detective. You're the expert.'

'You don't need to come along.'

'Are you kidding? Miss an opportunity for felony breaking and entering? Not on your life, young man – this is as close as I've come to getting arrested since Pink Floyd broke up.'

A trickle of sweat ran down my spine, pulling my flesh into goose pimples. 'I—'

'You all right, Sailor?' Moses' brow furrowed. 'You look a little pale.'

'I'm fine. Fine.' I reached for the bill. 'Can I at least leave the tip?'

He deftly slid the leather case into his lap. 'Nonsense: breakfast is on me. The evening's excitement is on you. But I must insist that between now and then you tell me what you're really looking for.'

'I'll let you know if I find it,' I said.

He pushed himself back from the table, his wrought-iron chair squealing in protest. 'Shall we walk a bit?'

'I should be fine,' I said, 'but I think it might rain on us – you sure you don't mind getting drenched?'

He dropped the bill on the table beside the hurricane candle as he got to his feet. He was an inch or two above six feet and probably tipped the scales at two hundred and thirty pounds. As the wind tousled what remained of his hair, he looked a little like Clint Eastwood.

Or like hanged men in a Clint Eastwood movie.

He ran a liver-spotted hand through his hair, pressing it carelessly back. 'Nope, I don't mind at all. I could use the exercise after that breakfast. Come on.' He started across the Persian rug, humming the same tune he'd been humming right before Hanley had crashed head-first through the awning.

'Moses!' I grabbed his wrist. 'What's that tune? I've been hearing it over and over down here and I can't place it, but I know I know it from somewhere.'

He tilted his head back, thinking, illuminated by the lights that shone from several of the hotel's toothy balconies. After a moment, he said, 'I think it's called "East Side, West Side", but don't quote me on it.'

I ran the title through my memory and came up empty.

'Yeah, that's it,' he said, and sang quietly, *'East Side, West Side, all around the town. The tots sang "ring-around-rosie"—'*

I joined him, off-key, but willing, *'—"London Bridge is falling down"—'*

Moses went on, *'Boys and girls together, me and Mamie O'Rourke tripped the light fantastic on the sidewalks of New York.'*

'I think that's it: "Sidewalks of New York".'

'Could be – it used to play on the boardwalk up in Asbury Park, the carousel, or maybe the bumper cars. Kate and I goofed off up there in '75 when the Ottawa manager placed me on the disabled list; we figured we'd finally have our honeymoon.'

150

'No money?'

'Sort of – her parents were loaded, but they didn't necessarily approve of their princess marrying a midlist baseball player. If I'd been a starter for the Yankees, it might have been different.' Moses took Rhett Butler's staircase towards the beach. 'We got married in the season, so we spent a weekend in the Provincial Arms Hotel in Ottawa, then I went back on the road.'

I stepped into the grass, but Moses waited on the bottom step. I stopped a few paces away. 'You coming?'

'You want me to?'

I chuckled, a little nervously. *What's with this guy?* 'Yeah, sure, why not? It's five-thirty in the morning and about to rain on us – it's the perfect time for some exercise.'

'All right, then.' Moses hesitated, as if checking his coordinates, then took charge. 'Come this way.' He gestured towards Spring Lake proper. 'I'll show you the sights.'

I looked up to room 6103 and the cross-looking gargoyle stared back at me. In the gathering dawn it appeared to be grinning.

Moses and I walked around the gigantic building and into the Rockwellian town of Spring Lake. Neptune was a mere four miles away, but Spring Lake might as well have been in another country, an absurdly wealthy country. Moses pointed out a lumbering neo-Tudor home large enough to accommodate the New York Jets and *tsked* like a schoolmarm. 'Whoever decided to build a n eo-Tudor castle at the beach either has the world's smallest penis or has been kicked in the head by one of his own Lipizzaner stallions!' He gave a huge belly-laugh, then asked, 'How's your leg doing?'

'All the moving parts seem to be moving well enough,' I reported. 'I hit the Naproxen pretty hard before I left this morning, so I may pay for all this activity later on.'

'I'll get you north in no time,' he said. 'You'll be back in Belmar before anyone at your house even rolls over.'

The rain swept in from the ocean; I heard it patter up Mercer Avenue and plop noisily into the lake. 'Here we go,' I said.

'No matter,' Moses said as he ushered me towards a tidy row of expensive-looking boutiques. We ducked from awning to awning as the rain got heavier – I wasn't bothered about being wet; it was Moses I worried about, in his six-hundred-dollar Italian loafers. He stopped beneath a forest-green awning, wiped his glasses and lingered, window-shopping.

'What's this place?' I asked.

'O'Malley's Jewellers,' he chuckled. 'I love the irony of it: an Irish jewellery store.'

There it was emblazoned across the window in a silly faux-Gaelic font: O'Malley's Fine Jewellery. 'Whaddya know,' I said, checking the other store fronts along Third Avenue, which appeared to be the town's main drag. 'The Irish Riviera, right?'

'Right,' Moses said, 'going back a hundred and twenty years.'

'So what's so special about this place?' I asked, cupping my hand to see inside the store. Black velvet display cases sat empty on both sides of the shop's doorway. There was no retractable grate or partition protecting the display windows – apparently Spring Lake was dangerous enough that all the jewels got put away at night, but not so dangerous as to merit window bars. I peered inside again. 'I can't see anything, just velvet shelves.'

Moses pointed towards the back. 'See that fancy clock on the wall behind the register?'

I looked again; next to the clock was a beautiful wooden display case illuminated from the inside, with what looked like a strand of black marbles. This was obviously a nice piece. 'What are they? Licorice gumballs?'

'The case is rosewood. The necklace is black Tahitian pearls,' Moses said, 'each one between 11 and 11.5 millimetres, and they may be cultured, but they are South Sea giants nevertheless. There are forty-five in the strand, so that particular necklace might fetch three hundred thousand dollars. See that one in the centre?' It was a monster, nearly twice the diameter of the others. 'With the centre pearl included, you're looking at three, maybe four.'

'Hundred thousand?'

'Million. Four million dollars.'

'Just hanging on the wall like that?' The cop in me was outraged.

Moses winked at me. 'Nice catch, Sailor. Mr and Mrs O'Malley would have you believe that's a copy; the real necklace is in a safe downstairs.'

'Is it?'

'I don't know,' he said. 'Probably. But in my mind they're the real thing.'

'Four *million* dollars? For pearls? I've only got eleven bucks on me. I'll have to stop back later this afternoon.' I had no idea why this was such a big deal to Moses. Pearls were supposed to be off-whitish – *pearl*-coloured – not black or cobalt-blue, or whatever these were. 'That had to have been the absolute granddaddy of all oysters. You'd think I'd have seen pictures of a thing that big in *Smithsonian Quarterly*.'

Moses spoke to the glass. 'It's natural – not cultured. It was discovered in a Marquesan lagoon in the waning years of the eighteenth century. That pearl, nicknamed Princess Cosette, is A-quality, and nearly seventeen millimetres in diameter, on a par with Russia's red spinel or the pearls in the Hapsburg crown.'

'I don't think I've ever seen a gemstone with its own nickname before. And you believe O'Malley's got the real thing out there for anyone to steal?'

Moses said, 'I'm sure he's thinking that no one but he and his wife know what they are. Any customers who ask about them are told that the genuine strand is locked away, so word gets out that those are resin.'

'You think he's an international jewel thief and he's hiding the goods in plain sight? I saw that in a movie once.'

Moses wasn't listening. To his ageing reflection in the display case he said, 'This strand of priceless pearls was given as a gift from a French Polynesian diplomat to Maybeth Baldwin, the wife of Canada's Prime Minister, back in the mid-seventies, after French Polynesia was granted partial autonomy from France. I guess the Canadians were one of the first nations to recognise them as their own partially autonomous government, whatever the hell that is.

'That centre pearl had belonged to a Tahitian chieftain's great-granddaughter. She had died of a heroin overdose in the sixties – and can you believe that Baldwin's wife wouldn't wear it? She didn't want to wear a pearl that had belonged to a dead woman – the damned thing was found in the *eighteenth* century, for Christ's sake: in 1796! Six or seven generations of dead people had already worn the bloody thing!'

I cupped my hands over my eyes for another look. 'It's beautiful, no question about that.'

'And mysterious and delicate and *improbable* all at the same time.'

'There's that word again.'

'Natural black pearls are just about the most improbable, precious jewel on this planet, Sailor. I bet you didn't know that.'

'I didn't, I confess. So … do you want to steal them or something? Because I'm free Thursday, but not Friday. I could probably work Saturday in if my mother comes down to babysit.'

Moses stared at the window, either at his reflection or at the strand of improbable pearls, for an unsettling moment. Finally, I nudged him. 'You all right?'

He sniffed loudly and brushed his Clint Eastwood hair back again. 'Sure, sure – I just enjoy looking at them. It's like gazing on a work of art, the Sistine ceiling or a Chagall stained-glass window, know what I mean?'

'Honestly, no,' I confessed again. 'I about managed to navigate my way through the Criminal Justice Program at Rutgers holding on to a B-average with my fingernails. I grew up working-class Freehold; if you put a knife to my throat and told me to list the differences between Monet and Manet, I'd tell you it was one vowel.'

He laughed again and slapped me on the shoulder, my bad shoulder this time, and set off along the street. We were no longer alone; the early workers had started to join us. Lights flickered on in some of the cafés and restaurants and an *Asbury Park Press* truck dropped two plastic-wrapped bales at the corner of Third and Jersey. They landed with a noisy splash. Moses produced a penknife from his pocket, sliced through the plastic and took a copy of the paper. He left a dollar. 'Ah, shit,' he said as he checked the headlines.

'What's the matter?'

'There was a riot last night in Neptune.' He read on silently. 'Looks like some folks think that shooter yesterday is a hero. Others wholeheartedly disagree.'

'Damn.' I gnawed on a knuckle. *Better get home; Hodges will be looking for you.*

'That's not too far from you, right? But when you think about it, racial trouble in Neptune City isn't likely to make it all the way out to your house – it might cause a bit of a stir up in Asbury, but not down by you.' He figured he could read my mind.

'Ah, that's not it, Moses,' I said. 'Listen, though, I'd better head home regardless. If Jenny sees this, she'll be nervous.'

'Of course.' He quickened his pace, the pearls entirely forgotten now. 'If you don't mind, I'll come along for another few blocks; stretch the old dogs a bit.'

'Let's go.' I started after him, willing more speed from my leg. 'Hey,' I said, to slow him down, just a bit, 'what did your wife do for a living? Did she grow up there in Ottawa?'

'Kate grew up in Halifax. Her family moved to Ottawa when her father got involved with politics and big business. She was a statistician, she'd almost finished her doctorate before we moved south. She worked for a non-profit – a bit of a rarity, back in the day. Nordic Rescue was a group with some heavy-hitter lobbyists – she'd heard five minutes of an inspirational speech from the company's founder, Charles Dunning, and was sold.'

'Young and idealistic,' I said. 'Nice. I remember those days.'

'Yeah, me too. So, Nordic Rescue's sole mission was the preservation of the Canadian Arctic. Kate spent years working on a project in the Nunavut Region, some kind of massive outwash plain way up near the Arctic Circle. The Hellmich Plain is ringed on three sides by mountains; it was left there by the Laurentide Glacier. Apparently it's the perfect nesting ground for the Eskimo curlew and back then it was threatened by oil companies and non-existent hunting laws. There were gazillions of these birds, living and breeding and prospering just fine on that outwash plain, until the Canadian government decided to cave in to the oil companies, which would have polluted the place back to the Stone Age and just about decimated the curlew population. Jesus Christ, but she fought like a crazy woman, months and months of shouting and calculating ...'

'Save a few birds while jacking up the price of gasoline, right?' I wiped rain off my face. 'That's an old song.'

'And all the while the Middle East was imploding. Carter couldn't find his ass with both hands. Americans were being taken hostage in Iran; a rescue mission failed brilliantly, and your parents were probably having a heart attack at the idea of paying a dollar or more a gallon for regular.'

'I was just a kid at the time,' I said, 'but I remember my father complaining all through the eighties. He'd never have blamed anything on Ronald Reagan, mind – everything was Jimmy Carter's fault, even ten years later.'

'Anyway, as a trained statistician, Kate was an immediate asset to the company. While Charles Dunning was charismatic in that rugged, leather-skinned-explorer kind of way, he couldn't calculate a covariate analysis or zero out a spreadsheet to save his life. Finding a wide-eyed, enthusiastic youngster with boundless energy and a Master's degree in statistics was like getting a visit from the Easter Bunny.'

I stepped off a curb, landed hard on my heel and groaned.

'You all right, Sailor?' Moses stopped to look down at my leg. 'We going too fast for you?'

'Nah, I'm fine,' I panted, 'it's just that you've got a bigger stride than me.'

He flashed an expensive smile. 'Uh huh, sure; and how many do you smoke a day?'

'All of them,' I said without hesitation, 'then I buy more.'

'Come on, then.' He ratcheted the tempo up another notch. 'Keep up, smoker. I'll do the talking; you just concentrate on not passing out.'

'Got it,' I said, 'but remember: you're a professional athlete. I'm an injured cop.'

'Horseshit,' he said. 'I'm an old man kicking your ass in imported loafers. Now close your mouth and pick up those Nikes.'

'Yes, sir! But it took years of neglect and self-abuse for me to get this way; that must count for something in life's great equation.'

'Sure; divide by zero.' Moses looked pleased with himself, then went on, 'Dunning about pissed his trousers when he learned of Kate's connection to Ottawa's political network. All of a sudden, Nordic Rescue's board of directors found themselves invited to cocktail parties with Canada's *real* power brokers. Research funding started rolling in, and grants. Kate was the reason, so Dunning took care of her – company car, nice office on Wellington Street, the works – *and* he threw his not-inconsiderable influence behind her Nunavut project. She was happy, and I was happy because she was happy.'

The rain was coming down harder now, and Moses slowed to cross the street. 'Let's go east. We'll part company at the beach, deal?'

'Done,' I said. 'Lead on.'

When we reached Ocean Avenue six-foot breakers pounded the beach mercilessly. The roar drowned out our footsteps; we might have been floating.

'What time tonight?' I called.

'Ten o'clock? I'll have Tony stick around, or come back, or maybe just slip me the key. Thomas and Mitch don't come on until eleven, and the three-to-eleven concierge will be busy with paperwork, wrapping up her shift.'

'Sounds good,' I said. 'That'll give me time to get my guys settled as well.'

'See you then,' he called and turned back towards the Warren & Monmouth's gilded cupola, now hidden behind scudding grey banks of thunderclouds.

'Thanks for breakfast,' I said.

'Thank you for the exercise.' He waved and strode south, head down, braced against the wind, with the confidence of a life-long athlete. I watched until he reached Brighton, then I turned and headed towards Belmar.

Riots in Neptune last night. That's not good. Hopefully the storm put a damper on those festivities.

I passed Lake Como. The wind had picked up considerably and now it swept the boardwalk with heavy curtains of rain. There'd be no swimming today. My thoughts drifted from plans for a trip to the library with Ben to Canadian baseball and Eskimo curlews, whatever those are. No cars passed, nothing punctured the damp shroud of white noise around me until I reached Seventeenth Avenue.

A teenage girl in a pink bikini top and a pair of cut-off shorts emerged through the door of a three-level place catering to large family reunions. She trotted down the sidewalk in bare feet, an umbrella in one hand, and dug around in the colourful fish-shaped mailbox.

'Morning,' I said, thinking it odd that a tourist would need mail.

She didn't answer.

Smart. Don't talk to strangers, especially the stupid ones wandering in the rain at six o'clock in the morning.

Three steps past the mailbox, I heard her sing, '—tots sing "ring-around-rosie", "London Bridge is falling down"—'

I spun around and felt a flare of pain in my leg. 'What? Hey!'

She glanced at me, her eyes wide, then took the porch steps two at a time. The skin of her shoulders and back was as white as a cadaver.

Go ahead, escape. Sorry.

I shook off the unnerving feeling that something weird had come looking for me this early in the day. *It was nothing, just a coincidence.* Marie appeared in my head. She always did when I felt like I was losing my mind.

'Leave me alone today, okay?' I said, dropping my head down against the rain. 'I'm taking your nephew to the library. Let me have a nice day, okay? Don't mess with me today.'

Marie shot me a look of affectionate disdain; no one I'd ever known could do it with such panache. 'It's not me, Sailor, not today. Nice to see you getting some exercise, though. You make the Sea Girt lighthouse this morning?'

'Not you?'

The pull-down security grate on a seashore gift shop slammed open noisily. The shop keeper flicked a cigarette butt into a puddle, looked me in the eye and sang, 'Boys and girls together, me and Mamie O'Rourke—'

My heart about quit. I turned away and tried to pick up the pace, though I couldn't jog, not yet; my leg wouldn't take it. I crossed Sixteenth, and as I passed in front of a baker's van it rolled to a stop and through the rain I heard its radio: a barbershop quartet or some old-fashioned choral group singing, 'East Side, West Side, all around the town …'

Now, I did run, just a few steps, though my leg felt as though someone had driven an ice-pick hilt-deep into the muscle. 'Jesus Christ,' I moaned, 'get me out of here!'

Only eight more blocks.

A gust of wind blew sand into my face and I sidestepped into a wrought-iron dining table in front of Seibert's Seafood. They'd replaced the Plexiglas tank outside, but there were only a dozen lobsters crawling around in there. I caught sight of a Belmar cruiser parked at the corner of Ocean and Fifteenth, keeping an eye on Seibert's. I was surprised I hadn't seen more docked along the beach. Maybe the rain had sent most of the revellers inside. I crossed in front of his car and offered him a wave; he ignored me.

Everything about me was wet, even my boxers. I tried to light a cigarette, but couldn't get it to take. The Belmar cop turned north on Ocean and paced me for a block, an intimidation ploy Huck and I had used a thousand times. Now I ignored him as he sneered through the window, keeping my gaze straight ahead and limping badly. From the corner of my eye, I saw his window open smoothly and I waited for him to call me over, as if one hobbling, drenched fool out before dawn was any threat to the town of Belmar's security. Whatever. I had my business cards, however soaked.

No badge, though.

He didn't call out; instead, he turned up his dispatch radio. Lots of cops keep them pretty well cranked to full volume; no one wants to miss a call, especially if they're out of the car – but this shithead was playing with me, creeping along at three miles an hour and watching me struggle through the rain.

I thought about giving him a business card and asking for a lift back to my house when I heard his dispatcher behind a burst of static. She sang, 'We tripped the light fantastic on the sidewalks of New York.'

Fuck. What's going on? I crossed Fourteenth Avenue and ducked beneath the Dunkin' Donuts awning. The twenty-four-hour artificial light inside might as well have been an oasis in the Sahara. 'Get your head on, Sailor; don't go to pieces today,' I told myself. 'You were doing fine.'

As I went in a blast of arctic air-conditioning chilled my bones to the marrow. The shop smelled of recycled air and sugary fried dough. An ancient codger with a scraggly beard wearing a flannel shirt and an oily NAPA hat was nursing a small coffee. He had a copy of the *Newark Star Ledger* open in front of him at a black and white advertisement for bras. I figured that was about as close as he was ever going to get to a handful of boob.

The toilet smelled like the Old Testament, one of the scary parts, but it was better than peeing on a street corner.

The pimply-faced teen behind the counter looked as vacuous as a pithed frog.

'Sorry,' I said, 'I know I'm a mess. Didn't expect the rain.'

'What can I getcha?' She had one iPod bud inserted, probably permanently, into her ear; the Dunkin' Donuts hat covered her greasy hair. Apparently work came before showers. I wondered why she wasn't home, finishing the last of her algebra homework before class.

I found a couple of crumpled singles and asked for a small coffee.

'Anything to eat?'

'No thanks.'

She slid the cup across the counter without looking up. 'One forty-nine.'

I gave her the two bucks. 'Keep it.'

The grizzled old-timer mumbled down at the brassiere models in his paper. I was glad I couldn't hear him, but he did at least have both hands on the table; that was a relief. I asked the girl, 'You need help with him? Want me to stick around?'

She glanced at his table as if noticing the old buzzard for the first time, and said, 'Nah, he's here every morning. Harmless.'

'Okay.' I took a long swallow and rooted around in my pack until I found a dry cigarette. 'Have a good day.'

She didn't answer as she pulled out a stained washcloth and began wiping down the counter. I dried my lighter on a napkin and hoped it would work, just once more. One would get me home.

Overhead, the muzak changed, modulating through a chord Mozart couldn't have duplicated in a hundred lifetimes.

Shit. Here it comes.

160

The girl behind the counter started singing before the opening beat: 'East Side, West Side—'

The homeless codger joined her in a three-pack-a-day gargle, '—all around the town—'

I hurried out, pausing beneath the awning just long enough to light my cigarette, then moved as fast as I could up the block. There was no sign of the Belmar cop, or the bakery van.

Five blocks, Sailor, just five: you'll make it, drink your coffee, smoke your cigarette and you'll be fine. There's a handful of yummy Nytol and a long nap waiting for you at home. You can take everyone to the library after lunch. It'll be fun. Just get those five blocks under your belt.

'Marie?' I asked the storm. 'Where are you?' *Nothing.*

At Twelfth Avenue, I hit the home stretch. It was 6:52 a.m. and the skies over New Jersey had brightened, though the storm still slammed the coast, the rain a steady downpour determined to hammer away all day.

At A Street, I silently apologised to my sister for dragging her into every one of my low days. *Not your fault – it was never your fault.*

At B Street, my leg felt better, still sore, but the promise of a hot bath had dulled the pain of the ice-pick. *A hot bath, almost too hot to bear: that's first on the menu.*

At C Street, I turned to look back at the ocean. The comforting sodium streetlights along the boardwalk were burning hazy yellow, like gas lamps in a Joseph Cotton movie.

Then bright light sliced through the downpour and Gabriel Lebow growled down at me from an upstairs window in a Cape Cod place two doors south. His made-up face, all white greasepaint with black hollows for the eyes and leering grin, was backlit by a ceiling fixture. Nothing else moved, no cars, no newspaper delivery trucks, just Gabriel, watching me.

Hopeless fear poisoned the air and I staggered a step, slipped off the curb and fell to my knees.

Slowly, Gabriel reached up to unlatch the window. The light behind him created a brilliant halo.

'Don't you do it, motherfucker!' I shouted. 'Don't do it!' I wished I had brought the Smith & Wesson.

Were you the one? Were you in my yard tonight, Gabriel, beneath my mother's pear tree? Outside my son's window? I'll fucking shoot you myself, I swear to Christ—

In a smooth gesture, the dead teenager pushed the window open. When he raised his arms, I saw two bloodstained holes in his sweatshirt, but the blood had dried, even the tiny rivulets that dripped down his chest, discolouring the hockey logo, a pissed-off raccoon on skates. Before poking his head out, Gabriel caressed the pane with one finger, leaving a thick trail of white greasepaint on the glass.

That'll be there later, Sailor; Christ, yes, you can check for it later and put this whole shitstorm behind you. Don't look now, though. Don't look up.

But I did.

Gabriel's mouth was opening wide, wider than anyone could possibly extend their jaws, even those freaks in the *Guinness Book of Records*, the ones who can eat eleven peaches in ninety seconds. Gabriel's mouth continued opening and I imagined I could smell the foetid aroma of decay from his throat. It was impossible, I knew, to detect anything from across the street but it was there, regardless, like the last breath of a dying animal.

'What do you want?' I whimpered. 'I'm sorry – I'm sorry about your leg, your face. I'm sorry. I didn't *know*.'

An awful sound like a soul consigned to Hell emerged from Gabriel's hollow throat and I pushed myself to my feet and turned my back on him, but his awful wailing followed me, chasing me down Twelfth and up the driveway to my house, where I ducked behind Jenny's minivan. I crouched on the porch, my head between my knees, and when I peeked out some time later, Gabriel was still up there, mouth still agape, incomprehensible gurgles still bubbling up from his throat, strangely musical but tortured, the soundtrack of death. I closed my eyes, covered my ears and waited for my breath to slow down, my heart to calm.

Inside, Jenny was standing over the sink, washing out baby bottles. Ben was having a heated debate with Anna's stuffed animals; whatever it was, it had Ben cracking up. With the lights on the house was warm, dry and welcoming; I inhaled deeply and smelled waffles, syrup and baby lotion.

Thank Christ.

Jenny turned. 'Well, there you are. I was just about to get worried.'

'Hey guys.' I had to flatten the wrinkles in my voice. 'Everyone eat already? You're up early for a rainy day.'

Ben bounded over. 'Look, Daddy, Annie's bear and dog can talk to each other.' He started them chatting, a tuxedoed bear in his left hand and a hat-wearing dog in his right, giving the bear a squeaky falsetto and the dog a dangerous baritone.

A three-pack-a-day garble.

'One second, monkey-man,' I begged. 'I need to change my clothes.'

'How far'd you go?' Jenny asked. In her khaki Capris and T-shirt she looked like everything I could ever hope to have out of life. 'No dead bodies this morning?'

I forced a grin. 'No, not today, just rain and wind.'

'There's coffee,' she said.

'Had some.' I untied my Nikes and kicked them across the floor. 'You guys didn't happen to hear anything strange outside this morning, did you?'

Jenny didn't look up from the sink. 'Strange? Like what?'

I downplayed my fear. 'Oh, I dunno, kind of like a broken Wurlitzer stuck on auto reverse, under water, with an amputee trying to play Beethoven.'

Jenny's eyes widened. 'No, no – we did hear something strange, but it was more like a broken Hammond organ under water, with a double-amputee trying to play Franz Liszt.'

'Not funny—'

'A little bit funny,' she said with a grin.

'So you heard something?'

'No, Sailor, not a thing. Does this have something to do with Ben carrying on about that tree outside his room.'

'Nah,' I lied, 'that was just the wind – the storm came in pretty hard.'

'I can tell. You look like you've been run over by a Zamboni.'

'I might have been. I need a shower, or maybe a hot bath – I'm frozen through.' I pulled a towel out of a drawer and dried the baby bottles. Jenny's coffee smelled like scorched earth, but I poured a swig into a mug, just enough to down a couple of Nytol.

'Leg hurt?' Jenny asked. 'Maybe you should take a day off from walking tomorrow.'

'I'll see how I feel.'

'Well, take a bath and a nap if you want. We're in no hurry to go anywhere today.'

'You want to go to the library?' I should have whispered it.

Ben jumped up, his bear-and-dog show forgotten. 'The library! Can we, Mommy?'

'Sure, buddy,' Jenny said. 'Daddy's going to rest for a little while, and then we'll go.'

Ben ran tight circles around the rug until he fell, giggling, and rolled to where Anna sat in her bouncy chair. 'Annie! We're going to the library!'

'Benjamin,' I said, 'you are one confounding little man.'

'Daddy' – he tickled Anna's feet – 'what's confounding?'

'Confounding is when five-year-old boys love the library as much as you do.'

'But, Daddy, they have books and videos and storytime and craft-time and sometimes puppet shows!' Clearly the children's section was the place to be.

'All right, monkey-face. But first, I have to take a bath and maybe a quick nap. Daddy's been up since your nightmare.'

'I didn't have a *night*mare. The shark was outside my window again.' Ben gripped my T-shirt with two small fists. 'Daddy, your shirt's *really* wet.'

'I know, monkey-man.' I dumped him on the coach and knelt down to kiss Anna's slobbery cheek. 'Morning, Smurfette.'

'You want the newspaper for the tub?' Jenny started for the door. 'It might be soggy, though.'

'No!' I stood too quickly; my leg nearly buckled.

'Jesus, Sailor, what's the matter?'

'Nothing,' I replied with forced nonchalance, 'It's just – well, it's raining so hard; I don't want you to get drenched just for the paper. You know.'

'I don't mind.' She draped her cloth over the back of a chair. 'I'll just run out for it.'

Think, shithead: think of something.

'Actually, can I borrow your iPod? I'd rather listen to some music.'

'Yeah, sure – where is it?' She moved away from the door, searching the kitchen for her bag.

'I'll find it,' I said. 'I think the beach bag's down here anyway.' *It's in your purse, Jenny, over by the television. Come away from the door and any thoughts of the* Asbury Park Press.

'Oh wait,' she called, 'here it is, in my bag.' She tossed it to me. 'Keep it dry, Sailor. There's a lot of downloads on there, hundreds of dollars' worth. You drop it in the tub and you might as well drown yourself along with all my ABBA songs.'

'If I happen across an ABBA song, I might just drown myself.' I untangled the headphone cord. 'You ought to steal the songs, like every fifteen-year-old on Earth.'

'I'm a lawyer, Sailor.'

'Tax attorney,' I said. 'There's a difference. Anyway, as a lawyer, what better reason do you need to steal songs?'

'And you're a cop.'

Was a cop, you mean.

'Okay, fine, pay for your ABBA tunes; I'm sure they need the eighty-eight cents.' I pulled my T-shirt off. 'I promise I'll keep your iPod dry and live to see another day.'

'Great.' Jenny gave me a smile that should have been illegal. 'We'll get ready for the library.'

'Hurray!' Ben shouted and took off running for his bedroom, 'I need long pants, Daddy. It's always cold there.'

I whispered, 'Did he say anything more about that shark?'

'Nope.' Jenny zipped her bag closed. 'That's the first he mentioned it.'

*

165

I leaned back against the chilly porcelain, freezing my shoulders while my body scalded in the steaming water. Riotous orchestral music blared through the iPod earbuds – Mozart, maybe, one of those guys; I turned the volume down to a whisper and closed my eyes.

Maybe I'll take a quick nap right here. This is pretty comfy.

I let my thoughts drift to eighteenth-century Vienna, well, the eighteenth-century Vienna I knew from Hollywood, and tried to sleep.

Barry Manilow slapped me awake; apparently, 'Mandy' followed 'Magic Flute Overture' in Jenny's alphabetical PLAY option. 'Yikes! I can't have this racket, not while I'm naked.'

I pressed the BACK arrow and started the Mozart over and tried to forget the words to 'Sidewalks of New York' and my vision of Gabriel Lebow with his face painted like a tribal death mask. The zippy strings part returned and I dried my fingers and reached back to crank up the volume while I looked down at my naked body. I'd lost a lot of weight since I'd been shot, and while I might not be a lean muscle machine, at least I wasn't the same Detective Flabzilla I'd been when I chased down Molly Bruckner on July fourth. Sunburned skin juxtaposed with scalded skin to make me look like a mammoth bratwurst, but I didn't care; I'd enjoyed the walking so far, the two dead bodies, OxyContin craving, gang shooting and lunatic musical hallucinations notwithstanding, and seeing I'd dropped some weight, feeling strength in my leg and grooving to a peppy Mozart tune, I scrubbed away my strange journey down Ocean Avenue.

Mozart finished with a noisy flourish and Barry Manilow started in, plunking piano keys with his elbows. I pressed and held the BACK arrow, one last time, just enough to hear the finale, and right on cue, the orchestra played backwards. 'Now that's a cool trick,' I said. 'Try that one, Mr Mani—'

I sat up too quickly, spilling water over the side of the tub. Staring down at the iPod's miniature screen I scrolled through Jenny's collection of songs until I found the right folder: PINK FLOYD, WISH YOU WERE HERE. RELEASE: SEPTEMBER, 1975.

I opened the folder with a wet thumb, cursed and dried it on a towel. *Where are you? Where—?*

I clicked on the song, turned the volume to full and listened. With the volume jacked way up, it was easy to hear every tiny scratch and finger-squeak. I nearly pissed the bathwater when I heard someone – it had to be David Gilmour – clear his sinuses. 'Goddamn. I can't believe they left that in there.'

After a few bars of guitar duet I could only describe as plaintive, Gilmour sang the same lyrics I'd known since I was a kid: *So, so you think you can tell, Heaven from Hell, blue skies from pain. Can you tell a green field from a cold steel rail? A smile from a veil? Do you think you can tell?*

I hummed along for a few seconds then pressed and held the BACK arrow.

Gilmour, Wright, Mason and Waters began playing backwards and there it was, those oddly arrhythmic, sustained resonant tones and incoherent vowel sounds I'd heard when Gabriel Lebow screamed at me from the upstairs window down the block. What was missing, what I didn't hear, was the sound of Mozart's violins played backwards, like the sound of a screaming child.

I released the BACK arrow and Pink Floyd started forward again, as genuinely heartsick or lovesick or homesick as they had been in 1975. I pressed BACK again, just to be sure.

In my mind's eye I saw him, his mouth agape, that inhuman shriek following me down Twelfth Avenue. 'Tell me this isn't happening,' I muttered. I pressed STOP, turned off the iPod, and got out. As I reached for a towel on the hook near the glass-enclosed shower stall I came face to face with an apparition, staring back at me with hollow eyes, mouth frozen in slack-jawed horror. It took me a shuddering moment to realise a suction-cup shampoo holder had once been stuck to the glass wall; those suction cups had left their indelible kiss on the glass and the steam from my bath brought the monstrous-looking visage into view. Its mouth, the bottom suction cup, was trapped for ever in a soundless cry.

I grabbed a towel and erased the ghost with a swipe, then fled, dripping, to the bedroom. Jenny came in and I grabbed my towel to cover up; if she saw me jump, she didn't say anything. I held my breath until the awkward moment passed, then said, 'What's up?'

'Did you see this?' She waved the paper at me, accusing me of lying and hiding something all in one fluid motion.

'No – what's up?'

'A riot, Sailor, a frigging *riot*, not three miles from here.'

'What? *Now*? What are you talking about?' *That* was more convincing. I'd known it would be just a matter of time before she found out. She read parts of the story aloud, describing the bar-room disagreement that thanks to the magic of modern cell phones had escalated into a street fight between community members and local thugs. The Neptune Township Police had broken up the mêlée, but groups of angry teens had spent the night throwing rocks through shop windows, looting, and fighting with police. They'd set two cars on fire and burned an abandoned home out near Route 18. The Neptune Township Police had made nineteen arrests, shot eight teenagers with rubber bullets and called in all available State Police officers and the Asbury Park Street Crimes Unit for assistance.

'Hold it,' I interrupted her, 'read that last part again.' I felt ridiculous standing there, hiding behind a bathroom towel, so I waited for her to look back at the page, then dropped the towel and stepped quickly into my boxers.

Part of me hoped Jenny would peek, but from the steady cadence of her reading, I doubted it.

'—*Neptune officials reported that by 11:30 p.m., surrounding jurisdictions had been contacted in an effort to round up the gangs ... um, here it is ... State Police officers from Holmdel Station and members of the Asbury Park Street Crimes Unit responded—*'

I pulled on jeans, then dived back into the laundry basket for matching socks. 'Interesting. I wonder if anyone will catch that.'

'What?' Jenny dropped the paper on the bed. 'You know, Sailor, if you put the laundry away, stuff's easier to find.'

'What? I can find everything I need right here.' I emerged with a white sock in each hand. 'See?'

'Those don't match, doofus.' She found a scrunchie on the bedstand and pulled her hair into a ponytail.

'They may not match each other, but they almost certainly match the socks I'll wear tomorrow.'

Jenny sighed. 'What do you wonder if anyone will catch?'

'That reference to Asbury Park's gang unit. Neptune Township called for help last night from Asbury Park, not Bradley Beach, Avon or Belmar.'

'So?'

'So, and I'm reaching, but it may mean that those two shitheads I met yesterday are hiding up in Asbury somewhere. I'm surprised I haven't heard from Marta Hodges.'

'Might it just mean that some of the kids running wild last night were from Asbury? Why the connection to the guys who shot Gabriel Lebow?'

I shrugged. 'Maybe it's nothing, or maybe they decided to squeeze a few of the thugs they pinched last night for info on my shooter. Someone might have seen something, heard something, caught sight of a tattoo. Who knows?'

She looked worried.

'What's the matter?'

'I don't like this, Sailor. This scares me. These kids are dangerous. I don't like being this close to— I mean, it was three miles away; how can you be okay with that?'

I pulled on a polo shirt with the VASP logo and immediately felt wrong, as if I'd suited up in someone else's uniform.

I started tugging it back over my head, but Jenny stopped me. 'Leave it on,' she said. 'You can wear it.'

'For me or for you?' I reached for her.

'For me *and* for you.' She took my hand.

'You want me to bring my gun?' I joked.

She didn't hesitate. 'Yeah, I guess. Yes.'

'Jesus, Jenny. It's the library.'

'What?' She didn't pull away. 'You think that much anger and hatred can't find its way down the street? This isn't you out patrolling Interstate 95 by yourself, Sailor. Our kids are here. Your son runs up and down the boardwalk like an escaped monkey. I can't keep a leash on him. So yes, I want you to bring your gun.'

I lied, 'We're fine here; this is an old Irish neighbourhood. There's not a criminal street gang within a hundred miles that would lay

169

claim to this corner of America. They deal in drugs, sweetie, not Smithwicks.'

She didn't answer.

'Look,' I went on, 'that riot was between shitheads who think that the shooter is a murderer who needs to go to prison and shitheads who think he's a hero who saved a bunch of middle-schoolers. Most of the rioters were either members of his own gang or rival thugs who showed up to stir the pot. It's animals against animals, backstreet shits who'll use any excuse to run rampant.'

'You're a racist.' Her nostrils flared; she was ready for a fight.

I eased off the tension in my voice. 'No, I'm not, I'm telling you the truth. You think there aren't white losers fighting over this same question today? I'm no racist; I hate all assholes equally; it comes with the job.'

'Don't talk to me like I'm a fourth-grader, Sailor.' Jenny dropped my hand. 'I understand the complexity of the situation, and I know as well as you do that there are people in Neptune – there are people all over the country this morning – who think that shooter saved dozens of innocent schoolkids, thug or not. That riot was—'

'No,' I cut her off and regretted it immediately, 'sorry, honey, but that riot was between extremists on both sides of an unfortunate incident. I don't give a damn what colour skin they have; that's not fair to any of the decent people trying to lead an honest life in Neptune. There are law-abiding folks over there who think that shooter is a hero and law-abiding folks who think he's a killer. But I'd bet dollars to Dan's Doughnuts it wasn't *any of them* looting stores last night. Plenty of people in Neptune want to live in a safe city. Making this issue about race isn't fair to any of them. Assholes come in all colours. Ask Huck.'

'So, what's it about, if it isn't about race?'

'It's about a depressed, suicidal teenager – a white, Jewish teenager, by the way – whose parents probably screwed him all the way up the totem pole until he was ready to off himself in a very public way. And it's about a teenager who turned to a street gang to feel safe in his own neighbourhood and then stuck with that gang as they affiliated themselves with a larger group, maybe a national or a global gang – I

170

understand the Bloods are big in Asbury Park – and then sold drugs, extorted money, evaded taxes, bullied locals and engaged in all the same kinds of nasty behaviours you'd expect from an Italian crime family up in Jersey City or a neo-Nazi group in Bumfuck, Arkansas. Skin colour has nothing to do with it. These are poor kids making a living by breaking the law.'

'So you don't think that shooter saved anyone yesterday?' She looked over the paper again, then dropped it in the wastebasket.

I took it out. 'I want to read it, Jenny. Throwing the paper away isn't going to—'

'Sailor.'

'Right. Sorry.' I tucked the paper under my arm. 'Sorry.'

Her brow furrowed. 'Well? Don't you agree that kids were saved yesterday? I mean, assuming you didn't know Gabe Lebow was committing suicide.'

Gabe. Why's she calling him Gabe?

'From the outside looking in? Sure: it looks like a street thug saved a bunch of little kids, and I'm sure there are news networks right now claiming that his younger brothers and sisters were all enrolled at Robert Morris Middle School, each of them in patent leather shoes and studying fractions or the American Revolution. But, Jenny, that loser shot Gabriel Lebow yesterday because Lebow was about to make national news on *his* street corner, thereby buggering drug traffic on Cameron Drive and Steiner Avenue.'

Her eyes widened. 'You believe that? He shot Lebow to keep police and the media *away*? How could that possibly work?'

I ran my fingers through my hair, taming the tangles. 'If he shoots one kid, the press is around for a few days; then everything's quiet, just another tragic day in America's cities. If he lets Lebow enter the building to shoot three dozen classmates, well, the police and the media and the researchers, social workers, federal investigators, and frigging Geraldo Rivera are all over this place for the next five years, writing case studies and celebrating the anniversary of the massacre.'

'Commemorating.'

'Whatever. You know what I mean.' I hung my wet towel on the closet doorknob to dry. 'If Lebow had shot up Robert Morris Middle

School yesterday, killing teachers and kids, the drug market along that whole block would be closed down for months. That's this thug's corner; I'm sure he's defended it before, probably dozens of times.'

'Killing people?'

'Maybe, but you've got to understand a criminal street thug. That guy didn't stop to think everything through; he saw a potential nightmare unfolding and he acted. It isn't supposed to make sense to people like us, who *tsk* and shake our heads and watch the news from the safety of the suburbs.'

'I want to go home,' she said, not to me, more to herself, to the floor, the laundry basket.

'Jenny' – I took her hand again – 'this could have happened at home, too. Fredericksburg isn't immune. No place is. Well, maybe one or two places, but I'm afraid of polar bears.'

She chuckled and moved closer to me. 'Ben would like it there.'

'Too cold. He doesn't have any fat on him.'

She wrapped her arms around my waist. 'I like this shirt on you.'

'I'll wear it every day for the rest of my life.' She smelled good, clean, like soap and happily ever after.

'It makes you look thinner.'

'I am thinner,' I said proudly. 'I managed an abdominal crunch last night and another one this morning.'

She snorted through her nose. 'Don't overdo it, Sailor. You don't want to hurt yourself.'

I buried my face in the nape of her neck and kissed her gently. Her earring, a white pearl, nothing Tahitian, brushed my cheek. She dug her nails into my back, just for a second, then let go, pushing me gently away.

'What's the matter?' I said.

'Nothing, well, nothing.' She took a step back.

'Jenny, I don't know when—'

'I'll tell you when, Sailor.' Tears tried to spill over her cheeks; Jenny didn't let them. 'When I'm confident that neither you nor I will spend even one second thinking about Sarah Danvers. That's when.' She backed towards the hallway. 'Take a nap if you like. I'll get the kids ready. We can go to the library when you wake up.'

'Jenny—'

'It's all right, rest for a while. I'll wake you up if Detective Hodges calls.'

Two hours later, I woke to the sound of Anna crying. I splashed water on my face, tried to fix my hair, and straightened the VASP polo shirt. Stepping back, I checked myself in the mirror: not great, but presentable. Sober. Thinner. *That's two in your favour, Sailor. Not bad.*

'Yeah, but you're seeing and hearing things, shithead,' I said to my reflection. 'That's the pills coming for you. Don't let your guard down yet.'

In the living room, Jenny was feeding Anna, while Ben channel-surfed at light-speed with the television set on MUTE.

'Hi, Daddy!' he said. 'Can we go now?'

'We sure can, monster-mash,' I said. 'What're you watching?'

'We watched a cooking show.' He didn't look up, content to watch the channels flicker by in a blur. 'A lady made a really big cake with yellow flowers all the way around the top.'

'Groovy,' I said. 'Did it make you hungry?'

'Not really,' he sighed, frustrated that nothing he wanted to watch had magically appeared on the screen. 'We had the sound turned off so you could sleep.'

'That was nice of you.' I sat behind Ben, letting him fall into my lap. I took the remote and switched to Channel 12 News. The word MUTE hovered ghostlike in green letters.

Mel-Ken stood outside the Cameron Drive entrance to Robert Morris Middle School, flanked by the stone steps and the basketball court. He gestured a handful of red roses on the court. Any sign of blood had been scrubbed clean by CSI techs or washed away by the torrent raging outside. Mel-Ken's mouth moved as he fake-frowned at the camera, huddling beneath an umbrella decorated with the news channel logo, yellow on white. *Like flowers on a cake.*

I pressed MUTE; the green letters vanished as Mel-Ken said, '—not far from where local teens rioted last night, indicating clearly that the city of Neptune remains divided on—'

Jenny said, 'Mute that, would you? I don't want to hear how the community narrowly avoided a tragedy of epic proportions only to have some Bible-thumper toss a bunch of roses out there to make everything all better.' Sarcasm puddled on the living room floor.

'No problem,' I said and pressed MUTE again as Mel-Ken cut to file footage of Superintendent Mihalko announcing that all Neptune Township schools would be closed until Wednesday, at least. She looked flushed in a wool suit, too warm for press conferences outside.

'Roses. Always roses. False sentiment, makes me want to vomit.' Jenny draped a burp cloth over her shoulder, hoisted up the baby and began patting her gently between the shoulder blades.

'Burp, Annie!' Ben said. 'Give us a good one.' He laughed and squirmed in my lap.

'A good one?' I asked. 'Who taught you that?'

'You did, Daddy!'

'I did?' I tossed him onto the couch. 'Actually, that does sound like me; doesn't it?'

Jenny nodded towards the television. 'Look at that, will you? People are so predictable. The next thing you know there'll be a candlelight vigil.'

'Nah, it's raining.'

'Mark my words,' she said, 'half the city will be out there later, holding candles and singing *Kumbaya* or some silliness, when they ought to be—'

'What, Mommy?' Ben was hanging on her every word.

Jenny blinked back tears. Her lip trembled. 'Nothing, monkey-man. Let's go to the library.'

On cue, Anna burped and Ben fell into the couch, clapping and laughing.

I watched Jenny a moment; she wouldn't make eye contact with me. 'Let's go,' she said to anyone listening, and I turned away, pretending not to see as she wiped her eyes on the back of her hand.

To Ben, I said, 'Raincoat, socks, shoes, buddy. We're rolling out of here.'

'Okay, Daddy,' Ben tumbled onto the floor, giggling, then crept quickly away.

I used the rolled-up *Asbury Park Press* to pat him on the butt as he hustled down the hallway. 'You've got thirty-seven seconds, monkey-man …' My bullshit warning trailed off as I caught sight of the story below the fold: a two-inch column, with a two-inch photo of a sandy-haired teenager. The paper noted that Neptune Township, Bradley Beach and Asbury Park police had no leads in their search for Jeremy Landon, the surfer missing from Ocean Grove since yesterday afternoon. Neptune Township Police had contacted the Coast Guard and begun a search-and-recovery effort.

My leg twitched involuntarily, reminding me how little it liked rising quickly from the floor, and I tottered to the sofa and let myself fall into Ben's pillow pile.

On the television was muted footage of the riot, three miles away. I can see why behaviourists suggest we are violent by nature: we move in packs, swarms, gangs, whatever the term, and look like animals, hunting, fighting, protecting. Some run, chaotic, but oddly predictable; others, many others, move with the ebb and flow of the crowd, towards and away from danger. Engagement is a group of five stomping another, kicking viciously at his head as he writhes on the pavement. Engagement is two women, both fifty pounds overweight, grabbing at each other's hair and blouses with one hand so they can pummel with the other, nothing like the movies, jab, jab, hook, uppercut: this is primal: rip, tear, claw, bite, stomp, then run. The police use rubber bullets and fire hoses. Nothing else, short of bulldozers, will divert the mob's attention. It is three miles away, and I started it.

An unpleasant wave of dizziness sneaked up on me; I had to lean forward and sink my head between my knees to keep from passing out.

'You all right?' Jenny asked, strapping Anna into her car seat.

'I'm fine,' I lied. 'A bit too much walking, too much Nytol, maybe. I've gotta lay off that stuff. I'll grab a smoke outside and be fine.'

'You sure? We don't have to go. It's shitty out as it is.'

'I'm okay – and besides, Ben'll self-destruct if we don't take him.'

'True,' Jenny agreed. 'But I don't want to go to the Belmar library. Is there one in Spring Lake?'

'Yup, on Third Avenue. I walked right by it this morning.'

'Let's go there.'

'Done,' I said. I needed to stop thinking about Harold Hanley,

Gabriel Lebow, thirty-five missing lobsters, one missing surfer, the curlew of the Canadian Arctic, minor league baseball, gang killers and a mutilated pig named Auntie Carla.

I stepped out of the driveway entrance, off D Street; I wasn't ready for Twelfth Avenue and Gabriel Lebow, not yet. I lit up, inhaled, and held the smoke until my head cleared, then blew out slowly, relishing the familiar tickle in my sinuses. I watched the smouldering red tip and coiling spirals of smoke, both impervious to the rain. *Christ, these are going to be hard to quit.* I inhaled again, then listened to the Belmar morning.

Rain chattered on the street, the sidewalk, the leaves, the hood of Jenny's minivan, swelling into a backdrop of squelchy noise. I listened for Gabriel, tuning my ears around the corner of the house, but there was nothing.

'You gotta go look; it'll only take a few seconds,' I told myself, and pressed the small button in the handle of Jenny's umbrella. It opened with a vinyl cough.

Armed only with the umbrella and emboldened by nicotine, I turned the corner towards C Street and the tidy Cape Cod house where I'd seen Lebow. A Taco Bell wrapper floated east like a paper boat that had been hit by a torpedo; I remembered the town's warning, that all the drainage gutters led straight to the ocean, and I snagged the wrapper and dragged it onto the sidewalk: clean-up duty was as good an excuse as any not to look up, not yet.

Overhead, a listless seagull wound its way east over the beach. It saw something disagreeable in the sand and cawed loudly before swooping south along the boardwalk.

I silently chided myself for stalling and, finally, lifted the umbrella and looked towards the Cape Cod's second-floor window.

A white smudge, like a line of finger-paint or a sloppy brushstroke, ran along the lower edge of one pane. Lebow had been there.

'That's not possible. He's in the basement at Jersey Shore Medical with his guts spread out over a wax-bottomed tray.' My voice did nothing to reassure me. For a moment, I wondered if I might be coming apart. 'A normal day,' I tried again, 'that's all I need, just a normal day, with no dead bodies, no gang killings, no tags scratched into trees, just a Regular Joe day with sandwiches and coffee, dirty diapers and stupid magazine articles.' I wanted another cigarette already, but I ignored the craving. 'Let's just have a normal day, huh?'

Ben burst from the house behind me; the screen door slapped shut in his wake. Leaping off the porch steps, he skidded across the sloping front lawn, with an excited, *'Whoa!'*

'Careful, buddy,' I warned, too late as Ben lost his footing and slid on his ass to the sidewalk. 'You all right, monkey-man?'

'Did you see that, Daddy? It was like the slide at the playground!'

'Nice work, crazy person, but now you're all wet.'

'I don't care.'

'Mommy does.' I corralled him beneath Jenny's umbrella. 'C'mon, we'll get you dry pants.'

'Will you read with me at the library, Daddy?'

A normal day, Sailor.

'I sure will, man-cub, but you'll have to help me figure out the hard words.'

'Okay, Daddy. We can sound them out, like in Miss Telegar's class.'

Spring Lake Library was camouflaged inside a sprawling neo-Tudor mansion just a little more tasteful than the behemoth castle Moses Stillman disliked so much. Ben located the comfy children's alcove five seconds after bounding through the entrance, ignoring the two-storey stacks and widow's walk balcony with its fine wrought-iron balustrade and Bruce Wayne fireplace. Jenny paused long enough to say, 'Wow! Check this place out, Sailor.'

'Nice,' I agreed, looking at the narrow wraparound balcony and spiral staircase. 'We ought to put one of these in our house. You know, open the place up a bit.'

'Right. What would we do with the upstairs bedrooms?'

'Dunno. I hadn't thought that far through it.'

'You want Reading Duty or Sleeping Duty?'

A normal day.

'Both, I guess.' I reached for the stroller. 'I'll start with Sleeping Duty. I've got a couple of things I want to look up online.'

Ben shouted from the Children's Room, 'Come *on*, Mommy. There's a jillion books and a big couch!'

The librarian, clearly retired from the Historic Documents room at the British Library, scowled at us through über-conservative quadra-focal lenses.

'Sorry,' Jenny whispered, hustling towards the Children's Room. 'Benjamin Owen, keep your voice down!'

I pushed Anna towards a rank of computers and parallel-parked her stroller between my chair and a rack of newspapers and magazines. On an adjacent table someone had left out a Rhode Island-sized coffee-table book called *Spring Lake: A Photographic History*, by one Rawlings Merriweather.

I leaned over Anna's stroller and whispered, 'We're not in Kansas any more, sweetie.'

Rawlings Merriweather's book sported two images of the Warren & Monmouth Hotel, one a black-and-white photo, the other, a current image. They looked like they'd both been taken from the air. The images documented a hundred years of 'improvements' and preserva-tion to the town's iconic façade.

From the Children's Room, I could hear enough to realise that Ben had found the same bicycling-bear book he'd read six hundred and eighty-three times already. Jenny tried to convince him to try something new, but he wanted no part of that conversation.

Jenny read. She was better at animal voices than I was.

Smiling, I clicked on the computer, figuring I'd fart around a bit on the Internet and check my email. An older woman in an expensive-looking hat clicked away on the next computer. Her silk blouse and never-say-die gabardine trousers clashed with her herringbone tweed jacket like chain-mail and macramé. Brittle salt-and-pepper hair hung loose over her collar – strange for a woman her age to have hair that long, I thought, but she obviously had enough money not to give a shit what I thought. She paused in her typing and looked down at Anna, offered a bright capped smile and said, 'Ooh, what a lovely little girl.'

'Thanks. I made her myself.' I slid my chair forwards with a shriek so loud I waved an apology towards the grim-faced librarian. 'Sorry about that.'

'Nothing to be sorry about,' Herringbone said. 'I think we're the only ones here today. Never made sense to me that the library has to be deathly silent when no one else is around.'

'I guess not,' I said, and dug in the bag until I found Eeyore. I spread-eagled him across Anna's legs. If she woke while I was distracted online she'd want the old donkey nearby.

'Eeyore?' Herringbone didn't bother whispering. The deep lines and leathery skin told of a lifetime near the ocean, much of it before the advent of sunscreen.

'Her favourite,' I said.

'My children were all rabbits: smart, energetic worrywarts.' A pencil-thin scar ran the length of her jaw, more evidence she'd seen some mileage in her day. 'They're older now.'

I'd never thought of Hundred Acre Wood characters as personality types, but it made sense to some degree. I said, 'I'm not sure she's an Eeyore; she just likes chewing on his ear. I figure that pegs her for a carnivore, if nothing else.'

Herringbone explained, 'Eeyores are dependable friends, loyal and predictable, but not in a bad way. Steady. There are worse traits to embody.'

'Okay.' I had no idea where this was going. Maybe she just wanted to chat.

'What are you researching today?'

I said the first thing that came to mind. 'Um, Canadian minor league baseball players.'

'What ever for?' Herringbone laughed, too loudly.

I looked over at the librarian, hoping she'd realise it wasn't me causing the ruckus. 'Well, I don't really know, except that I met a man recently who used to play in Ottawa, so I figured I'd see what kind of career statistics he tallied while he was up there.'

'Really?'

'Yup.'

She turned back to her own screen. 'I'll leave you to it, then. Good luck.'

'Thanks.' I checked on Anna, still sleeping like only a newborn can, and typed *Ottawa Pioneers* into Google.

Ten minutes later, I had skim-read a few articles about the Pioneers and their fifty-three-year history in Ottawa. I found old team photos, snapshots taken from Riverdale Park, their home venue until 1993, accounts of ageing major leaguers who'd spent time in Ottawa, *like a prison sentence, I bet*, before moving on to other Double-A markets or retiring into obscurity. I even found a legendary story about a Canada goose, killed by a line-drive during a two-out rally in a Governor's Cup play-off game in 1977. But nowhere did I find even one reference to Mark "Moses" Stillman, who, allegedly, played for the Pioneers for seven of his nine years in Double-A competition.

'That's odd,' I said to the screen, one of my incurable habits.

'Hmm?' Herringbone raised an eyebrow at me. 'Finding that hockey and curling outdistance baseball by a couple of furlongs?'

'Well, that, and I'm afraid my friend might have been fibbing about his background.'

'Is he old?' she asked. 'You mentioned that he *used to play*. I take it he's retired.'

'Um, not ancient or knocking on death's door, but he's a stretch on the dark side of sixty-five.'

'Ah.' She pursed her lips; her scar whitened as it stretched. 'Then he might be inflating his memories a bit. You know how it is when the shadows start getting long. The home run, the touch-down pass, the blue marlin, they all get polished up – and who can blame him? He'll never play ball again; it might be his only legacy, especially if he doesn't have children or grandchildren. Why not decorate it, just a tad, for anyone willing to listen?'

'Fair enough,' I said, 'but this guy doesn't exist at all.'

She hesitated a moment, then said, 'Then he's a liar … or a socio-path, of course. Given my choice, I'd take the liar. Sociopaths are so unpredictable.' She pulled her tweed jacket closed.

I had no idea what to make of her, and pretended to adjust something inside Anna's stroller, buying myself a second or two. 'Um, thanks. I'll see if maybe I'm spelling his name wrong, or perhaps I'm on the wrong website. Who knows?'

'Enjoy.' She went back to whatever it was she'd been typing. I pegged her for a wealthy protestant teetotaller, probably researching hymns for church. I didn't dare ask, for fear that I might have to explain to Jenny why I had tickets to a Sunday roast beef supper.

I found a site dedicated to archiving every last detail of every professional player in baseball history: career statistics, highlights, awards, injuries and even major disappointments. I goofed around for a while, looking up obscure players I remembered from my baseball-card days; I had no trouble finding players who'd spent the majority of their careers in Ottawa, playing for the Ottawa Giants, the Ottawa Athletics or the more recent Ottawa Lynx.

But no Moses Stillman, no Mark Stillman. Nothing, nada.

'Liar,' I said, clicking a link that brought up a page on the 1986 Mets. 'Why make up something like that? All those bullshit stories about restaurants, cheap weed and loose women?'

Anna didn't answer, but Herringbone did: 'When the shadows get long, you'll be surprised what people do.'

I nodded, and, to Anna, said, 'What's next, sweetie? Tahitian pearls? Let's see if those are bogus too.'

Now Herringbone did whisper, 'Ooh, those are lovely – did you know they are as rare as the rarest gems on earth? The legitimate ones, anyway.' She wrinkled her nose. I worried her glasses might slip off and shatter on the desk. 'These days most are farmed, like traditional pearls, bloody imposters.'

Coming from a woman with capped teeth, this made me chuckle. 'You don't like cultured pearls?'

'Pah!' she scoffed, flicking both wrists as if dismissing a bottle of bad wine. 'You can tell the difference in the smoothness. Natural pearls, particularly black pearls, have minor imperfections, wrinkles and ridges. That's how you know you've really got something special.'

After a minute or two, she peeked over again. 'If you'd like to see a gorgeous strand, there's one on display just down the street at O'Malley's, not three blocks from here.'

'No kidding?'

'They're exquisite, particularly the centrepiece, which I think is a fake; it's too large, too perfect, too impossibly glorious to be real.' Her voice now was a conspiratorial whisper, as if the two of us might snatch them and run for Mexico. 'And most of the phonies in this town have no idea what they are. I have *friends* who believe they're just costume jewellery, but I know better.'

'They for sale?'

'Everything's for sale, young man.'

'Right.'

'Legend has it this strand belonged to some Pacific Island princess who died of a heroin overdose back in the '60s. Tragic.'

'Heroin will do that to you,' I said.

'You should go and look; take your wife – I'm sure she'd love to see them.'

'I will.' I wiped a bead of sweat from my temple. I needed a cigarette. Something crashed in the children's room; I'd recognise it anywhere: the unmistakable sound of Ben dumping a kid's puzzle onto a wooden floor.

'Oh dear.' Herringbone looked up again.

'He's mine, too.' I stood, kicked the brake off Anna's stroller and started towards the children's alcove. 'Have a good day.'

'You too,' she said, and gave us a toodle-oo wave.

Just for fun, I left my computer screen open on a bomb-making site Huck had found during anti-terror training at Division Headquarters the previous spring. 'That'll teach her to mind her own business,' I whispered to Anna. Eeyore looked up at me with unblinking eyes.

We stayed in the library until the rain stopped. Ben had a minor meltdown when he learned that he couldn't take home the forty-three books he wanted to read – without a Spring Lake address we couldn't get a library card. Instead we promised that we'd hit the Belmar Library when Grandma came to visit on Saturday, which calmed him enough to enter into negotiations regarding lunch. Jenny wanted to go to Nagle's Café in Ocean Grove for burgers. Ben wanted ice cream. I just wanted to smoke. We compromised on Nagle's, loaded everything back into the minivan and drove north along the water, glad to see that the rain had kept most of the day-trippers away.

The beach, ironed flat by the deluge, looked like an exposed seam in the universe, an unfinished edge holding land and water together.

Three miles out, gunmetal waves continued to boil beneath an angry sky. Directly overhead, however, the capricious sun tried to burn its way through the storm.

'Look at the sidewalk, Mommy,' Ben said from his booster seat. 'It's like a river.'

'That's all the rain running away,' Jenny said.

'Where's it running to?'

'To those holes in the street.' I pointed out his window. 'There's a big pipe that takes the rain out to the ocean.'

'Are there sharks?'

'No sharks,' I said.

Ben wasn't convinced. 'I bet that's where the shark in the back yard lives.' He watched the beach, the boardwalk, the gutters for any sign of the shark he'd met in his nightmares.

We stopped at the lights and Jenny turned far enough to see him. Her hair fell over her face and I reached over to push it behind her ear. She took my hand, held it to her cheek for a second, then let it go. To Ben, she said, 'Buddy, there's no shark in the yard. Sharks have to stay under the water. You've read all those books about animals. You know that, right?'

Calmly, like an attorney making a point, Ben said, 'It's not that kind of shark, Mommy. It's different.'

'Is it mad or hungry?' I asked. 'Is it trying to get inside the house?'

Jenny shot me her death glare. *How about if we try not to make things worse, Sailor?*

Ben said, 'I dunno. I don't think so. It's just watching.'

'Watching what?' Jenny tickled his knee.

Ben giggled. 'The house, just watching the house.'

'You want me to stay up late tonight? Maybe see if I can catch it?' I asked.

'Sure, Daddy!' Ben yelped. 'And Mommy, if Daddy catches it – if he does, then can I keep it? Can we get a big bowl or a pool and keep the shark?'

Jenny chuckled. 'Of course we can, monkey-face – *if* Daddy catches the shark, we can keep it. But no reaching into its tank, because sharks love the taste of little boy fingers.'

Now it was my turn to glare. *Nice one – he'll never sleep again.*

Jenny tried to rebound. 'But they don't like the taste of little-boy pyjamas, so you're completely safe if you feed him while you wear your pyjamas.'

Good recovery!

Behind me, Anna woke with a start and howled. The minivan echoed childhood like a cavern.

'Uh, oh,' Ben said, 'Annie's awake.'

'Talk to her, monkey-man,' I said. 'We're almost there. See if you can get her to calm down.'

'Okay.' Ben leaned over as far as his seatbelt would allow. He sang, '*Ring-around-rosie, ring-around-rosie, ring-around-rosie.*' I gripped the wheel with both hands, as tight as I could; sweat dripped down my forehead.

Jenny said, 'That's not how it goes, buddy. Sing her the whole thing.'

'Help me, Mommy,' Ben said.

They sang together, and I loosened my grip, turned onto Main Street and found a parking place right in front of Nagle's. I could smell grilling beef and freshly brewed coffee and my stomach growled, reminding me how long it'd been since I'd eaten.

We only waited ten minutes for a table – Nagle's stayed busy year-round, rain or shine – and just as the teenage host waved us in, my cell phone buzzed.

'Damn.' I checked the screen. 'It's Hodges.'

'You have to take it.' Jenny hoisted Anna's diaper bag. 'Go ahead, I'll get the kids settled.'

'I'll be quick,' I said, and answered, 'Good afternoon, Detective Hodges.'

'How are you, Doyle?'

'Not bad,' I said. 'It's almost one o'clock, and I've yet to come across a dead body today.' I lit a cigarette and blew smoke out my nose.

'I knew there was hope for you.'

'What's doing? You find our thugs?'

'Not yet,' she said. 'Neptune Township is leaning on a handful of local losers, gang wannabes – actual gang members rarely talk unless they're looking at a stretch in the county lock-up.'

'I know that song, cousin. It's refreshing to see other cops wrestling with the same bullshit.'

'Just another day in paradise,' she joked. 'I'm calling because I didn't want you to worry about the fallout from yesterday, all that nonsense in the streets last night. I filed a report and the staff sergeant forwarded the Cliff Notes version to the local press. I've had reporters up my skirt since yesterday afternoon – getting goddamned crowded up there – and the fucking TV crews have been trolling for assholes up and down 71 all night. If they weren't such a pain in the ass, it'd be comical. They're here, but they don't know what they're looking for, not sure what to point the cameras at. You know?'

'I get it,' I said. 'But what do you mean about me not worrying?'

'Your name, your past, Doyle – I didn't release anything. I had to mention you in my report, but I made damn sure it didn't leak when we sent the scripts out to the newspapers. Neither Sergeant Collins from Neptune PD nor Bobby Harmon, the CSI guy from our office, spoke with the press; I promised them both a royal beating if they so much as breathed your name into their coffee cups. And only the Jersey Shore Med psychologist and I spoke with Gabriel Lebow's parents.'

'How'd that go?'

'Like a rainy weekend in Hell, but thanks for asking.'

'You mention my name?'

'Didn't have to; they were so distraught at the sight of us in the driveway they never asked, so I didn't spill. It'll come up though, eventually; they may get a lawyer, decide to sue someone – you, me, the county, the school district – and once they get past the initial shock, they may come looking for your head on a dish.'

'But not yet.' I stepped off the curb to avoid a teenage kid on a bike.

'They're pretty well crushed, Doyle. None of them saw this coming. While we were there, Lebow's aunt showed up, day off, I guess. She collapsed as well, but not before calling an uncle, a decent guy, some corporate lawyer up in Jersey City. The grandfather's got a law prac-tice across from the Prosecutor's Office; he's been a defence attorney around here for about a hundred years. I'm surprised we haven't heard from him. Another decent guy, runs in the family, I guess. Anyway, the uncle came down right away, and he talked to me for a while yesterday afternoon. He's going to make all the arrangements for the family. But no one had any idea this was coming.'

'That's strange,' I said, 'but it jives with what the assistant principal—'

'—Porter—'

'—right, C. Porter, what he said yesterday morning. This was a shocker for everyone involved. It'll be interesting to see what skeletons this kid had in his closet.'

'Fucked up,' Marta said. 'Kids today are all fucked up. It's the frigging Internet, you know? Too much access to too much information too young. When I was a kid, you got picked on at school – everyone did – so you either stood up to the bully bitch, met her on the sidewalk and got busy slapping, pulling hair, the works, or you shut up, found other ways to walk home, avoided the mall and prayed she'd find some other unlucky cow to torment.'

'Same with guys,' I said. 'It was the way of the world: you didn't like it, your only choice was to run away to Antarctica.'

'Exactly.' Marta sounded amused. 'You certainly didn't tell your parents or your teachers.'

'But you also didn't steal keys, download floor plans for the local middle school or lie about your age to order an RPG from an offshore dealer trolling for terrorists on eBay.'

'What a mess,' Marta said. 'And what's with all these goddamned cell phones – can anyone tell me why a twelve-year-old kid needs a cellular phone with Internet access, texting, email, Facebook and its own wi-fi cloud? What the hell are we thinking? You have a phone at age twelve, Doyle?'

I crushed my cigarette and tossed the butt towards a sidewalk trash can. 'Shit, we didn't even have quarters for the payphone! You needed a ride home, you called home, and when Mom or Dad answered you clicked the line a couple of times and they knew to come get us.'

Marta snorted. 'That's a good one, Doyle: we had it bad in Long Branch but not *that* bad.'

'Poor neighbourhood,' I said. 'Quarters were scarce; why waste one talking to my mother?'

'Anyway, the school superintendent has some psychologists and guidance counsellors assigned to deal with the aftermath over at Morris Middle. I guess a bunch of kids watched the whole thing from their classroom windows and now the poor bastards will be wetting the bed until their fortieth birthdays. Lebow's school counsellor is working with the Psych Division at Jersey Shore Medical to try and figure out why he decided to do himself in public. I can see how parents might not have known all the shit he had on his computer or in his notebooks, but I can't figure how a kid supposedly this depressed was walking around the house and no one noticed.'

'It's frightening how disconnected we can get, even living in the same house.' In my mind, I heard Jenny: *Sweetie, please tell me that we'll never, never miss something so obvious, so much pain in one of our kids, in Ben. Promise me that.*

'You said it, Doyle.'

'Anything I can do to help the family?' It felt like a lame request, but I offered anyway.

'No; they're planning some kind of memorial service at sundown. The temple's in Bradley Beach. We'll have plenty of uniformed muscle out there. If there's good news for me this week – and there has been very little – but if there *is* good news, it's that this shitstorm you cranked up is multi-jurisdictional.'

'How is that good news?' I asked. 'I'd have thought that would be a royal pain.'

'Oh, it is, don't get me wrong,' she corrected, 'but thanks to last night's antics I can dial up plenty of uniforms in case any irritated locals decide to crash the Lebow family's picnic.'

'Got it,' I said. 'So you've got a show of force in case anyone's up for another street fight. You letting the media know?'

'It'll leak, and that's fine by me.'

'Nice. Word'll get out: you riot tonight, you get your head busted. Effective public relations, Detective Hodges,' I teased.

'I'm hoping the rain'll keep them all inside,' she said, 'and keep things quiet for the Lebows.'

'You think I should—?'

'Hell no!' She cut me off. 'I've kept your name out of this – don't you

187

dare go showing your pasty-white Irish ass at any memorial service!'

'All right,' I said, 'I'll keep my head down.'

'Good thinking,' Marta said. 'Now, I gotta go. Don't skip town on me.'

'No problem. And again, I appreciate you keeping the media dogs off my lawn and my name off the Lebow family radar. Truly.'

'So far so good,' she said. 'Regardless, I think they're more pissed at me today than you, to tell the truth.'

'How come?'

'They're Jews. They're supposed to get him in the ground within twenty-four hours. The service tonight is only because—'

'—because you haven't released the body.' Gabriel Lebow would be at the Monmouth County Medical Examiner's Office, awaiting a post-mortem. Maybe shelved next to Harold Hardass Hanley – for a moment I imagined the two of them there, tucked into side-by-side drawers, not howling down at me from the neighbour's window.

'It'll be a few days,' she said, interrupting my vision. 'There are some things I just can't rush, even though the uncle's been phoning all morning, even had the rabbi call a couple of times, just to push us. I've got the county office trying to distract Lebow's parents with information from the Street Crimes Unit and progress tracking down our shooter.'

'How's that going?' I asked.

'We'll find him,' she said. 'You were right; there can't be too many places for him to hide. Neptune Township PD is squeezing a few of his customers now; your description of the buyer who crossed Cameron just before the shooting helped. Neptune think they know him.'

I remembered Tubby, in his tattered Jams and his flyaway hair. 'He won't be hard to spot if he's out on Steiner,' I said. 'He looks like a confused, half-naked back-up singer from an ancient reggae band.'

'We'll lean on him this afternoon, probably threaten him with thirty days. That long off the juice will scare him,' Marta said. 'Hopefully he'll give up a name, perhaps a gang alias.'

'Street Crimes Unit keep a database of those, too?'

'Can't make any real progress without one,' she said. 'Some of these kids spend twenty hours a day with one another and have no idea what their friends' real names are. William Tyler Bennett is Li'l T, or some shit.'

'Hard to spell on a résumé, I guess.' I wandered down the block and an old-time firehouse like something from lower Manhattan rose unexpectedly behind the restaurant. 'That's cool,' I said without realising it.

'What's cool?' Hodges asked. 'That I've got the Lebow family scratching at my office window? Because I beg to differ—'

'No, no. It's nothing,' I said quickly, 'I just never knew this old firehouse was back here.'

'You at Nagle's?'

'How'd you know?'

'That firehouse – it's still operational. It's like looking backwards through time, don't you think? Anyway' – she got us straight back on track – 'don't go thinking I did you any favours. The gang thugs around here are real assholes. We've got MOB, Double ii, G-Shine, B-Shine, SexMoneyMurder, Latin Kings, Black Haitian Pride and the ever-reliable Crips and Bloods all active: a regular hall of gang fame. Based on the tattoos you described and the street corner he was working, I'm guessing he's a member of the North Side Playaz. They've got a working relationship with the local Bloods to deal dope along Memorial Drive and 71. I can't imagine what the cut is for the Bloods, but it's gotta be significant. Anyway, your boy was a die-hard.'

'Why do you say that?' I asked. 'Aren't most of them die-hards?'

'Nah,' she said, 'we've got so many factions partially because you can't walk five hundred feet without crossing into a new town. Most of the thugs here don't get tattoos.'

I thought about that a moment. 'Makes sense, I guess. You move across the street and you've got to change your affiliation. That's a lot of money in ink and a lot of scar tissue where you've had the old ones removed.'

'I know that song, cousin,' she mimicked me.

'But the shithead who capped Lebow was painted up like the Sistine ceiling; so you figure—?'

'I figure him for North Side, hard core, a true Asbury Park homeboy, born and bred not a hundred feet from Memorial Drive. Trouble for us today is that the North Side Playaz have Blood allies against Black Haitian Pride, the Latin Kings, and a small faction of MS-13 trying to take hold up in Asbury Park, west of the tracks.'

'So our shithead could be hiding somewhere else?'

'A few places, Blood strongholds, but I don't want you to worry.'

'Because withholding my name—'

'Means nobody comes around to mess with your pretty wife or those two little babies you've got down the shore this month, Detective.'

God lifted the piano off my chest. I couldn't wait to tell Jenny. We were in the clear, for now. 'Thanks, Hodges. Truly.'

'No problem, Doyle, but you do owe me.'

'Name it.'

'I need you to ride along when we pinch him, if you're still around.'

'Done.'

'Good enough,' she said. 'Try the Reuben at that place. It's a miracle.'

'I will, Detective, thanks.'

She clicked off.

'Thank Christ,' I whispered. I lifted my phone to snap a quick picture of the old firehouse, promising myself I'd come back with the real camera later, then went to keep my promise: try the Reuben.

I found Jenny and the kids tucked around a table near a display case filled with old apothecary instruments and scales. It was the kind of stuff you figured the dealer might have used to measure out whatever Romeo and Juliet snorted to close the curtain at the end of the play.

No SWAT *snipers around to finish the job for them!*

Jenny waved and I sidled between crowded tables. 'Wait till you see what I found around the corner,' I called to Ben, who was kneeling on his chair and sucking milk through a long straw. I pulled up the photo on my phone. 'It's an old—'

I stopped short of the table, wiped the screen clear and peered down at the photo I'd taken not two minutes earlier. The Ocean Grove Firehouse sported twin cornices of brick and concrete, rising twenty feet on either side of the great sliding doors. On the flat top of the northern cornice, glaring down at my camera, was a vicious-looking gargoyle. The southern pedestal was empty.

190

I'd slept through European Art and Architecture so I had no idea what its facial expressions were intended to convey, but I inferred disdain, demonic aggression and a clear taste for human flesh. 'What the hell?' I said to no one.

'What's the matter?' Jenny asked, worried that I'd got bad news from Marta Hodges.

'Um, nothing,' I said, dragging a sleeve across my forehead. *So much for a normal day.*

'I don't understand why you feel you have to go down there, Sailor.'

'Sure you do,' I said.

'Okay, fine, I do, but I'd rather you stay here. It's late.' She held Eeyore up by his front hooves, forcing him to dance like Gene Kelly for Anna's entertainment. To the baby she said, 'Come on, sweetie, close your eyes. Will you? For Mommy? It's time for sleeping.'

Anna, wide awake in her bouncy chair, looked back without blinking. On the sofa behind them, Ben slept in his tangled Spider-Man blanket. Over Jenny's shoulder I watched Eeyore leap and twirl; I suggested, 'Maybe if we put the donkey to bed, the baby will follow.'

'Maybe.' Jenny draped Eeyore across Anna's knees. 'I'll try feeding her; that should shut her up.' She picked up the baby, slipped off one side of her tanktop and helped Anna latch on. While fundamentally maternal, it still made me want to have sex – I figured it wasn't so much the breastfeeding as the sexy slip out of that tanktop. All guys are thrilled when circumstances confirm that women are actually quite adept at getting out of their clothes on short notice.

Jenny slapped me out of it. 'Get me one of those burp rags, will you?'

Just the term *burp rag* was enough to quash my mood. I dug around in the bag until I found one. 'Jesus, Jenny,' I exclaimed, 'we've got to wash these – they're foul!'

'Your arm hurt?'

'A little, why?'

'Because mine are occupied right now.' She gave me a coquettish wink that brought my mood back full throttle. 'I figured if you weren't

191

in too much pain you might load the washer and push START. I imagine lots of people manage it one-handed.'

'Hey,' I warned, 'everyone loves a little ass now and then, but no one loves a smartass.'

'Well unless you get *your* ass in there and help me with *your* children's laundry, you can forget any hope of ever getting any ass at all, big-ass, striped or whatever.'

'Okay, okay.' I tugged the diaper bag over to the washing machine.

Behind me, Jenny said, 'Don't forget the hamper in Ben's room.'

'Got it,' I said without turning back.

'Thanks, sweetie.'

'Sweetie,' I whispered. 'Now I'm sweetie again. We'll have the cleanest goddamned clothes in North America if I can be *sweetie* again.' I began loading the dirty washing, without giving much thought to what I was actually stuffed in there – whites, colours, fabrics, synthetics, animal furs, the lot.

From the other room, I heard Jenny say, 'You'll probably need to do two loads.'

'Shit,' I whispered, 'too late.'

She went on, 'Or I can do the towels in the morning.'

I didn't answer.

'Sailor?'

'Um, no, it's okay. I've got it.' I closed the lid, killed the lights and went back to the living room. 'Why don't you put Anna to bed, I'll haul Ben down to his room and you can call it a day. I'll switch the stuff to the dryer before I run down to the Warren & Monmouth. I can meet Moses and Tony, get a quick look in Harold Hanley's room, get answers for all my irritating questions, and be back here in time to fold everything before it wrinkles.'

'I'm not going to be able to talk you out of it, am I?'

'Honestly?'

'That's the theme of our month here together, Oh Helpful Husband of Mine.'

'Any chance you're going to bed naked?'

She didn't even flinch. 'Nope.'

'Then no, there is no way you can talk me out of it, Jenny. I'm driving myself crazy over a couple of strange things which keep trying to line themselves up in my head. Five minutes in Hanley's room is all I need to get everything straightened out.'

Jenny flopped a cloth over her shoulder, lifted the baby upright and slipped back into her tanktop, covering her boob again before I could properly admire it.'Jackass,' she said.

'That's *horny jackass* to you, Celibate Wife of Mine.'

Jenny patted Anna's back until the baby burped like a Bavarian trombone player.

'Whoa,' I said, '*excuse* you.'

Jenny slipped the other boob free, adjusted the baby back into place and said, 'She's pretty milk-drunk now. I don't know how much more she'll take, but I'm betting she'll sleep for a few hours.'

'Then that cinches it.' I tallied points on my fingers, convincing the jury: 'You put the baby to bed. I'll take care of Ben. I'll switch the laundry; you don't need to bother with it, and you can go to bed early.'

She looked at me. 'Okay, Sailor, go. But if you call me to pick you up at one more crime scene, or if you get arrested—'

I offered my best *incredulous* face. 'I *can't* be arrested; I'm a State Police Officer. The only thing they arrest us for is shooting lunatics while stoned on stolen medication.'

Jenny's brow furrowed; I mentally slapped myself. 'Maybe a bridge too far?'

'Maybe.' She absently ran a hand over Anna's tiny head. 'No arrests and no dead bodies.'

'Not even a small one.'

On the muted television, an ambulance chaser in felonious pin-stripes told me to call if I'd been injured in a car accident. I couldn't hear him, but his lips were easy to read. Jenny finally said, 'Go. I'll be asleep when you come back to fold the laundry.'

'Done.' I leaned over to kiss her and this time she didn't turn away. Her lips tasted like a reprieve from every regret I'd ever known and I kissed her again, as deeply as she'd let me. Anyone who's never kissed his wife while she's breastfeeding their baby has missed something truly powerful. My insides softened to mush, and a swampy dizziness threatened to knock me backwards.

'Go,' she said again. 'Be careful.'

'You want me to stay?' I whispered.

'Yup, but no. I'll see you later. You taking a gun?'

That surprised me. 'Why?'

'Are you?' The ambulance chaser's commercial ended and a black and white movie came on, changing the light on Jenny's face.

'Am I taking a gun and turning one felony into about eleven? No, I hadn't planned on it.'

Like Anna, Jenny didn't blink. 'Take your gun, the big silver one I'm not supposed to know about.'

I did blink. 'Okay.'

'Thanks, Sailor.' Jenny went back to feeding Anna. 'And put your son to bed.'

'Got it.' I slid my arms beneath Ben wrapped in his Spider-Man blanket and lifted the whole bundle gently, managing to avoid straining my shoulder.

Ben groaned when I tucked him in. I was halfway into the hall when he said, 'Daddy? Will you check outside my window for sharks?' He pulled Spider-Man up beneath his chin and fell back to sleep before I could answer.

'I sure will,' I whispered, brushing his hair off his face. 'There's nothing to be scared of.' *Well, other than butchered pigs, stolen lobsters, criminal street gangs, armed drug dealers, suicidal history teachers, missing surfers, ghostlike Pink Floyd songs, and bomb-toting schoolkids waiting for an autopsy that will probably show that Daddy broke his leg and his jaw while wrestling him to the ground. And then there's his parents, who will read that autopsy report and come after Daddy with a lawyer who'll probably wear felonious pinstripes and appear in local cable commercials flanked by serious-looking books he's never really read. That's all, monkey-man.*

I loaded Uncle Paul's illegal Smith & Wesson with silver bullets, tucked it into my shorts and checked outside Ben's window. Dad's gnarled pear tree cut a foreboding silhouette in the O'Mearas' porch light. For a moment, nothing about me wanted to go out there, but I did, gun in hand. Of course I found nothing.

*

I arrived at the Warren & Monmouth about ten past ten. The weather was cool for September, but it was clear, and there was a bit of boardwalk traffic, kids mostly, walking, jogging or biking in the pleasant breeze. The morning's torrent had cleared the skies, leaving everything feeling uncharacteristically clean. As I drove south I caught the unmistakable aromas of the Jersey shore: pizza, coffee, grilling beef, cigarettes, even suntan lotion. I was all at once glad to be outside.

Moses Stillman, looking anxious, paced in and out of a pool of overhead light, wearing a groove in the weathered planks of the hotel's porch. In one hand he held a crystal glass with two inches of Scotch.

'That a single malt?' I asked as I crossed the Persian welcome mat.

'No.' He glanced at his drink as if surprised. 'It's an expensive blend. How'd you know?'

'I've been on the wagon for eighty-one days,' I explained. 'You could open a bottle of Oban in South Dakota and I could tell you how many kilos of peat they burned at the distillery.'

'You want one?' he asked. 'I've got a bottle right here. It's not Oban, but Johnnie Walker Blue, a decent potion if you like Scotch at $239 a bottle.'

'I do, and I do, and no thanks,' I said. 'I admit I'm a Dewar's man myself, the mule-piss of the Scotch family. But Jenny has a shortlist, eight hundred and seventy-one things I can't do without risking our marriage. Drinking any kind of Scotch is Number Three.'

'And numbers one and two?' Moses looked amused.

'Having sex with a twenty-seven-year-old histopathologist is Number One, and Number Two is killing the President of the United States with a chainsaw.'

Moses chuckled. 'Lovely. And where does OxyCodone fall on this list?'

I gave the question a moment's consideration. 'OxyContin is tied for fourth with grilling my mother-in-law's brain and eating it.'

He lifted his glass to me. 'Wonderful, Sailor! I promise we will do our best to avoid – well, all of those things this evening.'

'You all right?' I asked. 'You seem a bit tense, if you don't mind me saying so.'

'I'm fine.' He pushed salt-and-pepper bangs off his forehead. 'I'll just finish my bracer here and be right as rain, ready to go.' He took a long sip from the Johnnie Walker Blue, then gave my sling a tug. 'You all right?'

'Yeah, no worries. I'm just wearing this to keep everything in place. Shoulder surgery's a bitch.'

'Tell me about it.' He drank again, rotating his pitching arm with an exaggerated groan.

I said, 'You don't have to come with me, you know. I can do this by myself.'

Moses' craggy face fell. 'Are you kidding? This is the most excitement I've had in ten years; I wouldn't miss it for the world. I'm only pacing because I can't wait to get started. I've damned near pissed my trousers three times already ...'

I wondered how many Scotches he'd put away, though he was looking trim as ever in linen trousers and cotton sweater, and loafers worth more than my first car.

'All right,' I said, 'but I've got to warn you: we may not find anything; it could be a complete bust. I've been in pretty close contact with Marta Hodges over the past two days and she hasn't mentioned anyone finding anything there.'

'Why?' Moses asked, grasping the porch rail to steady himself.

'Why what?'

'Why have you been in close contact with Detective Hodges? Has she needed something from you? Because we haven't heard anything at all from her.'

Shit, Sailor, think fast.

'Um, I gave her a statement because I'm a cop who happened to be on scene when the body arrived. She's called a couple of times to discuss it, you know, follow-up questions.'

That seemed to placate him.

'Tony around?' I asked.

Moses turned towards the servers' entrance on the wraparound deck. 'He was just here. I think he's in the kitchen with Chef Sam. Apparently, she wants to meet you.'

'Me? Why?'

'You know.'

'Oh, that.' I grimaced. 'Okay, fine, but we'll keep it quick. The fewer people who know I'm here tonight the better.' The Sea Girt light passed overhead, watching our every move.

'Oops.'

'*Oops?* What do you mean, "oops"? How many others know what we're up to?'

'Um ... perhaps a few?'

'A few? Like six ... or *eighty?*'

'Sailor, you're something of a celebrity, so you stopping by to break into a room and investigate a crime that our own police have clearly mucked up is—'

'Whoa, whoa,' I cut him off. 'I *never* said the locals had mucked this up!'

He looked at me as if I'd just told him his mother was the Tooth Fairy. 'So why—?'

I ushered him towards a comfy-looking chair. 'That's a fair question, and I suppose the best answer is that there're a couple of things that aren't quite lining up on my mental scorecard, and I just want to be able to put them to bed, you know?'

'Um, no. Do you always speak in mixed metaphors when you're trying to confuse an issue? Does that sort of thing work with felons?'

I laughed unexpectedly. 'Actually, yes, generally it works pretty well.'

'Not tonight.'

'Fair enough.'

'What are you hoping to find?'

'Scratches.' *Phantom Pink Floyd and carousel music screamed backwards by the child I helped kill yesterday, dead farm animals, missing lobsters – who knows really?*

'Scratches? What does that mean?'

'That's not what I meant.' I let my mind race while I considered his drink.

'Want one?' he asked again.

'No, thanks, really,' I said with a sigh. 'Scratches: signs of forced entry, someone climbing from the roof to the balcony, maybe forcing the lock on the glass doors. I figure Hanley might have gone to sleep with the door open – he was on the sixth floor, so why not? Maybe someone came over the roof, dropped to the balcony, killed him and tossed him into your morning espresso.'

'But why? What would motivate someone to negotiate a precipitous slate roof to get to an old school teacher's balcony, just to make the body public a few minutes later? I'm no police officer, Sailor, but that doesn't make sense to me.'

'Me neither,' I admitted, finding myself eyeing the drink again.

Moses caught me. 'You sure you don't want one? I mean, I can appreciate your efforts to get clear of the OxyContin, but this isn't really drinking as much as it's appreciating art at its finest. We're not here chugging Molsons.'

I looked around, half-expecting to find Jenny spying on me. 'I'd better not.'

'Suit yourself.' He pulled an engraved silver flask from his back pocket and poured himself another inch. He'd obviously decided to drink his way through the evening's anxiety, and why not? By his age I'd probably be on my second liver.

He screwed the cap back, but left the flask out. 'Now back to my question.'

'I have no idea, and to tell the truth, if there'd been more blood and if Hanley's core temperature had been a bit higher we wouldn't be here. But I suspect he was plenty dead before he took the plunge.'

'But the Spring Lake officer mentioned drugs Hanley might have taken that could have brought his core temperature down?'

'Yup, there're a number of medications he could have been taking, or more likely he was hypoglycaemic, or maybe a diabetic who'd missed dinner the previous night. He was an old guy; he might have been taking dozens of pills every day.' I ran a finger along a frayed edge of the chair cushion. 'What the hell, call me curious.'

Moses leaned forward. 'Very well then. Who kills a seventy-something-year-old teacher?'

'Another fair question,' I replied. 'Unless it was random, just some sociopath, murders of older folks generally have their roots in love, power or money.'

Moses sipped. 'Three flavours I like!'

'I'm so glad you're enjoying this,' I said with a grimace. 'It might have been a lover, ex-lover, jilted lover, former-student lover or gay lover. That list also includes the angry spouse of said lover or ex-lover, particularly if that spouse is now the jilted spouse of the angry ex-lover. I can't remember if he was married or divorced, but that broadens the radar to include wife, ex-wife, jilted wife—'

'—angry wife, furious wife, wife who doesn't like wet towels on the bed, wife with credit cards, wife *without* credit cards, wife who chooses ugly curtains, wife who insists on putting the toothpaste back in the vanity mirror after every use, wife who can't parallel park—'

'—and a partridge in a pear tree.'

'I've been there, Sailor.'

'I can tell.'

Clearly a little tipsy now, Moses gestured towards my shirt pocket with two fingers, as if summoning a waiter. 'Can I bum one of those?'

'Sure.' I held out the pack, then lit one for him. He inhaled clear down to his ankles, then exhaled twin plumes out his nose.

'How many years?' I lit one for myself.

'Since I quit? Thirty-nine years, but I still crave them, especially when I get halfway to hammered.'

I considered the smoky snake coiling skywards. 'Yup, they might as well type it on my death certificate now. I know they're going to get me; it's just a matter of when.'

'Power and money?' Moses prompted.

'Power and money,' I agreed. 'That brings angry, cheated or jealous business partners, family members, investors, colleagues and students or former students into the equation. We'd have to look into what kinds of dealings Hanley had going on the side – real estate, drugs, Internet gambling, who knows? He had to be into something, though, to be able to afford this place. In the end it can amount to quite a list.'

'Keeps you employed, though.' He looked around for an ashtray and, failing to find anything, flicked ash beneath his chair.

'That it does.' I leaned on the porch rail and looked across Ocean Avenue. Joseph Cotton's sodium lights illuminated the boardwalk in symmetric puddles. I heard breakers in the distance, though I couldn't see them.

Behind me, Moses said, 'But you don't think that's the case here.'

'I don't. I admit it,' I said. 'Hanley probably just killed himself, though I don't know why and I wish I did. My sister liked him – she joked once or twice about becoming a history teacher and coming home to Freehold Catholic to work with him.'

Moses pointed at me with his cigarette, the pieces coming together in his head. 'And that's why you have a couple of things on a mental scorecard that don't line up before you put them to bed with all your other mixed metaphors.'

'You got me.' I finished the cigarette and flipped the butt into the grass. *But if there's a gang-tag scratched into the slate roof above that balcony, I'm packing up and moving to Costa Rica.*

Tony from Bergen County and a woman I hadn't met who had to be Chef Sam emerged through the servants' entrance. I couldn't quite tell from this far away, but for a moment it had looked as if they'd been holding hands. Tony couldn't be a minute older than twenty-three, and Chef Sam looked to be about thirty-five. Summer love.

'Evening, Detective Doyle.' Tony reached out his hand.

'Sailor, please.'

'Sailor.' In flip-flops and cargo shorts, his gold crucifix and a form-fitting Bon Jovi T-shirt, Tony looked like any of the hundred thousand tourists crowding Belmar beach in July. I caught sight of a New York Yankees tattoo near his ankle. Most of my dorm at Rutgers had the exact same one – so much for originality. He half-turned to the woman with him and said, 'and this is Sam Mancini.'

'Chef Sam?' I asked, shaking her hand.

'A pleasure, Detective Doyle. I know you'd rather not talk about it, but I gotta tell you my mother and father pray for you, like, every Wednesday and Saturday night. You could set your watch by 'em: wine, rigatoni, pray for Detective Doyle and his family. I'm not sure how long it's gonna go on, but they're not showing any signs of flagging.' Chef Sam wore her Corsica-black hair in a ponytail, and sported a floral-print sundress. No ring, so I figured her for a divorcée. She wasn't a beefcake, like most professional chefs, but she did tug that sundress into a healthy hourglass.

I said, 'Nice to meet you, Chef Sam, but please assure your parents that I didn't do much more than anyone would have done, given the same circumstances. And while dangerous, the odds that plague bacteria would have reached – where, Brooklyn—?'

She tugged nervously at one earlobe, as if checking for an earring she'd lost. 'Just off Fourth Avenue, down by Fort Hamilton.'

'—Brooklyn – are slim.'

Chef Sam said, 'Oh, you don't understand, Detective: most of my father's extended family is from Richmond, and he still has maybe thirty cousins down there. Your name around those dinner tables is like, *saintly*.'

'Ah, then I get it,' I said. 'Well, in that case, please let everyone know that you met me and that there is nothing at all special about me, but that my wife and I *definitely* appreciate all the prayers.'

She reached over and squeezed my forearm. 'I will, Detective Doyle. I'll tell them. They'll be thrilled that you were here when a dead body just goddamned fell out of the sixth floor. *Thrilled*.'

'It was one of the highlights of my week too,' I said, and laughed until she joined me.

Tony interrupted, saying, 'Det— Uh, Sailor, we figure it's about forty minutes until Thomas and Mitch come on duty. Mitch is no problem; he knows what's going on and he'll keep quiet.'

Shit, who didn't we tell?

Moses added, 'And Thomas sometimes arrives early, so we ought to get upstairs as soon as possible, just in case he arrives and wonders what we're all doing here so late.'

'I understand,' I said. 'Chef Sam, are you coming along for the ride?'

She looked disappointed. 'I figure I'll hang around down here – I can tell Thomas I came in to get a few things ready for the morning buffet. The late-night guys, they're just a short-order crew, they see me here late all the time, so they won't think anything of it. I've got my cell, in case Thomas happens to head up in the elevators.'

'Why would he do that?' I asked.

'Why does Thomas do anything?' Tony said. 'I sometimes think he's got a boyfriend he keeps tucked away in one of the empty rooms upstairs.'

I frowned. 'Any chance it was Harold Hanley?'

'Nah, nah, nothing like that,' Tony said. 'Thomas goes for them a bit younger.'

'Like middle school,' Chef Sam added.

'What?' I interrupted. 'What was that?'

'What was what?'

'Middle school?' I shook my head. 'Nothing, just something else that doesn't make sense trying to make sense, but only for a second. Sorry.'

Chef Sam looked confused; Moses wrapped an arm around her. 'Don't worry, Sam; I'm learning that Detective Doyle does that sometimes.'

I held up a hand, begging a moment, and as if reading my mind the Sea Girt light painted a stripe across the old hotel's midsection. 'Is there a chance that Thomas the Fop will come up to the sixth floor in the next hour?'

'Yes,' Tony said bluntly.

I pointed at Chef Sam. 'But you will watch out for him, because we don't want Tony getting fired or Mr Stillman getting kicked out into the street.'

'That's right,' she said, 'or you getting in any trouble either, Detective.'

I smiled. 'I'm not going to get in trouble from him; don't let that bother you.'

'But we're fine,' Tony said, 'because Sam has her cell and she'll text me if Thomas so much as moves from behind the desk.'

'Good enough,' I said. 'Who's got the keys?'

Tony held up a ring with about fifteen keys attached. 'Right here: I boosted the masters from one of the cleaning carts.'

I said, 'You guys still use actual keys?'

Moses said, 'It's part of this place's charm.'

'How do we get upstairs?'

Chef Sam said, 'The cleaning crews' elevator is down the hall behind the kitchen. No one's back there tonight.'

I discovered I was enjoying myself. I checked my watch – it felt like something William Holden might do before launching an attack. 'Nice job, everyone. Chef Sam, if you'll head for the lobby, the rest

202

of us will go in down there.' I nodded towards the servants' entrance. My cell phone buzzed; I peeked at it, didn't recognise the number. I pressed SILENT.

'Let's go.' Tony led me along the porch; Moses stopped him.

'Wait.' He produced his flask. 'Anyone need a quick splash before we go? For God and country?'

I shook my head as Tony and Chef Sam answered in unison, 'No thanks.'

Moses unscrewed the cap. 'I do: won't be a second.' He poured a sloppy splash, spilling a bit over his knuckles, and cursed in Italian. Tony and Chef Sam laughed together. 'Sorry.' Moses sucked his fingers clean, swirled the Scotch around the glass and downed it in one swallow. I caught another whiff of the booze; it smelled like a hard tumble off the wagon and a handful of expensive lies to Jenny.

Not tonight, Sailor. Fight this one off; it's not worth it.

'Mr Stillman's room in half an hour,' said Chef Sam, and she started across the Persian rug. She had a nice walk, and the flowery dress helped. The display had to be for our benefit, because those hips would do nothing to distract Thomas the Fop.

Moses left his glass perched on the porch rail before following.

I couldn't see much of the Warren & Monmouth's opulence from the hallway off the kitchen. Scuffed chequerboard tiles led between Chef Sam's stomping grounds and a huge laundry. The left side smelled like industrial-strength bleach; the right of garlic and burning cognac. A waiter had left a stack of leatherbound menus in a wall rack outside the kitchen and I snagged one as I passed.

At a T-junction Tony pushed open a fire door and turned right down a softly lit carpeted hallway both cleaner and classier than the service entrance. I listened behind us but didn't hear either Chef Sam or Thomas the Fop. I figured that for a good thing. Soft muzak wafted around us from hidden speakers. There were flourishing potted plants in each corner and miniature café tables set with monogrammed matchbooks and individually wrapped chocolates, even here in the employee area.

Nice place. I stole a handful of chocolates for Ben and Jenny.

Tony turned left, then a quick right through a fire door and along another chequerboard-tile hallway into a wide room so packed with cleaning carts it looked like a maid-army encampment. Beyond the cart lot I could see four elevators set in the plain concrete wall.

'So far so good,' Tony said, finding the elevator key on his stolen ring.

The cleaning crews' elevator made me want to buy a parachute. Three rusty metal walls were, I devoutly hoped, attached to the worn wooden base that was about as big as the dance floor at my wedding reception. Moses, Tony and I made our way inside and had enough room left over for my grandfather's '64 Buick. Tony pressed the SIX; I noticed the FOUR had been worn off entirely and the TWO and FIVE had cracks in their convex plastic covers. I read the menu I'd lifted from Chef Sam's kitchen just to keep myself distracted from the very real possibility that we were all about to plummet to the hotel's dusty basement. The elevator wheezed, groaned, and started up at about one mile every six months.

I flipped through the menu, reading the evening's specials. 'Tony, can you get Chef Sam on the phone?'

He produced a BlackBerry as fast as Otis, the gunslinger in my Louis L'Amour novel, did his Colt .45. 'Sure, Detective. Whaddya need?'

I glanced around our would-be coffin. 'Just a distraction from the ever-present thought that we're about to die in here.'

He grinned and handed me the phone.

Chef Sam answered. 'Hey, baby!'

I chuckled. 'Sorry, Chef, it's me, Sailor.'

'Holy Mother Mary, Detective Doyle, I'm sorry – I didn't—'

'It's fine, Chef, truly – I wish more women answered that way when I called.'

She giggled like a seventh-grader. 'I promise to answer just like that every time you call me, deal?'

'Sounds lovely,' I said. 'Of course, my wife will break both my legs so I'll be calling from the Jersey Shore Medical Center.'

'I hear they have a great emergency room, Detective. You'll be in good hands.'

'Chef—' I held the menu open with my sling hand. 'Who decides on the daily specials in the hotel restaurant?'

'I do.'

'All of them? Everything?'

'I'm the Head Chef; it's my restaurant. Why?'

'No reason,' I said. 'I just stole a menu on our way by and I'm wondering what is bobo duh camaro? I'm sure I'm saying that wrong. A *camaro* is what my sister's boyfriend drove in high school.'

She snorted through her nose, sounding shockingly like Jenny when I've really embarrassed myself. 'Sorry! Sorry, Detective, I didn't mean to laugh.'

'It's all right, Chef. I'm impressed I could even read the words.'

Chef Sam sounded suddenly different – educated, refined. '*Bobó de camarão* is a Brazilian shrimp stew made with coconut milk and *malagueta* peppers. We serve it over rice, but I've had it like a winter vegetable soup too. Do you like spicy food?'

'It's why God put me on Earth.'

'I'll send you home with some tonight,' she said. 'You'll love it. The hardest part is finding real Antarctica Beer around here.'

'Beer from Antarctica? C'mon, Chef, I've heard of esoteric menu items, but there can't be much brewing at the South Pole.'

Moses looked askance at me, snorted derisively.

'Actually, Detective, Antarctica Beer is one of the most popular and tasty, beers available in Brazil.'

'See?' I said, 'I knew that. I was just, you know, teasing. So, I've got to ask, what's potag woof duh kale? Might I find it on the late-night menu at Denny's? Can I get fries with that?'

Chef Sam laughed so hard I lowered the phone and said to Tony and Moses, 'She just needs a moment to catch her breath. Obviously, I've charmed her clear out of her panties.' I raised Tony's BlackBerry. 'Chef? You there? Any pulse?'

She took a few seconds to compose herself, then said, '*Potage oeuf de caille* is French: quail's egg soup, and one of the most delicious foods you'll eat on Earth.'

'Quails lay eggs?'

'All the time.'

'I've never even seen a quail – how the hell do you get quail's eggs?'

'I'm persuasive.'

'Chef Sam, I take back anything bad I've ever said about you.'

'Detective Doyle, you've only known me for about twelve minutes.'

'Then it can't be much, can it?'

'I guess not,' she said. 'Do you cook? Or is that your wife's job?'

I sighed. 'Chef, I wouldn't embarrass what we do at the Doyle household by calling it *cooking*. Most nights either Jenny or I strap on a flame-thrower and incinerate whatever we're eating – it's invariably lovely with mayonnaise.'

'Maybe we can arrange some lessons,' she said.

The elevator door opened on the sixth floor. I said, 'I'm going to hold you to that, Chef. But for now, we've got to go.'

She laughed again. 'Bye, Detective.'

I clicked off and handed the BlackBerry back to Tony. 'Marry that girl, Antonio. Do it tomorrow – hell, do it tonight; we'll be done soon. I'll stand as your witness and Moses can perform the ceremony.'

Moses shook his head. 'Only inside Saginaw City limits, sorry. Oh, and in Friesach, Austria.'

'Damn,' I said. 'And with a name like Moses, you'd figure he'd at least be able to get you to stomp on a glass or something.'

'Nope,' Moses said, 'the most I can do is to lead you through the desert and maybe across the Red Sea. But if a furious squall comes up, we'll all be screwed.'

'What?' Tony started down the hallway; Moses followed.

Furious squall?

We hadn't taken three steps into Harold Hardass Hanley's room, 6103, before I knew it'd be a bust. Someone had been through pretty thoroughly, on Marta Hodges' orders, I imagined – maybe Ed Hess and Kyle Cheese-Grater, earning Chef Sam's fine breakfast last Saturday morning.

As he opened the door, Tony swore, 'Shit! Sorry, guys, I forgot to bring a flashlight.' He ducked beneath twin strips of CRIME SCENE tape into the darkness.

'Nice thought, Tony' – I ducked as well – 'but this isn't the Water-gate Hotel. No one's outside monitoring the room through a zoom lens. Just turn on the lights.'

Tiffany-style stained-glass lamps blinked on.

'What's all that?' Tony asked, turning a full circle.

'Dust,' I said. 'Damn, look at that.'

'What?' Moses asked. 'Were you expecting something different?'

'Detective Hodges may be irritating, but no one can accuse her of skipping steps.'

'You didn't expect they'd thoroughly search his room?' Tony asked. 'Wouldn't they do that for a dead body?'

'Not for an obvious jumper, especially the fingerprint dust. Either Marta Hodges suspects there might have been someone else in here, or she's an insufferable OC.'

Tony held his hands up as if he'd suddenly realised he forgot examination gloves. 'Oh shit, Detective Doyle, should we not touch anything?'

'Hell, you can touch anything you like; they've lifted all they need from this room. Hodges might sit on it for a couple of days, just in case something comes up, something from his family, or maybe from a colleague they interview. Most likely she'll turn this room back over to the hotel without another visit.'

Tony clicked on the bathroom light. 'Anything he had in here's gone, including anything in the medicine cabinet. See?' He leaned back far enough for us to see that the vanity mirror had been dusted, searched and left open.

'Shit, I was hoping they'd left that stuff.'

'Stuff?' Moses flipped through a stack of local restaurant menus on the desk.

'Meds,' I said. 'I wanted to see what kinds of pills he was taking. Look like he puked in there, Tony?'

'No way to tell, Detective. The toilet's been flushed.'

'No dry splatter? Check the inside of the bowl, up around the edges.'

'Nope.'

'Any dirty towels?'

'Yeah, a bunch.'

'Check 'em out, would you? Sniff them, see if you catch anything odd.'

'Like puke?' Tony laughed.

'Puke, alcohol, antiseptic smells, chemical smells, anything that looks rusty-brown like dried blood, nasty spills he might have wiped up, clumps of hair, anything you wouldn't expect to find in your average bathroom.'

I heard him slide open the shower stall. His voice sounded like it might be coming from inside an elevator shaft. 'You do this every day? This is foul, Detective.' Clearly Tony wasn't over-enthused about his assignment.

'Most days,' I said. 'My old partner can smell a three-day-old joint in a dumpster full of rotting Chinese food. He's a human bloodhound.'

'Gross.'

'Yeah, well, I've gotta pay for college, and I can't dance or sing.'

Moses slid open drawers; most were empty. Two held a weekend's worth of conservative clothing: shorts, polo shirts, a braided leather belt and a baseball cap with a leather brim. Two pairs of trousers hung alongside a utilitarian navy blazer and a pair of rubber-soled Mephisto shoes, appropriate for a man who spent all day on his feet.

'Anything?' I asked.

'Nah.' He rifled through the clothing. 'No women's underwear, leather trusses or sadomasochistic armaments, if that's what you mean.'

'Condoms?'

'Two, actually, in one of those sealed packs you buy for a dollar at 7-Eleven or in the restroom at a truck stop.'

'Really?' Tony called from the bathroom. 'I didn't know him well, but he didn't strike me as a guy who was down here to wet the old wick, you know what I'm saying?'

Moses pawed drunkenly through Hanley's leftover possessions. 'Two condoms in a sealed pack. Who cares? Could be wishful thinking on his part.'

'True,' I said. 'Tony, you ever see him with a woman? In the bar, the restaurant, maybe walking on the beach?'

'Nope.'

'He out late drinking, cruising for older babes? I can't believe I'm saying it – this hotel doesn't look like the kind of place one comes to get hooked up –but maybe he had a squeeze down here, someone he met periodically?'

'Could be,' Tony said. 'I can take an hour tomorrow and sneak on the computer in the chambermaids' office. They don't care. I'll see if there were any women here, registered alone, maybe in his age bracket.'

'Good idea, Tony.' I hadn't planned on working Hanley's case this hard, but if someone else was doing the legwork for me I'd look it over, maybe nudge Marta Hodges in the right direction. I said, 'Of course, she'd have to be some kind of healthy woman to heave his dead ass out the glass door and over the railing at five in the morning.'

Moses chuckled and sneaked another blast from his flask. 'Maybe he liked them big.' He slid it back into his pocket and slumped into a nice-looking ladder-backed chair.

'Anything else in those drawers?' I asked, just to keep him focused.

'Oddments, bits and pieces, nothing outstanding.' Moses looked to be losing his enthusiasm for the evening's entertainment. He crossed his long legs and steepled his fingers. He might have been pretending to be contemplating Harold Hanley's last hours, but instead he appeared more wrapped up in the thought that it wouldn't be too long before detectives were going through his rooms in similar fashion. His eyes wandered out the sliding door and across the dark beach to the even darker sea.

I said, 'Moses, hey, you with us?'

He didn't look at me. 'Yup.'

'What was in that top drawer? Any medicine containers? Those weekly ones, you know, the days-of-the-week boxes so you don't forget or accidentally overdose?'

'I'm abundantly familiar with them,' Moses said, 'but no, nothing like that.' Still staring over the water, he said, 'Mr Hanley's got a Swiss Army knife, cheap-shit K-Mart sunglasses and two pens, one from a Thai restaurant in Marlboro and one nice one, a Waterman with FCHS engraved on the cap.'

'Freehold Catholic High School,' I said, opening the bedside table. A Gideon Bible, a handful of change, two packs of mints, half a

Hershey bar and three worn paperbacks. I pulled them out. 'Howard Zinn, Shelby Foote and Bruce Catton?'

'Yeah,' Moses said, 'perfectly normal for a history teacher – although I'm surprised a Catholic school would allow him to teach Zinn.'

'Seditious? Revisionist? Genius?

'Unappreciated in his time.'

'Aren't we all?' I murmured, bending to look under the bed.

'Not me,' Moses whispered.

Tony joined us in the bedroom, carrying a hand towel. 'Nothing much in there, Detective Doyle, just this, and I can't tell if that's blood or ink or an old stain.'

'Stink?'

'Can't tell.' He handed me the towel, indicating a dime-sized splotch of discoloration that might have been blood from a shaving cut.

'Nice work, Watson, but I meant more blood, like maybe if someone had mopped it up or spent three hours trying to scrub it out of the grout between the shower tiles.'

Tony's face reddened. 'Oh. No, nothing like that in there.'

'Nice job.'

Moses watched us. 'You find what you needed, Sailor? Is it Miller time?'

'Almost.' I flipped on the balcony light and opened the sliding glass door. 'Three minutes and we're out of here. Tony, please check with Chef Sam, make sure the coast is clear for us to get downstairs.' I stepped outside; surprisingly, Moses followed me.

From the balcony I could hear Tony talking in hushed tones. Moses said, 'You think Detective Hodges believes that something went on in this room, don't you?'

I slid a chair to one side of the balcony and got down on my knees.

Moses swallowed hard. 'Christ, he used that as a—'

'—stool,' I finished for him. 'Yeah, made it easier to get over the rail.'

'What are you looking for down there?'

'Blood splatter, blood drops, dried blood, anything really.'

'See anything?'

'Plenty of discoloration in the concrete, but that could be a hundred years of spilled drinks – gin, coffee, orange juice, whatever. It's too hard to tell what's fresh. And dried blood looks a whole lot like dried coffee, especially when it's soaked into porous stone like this.'

Moses asked, 'Any scratches, signs of struggle, someone getting dragged out here against his will?'

'No.' I appreciated him not asking me to elaborate what I was looking for. I didn't really want to explain that I was trying to match what might be gang-tags scratched into a dead pig's pen, a shattered lobster tank, a suicidal teen's hiding place and a dead history teacher's hotel room. Huck had taught me that one, too: never answer anything you don't want to see splashed across a newspaper billboard.

I dragged the chair against the rail, then paused, worried that if I slipped I wouldn't have the strength to catch myself, or to haul myself back onto the balcony.

Moses read my thoughts. 'You wearing a belt?'

'Yeah.'

'When you get up there, I'll hang on to your belt. I won't let you fall.'

Still I hesitated.

'What's the matter?' he asked. 'I can hold you, just don't lean too far over. You've seen what can happen on the other end.'

'That's not it.' I wiped my forehead dry on my shirtsleeve. 'It's just that I'm wearing a gun.'

'So? You're a cop.'

'I'm a suspended cop, three hundred miles from home. Technically I can't even carry a gun there.'

'You think I'm going to call the District Attorney's Office? I don't give a damn – in fact, I feel better knowing you've got a gun.'

I peeked over his shoulder. 'All right, but let's not tell Tony, okay?'

He gave me a drunken shrug. 'Suit yourself.'

I pulled the revolver from my belt and stashed it behind a potted plant.

Moses said, 'That's a .357, the one that shoots silver bullets.'

'Exactly. Don't let me forget it.'

'I'm sure one of us will remember.' He checked to be sure all four chair legs rested evenly on the concrete. 'C'mon, up you get.'

'All right, but don't let go.' Using my good arm, I held the balcony rail long enough to get on the chair – *the same one Hanley used to take a header from this very spot; this is a stupid idea, Sailor*. Crouching, I waited for Moses to grab hold of my belt with both hands.

'Got you,' he slurred.

And he's hammered. Lovely. At least if I fall, they'll probably prescribe me a whole sackful of OxyContin, maybe even some delicious and nutritious Demerol too.

'Okay, here I go.' I stood slowly, carefully keeping my balance. To Moses' credit, he kept both hands tight around my belt and one foot braced against the chair, keeping it pressed fast against the railing. 'You good?'

'Yeah, no problem.'

Behind him, Tony appeared in the doorway. 'Holy shit, boys, what are we doing? Detective, you gotta get down – Jesus Christ! You've already got one arm in a sling.'

'Antonio,' Moses warned, 'close your mouth and help me.'

'Right. Sorry.' He moved onto the balcony and he too gripped my belt with both hands. I felt better; Tony was beefy enough to haul me back over the railing by himself.

The chair was just tall enough for me to be able to see above the rusty gutter and onto the ancient slate roof. The tiles still held the afternoon's heat; they smelled of pitch, like a summer highway. Further up the slope I could see dark attic dormers, sooty brick chimneys, and the hotel's gilded cupola, which rose above the roof's peak in a seven-sided steeple, its cast-iron weathervane creaking in the breeze. The brightly lit cupola and surrounding widow's walk would be visible for miles. I, on the other hand, would not. To my right sat the same pissed-off gargoyle I'd seen on Sunday morning.

'Hold me steady,' I called down. 'I've got to let go for a second.'

'All right,' Tony answered in a harsh whisper, 'but, sir, we probably shouldn't be shouting. This isn't exactly on the list of regular evening activities here at the Warren & Monmouth.'

Moses grunted appreciation. 'B-nine; bingo!'

'Good point, Tony; sorry.' I let go, trusting the two of them to keep me from crashing to the porch below, and fished my BlackBerry from my pocket. A gust off the water hit me and as I swayed for a second, Moses and Tony renewed their grip, steadying me.

'You making a call, Sailor?' Moses sounded incredulous. 'Because I've got a landline in my room and a comfy chair where you can sit and talk all you like.'

'It's too dark to see much,' I said, 'so I need to take a picture of these tiles.' I snapped a few shots, trying to get as much of the area above room 6103 as possible. My flash hit the slates like lightning. 'Okay,' I said, 'I'm coming down.'

Tony and Moses were helping me down when I abruptly pushed myself back up.

'Sailor!' Moses tightened his grip again. 'What the hell are you doing?'

'Sorry!' I whispered, 'forgot one thing.'

'Try not to do that again, Detective. I'm pretty sure I just filled my boxers.'

'Won't take a second.' I aimed the BlackBerry at the cranky-looking gargoyle and whispered, 'Say cheese, motherfucker.' *I'll check to see if you're the one following me around, or if I just need to check into the nearest psych unit.*

This time I allowed Tony and Moses to help me, and once safely back on the balcony I pocketed my phone, moved the chair back, and took a long last look over the railing. A hundred feet down, the porch where Tony from Bergen County served Moses Stillman breakfast every morning at four-thirty—

4:37

—was a miniature boardwalk encircling the hotel. 'God damn, that's a long fall,' I said. 'I'm really frigging glad I didn't look down there first.' I tried not to think about Harold Hanley, standing here contemplating the ocean, the rising sun, the wind-carved dunes, before stepping onto a chair and tumbling head-first into oblivion.

Did he smell the coffee from Moses' breakfast table? I bet he did, his last aroma.

South of us, the Sea Girt lighthouse rose above the beach; to the north, the lights of Belmar brightened the beachfront where people

213

were walking along the boardwalk or the sand. Further north, historic Asbury Park lay quiet, almost entirely dark save for a few lights near the water which flickered like fireflies.

Another gust off the water carried the comforting smell of sand and salt. Time to go. I turned to Tony and Moses. 'Thanks guys; I really appreciate the help tonight.'

Moses helped himself to a celebratory sip of Scotch. 'Excellent. Antonio, see if you can get Chef Sam on that fancy phone of yours and we'll all meet in my rooms for a quickie nightcap, whaddya say?'

'Works for me.' Tony stepped inside to let Chef Sam know we were through.

'Thanks,' I whispered, and retrieved Uncle Paul's .357 from the shadows.

'You need a drink?' Moses seemed hell-bent on getting me inside that bottle with him.

Say no, shithead. Say no!

'Yeah, sure,' I heard myself answer, 'why not? One's not gonna kill me, right?'

'Exactly.' He slid an arm over my neck, more for balance than fatherly affection.

I'll have to hit Dunkin' Donuts on the way home. One quick $239 Scotch, then a $1.49 coffee to cover it up. No worries.

I figured Moses would have nice digs, but his suite would have swallowed my first apartment and left room for dessert. 'Jesus, Moses, how long you planning on staying?'

Tony chuckled, mimicking me, 'Jesus, Moses.'

'What, you never read that story? It's in the Bible: Moses had a grand-nephew from San Diego. Of course, they pronounced it Hey-soos.'

Moses slurred, 'Didn't he find an all-water route around the Cape of Good Hope?'

'Exactly,' I said, 'he walked the whole way.'

'You're headed straight to Hell, Detective Doyle.' Tony crossed himself and kissed his crucifix, punctuating the insult.

Moses crossed the tiled foyer to the sitting room and threw open a mahogany cabinet. He withdrew a velvet-lined box embossed with the Johnnie Walker Distillery crest. 'Anyone fancy a blast?'

'A small one for me, please.' Chef Sam appeared behind us. 'Thomas hasn't moved from his desk – apparently, the afternoon shift buggered up the computer audit and he's fit to be tied. He thinks a lot of himself for an overnight concierge. Isn't that, like, irony or something? Overnight concierge?'

'Yeah.' Moses withdrew the half-empty bottle. 'Who needs theatre tickets or dinner reservations at three o'clock in the morning?'

'You never know,' I said. 'Spring Lake strikes me as a place where a party could happen at any moment.'

Moses said, 'What irritates me about Thomas is that he says "and furthermore" when making an argument – what is he, thirty? I'm no expert, but that's gay right there.'

Tony said, 'Couldn't that tech person – Maryanne Something, you know, electric-purple fingernails and big hoop earrings? – couldn't she fix it in the morning?'

'Hey, don't make fun of big hoop earrings.' Chef Sam dropped a leather handbag on a small dining table that looked to have been carved from the same mahogany tree as the cabinet. 'My grandmother wears big hoops, especially when she's out clubbing.'

Moses shook his head. 'Baby seals. I remember when clubbing meant you were hunting baby seals.'

'Memories of your time north of the border?' Tony asked.

'Esatto, Antonio!'

Chef Sam slid back a chair that matched the ones in Hanley's room and sat carefully, as if afraid to break it. 'Actually, I'm not sure there's much difference between clubbing baby seals and what my grandmother does in her giant hoop earrings. It is Fourth Avenue in Brooklyn, after all.'

Tony snorted. 'Family tree? Or more trimmed family hedge?'

Moses dealt coasters like playing cards and placed crystal highball glasses on the table; at his insistence Tony and I joined Chef Sam. I sat up straight and remembered what my friends and I had dubbed the Death Chair in Sister Anne's office at Freehold Catholic – *just down the hall from Hardass Hanley's classroom.* These were dead ringers for that exquisitely unpleasant perch across from Sister Anne's desk.

'How d'you take it, my dear?' Moses waggled the bottle in Chef Sam's direction.

'Neat, please.'

'Sexiest thing in western culture.' Moses winked at her. 'A woman who knows how to drink whisky.'

'How about eastern culture?' Sam asked.

'Never been.' Moses poured for her.

I worried what he'd say when I told him I wanted mine over ice with club soda. He'd probably toss me out on my Scotch-craving ass.

'Just ice for me, Mr Stillman.' Tony tested dangerous waters.

Moses stopped, mid-pour. 'You sure?'

'Yes, sir. Just ice.'

'You don't want to try a sniff straight out of the bottle?'

'Do I?' He looked to Chef Sam for help.

'Drink it neat.'

'Neat?'

'Plain, unadorned.' She pulled her ebony ponytail out of the way and lifted her glass to her nose like a sommelier, inhaling the memory of smoky peat while the front of her dress fell open enough to awaken a whole host of memories for me. The crucifix she wore was dangerously close to dunking our Saviour in a vintage better than anything he'd ever swilled in Jerusalem. Chef Sam repeated, 'Drink it neat, Tony.'

Tony said, 'Neat, please, Mr Stillman.'

'Wise choice, Antonio.' Moses poured him an inch. 'Sailor?'

No, no thanks, Moses, because I'm horny, and sitting across from a sexy woman, and trying not to peek down her dress. My wife's home with my kids, sleeping soundly and trusting me not to do exactly – exactly – what I'm about to do.

'Sailor?'

'The same for me, just a small one, please.' My stomach knotted into a coiled nightmare. I'd be vomiting in the Spring Lake dunes again within the hour.

Christ, kill me now.

'Lovely.' Moses poured mine, dumped nearly three inches for himself and splashed another half-inch into Tony's glass. He sat heavily, the only one of us even remotely comfortable in those fragile chairs.

I didn't touch the glass, not yet. Through the amber whisky I could just make out the flag of Manitoba, a buffalo about to headbutt the Union Jack, on my coaster.

Chef Sam sipped. 'Goddamn, Mr Stillman, but that is good.'

'Isn't it, though?' Moses used both hands to prop his own glass on the gentle rise of his stomach. I hoped I looked even half as healthy when I hit seventy. 'Some luxuries are worth every penny.' He turned sideways to the table and stretched his long legs across the carpet, crossing his ankles. He sighed, perfectly content in this uncomfortable space. 'That's better.'

Trying to ignore my glass, I took in the rest of Moses' sitting room. The spacious living and dining area had been decorated more like a Hudson River mansion than some faggoty pastel cottage on the Jersey coast. Dark wood and burnished leather dominated the room, screaming *rich white guy lives here*. A small bookshelf near a leather sofa was crammed to bursting with Louis L'Amour paperbacks; on top, in a more ornamental role, were hardcovers, compliments of dead white men: Faulkner, Hemingway, Cheever, Dickens, and one I didn't recognise, Robertson Davies.

A closed laptop and some manila files had been stacked neatly beside a flatscreen TV and a pile of *Asbury Park Press* were held down by a nearly empty bottle of red wine; there were a dozen more in a wooden rack beside the television.

The walls had been decorated with old baseball memorabilia: framed programme covers, ticket stubs to dozens of ballparks, auto-graphed photos of major leaguers I remembered watching as a kid, and one large image of a youngish version of Mark 'Moses' Stillman, in an Ottawa Pioneers cap, sweating as he peered intently over the web pocket of his glove, ready to pitch. His glare, as intense as any I'd ever seen, said *Maybe I'll bring the heat, or maybe I'll bean your sorry ass back to the dugout*. I wondered why I hadn't found him on the encyclo-paedic website I'd searched at the library. Looking at that photo, enlarged and framed with care, Moses had either played pro ball and been overlooked by the Internet, or he had one vivid, damned-near-sociopathic imagination.

When the shadows get long, you'll be surprised what people do.

Apart from a couple of snapshots of a pretty woman in a canoe and a little girl in a soccer uniform, I didn't find any family photos in Moses' living room. I figured that he might have others in the bedroom, or the guest room, or the bathroom, or the library, or the frigging glass atrium he probably had down the hallway. *And this is supposed to be a hotel!*

'You not thirsty?' Tony asked, polishing off his Scotch.

'Not drinking too much these days.' I lifted the glass, saluted them, and sipped, just enough to get a taste. 'Jesus, Mary and Oprah, but that's yummy!' I sipped again, a bit more this time. It was easily the best-tasting thing I'd ever had to drink.

'How come you're on the wagon?' Chef Sam asked.

'Oh, I dunno; trying to live a little healthier, I suppose.'

Moses tousled my hair, like my grandfather might have done three decades ago. 'Sailor, this isn't drinking; this is appreciating the art of the blend at its finest.'

'Uh huh, yeah, right. I'll try that one on Jenny when I get home later.'

Chef Sam's smile faded and in the space of one breath she looked like a woman in the grip of some inner turmoil. 'Your wife not want you drinking, Detective?' It didn't take much to read her: Chef Sam wasn't going to be around if my marriage hinged on how much Scotch got poured at Moses' mahogany dining table. She must have been married to a grade-A jackass.

Wife's career taking off at that fancy hotel? Get shitfaced and beat her up. She put on a couple of pounds after squeezing out your kids? Head down to the local gin-mill and fuck a skank. Kids screaming? Smack 'em and drink in peace. The Yankees are on.

Chef Sam's brow furrowed. 'Detective? Are we going to get you into hot water at home?'

I held my hands up in surrender. 'No, no,' I lied, 'it's not like that. I think my wife is fine with my drinking. It's the OxyContin she worries about.'

218

Neither Tony nor Sam said anything for a second, then they both burst into laughter, clearly not believing a word I'd said. Tony reached for the bottle, then hesitated, cocking an eyebrow at Moses.

'Please, help yourself.'

'Thanks.' Tony poured for Sam, then himself. 'Sailor?'

'I'm good for now.' I swallowed another tiny mouthful. 'I've got plenty.'

'You sure?' Tony glanced down at my glass.

Empty. Shit. How the hell—? All right, all right, here we go. Fuck it.

'Sure.' I held the glass out. 'Hit me again.'

Tony did, finishing the bottle without refreshing Moses' glass. Abashed, he murmured, 'Sorry, sir.'

'Nonsense, Antonio.' Moses was already up and headed for the cabinet. He withdrew another velvet-lined case. 'Supply lines haven't run down yet.'

Chef Sam raised her glass. 'Eureka.'

I drank the Scotch, and had another. Three in less than ten minutes. *Ten weeks on the wagon, though, right? Ten weeks isn't bad.*

I tugged at my collar, but no one noticed. Moses' suite closed in on me as I slid my glass over. 'Just a bit this time, all right?'

'Sure, whatever you say.' Moses had gone round the bend; he was damn near sloppy. He poured me three inches, which I resolved to sip over the next hour while I slowly sobered up, got my flop sweat under control and found my way home.

All you need now is to get pulled over drunk and armed. You'll never work as a cop again, not ever. Isn't that nice? Stop drinking – push the glass away. Slip it to Chef Sam. She'll love you for it.

I didn't push it away. I didn't guzzle it either, but I couldn't leave it. I couldn't walk away. It should have been easy; the room was full of excuses to push myself back from the table. Hell, the photos on the wall alone were worth a visit. Half the guys up there had been idols to me as a kid. But I didn't do it; I sat with them, and I drank, fucking myself and my marriage up one expensive sip at a time.

$239 a bottle is pretty good shit, but it'd better be because I figure the divorce will cost you twelve thousand plus half of what you make for the rest of your life. Nice work, Sailor.

Finally Chef Sam distracted me when she asked Moses, 'Mr Stillman, did you and your wife ever stay here together at the hotel?'

Tony kicked her beneath the table – a corpse in the hallway outside would have noticed. Moses certainly caught it, his eyes moving quickly back and forth between them. For the moment I was sufficiently engaged to forget (or at least ignore) my burgeoning self-loathing. *What's going on?*

Missing only a beat, Moses unsheathed his winning smile like a rapier. His eyes cleared and he looked as sober as an Ocean Grove teetotaller. He said, 'Just once, Chef, back in October, 1975.' His slur, while still evident, had lessened. 'Kate and I got married during the season in '73, but I was pitching every five days that year, part of the Pioneers' starting rotation, so we didn't get to go on honeymoon. But by August of '75 we were eliminated from the play-offs, and I had a swollen elbow so I was sent down to Single-A – in those days that basically meant *go golfing; your season's over*.' He ran a manicured finger around the rim of his glass. 'Rather than spend the winter in Ottawa, which isn't nearly as miserable as it sounds, Kate and I decided to travel a bit. I had pitched all season as a starter; so I'd about thirteen extra dollars that month, and rooms here at the Warren & Monmouth were only about a hundred dollars a night back then.'

Tony interrupted, 'So an extended vacation here made perfect sense!'

'It did!'

Chef Sam sat up a bit straighter, narrowing the gap through which I'd been trying *not* to peek at her boobs for the past half-hour. 'Wait, I get it. Your wife had her own money! I love that – and in 1975, that was a big deal, wasn't it?'

'You bet.' Moses winked at her again. 'Kate wore the pants in the family. I wore the cleats.'

'So how'd you end up here?' Tony played along, but watching him, I could see young Antonio from Bergen County knew more than he'd let on to Chef Sam. I sipped the Scotch and silently promised to beat the truth out of him later on.

Moses played with the glass, but he didn't take another drink. Instead, he watched the amber liquid splash back and forth as he spoke. 'I grew up not far from here – I was a Jersey shore kid, salt water in my veins. Kate and I had been down this way a couple of times, visiting my family for the holidays, and she'd always said how grand she thought it would be to spend a honeymoon here, if we ever saved up the cash – Canadian money wasn't worth much back then – and found a week or two to spare. She'd been climbing the ladder at Nordic Rescue, a non-profit lobby firm she'd fallen in love with. So she wasn't often up for a long break – she wasn't a vacation-type of gal, my former wife.'

Former. Huh.

'I spent the winters of '73 and '74 away from her.' Now Moses did drink, gulping what remained and pushing the empty glass away.

'How come?' Chef Sam asked.

'I was a starter. There were Double- and Triple-A leagues in Arizona, Southern California, Texas, all over down here, and I needed to show the Pioneers that I was serious about making a difference, winning games, eventually getting to the big leagues, maybe even winning the Governor's Cup. I'd got a bit older and while I'd been blinking a whole bunch of pitchers ended up working in Double-A, most of them younger than me. It was a wake-up call: be a leader, teach these youngsters a thing or two. Show them how to win games, stay tough into the late innings. All bullshit.

'I hurt my elbow in '75 and never really got back to a hundred per cent.' Moses considered the Scotch bottle a second, then turned back to Tony and Sam. 'We spent two weeks in this very suite.' He gestured around the room and for a moment looked as if he hoped that we might transfigure, somehow, into his idyllic October 1975 visit. 'We slept late and made love and ate wonderful seafood over at Seibert's, and we planned our future. Kate wanted children, but she'd been so busy saving the Canadian Arctic from oil companies that we'd never got around to making a baby.'

Tony poured himself and Chef Sam another drink. 'So, did the old place work its magic?'

The colour left Moses' face. 'Magic indeed.' He slid his glass to Tony, who filled it and pushed it back. 'One night we walked up the boardwalk to Asbury Park for dinner. Kate loved boardwalk rides – I don't know why, probably because it's always so goddamned cold in Ottawa so a kid doesn't have but two or three weeks when it's warm enough even to think about a carnival. They still had a whole host of attractions in Asbury Park back then – I mean, the place wasn't gorgeous, but it wasn't the shithole it's become since the gangs moved in. Christ, what a waste. Some entrepreneurial New York developer could move in there, raise the rent and drive out all the hooligans. The beachfront up there could be a goldmine if it wasn't buried beneath four generations of failure.'

Tony said, 'There are some good things going on now, real estate projects and urban renewal stuff. Some nice buildings are going in near the beach.'

'We'll see. I always hoped the place would rebound.' Moses slugged down the Scotch as if it were water. 'But you've never seen a place fail with the sheer style of Asbury Park. James Bradley, the founder, came down from New York before the turn of the last century, looking for clean air, no booze, no blacks, and no Jews. Dumbass. Around here, can you believe it? I guess he wanted someplace clean for like-minded, sober Protestants to spend time with other uptight whities.'

'Guess it didn't work,' Tony said. 'Look at the place now.'

Drawing an arc over his head, Moses waved us all back in time. 'Hell, Antonio, that city failed on a grand scale, many times in the past ninety years.' He ticked them off on drunken fingers: 'One, Asbury Park died a little in 1919 thanks to Prohibition and corrupt city politics. Two, it died again in 1929 with the crash, when half the hotels went belly-up and no one could afford to vacation anywhere. It died third time in 1946, when most of the city came home from the war addicted to drugs. Fourth, in 1955, when the Garden State Parkway opened up the seaside resorts along the coast. It died, just a bit, in 1971, when seventy-five dollars could get you from Newark Airport to a sunny year-round vacation spot called Walt Disney World. I may be speaking out of turn here, but that place showed some promise.'

Chef Sam masked a belch. 'With a mouse as big as a Volkswagen, how could they miss?'

'Great Adventure opened in 1974,' Tony said, 'I remember it from school trips. They've got a drive-through zoo and the animals come

222

and sniff in the window for peanut butter sandwiches and third-grade fingers. What boardwalk could compete with that just twenty miles down the road?'

Moses started on the other hand. '1974, that's right. I remember that too, but it was game over for Asbury Park before that – shit, by 1975 the state was funnelling money into the city because starving hotel owners along the boardwalk had agreed to house 3,500 psychos – your full-on Looney Tunes from the state's psychiatric hospitals. Hah! It was a special place.'

'Holy shit!' Tony didn't know what to believe; Moses' story sounded too far-fetched to be fiction.

'My friends,' Moses said quietly, 'Asbury Park has died again and again over the past century, but its final death rattle sounded in July, 1970.'

'What happened then?' Sam asked.

'Samantha, my love, in July 1970 the angry blacks from the West Side followed the lead of angry blacks in Newark and Trenton when they rose up together.'

'The riots,' Tony said. 'My dad told me about them – the blacks had been forced to live west of the tracks while the whites they served strolled up and down the boardwalk, protected from the sun with parasols ...'

'They burned Springwood Avenue to the ground,' Moses said. 'I was pitching in Canada at the time, but my mother called that morning, July eighth or ninth, I think it was, and she told me about it. She and my father could see the smoke from their house; they could hear the explosions as gas tanks ruptured. Back then, a car could explode, not like today when they just burn up. Anyway, when the nightmare ended, almost fifty people had been shot and Springwood Avenue was a ruin – the city just bulldozed it all to the ground. And what was worse, the goddamned violence never once made it east of the railroad tracks. Can you believe that?'

I said, 'No matter. The damage was done.'

'That's correct, my young friend. You could never quite gaze up at the old Mansard roofs with their shingled cupolas and colourful pennants the same way again. ' Moses looked over his extended fingers as if forgetting what he was counting. He folded his hands in his lap. 'What the hell was I saying?'

'Asbury, 1975,' I prompted.

'Right, yes.' He pinched the bridge of his nose and closed his eyes, replaying the Technicolor reels in his memory. 'That night was perfect, breezy, light jacket weather. This place has a decent breeze for much of the summer, but nights can get muggy. Kate and I walked the Circuit, the boardwalk, we rode the rides, ate popcorn and candy apples, and drank Cokes we bought from a vendor on Kingsley.' He lifted his head suddenly and looked intently at us. 'We didn't have all this New Coke, Diet Coke, Coke with Vitamins, Coke Zero, Coke Four-Thirty-Seven bullshit back then, just Coke. The best thing to drink on the planet.' He frowned at the bottle of Johnnie Walker Blue. 'Well, almost.'

Tony wrapped an arm around Chef Sam who slid a couple of inches closer and leaned on his chest as she listened to Moses' recollections.

'The colours and lights and music and smells of Asbury Park that fall were like cocaine for us, only better. Coming from Ottawa, we couldn't help but get high on the place, especially after dark, when the shadows hid all the grime and cracked plaster, the broken glass, even the racism. There was a carousel up there – I don't know what ever happened to it, but it had hand-painted horses, each one different, and each one a masterpiece to make Walt Disney hide his face in embarrassment despite the cheap plane tickets. It was the last carousel built by the Philadelphia Toboggan Company – imagine that, a toboggan company carving horses! But if you rode the outside horses, you had a chance to lean over and grab rings from an automatic dispenser, and for every ten or twelve brass rings, there was a gold one.' His eyes closed, Moses reached into the air above the table and grabbed at nothing. 'If you could catch that gold one, you got a free ride. Jesus, but I must have gone round and round on that thing two hundred times trying for that frigging ring, but I never got the gold, never once. By the early 1980s and the Reagan administration the carousel was still up there, but the ring dispenser was gone.'

'Could you see them trying that today?' Sam asked.

'Hell no,' I chimed in, 'the Mothers' Mafia would never stand for it; little gifted-and-talented Haley or Joshua could fall and bust their head open. These days you keep your arms and legs inside; you're strapped right down.'

'It's the insurance companies,' Tony said. 'The premiums on an amusement park have got to be up in the zillions – I mean, you get one thirteen-year-old who has an arm ripped off, and poof: you're up in Bankruptcy Court.'

Moses chuckled. 'I had a lifetime of riding that carousel and I don't remember anyone falling off – and if they did, it was their own god-damned fault.'

'Times change,' Chef Sam said.

'They do.' Staring at the ceiling, Moses said, 'That old carousel was a masterpiece, though. I can still remember the song it played, over and over and over—' He hummed a few notes, then sang softly, '*East Side, West Side, all around the town. The tots sang "ring-around-rosie", "London bridge is falling down"* ...' His voice trailed off and a slow moment of discontent seemed to pass through him. No one moved.

'That's the one,' I finally whispered. 'That song again.'

'Yes,' he said. 'It is.'

'So what happened?' Tony asked, clearly nervous, wanting to move things along.

Moses picked up the story. 'We went to dinner at one of the big hotels, I can't remember which, and had lobster. You guys ever smoke really good grass (we called it grass back then too, or reefer) and then eat a lobster? You've got to try it – it's like eating kickass food *and* killing a monster in a Japanese horror movie.'

Everyone laughed and Tony took his cue and poured Scotch all around. I hadn't finished mine, but I accepted anyway.

'Did you make a baby that night?' Chef Sam prompted. Like Tony, she was anxious to get to the punchline.

'I think so,' Moses said, 'but not right away; I'll never forget what happened first.' He sipped politely, then said, 'The Bentley Hotel had a band.'

'Oh, is this a Springsteen story?' Tony leaned forward. 'Why didn't you say so?'

Moses wagged a finger. 'No, no, no, the E-Street Band was on tour,

Born to Run, by October of '75; they were long gone. Southside Johnny played three nights a week at the Stone Pony, frigging workhorses. But we went to dinner someplace further south, and I don't remember who the band was, just some local group, but they were atrocious.'

'So they were crap and you were stoned – what'd you do?' I asked, keeping his eye on the ball.

'We took our plates, our wine, our lobsters, whatever, and went to sit in the bar. At least we could talk without screaming over all the pain and suffering going on in the ballroom. After another hour, they finally took a break, but while they were off, these two guys from the bar, two young guys about my age, they got up and just walked onto the stage—'

Shit. Here we go.

'—who were they?' Chef Sam asked.

'Well, that's the thing,' Moses said, 'I'm not sure. They were tall, good-looking guys, thin, with long hair, and I think one of them had a beard, but what the hell, everyone had a beard then. Anyway, they just climbed up on the stage, strapped on two of the guitars that were up there, tuned them up – *thank God* – and started playing this song, and to this day, I cannot hear that song without flashing all the way back to Asbury Park, half a goddamned lifetime ago.'

'And?' Tony reached across the table, taking Moses by the wrist. 'Who was it?'

He shook his head. 'I don't know.'

'What did they play?' Chef Sam asked.

I interrupted, 'They played Pink Floyd's *Wish You Were Here*, didn't they?'

Moses sat bolt upright and his eyes widened. 'Why would you—? How did—?'

'Is that right?' Tony asked.

Moses stared at me and whispered, barely audible, 'Yes, it is. I can't say for certain, but I like to believe it was Roger Waters and David Gilmour. They released that album – and that's what it was, an *album*, not all this download crap, late that summer, and the songs made sense in order so you listened to them *in order*. And while it might just have been two local guys who knew how to tune a guitar and plunk out a—'

226

Plaintive.

'—plaintive melody, to me they will always be Waters and Gilmour. I've never bothered to look into it because I don't want to be disappointed, but Asbury Park in the early 1970s was a music mecca. Either way, they just played that one song, and it was perfect; an encore would have ruined it. It was almost like hearing Mozart: it was pure, perfect, simple, plaintive emotion.'

'And then?' Tony asked. 'Did you talk to them? Get a photo? Steal their green M&Ms?'

'Nope. They finished the song and went back to the bar. Kate and I ate our Japanese horror lobsters and walked back here to the Warren & Monmouth. We held hands and talked about love and children and baseball and the Eskimo curlew.' He laughed. 'God forgive me, but I hated that fucking bird, excuse me—'

'And you made a baby!' Tony hugged the empty Scotch bottle like a Barbie doll. I hoped the hotel had extra guest rooms tonight, because no way would Tony be able to get his drunk Italian ass all the way to Bergen County and back by four-thirty for breakfast.

'Again, I like to think so,' Moses said. 'We walked down through Ocean Grove, Bradley Beach and Avon, quiet towns, and all the way I kept thinking I could hear that Asbury Park calliope. Once we got to Belmar, the noise and bustle caught up with us and I lost track of Asbury. The wind was blowing Kate's hair into my face – I used to have to always walk on the ocean side of her because it drove me crazy to have her hair blowing in my face, but that one night I welcomed it. It tickled and tangled and got stuck in my mouth, and by the time we got back here, I was about ready to burst. We made love like lunatics on just about every inch of this room, and down that back hallway—'

'I'll let the maids know,' Tony said, and Chef Sam elbowed him hard in the ribs. 'Ow! Goddamn girl – what's with you?'

'Just shut up and let him tell the story, for Christ's sake.' Sam went back to resting her head on his chest.

'All right,' Tony said, 'sorry, Mr Stillman. Italian girls – what can you do?'

'That's it,' Moses said. 'It was the greatest time of our lives, up until we had Lauren and the whole universe changed, but before she was born we were young and innocent and stupid, and gloriously ignorant and passionate all at the same time. I'd give anything I have ever possessed, except Lauren, to go back for just one more hour with my Katherine. But time ruins all of us, doesn't it? Time and furious squalls, and never knowing what you've got in front of you because you're so goddamned busy looking for what comes next. Jesus, but if there's anything I hate about you young people, that's it.' Anger swept across his face and I thought for a second he might take a drunk's swing at me. If Huck'd been there he'd have cuffed Moses to the lamp and left him until breakfast.

Chef Sam sniffed and wiped her face on Tony's sleeve. At thirty-fiveish, with kids of her own somewhere, the young, innocent, stupid, ignorant, passionate days had passed her by as well; maybe why she was clinging so tightly to a muscle-headed, twenty-something Italian boy from a rich neighbourhood up north.

Moses was fading fast and the young lovers needed some alone time, either to make a baby or to get practising. I pulled the plug on the evening. 'I should get going.'

Chef Sam sat up, 'Me too.' She allowed her hand to linger on the back of Tony's neck, toying with his hair.

'So soon?' Moses used both hands to push himself to his feet and nearly toppled into me.

'Whoa there!' I gripped him beneath one arm and helped him to the leather sofa on the other side of the room. 'Here you go, take it easy there for a second.'

'Sailor—' He let the sofa swallow him up like a Raggedy Andy doll. 'How did you know? That's not fair, that—'

'Let's talk about it tomorrow,' I tried. 'We're both shitfaced, and that conversation will do neither of us any good tonight. Tomorrow.'

'Promise me.'

'What are we, eight?'

'Promise.'

'I promise.' And as absurd as that was, it appeared to calm him.

There were drunken hugs and handshakes all around, then, arms linked, Tony from Bergen County and Chef Sam stumbled down the hallway, shushing one another between warnings to watch out for

Thomas the Fop, who might be hiding behind the next potted plant with pink slips in hand.

As the door closed behind them, I tugged Moses' loafers off, tucked them beneath the sofa and asked, 'You want to crash here, or are you going to try to make it to bed?'

He ignored me. 'I'm afraid of her, Sailor,' he slurred; whatever sobriety he'd mustered to regale us with tales of his honeymoon in Asbury Park had run its course.

'Afraid of who? Chef Sam? She's harmless. Anyway, I'm pretty sure she's got her eye on Tony – and her hands, and probably her legs by now.'

'Not Sam, dipshit, *Kate*.'

'You're afraid of Kate? Sorry, Moses, you're not making sense.' I looked around for something to prop beneath his head. 'You got a pillow somewhere?'

'Bedroom. Second door. Leave your gun.'

'My gun? God, no, it's bad enough that I have it tonight – if you have it, we both get to go to prison, and prison is a couple of coats of paint less pleasant than this place.'

I staggered down the hall, flipped on the bedroom lamp and yanked two pillows from the neatly made bed. I was about to click off the light, but I lingered a breath or two. Something wasn't right: something I'd expected to find.

After a second, I realised: there was only one photograph of Kate and Lauren Stillman. They were sitting on a park bench which might have been anywhere. Lauren wore a yellow dress and held a vanilla ice cream cone, most of which had melted over her hands. Kate wore a lavender dress with an absurd straw hat with a black ribbon that looked like something she might have bought in Paris and then regretted. She sat with her knees spread, her dress pressed down between them, demure yet sexy. A macramé handbag rested near her feet. Both Kate and Lauren looked utterly happy, sharing a joke, laughing without a care. I guessed Moses had taken the shot, but Rembrandt himself couldn't have captured a more exhilarating image of mother and daughter.

'Nice-looking wife, Moses,' I said to the empty room. 'You outdid—'

I held my breath and leaned in to confirm what I thought I saw. I blinked back drunk confusion and forced myself to focus, if just for a second. Kate – Katherine – Stillman wore a string of black pearls, each one a near-perfect clone of its neighbour, all except for the centrepiece, a big bastard as wide across as a nickel. 'Sonofabitch.' I ran a fingertip over Kate's neckline, as if I might be able to feel the tiny imperfections Herringbone had promised would be there. All I managed to do was leave a smudgy fingerprint on Moses' photo. I flicked the light off and left the room.

On the sofa, Moses had just about punched his ticket. I tucked the pillows far enough to keep his head up in case he decided to hurl in his sleep like Jimi Hendrix.

'—afraid to die,' he murmured. 'She'll be there.'

'Heaven? Probably, depends on what you believe.'

'Waiting.' His lips barely moved. 'All changed when Lauren died – then Dunning.'

I found a blazer in the hallway closet. It reminded me of the Harris Tweed number Herringbone had worn to the library that morning. There were half a dozen jackets, all different colours and weights – too goddamned many for a guy visiting a hotel, even a rich guy. Shit, the temperature during the day still rose into the eighties.

I draped the jacket over him, patted him lightly on the chest and checked for my BlackBerry and keys. Before leaving, I took another look at the photo of Kate in the canoe. Like the one in the bedroom, it was secured to the wall. This shot had to have been taken in Canada, looking at the greying driftwood scattered along the lakeshore. Her happy yellow life vest was zipped all the way up, but she hadn't managed to hide the strand of perfect black pearls. *What was it you said, Moses?*

He snored indecorously from the sofa.

Improbable. That was it; right?

In the hallway, I realised I had no clue how to get out of the hotel. I certainly didn't want to choose the wrong door and end up at Thomas the Fop's concierge desk.

'Psst, hey, Detective,' someone whispered from my left.

230

'Who's there?' I didn't need to reach back to feel the .357 in the waistband of my shorts. 'Tony?'

'Yeah, come this way,' he whispered.

I went on tiptoe – I had no idea if the rooms on either side of the hallway were occupied, but if Tony was determined to whisper, I'd humour him and sneak around. I found him waiting in a doorway. 'What's going on? Where's Chef Sam?'

'Upstairs – we're in one of the empty suites a couple of floors up. We'll crash here and be able to get to work on time. Although I'm feeling that Scotch now; I'm going to be hurting unit at four-thirty.'

'Nah,' I said, 'sleep in. Moses isn't going to be interested in breakfast, certainly not at four-thirty.'

'4:37,' he corrected.

'Yeah, what the hell is that about?'

'Rich guy, loony needs,' Tony said. 'I don't care. He tips really well, and he seems to be decent, you know. We get an awful lot of hoity-toity pricks in this place.'

'I can imagine.' I followed Tony to the end of the hallway, through a fire door and down a short flight of concrete stairs to a dark entrance. 'Is this it?'

'Yeah, that streetlight's the corner of Essex and Ocean. Go out there and take a left. Your car's on the street.'

'Thanks, Tony.' I shook his hand. 'I appreciate the help tonight.'

'Are you kidding? It was the most fun we've seen in this place in months. Half of me is still a little sorry we didn't run into Thomas and have to beat his ass.'

'Well, the month is just getting started,' I said. 'I'll see you soon.'

'Good night, Detective.' He pushed the door open for me.

'Hey, one second.' I stopped. 'What was that with you and Chef Sam? When you kicked her under the table?'

I couldn't get a read on Tony's face in the half-light, but something changed – fear, anxiety, uncertainty; I didn't know what it was, but Tony's carefree countenance evaporated and his eyes narrowed. 'I'm not sure what you mean, sir.'

'Bullshit. I'm a cop, you're drunk and I can read you like a flashing highway sign. So what's with Moses and this hotel?'

He considered the question. I gave him time. Finally he pressed his lips together and said simply, 'Mr Stillman doesn't leave. Not everyone knows it, because he pays the management to cook the registration books every now and then. But apart from a few times a year when he's off to I-don't-know-where, he's here, in that suite. He doesn't check out.'

'Of the hotel?'

'Ever.'

Outside I circled the building looking for the minivan. For one terrifying moment I wondered if Spring Lake implemented some overnight parking regulation after Labor Day. The last thing I needed was to have to hump it all the way to some frigging car pound – but no, there it was, right where I'd left it: the only car on Ocean.

I breathed in deep, trying for a taste of the fresh breeze I'd felt on Hanley's balcony, but I got nothing but humid summer air.

'Sailor!'

I about wet my pants. Moses stood on the bottom step of Rhett Butler's staircase, backlit by the single light. He wore socks, no shoes. His face was in shadow, impossible to read. Once I managed to get back into my skin, he waved me over.

'What are you doing out of bed?' I couldn't guess what was holding him up. Three-quarters of a bottle of Scotch would have me gurgling less coherently than Anna.

'Come here.' Moses didn't bother whispering; Thomas the Fop must have seen him stagger by.

'What?' I waved *I don't wanna get caught* in drunk sign language.

Moses refused to step off the staircase, wouldn't put his shoeless feet in the grass, which was dusted with enough sand to look like snow in the dim porch light. 'They're not real, Sailor.'

I knew what he meant. 'I don't care.'

'They're a knock-off – two hundred dollars from a gift shop in the *Château Frontenac* in Québec City.'

'Moses, I don't care.'

'I saw you looking.'

232

'She was beautiful.' What the hell, nothing else came to mind.

'She was.' He slid his hands into his pockets. 'But the pearls were bullshit. She wore them all the time, but they were fakes, not like the strand at O'Malley's.'

Nice try, old man, but they're exactly like the strand at O'Malley's. You drunk enough to lie to a cop?

'Can you get back to bed?'

He swayed a bit and I worried. 'I had to tell Thomas I won't be at breakfast, if you were thinking about steak and eggs at four-thirty. I won't make it tomorrow; I'll be out for lunch. Maybe.'

'That's fine, Moses, because when Jenny smells Scotch on my breath, I will be in the Monmouth County morgue by four-thirty.' I chuckled unconvincingly.

He didn't appreciate the joke. *You're discussing his dead wife's jewellery and making morgue jokes. Nice work, Sailor. You should be a grief counsellor.*

'They were fakes, Sailor.'

'Okay, they were fakes. That's *fine*. Good night, Moses.'

WEDNESDAY

North Side Playaz

Belmar to Spring Lake and back: 3.3 Miles

Blue: *Jesus Christ, are you trying to kill me?*

I parked on the northbound side of Ocean Avenue, across from the Dunkin' Donuts. Garish purple and orange light spilled across the sidewalk and the silent roadway. At twelve-thirty on a Wednesday morning, Belmar had gone to bed, leaving the doughnut shop as an oasis of light and comforting aromas. Behind me, the incoming tide roared its perpetual howl, beating the beach senseless.

I crossed Ocean half-hoping a garbage truck might run me down. I'd fucked up monumentally, and now here I was, hoping that dropping a dollar and change on a blast of coffee would speed me up and stink me up just enough to get past Jenny without having to explain why I'd come home reeking of booze – albeit *really* expensive booze. There wasn't a workable explanation, not one that would keep me out of traction or stop Jenny from grabbing my parents' scuffed suitcases and heading for greener pastures. If the gods were smiling on me, Jenny would have been asleep for the past two hours. I tripped up the curb, stumbled, and decided to sneak into the O'Mearas' back yard and peek in the windows, just to check – although I'd have to navigate their fence without bleeding; blood would be as hard to explain as five Scotches.

The air-conditioning sobered me enough to order a coffee. Overhead, Kenny Rogers told me he knew when to hold them and fold them. Whatever.

I paid my dollar-forty-nine and tried to swish the fluid around my mouth and gargle it into the back of my throat to subdue the smell of Scotland on my breath. I stood in the wide front window and watched a couple of kids walk by, one carrying a basketball and apparently trying to rap. A bicyclist pedalled north on Ocean, looking ridiculous in Day-Glo spandex undies. Swirling another mouthful, I turned to make a crack to the Indian kid behind the counter, but he'd gone into the kitchen.

'Time to make doughnuts, I guess.'

The incandescent lights, as vicious as those in a high-school cafeteria, dimmed, not much, just enough to get me blinking and wondering if I might be about to pass out. I checked again for Gandhi, thinking maybe he'd turned the lights down in preparation for closing, but there was no sign of him.

I turned back to the street. Eventually, Kenny broke even or died or did some damned thing and the song ended. I sipped more coffee and waited to hear what would come on next, but nothing did; instead the speakers crackled out a rhythmic scratch, as if the needle on an ancient record player had got stuck on some dusty album – *and that's what it was, an album.*

I called, 'Hey back there, the record's stuck.'

The lights dimmed again, nearly to darkness now, with only the orange and purple letters to colour the Belmar night.

Outside, a young couple walked unhurriedly, arm in arm. I knew they couldn't see me, and like any cop I stood as still as a voyeur, waiting for something to happen. Wind off the water lifted the girl's hair, whipping it across her boyfriend's face, but he didn't mind, even had a few strands stuck to his mouth.

'Ah, shit,' I whispered. '*Shit.*'

As they came closer I saw they both wore patched bell-bottom jeans over leather sandals. The woman's macramé bag and knitted poncho nearly hid her paisley blouse, but did nothing to cover the strand of black pearls around her pretty neck, the centre gem as wide as a thumbnail. The pearls matched her eyes, so dark brown as to be almost black, depthless. Her young husband wore a waist-length leather jacket and a baseball cap pulled low over his forehead. He was

235

tall and wiry; a few inches on the north side of six feet, and he carried himself with the easy confidence of an athlete.

I looked backwards through time, watching Moses and Kate Stillman as they walked from Asbury Park south to their honeymoon suite at the Warren & Monmouth Hotel. They'd make baby Lauren that night, or at least get good at practising.

The cop in me elbowed the voyeur out of the way and I stepped quietly outside. Waiting silently on the concrete steps, I listened as Moses and Kate passed.

'—far you would swim for me?' Kate asked.

'To save you? I would swim a hundred miles.'

'A hundred!'

'Of course, and for me? How far would you swim to save me?'

'From drowning? Three miles.' She giggled and kissed his neck.

'Three! Only three? What's that about?'

She hugged him across his chest, her hair still whipping him like a cat-o-nine-tails. 'I'm not a professional athlete, Bozo. I can't swim any more than three miles.'

'I forgot,' Moses said, 'you're a statistician.' He slid an arm inside her poncho, hoping for skin on skin. 'So what's a statistician again?'

And they passed, happier and more content than they'd ever be again.

The lights inside Dunkin' Donuts came up. Behind the counter, Gandhi fussed with a napkin-holder, trying to pry it open with a butter knife, and overhead the old record player wound back to life, queuing up a new millennium and a scratch-free download of Taylor Swift's latest teenage dilemma.

'I gotta get home.' I drank the last of my coffee, burning my throat, gargled the final half-inch and spat it into the gutter. Jogging across Ocean, I fumbled Jenny's keys, bent to pick them up and winced as the shooting pain in my leg reminded me I wasn't up for late night jogging yet.

Shouldn't be climbing on chairs on sixth-floor balconies either, shithead.

I switched to sidelights and rolled to a stop at the corner of Twelfth and C, two doors down from the O'Meara place. I felt like an idiot – there wasn't anyone around, and no lights on for at least two blocks

– but I tiptoed to the O'Meara fence anyway. There was no sense getting busted because I was too noisy. If I was going to get caught, I preferred it to be for drinking, not for trying to sneak back in. Getting caught drinking said, *Sailor, you're an asshole!* But getting caught sneaking around said, *Sailor, you're a chickenshit coward!*

The corner of the O'Mearas' back yard fence was almost directly beneath the outstretched limbs of the old pear tree. I hadn't realised how long those branches had grown. I made an empty promise to prune them before Mrs O'Meara complained. The lawn had an oddly fishy aroma, as if the guts and heads of a fish supper had been left out in a torn trash bag.

All right, let's get this over with. I leaned over as far as I could but still wasn't able to see inside the bedroom. I pulled my sling tight, gripped the top of the fence and with all the confidence of a five-Scotch drunk I used my good leg to hoist myself up and over.

The fence might as well have been made of sharpened pikes; by the time I rolled over the top I was bleeding from a dozen splintery scratches along my legs, hips, ribs and neck.

Landing with a curse, I lay still, expecting diabolical pain to leave me paralysed, but it didn't; instead I was engulfed by an unholy stench, as if I had fallen into a cargo of rotting fish heads.

'What in the name of God and Ringo?' I found myself face down in a massive pile of half-eaten lobsters, dozens of them.

I dug for my BlackBerry, clicked the ON button and by the screen light examined this unusual compost heap. There were no rotting veggies, no mouldy breadcrumbs, no used coffee grounds, just lobsters, piles of uncooked, half-devoured lobsters.

God damn, Mrs O'Meara! What the hell's the matter with you? I got to my knees and checked the driveway across the uncut lawn, but it was empty.

I couldn't recall if I'd seen a car there all week; I didn't think so. I tried to remember when I'd last been near this part of the house; last night, when that pear branch had moved. I certainly hadn't smelled anything when I was outside this morning, standing in the torrential rain and trying not to look up at Gabriel Lebow.

Then Jenny, in my memory: *Who steals thirty-five lobsters?*

Fraternity brothers.

What's that scratching on the glass, next to the hole? Are those claw marks?

'Oh shit,' I said, 'not again.'

A blinding light shone in my face. '*Oh shit* is right, Detective Doyle. Mind telling me what you're doing back there? And what is that stench – you need a diaper change?'

I tried shielding my eyes. 'Who's that?' I whispered. 'Turn the light off.'

Darkness swallowed me. My eyes needed a few seconds to clear the stinging imprint the flashlight had left. 'Who's there?' I groped for the fence, my BlackBerry still tight in my fist.

'Come down here, kemosabe. I'll help you back over.'

Old voice – raspy. A smoker.

'Huck?' I found the fence and looked over the top, blinking to clear my vision. 'Uncle Hucker? What are you doing here? Why didn't you call me?' I checked my BlackBerry again: three missed calls. I forgot I'd silenced it at the hotel.

'I've been calling, shit-for-brains.' He reached over, hooked his arms beneath mine. 'I just got here a few minutes ago – I left Richmond after rush hour – and I saw you sneaking down the street like a drunken mailman. I about pissed my drawers when I saw you hurdle that fence ass-first. What the hell you thinking, Olga?'

'I'll tell you once you've busted me out of here.'

'Ready?' He tightened his grip.

'On three.' I wedged my toes against the lowest support slat.

'Three!' Huck heaved, I kicked and pulled myself and between us we managed to get my bleeding body back onto the sidewalk.

I rolled onto my back, laughing. 'Good to see you, buddy. Thanks for coming.'

'You smell, my young friend.'

'Found the seafood compost, just my luck.'

'C'mon.' He helped me up. 'I'll buy you breakfast.'

'Huck, it's one o'clock in the morning.'

'Lunch?'

*

238

Huck drove to an all-night diner west of Neptune. The coffee smelled burned, but I drank it anyway. Huck ordered a beer and a short stack of pancakes; I went with a pair of soft chicken tacos smothered in jalapenos and salsa. With the stench of rotting lobster, scorched coffee and Mexican food billowing around me like Pigpen's dust cloud, I didn't need to worry so much that Jenny'd catch a whiff of Moses' Scotch. Hell, it might be days before she dared to come near me again.

Huck lit a cigarette – New Jersey diners were the last place in the western hemisphere where you could still light up – and I bummed one too, as my pack had been crushed when I tanked the dismount into the O'Mearas' back yard. We smoked in silence for a couple of minutes. He tried for pensive but just looked tired. Huck was never one for poker; he clearly wanted me to ask the question that hovered over us like a storm cloud.

Finally I did. 'So. Have I got a job when I get back?'

He crossed his arms behind his head and leaned against the red vinyl bench. I noticed the torn seams had been patched with ageing duct tape. 'I wouldn't worry. Captain Fezzamo's got your back. He had Harper on the horn about six seconds after he heard about your heroics the other day. I'm not even really sure what I'm supposed to be doing here, but I was out the door before I knew what'd hit me.'

'Were they worried I was shitfaced when I tackled that kid?'

He crushed his cigarette in a gold ashtray that looked like it might have been left by Lyndon Johnson. 'Nope – actually, that might be a lie.'

'Whaddya mean?' I tried the coffee. 'Goddamn, that's bad.'

'Here at Fortnum & Mason? I'm shocked! You should order a beer.' Huck winked at a woman at the counter who was sopping up egg yolk with a crust of toast; she looked about ready to barf.

He untied the rawhide strip holding his salt-and-pepper ponytail in place, gathered his hair in one hand and retied it. 'I believe Lieutenant Harper is worried that you might have fallen off the wagon. Given your behaviour, aroma and overall appearance tonight, I can't wait to get back to Richmond and tell him just how wrong he is—'

'Prick.'

He gulped half his beer. 'But Fezzamo's convinced you're coming

239

back clean as a whistle, ready to get to work, and willing to stand up and take some of the credit for your silly antics last July. I tried to tell him that I didn't think there would be too many rubber-chicken dinners or hero ceremonies waiting for you, given the attention span here in the United States of ADHD, but he's the boss and I pretty clearly am *not* the boss.'

'But I've gotta worry about Harper?'

'Nah, Harper wants you to come back and do well – shit, he's the one who's been fielding all the ground balls coming out of Internal Affairs. Fezzamo just shuts the door and tells them to shove off. It must be nice being the captain.'

'You and I may never know, cousin.'

'True. Sad, but true,' he said.

'So no fallout on the shooting, nothing more on the civil suit?'

'Besides the normal bullshit: no gun until the IA guys are done, mandatory counselling, no *Star Trek* reruns – at least, not that I've heard,' he said. 'I mean, if you'd got yourself stoned and shot a parishioner at Our Lady of the Perpetual Boobies Catholic Laundro-mat and Truck Stop, you might have a problem, but you didn't. You shot a snake-wielding zealot determined to see a plague-infected Molly Bruckner reach Interstate 95 and – if he'd have got *his* wish – Reagan National Airport—'

'He *was* an asshole, that much is true.' I forced down a bit more coffee.

'So Burgess Aiken, dead and eaten by his own snakes, doesn't have too many credible advocates calling for your head on a plate. That's good.'

'But it doesn't make me a good cop in Harper's eyes,' I said, embar-rassed to hear the admission cross my lips, even in front of Huck.

'Forget that.' Huck finished his beer and waved the empty bottle in the direction of the kitchen. No one noticed. 'Harper's got five or six years on me. He's gonna retire as a lieutenant, and I'm sure it's everybody else's fault that he hasn't been promoted. He strikes me as a decent cop and a decent guy, and I'm sure that in the quiet moments when he takes two minutes to look in the mirror, the last thing on his mind is whether or not one of his detectives is an OxyContin junkie.

Shit, you pee in the cup a few times over the next year and he'll forgive you. He's done his time; he knows that life can bugger any of us on a moment's notice. Just pee clean and Harper won't think twice about you.'

Our waitress returned with the food. 'Soft tacos, chicken, and a short stack. Enjoy, boys.' At one-thirty in the morning and lit all over in disrespectful light she might have been twenty-nine or fifty-one. The brown and beige costume she'd been forced to wear did nothing for her.

Huck didn't care. 'Thank you, my love,' he said. 'I'll have another beer whenever you can get free.'

'Coming right up.' To me, she said, 'More coffee, honey?'

I held up my hands. 'No, I'm good, thanks.'

Huck took her wrist before she could clear the empty bottle. 'I'll keep that, sweetie. I like to peel the labels.'

She flashed yellow teeth and looked every bit of fifty-one. 'You know what that means?'

'That I like to hump ostriches? A guy's gotta have a hobby,' he sighed.

Fifty-One liked that and hung around a second, waiting to see what Uncle Hucker might say next.

As ever, he didn't disappoint. 'You know, I do own a little summer cottage in Fallujah. I'm just saying.'

Playing along, Fifty-One said, 'I get off at five a.m.'

'Damn,' Huck said, 'and the last plane to Baghdad leaves at four-forty-five.'

'I guess it wasn't meant to be.' She shrugged; her one-piece brown-on-beige polyester coverall-thingie rose and fell over her body like a theatre curtain.

'Maybe next time,' Huck said.

'Just the beer then?'

'Just the beer.'

She left.

I asked, 'Are you really like this all the time?'

'God wants me to flirt with ugly women,' he said. 'It's my penance for screwing up my marriage so righteously.'

241

'Jenny thinks Sandy would take you back.' I poured salsa over my tacos without looking up.

Huck snorted quietly through his nose. 'It's sad how much your wife drinks during the day, isn't it?'

I laughed and rerouted the conversation. 'So what's the timeline on Internal Affairs getting this wrapped up? They need to talk to me again?'

He skewered a triangle-slice of pancakes and talked with his mouth full. 'Dunno, don't think so. They already interviewed you. They're running around now confirming your side of things with me, Phil Clarkson, Doc Lefkowitz, Kay Bryson and—'

'Sarah Danvers,' I finished for him.

'Hey.' He held up a finger while he chewed. 'The way I see it, if the Internal Affairs investigator who flies out there to interview Sarah is a heterosexual guy, you're in the clear.'

'Who could blame me, right?' I made the joke, then instantly regretted it as Scotch-flavoured bile rose in my throat.

'Jenny, your wife.' Huck didn't let me wriggle away. He'd caught me with my hand in the cookie jar tonight and it was time to 'fess up. 'She might have some reservations.'

Reading his mind, I said, 'It was just tonight. I haven't had a drink or a pill since July fourth, I swear to Christ, Huck, I'm being straight with you. I had a few Scotches tonight because I'm kind of half-working this investigation and I needed to hang around and listen to this guy and I wasn't sure what he was going to say, and there's something going on with him and I can't figure it, and so I—'

'Whoa, wait – slow down, you're going to hurt yourself.' He poured more syrup over his plate. 'What are you talking about? What does this have to do with Gabriel Lebow and Robert Morris Middle School? You teaming with Monmouth County on this?'

'No, no, nothing like that.' I told him about Harold Hanley's death, about my conversations with Moses Stillman, and of the oddly similar scrapes and scratches I'd found in Auntie Carla's pen, on the lobster tank at Seibert's Seafood and in the elm tree Lebow had used to hide from Hannah Martin, the teacher on duty at the school gate. I made a half-assed attempt to connect the scratches with Hanley's suicide, explaining my desire to get a look inside that hotel room. I didn't mention the Pink Floyd music or the oddly clairvoyant manner in which I had known what Moses was going to say about that night back in 1975. In an effort to give my rambling, disconnected explanation some cohesion, I added that I'd searched the Internet but found no record of Moses Stillman ever playing professional baseball, but that there were photographs of Katherine Stillman – just a couple – showing Moses' former wife in a string of black Tahitian pearls, perhaps even the same strand on display at O'Malley's in Spring Lake. By the time I'd finished, even I didn't see any tenuous threads holding my suspicions together.

Huck tried to be a good guy about it though. 'Despite that nearly airtight summation of evidence clearly linking Moses Stillman to the great lobster heist of Central Jersey, I'm struggling to see any connections between anything you've just said.'

'Ass-wipe.' I ate more of my tacos. They tasted like warm wallpaper paste.

'I've been called worse' – he took in the diner's weary décor – 'and in nicer places than this, kemosabe.'

'I can't explain it, Huck,' I said, 'but something screwy is going on here.'

'And it isn't just you?'

I hesitated before answering, 'I suppose it could be.'

'Did you find matching scratches or carvings on the roof above Hanley's room tonight?'

'Dunno.' Heartened, I clicked through my BlackBerry's photo files until I found the few shots I'd taken earlier.

'Anything?' Huck shovelled more pancakes.

'Nah, shit.' The images showed no evidence that anything had been carved or scratched into the slate tiles above room 6103. 'Damn it, I was sure there was a connection, that Hanley was tossed out of that room after he'd died or been killed.'

'They doing a post?'

'Yup, over at Jersey Shore Medical, the place we passed on the way out here.'

'So you'll know soon enough.'

243

'I suppose so.'

Huck speared a bacon slice with his fork and I thought of Auntie Carla and wondered if her missing parts had been bacon. I clicked back and forth between the picture I'd taken of the gargoyle above Hanley's room and the gargoyle on the Ocean Grove firehouse, but I couldn't decide whether they looked identical or just similar, with eerily disagreeable concrete grimaces. Even with the phone right up to my face I couldn't determine if they were the same carving. *There you go, Sailor, even entertaining the idea that they might be the same gargoyle is spooky enough. Maybe you should go back on the pills.*

Huck asked, 'What's your gut feeling on Stillman?'

I clicked the phone off. 'For a good guy, he's a little odd. And maybe it's nothing recent, but he's got something indelible scrawled on his heart.'

'Really? Why do you say so?'

I shook my head to clear the cobwebs. I needed to make sense to Huck and have him think of me as a cop again, not just some charity errand he had to run for Captain Fezzamo. 'First, Moses is like a rich asshole, but he's not. I like him. He's pretentious as hell with his Italian loafers and his fancy breakfast routines, but he had a few drinks tonight and his working-class roots started showing. He knows wine and music, architecture and cultured food, Tahitian pearls, whatever, but at the same time, once he got half in the bag, his fake country-club façade cracked and he behaved like any one of us might after eight or ten drinks. When I first met him, he talked about Molly Bruckner; he even called her a *woman with a cognitive ailment.*' I made little curly-Q quotation marks with my fingers and felt like an asshole.

'Right,' Huck said, 'I remember; we can't call them retards.'

I went on, 'Yet tonight he talked about Asbury Park in the seventies, when the state gave money to hotel owners to provide housing for psych patients.'

'So?'

'So – instead of referring to them as *individuals with cognitive ailments*, he called them Looney Tunes, banana brains or some goddamned thing.'

Huck lit another smoke. 'That doesn't make him a felon.'

'I never said felon.'

'All right, so he changes colours when he's shitfaced. We all do.'

'And you know what's nuts? I put him to bed.'

'Decent of you.'

'We aim to please,' I said. 'Anyway, he'd fired down three-quarters of a bottle of Scotch—'

Huck toasted Moses with his beer. 'A man after my own heart.'

'—I got him to the couch, got his shoes off, whatever. I mean, I didn't hold his head while he hurled or anything.'

'Understandable. Honour among drunks. I get it.'

'And three minutes later, he's outside, pitching me this bullshit line about his dead wife's necklace, as if that'll distract me from the shit he'd said earlier.'

Huck cocked an eyebrow. 'While he was hammered or before that?'

'Hammered.'

'Ah, *in vino veritas*. Unless of course she's wearing a tank top and a Corona beer miniskirt, then it's pretty much *in vino bullshit*.'

'Cute.'

'What'd he say?'

'Disconnected stuff about his wife's non-profit, big oil companies, the Arctic pheasant or some frozen-assed bird, and his daughter's death.'

'His daughter's dead?'

'Yup, drowned with the wife, but tonight, Moses mentioned the change in his wife after the daughter died, as if they drowned on different days.'

'So he lied.'

'To a cop.'

Huck shook his head. 'Ought to know better. We're never, *ever* that drunk. But I ask you again: who cares?'

'Why distract me?'

Huck tried, and failed, to blow a smoke ring. 'He knows you're a cop – maybe he's sharper than he looks, he's trying to throw you off. Whatever.'

'I guess you're right. What difference does it make?'

'Then where're we going with this?'

'I dunno,' I said. 'Why would he lie about playing pro baseball?'

'Same question, different day: who cares? He doesn't know you from Elvis, and you're only going to be around for a couple of weeks. So he conjures up a fake past, some bullshit about bringing the heat at Riverfront Stadium—'

'Nope, the minors.'

'Minors?'

'In Canada.'

'Bullshit.'

'No bullshit, cousin. This guy lies about playing minor league baseball in frigging Ottawa. Call me crazy, but that screams *second best*. And to top it off, he's got a poster-sized photograph of himself peering nastily over the web of his glove, like he's ready to blow a fastball by Bucky Dent.'

Huck dropped his cigarette in Lyndon Johnson's ashtray and considered me as he might consider a bad painting. 'You looked him up?'

'Yup.'

'In NCIC? LInX?'

'Nah, just Google. Where am I going to get a login for NCIC? Fezzamo shut down my passwords.'

'Use mine, or I'll do it when I get home.' Smoke curled around us; Huck flicked a finger through the coiling tendrils, pulled a pen from his jeans and found a clean napkin. 'What's his real name? Please don't say *Moses*.'

'Mark.'

'Wife? Kids?'

I told him what I knew as he scrawled illegible reminders to himself. Afterwards, he folded the napkin, and stuffed it in his shirt. He stared again, a veteran cop on the lookout for bullshit. 'You haven't been drinking? Because you know you've got to get that shit out of your system before you piss for Harper. No weed; Jesus, that takes at least thirty days, and no pills, Sailor – who knows how long they can detect those chemicals. You might still piss dirty from all the shit you took in July.'

'I'll be all right,' I said. 'Stop worrying.'

'I'm older. I'll worry if I want to.' He finished his bacon, dragging the last bits through a puddle of syrup. 'No drinking?'

'Just tonight, Huck, I swear to Christ.' I eyed his beer and wanted one.

'And no pills?'

'Over-the-counter stuff,' I confessed, 'and plenty of it. I take Nytol as if they package it with me in mind. I don't sleep well, but I've never slept well, not since my sister died. Other than that I also hit the Naproxen pretty hard for my leg and shoulder—'

'They okay?' he asked. 'I hadn't expected you to still be in a sling.'

'I had an accident in the water the other day. Jenny heaved me out, but she pulled a bit too hard on this wing. I'm trying to keep it immobile – disarming middle school kids notwithstanding.'

'Okay.'

'Is that really why they sent you?' I asked. 'To report back on whether I'm hammered?'

'No one said as much,' Huck admitted, 'but why else would I be here? I figure I'll head over to the Monmouth County Prosecutor's Office tomorrow, just to show my face and legitimise you and your badge and your convalescence, but what else can I do?'

'Keep stopping by for our special pep talks,' I said.

He puffed out his chest. 'Nothing quite says *sobriety* like this physique, my friend.'

'I don't get it,' I said. 'I mean, if Harper and Fezzamo sent you, they must know – or at least suspect – that you'll go back and lie for me.'

'Thanks, shithead, I love you, too.' Huck took a swipe at my head.

'C'mon now, I mean it, there's not a chance in Hell that you're going back there to tattle and they must know that. Shit, you could kill the Pope with a chopstick and I'd swear in court that it was the one-armed man.'

He nodded towards my sling. 'Careful, kemosabe.'

'You know what I'm saying, Huck. Do you think you're here to bring back the message they knew you would bring back before they ever thought to send you?'

He thought this over, his slate-grey eyes following the curling trails of smoke. 'I suppose, but shouldn't that make me feel dirty? Somehow used?'

'In this place at two o'clock in the morning? We should all feel dirty.'

'Fezzamo's never struck me as stupid.'

'Right,' I said down at my half-eaten tacos. A frustrating tip-of-my-brain bit of information was eluding me, something that would make sense out of Huck being here. Then I said, 'Marta Hodges.'

'The detective? What about her?'

'Her timing.' I picked absently at a crack in the Formica. 'Two seconds after she arrived at Robert Morris Middle School the other day she asked me, in front of other cops, if I'd taken any pills that morning, trying to pick a fight.'

'She checked you out,' Huck said.

'She did,' I agreed, 'but beforehand – there's no way she could possibly have known I would be on that playground at seven o'clock in the morning. So she looked into my story after—'

'—after you met her at the hotel,' Huck finished. 'Why?'

'It was there, just now – I had it, Huck, I got a glimpse of it right at the edge of my vision, but I lost it.'

He didn't answer.

'She called Richmond after questioning me at the Warren & Monmouth Hotel last Sunday and someone there told her I'd spent four weeks puking up my guts at MCV.'

Huck didn't disagree. 'Fine – but what does that have to do with the price of lobsters?'

'I don't know.' I gave up. 'I can't figure it, Huck; I don't have a clue. But I'd bet you a beer it's why Fezzamo sent you. You're a sure thing; no bad news comes from Uncle Hucker.'

'He's right.' Huck finished his beer, found the napkin in his shirt pocket and scribbled another reminder.

'What's that?' I asked.

'Nothing.' He dug for his wallet. 'C'mon, let's get out of here.'

Seeing Huck brandishing his wallet, Fifty-One made her way back to our booth. 'You boys about done?'

'Yes, my love.' Huck gave her a twenty. 'It was an epicurean *fantasia*.'

'Uh huh, sure.' She took the bill. 'I'll get your change.'

Huck stood. 'No worries, my dear. We're all set.'

'Thanks, boys.' She walked with us towards the exit where a thirty-five-year-old cigarette machine featured a Marlboro Man who'd probably died of cancer while I was still in high school. Fifty-One held the door open for us. 'You boys hear about that missing surfer? Landon?'

'Yeah,' I said, 'I saw it on the news earlier. It's too bad – sounds like he was just a kid.'

As Huck led the way down the worn concrete steps to the nearly empty parking lot Fifty-One let the door fall shut behind her. She leaned on the cigarette machine and muttered, '*Sh'ma Yis'ra'eil Adonai Eloheinu Adonai . . .*'

'Are you kidding?' Huck lifted Ben high enough to sit on his shoulders. 'I was changing diapers before either of you finished middle school. I can handle this duty, no problem.'

Ben reached for the ceiling fan, giving the palm-shaped blades a spin. 'Look, Mommy, I turned the fan!'

'Careful, buddy,' Jenny warned. 'Are you sure, Huck? C'mon, you didn't drive all the way up here to babysit.'

'It's fine, really. Sailor and I talked about it last night and we're not entirely sure what I'm supposed to be doing here. At least this way I can report back that I did something productive.' He leaned down, slid Ben over his head and dumped him onto the sofa. Ben immediately bounced up and dived on for a piggyback.

'Benjamin,' Jenny said, 'get *down*.'

'It's okay.' Huck grappled with him, looking like a zookeeper trying to wrangle a monkey. 'When's the last time the two of you went out together, alone?'

Jenny didn't hesitate. 'June 27, last summer. We hired a babysitter, went to dinner and then to a movie. I think we both slept through it. Anna was about fifteen minutes old.'

'Three *months*?' Huck looked disappointed. Staring me down, he said, 'Are you *kidding*? Three months without a date? You two should go away for the weekend. I can stay.'

Jenny crossed her arms. 'Um, no—'

'Why not? Benji and I can whip up the old Fruit Loops and baked beans special – whaddya say, Benji? You wanna hang with Uncle Hucker for the weekend while Mommy and Daddy go to Atlantic City?'

'Is that far?' Ben stopped climbing, although he still had one hand wrapped tightly in Huck's ponytail.

'Nah, just down the street,' Huck said.

'Then, that's okay.' He resumed his ascent of Mount Hucker.

'Cool, we'll read the Torah and build a cottage out of whipped cream.'

'Two hours.' Jenny grabbed her bag. 'Can you three manage two whole hours without needing a trip to the hospital and without ingesting anything living or plastic or living in plastic?'

'Done,' Huck said.

'Done,' Ben echoed. 'We're going to read the Torah—'

'—and dance the Hora-Bora!' Huck said as Anna cooed in her bassinette.

'All right, if you're sure. The baby needs to eat in half an hour – there's breast milk in the fridge, on the left—'

'Whew!' Huck looked relieved. 'That's good, because I just ran dry!'

'I could pump real quick, if you like,' I said, but Jenny ignored both of us.

She kissed Ben on the forehead. 'Be good for Uncle Hucker, okay, buddy? I'll see you soon. And if you go outside, sunscreen. Okay?'

'Bye, Mommy,' Ben's face beamed in anticipation of the coming adventure. Uncle Hucker was the planet's greatest babysitter by a healthy margin.

I grabbed my wallet and cell phone. I had showered and scrubbed away the last of the rotten lobster; I thought I looked marginally presentable in cargo shorts and a polo shirt. I nodded thanks to Huck, kissed the kids and followed Jenny to where she waited on the sidewalk.

'Where do you want to go?' I asked. 'Your choice, you're the one trapped in the house most of the time.'

'Let's just walk,' she said, then, 'are you okay to walk with your leg and everything?'

'I'm fine,' I said. 'I've been getting in the miles; I'm pretty strong now, you'll see.'

She started towards the beach. 'It'll be nice just to walk – just us, no diaper bag, no beach bag or backpack full of toys and books, no stroller, no breast-pump, no blankets and wipes and pockets overflowing with Band-Aids, M&Ms and Cheerios.'

Jenny didn't realise that I'd have done about anything she wanted – anything to purge the guilt I had over the previous night's drinking with Moses. I wondered for a second if I'd have felt the same if Huck hadn't caught me, but I forced that from my mind: I'd drunk alcohol, and I'd no intention of telling my wife about it. Even worse, if Tony hadn't been around I might have hit on Chef Sam and tried to get her out of that pretty sundress. I didn't like thinking about it, but I had to admit: either way the evening had been a pretty clear step backwards for me.

Or at least a clear look in the mirror, asshole.

'Whatever you want to do,' I said. 'I just like that we're out.'

As we walked, Jenny took off the baseball cap she'd been wearing, loosened her ponytail and let her hair fall over her shoulders.

And she's trying to look nice for you.

We turned towards Spring Lake; the midday sun coloured the surf blinding white and the swells offshore emerald green. Light breeze tossed Jenny's hair into my face and I couldn't help but laugh.

'Sorry,' she said, pulling it together, slipping a scrunchie off her wrist.

'No, no.' I stepped around her to the ocean side. 'I'll just walk over here. Leave it down, it looks—'

'Whatever, Sailor.'

'No, it looks nice – I like it down, really.'

'Don't try to be too complimentary, love of my life, you might pull something.'

I took her hand and she laced her fingers together with mine. 'Actually, I was hoping that maybe later *you'd* pull something.'

She giggled. 'That's better; that's the Sailor I know.'

I exhaled hard. I hadn't vomited, but I should have; now my guts were all clenched up and I was seesawing between wanting more booze and regretting every ounce I already had sloshing around my

251

stomach. Embarrassing sweat broke out on my forehead and neck and I surreptitiously wiped my face on my sleeve.

'You all right?'

'Yeah, just a little warm.' *Fuck! Fucking Moses.*

'Come on.' She pulled me closer. 'Let's not try too hard and spoil it, okay?'

'Okay.' And I vowed never to screw anything up again, as long as I lived. I'd made that vow before, of course. 'Where do you want to go?'

'Back to Spring Lake,' she said. 'We only got to see the library yesterday. Let's go and find the house I'll buy when I marry a billionaire.'

'Alrighty. I'll help you pick out a nice one.'

Jenny had my undivided attention. She wore a yellow bikini top under a NY Giants T-shirt, enhancing the tantalising swell of her breasts, and she was probably wearing the yellow bottoms under her cut-off jeans – she'd been planning to hit the beach again this afternoon. I had to keep myself from peeking. If I was wildly lucky, *not to mention faithful and dependable and sober and supportive and a decent father*, I might find out first-hand at some point—

We walked comfortably side by side. Married people walk better together than dating people; dating people don't have the curves and rhythms down quite right. Married people have that all worked out and can walk for miles. Granted this is only when they can stand to be near one another, but for me, the afternoon's status held firmly at so-far-so-good.

At North Boulevard we turned west and took the path around Lake Como, another of Spring Lake's natural borders. Apart from a few bicyclists and joggers, we had the place to ourselves and enjoyed the stroll, watching the swans and revelling in the idea that someone else was on Diaper Duty. About halfway around the lake, Jenny asked, 'You hear from Detective Hodges today?'

'Not yet. Huck's going to see her later. I think he brought along a clean shirt and everything.'

'Why?'

'He'll offer to help, to meet with any lawyers or officials who might want my liver on toast. Actually, to tell the truth, I'm not sure. I think it's more that Fezzamo wants me to feel supported back home:

everyone knows I can't leave, not yet – Hodges may need more from me, or Lebow's family may file suit.'

'Hodges may not like him,' Jenny said. 'Huck's kind of an acquired taste.'

'He'll be all right. When it comes down to police work he knows what he's doing. It's the rest of his life that confuses him.'

'I still can't believe it's made national news – it was on again this morning, the *Today Show*, and then on some cable channel. That was a firestorm – they had an official from some anti-institutionalised-racism group and some stuffed-shirt executive from the Anti-Defamation League. Neither made any sense, neither could get a word in edgewise, and the jackass moderator just sat back and let them shout at each other. It's the perfect model for our kids: just yell and insult and nay-say one another until your five minutes run out and we have to go to a Viagra commercial. If anything, they made things worse. I really hope no one was watching. The ADL fool did everything short of calling criminal street gangs a black army engaged in a civil war, and the other buffoon went on and on about how Gabriel Lebow's Jewish heritage and religious traditions damned near *brainwashed* him into hating blacks enough to commit murder on a massive scale. I understand the cable news networks have to find something to fill twenty-four hours, and most days that's got to be hard to do, but they did more damage this morning than they're worth. And the goddamned Viagra sells itself.'

I mimicked the late-night advertisement: 'In the unlikely event of an erection lasting longer than four hours, find a gun and kill yourself.'

Jenny laughed out loud. 'Four hours! Jesus, you'd need a busload of women.'

My stomach eased up. Jenny's laugh helped.

At the far end of Lake Como we turned south on Main Street, walking towards the centre of town. In the distance, the Warren & Monmouth's gilded cupola refracted the golden afternoon light to all points of the compass. Jenny hummed a song, kicked at an errant pebble, then said, 'You know what I want?'

'Self-folding laundry.'

'Well, that – and a Coke. Is there anyplace in this town where you can buy me a Coke I can carry in my hand and not have to give anyone a sip, or to put it down somewhere to change a nappy, forget for two hours and then have to finish when it's all warm and flat?'

'Wow,' I said, 'your days must really suck.'

'You have no idea.'

I hugged her a bit closer. She rested her head on my shoulder, forcing us to slow down, find a synched step like high-school kids. 'Today, you're in luck, my love, because I, although not gainfully employed right now—'

'Don't remind me,' she interrupted.

'—have plenty of money to buy you a Coke, of your very own, that you don't even have to share with me, knowing, as you do, how much I love Coke.'

'And not Diet Coke. Real Coke.'

We didn't have all this New Coke, Diet Coke, Coke with Vitamins, Coke Zero, Coke Four-Thirty-Seven bullshit back then.

'Real Coke it is.'

'Unless you think I should drink Diet—?'

'Are you kidding? You're the sexiest mother of two walking the planet. Hell, there are mothers of one out there embarrassed to show their asses in public for fear of being compared with you.'

'I love you.'

'Wow,' I said, 'where did that come from?'

She stopped, turned towards me.

I froze, desperate not do anything that might bugger up this moment.

Jenny stood on tiptoes and kissed me, tentatively at first, as if figuring out if she still knew how, then deeper, as if fiercely determined to reclaim what I had thrown away.

I wasn't sure what to do at first; a voice in my head screamed *Wait! Is this all right? I don't know!* Then I gave in.

Jenny grabbed my hair and pulled my face level with hers and I ran my hands up beneath her shirt, finding the little knot where she'd tied the yellow bikini top. I tugged it loose, felt her back heave.

Jenny moaned, bit my lip and slid her hands down to my hips. Grinding hers forwards she pulled me hard against her. Still kissing me, she guided my hand under her bikini and as I caressed her breasts I felt her nipples tauten, heard her breath in my ear. 'Here,' she panted. 'Now.'

I looked around long enough to see that some gazillionaire had built a carriage house with its own narrow driveway behind his mansion. A ten-foot-high impenetrable hedge surrounded the property, jutting in just enough to create a space for cars and delivery trucks to pull up without being seen from the grounds.

Jenny read my mind. 'Back there.'

We fell onto the grass behind the hedge. I unfastened my shorts, yanked them down far enough to get one leg free, then stopped and watched as Jenny slid hers off and grasped the edge of her bikini bottom and pulled it to one side, just enough space for me to enter her.

I revelled in the silk-smooth velvet warmth of my wife; it felt like visiting a familiar place for the first time. I rocked forwards frantically as Jenny grasped my arms, pulled me down, and wrapped her legs around my back. We moved together in a perfect, maddening beat until, crying out, we collapsed beside the hedge, sweating and exhausted. I waited for God to take me. It would have been a fine time to go.

Jenny had other plans for me. She rolled me onto my back and straddled me. I ran my hand between her legs, caressing her through the yellow Lycra. She kissed me, long and deep, all the while grinding down with her hips, rocking on her own now, back and forth. It was far more than sex or self-stimulation; Jenny ground away all the anxiety and frustration, the fear and insecurity of the past ten weeks.

Still panting, she said, 'I love you, Sailor, I do.'

'I love you, Jenny.'

'Don't you fuck up my life, ever again, do you understand me?' She rocked again, harder this time. I'd have paid ten thousand dollars for a hard-on then, even a borrowed one, but I'd just come like a porn star and it wasn't happening again, not yet.

'I won't, Jenny. I swear I won't.'

I tasted salty sweat on her forehead and tears on her cheeks as we kissed, and at last Jenny slowed. 'Do you love me, Sailor? Our kids? Our life?'

'I do, Jenny, I *do*. Don't slow. Keep going.'

'Never again.' Redolent of summertime and desire, she panted into my face.

'Never.' I cupped both hands under her ass and pulled her forward onto me, not ever wanting her to get up. 'Jenny, I know you and I can—'

It began somewhere a little north of us, most likely on Main Street, out where we'd been walking. I heard it and tried to ignore it. My mind had played tricks on me before, and I was in the throes of reconciling with my wife so it wouldn't have surprised me. But when the music rose in volume and intensity, matching the threatening roar of the car engine, I knew something ugly was coming.

'Get up,' I said, scrambling for my shorts.

'What? What is it?'

'You hear that?'

Jenny listened. 'What, that music?'

This surprised me. 'You do?'

'Sure.' She tugged her shorts back on. 'That song – what is it?'

'*The Sidewalks of New York*,' I said. 'Please, Jenny, hurry up. Something's going to happen.'

'I don't underst—'

The bag was one of those cheap plastic supermarket deals that took the place of brown bags about fifteen years ago. I was still buttoning my shorts as I watched it sail over the hedge, obviously thrown from a passing car or truck. 'Get down!' I shouted, tackling Jenny, trying to cover as much of her body as I could with mine.

'What? Sailor! What the hell?'

The bag landed on the sloping fairway-perfect lawn about halfway between our intimate hiding place and the massive classical mansion atop the manicured knoll. It didn't explode or ignite but landed with a sloppy splash, a moist impact that tore open the bag and released about a gallon of runny, foul-smelling animal shit. They'd missed the house – I don't know how; it was huge – but only a few splatters reached the porch and the white wicker furniture.

'Fuckers,' I said, and hobbled towards the street, already reaching for my phone.

Jenny followed, absently knotting her bikini behind her back. 'What is it, Sailor? Who are they?'

A rusty pick-up truck, about as out of place in Spring Lake as a space shuttle, chugged unhurriedly along the street. As I watched, another bag was launched out of the passenger window to land with a foul splatter on another clean porch.

'Look at that,' I said, 'and in broad, frigging daylight, too.'

'Who are they?' Jenny pleaded. 'Do you know what's going on?'

'I think so.' I dialled the beach house as I hurried around the hedge. Between spotless Doric columns an equally scrubbed front door looked as though it had come from a tobacco plantation in North Carolina. A wide porch stretched the length of the house. 'Look up there.' I pointed for Jenny as the phone rang in my ear. 'Is that one of those things?'

'What things?'

'On the door!'

'A brass knocker? That thing?'

'No, no, on the side. What's that thing called?'

Now Jenny understood. She shook her head in disbelief and disappointment. 'It is, Sailor. It's called a mezuzah.'

Huck answered cheerfully, 'Uncle Hucker's Papal Artifacts.'

'Huck, get a pencil.'

His tone changed in a heartbeat. 'Go.'

'Late-model pick-up. Rusty, POS, Maybe '84 or '85. Chevy. Occupied two times, no description of the perps. Partial reg is: New Jersey, 568. I missed the rest of it.'

'What happened?'

'Call Spring Lake PD. There's a book next to the phone.'

'Got it.'

'Ask for Hess, Ed Hess. If he isn't on duty, go with whoever answers. The truck is headed south on Main, from Lake Como, tossing plastic bags of shit into—' I stopped and looked at Jenny.

Huck asked, 'Into what, Sailor?'

The colour had drained from Jenny's face. 'Jews,' she whispered. 'Goddamn. They're targeting Jews.'

'Jewish homes.'

'Ah, *damn* it,' Huck said. 'Okay, I'll call you right back.'

'Thanks, Huck.'

Jenny clicked on her own phone. 'Why aren't we just calling 911?'

I reached out to stop her. 'Because 911 calls are monitored and recorded and sent over the county's radio system for every jackass with a scanner to hear, including Mel-Ken and Tasteful Suit Barbie at Channel 12 News.' Her hands shook; I held them tightly. 'The last thing this place needs is more fuel on an already blazing fire.'

'Did you see them? Were they—?'

'I didn't; I don't know if they were black or white – they could have been either. But I can't imagine too many black thugs would drive around whitebread Spring Lake in the middle of the day tossing horseshit onto Jewish lawns; in my experience that level of stupidity is reserved for redneck Christians.'

And Hodges will love this one. Just my frigging luck.

Jenny wiped her eyes, hugged me and whispered, 'I want to go home.'

'Not yet, sweetie.' Her heart was racing beneath my fingertips. 'But soon. I promise.'

'Hey!' Now she backed off a step and held me at arm's length. 'How did you know something was wrong?'

'What?' I played dumb.

'That music, the song.' She stared me down.

I knew better than to lie. 'I dunno,' I said, staying as close to the truth as possible, 'just a feeling that weird song was out of place on this street.'

'You tackled me.'

'I heard their engine rev. I got scared.'

'Why?'

'Because anyone angry enough to throw shit at noon is probably willing to shoot out windows after dark.' This placated her – and why not; it was the truth, from a sane perspective.

Jenny started up the stairs. 'Come on, we'll tell them what we saw.'

'No, *no*.' I grabbed for her. 'Spring Lake PD can do that.' I kept my eyes averted from the house, knowing if I looked up I'd see him in one of the windows.

Jenny tugged her elbow free. 'Sailor – what's the matter with you? We are not going to stand by while some asshole tosses a bag of shit on their lawn and not tell them about it.'

'I – well—'

'I'll do it.' She climbed to the porch and rang the bell; I followed without looking at the house.

No answer. *Good.*

'C'mon,' I said, 'we can come back later, if you like.'

She pulled the elastic band off her wrist, yanked her hair into a ponytail. 'No, it's all right. The police can follow up.' She led the way towards the street.

I let her pass before I sneaked a glance up at the immaculate white façade. I knew better than to feel surprised, but I did. I closed my eyes to picture the upstairs window thirty seconds earlier; had it been there then, that narrow greasepaint stripe, like a rich white kid's gang-tag? It might have been; it didn't look like much. Someone could have slipped while painting the trim, just a sloppy brushstroke. But no, this place didn't have sloppy brushstrokes. Whoever lived here hired painters.

I looked again, hoping now to catch a glimpse of Gabriel Lebow staring down at me, dried blood on his sweatshirt. If he had decided to follow us, I might as well know. I checked out the second floor; five full-length double-door windows beneath the slate roof, each with its own miniature balcony and wrought-iron balustrade. The Spring Lake mansion could have passed for a Parisian hotel, albeit one haunted by a dead middle-schooler. Only one window, the second from the left, had the greasepaint smudge. I stared into it, waiting for him to appear, mouth agape like a python. A curtain billowed; the air-conditioning kicking on, or perhaps a housecat ...

'Sailor?' Jenny asked. 'You coming? You still owe me a Coke. Although after all this, I might have an Alabama Slammer.'

'Yeah, sweetie.' Bile rose in my throat and I turned from the manicured estate and its lawn stinking of animal shit. 'On my way.'

*

The house looked as though Thing 1 and Thing 2 had snorted a key of Columbian coke before running riot: every square inch of living room carpet had been targeted in an air-raid of plastic toys and stuffed animals.

Still unnerved, irritated, scared, and, I hoped, a little horny after our interrupted reconciliation, Jenny pulled up short on the linoleum entryway. 'Ah, Huck.'

He emerged from Ben's room, hands raised in surrender. 'Wait – wait, it's not as bad as it looks, and I have a multi-dimensional clean-up plan already drafted and charted in Excel. I'm on it; you two just came back about a week early.'

Jenny dared not step onto the carpet. 'The kids napping?'

Huck nodded. 'Ben just went down.'

'What happened?' I asked.

'Nothin' much. Ben was Geronimo. I was Custer.' He considered the carnage. 'Made sense at the time.'

'Sitting Bull,' Jenny sighed.

'Huh?'

'Did you get Ed Hess?' I tossed the car keys towards the ceramic Mickey Mouse on the counter.

'Staff Sergeant. Hess is on three to eleven. They sent a car, called on the cell.'

'Good. Keep it off the scanners.'

'And the AP wire,' Huck agreed.

'Thanks.'

'Whatever.' He sorted toys. 'Oh, hey, I forgot: Detective Hodges called.'

'Shit.'

'Nah, it's okay. They found your boy, Malcolm Smalls.'

'Who?' Jenny looked at me as if I'd been keeping secrets again.

'Hairy, shirtless, unwashed, chubby fellow, just finishing his Master's thesis on the Women's Christian Temperance Union.'

'Tubby!' I clapped. 'My witness, a dust addict from the looks of him.'

'Meth,' Huck said.

'Even better; that stuff cuts way down on the dental bills.'

Huck snowploughed a pile of Lego towards the toy box. 'Monmouth County detectives have a couple of Neptune Township road guys rubber-hosing him now, guys who work that street. Hodges didn't think it would take long. Smalls had an ounce of weed on him, a bullshit pinch. He claimed it was for personal use – no shit.'

I kicked an errant brick in Huck's direction. 'The promise of two weeks in the tank might motivate him.'

'Two weeks?' Jenny asked. 'For an ounce of pot? That's against the law.'

Huck stacked Styrofoam numbers as big as dinner plates. 'Yeah, I think Malcolm was absent the year they taught *habeas corpus*.'

I winked at Jenny. 'The thought of two weeks without a fix and he'll spill everything – they'll have our shooter in cuffs before the ESPN highlights.'

'Hodges can go to the Grand Jury this week – *zip bang boom* – and before you know it, Tattoo Boy is in the shower, wishing he'd brought a soap on a rope.'

'They still make that?'

'It's a top seller at Trenton State Prison.'

Jenny joined Huck on the living room floor, gathering up stuffed animals. 'They can't really hold your witness, you know – the Public Defenders' Office will have Hodges' head on a plate. *I* know that, and I'm a tax attorney.'

'They won't hold him,' Huck explained, 'they'll mention it in passing—'

'—to one another,' I finished his thought, 'not *actually* to Tubby.'

'He'll hear them, and he'll realise crystal meth is really hard to find in the county lock-up. Then he'll start singing.'

Jenny stopped and looked up. 'Those dealers might kill him.'

Huck gabbed a Barbie by the hair. 'Hmm, another American tragedy.' Twenty-five years on the job had jaded Huck Greeley to his marrow.

'Where're they cooking it?' I asked.

'Dunno.' Huck picked up the pieces of a wooden Eeyore puzzle. 'I'm sure that's on the list of questions Detective Hodges has all lined up for your Mr Smalls.'

'Did she say anything else?'

'She'll get the shooter's mugshot and priors off to the local news channels as soon as possible. I guess she's been having a hard time keeping order.'

I crossed through the carnage and took a seat on the sofa. 'You know it: black shithead kills white Jewish shithead who appears to be on his way to shoot up a middle school. It's a nightmare. Half the world thinks this kid's a hero; the rest have him pegged as a drug-dealing murderer, and everyone hates Lebow, who was *actually* on his way to a public suicide and likely didn't have the balls to kill anyone, himself included.'

'Hodges hopes your shooter's mugshot and rap sheet will speak for itself, and maybe shut up those locals busy sizing him for a hero's medal.' Jenny took the puzzle from him, completed it in twelve seconds. 'Huh. Whaddya know? That would have taken me half an hour.'

She started in on a crayon spill to rival Exxon's *Valdez*. 'What does she want Sailor to do?' To me, she said, 'Thank you for your help with this mess, by the way.'

Not moving from my seat, I looked at Huck. 'I didn't make this mess, sweetie. It sends the wrong message, you cleaning up after him.'

Huck growled, 'Fire me – oh wait, you can't: because you don't *pay* me!'

'Good point, cousin.' I joined them on the floor. 'So what does Hodges want me to do?'

'Call her,' Huck said. 'She wants you to come along for the pinch, hopefully tonight, which is good for me, too.'

'You don't need to,' I said, knowing nothing short of a nuclear attack would keep him away.

'Are you kidding?' he said. 'How often do they wrap up this neatly? Cop. Eye-witness. Easy ID. Perp in bracelets. *Wham, bam, shazam*: everyone goes home happy, and I report to Fezzamo what a nice job you've done helping out the Monmouth County Prosecutor's Office.'

Jenny looked sceptically at both of us. 'And to think, the fate of the Commonwealth of Virginia rests with you two.'

'Protect and serve!' I flipped a naked Barbie towards the toy box. She managed a double back-tuck before disappearing inside.

*

Huck and I rode together in the VASP Chevy he'd signed out for his trip to New Jersey. We both wore flak vests, and Huck had his VASP tin on a rawhide strip around his neck. Most everyone used nylon lanyards these days, but Huck remained old school – or no school, sometimes. My badge was conspicuously absent, still gathering dust on Captain Fezzamo's office shelf at Division Headquarters. Neither Huck nor I wore a gun, but I knew Huck had at least a snub-nosed .38 under his seat, much good it would do against the artillery that might be stored in the meth house. I'd brought along Uncle Paul's .357. I wasn't worried that I'd need it to defend myself against the North Side Playaz; SWAT would secure the street before Huck or I got within shouting distance. No, I was worried that Gabriel Lebow might show up. Here I was, heading into the most dangerous situation a city cop could face – a gang-fortified house on a gang-fortified street in a gang-fortified neighbourhood – and I was worried that the ghost of a dead eighth-grader might come looking for me. Lovely. *My head in the game, always with my head in the game.*

We followed Marta Hodges' unmarked Caprice. She rode with Bobby Harmon, the CSI detective from Monmouth County, and Sergeant Dave Collins, the Neptune Township cop who'd worked the Morris Middle School crime scene. Hodges and Harmon wore suits, and Harmon even had on a tie. He obviously wasn't going anywhere near the house until Asbury Park PD had it properly secured. Collins had traded his uniform for a MCPO windbreaker over a flak vest. I'd lay money that Hodges would be first through the door, vest or no.

Hodges was following three Asbury Park cruisers and a SWAT van. It might have been plenty dark at one-thirty a.m. but even in the rundown west side residents owned cell phones; Hodges and her team might as well have announced: *The Police Are Coming!* on one of those banners biplane pilots fly over the beaches all summer. A Monmouth County Prosecutor's Office van kept pace behind Huck and me. Inside, three lab techs were pulling on hazmat suits. Once the thugs were in handcuffs and the surrounding streets had been locked down, they'd don their hoods, enter the ice kitchen and hopefully just set the frigging charges.

The shops around here were either closed for the night or boarded up more permanently; FOR SALE signs hung from every third storefront. Several streetlights had either burned out or been broken by kids. In the half-light, we might have been in any low-rent section of any city in America.

James Bradley and his teetotal minions would have been both embarrassed and infuriated at the sight of their idyllic beachfront resort today. One place looked like a black-and-white snapshot of an abandoned business from the '70s. I tried to see inside the soaped windows and wondered why they'd not been broken.

Cruiser lights flickered brilliant blue in the darkness, islands of colour in an otherwise dark sea. They'd be here all night, monitoring Neptune's streets. There'd been race riots here before, but they'd not always been handled well. Having a police presence from the start sent a powerful message to those thinking they might stir things: act up, and you're leaving in bracelets, no flashy trial, just straight to lockup with the drunks, drug-dealers and wife-beaters.

We'd agreed to use the Wal-Mart parking lot on 71. Hodges sent four plainclothes men – filthy, bearded and tattooed – ahead of us; they were in a 1970s Grand Torino rustbucket that might not survive the night and on an old Honda Blackhawk with eight million miles on the clock and a seat that was more duct-tape than leather. Anyone who figured that crew for cops had to be clairvoyant.

The undercover team would take their positions on and around the property, then give SWAT the green light. An Asbury Park sergeant – I didn't catch his name – briefed Hodges; early intel suggested the target house was quiet, no late-night partying going on, in fact, there was no music playing at all, and no television or computer lights visible through the windows. The house directly across the street from our boy's place was also North Side Playaz, and probably full of thugs this evening. A neighbouring house, a perfectly normal-looking split-level ranch, was believed to be their ice kitchen; the entire place had been gutted and rigged for the cooking and packaging of crystal meth. No one lived there; it was, essentially, a factory in disguise.

The Asbury Park Street Crimes Unit had been watching the place for weeks, waiting for Richard B. Harris, a.k.a. Big G, of the Bronx, or Tejon G. Butler, a.k.a. Blade, of Newark, to arrive, preferably together. Harris and Butler were both in their thirties, North Side gang leaders, big fish. Busting a room full of thugs might feel righteous, but it would do nothing to slow the production or distribution of crystal meth in Asbury Park. Within a week the North Side Playaz would have opened another kitchen in another basement, maybe this time fortifying the surrounding buildings with actual firepower.

To take the head off the snake meant waiting for Big G and Blade to roll through town, checking on production, tightening up their account books, maybe handing out holiday bonus cheques to their faithful employees.

But Butler and Harris weren't in our crosshairs tonight; this raid had been drawn up hastily as a means to get cuffs on Roland James 'RJ' Mercer, the dealer shithead who'd shot Gabriel Lebow. And as irritated as the Street Crimes Unit might be with Hodges for buggering up weeks of surveillance, a murder pinch still trumped burning down an ice kitchen.

Huck said, 'So Hodges decided to bust the lab tonight, too?'

I rolled up my window and cranked on the air-conditioning. 'Yup. I think she's politicking some with Asbury Park. They've been sitting on this kitchen for a couple of months and they're not happy she's swooping in to pluck just one baby out of the nest.'

'And scare everybody else off.' He dug beneath his vest for a pack of smokes. 'Want one?' He lit up and went on, 'I don't understand why their chief's in such a snit about it. Shit, this is a frigging *murder* charge – this kid, RJ whatever, he's a *killer*. The good press alone from a collar like that is surely worth their cooperation.'

I added, 'They've probably got hundreds of cop hours on this lab, watching ice go out day after day, no bosses in sight, just teenage mules – Christ, with our luck, Harris and Butler will show up ten minutes after we lock the place down.'

I laughed. 'They'll drive by, waving, on their way to the beach.'

'Asbury Park needs this pinch, and the press – I mean, look at this place. It's like Beirut in the summertime.'

265

'I think it's always summertime in Beirut, Huck.'

'Yeah, I guess.' He adjusted the air vents. 'God, it's hotter than Richmond.'

'*Nothing*'s hotter than Richmond,' I corrected. 'Hell isn't hotter than Richmond.'

'This is close,' Huck said. 'Anyway, you watch: their chief will figure out a way to squeeze as much media coverage as possible out of shutting down this lab, even if Hodges doesn't get freaky lucky and find Harris and Butler jerking each other off in the upstairs bedroom.'

'Who knows? Maybe this bust will keep the two of them away for a while, drive them off someplace else.'

Huck leaned over to get a good look at me.

'What?'

'Sorry,' he said, 'just checking to be sure it was my old friend and partner, Sailor Doyle, sitting with me. For a second, I mistook you for some faggoty-assed liberal trying to inspire hope ... Harris and Butler – what do they call themselves? *Big G* and *Blade*? Douche bags! Anyway, *they* are not going anywhere: they'll stay clear for two weeks, then they'll be back with a vengeance. This place is a cash cow: you've got a hefty slice of the population already hooked on this shit, no import costs, no shipping losses, no middlemen bungholing you for thirty per cent. It would be like Starbucks pulling out after one of their seventy-nine million stores burned down – no way, one burns down, you build another across the street. Harris and Butler aren't going anywhere until Asbury Park PD either gets them indicted or, preferably, shoots the motherhumpers.'

'Lovely,' I said. 'You should be writing greeting cards.'

He blew smoke at the ceiling. 'I do: third shift over at Hallmark. *An unpleasant goddess named Isis had boobies of different sizes ...*'

The radio crackled and Hodges said, 'Sergeant Greeley?'

Huck clicked on. 'Yes, ma'am.'

'You and Detective Doyle pull up here on Whitman and wait. I'll radio when the subjects are secure.'

'Yes, ma'am.'

'The house is two blocks east on Third and one block north on Blake.'

'We'll find it.' He clicked off. Other cops might have been offended at being benched; not Huck, not now – maybe fifteen years earlier he'd have been the first one through the door, gun drawn, flak vest tight enough to restrict his breathing – but not tonight. Tonight we were in a demilitarised zone three hundred miles from home; waiting for the locals to take down the bad guys was fine.

Huck pulled over to let the lab techs in the van pass – why they were going in now, to a hot LZ, made no sense, but that was Hodges' problem. He looked along Third Avenue. 'Hmm. This is going to be more challenging than I thought.' He leaned forward and peered through the window.

I understood. 'Yeah. Would you rather get killed on the north side of the street or the south side?'

'We really are sitting ducks,' Huck agreed. 'We just gotta hope there aren't any duck hunters awake at this hour.' He stared down the street.

'Right, nothing quite says *Aim Here* like two white cops sitting in an out-of-state cruiser in the middle of the night.'

'Got it,' he said, and drove past a couple of houses to pull in behind a long brick building that might have been a warehouse eighty years ago. A narrow alley bounded by a chain-link fence ran alongside it. Huck backed into the alley, muttering to himself, 'Now, if we're lucky … all we need is—'

'What?' I looked around, then spotted it. 'The dumpster?'

'Yup, perfect.' He backed far enough into the alley for us to see across Whitman and up and down Third Avenue. Huck could use the side-view mirror to watch the alley and the fence while I kept an eye on the lots and lawns across Whitman.

'You think we're being overly cautious? I don't see much movement anywhere, and in ten seconds all Hell is going to break loose two blocks over.'

Huck sat back and lit another cigarette. 'Nope, this is fine. Who knows how long we'll be, or how many armed and pissed-off gangbangers might come running this way in the next five minutes.'

'You got cuffs?'

'Two pairs, and a couple of bundles of plastic ties in the back.'

'Should we pinch anyone running west?'

'Nope.' Huck checked the mirror. 'Taking down armed teenagers fleeing through Asbury Park at two o'clock in the morning is profiling, and profiling's wrong, kemosabe.'

'Sorry. Forgot.'

He cracked the window far enough to let the smoke clear. 'And we don't have any jurisdiction anyway. If we did, we wouldn't be sitting here like muppets.'

'Good point.'

'If we *do* see runners, though,' he said, 'we can always call them in.'

'Given the potential for inbreeding round here, I'm betting the North Side Playaz have dozens of middle school smurfs out buying cold medicine, matches and paint-thinner.'

'The Street Crimes guys will get it wrapped up,' Huck said. 'They need to work with the SROs in the schools, you know? Track 'em down on Facebook'

'Pop the trunk,' I said. 'I'll grab some ties, just in case.'

'Relax. Listen to the radio.' He reached for it.

'No, Huck— Wait ...'

'What?' He clicked it on. 'You don't want to listen to some music? I bet we can get all kinds of bitchin' stations out of Manhattan over here.'

Delbert McClinton filled the smoky cruiser with reminiscences of his *Sweet Home Chicago*. 'There we go,' Huck said. 'They'd better have this playing when I arrive in Heaven.'

I bummed another smoke and tried to relax.

'I thought you were quitting those.'

'One vice at a time, Uncle Hucker, please,' I said. 'My stomach still cramps up so bad I'm bent over and dry-heaving twice a week.'

'That's the pills.' It wasn't a question.

'Yeah, it's been tough. I'm taking the over-the-counter shit like candy – it doesn't do anything, but I'm tricking myself, you know?' My face flushed with embarrassment; I was glad we were sitting in the dark for my confession. 'Booze cravings are different; those make me sweat – it's weird though, it's just my face, forehead and neck. Like flop sweats. How fucked-up is that?'

In an uncharacteristically paternal gesture he reached over and pulled my head to him, a kind of half-hug. 'I'm proud of you, Sailor. I am.' He sniffed. 'I couldn't do it – screw that; if you told me I had to quit booze, even beer – I mean, it's all a joke, how much we drink, but when you stop and think about it, I've probably had a drink or two every day for the past twenty-eight years. Granted, I don't get blown out of the water too often – I'm maybe tipsy once or twice a week and full-on loaded a couple of times a month, but I have one or two with dinner every night. It's habit, as natural as reaching for these poisoned bullets.' He held up his cigarette. 'You're still in your early thirties – it's good, what you're doing. Quit the booze, then quit the nails.' He considered the tendrils of smoke coiling out the car window. 'Fuck it. I'll quit with you.'

'Bullshit.'

He tossed the half-finished cigarette into the alley. 'I can do it; watch me.' We sat in silence as McClinton's band roared from Texas to St Louis and back. After two minutes, Huck said, 'You got any smokes, Sailor? Jesus, I'm dying for a cigarette!'

I laughed and slugged him in the chest. 'You're not making this any easier, asshole.'

'It's not supposed to be easy, Grasshopper.' His "Asian" accent should have been against the law. 'But if you take a long look at old Uncle Hucker, divorced, alone, and alienated from his children, you'll learn something. You, my friend, are already three-quarters of the way down a road most of us are too frigging scared to take and you can't turn back now. Think about Ben and the baby. You'll be a better father for being a better and more sober husband to Jenny. Shit, you've got it made.'

'It doesn't feel like it,' I grumbled.

'It will.' He fussed with the radio. 'I remember when my father quit smoking – Jesus, but he was unbearable for six months. You've never seen anyone eat more candy, chew more gum, or gnaw their fingernails to bloodier stumps. I never paid much attention in psych class, but Freud had that oral fixation shit down cold.'

'What happened?'

'He just stopped.' Huck threw his hands in the air. 'After thirty years, he just quit. He was in agony for six months – after thirty years of Pall Malls, Jesus Jumping Christ, who wouldn't be? And you know what's nuts is that even twenty years later, when he was almost seventy, he still craved them from time to time.'

'Nice,' I said. 'I'm really looking forward to that – because I can promise you, if I'm still having OxyContin cravings in forty years, I *will* shoot myself.'

'Not to worry,' Huck said, 'quitting prescription meds is a hell of a lot easier than quitting the nails. Tobacco's diabolical, mixing chemicals and leaves so they get their hooks so deep you can't ever get away. OxyContin isn't made with that degree of ruthlessness in mind. You stay off another year and you'll be all right.'

'A year? Kill me now!'

'Easy peasy.' He leaned back again. 'Now, really – gimme a smoke.'

I tossed him the pack and we listened as Asbury Park's SWAT lieutenant and Street Crimes sergeant gave orders as calmly as if reading a diner menu. We knew everyone involved was charged up, with healthy, empowering stress coursing through their veins, but this team reeked of professionalism, even from half a mile away.

Snipers in place?

Schmidt go, LT.

DeJesus go, LT.

Alpha team?

Alpha go, LT.

Beta team?

Beta go, LT.

APSC?

Asbury is go, LT.

Huck turned down the car radio, silencing Albert Collins mid-riff; twenty seconds of strained silence passed. When the SWAT lieutenant finally broke in I jumped, and tried to hide it.

All units: go!

That was all it took. Huck rolled the window down and craned his head out to listen for gunshots, popping tear-gas canisters, screams. I nervously lit another cigarette, but it tasted funny, so I tossed it. 'Hear anything?' I asked.

'Nope,' Huck said, 'and that's a good sign. We'll just hang out right here, maybe even take a nap.' He cranked up the volume dial on the radio, just a smidge.

I heard three notes and hurriedly pressed the power button.

'Hey!' Huck sat up. 'That was Pink Floyd.'

'I know. I hate that song.'

'Philistine.'

Red and blue cruiser lights lit the streets and bounced off the houses and ruins along Blake Street. Porch lights blinked on over several houses and a faint glow brightened the morning watch in Asbury Park. Other than a delivery truck passing behind us, headed south towards Neptune, we heard nothing.

Another thirty or so seconds passed before the radio crackled again. Now there was a sense of hyped-up urgency and adrenalin flowing in the SWAT team's communications and I badly wanted to be there, getting my licks in, tackling some shithead, wrestling him into cuffs.

'Wanna go over?' I asked, trying to hide my own eagerness.

Huck checked the mirrors. 'Nope, not one bit. You survive the next hour and maybe I'll take you back to Fortnum & Mason for another late-night breakfast.'

'C'mon, Dad, can we? Huh, Dad? C'mon!'

The radio cut me off: *Alpha team, report.*

1715 is secure, LT. Occupied six times.

Beta team, report.

1717 is secure, LT. Occupied two times. And the pantry is full. Again, the pantry is full. Looks like a recycling plant in here.

'Nice,' I said. 'Sounds like they've got a batch ready to ship.'

APSC, report.

1716 is secure, LT. Occupied four times.

Ten-four. Good show all.

APSC to APLT.

APSC, go.

LT, we're requesting two female officers to assist with a search at 1716. Two female occupants. Disagreeable.

'Slumber party,' Huck teased, 'and I wasn't invited.'

APLT, two female officers en route. Ten-four.

'Think anyone's listening?'

'Yup. Press should be here in five minutes.' Huck checked the mirror again, then closed his eyes. 'Sounds like these local boys did a nice job; didn't need the state troops at all.'

'We'll see,' I said. 'If the North Side Playaz have been shipping crystal meth over state or county lines, which they probably have, this place will be crawling by tomorrow. The County Prosecutor will have to call the Attorney General.'

'I'm a little surprised Hodges didn't bring any state cops along tonight.'

'You don't know her,' I said. 'She likes to do things her way.'

On cue, Hodges' voice came over the radio. 'Sergeant Greeley, Detective Doyle?'

Huck answered, 'Yes, ma'am.'

'Please join me up here. I'd like Detective Doyle to assist with an ID.'

'On our way.' Huck fired up the Chevy and drove towards the blue and red carnival lights, but we'd managed no more than a quarter of the block up Blake before an Asbury Park police cruiser blocked our way.

'Looks like we're walking from here,' Huck said, and I piled out and joined him on the sidewalk. Ahead, I could see silhouetted figures clutching AR-15s or walking stooped over with their hands low behind their backs. High beams and searchlights turned everyone red, blue or blinding white. As we approached, several armed shadows brought order to the chaos, forcing handcuffed suspects to their knees along the sidewalk. Five, then seven, then eleven figures knelt down, shoulder-to-shoulder, some shouting fire-and-brimstone insults while others hung their heads, too tired, too stoned or too frightened to speak up. One female screamed and kicked wildly as she was wrestled into the back of a patrol car. Another came quietly and knelt beside the lengthening row of suspects.

Outside the perimeter an elderly woman in a nightgown held a flashlight and watched the proceedings like an inquisitive voyeur. She had a miniature dog on a leash; it lay near the old woman's bare feet, panting in the heat.

'You all right, ma'am?' Huck asked as we passed.

'Sure, I'm fine; it's them kids, though: they in a world of trouble. I knew it'd happen. I knew all along.' She gripped the flashlight like a club.

'You can head back inside your house, if you like, ma'am,' I said. 'We'll get this wrapped up shortly and be out of your way.'

'I ain't goin' in,' she said. 'I been scairt of them kids too long. I be glad to see 'em all go to prison.'

'Yes, ma'am.' Huck's mantra seemed to be getting him through the evening without a wrinkle.

The elderly woman lived three doors down from the meth kitchen. The two homes in between had been abandoned some time ago – in December, I guessed, because someone had left a fully decorated Christmas tree in the front window of 1720 Blake Street, its dusty tinsel, fake cranberries and brightly coloured baubles still on display despite the eighty-degree heat. A few bricks were missing from the chimney, and half a dozen roof shingles had been torn off like flakes of dead skin. Out front, the mailbox read HES ON 1720.

'He's on what?' I asked absently.

'Huh?' Huck asked.

'Nothing,' I said, 'just reading.'

'Well, I'll tell you what *he's on*: *he's on* the sidewalk, on his knees, regretting the day he decided to drop out of high school and pursue a career as a drug peddler. That's what *he's on*.'

'And he's probably also *on* some lovely local weed.' I stopped and sniffed, grimacing. 'Although this place smells more like an outhouse.'

We crossed over to 1715 Blake Street, close enough to see the suspects were all teenagers, in various stages of undress – Hodges had obviously caught them napping. None looked old enough to be Richard Harris or Tejon Butler.

As I watched an Asbury Park cop shone a light into one guy's eyes, asking questions while monitoring his pupils.

'Stoned,' I asked Huck.

'Probably that weed you mentioned,' he said. 'What the hell, it's a weeknight. You see Hodges?'

'Not yet.' I shielded my eyes from the SWAT van's glare. Dave

Collins, the Neptune Township sergeant, whistled and waved us behind a tattered hedge – nothing like the regal shrubbery Jenny and I had used for cover that afternoon. Once he was certain we had seen he disappeared into the darkness between 1715 and 1717 Blake.

I led the way, stepping over a graveyard of broken plastic toys, sea creatures mostly, and a massive turtle-shaped sandbox the local cats had evidently been using as a latrine. My eyes took a minute to adjust to the darkness, then Marta Hodges' athletic form materialised out of the gloom. Kneeling before her, his hands cuffed, was an angry young man prattling almost incoherently about Hodges and the Asbury Park police. It took me a second to realise that his ankles had been secured as well. Ignoring him, Hodges said, 'Detective Doyle, I believe you've already met RJ.'

As she clicked on a bright flashlight and shone it into the thug's tattooed face he closed his eyes tight and cursed, 'Yo! Get that fuckin' thing outta my face, bitch.'

My arms and legs went rubbery and my mind flashed back to the basketball court at Robert Morris Middle School and a sight I would visit in nightmares for the rest of my life: Roland James Mercer, his face a ghoulish tattooed canvas, saving my life, killing Gabriel Lebow.

'Not today, mothafucka.' Pop! Pop!

'It's him,' I said, forcing Lebow's death mask from my memory.

'No doubt?' Hodges asked.

'It's him.'

'Whaddya know anyway, whitey? Fuck all yas, ya don' mean nuthin' to me. Nuthin'.'

Hodges said, 'Shut up, RJ, and listen: you are under arrest for the murder of Gabriel Lebow.' She read him his Miranda rights.

RJ talked right over her. 'I neva hearda no Lebow, bitch – why ya lettin' this white boy tell ya I done someting I ain't? Ya know a nigga ain't been shootin' no whitey Lebow.' He writhed, struggling against his restraints, and I was certain if he'd broken free he'd have killed all of us with his bare hands.

Hodges scribbled notes in her ubiquitous spiral pad. 'I never said Lebow was white, RJ.'

He sucked his teeth. 'Now ya playin', bitch. Ya know ain't no niggas wid a name like that. Ya got nuthin'.'

'Where's the car? The Ford?'

'I don' got no car, nigga.' RJ rolled his head from side to side, trying to stare Hodges down but irritated by the flashlight.

'And the .32, where's the gun?'

'I ain't got no gun.'

'No gun? No .32-calibre pop-gun? Because if I find it, I'm going to tell every newspaper in New Jersey – hell, every newspaper on the Eastern Seaboard, that you carry a toy pistol, while the real badasses, the Bloods and Crips, they carry big boy guns, semi-automatic nines. How about that, RJ?'

'Fuck all ya.' He blinked against the makeshift interrogation light. 'I ain't sweatin' none of ya.'

'The Ford.'

'Don' got no car.'

'The .32?'

'No gun.'

'Your driver? Your bed buddy, what's his name? Oh yeah: PP. Is that because he's from Point Pleasant, or does he just have a big cock? Does it taste good, RJ?'

I looked at Huck, who pursed his lips and rocked his head back and forth slightly, suggesting: *Unorthodox, but effective given the circumstances.*

'I'll show ya cock, bitch, in that black ass a yours, teach ya some manners.'

'Manners? You? Really? Where's PP?'

'Don' know him.'

'You not hearing me, RJ? Because from where I'm standing, I see a thug piece of shit who shot a boy, someone's baby, on a school campus, in broad daylight, with a Virginia State Police Officer as a material witness.'

Damn, did you have to say that?

Hodges circled behind him. 'Now, you are either the dumbest thug ever to walk the face of God's green Earth, or you are dearly in love with whoever was in that car with you. PP. I figure he must have a horse dick on him for you to protect him like this. Huh, is that why, RJ? Roll him over, son, because if you fuck with me, there is nothing that's going to keep me from slathering you with mayonnaise and feeding yo' *black ass* to the judge, and believe me, RJ, I will pull every string in my power to get one with kids – no, even better: *grandkids!* – grandbabies at the Robert Morris Middle School, you hear me? You are going to fry, RJ, so it's time to turn off the attitude and start paying attention. Who was driving the car?'

'Fuck off, bitch.'

'Wrong answer, RJ.' Hodges shook her head. 'Look around: half your buddies will walk before lunchtime tomorrow; you know it as well as I do. So come on, where's the Ford? Where's the Fairmont?'

'Ya power-trippin' nigga bitch.'

Huck and I were a bit taken when Hodges sort of snapped. 'Do you have *any* idea how hard I've had to work, how much *shit* I've had to shovel as a black woman living in a community where the only role models kids have are dope-pushin' dumb fucks like you?' she screamed. 'I am gonna wear myself out ruining your life!'

RJ scowled at her in disgust. 'That make-up?'

'Don't you—'

'That black make-up on ya, bitch?' RJ smiled. His dentist had to have passed away fifteen years ago. 'Becuz, deep down, ya white, ya know it.'

'You wanna make this about skin colour?' She was truly pissed off. 'You're an embarrassment to your race, RJ; I wish *you* were white. Where's the car?'

'Fuck off.'

'Who was driving?'

'We wuzn't there. I told ya.'

'Bullshit. Security cameras in the dry-cleaner across Steiner picked up the car. Where's the .32 you used on the kid?'

'I wuz't there. None of us wuz.' He looked up at her again and spat.

'Did you get some sleep tonight, Roland James Mercer? Because you and I are going to go around and around and around this tree for the next few days.'

Hearing his real name threw RJ, just a moment's hesitation, but it punctured the tough-guy grimace that had served him so well for most of his misbegotten life. In that moment, he knew he was cornholed. 'I wanna lawyer.'

'You'll get one – when I say so.'

'Ya can' keep me from gettin' a lawyer.'

'I won't.' Hodges shot him a *What, me?* look. I wanted to kiss her full on the lips.

'Ya ain't black, bitch – I dunno what ya are.'

She leaned close to him. Huck reached for her, afraid that RJ might try to bite her nose off. I turned my head far enough to hear as she whispered, 'Neither are you, *mothafucka*.' She checked quickly over her shoulder, made certain Huck, Collins and I blocked the view from the street, and hit RJ hard across his tattooed face with the handle of her flashlight. He fell with a grunt, then started cursing and shouting again.

Huck stepped between them. He knew better than to touch her; *furious* emanated from her in fiery hot waves and if Huck'd put a hand on her, she'd have decked him, too. 'Detective Hodges,' he asked, 'can I check something with you?' He ushered her politely towards the turtle sandbox. 'We'll be just over here.'

She understood. 'Sure, Sergeant Greeley, that'll be fine. Sergeant Collins, would you come with us, please?'

They left me alone with RJ. Blood trickled from his temple, blurring already out-of-focus tattoos.

'Why ya care?' he finally growled. 'Huh, white boy? Why ya care I shot that kid? He wuz gonna shoot up that place – ya know it, so why ya give a fuck?'

'Shut up, *Roland*,' I said.

'I saved yo white ass, ya know it.'

I wheeled on him. 'You did, *Roland*. And I do appreciate it, because it means I will live long enough to see you go to prison for the rest of your life. So anytime you like, you can turn off the big gangsta act. I'm a Virginia State Police Officer, and I am quite happy for you to rot in a Trenton prison cell for the next eighty years. Hell, I'll send you a goddamned Christmas card each year to keep track.'

'I wuz the hero, mothafucka; I seen it on the news. You wuz the scared one.'

'Yup.' I nodded dramatically enough for him to see me through the darkness. 'And anything you say can be used against you. But don't shut up on my account. You just keep right on incriminating yourself, you frigging idiot. You think I won't be at the trial? You think I won't be deposed, that I won't remember every syllable of this conversation?'

That stung him; I don't know why. With that much prison ink on his face, I figured he had to have been arrested half a dozen times before, even served time. Roland James Mercer didn't make sense to me.

'Why ya ain't wearin' no badge, Larry Bird?' he taunted, using an elbow to push himself to his knees.

I walked a few paces off, tuned him out and tried to let it all go, but Gabriel Lebow wouldn't clear out of my head. He stared back at me, his hooded face slathered in greasepaint, wanting to die and afraid to do it himself. The very last thing on Earth he expected that morning was to get tackled from behind by a suspended recovering addict with a damaged shoulder and a marriage on the skids. What a way to go. *Lord, take him, please*.

Hodges returned, flanked by Dave Collins and Billy Harmon. 'This one goes to the county lock-up. Asbury PD can have the others. Sergeant Collins, please let them know that if they come across anyone answering to PP, any PP tattoos, references to PP in conversations they overhear or record, I want them to call my cell. And if they find a .32 semi-auto anywhere in this godforsaken street, I want it bagged up and delivered to the Prosecutor's Office. Got it?'

'Yes, ma'am,' he said respectfully, and trotted off.

Harmon and Huck took RJ beneath his arms and half-carried, half-dragged him to Hodges' Caprice. When they passed me, he said, 'You wuz the scared one, white boy.'

'Yup. Have a good night, Roland.' I lit a cigarette.

With RJ locked in the back of her car, Hodges said, 'You two can go. Thanks.' She shook hands with each of us.

'You need any help?' Huck offered, knowing she'd turn him down.

'Just for you to let your Captain Fezzamo know that Detective Doyle has been essential in our apprehending a murderer and drug dealer.'

Huck smirked. 'I'll do that.'

'Doyle.' She turned to me. 'I'll call you tomorrow or Friday with an update.'

'You know where to find me.'

'The County Prosecutor's got a team of lawyers assigned to this one. We'll get you interviewed, maybe some afternoon when the kids are napping.' She smiled, and I wanted to kiss her. Her teeth, red, blue and white in the rolling lights, were clean and straight, nothing like RJ's mouthful of cracked, yellowing fangs.

'Good night, Detective Hodges.'

'Good night, *Sailor*.'

Huck and I walked back to his car. He wished the elderly woman a good evening then opened my door for me. 'Well, my friend, that was easy.'

'Yeah, nothing to it. RJ seems like a nice kid, just misunderstood, you know?'

Huck choked. 'Oh, yeah.' He coughed. 'A model citizen. Three hundred million sperm, and that cloven-hoofed retard was the fastest.'

'You still want a late breakfast?' I asked. 'On me.'

'On you? Certainly. I'll drive.' He managed a three-point turn, his lights momentarily bringing holiday colour to the forgotten Christmas tree in the window at 1720 Blake Street.

THURSDAY

Sh'ma Yis'ra'eil Adonai Eloheinu Adonai Ehad

Belmar to Bradley Beach: 2.4 Miles

Red: *Just harpoon me and finish me off, why don't you!*

We made it home by three-thirty. Huck figured he'd sleep a few hours, coffee up and then head for Richmond, missing the morning rush on the Turnpike and the afternoon rush through DC.

Jenny'd waited for us. She sat curled up on my mom's old sofa, reading a law journal several grades above my Louis L'Amour novels, wearing the powder-blue pinstripe shirt she'd bought for me when I got called up to Homicide. Huck didn't know, but Jenny in one of my shirts was code around our house: sex had been pencilled onto the agenda. We could finish what we'd started behind the hedge in Spring Lake; that was fine by me.

I couldn't quite see if Jenny was wearing shorts beneath the shirt-tails; I imagined her there in only panties and felt plenty compelled to hustle Huck off to the guest room downstairs.

'You guys all right?' She left the law magazine on the sofa and fiddled with her hair, embarrassed that Huck was seeing her this dishevelled.

'Yeah, we're fine,' I said. 'You didn't need to wait up.'

She yawned. 'I didn't really. I've been in and out for the past few hours.'

In and out. I get it. Tease.

Huck and I told her about RJ's arrest, his essential confession, and Hodges' plans to report good news back to Fezzamo. Relief rose like a flush in Jenny's cheeks as her life – *our life* – came slowly back into focus.

She'd left one too many buttons open on my shirt. I peeked at it, trying to warn her; Jenny didn't care. We were married again as of that moment and naked wrestling would commence in five minutes. We had months of awkwardness, distrust, dishonesty, and just plain shitfacedness to make up for.

I said, 'Go ahead in to bed. I'll get Huck settled downstairs then check on the kids.'

Huck gave her a hug. 'Good night, sweetheart.'

She kissed his cheek. 'Thanks for coming, Huck. Please say hi to Sandy for me.'

'I'll tell you what.' Huck scratched his chin. 'How about if *you* tell her *I* said hi. I'm pretty sure she'd prefer that option.'

'Go to bed, hippy.'

With Huck settled in the guest room, I looked in on Anna and Ben, a token gesture on my part and starkly unfatherly: I'd had a granite-hard boner from the moment Jenny disappeared into the bedroom.

Anna slept on her back in baby paradise, her arms and legs spread-eagled, while Eeyore stood guard. I leaned over her bassinette, my cheek nearly touching her nose as I waited to feel one of her infinitesimally small breaths. 'Good night, baby. Daddy loves you.'

In Ben's room, he'd won another skirmish with two sheets, a blanket, two pillows and a farmyard full of stuffed animals; The evidence lay strewn across the floor as he slept soundly, curled up on an empty bed.

'Jeez, buddy,' I whispered. 'What're you dreaming?' I tucked a pillow under his head, draped a blanket over him and kissed his temple. 'Good night, monk—'

Stark, unbridled terror lanced through my chest while a gurgling sound rose from my throat; I heard it, as if from across the room. Ben's window, the one that looked onto the old pear tree and the remains of three dozen lobsters, sported a horizontal stripe of white greasepaint.

Could a bad guy get in, Daddy?

'No!' I crossed to the window, cupped my hand to see outside. 'I only heard three or four notes, not the whole song – I turned the radio *off*.' Anger welled up in me. 'I'll kill you again, motherfucker. I'll kill you myself.'

I kicked off my Nikes and gathered up another blanket and pillow from the floor. Nudging Ben, I climbed into bed beside him; he groaned and rolled against the wall, making room for me. I hid the .357 behind my shoes, but within reach if I needed it. Closing my eyes, I pretended to sleep.

Jenny peeked in five minutes later and whispered, 'Ah shit, Sailor.'

I didn't move. She kissed my forehead, shut off the hallway light and padded back to bed.

Dawn had whitened Ben's window when I finally drifted off.

I slept until nearly midday. Cramped and stiff, I rolled onto my back, propped my head on a stuffed elephant and took stock of my aches and pains. I'd forgone my sling the previous night and I regretted it now. The combination of activity and sleeping curled up next to a sugar-charged Tasmanian devil had left me sore, my shoulder throbbing. Pain also thundered through my lower back in perfect sync with my heartbeat. I needed a day off, and maybe a round or two with Amanda the Amazon's rubber bands.

Red: Just harpoon me and finish me off, why don't you!

I was a little proud of myself, though: I'd managed to exercise every day, lose a few pounds, and connect with my wife. I wanted to keep going; success was proving to be an outstanding motivator. With RJ safely behind bars, I could now focus solely on Jenny and the kids; I hoped the mayhem of the past few days would finally fade away. And yet imagining Gabriel Lebow at every turn, finding stripes of white greasepaint tagged on windows, left my stomach in disconcerting knots. I'd cracked up once this summer; spiralling out again would cost too much. I'd been frightened I'd lost Jenny and our marriage, nervous about gang-bangers killing us in a drive-by, worried that the local media would find me, scared for my job, our future, hell, just about everything ... Finding Jenny again and putting Lebow's killer away should have cleared up most of my problems.

But there it was: Ben's bedroom window with a greasepaint stripe across the pane. Part of me hoped that I'd wake to find it gone, just another figment of my over-active imagination, but with *Phantom of the Opera* make-up smeared over the glass, now, in daylight, the tumultuous questions of the past week gelled into something unexpectedly real.

I checked the floor; Uncle Paul's cannon was still there, tucked behind my shoes.

Jenny and the kids had gone out; I didn't know where to. The sun shone, so I guessed they might have walked down to the beach or over to Avon. The house was quiet. I braced for pain, clenched my teeth and rolled out of Ben's bed. Surprisingly, my legs kept me upright and though my back growled for a moment, it wasn't unbearable. I dug in my pockets for a couple of Naproxen and swallowed them dry. All the while I stared at the window stripe, Lebow's white-boy gang-tag.

I craved a cigarette, a beer, a $239-dollar Scotch and an OxyContin, the suspended cop's self-medication regimen of choice. But none of those antidotes materialised, sadly. I unlatched the window, reached outside and dragged a fingertip through the smear. It had the consistency of congealing mayonnaise. I sniffed the pasty substance, and it took only a whiff to be certain that this was the same shit Lebow had painted over his face as he hid behind the elm tree on Cameron Drive. Whatever it was, it had already been indelibly etched in my memory. Nothing I'd smelled so far in my lifetime quite matched the aroma of a suicidal teen in stage make-up.

'Shit.' I exhaled slowly, hoping to keep things in reasonable perspective. 'What now?'

Wiping my hands on my leg, I knew I couldn't send Jenny and the kids home to Virginia, even though that decision made the most sense. I both wanted and needed them with me as Jenny and I re-forged what hopefully would be the life-long bond I'd carved up last winter. We'd be stronger now where we'd broken, like calcified bone. I took heart, though, knowing that they'd be away this weekend, just for a couple of days. We had made plans to visit Jenny's parents, and if she took the kids and went alone, I'd feel better about going out hunting for Gabriel after dark. I'd have to lie again, insist that I had to stay here for Hodges, maybe. Hopefully, she'd buy it.

I didn't have the strength to tell Jenny that I'd been seeing and hearing and imagining things again – actually, with fifteen inches of greasepaint slathered on the window, perhaps I *wasn't* imagining things. My options dwindled, draining through the floorboards of Ben's bedroom as I stood there watching the breeze rock the branches on Dad's old pear tree.

I had to find Gabriel.

I dug my BlackBerry out of my pocket and dialled Huck.

'Good morning, Mary Sunshine!' Even through the cell phone, I could hear that his windows were open, his radio cranked up.

'Hey, Uncle Hucker,' I said, then cleared my throat.

'You all right? You were racked with Ben when I left.'

'Yeah, I'm good,' I said. 'How far are you?'

'Exit 3 on the Turnpike, not too far. I rolled out of there about ten o'clock, ought to get south of DC in plenty of time.'

I wasn't sure why I'd called him; I just needed to feel connected to Earth, I guess. 'Thanks again for coming up.'

'No worries, kemosabe,' he shouted above the radio. 'You'd have done the same for me.'

'Maybe.'

'Yawn.'

'Hey, if you think about it—'

He cut me off. 'I know: check out Mark "Moses" Stillman in NCIC and LInX.' In my mind's eye it was easy to see him shaking his head, thinking I was incapable of just relaxing on the beach with my family. 'I'll get to it tomorrow morning, give me a reason to run down to Division. I'll call you if I find out he's wanted for hacking up nuns with a machete.'

'Yeah,' I snorted. 'Make a note of that, please.'

'You all right?'

'You asked me that already.'

'Well ...'

'I'm good, Huck. Thanks. I'll see you at home in a couple of weeks.'

'I'll track you down if I hear anything back from Fezzamo, but your antics up there will go a long way with Internal Affairs. Nothing like

284

saving a school full of kids to pad your résumé.' Huck whipped the snot out of any therapist I'd ever known.

I said, 'We both know I didn't save anyone – *again*. Lebow couldn't have killed a sinus infection.'

'Yeah, but you *didn't* know that when you tackled him,' Huck said. 'That counts, Sailor. Points for stupid hero tactics.'

'Drive carefully. And put the damned beer down when you're talking on the phone. Jesus, you're going to hurt someone.'

'It's before noon,' Huck corrected. 'I'm drinking orange juice with my vodka.'

'See you.'

'Peace on Earth, buddy.'

I clicked off, checked the screen: two messages.

Coffee first; had to keep my heart beating. Jenny'd left the pot on and the kitchen smelled good, like a Maxwell House commercial. Sadly, it tasted like ashes. I scooped two extra sugars into the mug and drank it anyway, then clicked on Channel 12, hoping to catch the midday updates. With the volume up loud enough to hear in the kitchen, I went foraging for food. Evidence of an egg-toast-bacon-and-Fruit-Loops breakfast lay piled on the counter like war carnage.

I bet Huck had the Fruit Loops.

As I toasted bread, I ran hot water into the sink and slowly washed and dried the dishes. Behind me, news reports filled the empty house:

'—*losing hope of finding Jeremy Landon, the teenage surfer missing since Monday afternoon … in a prepared statement the Landon family asked all of Monmouth County to pray for their son. Anyone with information on Jeremy's whereabouts should contact the Neptune Township Police Department at—*'

I scraped bacon gristle off the frying pan and rinsed it under the faucet. The cast iron held the water's heat. It'd be warm three days from now, tucked into the metal drawer beneath the oven.

'—*a joint effort, members of the Asbury Park Street Crimes Unit and the Monmouth County SWAT team raided several homes in northwest Asbury Park late last night—*'

I craned my neck to see the television. Surprisingly good footage from the lawn at 1717 Blake Street had four Asbury Park officers ushering handcuffed gang bangers into the back of a cruiser, its blue and red lights still rolling, half an hour after the raid.

'—*also taken into custody was this man, Roland Mercer, a noted North Side gang member, suspected drug dealer, and key suspect in Monday's shooting at Robert Morris Middle School in Neptune. Mercer is said to have been identified by an eye-witness to the shooting, now believed to be an off-duty police officer. Sources inside the Monmouth County Prosecutor's Office have withheld the Samaritan's name in the interests of protecting him and his family from possible gang retaliation. Roland Mercer is due to be arraigned Monday on charges of second degree murder—*'

I washed out Jenny's coffee mug, a ceramic atrocity Ben made on a preschool field trip to a local pottery studio. Jenny loved it; so I treated it like a Smithsonian treasure, drying it by hand and stashing it safely behind the plates.

'—*despite his criminal history, some citizens of Monmouth County and the state of New Jersey feel that Roland Mercer acted as a hero and should not face charges for shooting Gabriel Lebow. Monmouth County officials plan to have increased police presence at the courthouse before Monday's hearing, in anticipation of demonstrators from both sides of this troublesome issue. Civil unrest continues to be a problem in Neptune, Neptune Township and Asbury Park: pockets of protestors battled with police throughout the night. There were seventeen arrests on various charges. However, a tense peace seems to have fallen over the city this morning. Neptune Township Police Chief James McCormick spoke with Channel 12's own Charlie Webber—*'

Two mugs of burned coffee, two pieces of toast with jelly, a sink full of dirty plates, and two sore hands later, I'd found my rhythm, a steady pace I'd use to get through the day. An explanation existed somewhere for my unexpected visits from Gabriel Lebow. I simply had to find it, or find him.

'—*finally, a disturbing story out of Spring Lake, where Jewish home-owners have been the victims of anti-Semites. Spring Lake Police have stepped up their patrols in response to the drive-by attackers, who have been throwing bags of animal faeces onto properties in what appears to be anger at the Jewish community for Robert Morris Middle School student Gabriel Lebow's apparent plans to engage in a Columbine-like massacre earlier this*

286

week. No injuries have been reported, but Ira Comite, spokesperson for the Anti-Defamation League, was in Spring Lake this morning, speaking out against these ugly—'

I brushed my teeth, changed into my bathing trunks, collected a towel and headed for the beach, Uncle Paul's .357 tucked in my backpack.

Outside, I checked the messages on my phone. The first was from Ben: *'Hi, Daddy. Mommy says to tell you that we're at Bradley Beach. She says to stay home and rest. We'll be back after lunch. Bye, Daddy. I love you. Bye.'*

A few seconds of background noise, then: *'Daddy, this is me – Ben – it was funny to wake up and find you in my bed.'* Ben laughed. *'Mommy said you got lost on your way to bed last night. That's funny. Okay, bye, Daddy.'*

My second message was from Detective Hodges, who sounded tired, but confident: *'Doyle, it's Hodges. I spoke with the county prosecutor this morning, got him out of bed – heh. He's going to push to hold RJ without bail. I figure with a gun and a carload of meth, I can put him on that street corner with intent. He didn't run onto that basketball court to save a white cop from a white kid with a shotgun – although that's what the public defender will argue when they paint him as a local hero. They're probably fitting him for an Abercrombie & Fitch suit right about now. I let Media & Public Relations have everything on him. They'll get his ugly tattooed mug and colourful rap sheet on every cable and news channel from here to Seattle. That'll quiet things down in Neptune. I've got nothing back yet from lead counsel on the Lebow shooting, so I don't know when they'll come looking for you. You're logged in the murder book from Monday morning, so you'll be on the list before too long. When I hear back, I'll call. Um, I guess that's the update so far. Thanks again for your help pinning this on RJ. He's a first-class piece of shit. We could do worse than send him away for sixty years. All right, call if you have questions, I'm off to find a rusty old Ford Fairmont with a used .32 in the glove box – mind you, it's probably under fifty feet of water by now. See you.'*

As I passed Twelfth and C, I avoided looking up at the place where Gabriel had left his tag Tuesday morning. The Naproxen seeped through my lower back and I tried hard to lose myself in the steady rhythm of my steps.

Bradley Beach. Two miles. Perfect.

At Ocean Avenue and Twelfth, I let the onshore breeze blow through me, cooling the sweat on my face and reminding me that no matter how often I returned to these neighbourhoods, some things would never change.

I turned north, but not before glancing south to Spring Lake. The cupola atop the Warren & Monmouth Hotel radiated the midday sun like light from a fallen star. Growing up here, I had never realised how curious it was to have a snooty millionaires' playground less than five miles outside a veritable demilitarised zone. Standing on the board-walk in Belmar, I could see – hell, in an hour, I could *walk* – from the affluent glory of Spring Lake's estates to the deadly streets and abandoned houses on Asbury Park's west side. At the Shark River drawbridge I took a break and watched the fishing boats winding their way through the narrow channel. I dialled Doc Lefkowitz at his office in Chesterfield County.

His receptionist put me on hold, promising to pull Doc away from whatever boil he was lancing for twenty-four hundred dollars an hour.

'Detective Doyle!' he shouted. 'What a surprise. How's your leg?'

'I'm all right, Doc. Thanks. I've been putting quite a few miles on it, trying to get my strength back before Jenny and I go home.'

'And your shoulder?'

I winced. 'I had a bit of an accident in the ocean,' I said. 'Jenny hauled me out of the surf quickly enough, but I think she might have untied some of the knots holding me together. I've kept it in the sling, hoping it sorts itself out—'

'Sailor, get yourself to a doctor,' Doc interrupted. 'Shoulders don't fix themselves. You'll be sixty years old and unable to open a mayon-naise jar.'

'Well, mayonnaise is bad for me, right?'

'Doctor,' he ordered, 'and don't dilly-dally on this one, son. That wing was in decent shape when you left MCV.'

'All right, I'll find someone up here and have it checked out,' I lied.

'Ah, goyim! All goyim are the same. *Meshugoyim!*'

288

'Doc—'

'So did you call me for a reason, or just to say hello to an old man trying to get through another workday?'

'Just to chat, I guess.'

'Sailor—?'

'I don't know,' I admitted, and started walking again. 'I've managed to get myself involved in a bit of a mess up here: black and white and Jewish and rich and poor and I don't know.'

'You need help? You want me to call Captain Fezzamo? I think he owes me a dozen favours.'

Nah,' I said, 'Huck's already been here, helped me wrap some things up. I'm just feeling a little unsettled. I hoped if I ran a couple of thoughts by you maybe some answers would line up in my head.'

He laughed. 'I've never known anything to line up in your head, Detective Doyle.'

'Funny.' I climbed the steps to the boardwalk in Avon. 'Doc, what do you know about Canada in the 1970s?'

He hesitated. 'What kind of question is that? First of all, I don't know how that relates to black and white and Jewish and whatever else you said. And second of all, I'm *Jewish*; I don't know anything about Canada. It's the big one north of us, correct? The one with all the mooses and the geese that poop on the golf course at the Short Pump Country Club?'

'That's the one,' I said. 'I'm wondering about Canadian politics, back in the seventies, maybe something related to a huge area of permafrost and tundra near the Arctic Circle called the Hellmich Plain, or Shelf, or something. Ever heard of it?'

'You're kidding, right?'

I squinted against a sandy gust of wind. 'I didn't think so. Anyway, there's some kind of bird, a rare, endangered bird, that nested up there, the Eskimo curlew. And back in the seventies a guy named Dunning – I forget his first name – led a non-profit group called Nordic Rescue in an effort to protect this Hellmich Plain. I think Dunning was on the up and up, actually concerned for the environment and wanting to see this area of land protected—'

'But the cop in you—?'

'Exactly. The cop in me thinks there was something else going on, something involving Canadian politics, pay-offs, maybe the Prime Minister's staff, oil companies, and possibly even a minor-league base-ball player from Asbury Park pitching in Ottawa at the time.'

Doc listened patiently, despite the fact that every minute on the phone probably cost him forty dollars in patient fees, then said, 'Okay, not that any of this is ringing any bells, but I do know that the 1970s were a time of significant unrest here in the US, and the two major contributors were—'

'The Soviet Union,' I said.

'—and America's unhealthy reliance on foreign oil,' Doc finished.

'What would you bet that this Hellmich Plain sits on top of massive oil reserves?'

Doc said, 'You want me to dig a bit, see what I can come up with?'

I watched a young couple kicking a ball on the sand; she missed and it bounced over the railing. I snagged it with my good arm and tossed it back.

'Sailor?'

'Yes, actually – would you see if you can find anything? It's not pressing really; I guess I'm just a bit out of it up here. Part of me came undone in the water the other day; part unravelled outside a school on Monday morning, and part of me can't seem to come to grips with the fact that an ageing baseball player has been lying to me all week and I can't figure out why.'

'Maybe he's just a jackass,' Doc offered.

'Maybe,' I said, 'but he doesn't seem the type – I mean, why? What's the point in being nice to me just to make up a pack of lies?'

'Sociopath. Stay away from him,' Doc said, sounding like Herringbone from the Spring Lake library.

'That's probably it,' I agreed. 'Hey, listen, I've kept you from your patients too long. I'll come and find you when I get back, all right?'

'Have you heard anything from Lieutenant Harper? Internal Affairs?'

'Not yet,' I said.

'That may be what's got you so *shroyft*.'

I didn't have a damned clue what *shroyft* meant, but I guessed it was pretty much what Jenny had been thinking too. 'I suppose so. It'll be nice to have a verdict – one way or the other – although I *really* need it to work out in my favour. Being a cop is about all I know, though most days I'm even not so good at that.'

'Let's hope it's the right way,' he said. 'I'm sure it will be.'

'Thanks, Doc. I'll see you.'

'Take care – and I'll call if I uncover evidence of a great goose-poop conspiracy up north.'

'Thanks again. And don't forget to—' I stopped short.

'Sailor?'

'Doc, what happens when a Jew commits suicide?'

'We die, just like anyone else.'

'Smartass. Everyone's a smartass. You know what I mean.'

Doc thought for a moment, then said, 'There are those who consider suicide a crime against God's law, because it is the deliberate taking of a life, and all life belongs to God. That's why most Jews aren't organ donors; the whole shebang belongs to *Adonai*. However, if you look closely at the *Torah* and the *Talmud*, you'll find that there's not much written on suicide.'

'So – it's okay?' That didn't come out right, but what the hell, it was Doc. He'd understand.

'Oh no, it's far from okay, Sailor,' Doc said. I'd have bet a thousand dollars he was frowning and holding a finger aloft, like an irritated professor. 'Without much mention of suicide in our sacred texts, it makes things worse, because—'

'—because it's unaddressed.'

'Exactly. You see, the souls of the wicked spend more time in *Sheol* than the rest of us, and I say *us*, although Esther and I are clearly among the Chosen who won't spend any time there at all.'

'Right, right. Feel free to forego the bullshit any time now.'

He went on, '*Sheol* is described as a shadowy place, a holding centre for Jewish souls – some stay a short time; others hang around for longer, until their souls are cleansed – another sticky subject – to welcome the Messianic Age, when the Messiah will finally come to Earth and empty this rubbish bin once and for all. It's actually a pretty accurate metaphor for life: real redemption only begins after the fable ends. That's when the real work starts.'

291

I tried for a connection. 'So Jews who commit suicide might spend more time in this *Sheol*-dark-scary-pit place while waiting for Jesus—'

'—or whoever ends up being the Messiah, yes.'

'And they might never get out of there?'

'That's correct,' he said. 'I'm no scholar, Sailor, but an eternity in *Sheol* and the possibility of being ignored at the advent of the Messianic Age ought to be enough to scare any God-fearing Jew away from suicide. But you know what complicates things is the Jews who killed themselves on top of Masada to avoid persecution by the Romans, a story of bravery and religious martyrdom going back two thousand years. I can't imagine many Rabbinical documents suggest those people, Jewish heroes to a great many, will spend eternity in some noisome limbo.'

I remembered something Jenny had said to Hodges. 'Would a Jew killing himself say the – the whateveritis prayer before dying?'

Doc filled in the blanks. '*Sh'ma Yis'ra'eil Adonai Eloheinu Adonai Ehad*. Of course. To steal a phrase, it would be a Hail Mary pass to string a lifeline out of *Sheol* one day. It is God's wish that all Jews live out their lives performing *mitzvot*, pro bono work, until the day He calls us home. Suicide is a crime against God's wishes, if you'll permit me to suggest, however humbly, what God might be thinking.'

I pinched the bridge of my nose, trying again to expel Gabriel Lebow's death mask from my mind. 'If anyone can tell what God's thinking, Doc, it's you.'

'Nonsense,' Doc said. 'But when the smoke all clears, Sailor, I'm of the Jewish faith enough to know that suicide is a direct crime against God's will.'

'Jesus,' I muttered.

'Nope, Jesus doesn't enter into the conversation,' Doc chuckled. 'Google Psalm 88 when you get a chance. That'll clear things up for you.'

'Thanks again,' I said. 'I appreciate the help.'

'Get that shoulder examined, Sailor. Don't drag your feet.'

'I will. See you, Doc.' I clicked off.

*

At Bradley Beach, I found the minivan parked next to a miniature golf course. Jenny wasn't on the course so I headed for the water, though my leg disagreed with this decision the moment my foot sank into the sand. In my head I could hear Marie encouraging me to keep working out, keep building that muscle – it was easy for her to say; when she died she was an élite athlete. I was thirty-two years old, and ten years since I'd last run with any conviction. But I found hitherto unknown reserves of strength and energy when I spotted Jenny in her yellow bikini, standing ankle-deep in the froth, holding Anna and watching Ben tear around like a madman. Beside her Curt the Blurry Lifeguard held a bright red flotation device and sucked in his non-existent gut. With only a few other visitors to the beach on a Thursday in September, Curt was able to give Jenny his undivided attention.

Glad I brought a gun after all. Douche-bag.

My mood shifted when Jenny saw me and, calling to Ben, turned and definitely sort-of-hurried to meet me, leaving Curt alone with his fancy red water wings.

Ben saw me as well. 'Daddy!' he screamed and dashed up the beach, passing Jenny as if she'd been standing still. *Wow. They're all happy to see me. Hang on to this one, Sailor. These moments are rare.*

Three feet away, Ben shouted, 'Catch me, Daddy!' and dived, before Jenny could stop him.

I did – although my arm and leg both threatened to mutiny.

Ben, chattering nineteen to the dozen, said, 'Daddy, we saw you on the news.'

'Really?' I looked at Jenny.

'Hey, sweetie.' She kissed me, which helped to quiet my throbbing pains. 'You didn't need to come all the way up here – did you walk?'

'Yeah,' I said. 'I feel pretty good.'

'I'll be the judge of *that*,' she said, with a coquettish grin.

I laughed. 'That was funny. You just made a joke about – what are they? Adverbs?'

'Jesus, what you didn't learn in school is embarrassing.'

'What?' I hefted Ben on my good hip. 'I can make adverb jokes with the best of them. Right, monkey-man?'

Ben didn't care. 'Daddy, we *saw* you, on TV. Well – we didn't see you, but Mommy said that's where you were, with Uncle Huck last night, on TV!' To Ben, being on television was right up there with performing miracles or saving lives.

'I know,' I said, 'I saw it, too. But you know what we're not going to talk about or think about for the rest of the day?'

'What?'

Jenny said, 'Those men on TV, buddy. We're just going to have fun and swim and teach Annie how to say *Walter von der Vogleweide*.'

'What?' Ben and I asked in unison.

'Never mind.' Jenny smiled. 'Let's go.'

I dropped Ben to the sand; he took off as though he'd been fired from the deck of an aircraft carrier. Jenny wrapped an arm around my waist, kissed my cheek and whispered, 'What happened to you last night? I used shirt code and everything.'

'Dunno,' I lied. 'I lay down next to Ben for a second, and the world just stopped spinning.'

She nibbled my ear; I checked to make certain Curt the Blurry Lifeguard was looking at us. *Take that, skinny!*

Jenny said, 'Well, you'd better find a way to keep it spinning tonight, even two or three times around, love of my life.'

'Am I?'

She stopped, shook her head. 'Yes, you infuriating shithead. I love you.'

I kissed her. 'I love you, Jenny.'

We walked together down the beach. She passed Anna to me and she and Ben kicked a ball back and forth in the surf. When the breeze died down a moment I tuned my ears towards Asbury Park, but heard nothing, no calliope, no Pink Floyd, no screams played backwards on an iPod, just waves on the sand and gulls screeching.

I wasn't old, not yet, but I'd lived long enough to know that there are days we live for. This had been one of those days: my wife loved me; my kids loved me, and the sun and sea and sand had collaborated to bring a moment's grace to the turmoil that had been my life for the past couple of years. I'd found the right path, where I could let go of the nightmares that followed me after Marie's death, where Jenny – the right woman for me, thank Christ – could become everything she hoped to be: lawyer, mother, wife, independent, powerful, beautiful, coveted. If there's a Heaven (and there'd better goddamned be), it would suit me just fine if it looked like Bradley Beach, New Jersey.

Jenny made corn on the cob and sliced blood-red Jersey tomatoes, one of the planet's only perfect foods. I grilled burgers and drank lemonade instead of beer and we ate outside in the waning hours of summer, smelling the first chilly breezes of fall and watching as the sun fled behind us. Ben sang songs about magic bears and Anna gurgled approval. If I'd have been given one wish from a genie stoned or stupid enough to wash up on a New Jersey beach, I'd have wished for that afternoon to go on for ever.

But that'd be a silly wish.

After dinner, Jenny and I washed dishes while Anna napped and Ben coloured pictures. He finished two, then begged permission to watch TV. I said, 'Okay, buddy, but no *SpongeBob*. I don't think I can be in the same room with *SpongeBob* tonight.'

'All right, Daddy.' He grabbed the remote and lay spread-eagled on the carpet in front of the television, fifteen years and a beer all that separated him from some ratty basement flat.

Jenny looked dismayed. 'Where do men learn that? I didn't teach him that. Did you teach him that?'

'Hell no,' I said, 'I don't watch TV. I hate TV.'

Ben clicked through the channels with alacrity, skipping commercials and boring adult programmes after only a second or two. He finally stopped at a grainy film, in colour but already a few decades old. 'What's this one, Mommy?' he asked.

I watched as a skinny man in an open shirt used a screw-together crowbar to dig handholds in a concrete wall outside a fortified mansion. Fake sweat sprayed on the actor's arms and chest preserved the illusion of summer heat, despite the late hour. 'I've seen this one,' I said, unable to remember the title. 'He's going into that house, up there on top of that wall, and he's going to—'

'To what, Daddy?' Ben rolled over far enough to see me.

Jenny glared.

'Nothing, buddy,' I said, 'but change that one; that's not a kid movie.'

Ben pointed as the actor, whoever he was, climbed towards the mansion. 'Look at that; he's on the wall like Spider-Man.'

'Change it, buddy,' Jenny ordered.

'Okay,' Ben said obligingly and clicked onwards – there were too many channels to explore; getting stranded on one made no sense to him anyway.

'What was that?' Jenny whispered.

'I can't remember the name of it,' I said, 'but that skinny guy with the crowbar is about to clobber whatshisname, Joseph Cotton, the guy from *The Third Man*.'

Ben heard us. 'That guy was going to *kill* someone, Daddy? Could a bad guy get in? Did that bad guy get in?' He clicked backwards, looking for the film again.

Jenny stopped him. 'You don't need to watch that, monkey-face.'

'But I *want* to, Mommy.'

'No.' Jenny took the remote, surfed through a few options and settled on a Disney Channel screening of *Old Yeller*. 'Here you go. Watch this dog. He fights a bear, then – then he wins the Korean War.'

'Really?'

'Yup.' Jenny rejoined me in the kitchen.

'You gonna let him watch that?' I whispered. 'You know how that ends?'

'He'll be asleep in ten minutes,' she said. 'The dog will live through the next ten minutes.'

I sat on the sofa, Googling oil companies and the Canadian Arctic, the Eskimo curlew and the Canadian Prime Minister's cabinet from 1975. I checked out Charles Dunning, who'd actually died in the Arctic back in 1994. He'd frozen to death on a glacier after his seaplane sank during a storm – a shitty way to go if you ask me. His company, Nordic Rescue, had moved to Manhattan in the late eighties. I found a few articles written by the company's COE, a geologist called Emmit

LeFevbre, who'd been appointed a few years earlier. I was about to move on to Moses and Katherine Stillman, when Jenny walked into the living room wearing only my pinstripe shirt – no shorts. She avoided eye contact as she lowered herself into the old Barcalounger and I pretended not to notice as she retrieved the remote from the floor and began switching idly through the channels. With her bare legs stretched out, she could have found live footage of a gorilla humping Fred Flintstone and I'd have ignored it.

Jenny landed on the film Ben had been watching: Charlton Heston was chasing Edward G. Robinson's dead body through a processing plant, where dead bodies were emerging as food.

Edward G. Robinson? I'd rather eat Fred Flintstone – or the frigging gorilla!

I sat up. 'Hey, that's it.'

'What?' Jenny turned the volume up, just a pinch.

'The movie where the skinny guy kills Joseph Cotton with a crowbar. What the hell's it called? C'mon, Jenny, you know this one. They're turning dead people into food to feed people before they die to become more dead people to turn into food. And Charlton Heston is figuring the whole thing out about two hours after the rest of us, because they've already established that nothing grows or lives or thrives on Earth any more, except humans who procreate like rabbits.'

'Ooh,' she teased, crossing her legs, 'let's watch that part.'

'Shit, what's it called? They spoofed it on *Saturday Night Live* a hundred years ago.'

She raised her eyebrows at me. 'Sorry.'

'*Soylent Green!*' I blurted. 'That's it! Interesting politics, cheesy 1970s movie.'

'Congratulations,' she said without inflection, 'can we have sex now? Because either your son or your daughter could be up in the next eight minutes.'

I slapped the laptop closed. 'Don't you worry, my love; I don't need eight minutes!'

'You may not, but *I* do, Sailor.'

I crossed the room on my hands and knees, kissed her ankles. 'Well then, I'll just have to take my time, won't I?' I slid my hands up her legs.

'You'd better.' She flashed me a quick glimpse of the promised land, then hustled down the hall into our bedroom.

I stood slowly, watching Charlton Heston ride a conveyor-belt full of nutritious and delicious Soylent Green squares. 'Tell the world, Chuck. I'm going in.'

I clicked the television off, and followed Jenny in to bed.

FRIDAY

King James Island

1838 Blake Street to 1720 Blake Street: 0.6 Miles

2400 milligrams of Ibuprofen.

Two a.m. Jenny'd pulled on a T-shirt; I wore boxers. She looked like a goddess fallen from Olympus, but snored, sounding like a '79 Chevy Nova.

I rolled over, then back, searching for a comfortable position where I'd be able to fall asleep before my arm or leg or shoulder or hip started cramping up. Curse ageing – what happened to the seventeen-year-old me who could sleep through an air-raid curled up on a concrete floor?

Jenny groaned and rolled onto her back.

I sat up again, just to look at her, this time coveting without regret.

She lay with one arm over her head, the other tucked beneath the sheet. Her T-shirt rode above her navel, and I leaned down to kiss her belly, close enough to feel downy-soft pubic hair tickle my lip. She smelled like sweat and lust and till death do us part. And she was right: through it all, our reconciliation

fuckingsuckinghumpingscratchingbitingpullingpushingkissingholding-sweatingmoaning

neither of us had thought about Sarah Danvers. That was good.

I lay down again and tried my right side, then my left, then sat up. I thought about raiding the fridge for some post-coital chicken wings, but decided instead to listen to my wife as she snored, shifted and slept her way through the night.

The image of Ben flooded back to me: sprawled on the floor, clicking through channels like an unemployed welder. I hadn't mentioned it to Jenny, but he looked so much like my father, I couldn't shake the memory.

Look at that; he's on the wall like Spider-Man.

Could a bad guy get in, Daddy?

He's on the wall . . .

Then Huck, in Asbury Park: *I'll tell you what he's on: he's on the sidewalk, on his knees, regretting the day he decided to drop out of high school and pursue a career as a drug peddler. That's what he's on.*

He's on. The mailbox in Asbury Park. 1720 Blake Street, their Christmas tree decorated and waiting for a missing family. He's on. No, Hes on. No apostrophe. Hes on.

A letter missing.

Charlton Heston.

Moses.

'Holy shit!' I sat bolt upright. 'Holy *shit!*'

'What? What is it?' Jenny murmured without waking.

I kissed her temple. 'Nothing, sweetie. Go back to sleep.'

I tiptoed to the kitchen, powered up the laptop and logged on to the Internet. The few seconds it took to connect felt like hours. *I cannot frigging believe this: one check, that's it. I just need to check one place.*

I heard Moses Stillman's echo: *I grew up not far from here, north of Asbury, back when you could still walk around up there.*

I navigated my way to the website Anna and I had discovered at the Spring Lake Library. It archived the life and statistics of every baseball player from every league throughout the game's history.

I typed *Moses Stillman*, just to double-check, and got nothing.

I put in *Mark 'Moses' Heston*.

I didn't hit paydirt right away; there were no bells and whistles or flashing lights. First a link appeared for a window cataloguing statistics tallied by a minor-league pitcher who'd worked his way through the Double-A farm system back in the early '70s. The name, highlighted in blue, read *Martin 'Moses' Heston*. I clicked on it, and my heart froze solid in my chest. There, in tiny font, beneath his name: *Ottawa Pioneers*. Three lines down, the tumblers keeping the enigmatic Moses Stillman safe inside his hotel prison slid into place. In equally small letters, the Internet noted Martin's hometown: *Asbury Park, New Jersey, USA.*

I was tired beyond description, but I jumped up when Anna cried for formula at 5:15. Jenny and the kids would only be gone until Sunday morning, but I wanted as much time with them as possible before they left for her parents' place in Morristown. I'd begged off, claiming that I had to stay in Monmouth County.

'Why?' Jenny asked, shuffling official-looking documents into her laptop case. 'What're you going to do here by yourself?'

'Read. Walk. Nothin' much,' I said. 'But I don't want to get out there and end up with some judge filing a bench warrant for my arrest.'

'Wouldn't Detective Hodges just call you in?'

'Probably,' I said, 'but I can feel the ice thickening beneath my feet. Things are headed in the right direction, here and with Fezzamo, and right now I'm not up for tempting the fates. That sergeant from Neptune Township – Collins – he signed me in to the murder book at Morris Middle the other day and it'd be just my luck that the Prosecutor's Office – or worse, the Public Defender – would come looking for me in the next two days. I don't want it to look like I'm skipping town.' It might have been bullshit, but it was shiny bullshit.

Jenny didn't buy a pinch of it. 'Uh huh, sure; pull this leg and it plays a song, Sailor. Just say you get bored at my parents' place.'

'I get bored at your parents' place,' I confessed, then added, 'and I'd rather not have a bench warrant issued in my name.'

'Okay,' she sighed, 'but you're telling Ben.'

'I will,' I said. 'He won't mind. With your father and the dogs and the pond and fishing, he won't have two minutes to realise I'm gone.'

Now, changing a diaper in the tiny glow from Anna's nightlight, I whispered, 'I'll see you in a couple of days, okay, sweetie? Daddy's gotta find a bad guy this weekend, before he decides to come inside the house after me.' I tweaked her nose. 'I love you, Smurfette. Be good for Mommy, and stay away from Grandma's pot roast. The Russians used that stuff against Hitler.'

Jenny appeared in the doorway, still in her T-shirt. She'd pulled on a pair of Morristown High School PE shorts. I hadn't noticed her toenails the previous night. She'd painted them Kelly-green. *Erin go braless!*

Leaning against the doorjamb, Jenny said, 'What are you two whispering about at this hour?'

'Nothing much – just her latest blog, the triumph of the empowered woman in the new millennium, and Beethoven's twelfth symphony.'

'Beethoven only wrote nine symphonies, doofus.' She knelt beside us. 'You want me to feed her?'

'Nope, you go rest. We're going to get a bottle now. You can feed her before you get in the car.'

Jenny's mouth turned down at the corners. She looked ready to protest, then yawned instead. 'Okay. But if your son makes a sound in the next hour—'

'We'll lock him in the basement,' I said.

'Excellent.' Jenny started to shuffle down the hall. 'It's ten, actually.'

'Ten what?'

'Ten symphonies, or at least part of a tenth. I'm pretty sure.'

I looked at Anna. 'No one out here cares, honey.' I found my Louis L'Amour novel under two days' discarded newspapers and settled down on the sofa with Anna in one arm, the paperback and the bottle in the other.

I popped the bottle in her mouth, opened to my bookmark – Otis the *deus ex machina* was encouraging Buck to turn the herd south-west – and started reading. 'You're going to love this: the good guys don't know if the new guy is good or a—'

Could a bad guy get in, Daddy?

I tossed the novel aside. *The new guy, Emmit LeFevbre: the geologist from Ontario . . .*

Jenny and I had loaded the kids into the minivan by eight a.m. I lugged out the scuffed old suitcases Jenny had packed last weekend – it took me two trips to get them both outside, but I didn't mind; the fact that she hadn't loaded them herself, in the middle of the night with divorce papers in hand, made me happy to help out.

Ben protested a little when I told him I had to stay, but once I'd reminded him there would be fishing and dogs and frog-hunts and duck-chasing he was happy to climb in the back; he even strapped himself in. Anna slept in her car seat beside him. Hopefully she'd sleep all the way.

'You want a bullfrog, Daddy?' he asked.

'Of course – the biggest you can find.'

'One named Rufus?'

'Is there a better name? I don't think so.' I kissed his nose.

'Okay.' He tugged anxiously at the seatbelt. 'C'mon, Mommy, let's go.'

Yes, Mommy. Get going. I've got to get a move on myself.

'You all right?' Jenny started the engine.

'Yeah, fine,' I said. 'I'm going for a long walk today, maybe ten miles – make Aunt Marie proud. Call me on the cell if you need me.' I spoke nonchalantly, working hard to hide the tension in my voice.

She leaned over to kiss me – we had a tacit agreement that we wouldn't snog each other too furiously in front of the kids – but as long as she was leaning out of that window, I wasn't going anywhere, despite my sublimated anxiety. Finally, she pulled back, just far enough to give my chin a nibble. 'Bye,' she said.

'Bye. Be careful.' She had a couple of runaway hairs stuck in the corner of her mouth. I pulled them out gently.

'You, too.'

I watched them drive off, watched Jenny turn north, headed for Route 35. As soon as the minivan had disappeared around the corner, I ran for the house, my leg already complaining.

Too bad. We're going to get some mileage today.

Inside, I stripped down, stood beneath the shower for fifteen seconds, dried off and hunted in the closet for the one pair of decent trousers I'd brought. I revelled in how baggy they'd become, then went spelunking for my other decent shirt – the powder-blue pinstripe number, Jenny's favourite, was tangled up beneath the bed.

Cleaned, pressed, shaven, tucked into the same shoes I'd worn across fifteen miles of plague-threatened Virginia countryside, I knotted a blue silk tie over my crisp white shirt and could not have looked more like a cop if I'd tried.

To my reflection, I asked, 'Sling, or no sling?'

'No sling. And no gun, not across state lines.'

I checked the time: 8:27. I had twenty-six minutes to catch the 8:53 from Asbury to Penn Station in Newark; from there, I'd catch the Path Train into the city. Jenny'd taken her laptop – she figured she could work while her parents played with the kids – so I'd have to do my basic research on my BlackBerry. It would be a pain in the ass, but I'd be spending an hour on trains into Manhattan.

I grabbed a pen with *Seibert's Seafood* scrawled up the barrel, tore a few sheets off the message pad beside the phone and went out front to wait for my taxi.

I napped for the three miles between the beach house and Asbury Park station.

In the city, I took the Thirty-Fourth Street exit from the Path station, near Macy's and the Empire State Building. I had to get to East Ninety-First Street, a nice address, but not one I'd ever have associated with a corporate office. The Upper East Side, particularly way up there, was generally reserved for rich doctors with offices near Mount Sinai Hospital, or political snots jockeying for the Mayor's attention. I could have taken the subway and saved ten bucks, but fuck it, I was in a hurry.

I called Huck at CID from the cab.

He answered, imitating Lurch Addams. 'You *rang*?'

'Hey, shithead.'

'Lovely to hear from you, too, Sailor. What's doing?'

'Just putting the pieces together.'

'Pushing the rock up the hill?'

'You know it.' I steered him back on course. 'You have a chance to run Moses Stillman for me?'

'Yup, and you know what?'

'Nothing, right?'

'How'd you know?'

'Because his name isn't Moses Stillman.'

He feigned irritation. 'You might have mentioned that before I slaved over a hot laptop for six minutes this morning. You just don't appreciate me. Sailor, I don't think it's going to work out between us.'

'Hey, shithead!' I said again. 'Pay attention.'

Now he imitated Clint Eastwood, badly. 'My friends and my mother call me "shithead". And you're neither, punk.'

The Eastwood thing made me think of Moses' hair. 'Huck – *focus*.'

'Okay, okay; it's just *boring* down here today.'

'Martin Heston.'

I heard him hunt around for the gnawed bit of pencil which was always all he had on his desk. 'Spelled like the dead ape guy? With all the guns?'

'Exactly.' The cab pulled up in front of a three-storey brownstone that was probably worth more than the gross national product of Lithuania.

'Seventeen-fifty,' the driver said through the Plexiglas partition.

'Where are you?' Huck asked.

'Manhattan.'

'What's going on?'

'I don't have time to talk now, Uncle Hucker, but do me a favour and I'll call you back in two hours.' I gave the driver a twenty and stepped onto the quiet sidewalk. Most of the planet had no idea that streets like this existed in New York City. I might have been in an affluent corner of Boise, Idaho.

Huck said, 'Whaddya need?'

'Run Martin Heston, Charles Dunning and Katherine Stillman everywhere you can get access. Send basic notes on anything you find to my work address. I'll get it on my phone here and call you back. I was going to Google Stillman last night, but I – I got distracted.'

'Got it,' he said. 'What're you doing in New York?'

'Visiting a place called Nordic Rescue, Dunning's old company.'

'Why?'

'I'm not sure,' I said, then confessed, 'I think it might have something to do with the suicide I told you about, Hanley, the one from last Sunday morning.'

'How?'

'Don't ask me that yet.' I hesitated, taking in the sculptures, the decorative cornices and ornate miniature balconies.

'Sailor?'

'Yeah, okay, and the shooting at Morris Middle. I know – I know I'm nuts, but there are too many threads tying all of this together, and I can't explain it but I've just gotta dig a bit deeper before I can let go.'

'Wait a minute,' he said, 'you're trying to link the hotel skydiver with the dead kid at the school? The Lebow shooting?'

'Yeah. I know it sounds nutty.'

'How are Dunning and the baseball player, whoever he is, involved? All that scratching nonsense you were talking about?'

'Maybe they're not,' I admitted, 'maybe I've just got too much time on my hands.'

'Whatever.' His chair squeaked as he leaned back and thunked his boots on the desk. 'I wasn't doing anything anyway.'

'Thanks, buddy.' I started up the steps to the brass-studded oak doors beneath the etched-glass window reading *Nordic Rescue*. 'I'll call you later.'

'All right, but not during my nap time, kemosabe.'

The lobby at Nordic Rescue looked more like an élite gentlemen's lounge than a place of business. I half-expected to encounter some chubby British businessman, cigar in hand, reading the *Financial Times*. Delicate chairs lined one side of an intimidating walnut desk set with a leather blotter and a green banker's lamp. Behind the desk the floor-to-ceiling windows stood open. A leather-topped coffer stood against one wall, just beneath a stately sideboard sporting framed photos of masked and goggled explorers on top of various barren Arctic peaks. A small table sat, café-style, near the opposite wall, also with two of the spindly chairs. Over a miniature bar a caribou head glared down. He looked parched.

Forest-green carpet ran the length of the room and darkly stained panelling rose as high as the decorative chair-rail. The room's centre-piece was a globe the size of a VW Beetle, fashioned out of polished stone and laser-etched with major geographical features. I watched, transfixed, for a few seconds before realising that it rotated. I wasn't smart enough to calculate if it spun in scale-time to the actual Earth, but for what it must have cost Charles Dunning, probably.

The dun-coloured walls had been covered with framed maps, charts and dozens of aerial photographs of what I guessed were Dunning's successful expeditions and rescues. I took my time moving through the room – no one was at the desk, anyway – and looking over the photos. Each frame held a rectangular brass plaque inscribed with the name of the area pictured.

To me, most of them looked alike.

Réserve Faunique Manicouagan, Québec. Green, white, brown, black, cold.

Stanley Mission Regional Park, Saskatchewan. Green, white, brown, black, cold.

Wimapedi Creek Provincial Reserve, Manitoba. Green, white, brown, black, cold.

Hellmich Outwash Plain, King James Island, Nunavut. White, black, holy-shit-cold.

In a subtle gesture, the lower corner of this last frame had been crossed with a thin bit of black fabric, denoting, for inquisitive visitors, that this was where Charles Dunning had signed his bill. From what I could see in the photograph, the Hellmich Outwash Plain could not have been more than ten or fifteen minutes from the North Pole. I figured there must have been some green somewhere, a few trees stunted by vicious winds, or at least a bit of lichen or tundra brush for the curlew to use when building nests. But other than that, the whole place didn't seem worth saving. Who would want it?

'Damn,' I whispered, 'what a place to die.'

'King James Island.'

I jumped, shrieked like a teenage girl. 'Jesus Christ, you scared me!'

'Sorry. Didn't mean to.' A sepia-skinned bald man, mid-twenties, with what looked to be Asian characters tattooed in a two-inch collar around his neck, stood in front of the receptionist's desk. He leaned on one of the chairs and lifted a Starbucks' cup to his lips before biting into a Brooklyn-sized bagel sloppy with cream cheese. He was thin and wiry, but he was in good shape and wore clothes to match the

Hemingwayesque feel of Nordic Rescue's lobby: leather boots, cargo pants, decent shirt open at the collar, and a heavy-banded wristwatch, one of those complicated fuckers for people who absolutely have to know Zulu time, New York time and Yukon time all at once.

I caught my breath. 'Just checking out the photos and maps.'

'King James' – he gestured with the bagel – 'my favourite. Seventy-four degrees twelve minutes north by ninety degrees forty-two minutes west. It's the dead centre of the Northwest Passage as you sail from Baffin Bay, deep water all around.' He joined me beside the frame. 'William Baffin himself named the place. I figure he must have bumped his nose on her headlands three or four times trying to find a way through there. He can't have thought much of King James to have named that pile of rocks in his honour, though. It's a pretty disagreeable place to visit.'

Distance was this guy's friend; up close you could see the grim acne scars across his face, and one eye hung halfway closed, the lid thick with pink scar tissue.

Damn, this guy couldn't have wrangled a prom date at a school for the blind.

'Have you been up there?' I asked, then said, 'Sorry. My name's Sam Doyle. I'm visiting from—'

He nodded. 'Thought I recognised you, Detective Doyle. Quite a summer you had.'

Shit.

'Yeah,' I said, 'a regular hootenanny.'

He backed away a step, playfully raising his hands. Two fingertips were missing from his bagel hand. 'You're not contagious, are you?'

I pretended to calculate on my fingers. 'Not for at least the last twenty minutes. No worries.'

He placed his cup on the bar and extended his hand. 'Emmit LeFevbre.'

'LeFevbre? So you're obviously from Hoboken.'

'Toronto.' He laughed. 'Grandpa was from Rouen, Grandma was Wahta Mohawk. Scandalous.'

'Young love won't be denied.' I turned back to the photograph. 'What's it like?'

'Dunno. I've not had the chance to go yet,' he said. 'I planned a trip up there with friends during the summer of '07: fishing, camping, exploring, you know. Hudson's Bay ran a trading post on Somerset Island to the southwest seventy-five years ago – it's abandoned now, but it's still a good place to launch boats for King James. Both islands are uninhabited. Actually, I think Charles Dunning, our founder and former CEO, might have been the last person to step foot on King James, back in 1994, apart from the occasional fisherman out of Resolute or Arctic Bay, I guess.'

'What happened in '07?' I asked, just to make conversation. I needed information on Charles Dunning and Katherine Stillman, not Zitman's failed camping expeditions.

He surprised me. 'That spring I tried Everest.' He took a bite of bagel, chewed for a few seconds. 'It didn't go well—' He indicated the scars on his face with a truncated fingertip.

My respect for him grew exponentially. 'No shit?'

'It's a bitch of a hill.' He waggled ruined fingers at me. 'I spent thirteen hours trying to walk two hundred feet while my fingers and face froze off – literally. They're still up there somewhere.'

'Why not turn around, head back to camp and warm up?'

He half-shook his head. 'Don't know. You're up five miles; it's hard to think straight. Your IQ drops to around forty. But I'll try it again some day.' He moved to a large wall-map of the Canadian Archipelago. 'Gotta finish my doctorate first.'

'Really?' I crossed to the map. A decorative legend in the lower corner credited the Hudson's Bay Company. At eight feet wide, it looked like something from an Errol Flynn movie. 'What are you researching?' I'd learned to speak a bit of PhD committing adultery with Sarah Danvers for seven months.

'You're looking at it.' Using a proper finger this time, Emmit drew an imaginary circle around an irregularly shaped splatter tucked between three massive islands just south of the Arctic Circle. 'There she sits.'

'Is that King James Island?' I pressed forward to take a closer look.

'Eighteen hundred and sixty-two square miles of gneiss and shale moraine and loamy outwash plain, soil probably dragged there by a glacier, hauled all the way from Ontario. It's uninhabited, except as the spring nesting grounds for a growing flock of migratory curlew—'

'The ones Charles Dunning set out to save back in the seventies.' I tried steering him back on course.

'You've done your homework, Detective Doyle,' he said. 'I'm impressed. But what brings you in today? What can I do for you?'

'Are you—?'

'I'm it: the skeleton crew's skeleton. What the hell, it's Friday, right?'

I wasn't sure how to broach the topic of Kate Stillman and could have kicked myself for not practising a catchy opener on my way into the city. I stammered, 'Well— I, uh – I'm looking into—'

'Hey.' His face brightened. 'Is this some kind of investigation? Are you following up on that mess from this summer? Is Nordic Rescue involved somehow?'

'No, no!' I backed away a step. 'It's nothing like that.' My mouth tasted funny. I glanced at his coffee cup, then up at the caribou glaring down at me. 'I've been laid up for a while – you might have read that I managed to get myself shot a couple of times back in July—'

'I heard that, yeah.' He nodded, pressing his lips together. 'Secret Service?'

'Twice,' I said. 'Anyway, I've been doing a lot of reading over the past couple of months. I've always been interested in explorers, and I came across Charles Dunning's work in an article I'd found on William Baffin ...'

Too deep, Sailor. You're in over your head!

'Really?' Emmit looked incredulous. He nodded towards one of the antique chairs beside his desk. Digging for a pen, he said, 'I thought I'd read everything there was to read on Baffin – but I've never come across anything about Dunning or Nordic Rescue. How cool is that?' He found a slip of paper, fell into his own comfortable leather chair and asked, 'Who was the author? I've got to get a copy.'

Of course. Of frigging course ...

I lied like a career criminal, keeping eye contact with Emmit LeFevbre. 'I'm pretty sure it was a researcher named Harold Greeley. If you give me a business card, I'll send you the link when I get back to my hotel.'

Huck is gonna kill you, shithead.

'Greeley?' he scribbled. 'Are you sure? I've never heard of him.'

'Yeah, pretty sure,' I lied. 'I mean, I've done a lot of reading recently, so I may have it wrong, but I've got the reference and I'll make sure I send it to you.'

He pulled a BlackBerry from a polished case, probably L.L. Bean, and started typing. 'I'll see what comes up.'

'Hey,' I interrupted, too loudly, 'um, can I talk you into a cup of coffee? Maybe a glass of water? I'm still working on this leg, and it was kind of a long walk out here. I never realised how far it was to the East River.'

Put the phone away. Put the goddamned phone away.

He holstered the BlackBerry; I sighed quietly.

'Yes, sir.' He started towards a side door off the lobby. 'Cream and sugar?'

'Thanks.'

'I never drink it, tastes like monkey piss.'

'Well, I'm a cop. If you can't stand a spoon in it, I won't touch it.'

'I've got just the vintage for you, Detective. Back in a second.' Emmit moved with powerful, lithe grace. I'd never met a mountain climber before. He was an impressive kid, even with Everest's signature across his face.

He returned a few minutes later and settled into his chair, hopefully with any thought of Huck Greeley's bullshit writing career forgotten. He handed over a Nordic Rescue mug and a delicate porcelain sugar bowl, entirely out of place in the masculine room. Somewhere, Nordic Rescue employed at least one woman.

'Here you are, Detective.'

'Thanks.' I stirred a sugar in, buying another couple of seconds before asking, as nonchalantly as possible, 'So: why King James Island? Why choose that battle? Was it really about endangered birds?'

Emmit stared at me, daring me to look into his ruined face. 'Well, that's an interesting question for a Friday morning, Detective Doyle.'

I feigned indifference, badly. 'I just wonder if there was something else going on, you know? Maybe something under the radar.'

He watched me squirm uncomfortably for a few seconds before

answering, 'There might have been. What do you think, after all your reading?'

'Oil?'

Emmit wiped the back of one hand across ridges of frostbite damage on his cheeks and nose. 'Inuit legend – actually, it might be Thule – tells of a group of fishermen blown off-course who sought shelter on King James Island, long before William Baffin's grandfather was even born. Anyway, these fishermen noticed two stark characteristics of that pile of rocks. First, there was soil, real dirt, that smelled faintly saline—'

'Was that oil?'

He shook his head like my high school chemistry teacher, disappointed. 'Petroleum compounds don't have a pH, Detective. Anything with a saline aroma would have been essentially salt.'

'Salt?' I didn't get it, and I made a mental note to quit hanging out with graduate students.

'You know how the earliest geologists and oil-drillers found reserves beneath the ground?'

I guessed. 'Electricity? Chemistry? Indigenous plants? Oily sheen on lakes or ponds?'

Emmit gave me a thumbs-up. I was pleased to see all of it there. 'Not bad, Detective; all pretty good guesses. These days we have seismic waves, electric probes and geo-chemical experts who examine soil samples, but back then techniques were less complicated.'

'They dug a hole?'

'They dug a hole!' Emmit toasted me with his Starbucks' cup. 'Pretty cool, huh?'

'Oh, yeah.' I reciprocated with my own mug. 'Edge-of-your-seat stuff.'

'But I'm half-lying to you because they didn't often dig a hole as much as they *borrowed* a hole.'

'From salt-miners?'

'Now you're catching on,' Emmit said. 'Salt-miners used to strike oil all the damned time and it pissed them off more often than not. Edwin Drake wasn't any more qualified to prospect for oil than you or me; hell, the guy was a railroad conductor, for pity's sake. Come to think if it, I'm a boat-load more qualified than Drake. But what he had was information from salt-miners in western Pennsylvania. If he'd been in Texas, he'd have shat his pants.' Emmit was a bit carried away. Composing himself, he said, 'Excuse me.'

'Oh no,' I said, 'keep going. I'm right with you. But back to King James Island, please.'

'Thules and then Inuits used whale-oil and blubber to fuel their fires because whales were all over the place. But whaling, despite the astonishing efficiency with which we decimated most whale species, was wicked dangerous, especially in the centuries before the big European and New England ships plied those waters. A forty-foot sperm whale dragging three Inuit longboats could make a village full of widows with a couple of sweeps of its tail.'

I tried to make connections, but I still couldn't tie salty soil to dead Eskimo fishermen. 'I've got to admit, Emmit, you're losing me; where does the salt come in?'

He went on as if it were obvious, 'Salt is what brought Arctic nomads to the Qikiqtaaluk Region, hundreds of years before Baffin named it for King James.'

'They dug a hole looking for salt and found oil,' I said, still not sure how the goddamned whales got involved.

'Even better.' Emmit found a piece of scrap paper on his desk. Flipping it over, he drew a makeshift map of a crescent moon, then lightly coloured the space inside the crescent. 'The stranded fishermen climbed up here' – he indicated the top of the crescent – 'which we now know is a moraine left by a passing glacier.'

'Glaciers move around that far north?'

'Oh, sure,' he said. 'Granted, it takes longer, but they're always shifting here and there.'

'Okay,' I said, 'so that's the high ground?'

'Correct. And down here' – he ran his pen tip through the area he'd coloured – 'is a vast plain of dirt and permafrost, twelve hundred square miles, and fairly level all the way down to where it runs into the sea.'

'The Hellmich Outwash Plain.'

'Exactly,' Emmit said, 'home to a veritable legion of endangered Eskimo curlew for three months out of the year.'

'Salt?'

'We'll get back to that.' Emmit returned to his map. 'This part's better. And I know this is legend, but, man, I hope it's true.'

'So what happened?' The Virginia State Police Academy didn't have a course on how to connect a thousand-year-old Thule fisherman with a school shooting and a gang thug's meth kitchen. Right now, Emmit LeFevbre had my undivided attention.

'Apparently the scouting party scrabbled their way to the moraine's highest point, somewhere around here.' He made an X on the map. 'And once there, a fisherman slipped and fell, and dropped his torch, which was nothing more than a length of wood wrapped in strips of cloth dipped in whale-oil. It'd burn pretty well, but it smelled awful and made quite a bit of smoke.'

'So – he fell and—?'

Emmit stood, apparently too excited to tell this bit sitting down. 'And his torch caught the very rocks on fire.'

'That's it?' I waited for the punchline. 'Burning rocks? Old Testament bullshit?'

Emmit shook his head again.

Hey, the world is full of stupid people; you'd better get used to it.

'What am I missing?' I asked.

'The *rocks* didn't burn, Detective Doyle.' As he leaned across the desk the muscles in his neck made the tattoo expand and contract eerily. 'What burned was the *oil*, trapped inside the shale.'

'Duh,' I said. 'Sorry, should've seen that one coming.'

He reached over and put a hand on mine.

Wait a minute.

'It's all right, Detective.' He squeezed my hand. 'You're new to this. I've been studying the geology of the Nunavut Territory for years.'

Deftly I worked my hand free, reached for the spoon and stirred my coffee again, just for the exercise. 'And where does Dunning come in?'

Emmit summed up quickly: 'Arctic nomads mined for salt to preserve meat, but they also discovered oil, plenty for their meagre needs. They'd make their seasonal trips over from Somerset or Devon

Islands and soak hundreds of feet of material in oil which they'd later trade with trappers, hunters and seamen. Eventually, they started trading casks of the stuff, and then big barrels of oil – imagine that, five hundred years before the world's first supertanker!' He picked up his sketch, looked at it, then tossed it in a bin behind the desk. 'The Inuit still hunted whales, but King James Island helped them prosper in an unforgiving part of the planet. Oil's addictive; there's no question about it. Anyway, Charles Dunning came along in the late 1960s, a dyed-in-the-wool environmentalist who genuinely gave a damn about the dwindling curlew population on the island. He lobbied and argued and cajoled and begged – but let's not kid ourselves, Detective, it wasn't until the Yom Kippur War that anyone in the Western Hemisphere began to give a damn about that pile of rocks.'

'Oil companies,' I said, hoping finally to get something right.

'In disguise,' Emmit said. 'Oil companies have done that for the better part of the last century.'

'Sure. Send in the chemists and geologists and botanists—'

'—looks like science, smells like science, acts like science, and then—'

'—drill a hole, pollute the planet, kill the curlew, because Mama's gotta drive the SUV to McDonald's for a double Whopper.'

'Nice one, Detective Doyle, but the Whopper is Burger King.'

'Don't make me shoot you, Emmit.'

His smile evaporated. 'Sorry. I was just—'

I grinned. 'It's all right. Jaded and grumpy, I can do. You take care of the chemistry.' I finished my coffee and said, 'You don't happen to smoke, do you?'

Emmit's face flushed. 'Closet.'

'Outstanding.' I stood, shook the stiffness from my leg and pulled the pack from my shirt. 'Out on the balcony all right?'

Nordic Rescue's balcony overlooked a fairytale courtyard with a lush green lawn in the centre and pots of flowers everywhere. Two patio chairs sat beside a matching wrought-iron table. Emmit led me down fire escape stairs and motioned to one of the chairs. 'No one else out here this morning. We're lucky.'

I lit up. 'Your little slice of Heaven?'

He pulled a single cigarette from a slim silver case. 'Yeah; it's amazing what four hundred square feet of lawn is worth in this city. Probably twenty people in four buildings share this bit of grass and we protect it like the sunken road at Antietam: no dogs, no parties, no barbecues.'

I tried to relax in the classy but uncomfortable iron chair. 'So, if I understand right: back in the seventies Charles Dunning went head-to-head against powerful oil prospectors – after the Yom Kippur War? What was that, '73?'

Emmit nodded. 'The US government supported the Israelis, largely to piss off the Soviets. And OPEC promptly slapped an embargo on the West. Nixon sent Kissinger to pull the Israelis out of the Golan Heights and Sinai, but by 1974 the damage had already been done. Panicking oil companies spent hundreds of millions of dollars looking for oil outside the Middle East: in the Arctic, South America, Mexico, deep-water drilling, and all at full throttle. The Ford and Carter administrations and the American people *demanded* oil. The price of a gallon of gas hit one dollar and people thought the world was going to end.'

I began wishing I had stayed awake in history class. 'So what happened? Did Dunning get his ass kicked?'

'Nope.' Emmit crushed his cigarette on the sole of his shoe, then stashed the butt in the silver case. 'He won – and this is the stuff of legend around here, but I tend to believe it – Nordic Rescue probably wouldn't have survived this long if Dunning had given up on King James Island.'

I waited.

'You see, Charles Dunning was a dedicated environmentalist – one of the first of the real tree-huggers – but he wasn't a politician; he'd as soon ram a Japanese whaling ship with a canoe as don a suit and argue his case in the halls of Parliament.'

'How'd he manage it?' I asked, crushing my own cigarette. I pulled out the pack and offered him one.

'No, thanks. I don't normally smoke more than one.'

'Really? Damn – you do realise they sell them in these handy packets of twenty?' I left the pack on the table.

Emmit laughed. 'All right, if you're buying.'

I watched him choose one with his intact fingertips, delicately, like an uncertain high-schooler. I said, 'So how'd he manage to keep the drillers off the island?'

'He had help inside the Canadian government.'

'Well, duh,' I said, 'nothing gets done without a hand-job here and there.' Emmit blushed and I apologised. 'Sorry – I don't always think before I open my mouth! My wife says it's her most favourite and least favourite thing about me.'

'It's all right, Detective.'

I tried to put the conversation back on safe ground. 'So who helped him? Any names I'd recognise? And remember: I failed US History twice despite a girlfriend with a 3.85 GPA and a D-cup.'

Emmit laughed out loud. 'You're a real kick in the teeth, Detective. I can't tell you how pleased I am you came in today. I'm not sure what your plans are, but I really hope you can stick around for lunch. There's a great Vietnamese place over on Second Avenue. Okay, so Dunning found out that a conservative MP from Ontario was drafting a bill to allow a British-based multinational access to Somerset, Devon and King James Islands – that's deep water there, and big boats can carry *lots* of oil. Jimmy Carter's presidential campaign was gathering strength in the US, balancing bullshit promises for oil exploration with bullshit promises to protect the environment.'

I interrupted the history lecture before Emmit got even more carried away. 'So how did Dunning do it? How did he manage to save King James Island from the evil British oil barons?'

Emmit stood and stretched, maybe for my benefit; I was too confused to know. 'Dunning hired good people, and his right-hand man – well, woman – she knew everything about politics that Dunning didn't—'

'Katherine Heston,' I broke in, and Emmit rewarded me with a beaming smile.

'Half right, Detective, but she kept her maiden name, as lots of educated women did back then. You know: NOW and bra burning and hyphenated names.' He reached for the smokes. 'One more?'

'Absolutely; help yourself.'

He picked up the pack. 'Katherine Stillman was the Assistant

Principal Secretary's daughter – and she was Dunning's inside man. She was a numbers whiz, doing a PhD in statistics, and she had major connections on Parliament Hill.'

'So what's the Assistant Secretary whosis?'

'The Assistant Principal Secretary is kind of like the Deputy Chief of Staff.' He blew smoke out his nose like a pro. 'The Principal Secretary is Chief of Staff to the Prime Minister' – he threw his hands up as if to say *dumbass!* – 'to Prime Minister Baldwin.'

I'd stopped listening. *Holy shit. Holy shit. I've got to get— I've got to— Shit, I don't even know what to ask.*

Emmit, oblivious to my excitement, carried on, 'Kate Stillman was a powerhouse back in the old days, and her timing couldn't have been more perfect. She came along right when Charles Dunning needed access to powerbrokers on Wellington Street. But Dunning didn't hire her because she was smart; he needed her for insider information on the ebb and flow of parliamentary sentiment over the environment, and first and foremost, Parliament's perspective on King James Island and the welfare of a few thousand curlew versus Jimmy Carter's willingness to sacrifice an unknown Canadian island for a bit of campaign momentum on environmental issues back home. You know, it's a heck of a lot easier to get behind oil-drilling on a frozen bit of Arctic rock where a handful of birds might get greased than it is to come out in support of drilling in Yellowstone National Park.'

'Yeah,' I said, my head still spinning, 'those hand-jobs again.'

'You bet.'

I paced the courtyard. 'So, let me try to sum this up, just to be sure I've understood everything.'

He sat, laced his fingers behind his head. 'It's all yours, Detective.'

I tried to ignore the distinct possibility that Emmit LeFevbre was appraising my ass, 'Charles Dunning emerges on the Canadian environmental scene in the early seventies. He's smart, committed and charismatic, but devoid of political acumen. His passion is compelling, particularly to Katherine Stillman, a young doctoral student – who *is also* the Deputy Chief of Staff's daughter, who does his books, crunches his numbers, organises his lobbyists, maybe even writes his speeches.'

'Close enough.'

I stopped pacing, looked at Emmit. 'You think they were sleeping together?'

Emmit looked at me. 'Never thought about it – but why do you ask?'

'I'm a cop; I suspect everyone, all the time. Men and women who work that closely together generally want to hump each other.'

Emmit gaped. 'That's a pretty cynical view, Detective.'

'Sure is,' I said, 'but people can be disappointing.'

'Go on.'

'So Dunning gets wind of the fact that the Canadian government is thinking about giving drilling rights on King James Island to a British oil company. He doesn't like the idea, because the island's home to a hundred thousand endangered chickens. So he marshals his resources – Kate Stillman foremost among them – and leans on the Canadian Parliament to kill the bill and send the Brits packing.'

Mimicking me, Emmit twirled the burning nub of his cigarette. *Get on with it.*

'So Stillman runs to Daddy, who rallies enough support for Nordic Rescue to get the Hellmich Outwash Plain listed as a national game reserve or some damned thing. Meanwhile, Dunning's reputation as a man who can get things done is established.'

'Top marks, Detective.' Emmit clapped.

I held up a hand. 'Not done yet.'

'Sorry!'

'Because this is the part that bugs me,' I said. 'Down south, Jimmy Carter promises the American people that he'll find oil outside the Middle East. You said yourself that he wasn't about to go looking for it in the Rocky Mountains—'

'—they *are* purple and majestic, after all!'

'True,' I said, 'but you'd think the Carter campaign would have got behind a bill to allow the Brits to drill on King James Island – I mean, what the hell did Carter care? It's a pile of oily rocks. You can't convince me that Carter actually gave a damn about a flock of pigeons freezing their asses off up there.'

Emmit scratched at his scar. 'Apparently, he did, or, if not, he had some motivation to keep his mouth shut.'

'But why? It doesn't make sense.'

'Dunno.' He stood up. 'It was a long time ago, Detective. I've read about everything ever written on that project, short of your Greeley article, and I've not seen anything definitive on that question. My guess would be that the Carter campaign found what they needed elsewhere. They had momentum on oil; they might have been flagging a bit on the environment, so getting behind Nordic Rescue probably gave Carter four or five good sentences for a stump speech in a key New England state. If the liberals were upset with him for encouraging oil companies to drill holes in the Gulf of Mexico, maybe he earned a couple of points back by agreeing to help save a few thousand Arctic curlew.' Emmit started towards the stairs. 'Another cup of coffee, Detective?'

'No, thanks,' I said. 'I've taken up too much of your time already.'

He stepped aside to let me move past and as I did, he clapped a mutilated hand on my wrist. 'How about lunch?'

'I appreciate the offer, Emmit' – I turned far enough to escape his grip – 'but I've got to get back to Jersey. I've got a breaking-and-entering appointment tonight.'

He chuckled, then stopped. 'You're not kidding.'

'Nope.' I pocketed my smokes. 'Not really sure what it is: meth lab, gang stronghold, or maybe just an abandoned house with an old Christmas tree in the window.'

He looked at me as if I'd told him I had plans to assassinate the Pope. 'Why?'

'Just curious, I guess.' I started up the stairs.

Emmit didn't follow. 'Does it have something to do with Charles Dunning?'

'It might.'

'Will you let me know what you find?'

'Sure,' I said, 'if I find anything.'

'So that's why you're here; you're trying to connect King James Island with a crack den in New Jersey?' His face scrunched in consternation. 'I don't understand.'

'Neither do I, Emmit, not yet – but I promise I'll let you know if I discover anything unexpected. It'll make a hell of a chapter in your dissertation.'

'Jesus,' he whispered.

'Oh, and I'm pretty sure it's a meth lab, not a crack den. Thanks again for your help.' I handed him the coffee mug and showed myself out.

I walked towards Central Park, the cacophony that was Manhattan growing with each block. My thoughts tumbled over one another, refusing to gel into anything coherent, and I committed myself to walking until I had made sense out of my visit to Nordic Rescue. I couldn't get free from the nagging sensation that I'd missed something, but I couldn't get my hands around it. My frigging brain didn't want to work right.

Get a beer.

One too many hits of OxyContin had left me stuck somewhere east of stoned-and-happy but west of sober-and-sensible. Dr Krandall explained it during one of our sessions; scared witless, I'd tried to ignore her. She told me my brain had changed: it'd got used to periodic visits from the Oxy Fairy; and once changed, it would never be the same. So getting sober meant learning to use a new brain, one with tyre tracks all over it.

As hard as I tried to see some connection between Moses' cryptic stories and my strange encounters with Pink Floyd and Gabriel Lebow, and even learning that Katherine Stillman was the daughter of someone high up in the Canadian government, I hadn't really anticipated finding anything of substance. I figured I'd simply been on another breakneck downhill, a final *fuck you very much* from this summer's rollercoaster. And things would either clear up on their own, eventually, or they wouldn't, and I'd spend the rest of my life paying for one stupid, desperate decision I'd made as a Vice cop in a drug dealer's closet.

I crossed Madison Avenue, still walking, still thinking, when my phone buzzed. 'Uncle Hucker!'

'Hey, kemosabe,' he said. 'You still in the city?'

'Yeah, on my way to find a cab now.' I leaned against a maple tree growing through a small hole in the sidewalk. Three lengths of taut wire held it fast, like Lilliputian restraints. 'Actually, I'm glad you called. I was just thinking about getting a beer or nine. You can talk me out of it.'

'Don't do it.'

'That all you got?'

'You need more than that?'

'I guess not,' I said.

'Good. Now, you got a minute?' He sounded concerned.

'What's the matter?'

'You know how I was only half humouring you on this crazy non-existent connection you're trying to make?'

'Uh huh. And?'

'And you know how I kind of figured this was all in your head, because you'd had a hard time these past couple of months?'

'Huck, I will take a plane down there just to beat your ass if you don't get to the point.'

'I did some digging the past couple of hours—'

'NCIC? Google? CORIS? *What?*'

'A little bit of all that, yeah,' he said. 'And you're never going to guess who this Moses – Mark – Martin Stillman Heston was married to.'

Without missing a beat, I said, 'You're probably right, but if I had to guess, I'd take a wild stab that he might have been married to Katherine Stillman, the daughter of the Assistant Principal Secretary to Canadian Prime Minister Baldwin back in the mid-1970s.'

'Assistant Principal Secretary?'

'Think of it like the Deputy Chief of Staff,' I said.

'Jackass. No one likes you.'

'That's true, but I'm working on Jenny this month.'

'You know who Stillman worked for?' Huck tried again.

'Nordic Rescue. They're a non-profit group dedicated to the preser-vation of land and species in the Canadian Archipelago.'

'Okay, so you get an A for effort,' he said. 'You're also aware of the enormous conflict of interest if Stillman had used her influence to alter public policy decisions in Nordic Rescue's favour?'

'Yup – but what the hell, it was Canada in the 1970s. Who gives a shit?'

'True.' He paused.

'Huck, come on, spill it. What am I missing?'

He sighed. 'Dunno, buddy. Maybe it's nothing – maybe it's just an insane coincidence—'

'Huck, I'm loading my gun right now.'

He said, almost to himself, 'You were hearing things and seeing things this summer, and I figured you were stoned and crazy, or stoned and drunk and crazy, or depressed and stoned and drunk and crazy ...'

'Okay, and I still love you, but if you don't start making sense—'

He cut me off. 'Do you know how Katherine Stillman died?'

I thought for a second. 'Um, sure: she was in a sailboat with her daughter, Lauren; they were tanning, goofing off, when a storm came up. Moses called it a squall – a *furious squall*. Anyway, they drowned.'

'No, Sailor, they didn't.'

'What happened?' Around me the natives of Manhattan's Upper East Side, all looking like they had raided Steven Seagal's wardrobe, bustled about their daily lives. 'Huck?' I stood still, waiting for the world to spin, like the globe in Emmit's lobby.

His voice settled into a steady cadence as Katherine and Lauren's story took shape. 'Lauren Heston died in September 1993, cause of death: drug overdose. But you don't have to be a Nobel Laureate to read something crooked on this one. I pulled the file in NCIC, and the whole thing stinks. She'd never been in trouble, no priors, got good grades in school, varsity softball player, church youth group: a nice kid. The ME's report says 750 mg of heroin in her blood, no note on the purity, but only three injections, no tracks, no scars, no history of even smoking grass with her girlfriends, never mind shooting up under the boardwalk.'

'Where'd they find the body?' I asked.

'Near the lighthouse in a place called Sea Girt, New Jersey – I'm not sure if she died and was dumped, or if she died in the sand and the tide pushed her around for a while, but she didn't drown. There was nothing at all in her lungs, and just that blue-green shit, you know, intertidal algae, in her throat.'

*That lighthouse, painting its prison stripe across the Warren &
Monmouth's façade, day and night. How does Moses live there?*

'It doesn't add up,' I said. 'The girl next door goes out and pumps herself full of smack?'

'And engages in anal intercourse,' Huck added.

'Jesus, Huck, how about a little warning! I've got a daughter, you know!'

'So do I, kemosabe, two of 'em.'

'So who did her?'

'Dunno,' he said. 'The initial investigation points to a local loser, Michael Bartollo, an Italian beach bum and part-time mob enforcer from Point Pleasant. He's got multiple priors – drugs, malicious wounding, B&E, mob activity: a Christmas list of felonious behaviour.'

'So what the hell was Lauren doing with him? Tough-guy boyfriend from the other side of the tracks to piss off Mom and Dad?'

'Nah,' Huck said, 'Mikey Bartollo was a piece-of-shit high-school drop-out and Lauren Stillman, the goddamn homecoming queen, would have pissed her little lacy panties at the first sight of him. I'll email you the file; this ain't no James Dean good-looking rebel: Mikey Bartollo was a monster from a Rob Zombie movie.'

'*Was*? Where is he now?'

'No idea,' Huck said; 'doesn't say here. But he never went to trial. It looks like he was questioned and held until he made bail, then he disappeared.'

'So who ponied up the cash to get him out?'

'No bond record here,' he said, 'but I can probably find it if you want me to.'

'Nothing on him since? He hasn't been pinched for *anything*?' That didn't make sense: once a shithead, always a shithead.

'Nope.'

'He dead?'

'Probably,' Huck said, 'or he figured out a way to change his name, fingerprints, birth certificate and the pictures of his old Italian grandmother on the visor in his I-ROC.'

'So he jumped bail and never got arrested again? I'm just not buying that, Uncle Hucker.'

'Me neither.'

'So what you're saying is that Lauren Heston went out on the boardwalk in Point Pleasant by herself – which has *never* been a good idea – and she met Mikey Bartollo, a.k.a. *The Creature from the Black Lagoon*, and she agreed to have anal intercourse with him in the sand, after taking three hits of happy horse, the first time she's ever touched drugs ...'

'Correct,' Huck said. 'Why sneak a beer from the fridge when you can fly nonstop to Planet Stupid?'

'God bless you, Huck. My daughter's never, ever leaving home without me and a gun and a guard dog and the Seven frigging Samurai.'

'Can't wait to see her prom dress,' he laughed. 'Chain-mail?'

'Electrified,' I answered. 'So what's with Kate Stillman?'

'Oh, right.' He paused. 'Well, here's where it gets weird.'

'Anal rape and heroin murder isn't weird enough for one day?'

'Not even close, buddy. This one's scary.' I heard him take a deep breath, then jump in. 'Because it involves you.'

'*Me?*'

'Katherine Stillman didn't drown on a sailboat, Sailor, but she did drown,' he started. 'In August 1994 she walked into the ocean at Spring Lake, swam out as far as she could, and waited for God or David Hasselhof to bring her home.'

Jesus Christ – I know where this is going ...

Huck continued, 'Her body was out there for a few days until she washed up onto the beach at—'

'—Asbury Park,' I finished for him. 'Just north of Convention Hall, a couple of hundred yards up the sand towards Allenhurst, near the jetty.'

'That's the spooky part,' Huck said. 'And you know? I've heard you talk about it a few times and never thought anything of it; it's just another story from your youth, like a home-run ball, or a boob grab after the prom, whatever.'

'I'd been jogging on the beach,' I whispered. 'Marie and I used to run out there all the time. She went south towards Spring Lake – she was much faster than me and I let her go on her own, but I wasn't ready to quit and I didn't want to wait around on the boardwalk in Asbury, because it was always a convenient place to get mugged, if you know what I mean.'

'I do, my friend.' I heard him shuffle pages. 'I found the police report online, and this piece in *The Asbury Park Press*.' He read out loud, 'A police spokesperson reported that Katherine Stillman, 51, of Asbury Park, was last seen Tuesday morning on the beach at Spring Lake, by Maile Bond, a concierge at the Warren & Monmouth Hotel. Ms Bond, 27, was not on duty when she saw Mrs Stillman, strolling near the surf. Ms Bond identified the clothes Mrs Stillman was wearing when she either fell into the waves, went swimming, or possibly decided to take her own life. The Monmouth County Medical Examiner's Office has not yet released details of the post-mortem.'

'I remember that article,' I said. 'My sister taped it to the refrigerator until my mother finally tossed it. She said it was unsettling to have that photo on display in our kitchen.'

Huck read, 'Mrs Stillman's body was discovered by a Freehold teenager, Samuel Doyle, who was jogging on the beach in preparation for the coming football season at Freehold Catholic High School— You played football? I gotta admit, Sailor: I don't see it.'

'That's not entirely accurate,' I said, 'but I guess it's close enough.'

'You didn't remember your corpse's name when you met Moses? Didn't connect the two?'

I started walking again. 'Shit, Huck, that was half a lifetime ago – these days I barely remember my own name. I *do* remember her smell, though: *Jesus*, but she was rank!'

'I don't get it,' Huck said.

'Neither do I,' I admitted.

Huck sounded stern. 'That's not good enough, Sailor; you need to do better. This is fucked up; this *can't* be a coincidence. I want you to try and explain this.'

'What are you suggesting, Huck? That the sublimated memory of Katherine Stillman has come back to haunt me seventeen years later? Am I truly that neurotic?'

'No,' Huck gave up, 'I guess not, but …'

'It's messed up, Uncle Hucker, I know, but I can't tell you what it means – or if it means anything at all.'

'Maybe she offed herself because of the kid, Lauren – think she was depressed?'

'Wouldn't you?'

'Yeah,' he said. 'Funny that the old man still lives there, you know?'

'I was just thinking that,' I said. 'The Sea Girt lighthouse shines a beacon across the face of that hotel every thirty seconds. I couldn't do it; I'd have packed up and shipped myself off to Tijuana or Bucharest, anywhere but there.'

'And to stay for all those years, after losing your wife and your daughter in just a couple of months? Yikes, but that takes some serious—'

'Wait a minute,' I interrupted, 'give me those dates again, Huck.' I groped in my pocket, but I'd left my *Seibert's Seafood* pen at Nordic Rescue.

Huck shuffled pages again. 'Here it is: Lauren Heston, died in September 1993. Katherine Stillman died eleven months later, in August 1994.'

'And Charles Dunning died in the middle. Huck, don't you think it odd that the founder of Nordic Rescue – Stillman's boss – died of exposure on a glacier in the Canadian Arctic *after* Lauren but *before* Katherine? Or am I just reaching?'

'At this point, cousin, what I think is reaching doesn't matter any more. This is as buggered a rodeo as I've encountered since the last time we let you go out on your own. And you know how that one turned out.'

I crossed Fourth Avenue and saw the impregnable treeline of Central Park in the distance. 'Yeah, I know. My leg still hurts when I get up in the morning.'

'Don't get old, kemosabe!'

'Thanks for your help, Huck,' I said, meaning it. 'Call me if you figure any of this out.'

'I will. And no beer.'

'No beer.'

'Peace on Earth, buddy.' He hung up, and I crossed to the sunlit side of the city canyon. Engines rumbled. Horns sounded. Noisy gangsta rap battled noisy Neil Diamond. People jostled; and a breeze, redolent of pretzels, pizza and muggy exhaust brushed the street with its grimy breath.

Kate and Moses in Asbury Park in 1975. Music on the carousel. Music in the hotel bar, maybe even Waters and Gilmour themselves. The Warren & Monmouth Hotel, their honeymoon destination, where they'd been happy, now Moses' home, lit night and day by the Sea Girt lighthouse, where Lauren Stillman's body was dumped by a missing drug-dealing mob enforcer. Mama Stillman can't take it, so she jumps in for the long doggie-paddle back to Halifax. Moses is broken up, so he sells her Tahitian black pearls to a local dealer who pays him enough to buy the honeymoon suite at the Warren & Monmouth. It's screwball, but believable. So how's Charles Dunning related? Was he fucking Kate? Was he Lauren's real father?

I went into the first bar I could find, some faggy hotel place with a grand piano, a huge crystal chandelier and a bored, tuxedoed bartender polishing already spotless glasses. I grabbed a stool. Except for an elderly couple eating thirty-dollar salads near the window, I had the run of the place. Not much of a lunch crowd.

'Yes, sir?' As the bartender placed the polished glass on the shelf I caught a glimpse of a silver-and-turquoise bracelet on his wrist. It looked out of place in Manhattan, like something he'd bought from a roadside peddler in New Mexico.

'Beer, please.'

'Which one?'

'Whatever you're pushing.'

He drew me a pint in an etched glass, and I watched the bubbles gather into a perfect head and followed an errant drip as it tracked slowly towards the granite bar.

'That'll be $8.50.'

I pulled a ten from my wallet, inhaled the hoppy aroma and tilted my head to catch the chandelier's light through the amber lens. *That's how to view the world, through a hops filter.* The bartender, the elderly couple, the glasses, all took on a funhouse-mirror quality, stretching and morphing comically on the other side of my glass. But I didn't drink the beer. Not yet.

'Have you a pen I can borrow?' I asked.

The bartender found one by the register, slid it down the bar.

'Thanks.' I scribbled a few words on a cocktail napkin embossed with the hotel's crest and let my thoughts find their way back to Moses and Kate. As unlikely as the Stillman-Heston story seemed, the only link to everything – 1720 Blake Street and the North Side Playaz' ice lab, Lebow's shooting, lobsters rotting in the O'Mearas' back yard, all of it – was me, and a pair of songs Moses and Kate had heard while out for the night together thirty-six years earlier.

'Fuck it.' I reached for the glass, made eye contact with myself in the mirror above the bar, and left it alone.

'Sir?' The bartender's chamois froze, mid-polish.

'Nothing.' I turned the napkin over and wrote:

Lauren Heston, September 1993

Charles Dunning, May 1994

Katherine Stillman, August 1994

And still nothing gelled.

'Give it up, Sailor,' I said quietly, not wanting to arouse any more suspicion in the bartender, who was already eyeing me a bit strangely, obviously wondering if I was planning to drink my beer, or just use it as a kaleidoscope. I rotated the napkin and in an empty corner, wrote:

Asbury Park to King James Isl—

Behind me, the piano woke with a jazzy flourish, a rising scale, clearly an introduction to some old standard, and I spun on my stool to find the elderly woman, her salad half-eaten, sitting behind the titanic instrument. The old man – I figured he had to be her husband – was watching like a seventh-grader hoping for a good-night kiss.

Nana Beethoven plinked through a series of complicated-sounding chords.

The bartender joined me. 'She's pretty good, huh?'

'Yeah,' I said, 'she's breakin' windows.'

'They come in all the time, weekdays, you know: nothing else going on. Always white wine and Cobb salads.'

'How long have they been married?' I asked.

'Oh, they're not married,' he said.

I turned back to him. 'Eighty-year-olds in a tryst? *Bullshit*.'

'I'm not lying,' he said. 'Is something wrong with your beer?'

I reached for the glass, slugged half of it. 'Nope – actually, I'll have another when you get a second.'

'Got it.' He reached for a clean glass. 'As you can see, I'm not exactly overwhelmed this afternoon.'

I finished the pint in three swallows, closed my eyes and exhaled slowly, feeling nearly nine dollars of cold brew filling the hollow nooks in my soul. It was altogether too familiar, and entirely too comforting.

What're you doing, Sailor?

I grabbed the fresh beer, guzzled half.

Nana Beethoven finally finished showing off and settled into the tune she had been planning to play while her boyfriend's Viagra kicked in.

Here it comes—

Jazzy, syncopated, as light on its toes as Fred Astaire, the music filled the opulent room. 'The Sidewalks of New York' had never sounded so charming.

I raised a finger to the bartender. 'And a double Glenlivet, please.'

'Coming right up.'

Before the last ten weeks' cold turkey, I'd been a Dewar's drinker. These days I couldn't stand the smell of it; I couldn't even bear to look at the label. Rehab is a dangerous place. For every two wounds I bandaged, one opened, bloody and sore.

Dewar's might have been foul, but other Scotches, like Moses' Blue Label, somehow managed to retain their smoky allure. The bartender set the stocky crystal glass down while Nana Beethoven continued to trip the light fantastic.

'Would you like to start a tab, sir?' he asked.

'Um …'

Shit. Shit. Shit! I can't put this on a credit card; Jenny'll bust me. And I can't take money out of an ATM, not here, not today. I've got to live on cash, at least until I'm back in Jersey. Fuck. Fuck. Fuck!

I tapped the bar with his pen. 'What am I up to?'

'That's another $8.50 for the beer, and $19 for the Scotch: $27.50.'

'Outstanding.' I handed him thirty dollars. 'Flag me. It's too early to get stinky today.'

330

'Got plans while you're in the city?' he asked, looking for more than a $2.50 tip.

'Sobriety.' I raised the Scotch to him and tossed it back. He left me alone.

With Nana Beethoven in the background I imagined the Asbury Park carousel, spinning on through the decades, while kids and tourists, drunks and punks, lovers and losers, all rode the fancy painted wooden steeds around and around for ever. I'd ridden it myself thirty years earlier, but they'd removed the old ring machine. Too many cracked skulls, I guessed.

Moses and Kate. October 1975. No gas. No oil. OPEC's pissed off with the West, but the sheiks need dollars to buy their solid-gold toilet seats. Charles Dunning uses Kate to get inside the Prime Minister's inner circle and they sway public policy –and save a bunch of birds from the Big Bad British Oil Company. Who gives a damn? King James Island is just a pile of rocks in the middle of nowhere. And Kate's dead. Dunning's dead. Lauren's dead. And Moses is a fucked-up old man, a nice fucked-up old man, but a fucked-up old man nevertheless. Why's he living in his honeymoon suite, dead smack between the place where Bartollo dumped his daughter and where I found his wife? That's a mystery, but not an important one, right? Who cares? Kate's dead. Dunning's dead. And Lauren's dead—

Wait, no, not dead – murdered.

And that's the kick in the balls: Lauren's murdered, Dunning's death is suspicious and Kate offs herself – why? Guilt, depression, addiction: our top three choices when a fifty-year-old woman takes a header—

Shit, I forgot: Hardass Hanley's dead too: he took a header into my breakfast.

Round and round the carousel spun, lights flashing, colours blurring – nothing like the digital super-duper colours of today, all those computer-enhanced high-definition Crayola shades, but the colours of a 1970s amusement park, flickering bulbs casting shadows, the calliope coughing out its tune – sounding nothing like a grand piano, not by a mile – Kate and Moses kissed, danced, sang, and held one another beneath a broken sky, in a broken city, along a broken midway that smelled of creosote and pulled taffy. They were young and in love; to them, it was Heaven.

I scrawled on a clean napkin, still watching the carousel in my imagination: Moses, tall and wiry, reaching for the gold ring, and Kate, thin and pretty, her Tahitian pearls matching her dark eyes but clashing with her cheap macramé bag.

'Holy shit.' I stood up, grabbed my beer and started pacing as Nana Beethoven's music swelled and filled my head with the sounds of October 1975. I ran my hand over the smooth piano, felt the faint resonant vibrations as 'The Sidewalks of New York' recalled a forgotten age. 'Holy shit.'

'You all right, sir?' the bartender asked.

'Yeah,' I said, 'yes. I'm just trying to remember something.'

'Can I help?' he said. Still fishing for that tip, then.

'Nah,' I said, 'it's from a while back. October 1975.'

'Greatest series ever: Reds – Red Sox – went seven. The Big Red Machine won it at Fenway. Unbelievable team: Bench, Gullet, Perez, Rose—'

Then Moses, in my head: *I was going to strike out Pete Rose on three pitches.*

Never faced him?

Never even encountered him.

Nana Beethoven leaned into it, her notes sending spikes through my head. 'I'm close, goddamnit, I'm *so* close.'

'Sir?' The bartender inched near the phone. Beneath the bar, his finger was poised to summon hotel security.

The music stopped; Nana Beethoven accepted the modest applause from her octogenarian boyfriend with a polite curtsey. The old dude laughed and cheered, sixty years of cigars rasping in his throat.

I stopped as well and to no one, I asked, 'How'd she get the pearls?'

'Sir?' The bartender was alarmed now. He was watching me closely, watching my hands.

'The pearls,' I said again. 'If Herringbone was right, those pearls were a gift to the Canadian Prime Minister from some French Polynesian princess. The legend – even if it's bullshit— Sorry, even if it's *nonsense*, the legend says that Maybeth Baldwin refused to wear them because some South Pacific princess had died of a heroin overdose while wearing them. I'm not buying that part because there's not a chance in Hell the Tahitian government would have gifted that particular strand on an ambassadorial trip. So let's say that's all baloney ...'

No one answered.

'The pearls hanging in O'Malley's in Spring Lake: how did they get around Kate Stillman's neck?' I started pacing again. I finished the beer, felt it chase the Scotch into my bloodstream. 'They *can't* have been a gift – she didn't do Prime Minister Baldwin any favours. What did she accomplish? In a roundabout way, she kept the Canadian government from granting its approval for a British company to drill on King James Island. Big frigging deal: you don't earn a four-million-dollar necklace eliminating massive kickbacks from the energy lobby.'

I paced. I felt the booze clamp down on my capillaries, jacking up my temperature, raising my blood pressure, making me sweat. I loved that feeling.

It's a drug. You're addicted. Deal with it later.

I wiped my face on my sleeve and repeated, 'You don't get a four-million-dollar necklace for evicting a major oil company. Insiders must have lost *millions* – they'd want to kill her themselves, right then and there, not twenty years later. So someone must have made money. Dunning got his reserve. Kate got a necklace for her troubles, and the Canadian government got – what?'

Again, Moses sidetracked me: *They're a knock-off, two hundred dollars from a gift shop in the Château Frontenac in Québec City.*

'No, they're not, Moses,' I said in the bartender's direction. 'They're not a knock-off at all. But why did she have them? How did your wife get those pearls?'

'Moses?' The bartender accepted the empty glass. 'Sir, are you all right?'

'I'm fine, buddy,' I said. 'I haven't felt this good in months.' I dropped a five on the bar. 'Thanks for the drinks.'

Any plan to call the Department of Homeland Security to report a babbling terrorist forgotten, he pocketed the bill and said, 'Very good, sir. Have a nice afternoon.'

As I turned to leave I waved to Nana Beethoven. 'Love that song, Grandma. Nice work.'

'Thank you,' she beamed, and waved her own liver-spotted fingers.

Beside the Fifth Avenue entrance – oak double doors with cheesy ornate fittings – someone had hung a shoulder-high oval mirror, probably because its frame nearly matched the absurd gilded door handles. Approaching past the hostess station, I caught a glimpse of myself: tired, half-drunk, but moving well under my own power.

I pushed my hair back from my face and started for the street when I saw his reflection; Gabriel Lebow, sitting on my stool at the bar, propped his elbows on the polished granite and with both hands rammed a live lobster into his mouth, tail first. For a fraction of a second I tried to remember if I'd seen Lebow's teeth before, perhaps when he'd gaped at me on C Street, howling Pink Floyd in reverse. I couldn't recall seeing them, but they were bared now, rows of needly teeth, silvery-white, like mercury. When he chomped down on the struggling lobster, its legs and claws flailed, scrabbling futilely for mercy.

Lebow crunched his way through the lobster while I watched, my feet stuck numbly in place beneath the ugly mirror.

I caught a cab south on Fifth Avenue. Outside Madison Square Garden I bought two 40-ounce Budweisers, each in its own brown paper bag. At $4.00 each they ranked among the greatest bargains I'd ever found. Two Power Bars ensured I wouldn't starve on the trip back to Jersey.

On the Path Train to Newark I found a quiet seat away from the early commuters and drank surreptitiously all the way to Penn Station.

I did the same on the 4:01 NJ Transit to Asbury Park.

To kill time on the journey home I tried to Google the Bible on my BlackBerry. I wanted to see what Doc Lefkowitz had meant about Psalm 88, and Jews who commit suicide. Knowing Doc, trying to work out any connection by myself would leave me with a headache. 'Whatever, Sailor,' I said, 'you're on your way to a headache regardless.'

I tried not to curse out loud as my clumsy fingers fumbled the minute keys, or start talking to my phone; *that* would attract the Transit cops, and I didn't have time to explain myself – not that they were famous for their listening skills.

On a Bible site – one of more than forty-two million, apparently – I scrolled through an alphabetical listing of links, looking for Psalms. I hadn't paid much attention in Sunday School, Catechism, First Communion, or Mass; I wasn't entirely sure if there were Psalms included in each of the Gospel chapters, or if they merited their own section like Peter, John, Paul or Ringo, so I started clicking on chapter headings, hoping to luck onto the Psalms, maybe even find out what the hell a Psalm was.

I didn't find any in the *Book of Ecclesiastes* – and I couldn't tell if that was a person or some Old Testament recipe for slaying a farm animal. In the *Gospel According to Peter* I scrolled through lots of stories about Jesus. In *Luke*, I found the same thing, and almost gave up, when I suddenly realised it would make sense if I just entered *Psalm 88* in the search engine. But there I was at *Mark*, and I hesitated, my inebriated thumb poised over the ENTER key. Staring down at the miniature screen, I whispered, 'Nah, it can't be that easy.'

I pressed ENTER and scrolled down until I got to Mark, Chapter 4, Verse 37 and read, 'A furious squall came up, and the waves broke over the boat, so that it was nearly swamped.'

Furious squall.

Forgetting Psalm 88 I clicked off the BlackBerry, cracked open my second Budweiser and watched out of the window as the train pulled in to South Amboy Station. Nibbling a Power Bar that tasted like a peanut-butter-and-barbed-wire sandwich, I swilled beer, content to let it addle my thoughts, at least for now.

At 5:26 p.m. I disembarked, shitfaced, onto Memorial Drive in Asbury. The late-afternoon humidity almost toppled me over as I made my way to the taxi rank. I leaned on a dented *Asbury Park Press* rack for support and a rusty corner sliced a jagged tear in my forearm. I sucked the blood clean – I was just sober enough to know I didn't want a stain on my sleeve – and glanced through the scratched Plexiglas to read the day's headline: *Surfer's Remains Found.*

I didn't bother buying a copy, or even trying the rusted catch to steal one. I knew what the article would say. Monmouth County, New Jersey, would make the national news again tonight as descriptions of Jeremy Landon's mutilated body leaked from the basement morgue of the Jersey Shore Medical Center.

I wouldn't watch, though. I had other plans.

Safe at home I threw up, changed clothes, and dug in Ben's closet for his art supplies. On a sheet of white construction paper I drew a circle at the upper edge of the page and labelled it *King James/curlew/oil/Dunning*. Halfway down the page, I drew a maple leaf, coloured it red – what the hell; I was drunk – and wrote *Ottawa/Stillman/Moses/pearls*. Near the right edge, I drew a passable rendition of the dome of St Paul's Cathedral; that was *London/oil company/$$$*. Finally, at the bottom edge, I drew the seven-sided cupola from the Warren & Monmouth Hotel and noted it *Spring Lake/Moses/Lauren/Kate*. Down the left margin, I wrote a column of apparently unrelated words and phrases:

'Wish You Were Here'
'Sidewalks of New York'
October, 1975
Tahitian Pearls
Auntie Carla's Pigpen – Matching Tags
Stolen Lobsters – Half-Eaten and Dumped
Lobster Tank – Matching Tags
Kate Stillman's Suicide – Sailor Doyle
Environmental Protection Legislation
Oil Prospecting
Gabriel Lebow
Harold Hardass Hanley – Sailor Doyle
Black and White Greasepaint – Death Mask
Rednecks & Jews
Jews Avoid Suicide – Eternity in Sheol
Thugs & Riots
Roland James Mercer – RJ

Sea Girt Lighthouse
Deputy Chief of Staff
Doc – Soviet Union & Foreign Oil
Dead Surfer – Jeremy Landon (Matching Tags?)
Lebow's Tree – Matching Tags
Michael Bartollo – Missing

I left space beneath Bartollo's name for additional terms, dates, anything else that might come up while I endeavoured to convince some meaning to emerge from my experiences and conversations this week.

With a red marker I drew a two-headed arrow from London west towards King James Island and towards Ottawa. Along the crooked shaft, I wrote: *Oil Pay-offs – NO.*

With a green marker I drew an arrow from Ottawa, north to King James Island. Along that shaft, I wrote: *Env. Protection Legis. – YES.*

With a black marker, I drew an arrow south from Ottawa to Spring Lake. Along that shaft, I wrote: *Pearls to Kate – YES. Pay-off? Dunning? Why?*

The arrow from King James Island south to Spring Lake was orange; the parallel arrow running in the opposite direction yellow, and beside those two, I wrote just one word: *Connections?*

Craving nicotine, I took my makeshift map, my lighter and my smokes outside and sat on the steps and considered those pesky lingering questions:

Did Dunning's death have anything to do with Kate's suicide?

Did Kate love him? Did she kill herself over him instead of Lauren?

Did Dunning get the pearls from the Prime Minister in return for his work on King James Island?

Did Dunning give them to Kate for solidifying his position as a lobbyist?

Where did the money come from? If Canadian legislators and lobbyists lost huge kickbacks from a British oil company, what made King James Island worth the effort? And the cost?

'That's the million-dollar question, my friends.' I flicked my cigarette butt towards the street, got up and paced back and forth across the driveway. 'An oil company would pay lunatic dollars to see that legislation pass. Prospecting rights there would have been worth millions, even back then – *especially* back then. So what motivates Prime Minister Baldwin to come out against it? His Deputy Chief of Staff, Stillman? Stillman's daughter? Nah. Jimmy Carter? Maybe.'

I paced another lap in silence, then pulled up suddenly. 'Wait a second, shithead!' I looked down at my map, the drunken writing, the two-headed arrow coming west from London. 'That's *it*!'

I ran back inside and dug around for the green marker, and drew half a dozen arrows, all pointed towards Ottawa from different points of the compass. With a black marker, I made an X on the shaft of the green arrow pointing west from London. *No money there.* I considered the other green arrows. *So where'd the money come from?*

With the green marker, I made another half-dozen arrows, each ending within a half-inch of my bright-red maple leaf. *Ottawa.*

'No one gives up millions in energy kickbacks to save a couple of hundred birds, no way. Charles Dunning might have been the planet's most charismatic tree-hugger but there's no way in Hell he – and Kate – could have convinced the Canadian government to forego that kind of money, unless— Unless—?'

I stepped outside and lit another cigarette. The sun had dropped behind the trees; it'd be dark soon. I took a long drag, revelled in the warm stupid-all-over feeling that came from too much beer and watched night creep across the ocean. I tried not to fight the veil the alcohol had dropped over my mind's eye; rather, I tried to work with it, to let it eliminate extraneous information, to focus my attention on just the meaningful details.

The only way the Canadian government would give up millions in oil pay-offs was if there was more money coming from somewhere else. Darkness gathered over the water. *No amount of love for the environment could ever convince a room full of legislators to pass up that kind of money. Simple as that.*

'Huh. Maybe Charlton Heston had it right: when nothing else grows, when nothing can survive, we'll eat each other. Groovy.' I had no idea if any Eskimo curlew still nested on King James Island, but if they did, they were the luckiest birds in evolutionary history.

I went inside, left my makeshift map on the table and called a taxi.

'Who paid?' I asked out loud, watching for my cab. 'Who could have *outbid* a British oil company? And who knew about it?'

The question hung in the air like a grim smell, and I left it there when the cab pulled up. I didn't wear my sling – I'd regret that later – but I did bring the .357.

The cab driver, an Arabic guy with a knife scar on his cheek, thought I had lost my mind. With the promise of continued unrest in Neptune and news of a major drug bust on Asbury's north side, the fact that I would want to be dropped off (after dark) at the corner of Fourth and Langford was as mysterious as it was suicidal. For five blocks he tried to talk me out of it, noting the myriad ways in which I might find myself dead by lunchtime Saturday.

I ignored him, insisting I had the address right; I even offered an extra five bucks if he could get me there with no further description of my impending dismemberment. He tried not to look nervous and cranked up the Arabic dance music playing on the radio. To a drunken Catholic from Freehold it sounded like someone trying to extract one of those cobra-charmer flutes from his rectum.

But I'd never been much of a musician.

As we turned across the railroad tracks, I knew I'd made a mistake: a brightly lit Quick-Mart on one corner of the intersection illuminated Fourth and Langford as if it were midday. The parking lot was playing host to at least two carloads of teens, who were taking advantage of the overhead lighting to check out the bodywork and interior detail of the other crew's wheels. One car, an Eldorado convertible from the late 1970s, looked as though it had had a twenty-thousand-dollar facelift. The other, a much younger Escalade, looked as foreign on Asbury's west side as an Amish Ferrari. Why thugs spent thousands of dollars on their cars but wouldn't move out of their stinking neighbourhoods mystified me – I suppose if the money came from drug trafficking, sticking to the streets they knew, however appalling, made strange sense.

The Quick-Mart, one of the only businesses open in this part of town, sold rolling papers, beer and cheap food: all the fixings for a late summer party. I'd stand out brighter than the Sea Girt lighthouse; they'd spot me in five seconds.

'Drive on,' I told the cabbie, 'up to the next block.'

'I try to tell you,' he said, 'but you no wanna listen.'

We rolled slowly past the Quick-Mart where thugs drank beer from brown paper bags and smoked blunts full of imported weed. They passed stubs of cigars back and forth between the half-naked teenage girls looking for a party, or a way out of Asbury Park. Loud hip-hop thudded from massive woofers fixed behind the Escalade's back seat and through the open window I could just see a young woman's head bobbing up and down in time to the music. Lovely.

Some were thin, some muscular, few overweight; most of them were dangerous-looking in their colours – baggy jeans, tattoos and cheap bling. These were the North Side Playaz. Some had spent the night in the Asbury Park drunk tank awaiting their morning meeting with a judge who'd slapped their wrists, fined them, then released them with the understanding that an arrest in the next six months would mean jail time. The Monmouth County Prosecutor's Office had such a back-log of underage misdemeanor drug pinches on the books that slapping wrists and establishing six-month recidivism timelines was the only way to separate the party kids getting stoned from the import-export specialists bringing drugs into the schools.

I recognised several from Blake Street; so this was likely their get-out-of-jail rave. Some of the girls sported brightly coloured Glo-Sticks on lanyards – Ecstasy, yummy – while others passed joints or sipped from clear wine bottles.

'Mis en bouteille au château, obviously,' I said.

'Huh?' The driver glared at me in the rear-view mirror.

From the look of things the rave was just getting airborne – and no one seemed to care that the Asbury Park police might notice. I hadn't seen any lookouts, but they'd be there somewhere, watching for cruisers, unmarked cars or rival gangs, anything that might need a beat-down or a bullet.

Not a one of them looked to be over twenty-one. It made me won-der if the fancy wheels really belonged to any of them, or if there was a car dealer or two tied up in the trunk of that Eldorado.

'Where to now?' the driver asked. 'Maybe we stop in your Christian Hell, huh?' He laughed at his own joke. I thought about cracking back about suicide bombers, but couldn't come up with anything.

'Take a left at the next corner,' I said, 'onto Blake.'

He signalled and turned into the darkened street. 'This is better, huh? No one sees you get out, right?'

I gave him a ten and punched his cell number into my BlackBerry. 'I'll call in about an hour.'

'I'll pick you up right here, huh?'

'Perfect,' I said, and slipped him another five. 'Don't dilly dally.'

This wasn't perfect, being dropped off on Blake; though it looked quiet, the old woman Huck and I had met might be on her porch, enjoying the evening without worrying about stray bullets or stoned burglars for once, thanks to our little arrest-fest.

I closed the cab door quickly, dousing the interior light, and as the driver pulled away I ducked behind a hedge, staying low. My stomach ached from vomiting, but I kept down, moving from bush to trash can to abandoned car to storage shed, moving towards what I hoped was Moses and Kate Heston's former home. Most of the streetlights had been shot out, but three remained, unwelcome stars spilling puddles of light in front of 1717 and 1718 Blake Street, directly in my path.

At 1715 Blake I cut across the lawn, moving as quickly as my throbbing leg would allow, skirting the plastic turtle sandbox full of catshit and sneaking behind the hedge where Hodges had clobbered RJ with her flashlight. I scrambled inelegantly over the hedge, reopening the cuts from Mrs O'Meara's fence and adding a few new ones for good measure. As I rolled over in the grass I felt more like a kid playing war with his friends than a cop trying to avoid getting killed. I had some vague recollection of my instructors at the Police Academy suggesting operations such as this be conducted only by sober officers.

I cut behind 1717 Blake, another wood-panelled split-level ranch, once Gerald Ford's American dream house, now, forty years later, a meth kitchen and North Side Playaz' flop-house where a thirty-year-old gang boss could get regular head from fifteen-year-old girls desperate to move to Manhattan. Picking thorns out of my hair, I couldn't help but think about the women I'd seen on the boardwalk in Spring

Lake: tall Northern European women, big-game trophy wives with high cheekbones and even higher silicone implants. Botox injections made it nearly impossible to tell the fifty-year-olds from the twenty-five-year-olds. Down there, they fucked to stay; up here, they fucked to leave. Jenny'd call that sexism. She was probably right.

Huck'd call it America. He was probably right, too.

There was no good way to get across to 1720 Blake without being seen so I cut behind 1721, the old lady's house. She had left lights on her back porch, but I didn't see any sign of her as I jumped the flower bed she'd planted to mark the edge of her lot. I was thankful to find a break in the hedge rather than have to attempt another high jump, and finally, I hit pay dirt.

Two doors down from the ice lab, Blake Street fell into darkness again. I crossed quickly, staying low, and backtracked to 1720 with its Christmas tree in the window and *Hes on* still legible on the mailbox out front.

Two blocks away, the Quick-Mart party raged on, and I was glad for it. The thudding hip-hop, cranked as high as the amplifier would go, sent rhythmic thunder across the neighbourhood, like tribal drums in a western movie. I pulled off my T-shirt, wrapped it around my fist and broke the glass, then reached through and unlocked the door.

Once inside I quickly shook out the T-shirt and put it back on, counting breaths and listening. After thirty, hearing nothing, my heart began to slow and I pulled out my penlight to check my surroundings, careful to keep the beam below the window.

I'd come into a kitchen with an old Formica table, rusting chairs and gas stove, and a stained old Frigidaire that might actually have done time in the *Partridge Family* kitchen forty years earlier. Scattered over the peeling linoleum floor were hundreds of plastic water bottles, obviously dumped here by young gang wannabes smurfing the bins along the boardwalk, together with a clutch of plastic nasal inhalers.

More Ecstasy. Nice, and so good for you, bursting with vitamins and minerals!

I sniffed the air. Apart from the musty aroma of mouldy carpet and general neglect, 1720 Blake didn't have that gristly, scorched-plastic smell like a burned-over meth lab. The water bottles might just have been stored here for use across the street. I took that as a good sign; hopefully, no one would be coming to open the store.

I crawled through the kitchen to the front room with the bay window and the dusty aluminium Christmas tree; I clicked on the penlight again. A few holiday packages, torn open, had been left beneath the tree. Someone left in a hurry.

To the right of the tree stood a dusty baby grand piano. I remembered Moses telling me about his mother and the silent movie era in Asbury Park.

These days she'd be swept off to Julliard or the Paris Conservatoire.

The piano must have been hers, passed down to Moses when Lauren was old enough to take lessons. I closed my eyes and saw her there in a green velvet holiday dress, her hair in a red-ribboned ponytail. Lauren would play 'Deck the Halls' and 'Good King Wenceslas' while Kate sang along and Moses nearly burst his shirt buttons with pride. It would have ruined them, Kate and Moses, to know that only a few years down the road Lauren would be anally raped and pumped full of heroin by a mob enforcer. I trained the penlight around the room and silently promised never to let my kids go anywhere alone. Ever.

When I saw the books, I exhaled in satisfaction. I hadn't wanted to be right, but I'd expected it. Beside a comfortable easy chair were dozens of dog-eared Louis L'Amour novels, stacked neatly together. It was all I needed to see.

All right, this is the place: now what do you hope to find face down on the floor?

I clicked off the light and slipped towards a hallway I hoped would lead to the bedrooms, but I'd not taken three steps before I smelled burned sterno, melted plastic and summertime at the dry-cleaner's.

'Ah shit,' I whispered, 'it's an alternate frigging site. Sailor, you've got to let Hodges know somehow – you can't just tell her what you found during a B&E.'

I tried one of the doors and it opened into what must have been Lauren's bedroom, given the *Def Leppard* poster that still hung on the panelling and the Apple II-E computer in the corner. The curtains were drawn so I risked the penlight again; a quick sweep confirmed my suspicions: two ping-pong tables, both littered with plastic bottles with the tops cut off; several discarded sterno cups; two butcher's knives; three disposable cigarette lighters; five boxes of wooden matches; dozens of Ziploc baggies; three hot plates plugged into a surge protector, and piles of empty over-the-counter cold medicine packets. On the floor beneath the window, someone had left two five-gallon containers of dry-cleaning agent, which accounted for the smell.

In the next bedroom I found even more trash – no surprise; meth chefs can hardly leave their rubbish by the curb for the garbage truck: the curb is public property; every cop knows that. So what does any self-respecting meth chef do? He just tosses all his rubbish onto the floor – buggers the resale value.

Back in the hallway, I shone the light on the last two doors. One proved to be a closet; two pairs of snow boots had been left, along with a dozen wire hangers and a knitted New York Jets hat.

The second door surprised me; I'd expected it to open onto the master bedroom, but instead I found a staircase to a Stygian basement.

I'd wanted to see if anything had been left – I'd guessed the master bedroom had been converted to a gang-banger's love-nest, but I hoped there might be personal papers or old documents overlooked, maybe left in a bedside cabinet or wardrobe.

I so didn't want to go down into the basement ... but I did. Closing the door behind me, I creaked down the thirteen wooden steps. I counted. I used the penlight to check the room, but it was disappointing: a rusty, dripping water-heater, an ancient furnace, a few hundred empty beer cans and wine bottles. The concrete floor sloped towards a drain near the water-heater; these places must have flooded enough back in the sixties that the builders started off with a drain before ever pouring the foundation.

The walls on three sides had been padded with filthy mattresses; the fourth wall was mostly covered in old egg cartons, a poor man's recording studio. Beneath the egg cartons, near the floor, was a four-by-four concrete block, with metal rings set at either edge. A coiled length of chain lay on the floor for Fido's return.

'Whaddya know,' I said, 'the boys keep their dog down here.' I looked again at the mattresses. 'Goddamn thing must bark all day to need that much padding.'

Above the water-heater was a corkboard, dangling like an empty frame. The new residents had torn down whatever notes or photographs had once been affixed to it, leaving only a torn bit of yellowing newsprint in the lower corner. Enough of the masthead remained for me to see the page had come from the *Asbury Park Press*, but there was no date. I carefully removed the paper and scanned the few sentences that remained, but stopped dead when I read: *Attorney Isaac Lebow refused to comment on the nature of*

It ended in a ragged tear.

Of all the things I had expected to find in Moses and Kate's old house, Gabriel Lebow's grandfather hadn't been on that list.

Shaking, I crossed to a metal chair near the drain and sat down. I examined the bit of paper again, but found nothing more. Nonetheless, I folded it and put it in my pocket. I looked at the acre of empty beer bottles. In a far corner was another plastic bottle of dry-cleaning fluid, along with half a dozen cans of paint thinner. *I wonder why Hodges didn't mention this place last night.* I leaned back in the chair. *She said Asbury's been watching these guys for weeks. They must have had warrants, must have known that—*

The chair wouldn't lean.

I trained the penlight down between my feet. The chair had been bolted to the floor. I didn't envy the rival gang members who ended up down here. Moses' and Kate's basement had been converted into a convenient place to have fingernails wrenched off – I didn't see any dried blood or significant stains, but I figured the drain had carried much of the evidence out to sea. I started up the stairs. I still needed to find Moses' bedroom.

Near the hallway door, I clicked off the penlight. Something was missing.

I waited, listening to the silence. *No music: the cops must've come by.* I stepped into the hallway and turned towards the front room. *All right, Moses, now where's your—?*

Something solid, a bat or a heavy stick, slammed down on my shoulder from behind, undoing ten weeks of healing in an instant – whoever it was had been trying to crack my skull, but missed in the darkness, glancing off my ear and hitting my shoulder instead.

A primitive need for survival took over – whoever hit me had unloaded without remorse and if I did not get to safety, I would die. Reaching for my gun never crossed my mind.

I felt him coming, heavy footfalls through the carpet, and a second man materialised out of the kitchen, took two steps and kicked me in the ribs. I heard them crack. I rolled onto my back, unable to breathe, unable to move, the brilliant agony in my shoulder matched by the crippling pain in my abdomen. I was broken; it would be weeks before I could move again, never mind get away.

The first man – tall, black, muscular, *enraged* – emerged from the hallway, a wooden baseball bat held above his head. He stood over me, screaming, his tattooed face, like RJ's, a mask of raw hatred.

I rolled to my right, saw the Christmas tree, the forgotten packages. *What's in them?* I wondered dully, waiting to die. *Ben. Anna. Can you hear me? Daddy loves you.*

Then a roar, deafening in the small room, and a shriek to match mine, I saw the baseball bat clatter onto the floor and roll beneath the table.

One man was gone. The porch door slammed open, then shut, and another pane of glass broke, tinkling onto the steps outside. I heard it through my left ear; my right was useless.

The second man, the tattooed bat-wielder, had fallen to his knees and was watching, his eyes bulging, as blood spurted from the ragged stump of his wrist. When he finally looked away, it was to search for his missing hand. He patted the blood-soaked carpet like a drunk who'd lost his car keys.

It's Blade and Big G – the cars are theirs, the Eldorado, the Escalade.

Someone kicked the screaming man towards the kitchen and firm hands helped me up. They smelled of cordite and gun oil. I let them half-drag me outside to a car I'd seen before but couldn't place. My shoulder was screaming; my arm hung limply at my side. 'Jenny,' I groaned.

'Shut up now and get in.'

Inside, I knew at once that I was in a police car; that made me feel better. At least I wasn't going to die. I lay sprawled over the back seat, tried to ignore the pain, and focused on catching my breath.

Up front, the driver stowed a 12-gauge in the rack between the seats. He'd used it to blow my attacker's hand off, one perfect shot; an inch lower and his head would have come apart, his prison tattoos ripped away.

I concentrated on sucking in air, wondering if I'd broken more than two ribs.

The cruiser's powerful V-8 roared as we careened towards Neptune City. No lights, no sirens: *whoever it is isn't supposed to be here either*. I rolled over and puked on the floor.

Feeling bad about it, I tried to apologise. The unseen officer said, 'Don't worry about it, Detective Doyle.' I recognised his voice, but I still couldn't remember from where. 'I'll get you to the hospital, but we need to come up with a story, okay? I'm thinking you tripped on the boardwalk, fell backwards down some concrete steps and managed to take a metal handrail or maybe a bike rack, one of those heavy ones, right on that shoulder. I think we can sell that.'

'Okay,' I wheezed. 'My ribs are broken. Can't tell how many.'

'Concrete steps will do that, too.'

'Who are you?' I tried lifting my head but couldn't summon the strength.

'It's Ed Hess, Detective. From Spring Lake PD.'

'What are you doing up here?' I fought for each breath; finally, they started coming easier.

'Supp assignment for the county.' He drove with two hands, like my mother. 'I was watching the street for the Prosecutor's Office, thirty-two an hour. Hodges tosses them up; I grab them when I can.'

I tried to shake my head, but every inch of my body hurt. 'Don't kid a kidder, Officer Hess: you're an old white man in an unmarked police car; the only way you're here is if you're lost on your way to a supp assignment outside a shopping mall. So what's going on?'

He pulled off his baseball cap and tossed it onto the passenger seat. 'I'm keeping an eye on you, Detective.' He said that as if the answer had been obvious all along. 'Your friend Greeley—'

'Huck.'

'Right, Huck, well, he asked Detective Hodges to watch you over the next couple of days. Said your wife and kids were away; you might find some shit.'

'Did he now.' *Huck, my own gunslinging Otis ex machina.* 'So why you?'

Hess said, 'Hodges and I, we served in the Coast Guard together, twenty years ago. I was a master chief, a twenty-year NCO; she was just out of the Academy. We both ended up down here after I retired and she had kids – funny how shit works out, huh? Anyhow, she calls me every now and then for off-the-books shit.'

I remembered Hodges calling him *Master Chief* over breakfast last Sunday morning. 'Your tattoo,' I murmured, 'saw it last weekend.'

'Yup,' he chuckled, 'picked that up in Key West when I was young and stupid. But hell, we were fighting the war on drugs: *Just Say No* and all that shit.'

My ability to speak lagged three paces behind my brain. I took a deep breath, felt my ribs like steak knives in my side, and said, 'You just shot that guy.'

Ed's voice dropped a register. 'Yeah, I did. I mean – I didn't want to, but you know, that boy was going to kill you, Detective.'

'I know.' I clenched my teeth, got my good hand beneath me and pressed upward. With another embarrassing shriek, I managed to sit up. Around me, Neptune City spun and tumbled. I breathed in great gulps, waiting for the pain to subside. It didn't. I asked, 'You've got a 12-gauge in an unmarked Spring Lake cruiser?'

'I do when I come up here, Detective. If you hadn't noticed, we're not in Kansas any more. Hell, we're not even in Oz.'

'Fair enough.' I didn't know what death would feel like, but it could only be a couple of degrees worse than this.

Ed found me in the rear-view mirror. 'You mind telling me what you were doing in that ice kitchen?'

I couldn't get my thoughts together. My vision blurred and I slumped back in the seat. 'No pain meds,' I said, fighting to stay awake, 'tell them no pain medication – no prescription meds. Just Ibuprofen.'

Ed laughed. 'Okay, Detective, but by morning you're sure going to regret that choice.'

'None,' I managed, and felt better for having been understood.

'And don't let them call my wife. Don't ...' The back of Ed's head swam in and out of focus. I rested my head against the window, closed my eyes and tumbled away.

I had heard the news of Blade's murder the following day before my mind finally registered the fact that Ed Hess' car window had been striped with white greasepaint.

Then there is noise, and aggressive light. I'm rolling around on a gurney, trying to sit up, but a nurse with a thin scar across her chin and one of those Cindy Crawford moles above her lip pushes me back down. 'Just relax, sir,' she says.

A doctor, younger than me, too goddamned young, looks at my shoulder, my ear – two minutes, tops. 'Get film on this.' And he's gone. A baby's screaming behind a white curtain and a homeless man as grizzled as any ancient codger in the Old Testament mumbles something about having to take a piss. He's on a bed beside mine. The curtain's open.

Things roll by: gurneys, wheelchairs, nurses, paramedics. Two cops, Neptune Township guys, are helping a teenager in cuffs into a room across from the nurses' station. His face is bloody, his nose crooked, I can see that even from this far away. The nurses' station is the nerve-centre of this whole place. Asbury Park, Neptune City, Belmar. Everyone's here, bleeding, battered, broken, drunk, drugged, stoned and scraped. There's yelling, pleading, crying, and all of it underscored by whispers: there's plenty of bad news whispered around this place; plenty of encouragement too, I suppose.

Condom rubber around my upper arm. 'Just something for the pain, sir.' Scar-chin is back.

'No pain meds,' I tell her, 'just Ibuprofen.'

'It's only a mild dose—'

'Do not stick me with that needle. Do you understand?'

'It's just a little sting, sir; a big guy like you won't feel a thing.'

'It's not the sting, sister: it's the ten weeks of rehab. If you inject anything other than saline into my arm, I will have the Morris County Prosecutor's Office deport you.'

'I'm from Parsippany.'

'Then it'll be a short trip. Now shove off and I'll try to sleep.'

'Sir, you may be waiting for radiology for a while.' She leans over me, whispers, 'It could be a couple of hours.'

'Ibuprofen.'

She looks down at me with sullen petulance, and I want to slap the shit out of her. It bugs me because God made nurses for flirting: that's troopers' Holy Writ.

'I'll get the doctor.'

'Whatever.' I try to roll onto my side. 'Can you turn on the TV?'

But she's gone.

Ed Hess peeks in. He's on a cell phone; I figure it's Hodges. He half-waves, then crosses to the nurses' station, a safe harbour in a storm, as the doctor returns and starts asking me a list of inane questions, all the while looking at my shoulder, rolling the socket around while I wince. 'What about that?'

'Eight.'

'Eight! That's pretty bad.' He holds my elbow parallel to the floor. It would hurt in this position even without having been clobbered with a baseball bat.

I try for a joke. 'Eight. Better than nine, though.'

'How about now?' He lowers my elbow and rotates it out behind my back as if moving me for stop-action photography.

'That's a nine,' I say through clenched teeth.

'Hmm.' He scribbles on a chart. 'I understand you're giving the nurses a hard time.'

'Just the ones who want to inject me with prescription pain medication.'

'You have a problem with pain management? Christian Scientist?'

'Addict.'

'Ah.' He nods as if we're commiserating. Now I want to slap him too. 'How about something to sleep? Give the Ibuprofen some time to take hold?'

'Melatonin?'

'Ambien – it's like melatonin, maybe a bit stronger; prescription-strength stuff, but I'll keep the dose light. Agreed?'

I'm off to radiology. Why those rooms have to be kept Arctic-cold I don't understand. The cold table slaps me lucid and I lie as still as possible while the techs do their thing. I want to stay awake until I'm back in the examination room – I want to know if any gang overlords have checked in with a bloody stump where they used to hold their chopsticks, but I drift off thinking about Ben, Jenny and Anna.

I wake later, in a different room. A nurse, not Scar-chin, checks my blood pressure and temperature, ramming that cone-thingy into my ear. I want to ask why, but I guess it's just a drill, a means to zero out my chart before letting me go home. My arm's wrapped against my chest, my ribs constricted so tightly with bandages and surgical tape that I figure I'm done breathing for six weeks.

'What time is it?' I ask.

'Just after three.'

'No kidding,' I look around for Ed. 'The Spring Lake cop—?'

'—is waiting for you in the lobby.' She checks the bruises on my ear, the tape around my midsection. 'You're all set to go.'

I notice the wheelchair. 'I can walk.'

'I've got to wheel you out. Hospital policy.'

'Okay.' I struggle to pull shivery legs over the side of the bed. 'Ambien? Maybe it's a pinch more powerful than melatonin?'

'The doctor's written you a prescription, just a week's worth.' She prattles on about paperwork, key signs to look for that could signify an infection, an unassisted triple-play, an invasion of Russia, whatever. I've got two broken ribs – it feels like thirty – and my shoulder is too damaged for surgery tonight. I've got to come back Monday, maybe Tuesday. Until then, 2,400 milligrams of Ibuprofen a day.

That'll clear up the swelling. I might just drop my liver in the bathtub, too.

I sign my name thirty-six times and get wheeled out into noise and aggressive light. Ed Hess is there, reading a magazine and drinking from a water bottle.

'Thanks for waiting,' I say.

'No problem, Detective.' He drops the magazine on a table littered with them.

'Where's my gun?'

'In the car.'

'Did our friend show up? Lefty McShithead?'

He shakes his head. 'Nope, but . . .'

'But what?'

He raises a hand. I'll wait. He helps me up and out the door and I sit in the front of his cruiser on the way home. The back smells of my vomit. I cringe a little.

He snaps his seatbelt. 'What were the names of those two losers, the North Side bosses?'

I can't think. 'Um . . . Blade and Big G. I think Big G is Richard Harris—'

'Who's the other one? Blade?'

'Something Butler. Some strange name, Techtron or Teflon.'

'Tejon?'

'That's it!'

'He came in, about an hour ago; I guess I should say that he was brought in.'

'Down one hand?'

Ed rolls his window up, turns on the air-conditioning. 'Nope, the other one, the one who kicked you.'

'What happened to him?'

'Dead,' he says as we turn south on 71. 'I know the on-call doc for the overnight, the one who pronounced him. She let me peek under the sheet.'

'Shot?'

'Head caved in like he was hit with something sharp, a garden rake, a ball-peen hammer, something with points.'

'Goddamn.' I adjust vents, let the AC tighten my skin into gooseflesh. 'Where'd they find him?'

'1717 Blake, on the lawn. Some old lady walking her dog. Asbury Park PD's got it so I didn't hang around too long – didn't want to look like I was too interested, you know.'

'That's just across the street.'

Ed blows the horn at a late-model Caddy creeping along in the left-hand lane at twelve miles an hour. 'Something hit Tejon Butler hard – we're talking brains and skull omelette, a real frigging mess. But otherwise, there's not a bruise on him.'

'I don't get it,' I say. 'Who else was up there? The rest of the crew was raving over at the Quick-Mart on Fourth.'

Ed pulls into my driveway. 'I'll get Hodges up to speed in the morning, but for your two cents, my friend, you—'

'—fell down the steps, backwards, on my shoulder, ribs and ear. Got it.'

'Nasty tumble.' He laughs. Only a lifer can blow a drug-dealer's hand off and then laugh while lying about it. I remember why I don't live in New Jersey any more.

Without Jenny around, I still sleep on my side of the bed. I prop three pillows beneath my shoulders, hoping for a comfortable spot. Sweating in pain, I practise how I'll tell Jenny that I fell, sober, down the boardwalk stairs. There's not a chance she's going to believe me.

Ed's in the house when I fall asleep. I figure he'll let himself out.

SATURDAY

Mikey Bartollo

Belmar to Spring Lake and back: 4.6 Miles

Ambien: Marked drowsiness may occur.

I heard noise from the kitchen before remembering that I was supposed to be alone. I listened for a few seconds: drawers opening, closing; the refrigerator door; water in the sink.

'Ed?' The very act of calling out sent pain spiralling through my ear, my shoulder, my ribs. I groaned and let the pillows take me. My eyes closed and I inhaled until the bandages hugging my chest conspired against me. The pain was diabolical: laser-sharpened on the outside, throbbing within. 'No painkillers, Sailor. You've gotta earn this one.' I pushed myself up and recalled what Doc had said: *Real redemption begins only after the fable ends*.

I didn't have a frigging clue what that meant, but I figured this is what it felt like, ten – no, eleven – weeks later and fighting for my life, my marriage, my future as a father and a cop. A little pain would clear my head, do me some good.

'Ed?' I tried again. 'How about a little help.'

The aroma of freshly brewed coffee snaked down the hallway from the kitchen, but there was no answer. 'All right,' I said to the empty room, 'I'm coming.'

Using the wall for support, I shuffled past Ben's room, took heart that his window hadn't been striped again, and cut across the living room into the kitchen. 'I didn't know you'd crashed here,' I said. 'I would have been a better host if I'd—'

Martin Mark Moses Stillman Heston, whoever the hell he was, rinsed a coffee mug in the sink.

'Good morning, Sailor!' He handed me a cup of coffee. 'I think I've fixed it just the way you like.'

I took the cup. 'Moses, what's going on? What're you—?'

'Oh, right, that,' he interrupted. 'Sorry. I was out for a walk after breakfast, and I made my way up here, so I stopped by to say hello.' He pulled a chair back for me and I sat, grudgingly, uncertain what the next few minutes would hold. Moses helped me slide the chair forwards. 'I knocked, but there was no answer. So I figured you were out, but then I noticed the door was unlocked and I didn't want to leave your house open so I peeked in and called for you, but I didn't hear anything.'

'You checked the place over?' I sipped his coffee. It was better than Jenny's by twenty thousand leagues.

He nodded. 'That's when I saw you, propped up, taped up, wrapped up as tight as a Tijuana tamale. It was clear that you'd reinjured yourself so I looked around for your wife – just making sure you had someone to look after you.'

'She's away for the weekend,' I said, really wanting to believe him. 'Sorry, Moses, have a seat.'

He slid his own chair back. 'Anyway, I apologise for breaking into your house, Sailor, but if you don't mind my saying so, you're a train wreck.'

'Thanks.'

'Don't mention it.' He waved airily. 'Anyway, since I don't have any plans, I can hang around here and help out – if you like.'

'Really, I appreciate the thought, but I'll be fine here on my own. I'm not planning on going too far today.' *And I need you out of here until I'm a bit stronger, a bit sharper. Why was Gabriel Lebow's lawyer grandfather quoted in a newspaper article that I found tacked to a corkboard in your basement?*

If Moses read disquiet in my face, he didn't show it. Rather, he fastidiously collected and stacked a clutch of paper napkins Ben had scattered over the table. 'What on Earth happened to you, anyway? I'm glad I came by – I mean, I've been— Well, things were a bit

355

awkward when we last spoke so I thought I'd stop in, and I'm damned glad I did.'

'Don't worry about it, Moses,' I said. 'We were both pretty shitfaced the last time we talked.'

'I more than you.'

'Whatever.' Now it was my turn to wave airily, one-handed.

'No, no, now, let me explain—'

'That you had a few too many Scotches?' I asked. 'Please, that's not a problem with me; let me assure you. I've been in a glass house for the past eleven weeks; I'm not about to start throwing anything.'

'So what happened?'

'I fell down the stairs, out by the boardwalk, just slipped. Goddamned embarrassing more than anything. I went over backwards, blacked out. The Belmar cops took me over to Jersey Shore Medical. Jenny's at her parents' place with the kids until tomorrow, so I'll spend the whole day on the couch, the first time since Ben was born. It'll be like a painful treat.'

He looked incredulous. 'You single-handedly saved the Eastern Seaboard from the devastation of plague and you're undone by a set of stairs?'

'They were slippery.'

'Did it rain up here?' He stared.

'Sprinklers.' I stared back. 'Down on Twentieth, that little patch of grass with the bench and the fisherman sculpture.'

'Well, I'll be damned.' He opened the fridge. 'What can I fix for you to eat? You must be hungry.'

'Woozy more than anything,' I said. 'I'm not taking any pain meds.'

'Makes sense, I'm sorry to say.' He leaned on the open door. 'So – no breakfast?'

Screw it. 'Moses, have a seat – after filling me up, please.' I waved my mug.

'Sure, Sailor.' He poured out, then sat. 'What's on your mind?'

'You are.' I let my toes dangle over the edge of the high board, then dived in. 'Yeah, you see, I know you've been lying about your past, but I don't know, is it because you don't want anyone to know your wife killed herself, or maybe you don't want to relive that devastating time for you and Kate when Lauren—'

'Don't!' He held up a trembling hand and covered his eyes with the other. 'Don't say it, Sailor; I can't bear to hear the words. Please.'

I waited, and Moses sobbed quietly to himself for a few seconds, then wiped his face on some of the napkins he'd just tidied. 'Go ahead, Sailor. Go on.'

'Maybe none of this is my business, but I've gotta be straight with you. The other night, when you were telling me about you and Kate in Asbury Park back in '75, I knew you were going to talk about that old carousel, and I knew – and I can't believe I did, but I knew—'

'—about the bar,' he said. 'About Roger Waters and David Gilmour.'

I frowned. 'Right. And I wouldn't have looked any further into it – I wouldn't even have cared – if I hadn't been haunted by the perfect impossibility of how and where that knowledge came from. Am I making sense?'

'No,' he said, 'but at least you're not mixing your metaphors.'

I went on, 'And I know about Charles Dunning, and Kate's connections, and King James Island – I don't know how she swayed that vote, to keep the oil company out, unless Jimmy Carter had promised prospecting rights to an American firm—'

'That's not the reason,' he said into his coffee cup.

'But I figure that's where she got the pearls, that you sold after she died—'

'That's not the case, either.'

'I'm sorry, Moses, but something's going on around here. People are dying, and maybe it's all connected; it feels like it is – but maybe it's not; maybe I'm just struggling to drag my broken – *changed* – ass back from the brink of death. I was seriously fucked up this past summer and I'd love to put it all behind me, but I can't, because the scars I picked up making stupid, *selfish* decisions are going to be with me for the rest of my life. And perhaps that's all this is: the first few weeks of the rest of my life.' I chugged the coffee. 'If that's the case, then I'm scared and embarrassed and truly sorry. But if not, then something strange and unnerving and somehow wicked is at work here – and I mean *here*, between Asbury Park and—'

'—Spring Lake?'

I considered that. 'The Sea Girt lighthouse.'

Moses shut his eyes tight against the memories. Holding his breath, he sniffed and choked, all at once, and twin rivulets of snot ran from his nose. He grabbed more napkins, wiped his eyes, blew his nose. 'Sorry.'

'And what's worse,' I said, looking away from him, 'is that I don't know if any of this would have happened if I had stayed in Virginia. I feel like the only real connection between any of the strange occurrences of the past week is me.'

'Is that what you were after with this?' He reached over and retrieved the map I'd drawn the previous night. He'd even cleaned up Ben's art supplies while I slept.

I took it from him, looked it over, then put it down. 'Yeah, I suppose so.'

His tone shifted from innocent confusion to accusatory query: 'What do you mean by this line here, where you've written: *Katherine Stillman Suicide – Sailor Doyle*? What does Kate's death have to do with you, Detective?'

When he said the word 'Detective' he sounded like the villain in a bad movie, trying for some control over the conversation. I just told the truth. 'Moses, I'm pretty sure I was the teenage kid who found your wife's body, that day back in 1994, on the beach just outside Asbury Park.'

'*You?*'

'I was jogging with my sister,' I explained. 'She used to run on while I farted around up there, waiting for her to get in her miles. I ran north from Convention Hall and found Kate on the beach. I was with her for a while, waiting for the police to arrive.' I watched Moses' eyes grow moist again. 'I'm sorry.'

As if distracting himself, he said, 'And you've discovered Mikey Bartollo.'

'A friend helped me with the research.'

'Why?'

'Because I'm trying to make sense of my experiences this week – or I'm trying to confirm that I've lost my mind; either one is possible, but I'd like to know which it really is.'

'Is that all?'

'No,' I said, 'as a matter of fact, it isn't. I'd like to know why you're here, living halfway between the two most tragic events of your life. Is it a choice, some kind of crazy penance? Guilt? All of those? None?'

Moses leaned forward and exhaled slowly; I watched his whole body deflate, just a bit. He sat that way for almost a minute before lifting his head to look at me. 'You want to know about Mikey Bartollo?'

'Actually, I do,' I said. 'I know it's an invasion of your privacy, but yes, I do.'

Pursing his lips, he nodded slightly. 'All right. I'll tell you.'

My cell phone buzzed on the coffee table: Jenny. I let it go.

Moses toyed with my map, folding and unfolding one corner. He traced the circle of green arrows I'd drawn, each pointing to Ottawa, each another potential source of anonymous pay-off money orchestrated by Kate Stillman, her father or Charles Dunning, then started, hesitantly, 'I can see you're trying to connect Kate and Lauren's death with illegal kickbacks to the Canadian government, specifically, I'm guessing, the Prime Minister himself, his Chief of Staff, or certain key MPs back in the mid-70s. That's' – he rotated the page a quarter-turn, considered it from a different angle – 'not quite right, Sailor.'

I didn't answer.

'You're wondering if there was some grand conspiracy in Ottawa that led to all of this but there wasn't. Did Charles Dunning use Kate to gain influence on Parliament Hill? Sure; I'd be fooling myself if I pretended he'd hired her for any other reason. Kate was great with numbers, but most of all she had the key to the Assistant Principal Secretary's office. Her father was a powerbroker who adored his daughter and hated the limelight – I saw him on the television news once, maybe twice – yet he had access to information, money, dealmakers – it was perfect for Dunning.'

'Who paid when Baldwin forced the vote that kicked the British out of King James Island?'

Moses sighed. 'I don't know – I'm not sure anyone did. I was pitching in Arizona that winter, trying to salvage my career. Kate helped Dunning get inside; he needed his hands in the pockets of a few powerful MPs and a few noisy lobbyists. Down here, Jimmy Carter had all the momentum he needed on oil exploration; Americans would have let him drill in their back yards – their *front* yards, even. It was easy for him to turn the other cheek on the King James question. He didn't have to do anything, just keep his mouth shut and collect the support from the environmental lobby. I figure that night Carter's Executive Staff probably sent Dunning roses and bourbon tucked inside a hooker's G-string.'

I didn't know whether to believe him. I'd decide later, after he told me about Lauren and Kate. 'So you're saying it's just a coincidence that your daughter, your wife and her former boss all died within a year of one another?'

'I am,' Moses said, then, 'well, not Lauren and Kate, no: there were clearly heart-wrenching ties between those two funerals. But Dunning? To hell with him – he was dumb enough to fly up there alone, a sixty-eight-year-old man. Dumbass believed too many of his own press releases.' He glanced at me, then looked down again.

You're lying! Why? It was eighteen years later. I didn't want him to read accusation in my face so I limped to the window, tugged the curtains back one-handed and let in the morning sea breeze. 'That's better,' I said.

Moses asked, 'You want any help with anything, Sailor? I can lug stuff around with the best of them.'

'I'm all right,' I said. 'The tide's coming in, is all, and I want to air the place out a bit, catch the breeze while it lasts.' I took my seat. 'So Bartollo was a coincidence, a mob enforcer who just happened to meet Lauren on the boardwalk?' I didn't mention what had happened between them, what Bartollo did before killing her. If it had been my daughter, I'd have shot anyone who ever mentioned it out loud.

'The worst night of my life,' Moses whispered. 'You can't imagine it, burying a child, unless it happens to you.' His voice dropped further, as if someone outside might be listening. 'You mentioned your sister, Sailor. Did your parents survive it?'

'My mother did. She's still in Freehold, in the old house. It killed Dad.'

'I'm not surprised.' He fidgeted with the napkins. 'That father-daughter connection, it's so laden with expectations of protection and security, right up to the moment you give her away at the altar, hopefully to a strong, handsome, gun-toting young guy who will kill and die for her. That's a father's gift and burden, you know?'

I nodded, not wanting to interrupt him.

'And then if the husband fucks things up, you get to kill him, too.'

I laughed, though I didn't want to. 'You're right,' I said. 'Anna's only five months old, but I'm already accepting résumés from potential husbands.'

'Sailor, my Lauren was graceful, smart, beautif—' He started sobbing.

'Moses,' I said, 'you don't have to— Bartollo.'

'That cocksucker!' he shouted. 'You should have *seen* him. It would have driven you mad to see him sitting in court, all smug and sneering at the judge. Christ, but I wanted the bailiff to pull a gun out and blow his nuts off. He took my baby and did those – those dreadful things to her, and he had the stones to sit and stare at the judge as if forty years in Trenton State Prison would be a trip to Palm Beach for him.'

'So he made bail, and took off?'

Moses slowly lifted his swollen red eyes and glared at me across the table. Tears streaked his leathery cheeks as he said, barely audible, 'Bartollo didn't take off anywhere.' He pressed his lips together in a vicious smile, and I finally understood.

'You killed him.'

Moses wagged a finger. 'I *collected* him.' He crossed to the coffee-maker, filled my cup, then his. Sliding sugar and a spoon to me, he said, 'I collected him from a filthy studio apartment over a Mexican restaurant on the Point Pleasant boardwalk. It was easy once I'd set my mind to it. I knew where he'd be; he didn't have anyplace else to go.'

'Why not just kill him?' I asked, not sure where this was going. 'He was a thug with known mob ties – they had fifty different reasons to kill him.'

'Because, Sailor – and you'll learn this as your children get older; trust me – as devastated as I felt in the wake of Lauren's death, as crippled as I was – *collecting* Mikey Bartollo was my job, but—'

Jesus Christ, now *I get it.*

'—*killing* him was Kate's prerogative.' He picked up one of the paper napkins, wiped his face, and said, 'Papa Bear might clobber you, but Mama Bear will rip your heart out and eat it while you watch.'

'What'd you do with him?'

'You don't want to know.'

'I do,' I said, as doors opened in my mind; this was all about to make sense.

'Kate and I had a little place up on Blake Street in Asbury Park, just south of where my parents used to live – it wasn't the best neighbourhood back then, but it was all right – it's a nightmare these days. We hadn't spoken much after the funeral. There wasn't anything to say … but the silence, with both of us sitting around staring at nothing, was backbreaking. So I smoked a lot of pot; Kate popped her share of Quaaludes – they were candy compared to the shit you were taking this past summer, but they got the job done. Anyway, when Bartollo made bail, we figured his lawyers would put him up somewhere and groom him for the trial, get him sober, shaved and cleaned up – but they didn't. Or if they did, they let him go back to his apartment to pick up stuff, socks and underwear, whatever—'

'—and you were waiting?'

'I was.'

'How'd you get in?'

'I was sitting at home listening to Pink Floyd – man, I loved those old records; I bet they're still up there in a box, maybe in the attic.' Moses massaged the back of his neck. 'I couldn't stand the silence between Kate and me so I played a lot of music. Floyd never let me down, them or Foghat, when things really got noisy. I'd just finished a couple of beers and was thinking about heading to bed when Kate came in, turned the stereo down and just looked at me. I wasn't sure what was happening so I didn't say anything. She looked good for a woman in her early fifties, and I realised that I would love her for ever, though I could see the anguish in her face. We might never speak again, but I would love her until the day I died.'

'She sent you out?' I asked, already knowing the answer.

'She stared down at me, a depressed drunk sprawled on the couch – I remember it as clearly as anything in my life, Sailor. She pushed a lock

362

of hair behind her ear and said, "Bring him to me, Moses. Go, right now." I found a crowbar in the garage, snorted two lines of decent coke a friend had left for us, and drove down to Point Pleasant in our old Buick. I used the crowbar to pop the trim off his doorjamb and a bit of cardboard to open the latch – there was no bolt, no chain, just the el cheapo lock on the knob. I pressed the trim back into place and waited for Bartollo to show up. He came next morning,' Moses said. 'I was pretty wiped out when he finally got there – I'd crashed from the coke and had a hangover to boot; I was hungry and tired and dehydrated and thinking about heading home before it got too bright and I might be seen sneaking down the back steps. The Mexican place didn't open until lunch, but I worried maybe one of the waitresses or cooks might come in early.

'And then Bartollo showed up, like it was the most natural thing in the world, no worries, no sneaking around like a murderer on the lam, no hood pulled over his face, just another dumb muscle-headed chicken coming home to roost.'

'And you clobbered him,' I said.

'Not at first,' Moses said. 'I wanted to – I tried when he came through the door – I'd wanted him dead for weeks, but I couldn't make myself take the swing. And me a fucking baseball player. It should have been easy.'

'It's hard when you're in close,' I said. 'It's why cops are as afraid of knives as guns. A knife means you're either Looney Tunes or deadly serious.'

'He came through the door, tossed his keys and started taking off his jacket. I watched – it was several seconds before he realised I was there. It felt like a goddamned eternity to me.'

'So how'd you manage it?'

'I remembered Lauren at the hospital, all those tubes sticking out of her throat, her nose, her arms, and a great rage just overtook me. I swung for the fences.'

'Did he die right there?'

'Oh no, Sailor, not even close.'

'But you tagged him with a metal bar?'

'A few times,' Moses said, 'I'm not sure how many, but it was

363

enough to knock him senseless – I know I broke one of his arms; it hung crooked from his elbow and swelled to the size of a dachshund. I think it did some internal damage as well. He shrieked a couple of times, then fell – and you know what's funny? When he finally lay there huddled in a foetal ball at my feet, the fire went out. I had to really force myself to hit him again, right at the base of his skull – it made me sick to do it, but I needed him out cold.' Moses chuckled. 'People don't realise how hard it is to knock someone unconscious, not for any stretch of time. You can blast the shit out of them, then the sonofabitch wakes up five seconds later!'

'Couldn't keep him out?' I asked, crossing the kitchen to open the front door.

'Where're you going?'

'I need a cross-breeze,' I explained. 'If we're going to sit here, I've got to be able to smoke. I'm already feeling the torn tissue in my shoulder: if I don't smoke, I'm going to be jonesing under the boardwalk, begging opium from some HIV-positive circus clown ... and Jenny'll have my ass in a sling.'

I lit my cigarette and felt soothing familiarity ease the pain and tension in every battered corner of my body. 'Ah, that's better.'

'Gonna die, Sailor.'

'Yup, but not today,' I said, handing him the pack. 'Go on.'

Moses found a plastic water bottle in the recycling bin, took out a small penknife and sliced the top off. He flicked his ashes into the base. He leaned back, the cigarette dangling from his lips, and stretched his long legs towards the living room. 'Bartollo was out, but just for a few seconds, then he started groaning again. He was a big kid, maybe two hundred pounds. I knew I could lift him, but the last thing I needed was to have him struggling while I was trying to get him into the trunk of my car – and in broad daylight at that.'

'Felonies are a bitch, Moses,' I said, 'and I'm not making fun of you; I promise. But every single person who thinks they won't ever get caught fails to consider hundreds of variables, any one of which might send them up the river. By the time I arrive on the scene I've got all the time I need to pick things apart, one by one, until I find the one that leads me right up your skirt. So: how'd you manage it?'

364

Moses raised his hands. 'I admit I got a bit frantic. The sun was up, for Christ's sake, and there were already people out on the boardwalk – joggers, an Islamic prayer group, even old men playing boules, if you can believe it.'

'Where was your car?'

'Half a block down, a long way to carry a bleeding Italian shithead, let me tell you. And I wasn't a young man any more, either. So—'

'—so you searched his room, found a stash of smack and pumped him full of it right there on his own floor, didn't you?'

Without hesitating, Moses said, 'I did: I cooked it at his table, in a dirty spoon next to a plate of stale refried beans. He had on a long-sleeved shirt so I stuck it into his neck. And while he didn't pass out entirely, he wasn't in any state to fight me.'

'How much did you give him? I asked.

'All of it,' Moses said. 'I didn't know anything about heroin, still don't: I was a pot-smoker, a beer-drinker. I'd done a bit of coke after Lauren's death, but that was just to get through the day without hanging myself in the bathroom.'

I flicked ash into the water bottle. 'So Bartollo faded in and out of drugged bliss, you pulled the car up to the front door—'

'—back door,' Moses corrected, 'and popped the trunk. You could fit the population of Rhode Island in the trunk of an '88 Buick. Back in the apartment, I waited until it looked like no one was around, then I hefted Bartollo over my shoulder – he moaned a bit when the broken bones in his arm scraped together, but I didn't care. I kicked the door open, hauled him down the steps, dumped him in the trunk, then drove around the block and parked behind a Point Pleasant police car outside a McDonald's. Hide in plain sight, right?'

'Risky.'

'But it worked,' he said, 'and I walked back to the apartment thinking I'd wipe the place down, deal with fingerprints, hair, whatever – I used to watch a lot of TV crime when there was no baseball on and they were just getting their shit together on DNA testing. So I tried cleaning up that pigsty a little, you know—'

'You burn it down?'

'I didn't mean to take out the whole restaurant, swear to God – but those old wooden places along the Point Pleasant boardwalk, the wood's been drying out in the sun for a hundred years—'

'Went up like a matchstick?'

'Three buildings.' He grimaced.

'Nice, Moses,' I said. 'I was trying to keep track of the felonies, but I lost count after five, maybe six.'

He dropped his butt into the makeshift ashtray, then gestured for another. I tossed him the pack.

'As much as I regretted burning down those buildings, it did give me a free pass out of town: every police car, fire engine, ambulance and paramedic was there within three minutes. I walked back to the McDonald's, ordered breakfast, then drove away at the speed limit, fifty-five, that old double-nickels campaign. I had no idea where I was going so I just drove west until I got into the farmland out there in Warren County. I wasn't sure exactly what I was going to do with him, but I knew I'd need rope, duct tape and water at least, which I picked up in a store on Route 46, west of Hackettstown. I'd started towards the Delaware River, only a couple of miles out from that store, when a state trooper pulled in behind me.'

'Uh oh,' I said.

Moses smiled. 'God was with me that afternoon. The cruiser followed for about half a mile and then I saw a back-country road – I would never even have seen it normally, let alone taken it – but I signalled and turned off the highway as if I'd always planned to, as if I knew where I was going.'

'And you found a cave?'

'A barn, about a mile up. A real estate sign had been stuck in the ground for so long the grass was as tall as the placard. Part of the roof had caved in and there was a bit of bailing twine holding the doors closed. The place was perfect, so I hid the car inside.'

'Jesus Christ, you left him there?'

'Just for a few days,' Moses explained, all matter-of-fact. 'Kate and I had some stuff to do if we were going to host Mikey Bartollo at home …'

Holy Mary, mother of God! The mattresses and egg cartons on the walls; that dog chain, the chair bolted to the floor over the drain — that was all for Bartollo . . .

I didn't let on to Moses that I had been in his house, but I swallowed dryly and asked, 'What do you mean, *host* him?'

He looked away from me. 'Kate changed that winter: something fundamental and good inside her broke and she started down a path I worried she'd never come back from. I tried to help her; I swear I did. After it was done I took her to Italy, and we stayed for six months, eating, drinking, visiting museums, and praying for forgiveness in every church and chapel, every cathedral and roadside shrine we could find, until Dunning contacted Kate from New York—'

'What did he want?' I asked.

Moses waved me off. 'Nothing; it didn't matter, it was immaterial.' He turned back to the window. 'I left Bartollo in the barn for five days – I went back a couple of times, I fed him, and gave him enough water to keep him alive. On the third day I realised I'd have to set the broken bones or he'd get an infection and die on me, so that night I went out to the boardwalk and scored some smack, not much, just enough to send him over the edge while I tugged his bones back into place.'

'Holy fuck,' I whispered.

Moses didn't hear me. 'That was the worst of it for me, driving out there after midnight, setting his bones by candlelight. Even starving and high, the pain must have been excruciating. I'll never forget Mikey Bartollo screaming for God to call him home before he passed out. After that, it was easier. I splinted the arm, taped him up, emptied his bucket, and left him water for when he woke.'

'Decent of you.'

'Hey,' Moses snapped, 'you have *no* idea, okay? No idea. So— Just keep your editorial comments to yourself, all right, Sailor?'

'Sure, Moses,' I said, 'but anytime you like, you feel free to fuck yourself and your guilty conscience.'

He looked at me and for a moment I thought I was going to have to fight him one-handed. He was old but still tough, and a good fifty pounds heavier than I was. He glared, then flashed his neatly capped smile. 'You're all right, you know, Detective.'

I twirled two fingers. He knew what it meant.

'Okay, so on day five talk of Mikey Bartollo's disappearance had quieted down. The police had been to the house to question Kate and me, but we didn't even need to play dumb, really; all the signs pointed to Bartollo torching his own apartment and taking off. The police ran his picture in every newspaper in the state, and the FBI helped out by listing him as one of their "Most Wanted". And after a few days, the media moved on to the next big story: two Blackhawk helicopters crashed in Mogadishu and a bunch of US soldiers died. But that was it: Bartollo was gone, and no one, particularly not the Asbury Park Police, gave a shit.'

'What did you mean when you said you and Kate had preparations to make?' I wanted to see how much of the truth Moses would tell me. 'How did you *host* him?'

'We had him tied up naked in our basement for two months that winter.'

'Good lord, Moses! How could—?'

'Stop!' he shouted, then lowered his voice. 'Please, stop for just a moment and ask yourself the question: what would you do if you had your hands on the man who had poisoned – *defiled, murdered* your daughter, your baby girl? What would you do, Sailor? How long would you torture him – or would you just shoot him? Or is that too easy? Would you cut his toes off, his fingers, his cock – that same filthy piece of flesh he'd rammed into your daughter's ass? Would you starve him, drug him, beat him nightly with a chain? Would you make tape recordings of him crying for his mother, begging for his life? And would you listen to those tapes as you drove around in your car? Would you cut off his pinkie and wear it on a string around your neck for the weekend like a macabre pendant? Would you brand him with a fireplace poker? I've gotta tell you, that stench, it gets on your skin, in your clothes; it *lingers*. I don't want you to answer me now, Sailor; next time you're alone, you look in the mirror and answer those questions for yourself. *What would you do?*'

He started crying again, then said, 'I didn't *need* it. I would have been happy just to put a bullet in his head, but Kate, my lovely Kate, she needed more. She sold her soul to the Devil to torture that boy,

Detective: my wife, the most beautiful, wonderful, caring wife and mother, changed into a brutal monster that winter, to ease her own pain. The anguish would come over her, and rather than seeking solace in my arms, or counselling, Kate would go down to our basement ... I can still hear those wooden treads creaking – that sound must have driven Bartollo mad – crazier than he'd already become, suffering through Kate's torture.'

'Moses,' I said carefully, 'why didn't you intervene? Could you not convince her how insane this was?'

'Don't you think I *tried*, Sailor? But until Kate had sated that wrath with Bartollo's suffering there was no talking to her. Those stairs would creak, and I'd run for the stereo, to play my Pink Floyd records as loud as I could without attracting unwanted attention from the neighbours or the police.

'Bartollo screamed down there; sometimes I could feel his pain, resonating in the floorboards.'

'*Two months?*'

'Just about.'

'How did it end?'

'I went down one morning to give him some water and to clean him up. We kept him naked most of the time – the furnace was down there so he didn't freeze – but he'd struggled through some pretty vicious colds, plus he had a nasty infection in his mouth where Kate had torn out some of his teeth. We generally just hosed him off – we had a drain in the floor, the builder had put it in when the house was built – so that was about the easiest way to deal with all the blood and shit. Anyway, this morning, he was dead, thank Christ. He looked like something that had been hit by a garbage truck. We'd rigged up two places to hold him, either chained to a concrete wall beside the boiler or strapped to a chair I'd bolted to the floor. Kate had left him strapped in the chair – he hated that.'

'Why?' I asked, not really caring what the answer might be.

'From the chair, Bartollo could see a corkboard Kate had hung up – nothing special, just something she'd bought for Lauren, you know, to hang in her dorm room. Anyway, Kate had hung it up with piano wire – I can't remember if I told you, but my mother was quite a piano player—'

'You mentioned it, yes.'

'Well, Lauren played too; I insisted.' Moses wiped his eyes again. 'So one night Kate and I were decorating the Christmas tree – we weren't really in the mood for it, but we didn't want to attract attention, and not having a tree would've looked weird. I was trying for a sense of normality in the middle of an emotional firestorm, and I poured us each a glass of nice wine and for the first time in weeks we talked. I started to feel like we might be getting somewhere – I swear, that night there were maybe twenty minutes when both of us forgot that Mikey Bartollo was sitting naked, gagged, and lashed to the wall downstairs, freezing his battered nuts off.'

'I understand,' I said, not understanding at all, but waiting to see where this led.

'Anyway, my wife dropped an ornament, one Lauren had made for us back in pre-school. Kate treasured stuff like that, and when she reached to catch it, she knocked over her wine glass and it spilled, blood-red, over the piano keys, dripping onto the carpet. And that was it, the switch flipped, and the next thing I knew Kate was clipping a length of piano wire right out of the old Chickering, the same piano my mother used to practise Franz Liszt and Frederick Chopin, and then she was off, creaking down those stairs again.'

'She used the wire to hang up the bulletin board?' I asked.

Moses nodded. 'After whipping Bartollo with it until her arms ached.' Almost as an afterthought, he added, 'He lost an eye that night.'

I'd heard enough. 'Back to the chair and the bulletin board, please.'

'Kate used to strap him in the chair and leave him staring up at that board.'

'Why?' I asked, as one significant puzzle piece finally clicked into place. 'What was on it?'

Moses ticked the list off on his fingertips. 'Newspaper stories, court documents, old drawings of Lauren's, photos of Lauren – and of Bartollo's family, his mother coming out of church up in Allenhurst, his sister, waiting on tables at a diner in Wall Township. Kate used to whisper to him how she was going to kill his family, torture his mother, bring his sister here to join him in our happy suburban dungeon.'

'She pushed Bartollo over the edge,' I said. 'Sleep deprivation? Psychological torture?'

'Oh, yeah, badly; I found him a few times after he'd tried to bash his brains out on the floor. Kate shortened the chain when she came home from work and found him trying to choke himself to death with it. He almost succeeded, too; he'd got a coil around his neck and then stretched out as far across the floor as he could – only six inches off the concrete – trying to use his own body weight to hang himself. Pretty creative – and he would have succeeded if Kate hadn't found him. That was the night she cut off his earlobes with her sewing scissors.'

'Okay, enough.' I held my hands up. 'Please, Moses, stop.'

'Too much for you, Detective?'

'Actually, it is,' I admitted.

'It was for me too,' he said. 'I was relieved and sickened the morning I finally found him dead.'

'Where'd you dump him?'

'Out there.' He pointed towards the ocean.

'In the winter?'

'I had an old catboat moored at a pier in Belmar, west of the Shark River bridge. It was freezing, much too cold for anyone to be on the beach after dark other than a few drunks and stoners on the boardwalk, but they all huddled over their campfires and didn't give a rip. They weren't good witnesses.'

'How'd you keep the body down? You know that once bacteria gets to work, any self-respecting corpse fills with gas and pops to the surface after a few days.'

'Not this one,' Moses said. 'While I sailed up the beach, Kate fixed three concrete blocks to Mikey's chest and legs with duct tape. It took both of us to get him up the basement stairs and into the trunk; even though he'd lost half his body weight, with those three blocks on him it was a real chore. We backed onto the sand beside the Casino ruins and dragged his body down to the boat, then Kate moved the car while I got ready to sail. No one came by, no close calls, no late-night joggers, no die-hard cops walking the beachfront beat; it was just Kate, me and Mikey.'

'How far out did you go?' I wasn't even sure why I was still asking questions.

'A couple of miles,' Moses said, 'with Kate sitting in the bow, the same as she had on a thousand sailing trips with Lauren and me. It was ungodly cold and windy – I'd originally wanted to get out ten, maybe fifteen miles and dump him in deep water, but it was too much so we came about and rode the wind north to Allenhurst. Kate decided she wanted to dump him where his mother would look out over the ocean every Sunday when she came down the church steps after Mass. It was her penultimate act of revenge for Lauren.'

'Penultimate?' I said. 'Was there more? Could there be?' My phone buzzed again.

Gotta call your wife before she calls out the cavalry!

Moses finally turned back to the table. He folded his arms and rested his forehead on his wrists and said quietly, 'Kate understood about gas build-up in decomposing bodies …'

Again I finished for him. 'So she poked him full of holes.'

God, please forgive him. He's a tired old man. Give him some peace.

'I couldn't watch – I don't like thinking about it, even now, but I can't forget the sound of that knife over the breeze and the flapping sails. Sailor, she was a middle-aged woman perforating the corpse of the man she'd tortured mercilessly – *mercilessly* – for two whole months.

'Eventually I heard the knife splash into the water and I waited while Kate washed her hands. Then we dumped his body, sending the man who had raped and murdered our daughter to the bottom of the Atlantic with fifty pounds of concrete taped to his chest and fifty holes punched in his stomach. We sailed back to Shark River, and I scrubbed every inch of that boat.'

'You were thorough. That's good,' I said without a hint of judgement in my voice. If Moses lost his temper again this morning I'd be back in hospital. He hadn't mentioned Lebow, the lawyer, or why that name was tacked to Kate's torture board, but I didn't ask; it would do him no good to learn that I had already been in his basement. I'd have

Huck look for that connection later. If Gabriel Lebow's grandfather had defended Mikey Bartollo, had helped him make bail, then I was back chest-deep in either an inexplicable coincidence, or something worse.

Moses interrupted my thoughts. 'The next morning, I made breakfast: eggs, pancakes, bacon, coffee, juice, the works. I wanted to find my wife again, somewhere on the other side of God's cruel looking-glass. I hoped she'd be – if not happy, salvageable. I was ready to spend the rest of my life helping her deal with what had happened to Lauren, to us, to Mikey Bartollo.'

I said, 'Breakfast is a good place to start, Moses. I often bring Jenny a couple of crullers after I've screwed up.'

'And it worked.' He perked up, his eyes bright despite the redness and swelling. 'Kate had a couple of pancakes and a few slices of bacon and said, "Let's go to Italy." Just like that! I had eight dollars to my name, but her family was loaded, and they'd left a ton of money for Lauren's college fund, a twenty-one-year-old trust fund, car fund, house fund, you name it. Kate showered, put on a nice dress, made her face up, arranged for a semester off from her classes at Monmouth County Community College and drove to the bank while I scrubbed down a basement she would never again enter as long as we lived in that house.'

'Was that when you learned Italian?'

'*Esatto!*' For a brief moment he was back on the porch at the Warren & Monmouth, ordering steak and eggs for breakfast. 'But I also learned guilt and penance and redemption – there's no better place for a Christian to deal with guilt than Rome.'

How about a honeymoon suite in a Spring Lake hotel?

'I've never been to Italy,' I said, 'but I do have a friend, a Jewish friend, who claims that redemption begins only after the fable ends.'

Moses laced his fingers behind his head. 'He's right: the hero at the end of the story never really gains redemption; he maybe gains a *measure* of redemption, enough to motivate him to get off his ass.'

'Real redemption is a longer road.'

'Don't you know it, Detective Doyle?'

'I do,' I said.

Moses pushed his chair back, stood. 'Sailor, I read about you this past summer, saw your interview on television. What you did down there in Richmond strikes me as heroic. I know you disagree, but you're a person of decent character—'

'Moses, I—'

'Please, let me finish.' He moved shakily to the window and let the curtains billow against his outstretched fingers. 'I've told you enough today to get myself locked up for the rest of my life. As you decide what to do with my confession I hope you'll believe that I have struggled to atone for the decisions Kate and I made that winter. The guilt and self-loathing permeate my dreams most every night. I've not dated nor remarried, nor have I moved away, because I want to be reminded – I *need* to be reminded, every day – of what happened here.'

'I'm not going to tell anyone any of this,' I said, stopping him. 'You were parents. You found the man who'd killed your daughter, and you exacted a vengeance most parents would find enviable. Do I agree that was the right choice? No – but with two healthy, happy kids living in my house, I won't judge you either.'

'I appreciate it.' He shook my hand. 'But now I should be going. Sorry to have broken in this morning; please pass along my best to your family.' His urbane, rich-guy exterior returned. Further discussion would have to wait until our next meeting.

'You all right to walk home?' I asked, escorting him to the door.

'I am, thanks,' and he left, strolling east on Twelfth with his hands in his pockets, his face turned to the breeze.

I ran for the phone, called Jenny, and told her I'd fallen down the steps at the boardwalk; that I had been in the hospital half the night. She wanted to come home right away, but I told her not to worry; I'd be on the couch all day, watching college football. She never asked if I'd been drunk, stoned, chasing women, any of it – just genuine concern, then a healthy dose of mockery when she realised I was all right.

'But surgery, Sailor? Do you really want to do that here?'

'From what the doctor told me last night, it's a simple procedure. If you like, we can have it done up in Freehold, at Centra State. I can't remember how many orthopaedic procedures I had done there as a kid. You know: football, baseball, arrow catching, the works.'

She didn't sound convinced. 'All right, but stay on the couch today. Don't do anything. We'll figure all this out tomorrow. I'll get the kids packed up after breakfast.'

'I should've come with you.' I sat gingerly on the sofa, a mountain of pillows behind me. 'It would've been more fun.'

'Your loss, Navy boy,' she teased. 'We could have gone a couple of rounds in my old bed, pretended we were back in high school.'

'I didn't know you in high school, Nutsy.'

'Oh, right, that was someone else.'

'Bitch.'

'Cripple.'

'I love you.'

'Prove it tomorrow, Sailor.'

'I will,' I said, 'but you'll have to be on top. I'm not too mobile.'

She hesitated a second too long, and I filled in the blank for her. 'No, nothing, Jenny, I wouldn't let them give me anything. I've got a prescription for Ambien, but only a week's worth. It's just Ibuprofen, a lot of it to take the swelling down before Tuesday.'

I could hear the relief in her voice. 'Okay. Well, take the Ambien and sleep. That's a good idea. We'll see you tomorrow.'

'Kids okay?'

'Fine,' Jenny said. 'Ben's been chasing ducks around the pond for twenty-four hours, but Dad hasn't let him out of his sight since we got here. They even had a camp-out on the bedroom floor. He's going to sleep for three days when we're gone.'

'Great,' I said. 'Tell everyone hello. Sorry I'm missing the duck hunt.'

'I'll call you later.'

She clicked off and I dialled Huck's cell. His voicemail picked up: *Hello, you've reached Huck Greeley at Huck Greeley International Enterprises. If you're a venture capitalist or an investor leave your contact details after the tone. If you're one of my daughters, leave me a message. If you're Cameron Diaz, I'll be right over.*

The phone beeped; I spoke quickly: 'Huck, it's Sailor. Fall of 1993,

Ocean County Court or New Jersey State Superior Court. Perp's name was Michael Bartollo, up for rape and murder of Lauren Stillman or Lauren Heston. I need to know his attorney's name; could be Isaac Lebow. Check that if you can; I want to see how and why this shithead made bail on a rape-and-murder charge. What the hell's this guy doing getting bail? And how did he come up with the bond? Got it? Dig for me in NCIC, LInX or CORIS if you can bum a login off one of the probation officers you pretend you're not seducing. I'll be around all day. I've got some research to—'

The line beeped again, cutting me off. I hated that – I never knew if the whole message had got through, or if it had got lost between me and some satellite floating over Uruguay. 'Shit.' I looked at the phone as if it might tell me what to do. 'Ah, whatever.' I flipped it off and tossed it on the coffee table. 'Okay, what's next?' I closed my eyes, thinking back over everything Moses said. *It's too much right now. Just get some Ibuprofen, 600 milligrams to start, and then walk down to the library. That'll hurt, but what the hell. It'll give you time to think.*

On Ocean Avenue headed south, my arm in a sling. Press PLAY, REWIND, PLAY, REWIND on Moses: lots of big pieces fell into place, but not all; there's still too much scribbled in the margins on this one: a dead pig; half-eaten lobsters in the yard; a dead surfer, and now a dead gang-banger, Blade – Christ, what a stupid frigging name. Hardass Hanley. Gabriel Lebow – that one scares me; that's too coincidental. If Bartollo's lawyer was that kid's grandfather and he's scratching a lunatic's pattern into a big old tree on Cameron Drive, the same pattern on Auntie Carla's pigpen, on the Seiberts' lobster tank, on Landon's surfboard . . . I didn't even see that one, but I'd bet a year of my life they're a dead ringer.

And greasepaint. On Lebow, on the Cape Cod place over on C Street, on the mansion with the bag of shit on the lawn, on Ed's cruiser last night . . . and on Ben's window.

Scratches – claw marks; that's what they are, Sailor. And missing pigs, lobsters, surfers, gangstas . . . and Blade, dead two minutes after kicking me in the guts. He crosses the street, probably at a full sprint, and gets his head caved in . . . no other bruises on him. Dead.

Could a bad guy get in, Daddy?

Yes, Ben, a bad guy could get in.

I wonder whether Moses glared off the mound like he does in that photo hanging on the wall of his room – prison, whatever the hell that place is. I mean, Jenny and I have been to some hotels in the past ten years, but we've never brought along posters of ourselves.

Of course, we don't have posters of ourselves.

Scratches. Greasepaint. Dead meth pushers. Oil barons. Inuit salt-miners. Environmental lobbyists. Dead surfers. A suicidal history teacher. And a minor league baseball pitcher.

It all makes perfect frigging sense.

The walk to Spring Lake was painful, but thankfully uneventful. I didn't spot any telltale tags scraped into high-end sports cars, or have to duck flying bags of shit, or have to fight my way out of any crack dens. The Tudor-style library hosted Saturday story-time for kids and the parking lot was overflowing with honking great Yukons and gas-guzzling Sequoias. A limousine waited half on and half off the lawn. I pushed aside a colourful bouquet of spritely helium balloons as a clown in a lively version of the same greasepaint that Lebow wore to his suicide handed me a balloon animal– it might have been a hippo or an aardvark. Miss Quadrafocals from the British Museum stood her post behind the circulation desk.

While the crowd in the Children's Room rivalled the masses at a U2 concert, the main floor sported only a dusting of bored-looking dads dressed smart casual. A few of them looked at me with my greasy hair, my arm in a sling and my ribs taped up like a mummy, but I didn't care. There was an open cubicle and I ducked into it.

I had no idea what the main sources of news were for Ottawa, Ontario in the mid-1970s so I started in Google, and two clicks led me to the *Ottawa Journal*. I typed a few key words into the search engine, hoping I might be able to dig up forty-year-old pieces directly from the home page, but the archive was only ten years old.

'Shit,' I murmured, too loudly, and looked around for Miss Quadrafocals. 'This isn't going to help.' I scrolled over the home page, looking for contact details for the paper's archivist, pasted her address into a message and typed a few brief lines about conducting research for the Virginia State Police and needing access – or at least a bit of assistance – digging up news from the mid-1970s. It didn't sound too convincing, but what the hell, I was typing one-handed. I didn't have time to be eloquent. With a silent Hail Mary, I clicked SEND.

At the circulation desk, Miss Quadrafocals explained that because I was from Belmar and not Spring Lake, I'd have to invest in a four-million-dollar mansion within the town limits to qualify for a library card and unlimited printer access – or I could pay ten cents a page like any other out-of-town loser. Since I was four million dollars short (minus the eleven dollars in my pocket), I opted for the payment package. I silently promised to print only critical pages; dimes were hard to come by for a jackass who'd spent nearly fifty dollars getting drunk in Manhattan the previous day. I figured I'd email any useful links to myself and read them cover-to-cover on Jenny's laptop when she got home. That'd show the greedy misers.

A roar of approval resounded from the Children's Room, clearly pissing off Quadrafocals.

'Sounds like the hero won,' I said, stealing a miniature golf pencil from a box on her desk.

She scowled, grim-faced, at the Children's Room and said, 'Sometimes the dragon wins.' She fingered a silver brooch with a wine-coloured stone that held a pretentious scarf in place around her narrow neck.

I laughed despite my aching ribs and mangled shoulder; I hadn't expected Miss Quadrafocals to be funny. 'I'm sure he does.'

I wandered back to my computer and opened the *Ottawa Journal* homepage again, looking now for Charles Dunning's death. A few articles and an obituary from the summer of 1994 described Dunning's work preserving vast tracts of Canadian territory as wildlife sanctuaries and parks. As far as I knew, northern Canada wasn't on many too many shortlists for urban development, so I had no idea why he was such a hero – saving it didn't strike me as all that challenging a job.

You want to impress me, sort out a game preserve in southeast DC. Here pheasant, pheasant, pheasant . . .

Details of Dunning's death were sketchy; he'd flown his seaplane up to King James Island, filing his flight-plan with Nanisivik Airport near Arctic Bay. He'd been flying around the area for years, and he'd found a suitable place to land. On this occasion he intended to moor his plane, then kayak to shore. He'd planned to spend five days exploring the island. When he failed to make contact with Nanisivik, the air-traffic controller contacted Dunning's office in New York City. After three days with still no word from Dunning, Nordic Rescue alerted the Canadian Coast Guard, but a violent storm kept them from landing a helicopter on the windswept plain for another four days. Satellite photos showed what was left of Dunning's camp, but his plane had disappeared. The Coast Guard speculated that it had either sunk or crashed, probably as Dunning tried to escape the storm.

The Directors of Nordic Rescue begged the Canadian government to conduct a thorough search of the island, but without Dunning's plane, there was little hope of recovering the body, so they contracted a Nunavut seaplane pilot to fly over the island for several days, hoping their CEO might manage to signal from the ground with a fire, rock formation, pistol or flare gun. But a cold front cut the search effort short and Dunning was listed as missing, feared dead, lost for ever in the waters off his greatest political victory.

I sprang for the sixty cents and printed Dunning's one-page obituary and an article on a Danish cargo ship that had foundered in the waters off Devon Island in 1981. Then I clicked back to Google to search for the string of Tahitian black pearls once given to Prime Minister Baldwin's wife as a diplomatic gift, and now – I firmly believed – gathered dust in a jewellery store not three blocks away.

I had to wade through about sixty thousand websites immortalising Johnny Depp in that ridiculous get-up he wore in all fifty-four of those pirate movies – I'd forgotten his ship was called the *Black Pearl*. After twenty minutes of searching, I gave up, emailed a couple of worthwhile links to myself, and clicked the Internet closed.

Before quitting, I checked my email one last time, just out of habit. Surprisingly, I had a message from an archivist at the *Ottawa Journal*: g.bailey@ottawanews.net had replied not five minutes after I'd contacted the paper – on a Saturday afternoon, too.

That's dedication to forty-year-old news: Miss Quadrafocals would be proud!

I opened the email and read:

> *Dear Detective Doyle,*
>
> *If you fax a copy of your police credentials to my attention at the Ottawa Journal, I will be happy to provide you with a 24-hour login/ password to our comprehensive archives. You should be able to find what you're looking for there. The paper's search engine is fairly self-explanatory; however, feel free to contact me with any questions. I am happy to assist with your investigation.*
>
> *Best wishes,*
> *Gretchen Bailey, Assistant Archivist*
> *Ottawa Journal*

She'd listed fax and phone numbers as well, in case the newspaper's website failed to answer my questions. I rose to beg Miss Quadrafocals' permission to use the library's fax machine and was halfway to her desk before I remembered that Captain Fezzamo had confiscated my badge when he'd placed me on administrative leave.

'Fuck,' I hissed, covering the obscenity with the back of my hand.

Miss Quadrafocals glared at me over her glasses as if to ask, *What now?*

'Sorry.' I raised my hands in surrender. 'Nothing.'

She returned to frowning towards the Children's Room and the screeching sound of balloon animals being wrestled to death.

I clicked REPLY, and wrote:

> *Ms Bailey,*
>
> *Thank you for your quick reply. I will ask my supervisor, Sergeant Harold Greeley, to fax his ID to you a.s.a.p. He's spearheading this investigation for our Criminal Investigation Division.*
>
> *I appreciate your assistance.*
> *Detective Samuel Doyle*
> *VASP*

I was beginning to lose count of the number of times I'd used Huck's name this week. When he wasn't writing research articles connecting Charles Dunning to King James Island, he was supervising a phantom investigation into a seventeen-year-old death fifteen hundred miles outside his jurisdiction. Lovely.

I called Huck, left a message for him to check his email and find a fax machine on a Saturday afternoon. Maybe they'd have one behind whatever bar he was propping up while he watched college football. I forwarded the email from Gretchen Bailey to him, then logged out and tried to stretch my leg against a rack of non-fiction.

Blood throbbed through the damaged tissue in my arm, and I swallowed another 600 milligrams of Ibuprofen. I'd have burned Atlanta for a hit of OxyContin, but I tried to shake the craving. As sweat dampened my face and body I held on to the newel post of the spiral staircase with my good hand, no longer fighting the tunnel vision, the yellow sunbursts, the shortness of breath.

'Screw this,' I whispered, my stomach already cramping around the Ibuprofen. 'No puking, Sailor: you *cannot* hurl in the public frigging library.' I gave a moment's serious consideration to breaking into the first mansion I passed – they'd have OxyCodone in their medicine cabinet. Half the homes in America had pills for skittling; these rich bastards would hand round handfuls like mixed nuts.

Feeling dizzy, I decided to wait in the men's room. I shouldn't have walked down here; that'd been my mistake – all that bullshit about pain and redemption was exactly that: bullshit. To make myself feel better I silently vowed to bust Moses one right in the snout the next time he started with any of his uptight, philosophical hooey.

Using the stacks for support, I staggered towards the foyer and the restrooms. As I passed the newspaper rack I grabbed the *Asbury Park Press* – I had no intention of reading it; I just didn't want Miss Quadrafocals getting suspicious. I'd rather look like a guy who had to drop a significant package than a guy craving pharmaceuticals.

The restroom was cold. I dropped my pants awkwardly with one hand – with no frigging clue how I'd get them back up again – and sat on the toilet seat, waiting for my temperature to drop. Sweat stained my bandages and the sling around my neck felt like a hangman's noose. I squeezed my eyes shut and breathed in through my nose and out my mouth, wincing, trying to ride out the storm as I emptied my bowels in a grim rush.

When my vision cleared, I noticed the front page of the paper: Jeremy Landon's body, missing since Monday, had been carried all the way south beyond Sea Girt by Tuesday's storm. My breathing slowed as I read the few details the *Press* had been able to wrangle out of the ME's office. The Monmouth County Medical Examiner reported that Landon had injuries consistent with a boating accident, and evidence of posthumous contact with bluefish or small sharks. Jenny had probably tossed last Saturday's paper by now but I would have bet a month's salary that the pattern of scratches inside Auntie Carla's pigpen would match those crisscrossing the missing surfer's body.

The stall stank like a season in Hell and I worried that I'd not be able to clean myself up and get dressed without dropping my gun, my phone or my waning dignity into the toilet.

Fifteen minutes later I emerged red-faced from the men's room, replaced the newspaper in the rack and hurried outside. Thankfully the wind had picked up; it chilled my flushed skin and helped to dry my sweaty clothes. Pain thudded steadily at my temples: I'd beaten back another craving, but I felt worn to the nub with the effort.

I thought about getting a cab, but I shook the feeling off, bought a two-dollar bottle of water, drank deeply and started for home. My legs felt numb, almost disconnected, but they managed to keep me upright as I trudged past Lake Como and down the slight incline to the Twentieth Street boardwalk entrance, where I had allegedly fallen backwards down the stairs. As I crossed into Belmar I gave myself better odds of making it home in one piece, and with the rhythm of the wind and the waves setting the tempo for my slow but inexorable journey, I let my mind drift again.

Katherine Stillman – Mama Bear – chained Mikey Bartollo to the wall, yanked his teeth out, broke his bones, cut off his ears and tortured him with photos of his own mother coming down the stairs after Mass. No pictures there the other night, but I'd bet she wore black, even all those years later. Italian women are like that.

'—*stop for just a moment and ask yourself the question: what would you*

*do if you had your hands on the man who poisoned – defiled, murdered –
your daughter, your baby girl, what would you do, Sailor? Would you cut
his toes off, his fingers, his cock . . . Would you starve him, drug him, beat
him nightly with a chain? Would you make tape recordings of him crying for
his mother, begging for his life? And would you listen to those tapes as you
drove around in your car? Would you cut off his pinkie and wear it on a
string around your neck for the weekend?'*

*What would I do? What would Jenny do? Would we really keep him
tied up all that time, exacting our vengeance one torn fingernail at a time?*

*No, that's too barbaric, primitive, whatever. Or is it? Could it be worse?
What about burning him, chopping off, cooking and eating bits of him while
he watched?*

Nah, not us: just shoot the bastard, right?

While my imagination distracted the pain receptors in my brain,
my diligence carried the rest of me home. At Twelfth and A I lit
a celebratory cigarette and damned near reinjured my shoulder as I
waved a high-five to the haunted Cape Cod on C Street.

Inside, I tossed the keys on the kitchen table, dug in the fridge for
a Diet Coke and guzzled half on my way to the bedroom. I needed a
clean shirt and wanted to rinse out my sweaty sling, even if it meant
sitting immobile on the sofa watching college football while the dryer
tumbled for half an hour. I didn't really care who was playing. I'd
made it home, and still had plenty of time to get—

—white greasepaint, thick and fresh, marked Ben's bedroom window in a crooked stripe, like a slash. I pulled up, mid-stride, the throb
in my arm and forehead the only evidence I was still alive.

'Ah, no,' I murmured, drawing the .357 from my waistband, 'not
today, not already. *Please.*' Scarcely thinking, I went out front, keeping
the gun hidden, and moved tentatively around the house. Whoever
had jumped the O'Mearas' fence to tag my house with stage make-
up had crushed the leaves under the old pear tree. The wind off the
water freshened, rustling the branches, but not shifting the cloud of
putrefaction from the rotting lobsters which swaddled the back yard.

Jesus, those fuckers stink. I inched towards the fence, listening.

Nothing moved, yet something was there, a presence. Near the
corner where I'd fallen, drunk, into the pile of lobsters, the stench

permeated everything; my skin would reek of rotten crustacean until I'd scrubbed every inch in the shower.

Now invisible from the street, I lifted Uncle Paul's heavy revolver, ready to fire should Lebow, a gargoyle, a British oil prospector, Puff the Magic Dragon, whoever – *whatever* – came over the fence after me. 'You there, Gabriel?' I called, bracing myself for another assault by Pink Floyd backwards, wailing children backwards, maybe even a bit of that *Magic Flute* backwards.

But he didn't sing to me; instead Gabriel or whoever hid behind the fence—

I can feel you there, you cocksucker, I can feel your weight on the grass.

—scraped a fingernail – a *claw* – over the planks of the O'Mearas' fence. The scraping continued, skittering over my head to the top of the fence and back down again, dragging a ragged tear through the weather-beaten planks—

I tried running for Twelfth Avenue; I could climb the short rise, see over the fence and maybe even get off a shot before the Belmar Police and County Psych showed up to carry me off, safe inside a made-to-measure straitjacket. I huffed my way up to the sidewalk and craned my neck, straining to see into the O'Mearas' yard.

What I saw about undid me – and while Mr and Mrs O'Meara would probably call the city PD to report a vandal, no one else would realise what had been clawed into the wood, no one but me. There, above a stinking pile of decomposing lobsters, someone had scratched a half-moon shape over an oval. Ten million people could look at it and not recognise it, but I did, in an eyeblink. I was looking at a rough map of King James Island, just like the one Emmit LeFevbre had drawn, then crumpled up and tossed into his bin at Nordic Rescue.

Whoever had scratched the map was gone.

That night, I skipped the Ambien and slept on the sofa in the living room. Propped up with pillows to accommodate my shoulder, I cradled the .357 beneath Ben's Spider-Man blanket and watched the hallway. I kept the front door, my only exit, safe behind me. The wind blew hard all night, sweeping a stormy front down from the northeast.

SUNDAY

A Camp out

Giants Win. Jets Lose.

Yellow: *Okay, I can almost do this.*

Morning found me as stiff and crooked as a ninety-year-old man. I hadn't slept well: fear and pain can be inspirational motivators when I need to stay awake. I found a carton of orange juice in the fridge and guzzled down the day's first dose of Ibuprofen. The icy juice chilled my bones and a false sense of wellness suffused my body. As I tossed the carton towards our recycling bin I caught a whiff of myself and considered unwrapping long enough for a shower, but after only a few seconds searching for the end of the tape around my midsection I gave up.

'Screw it.' I replaced the .357 in my belt. 'Jenny'll help me get it figured out when she gets home. No sense tempting the fates now – fall and break another bone, have Lebow show up while I'm naked. Ain't worth it.'

I checked Ben's room to be sure no one had turned up overnight, but there were no more stripes on his window, so I brewed a pot of coffee, found the pages I'd printed on the Danish ship and settled myself at the kitchen table.

Captain Georg van Heltzel and his ship, the *Kanal Fugle*, headed west through the Northwest Passage in late April 1981, carrying German trucks to Nome, Alaska. The ship encountered powerful headwinds from the west-northwest just as van Heltzel adjusted their course north into a deep-water channel around King James Island.

Twenty-five-foot waves battered the port rail for nearly two hours as she clawed her way north through unforgiving waters, but van Heltzel had burned too much diesel keeping his ship off the headwind, and turning west, into the wind, would swamp him. Instead, he decided to seek refuge in the lee of a large promontory jutting from the southeast corner of Devon Island, only twenty miles away; the charts showed ample depth for the *Kanal Fugle*, and a southeasterly tide would help to slow the heavy cargo ship.

But when van Heltzel turned the *Kanal Fugle* northeast, her exposed beam took the brunt of the storm, the cargo shifted and fifteen two-ton trucks broke free from their moorings and slammed into the starboard bulkhead like a tidal wave. The *Kanal Fugle* rolled onto her side and foundered.

Of the fifteen crew on board, eleven made for Devon Island in two lifeboats, as the storm raged in the east like a mythological nightmare. The remaining four, including Captain van Heltzel, were last seen struggling to start their own lifeboat's engine; they were carried east and then south with the tide, rushing past King James with no way to stop.

The eleven crew members who did reach Devon Island survived, finding shelter until a Canadian Navy chopper was able to airlift them to the cruiser waiting out the storm near Spence Bay.

The other four men were never found, though the remains of their lifeboat washed up on a rocky shore on the northeast edge of King James. The ship's log, locked in a watertight box, was recovered from the wreckage. Its final entry, dated April 8 at 4:12 a.m., noted that with land in sight and the boat's motor finally operational, Georg van Heltzel had ordered his men to make for King James, where they hoped to signal any rescue plane or ship responding to the mayday van Heltzel had sent before relinquishing the *Kanal Fugle* to the Arctic waters.

I set the pages aside. *I'll never complain about my job again.*

Someone knocked, and I figured it wouldn't be Lebow; that prick was planning to come in by the window. I pushed myself onto my feet, swearing, and staggered, stoop-shouldered, for the door.

Ed Hess waved at me through the window. 'Good morning, Detective Doyle,' he said as I let him in.

'Good morning – and what brings you to my door this fine morning?'

'Oh, nothin' much.' He glanced at the coffee-maker.

'Help yourself,' I said, left the door open and cracked open the living room window: the perfect smoker's lounge. I lit a cigarette and offered the pack to Ed, who was stirring six sugars into his mug. He poured in enough milk to make a frappe and shook his head. 'No thanks,' he said.

I blew smoke into the cross-breeze and as it roiled out the front door I watched it go, wishing I had paid attention in physics class. 'How're you doing, Ed? I don't think I ever thanked you for saving my neck the other night.'

'Don't mention it.' Ed was wearing his gun, but he wasn't in uniform; I guessed he was either just coming on duty or just heading home. 'How're you doing? Feeling all right? All put back together?'

'I've got to have more surgery,' I said glumly. I flicked ash into my empty mug. 'I guess I knew I'd have to after Jenny hauled me out of the ocean last weekend, but this clinches it. No chance of skipping out now.'

'Sorry to hear that,' he said. 'Shoulder surgery's a bitch.' He rotated his own muscular arm as if remembering weeks of painful physiotherapy. His chair creaked beneath him; I worried that it might collapse. Ben had been the largest person to sit there in years. 'Otherwise, you feeling better?'

'Not bad,' I lied. 'So what can I do for you, Ed?'

'Nothin' much,' he said again, 'but d'you mind telling me what you were doing up there the other night?'

'You wouldn't believe me.'

'With an unregistered .357 big enough to bring down a pterodactyl?'

'You wouldn't believe me.'

'Try me.'

I took a deep drag on my cigarette, pretending I needed a second to decide whether or not to tell him the truth. Smoothly, I lied. 'I noticed that place the other night when we were up there with Hodges and the Asbury Park SWAT guys. I saw that Christmas tree in the window, so it was obviously abandoned, maybe those North Side thugs were using it for their meth lounge, brothel, whatever – who knows?'

I stopped and looked at my shoes, then looked Hess in the eye. 'I'm not sure how much Hodges told you, but I've been kind of at outs with my captain, my lieutenant, my wife, shit, most everyone important in my life these days. I thought – yeah, I know it was dumb, but I might sneak in there and earn another couple of points for myself, my career, whatever reputation I have left as a cop.'

'Bullshit.' Ed didn't hesitate.

'No bullshit.' I held the eye contact and stared Ed down. 'I knew there was at least one house between the Christmas tree place and the meth kitchen, where the old lady with the little dog lived.'

'Why the gun?'

'Did you go up there without one?'

'Good point,' he conceded, 'but why didn't you tell Hodges?'

'You think she would have let me go on my own?'

'No.' His skin had been tanned for so long it looked permanently dyed, the colour of dirty pennies. 'No, I guess not. Knowing her, she'd have gone herself—'

'—or sent the Seventh Cavalry,' I added.

'Or that.' He finished his coffee and stood. 'You need anything, Detective?'

A puzzle piece clicked into place. 'She sent you today, didn't she?'

Abashed, he glanced down at my notes, scattered about the table.

'She did, damnit,' I said. 'I wonder – I can't figure it— Wait, of course, of frigging course!'

'What?' Ed pretended he didn't get it.

'You don't work for the county!' I pointed up at him with my good hand. 'You work for Spring Lake, you're a townie. You and she are buddies from way back, so she can ask you to do just about anything, and she doesn't have to write it down, or report it. If *she* came in here this morning and asked me what the hell I was doing in Asbury Park the other night, she'd have—'

He interrupted, 'She'd have to note anything you told her in Tejon Butler's murder book, perhaps even drag your ass in on suspicion of murdering the very douche-bag who'd just broken your ribs with his size 11 Ali Haji-Sheikhs.'

I dropped my cigarette in the mug and made a mental note to get

388

rid of it before Jenny got home. 'Right. Clever girl, that Hodges.'

'She is,' Ed agreed.

'Where is she? Outside?'

'Just down the block, sitting in my cruiser. I'm on eleven-to-seven today. We had breakfast and tried to figure out what you were up to – I didn't have the first idea – I mean, I'd seen you get on the train from Asbury. I didn't follow you—'

'I went to the city,' I confessed, 'visiting a friend – nothing connected to the North Side Playaz.'

'Whatever; I hung around the train station until you got back, then followed you in the cab.'

'And watched me break into 1720 Blake Street.'

He sat back down. 'I had some trouble following you up there; you were sneaking all over the place, then I finally saw you cross the road beyond the streetlights, where it was dark. I actually figured you were headed south to the Keys – and then I noticed the penlight in the window at 1720.'

'Damn,' I said with a laugh, 'and there was me thinking I'd been all James Bond-sneaky.'

'I almost missed it,' he admitted, 'but two seconds earlier Jackass 1 and Jackass 2 pulled up in an Escalade big enough to carry *all* the Green Bay Packers.'

I frowned. 'Yeah, I'd seen it at the Quick-Mart on Fourth.'

'Anyway,' Ed went on, 'either they saw your light, or they're the dumbest thugs in North America, because they went in as if they owned the place – hey, they don't own the place, do they?'

'Not that I know of.'

'Whew!' He feigned relief. 'That's good – if they did I'd be in a world of trouble in civil court.'

'Do go on, please.'

'There's nothing to tell, Detective: they went in; I waited a couple of seconds, didn't see your dead body get tossed onto the lawn and figured I'd better hustle in there to help you out.'

I said, 'Good thing you weren't at that shopping mall.'

'Good thing.'

'So what does she want?' I nodded towards the street.

Ed shuffled the papers around on the table, not really looking at them. 'I'm pretty sure she'd be happy to know that you're going to be here today, on that couch, watching the Jets game, and enjoying whatever meds that seventeen-year-old doctor prescribed you the other night.'

'I'm glad to be able to make her happy,' I said. 'He *was* young; wasn't he?'

'I have T-shirts older than that kid,' he said sadly.

I laughed, and my ribs reminded me laughing was off the menu. 'Stop, Ed – damn, you're going to have to take me back to Jersey Shore Med.'

'I'm not kidding!' He threw his hands in the air. 'I've got T-shirts from the 1977 Boston Marathon, one from the Reagan campaign in 1980, and a victory T-shirt from the Lake Placid Olympics when the US beat the Soviets in hockey!'

I flicked my lighter on, played with the flame. 'So what's the news on RJ? Has he rolled over yet? Or is Detective Hodges waterboarding him for a confession?'

Ed said, 'Nah, this one's going to be a headache. The Public Defenders' Office has sent in some kid with a head full of law-school knowledge and about as much experience as the new socks I'm wearing. He's already on the news, right on the goddamned courthouse steps, talking up RJ as if the kid's really a hero; he's looking for his fifteen minutes big time. Did you see it?'

He went on, 'I haven't seen anyone this in love with the spotlight since William Kunstler died. NAACP, ACLU, the Rainbow Coalition – none of them want anything to do with RJ. The whole world seems to understand that he's a cold-blooded killer peddling lethal ice to middle-school kids, and yet the Monmouth County Public Defenders' Office manages to find the one idealistic douche-bag out there hoping to save black America, starting with Roland James Mercer, a black American that even black America wishes would go away for ever.'

'Not anyone Jesse Jackson's inviting over for tea?'

'There are guys in the state lock-up in no hurry to spend quality time with RJ.'

'But the extremists—'

'Exactly,' Ed said, 'RJ's lawyer's either too idealistic or too god-damned stupid to realise that if you want to change the world, you've gotta have at least a couple of redeeming qualities, and RJ's got a grand total of nothing in his favour.'

'But if you keep calling him a hero on television—'

'—Americans will believe you, because the American media never lies to Americans with an IQ in the eighties.'

'Which is most of us.'

'Speak for yourself, dummy; I'm a genius.' He slid his chair back; I waited for it to come apart. 'In case you hadn't noticed.'

'I had noticed, Ed: clearly, your unparallelled wisdom is what keeps you punching in eleven-to-seven as the town fuzz.'

'Fifty-two-five a year, plus my Coastie retirement.'

'Just until your career as an underwear model takes off, right? That is – if Ted Kennedy underpants ever catch on.'

'Yankees, Doyle; I'm gonna play for the Yankees.'

'Good luck with that.'

'Stay put today.' He started out.

I followed him. 'Okay. Tell Hodges I won't go anywhere.'

He opened the door for himself. 'Call Spring Lake PD if you need anything – popcorn, ice cream, Cameron Diaz, whatever.'

'She in town?'

'No,' he said, 'but the popcorn's pretty good.'

'Thanks again, Ed,' I said, and watched him shuffle down the sidewalk, his hands buried deep in his jacket pockets. He looked un-nervingly like Moses.

With the door closed behind me, I sniffed the air. A faint vestige of cigarette smoke hung like a bad memory. I chucked the rest of the coffee and the butt I'd already smoked and promised myself I would smoke outside from now on. I couldn't wait to see Jenny, and the kids. Being broken – now badly broken – had moulded those needs into tangible shape.

I *had* to behave myself ...

Just as soon as I figured out what was going on with Gabriel Lebow, Moses Heston and King James Island, I'd start behaving myself.

I switched on *New Jersey News*, hoping for an update on Jeremy Landon, RJ's fame-hungry lawyer or Tejon 'Blade' Butler's murder; instead I got a pre-game show for the Jets. I hiked the volume up and went to the kitchen, thinking about brunch.

I grabbed a sponge and turned to wipe down the table. My papers, the article on the *Kanal Fugle* and the crazy scribbles I'd drawn from the Canadian Arctic south to Ottawa and down to Asbury Park had been stacked neatly.

Ed Hess.

I wondered if he'd read them.

Why would he? They don't seem to mean anything; they're just scribbles, names he doesn't know with places he doesn't know. What would Ed care, Ed, in his thirty-year-old T-shirt from the US–Soviet hockey game, he wouldn't give a shit.

Right?

I ate a couple of eggs with toast, and drank funny-tasting water from the tap. I didn't need more coffee. With my second glass I took a hit of Ambien, just to see if it'd work during the day. Outside, I smoked a cigarette that had almost no taste. I blamed the wind whipping off the water. The Sunday edition of the *Asbury Park Press* waited in the driveway, but I left it for later. As the first tendrils of Ambien blurred my vision and tugged at my eyelids I decided it most certainly did work during the day and I headed inside to crash on the couch. With the TV muted and Uncle Paul's .357 beside me, I watched silent high-lights of last week's Jets game. Chilly air blew through the living room and I wondered for a moment if Hodges and Hess were still staked out on Twelfth. But I didn't really care; I wasn't going anywhere – and if Lebow showed up looking for me, I'd welcome their help.

Sleep took me quickly.

I woke to the visceral shriek of the phone. It'd been so long since I'd heard an actual phone ring, as opposed to buzzing, chirping, giggling, or playing the opening bars of Beethoven's *Fifth* that I nearly rolled off the couch.

'Holy cats!' I tried to shout, but didn't have the strength. 'What the hell?' I blinked my vision clear and shook cobwebs from my brain as the phone continued to howl at me from its perch on the kitchen wall.

'Hello!'

'Damn, sweetie, you don't need to yell.' It was Jenny, in the car. 'You all right?'

'What? Hey, honey,' I tried to sound lucid, pleasant, 'where are you guys? What time is it?'

Mental note: do not take Ambien during the day. Like melatonin, my pink ass! That shit ought to have a kick-stand.

'Oh, did I wake you, Sailor? Sorry – Ben wanted to tell you about the ducks, and I needed to see if you'd had a chance to go grocery shopping.' In the background, Ben sang to Anna.

'Why are you calling on this line?'

'I tried your cell a few times but you didn't answer.'

'I think it's down the hall. I'll go get it.'

'Anyway, did you go grocery shopping?'

'Did I go grocery shopping? Me? Jenny, I don't have a car.'

'I thought you might have walked, you know, got some exercise.'

'My arm's in a sling and my ribs are taped up like a mummy and I'm waiting for you to get home so I can get into the bathtub without crying for my mother.'

'Oh, sweetie, I'm sorry. I guess I didn't realise it was all that bad. You should have said something. We could have come home yesterday.'

'I'm okay,' I said, 'just tired. But no, I didn't have a chance to get groceries.'

'What do we need?' I heard her shush Ben: *I can't hear Daddy, buddy.*

I said, 'I don't have any idea what we need, Jenny.' I looked around the kitchen, as if something might come to mind. 'Orange juice,' I said finally. 'I finished the orange juice.'

'That's it? No other food groups?' Jenny was in a good mood. Two clean and fed kids in the car, laundry done, bags packed, and she was still in a good mood. I couldn't wait for them to get home.

I fought off another yawn. 'And meat. Lots and lots of meat. Venison, quail, pheasant, hippo, giraffe – actually, we have plenty of giraffe in the freezer – so, just the hippo and the chicken-fried hamster.'

'Look in the fruit drawer and tell me what you see.'

'What I see or what I don't see?' I opened the fridge. 'We have three oranges, a tomato and a plastic container that's either filled with chopped melon or severed body parts.'

'You know what?' She changed her mind. 'You want lobster tonight? We can splurge. I'll get potatoes and – I dunno – something green.'

That woke me up. 'Actually, Jenny, I most assuredly *don't* want lobster.'

'Why? I thought you liked lobster. What the hell, we're at the beach.'

'Get shrimp,' I suggested, trying to sound positive. 'They're like small lobsters. The full-sized versions scare me – it's too much, you know, like eating kick-ass food and killing a monster in a Japanese horror movie.'

I could see her shaking her head. 'Go back to bed, weirdo. I'll deal with the groceries. We'll see you in an hour.'

'Bye, honey.' I clicked off. The Ambien bottle sat on the table beside the printouts on King James Island and the *Kanal Fugle* disaster. I read the label: 'Not to be taken with alcohol. Marked drowsiness may occur – they ought to edit that: marked slobbering may occur, dumbass.' Then I remembered my cell phone and hobbled down to retrieve it from the bedroom. When I clicked it on, the screen blinked: THREE MISSED CALLS.

The first was from Ben: *Daddy! We're coming home, but, Daddy, I have to tell you about the ducks at Granpa's pond! They were—*

I pressed SAVE; I'd listen to it later when I could appreciate it.

The second was from Jenny: *Good morning, sweetie. We're on our way, but I wanted to ask if you'd had a chance to walk out to the—*

I hit DELETE.

The third call was from Huck: *Hey, kemosabe, call me back. I've got news for you on Mikey Bartollo and Isaac Lebow, interesting relationship, that one. Maybe you can shed some light on it? I'm sorry if I called you crazy – you may be on to something here. I'm at CID, but hit me on the cell if you get this after one; I've got a date with a bartender for the Cowboys game.*

I pressed Huck's speed dial and he picked up immediately. 'Good morning, lazybones. Any pulse this morning?'

'Barely,' I said. 'Whaddya got on Bartollo?'

'Well, hello to you, too, Uncle Hucker – yes, I'm fine; thanks for asking—'

'Jackass!'

'So why are *you* grumpy? I'm the one at work on a Sunday morning; you're the one sprawled out on the beach reading westerns and smoking cigarettes.'

'Huck …'

He cleared his throat. 'Uh, let's see, where to start – okay, so: Mikey Bartollo, world-class loser and *cappo di tutti cappi* of Jersey Shore assholes. From Point Pleasant. His priors were so long before he fell off the radar in '94 that I damned near fell asleep while waiting for the printout. He's done it all: grand larceny, rape, malicious wounding, assault, peddling, possession, usage, conspiracy, auto theft and singing disparaging limericks in the presence of the *Torah*, you name it; it's here. What this kid was doing walking around off his leash just defies logic.'

'Go on.' I looked for a pen and settled for Ben's orange marker. 'So what's Bartollo's connection to Isaac Lebow? And how'd you get this stuff anyway?'

'I have my ways,' Huck said with a filthy little laugh.

'What's her name?'

'Margie,' he answered after a moment. 'She works for St James County – I actually met her after your little jaunt this past July. She lets me use her login.'

'That's against the law,' I said, mock-sternly.

'What law?' he defended himself. 'You show me the law and I'll follow it – well, maybe.'

'Anyway, Lebow?' I walked outside, lit a cigarette.

'This is the part I don't get, cousin. You see, Isaac Lebow was a pretty active defence attorney down there in Monmouth County, but he had no track record working with thugs or dope. Looks like his employees – mostly Jewish kids in their first year after passing the bar – were trolling the courthouse looking for paying customers to clear their school fees, but Lebow himself, he hadn't been in court with an honest-to-God street felon in twenty-five years.'

'White-collar shit?'

'Big-time Jews: rich New Yorkers living in Jersey, tax stuff, all the illegal machinations of money, those Richie Rich bastards shovelling it into their bank accounts, whether it belongs to them or not—'

'Easy there, Uncle Hucker, your prejudices are showing.'

'So what I'm trying to tell you is that Isaac Lebow had absolutely no business being in that courtroom with Mikey Bartollo. These two didn't even speak the same language – it made no frigging sense whatsoever!'

'So – what?' I was at a loss to make any sense of this. 'Lebow works a deal for bail, and then assigns Bartollo to a twenty-two-year-old first year in his office?'

'Or—?'

'Or – or what? I'm lost.'

'Or he washes his hands of the whole affair when Bartollo disappears three days after posting bond.'

'Lebow couldn't have known that Bartollo was going to get picked up.'

'Why not?' Huck said. 'He ran in some pretty powerful circles. Who knows what he might have got wind of?'

'But that implies some powerful figure wanted Bartollo gone, and for what? Killing a teenage girl on the beach?'

'The granddaughter of the Assistant Principal Secretary to Prime Minister Baldwin.'

'Nah, that was twenty years earlier and in another country; there's no way Isaac Lebow could have figured that—'

'Yes?' Huck prompted.

I started pacing across my driveway, stretching over the folded copy of the *Asbury Park Press* with each turn. 'Huck, what if Lebow knew that Bartollo was going to jump bail, or that someone was going to off him in the weeks before the trial?'

'Sounds like a New Jersey fairytale to me. All you're missing is a pregnant alcoholic teenage princess,' he said. 'Go on.'

'Lebow personally handles the arraignment, posting bond, there in his five-thousand-dollar bespoke suit. Bartollo's released, against astronomically ridiculous odds—'

'And he jumps?'

'No,' I said. 'Before he has a chance to jump—'

'He gets whacked.'

'Colourful.'

'What the hell, we're talking about New Jersey here.'

I ignored him. 'Before Bartollo disappears, gets killed, transported to Italy or Rio de Janeiro or the bottom of the deep blue sea, he is kidnapped unexpectedly—'

'—by who? Whom? Oh, wait a minute, not your boy, the baseball player, Nolan Ryan and the Planet of the Apes.'

'Martin-Moses-Heston.' I stopped, listened, waiting in my driveway for Huck to tell me I was nuts.

Huck didn't reply.

I asked, 'Who made Bartollo's bail? Who actually paid? You got it there?'

'Um, one second.' He shuffled papers. 'Here it is: one hundred and fifty thousand dollars, posted by one J.M. McMichael. No other information available.'

That couldn't be right. 'A buck fifty? Are you shitting me? He anally raped and murdered Lauren Stillman, and he got off for a *buck fifty*?'

'Hold on,' Huck interrupted. 'It says here that Lebow's argument at the arraignment was that Bartollo and Stillman were partying under the Point Pleasant boardwalk and things just got out of hand; Stillman took a bit too much smack. The butt party, Lebow suggests, was mutual.'

'That fucker.'

'It's why I never went to law school, kemosabe.'

My head swam. Wind off the water made it hard to hear, to think. 'Um, Huck, I'm not sure what—'

'You all right, cousin?'

'Who's McMichael?'

'Somehow I knew you'd ask that very question; so I did a bit of digging in the New York, New Jersey area.'

'And?'

'John McMichael is a high school history teacher in Somerville who hits his wife from time to time. James McMichael owns a plumbing company in Queens and was picked up for trying to sell coke to an undercover cop in a Manhattan bar. Jerrold Manfred McMichael was arrested at Newark Airport for trying to smuggle kiddie porn into the US from Heathrow Airport. And J. Martin McMichael works in a scuba dive shop in Wildwood and has been arrested four times: twice for drunk and disorderly, one DUI, and one driving on a suspended licence. Otherwise, the cupboard is bare.'

'Shit,' I said. 'None of them are even close.'

'You figure it's someone from out of state or a bullshit ID?'

'Dunno, Huck; you've been in a bail bondsman's office. Even with the Internet not all those guys keep the cleanest records. Someone could have come in with a bullshit ID, a fake driver's licence from another state, whatever. As long as he's paying for the bond, who cares if his ID photo is a little blurry?'

'This stinks, Sailor.'

'You know it, cousin.' Jenny's van turned from Ocean onto Twelfth Avenue. 'Hey, I gotta go. Jenny's home.'

'Good luck,' he said. 'You need me up there?'

'Maybe,' I said. 'If I do, I'll call you back. But thanks, Huck. You've helped stir plenty of mud into already muddy waters.'

'We aim to please here at Uncle Hucker's Illegal Investigations.'

'See you.'

'Peace on Earth, buddy.' He hung up.

Ben burst from the minivan. 'Daddy!' He ran at me, full tilt.

This is gonna hurt.

'Daddy, you should have seen the ducks at Grandpa's pond. They were—' He pulled up short, stopping dead in his tracks. 'It sure is windy here, Daddy.' He turned his face into the breeze, like an Irish setter. 'It wasn't this windy at Grandpa's. Do you think it's a tornado coming, Daddy?'

I knelt down to give him a gentle hug. 'A tornado? No, monkey-man, it's just a strong wind off the ocean. It happens sometimes, nothing to worry about.'

Jenny emerged laden with grocery bags. 'Hey, sweetie, can you lift anything?'

'Sure' – I waved my good arm – 'one-handed.'

'Then get your daughter, all right? She may need a diaper.'

'Got her.' I unlatched Anna from the car seat and lifted her out; even that small weight made my ribs hurt. 'Hey, baby, did you miss me?' I bent over her and sniffed. 'Yikes! Jenny, when's the last time you changed her?'

She propped the porch door with a bag of bananas. 'Before we left Mom's. Does she stink?'

'No, not at all – sheesh, this has to be how they destroyed the Death Star. The movie had it all wrong.'

'Just change her, Sailor,' Jenny called from the house. 'I promise her next poop will be like a whiff of French perfume.'

'Promise?'

Ben started pulling my T-shirt. 'Were you here by yourself last night, Daddy?'

'Sure was, buddy. Why?'

'I would be scared by myself. Were you?'

'Nope,' I lied, 'I slept on the couch – and you know what? I was thinking that maybe tonight I'll sleep on the couch again and you can sleep on the floor next to me. You want to? It'll be like a camp out.'

His eyes widened. 'Can we really, Daddy?'

'Sure,' I said. *You're sure as hell not sleeping in your room tonight.*

'With Mommy too?'

'If she wants.'

Jenny appeared on the porch. 'If she wants what?'

Ben ran to her. 'Mommy, do you want to camp out with Daddy and me in the living room tonight? We can watch TV late and have popcorn.' He turned to me. 'Do we have popcorn?'

'We can get some.'

Jenny looked back and forth between us. 'You're having a camp out in the living room?'

Ben said, 'Daddy has to sleep on the couch for his hurt arm and I'm going to sleep on the floor next to the couch. Can I take the blankets off the bed, Mommy?'

Jenny frowned, a sly, chiding glance that said, *And I was going to be on top tonight, dumbass.*

I smiled back at her. Anna was getting heavier by the second. Without breaking eye contact, making it as intimate as I could manage, I said, 'Maybe for a little while, buddy; we'll see how well you can sleep on the floor, okay?'

'Okay, Daddy!' And he scurried past me, ready to tear the covers off his bed.

Jenny kissed me lightly on her way back to the minivan. 'Hi.'

'Hi – welcome back.'

She ran a hand over my shoulder like a sculptor checking her lines. 'You all right?'

'Assorted cracks and bruises, nothing much new – surgery's on for Tuesday, if the swelling goes down.'

'Clutz,' she said fondly. 'That's going to sting. But at least we're here for another few weeks so you'll have plenty more recovery time.'

If you only knew.

'Yeah.' Without thinking I tried for a shrug, but it hurt too much. 'It was pretty embarrassing – the Spring Lake cops took me to the hospital.'

Shit! How stupid am I?

'Spring Lake?' She locked the car. 'I thought you said you fell down the steps by Twentieth Street.'

'Yeah, I did. But I lucked out – one of the guys I met last weekend at the hotel was parked up there – don't know why – and he drove me over to Jersey Shore Medical. I guess he must live up this way. I bet there's not many cops can afford to live in Spring Lake.'

'Sure, whatever.' Jenny was going to assume that this month especially I would be telling her the truth. I hadn't forgotten my parents' old suitcases, sitting locked and loaded outside the bedroom. Jenny wouldn't just leave; she'd downright kill me if she knew all the shit I'd been keeping from her this last eight days. And even if I'd wanted to tell her what'd been going on, I didn't have a clue how, not without her calling Dr Krandall and having me hauled back to Richmond for another ten weeks of intensive psychotherapy.

Jenny tucked us in at nine, Ben on the floor and me on the couch, with a spooky candle burning in a water glass on the coffee table. It reminded me of the hurricane candles Moses used for his pre-dawn breakfasts.

I hit the Ibuprofen pretty hard, but I skipped the knock-out pills – I badly wanted to be lucid if Jenny really did want to go to the pony-ride later. But she'd had the kids for two days on her own and I was betting she'd hit the pillow and be long gone until morning. That was all right; she deserved the rest. I hoped she'd sleep well; it was a perfect fall night for sleeping deeply, without a care.

Tucking Ben in, she kissed his forehead and said, 'Good night, monkey-man. You need anything?'

On the rug, Ben pulled his blankets into a bunch, and said, 'Just the remote. Daddy and I are going to watch TV all night.'

'Are you?'

'Yup!' He laced his fingers behind his head, blew an endearing kiss to her, and was sound asleep by nine-fifteen.

Jenny kissed me good night too. 'You gonna watch TV for a while?'

'A little while,' I said. 'I want to be here in case he wakes up. I'll be in later.'

'You want any Ibuprofen?' She sat on the couch, rested her head on my chest.

'Nah, I'm good.'

'Need anything?' She was wearing cut-offs and an old Innsbruck Tavern T-shirt. She'd tied her hair up to do the dishes and smelled of soap and baby lotion.

'Just a girl from Jersey who'll love me for ever.'

'Woman, shithead,' she said without lifting her head.

'Right. Sorry.' With her on my chest and my arm in a sling, I didn't have a free hand to hold her.

Jenny kissed me softly, tucked my blankets in, and said, 'Good night, Sailor.'

I flipped through the channels. The Jets had lost; the Giants had won. I'd eaten shrimp and watched my son tear a lobster limb from limb – it was like watching a hero dismember a monster in a horror film. He'd even let it loose on the kitchen floor before Jenny boiled it alive. That prehistoric sonofabitch had scurried furiously across the linoleum, making a final break for freedom and the thundering surf in the distance, before Jenny finally scooped it up and dunked it head first into the pot. Ben closed his eyes and plugged his ears. He might have been willing to devour it, but he didn't want to have anything to do with its murder. Good-hearted kid.

The Jets had lost; the Giants had won.

Ben snored meekly through his nose.

I watched football highlights for an hour. Every other commercial was a political ad for this November's presidential election. I watched a few before pressing MUTE whenever they appeared on screen: President Baird promised four more years of improved test scores in America's schools while Bob Lake swore he'd keep us all safe from the imminent threat of a terrorist attack.

Neither mentioned the imminent threat from America's criminal street gangs, our own army of domestic terrorists.

I closed my eyes but kept seeing Big G, Richard B. Harris, standing over me, full-throttle homicide in his face as he brandished his bat, ready to crush my skull, until, with a flash and roar, Big G's countenance changed, morphing from rage through shock to agony after Ed Hess blew his hand off with a 12-gauge.

Who was going to protect us from Big G? Hess? Huck? Me? Not the President – not Bob Lake. His men had already shot me twice. It'd be hard to vote for him after that.

When I opened my eyes, Jenny stood in the hallway. Light from the candle painted her tan legs the colour of fire. She'd taken off the cut-offs and clearly wasn't wearing a bra. She'd slept, at least for a little while; it showed in her face. Hopefully, she'd rolled over horny and thought of me.

'You coming?' she whispered.

'Not yet, but I can be convinced. You'll be gentle with me?' I pushed my blankets back. 'I might break.'

'No promises, Sailor.' She turned and padded down the hallway, the T-shirt just covering the light swell of her ass. My ribs hurt, but I couldn't have cared less. Sex with broken ribs was going to be like getting the shit kicked out of me by Rita Hayworth.

'C'mon, Navy boy,' Jenny said softly.

I couldn't think of anything to say. 'The Jets lost; the Giants won.'

'I don't care,' she called from the darkness.

I clicked the television off and hurried after her.

Ben didn't move.

MONDAY

Hopelessness, Disillusionment & Silver Bullets

When the shadows get long ...

'Mommy!'

I heard Ben as if from inside a locked room in a house across the street and my mind flashed through a slideshow of lighting-quick images – dreams, snapshots, daguerreotype photos. Ben in a room with the door locked. Ben in a basement, the walls padded with egg cartons and old piss-stained mattresses.

'Mommy!'

Ben again, closer now.

Jenny moved, groaning, and rolled over, shifting the blankets.

We're in bed. I'm in bed. With Jenny. Where's Ben? Where's the baby?

'Mommy!'

'I'll go,' Jenny murmured. It might have been me who said it, but Jenny rolled back, sighed, kissed my cheek and slid softly away.

The blankets whispered, remembered her warmth, the smell of her beside me.

She stood, wobbled, her hand on her forehead. 'Mommy's coming, buddy. One second.'

I picked my head up, saw Ben, backlit by the distant glow of a streetlight somewhere outside. He shuffled in the doorway. 'Mommy?'

'Yeah, buddy. You okay?' The wind huffed through the window.

'There's something ...' he started.

'Come here, buddy.' Jenny knelt on the rug. 'Did you have a bad dream?'

'No.' Ben dragged his feet, his socks whispering in time with the blankets, the breeze. 'There's something funny on my face. I think a bad guy got in, Mommy. Did a bad guy get in?'

My blood froze. *No, please, God: he didn't just say that*—

Then Jenny's voice, stark in the darkness: 'Oh my God! What is—? Sailor! Wake up!'

Jenny's feet thudded on the floor, two quick, harried steps, out of place after sex, love, deep sleep. Then the soft, yellow glow of her bedside light clicked on. 'Oh Jesus – what *is* this? Jesus! Sailor, help me!'

Ben's face had been slathered with black and white greasepaint as thick as the stripes on his bedroom window. He'd been painted, decorated with a deathmask identical to the one Gabriel Lebow wore to his suicide.

You broke your cane over his leg, snapping them both together.

Jenny shouted. I didn't hear.

Ben cried, nervous at seeing his mother so upset; he was scared, but not hurt.

'Okay, cocksucker.' I rolled out of bed, tugged on my sweatpants. 'I'm on my way, *right now*. I'm *coming* for you.'

'Sailor, what is it?' She hugged Ben close, wiped his face on her Innsbruck Tavern T-shirt. 'Who's here? Is someone here— oh my God, the baby! Get Anna!'

'There's no one here, Jenny.' I crossed the hallway into Anna's room. She was lying on her back, silent, unmoving. I leaned over, my cheek half an inch from her tiny nose. There was a faint gust, like silk – every parent knows it: the three a.m. confirmation that everything's fine. Across her little legs, Eeyore stood guard. Old Herringbone had been right: *Eeyores are dependable friends, loyal and predictable, but not in a bad way. Steady.*

I patted the worn donkey on the head. 'Good job, buddy. You stick with her. I'll be back.'

From our room came the sound of Jenny comforting, struggling to banish the terror from her own voice. I went around to my side of the bed, retrieved Uncle Paul's cannon and jammed it in my waistband. 'I'll be back. Stay here. Stay together. Anna's fine. She's sleeping.'

'Sailor.' Jenny's eyes found me in the half-light. She looked frightened. 'Who did this?'

'Gabriel Lebow.' I left my sling on the floor. Once again torn tissue flooded with blood, throbbing with every footstep.

'What—? Wait!'

'Just stay here,' I said. 'Don't call the police.'

In the kitchen I flipped on the stained-glass lamp. The porch door had been left open and deep scratches marked the woodwork around the doorknob. I grabbed the keys and with a muffled curse climbed into the minivan. 'Where you going, Gabriel? Neptune? Spring Lake? Asbury Park?'

No one answered, so I turned towards the beach on Twelfth Avenue. I checked the dashboard clock: 3:29. 'Asbury Park,' I said grimly.

I hit Ocean Avenue, four blocks away, at sixty miles an hour, and nearly roll over making the turn north. There's no one on the boardwalk: no cops, joggers, vagrants – and no thirty-five-year-old apparitions, Kate and Moses Stillman, arm in arm, she wearing priceless pearls and a cheap macramé handbag. I press the POWER button, crank up the volume. David Gilmour plunks his sorrowful melody, sings—

So – so you think you can tell – Heaven from Hell ... blue skies from pain ...

Careening north as fast as the minivan will go, I crest the elevated drawbridge over Shark River, and see Gabriel, off to my right: little more than a hunched shadow in flight, running in impossible four-legged bounds, like a panther, hurdling from the boardwalk to the sand, speeding into the surf for a fraction of a second, then back up the beach and across Ocean Avenue in one colossal leap.

He crashes through a hedge, out of sight, and I figure he's injured, having flown so far. I swerve through the oncoming lane – no one's driving at this hour – and onto the sidewalk, Uncle Paul's .357 in my lap. I can't drive and shoot simultaneously. With my high beams trained on the fresh tear through the neatly trimmed hedgerow, I cock the pistol, open my window, and aim, waiting for Gabriel to leap out at me, spindly teeth bared, face painted, this time for war.

On the radio, Pink Floyd continue singing the soundtrack to this nightmare: How I wish, how I wish you were here ...

Loud scrabbling sounds come from across the street, again to the north and I look up in time to catch Lebow's shadow clawing its way up the slate roof of a three-storey house, headed for Ocean Grove.

Nagle's. The old firehouse with the gargoyle perched on the decorative cornice.

I stomp on the gas; the tyres squeal. Lebow leaps wildly back across the street, near the Ocean Grove jetty. He looks like a massive bird of prey, black and nefarious, as he dives, somersaulting through the air, and lands lightly on the sand. He bounds madly towards Asbury Park.

And now I know what happened to Auntie Carla, the prize-winning pig, to Jeremy Landon, the missing surfer, to Mrs Seibert's stolen lobsters, the remains of which rot in the grass behind my house. Gabriel Lebow, this creature, has taken them, torn them to pieces, eaten his fill.

I'd do anything for a loaded cruiser, a V-8 with a 12-gauge and half a dozen clips for my .45. With the .357, I've got six shots, left-handed.

I lose sight of him – he's not been more than an inky blur – at the north end of Ocean Grove. Across Deal Lake, Asbury Park is completely dark, a veritable rip in the fabric of the universe. My tyres scream, waking the dead, as I turn around the lake, bouncing over the pedestrian walkway towards the beach, the old Casino—

—where Kate and Moses hauled Mikey Bartollo's body—

—and slow to a crawl, my injured hand resting uselessly on the steering wheel, while I grip the .357 with shaking fingers. I turn off the radio and the lights, watch the shadows, the abandoned hotels and businesses along Cookman Avenue, waiting for Lebow to strike.

I crane my neck out the open window to listen.

The silence breaks: wood on wood, planks falling onto a pile of old pallets in an alley between the burned-out shell of a Roaring Twenties movie theatre and a dilapidated Art Deco hotel, The Bentley. The planks fall from an upstairs window, where they'd been nailed into place like makeshift shutters.

'There you are.' I pull over, kill the engine. 'Oh shit, Sailor, don't tell me you didn't bring a flashlight.' I check the glove compartment and find a battery-powered emergency light, a cheap Wal-Mart light. 'It'll have to do.'

I can't remember where I left the penlight, probably beneath the Christmas tree at 1720 Blake.

Crossing Cookman Avenue towards the empty relic, abandoned for thirty years and haunted by the ghosts of gangsters, film stars and crooked politicians, I look like a smallish version of the Sea Girt lighthouse, blinking red against the coastal night. I consider dousing the light, but in the end I leave it illuminated. If Lebow can't see me, he can still smell me, hear me, feel my heart thud through the misty darkness.

I kick the old double doors; they shatter to dust and two teenage junkies rush out. They're both dark, thin, ragged. 'Don't shoot, mister!' one of them yells.

'Beat it!' I shout, then go inside.

It is too dark to see well, but in the blinking red light of the emergency lamp I realise I'm centre stage in a once-grand foyer. A vast oceanfront restaurant stretches beyond a cracked archway to my right. A bar, also Art Deco but rotting and forgotten, connects the restaurant with a patio in the courtyard. A broad staircase with a carved banister and the mouldy remains of what must have been plush red carpet spirals to the second floor.

I ascend as quickly as my tired legs can carry me, the blinking light in my worthless hand, Uncle Paul's cannon in the other.

'Gabriel,' I call into the darkness, 'come on out, Gabriel.'

Sweat stings my eyes, but I don't pull my gaze away from the top of the stairs, where a heavy, red curtain hangs between the landing and the hallway beyond.

Two steps from the top, I call again, 'You in there, Gabriel? Because I'm coming to kill you, jackass. You shouldn't have come near my son. I told you I was sorry. I told you I didn't mean to hurt you – I would have helped you if I'd known – but you made a mistake tonight, motherfucker.'

Nothing.

On the landing I hold my breath and duck to one side. I fully expect Lebow to explode like a panther through the musty velvet curtain and carry both of us backwards down the ostentatious staircase. My throat is coated with dust; I hold my breath and fight the need to cough. I reach out with the gun barrel and slide the curtain aside, peek through, and then inch in.

It isn't a hallway, but what must have been a private party room, complete with a permanent dance floor, a small stage, a dining area, and a comfy mahogany bar. In the cracked mirror I see my face, pale in the intermittent flashes of light. Uncle Paul's gun gleams silvery-red. This is the room; I know it as soon as I creak from the landing onto the smudged dance floor. This is where Moses and Kate heard Rogers Waters and David Gilmour back in 1975.

Just two lost souls swimming in a fish bowl, year after year. Running over the same old ground, what have we found? The same old fears. Wish you were here.

'You in here, fuckface?' I lower my voice. If he's come in the upstairs window, he can hear me. 'Huh?' Two steps forward, then three. My toes reach the edge of the dingy parquet floor. 'Gabriel?'

There's a crash from behind the bar and a flash of mercurial black, followed by two explosions as I fire, wildly, towards Lebow's low, powerful shadow. He bursts seawards out the picture window overlooking Kingsley Avenue and the boardwalk beyond.

I fire another shot through the shattered glass at Lebow's falling, flying form. This will kill him: the fall from up here, that'll get him, at least it'll injure him, slow him down long enough for me to get downstairs and put a bullet in his head.

I try not to think about RJ, currently languishing in the county lock-up for shooting Gabriel Lebow. I identified him for Marta Hodges; it was easy with those tattoos on his face. Yet here I am, trying to shoot Lebow all over again, to kill him in cold blood.

When I shoot, the muzzle-flash blinds me; I blink rapidly to focus.

I peer through the gaping wound Lebow has torn through the hotel's upstairs windows and search for him outside. To my surprise I find him, a mere shadow, hunched over, on a one-storey roof across the street.

I heave the blinking red light, hoping to brighten my target enough to finish him from here. Miraculously, the bulb survives its crash-landing and the lamp rolls to within a few feet of Gabriel's ghost. Taking aim, I fire.

Another explosion, and another flash blinds me, but I can hear him, whatever it is, scream in pain: the sound of a tortured child, a backwards-played violin—

That's right, fucker. If you can scream, I can kill you.

I blink, trying to clear my eyes. I need to shoot again, to wing him, if I am to have any hope of keeping him down long enough to drag my own *broken body over there. Wiping my eyes on my sleeve, I strain to see, but it's no use; I'll need a few seconds more.*

Through my blindness, I find the blinking light, its red pulse a heartbeat in the empty city. It rises, turns a lazy circle, then flies at me with astonishing determination.

He threw it back, the *shithead*. He heaved my own light up—

'Oh Jesus Christ!' I step backwards and my ankle breaks through a rotten board in the dance floor; I am trapped, not two steps from the precarious ledge.

Sirens wail in the distance: someone's heard the shots, but they're coming too late. I won't make it another fifteen seconds.

Gabriel Lebow's inky, acrobatic form rises like a demonic nightmare, flying up at me from the roof across the street, closing the distance between us before I can run, shoot, even cry out.

Then he – it; Gabriel Lebow – is there: clinging to the edges of the shattered glass, the splintered sill, all black, arms outstretched like wings, fingers gripping like talons. I fire blindly; there's no shriek of pain this time.

The muzzle-flare blinds me again, and I fall back hard, my ass fracturing more floorboards, trapping me even more. Like a pig in a pigpen at the Monmouth County Farmers' Fair.

I raise the .357; it wobbles in my hand. With my eyes closed tight, I aim with my mind, cock the hammer—

Lebow leans in, his torn clothes billowing, and brings his face close to mine. Mere inches separate us now. I can kill him, blow his head off, but I can't make myself pull the trigger. I'll never be this frightened again. This is more terrifying than all my childhood nightmares fused together: I want to kill him, but I don't have the strength to pull the trigger, not now that we're face to face.

I can't see. I blink as fast as I can, frantic to take in this monster that's haunted me and threatened my son, but I can't.

His breath redolent of rotting pig, dead surfer and week-old lobster, Lebow howls into my face. I hold my breath, but I can feel tiny splashes of hot spittle dance across my cheeks and lips.

His desperate cry drives me mad and I drop the .357 and scream, struggling to cover both ears with one arm. My injured arm is completely useless now, and I press myself as far as I can into the broken dance floor,

*squeezing my eyes shut, howling like a madman as I wait for Gabriel Lebow
to crush my skull with his talons, those same claws he used to kill Auntie
Carla, Jeremy Landon, Tejon 'Blade' Butler and the lobsters outside Ben's
room.*

*Then there's silence. I'm alone. I've stopped screaming. The wind blows
over the boardwalk, washing away the stench of Lebow's breath, and I rest
on my back, panting, until my heart slows.*

*When I open my eyes, Jenny's flashing red light is on the floor beside
my foot, just inches from the broken window and the long fall to Kingsley
Avenue.*

*Gabriel Lebow, or whatever remains of him now that his cursed soul has
returned from Hell, is nowhere to be seen.*

*I click the LIGHT button on the Ironman running watch Jenny bought
me when I decided to get into shape.*

3:52 a.m.

*I extricate myself carefully and stumble to the minivan. Asbury PD
cruisers crowd the corner of Kingsley and First, two blocks over (thanks
possibly to the two teens I spooked earlier). I drive dark until I'm clear.
When I turn on my headlights they illuminate deep, irregular disturbances
in the sand, like a giant's footprints. I park again and follow them a quarter-
mile beyond Convention Hall, where they simply stop.*

'He's in the water,' I say to no one, and in my head, I can hear Ben: It's
not that kind of shark, Mommy. It's different. *And I see his drawing: a
shark with vaguely human arms. It's chasing a bad guy through the water.*
Could a bad guy get in, Daddy?

'Yes, buddy, a bad guy could get in.'

*I don't know how many bullets I have left; I can't recall how many I've
fired, and yet I watch the ebony surface of the water as I back slowly down
the beach to the car.*

*Inside, I crank up the air-conditioning and drive home. In our driveway,
I wipe my face with my T-shirt. My breath has slowed, my heart, too. I've
got to keep it together, I've got to come up with something to tell Jenny.
I've been lying to her all week, the very week I promised never to tell her
anything but the truth.*

*She'll see through any lie I tell her now, unless it's a good one, a gold-
medal winner. My mind is racing as I pocket the keys and stuff the still*

411

warm .357 back into my waistband. In the porch light, I can see that I'm filthy, a mixture of blood, sweat and sand, in layers, like an artist's sketch of misfortune.

'What're you going to say, Sailor? What're you going to tell her? You've got to tell her something – Jesus Christ, she saw the greasepaint shit on Ben's face. She knows someone was in the house. It's a frigging miracle she hasn't called the police already. You've got to come up—'

Crossing my driveway, I step on the Sunday edition of the Asbury Park Press, the one I paced back and forth over earlier while talking to Huck. 'When was it?' I turn my face towards the beach, relishing the cool breeze. 'Was it Monday?' I need a smoke. 'Not Monday, Saturday: our first day here. Anna and I went walking. Jenny was pissed off about Sarah. She'd—'

I bend down to collect the paper; I should have done it this morning. With it tucked under my arm, I take the last few steps towards the porch. 'Saturday: it was last Saturday that I read about Auntie Carla.'

Standing board-stiff on my mother's old porch I look at my exhausted, sweaty reflection. It's two, perhaps three breaths before I'm willing to admit out loud what I know: 'The pig, Auntie Carla, died at the fairgrounds before you ever tackled Gabriel Lebow at Morris Middle School. That – thing – isn't Gabriel.'

I check my watch: 4:23 a.m. 'All right, Moses, I'm coming. I'll be right there.'

Inside, Jenny had slid the kitchen table and chairs behind the door. I pushed against the barrier, managed to crack the door an inch or two, then whispered, 'Hey! It's me.'

She must have been hiding in the kitchen because within seconds I heard chairs slide over the linoleum. 'Where'd you go, Sailor? And what are you talking about Lebow? How could it be Lebow? He's dead.'

'Right, I was thinking Lebow, but what I meant to say was ...'

Okay, shithead, what did you mean to say? Hurry up!

Jenny slid the table back and I pressed the door the rest of the way open, buying myself another precious second to think of something creative that might fool my extremely intelligent wife.

412

'Was what, Sailor? Who broke in here – and why can't I call the police? Your *children* are here, for Christ's fucking sake.'

'I already called them, Jenny,' I said. 'I needed to call the Staff Sergeant from Asbury Park: he's the one who helped us the other night, he was on point for the raid. He knows all the players up there, he's got all the road guys in the city out looking.' I cleared the absurd barrier, hugged her close. 'How's Ben?'

Not to be deterred, Jenny pressed on, 'Who broke in here and painted my son's face? Do you have an actual suspect? You stink of gunpowder, cordite, whatever you call it. Did you shoot someone?'

'At someone,' I admitted.

'Who?'

'Jenny, I haven't told you because I didn't want you to worry, but the other night, when Huck and I went up to help Hodges, the raid turned up loads of assholes, but we didn't net the two biggest fish, the thugs who oversee the meth kitchens up here, bad dudes, both of them. It's why I didn't go with you to your parents' place.'

Oh, we're lying now, kiddies.

'They're *here*? Now?' In the light from the streetlamps, Jenny's face shone pale, and I worried she might collapse.

'Not right here, no,' I lied. 'We have one in custody; the other was running up the beach towards Allenhurst when I came back to check on you. I've got to change my clothes and get over to the North Side station. I want to be there when they're questioned.'

'Okay.' She backed away a step, her interrogation ratcheted down one notch.

'How's Ben?'

'Fine,' she said, 'I lied to him, told him it was Poseidon coming out of the ocean to paint his face for doing such a good job learning how to swim.'

'What the hell—?'

'Hey!' She jammed a finger in my chest. 'It's all I could think of to keep him from having a complete meltdown.'

'No, that's not what I meant!' I hugged her again. 'That was great, Jenny. I'd never have thought of anything like that.'

'And I told him that if he went to sleep, there was a good chance

413

Poseidon would send a mermaid with treasure for him. So I stuck a twenty under his pillow.'

'Twenty? Wow,' I teased, 'that's more than I get all week.'

Jenny wasn't in the mood for goofing around. She frowned. 'I want to go home, Sailor, tomorrow – tonight. Right now if we can.'

'You know I can't, Jenny. C'mon; we've got both these assholes. I'll go and help Asbury PD with the booking, and we'll be in the clear.'

'How'd they know where we live?' she challenged. 'I thought Hodges was keeping your name out of this.'

'She got pretty mad when they took RJ – Lebow's shooter – into custody. She used my name; I figure he must not be nearly as dumb as he looks, because that's the only time anyone mentioned me at all – RJ must have told his lawyer that a Virginia trooper was the one who ID'ed him. Ed Hess described the lawyer as "a civil rights activist without a clue" – he must've mentioned my name to Big G and Blade. It's not that difficult to find the house – Mom's name is in the phone book, for Christ's sake.'

'"Big G" and "Blade"? Really?'

I nodded. 'Not in any danger of getting shortlisted for the Nobel Prize, either of them.'

'Well, what if they tell other gangsters where to find us?'

'They won't.'

'How do you know?'

'A few reasons.' I was lying so fluently now I just opened the valve and let the bullshit flow. I'd beg for forgiveness, *again*, when we got back to Virginia. 'First, they didn't break in here to kill us. They came to terrorise us—'

'Well, it worked.'

'No, it didn't,' I explained, 'I'm fine; you're going to be fine. Anna never even woke up, and Ben's twenty dollars richer. We're okay, all of us.' She pulled up a chair, sat down. I stayed standing; I was afraid that if I sat down, I'd not be able to get back up. 'If Blade or Big G tell any of their street soldiers where we live, we might be killed in a drive-by shooting while those two are in lock-up.'

'Whew,' Jenny feigned relief, 'that makes me feel better.'

'You don't understand,' I said, 'killing a police officer is enormously bad for business. Right now Blade and Big G will kill, cook and eat anyone who comes near us, trust me on that.'

'And?'

'And— And given how furious Hodges was when she put the cuffs on RJ the other night, I don't think Blade or Big G are going to be seeing the light of day any time soon. And when they do, it'll be with an attorney she *recommends* from the Public Defenders' office.'

'She can do that?'

'Happens all the time,' I said.

Jenny shook her head. 'I can't believe how lightly you cops take the law.'

'What?' I said. 'You tell me you wouldn't rather have an old, conservative, *religious* lawyer working with them than a young, hungry liberal activist out for cop blood?'

'I want to go home.'

'Not yet.' I knelt down in front of her, placed my hands gently on her thighs. 'We have to stay here at least until Hodges wraps up the arraignment on RJ, maybe until I get deposed by his attorney, depending on how quickly they get their shit together. After that we'll go home, and I'll come back by myself for the trial.'

'How long?'

'Couple of days, tops.' I was lying again; I had no idea when the Monmouth County Court would get around to RJ. 'But now, Jenny, I have to change and get back to Asbury Park as quickly as possible. I'll call you when I know what's going on.'

'Okay,' she said, 'but leave me the gun.'

I only hesitated for a second. 'Okay. I'll load it for you. You remember how to shoot?'

'No, but I'll look it up on YouTube. Not much chance I'm getting back to sleep tonight.' She rubbed her eyes.

I kissed her lightly on the forehead. 'Poseidon? Not Neptune?'

'It's a town three blocks away; it'd confuse him.'

'Okay.' I left her the gun, changed clothes, took a handful of Ibuprofen and wrapped my arm back into my sling. 'I won't be long,' I said before leaving. 'Lock the doors, and don't go anywhere. I'll call you.'

'Be careful,' she whispered, leaning in to kiss me again.

'What could go wrong? And when I get home, maybe a mermaid will be waiting in my bed too.'

'Not funny.'

'I'll be back,' I promised, and hurried to the minivan, then, 'Fuck, fuck, fuck!' I shouted, pounding the steering wheel as I headed south for Spring Lake and the Warren & Monmouth Hotel. In seven days, I'd been drunk twice, jonesing for pills so bad I'd got myself sick twice, lied to Jenny more times than I could count, and been intimately involved with three dead bodies and a seventeen-year-old murder confession.

The dashboard clock read 4:41 a.m.

I found Moses sitting at the same table where I'd met him a week earlier. A custodian I hadn't seen before busied himself with a vacuum, cleaning the acre-wide Persian carpet at the top of Rhett Butler's stairway. Moses, in neatly pressed trousers and a cotton sweater, tapped his Italian leather loafers in time to whatever song was playing in his head.

He stopped when he saw me. 'Good morning, Sailor! Out for a bit of exercise this morning? By God, but it's good to see you up and around.'

'Good morning, Moses.' Without waiting for an invitation, I pulled back a chair and sat myself. 'What's on King James Island?'

My question instantly erased Moses' normally cheery disposition. 'What do— What do you mean?'

'What I mean is: there are people dying all over Monmouth County this week, in strange attacks, brutal killings and improbable suicides. The county detectives can't possibly connect them – *if* they're connected – because they can't possibly know about the few insignificant threads that link them. But I do.'

He fussed with his napkin. 'Forgive me, Sailor, but I'm not sure I follow you. How is it that you believe I have—?'

'Knock it off, Moses,' I said without raising my voice. I'd calmed down on the brief drive south; I knew I wouldn't get what I needed

416

screaming at him. 'I know that Gabriel Lebow was Isaac Lebow's grandson. I know that Isaac acted as Mikey Bartollo's attorney. I know that Isaac was – *is* – one of the highest-paid defence lawyers in North Jersey, and I've learned enough about Mikey Bartollo to know that he didn't have the liquid assets available to buy Lebow a cup of coffee, let alone retain him as counsel on rape and murder charges. I don't have any idea who J. M. McMichael is, or why he posted bond for Bartollo, but I'd bet a month's salary it was to get Mikey back on the street, where the Jersey mob could put a slug in the back of his head. Lebow made a mistake taking that case; he'd built his career defending rich Jews and businessmen against the Feds in high-profile tax and finance charges. His idea of *pro bono* would have been finishing up the paperwork for a new wing at the hospital, not dirtying his fingers with a nasty piece of shit like Mikey.'

Moses looked like an animal with its leg in a snare; his mind clearly raced for a reply. I gave him another minute, then said, 'Whoever had Mikey in their crosshairs probably left a load in their pants when he went missing. So here's my question: why? Did Bartollo know something he wasn't supposed to? Had someone paid him to murder your daughter? If so, who was it? If you and Kate had him tied up and tortured in your basement for two months, you must have learned all about what motivated Mikey. Did your daughter's death have anything to do with Charles Dunning's decision to visit King James Island that spring? Or am I the only one who finds it odd that Lauren, Dunning and Kate all died within a year of one another?'

'Sailor, I—'

'Hold on a second,' I said, needing to move more puzzle pieces into place. Moses was no doubt about to engage his ridiculous, rich-old-man smile and try to put me off; I had to get enough of these disconnected pieces into line that he'd realise that there was no reason to bullshit any longer, not when he was alone with me. Whatever haunted his dreams between 4:00 and 4:37 a.m. had shown up at my house and assaulted my son. If I had to ram a fucking fork into Moses Heston's chest to get some answers, I'd do it.

I said, 'Kate had influence inside the Canadian Parliament. Granted, it was indirect, but I'm betting the flow of information around the

Stillman dinner table was pretty fluid. A few bottles of wine, a nice piece of roast beef, and before you know it, Daddy's spilling everything to Katie and her nice new hubby, that talented young man who's slated to pitch in Arizona this winter, maybe even hit the big time.'

Moses stared down at his plate.

'Dunning needed the King James Island vote to solidify his company's position as a powerful lobby and Kate knew that. But I don't believe for a second that lawmakers in Ottawa gave up a lucrative connection to a British oil conglomerate in the interests of saving a few fucking ducks. Now, I don't want to get upset with you this morning, Moses, because maybe all you're guilty of is falling in love with a woman in politics. What the hell, we don't blame guys for following their dicks. But Dunning walked away with an island and Kate with a strand of Tahitian black pearls; someone on the other side of the desk had to win.

'I've spent some time researching and so far what I've learned is that one hundred per cent of the people I can find who've visited King James Island in the past thirty years have ended up dead. So why is that? What's there? Are the deaths connected? – I think they are. Who paid to keep them covered up? Jimmy Carter in 1976? Later? Why would he? Vietnam and Richard Nixon were goddamned embarrassments for the conservatives; did Carter really need to kick oil prospectors off a pile of rocks that no one cared about?'

Moses slid his plate to one side, propped his elbows on the linen tablecloth and buried his face in his hands. 'You don't understand.'

'So help me understand,' I said. 'Whoever *compelled* Gabriel Lebow to slather on the war paint and kill himself at Robert Morris Middle School last week has visited my house, several times.'

He looked up at that, his face a mix of grief and disbelief.

'Last night my *son's* face was painted with the same greasepaint Lebow wore when he attacked the school. My *son*, Moses. He's five years old.'

Moses' hands were shaking. He gripped the edge of the table to hide it. To himself, he said, 'This has to stop.'

'I agree. And I can help you, just as soon as you start giving me some answers.' I helped myself to a glass of his orange juice. My ribs, shoulder, hip, legs, back, every inch of my body felt as though I'd been hit by a car. I gulped the juice and poured another. 'Moses, what's on King James Island? Why is it so important that seven, maybe more, people have died because of it?'

'Seven?'

'A shipwrecked crew from a Danish freighter made for King James in 1981. Those who sailed for Devon lived. Everyone who made for King James died.'

From the service entrance, Tony from Bergen County emerged carrying an empty tray. Seeing me, he waved. 'Good morning, Detective Doyle? You hungry?'

'Not today, Tony.' I shook his hand. 'Just out for my morning constitutional.'

Moses and I watched him clear the plates in silence. Finally, Tony tried again, 'You sure, Sailor?'

'I'm good, thanks.'

'Mr Stillman?'

'*Sto bene, grazie, Antonio.*'

He started back inside, then paused. 'Just give a shout if you need anything. I'm helping the sous crew get ready for breakfast.'

When the door closed behind Tony, Moses asked, 'You have any cigarettes?'

'Always.' I handed him the pack. He lit one from the hurricane candle on the table. I joined him, then waited. The silence between us grew uncomfortable. Moses wore three decades of fear and frustration like a latex mask. Finally, he asked, 'How did you know the name of that song the other night? When I was telling everyone about Kate and me and our night at the Bentley Hotel.'

'Every time I turn on the radio, every car that drives by with its windows open, every grocery store or restaurant I go in, Moses, that song is playing. Do you know why?'

'Yes,' he started, then shook his head, 'actually, no, I don't know, Sailor.'

'That's not helping,' I said. 'Who paid Kate's father to influence public policy regarding King James Island? Do you know?'

'I *was* there,' he said. 'You might have been making the point, just

419

now, but you weren't that far off. Kate's father didn't like the idea of her marrying a minor leaguer, but I was good and I had a solid shot at making the majors. Those winters in Arizona – they were awful, being away from Kate and Lauren, especially Lauren, she was so little – but as a son-in-law, it was a wise decision. It sent a strong message to Kate's parents: I wasn't a fortune hunter; I was a major league talent, someone they could brag about at parties.'

'Who paid?'

'When I hurt my arm—'

'Who paid, Moses?' I rose a bit from my chair.

He rose as well. As angry as I was, I didn't want to fight him – with a good fifty pounds on me, he'd kick my crippled ass halfway to the beach. But with the image of Ben's deathmask fresh in my mind, I stood my ground. 'Tell me who paid off Kate's father? Was it Charles Dunning? Did Nordic Rescue have connections outside Canada? Another oil firm?'

'Okay, so you do need to hear this.' Moses waved a finger in my face; I nearly bit it. 'It'll make sense, I promise, but you've got to be patient.'

I sat. 'Fine.'

Moses looked contemplative for a moment, then said, 'When I hurt my arm, the future got pretty ambiguous all at once. We needed money – no, *I* needed money. Kate had money; her parents were stuffed full of it. But I needed to show that I could take care of her and Lauren.'

I started to speak, then stopped myself. Let him tell it his way.

'I had no training, no education – I told you before: I majored in baseball,' Moses said. 'Kate's father could have helped me, but the idea of going to work in an office made me want to gnaw off my own leg. I was a ballplayer, a pitcher, and the only time my world made sense to me was when I stood on that mound. My life had always revolved around baseball, until I met Kate and we had Lauren, after a perfectly wonderful night together on that shitty old boardwalk in Asbury Park.'

'Lovely, Moses.' I lit another cigarette. 'Who paid?'

Now he did stand, leaning over the table and looking as intimidating as the poster hanging in his suite. 'The fucking Department of

420

Defense paid, Sailor!' His voice sounded slow, toneless. 'The United States Department of Defense – masquerading as environmental lobbyists – paid Kate, Charles Dunning, Kate's father and half the fucking Canadian Parliament to set King James Island up as a permanent game preserve, government-sponsored for ninety-nine years. Kate's father knew, and probably the Prime Minster, Ben Baldwin himself, but the rest of them? I don't know.' He sat heavily. 'By 1977, the Carter administration was neck-deep in talks about the Strategic Arms Limitation Treaty, embarrassing the American people with its pleas for arms control, all the while the rest of the goddamned world knew full well the Soviets weren't about to decommission their Intercontinental Ballistic Missiles – no one was. It was the biggest farce you've ever seen. But none of it mattered, because while President Carter was on TV convincing the world that we needed to limit the production of nuclear warheads and maybe, what the hell, stand a few of the other silos down, the CIA was busy locating sites for first-strike MIRV ICBM silos all over the place. King James Island was absolutely perfect: an endangered flock of Eskimo curlew roost there every spring and summer, so a splashy public policy battle keeps out a foreign oil company. Just for good measure there's a nice little kickback for everyone who votes to kill the British prospecting proposal, and a good-looking environmentalist takes the credit for liberal-minded Canadians everywhere. *Perfect!*'

I remembered Doc Lefkowitz saying, 'The 1970s were a time of significant unrest here in the US, and the two major contributors were the Soviet Union and America's unhealthy reliance on foreign oil.'

'Prime Minister Baldwin was so pleased with Kate's work that he gave her the pearls. Back then things were a bit looser – yes, the civil service was supposed to keep a record of every gift ministers received, whether from a foreign diplomat or a visiting Hollywood movie mogul, but sometimes, shit got thrown in a drawer and forgotten – paperwork got misfiled and gifts got passed around. You can't tell me it didn't happen in Washington, too; hell, I bet it still does.' Moses was definitely agitated now. He poured himself some water and stole another cigarette from my pack. 'Kate loved those pearls, and Maybeth Baldwin had never even put them on, can you believe that? You've

421

got a priceless piece surrounded by the rarest, most *improbable* jewels on Earth, and you won't wear them because some Tahitian princess OD'd on heroin when she wore them to her boyfriend's for a blowjob party. Jesus Christ. It's a disappointing world, Sailor, a disappointing fucking world.'

Time to get him back on track. 'So the CIA wanted King James Island for missile silos? Is that all?'

'*All?* Are you kidding me? Do you have any idea what a big deal it is for a NATO nation to run interference for a NATO ally while all of NATO watches the SALT talks like they mean something? Is that *all?*' The disdain in his voice was as thick as syrup.

'Is it?' I steepled my fingers, waited.

Moses crossed and uncrossed his legs, buying himself a few seconds. Finally, he murmured, 'Actually, no.'

'So?'

'As it turns out the MIRV ICBM silos—'

'Wait,' I interrupted, 'what's a MIRV?'

'Multiple Independently Targetable Reentry Vehicles, Sailor, what every growing boy needs to take care of the school bully. While Carter negotiated with Brezhnev on how many warheads to dismantle, the United States government was designing a first-strike missile that would dump eight, even ten warheads at once – in fact, I remember reading that the Soviets had plans for single ICBMs that could deliver thirty thermonuclear warheads simultaneously. That'll ruin your baby shower,' he added sarcastically. 'But sixteen years later it turned out that the King James silos weren't designed just to target the Soviet Union.'

'China,' I guessed.

'And we have a winner!' Moses cheered sardonically. 'Why the hell not? Most Americans still fail to grasp that the Vietnam conflict wasn't a war between North and South Vietnam over Communism – sure, that's a convenient excuse to go in and bully the natives, but twelve years is a long time to fight over a bit of swampy jungle, don't you agree? No, Vietnam definitely was a war between the United States and the Soviet Union and China, and you can bet your backside that after that little débâcle CIA spies started combing our corner of the world for convenient places to hide warheads ready to take out the Chinese. And you know what's really amusing? Before it all ended, there was even talk of filling those tubes with all sorts of nasty shit – biological weapons designed to infect China, bacteria that come with a user's manual and a crash helmet. And yet we're the United States, Sailor: we're supposed to be above shit like that! We're *supposed* to be an example to the rest of the world!'

'Why?' I asked, without thinking. 'Why wipe out China? Hadn't Nixon been there? Weren't relations improving?'

'Sure,' Moses teased, 'they were about as swell as our relations with the USSR during the SALT talks. The problem with China is that there are so goddamned many of them, and the country's so big that plain old thermonuclear warheads just wouldn't get the job done; nope, we needed to *infect* those sons-of-bitches before they organised an army as big as the population of the United States and sailed over here to whup our backsides.'

I stood up, walked to the porch rail and leaned against it, listening to the breakers thundering like a cannonade in the distance. 'What a mess,' I said. 'And somehow this all goes back to your arm injury? How is that possible, Moses?'

He joined me, a burning cigarette in his mouth and a cup of tepid coffee in his hand. 'Ah. That's where the wheels come off the wagon, my friend.'

Moses clearly had some momentum; he was finally prepared to spill everything he could recall. A struggle, a *furious squall*, had been raging inside him for the past thirty-six years; this morning, good or bad, one side would finally win.

He nudged my ribs with his elbow. 'You all right?'

'Little battered, but yeah.'

'I was pretty impressed with you this past summer, Sailor.'

'Moses ...'

'Hear me out,' he said, 'just for a second, because it's important to me that you know how – yeah, *impressed* I was with what you did for Virginia, the country.'

'Okay – thanks. Why?'

'Where do you suppose a spy comes from? What makes a spy?'

423

I really wasn't up for word games, but I said, 'Money, politics, disillusionment, idealism? I'm not sure I've ever thought about it, but if I had to guess, I'd say it's something more than just money. Maybe some combination of money and disillusionment probably work together over time more so than patriotism, which is a form of idealism, if you ask me. But what Kate and Dunning and the Canadian Parliament did, that was politics, not espionage. When the whole government does it, I don't think it's spying; it's more like foreign policy.'

'I suppose you're right,' he conceded, 'but for my two cents, I believe all spies come from a place half-buried in hopelessness and half-covered with disillusionment.'

'Careful,' I mimicked him, 'your mixed metaphors are about to show!'

'Go easy on me. I'm old.' He took a last look at the gathering dawn and returned to the table. 'American culture has become something of a global joke.'

'I don't understand,' I said. 'I'm not all that much of a philosopher.'

Moses tried to explain. 'I think of the soldiers who died in the Civil War, the Second World War: hundreds of thousands of Americans dead, and for what?'

I answered his rhetorical question. 'Freedom? Liberty? The preservation of the Constitution? Again, I don't see how this gets us back to your arm injury and Chinese people targeted with biological warfare.'

'Do you really think all those soldiers should have died so that Sylvester Stallone could play Rocky Balboa six times? Or so that Americans could be free to worship at the church of Wal-Mart before gnashing five thousand calories a day, all the while happily believing that the American ideals we're sold by Walt Disney, Frank Capra and Garrison Keillor are accurate? American history textbooks are bullshit; the *Glory, Glory Hallelujah* version of this country doesn't exist. It never has existed, yet most of the obese fuckers walking around out there fervently believe that their vote counts, that their president gives a shit about them, and that he is going to sober up their drunk uncle or heal their pregnant teenage sister, or convince their father to stop getting shitfaced and beating their mother. Did six hundred thousand really die in the Civil War so that we could have the George Foreman

424

Grill, eight hundred television channels, fat-free bacon, twenty-four-hour news voyeurism and meth labs in the suburbs?'

'Whoa, wait a minute, Moses.' I'd lost him now. 'If you want to convince me that the American ideal depicted in Frank Capra's movies or Walt Disney's *Hall of Presidents* is a crock of shit, I'm right there with you, but I'm pretty sure most Americans would agree – I think it's just the opposite, we pay our ten bucks to go to the movies so that we can *escape* for two hours, not so that we can be sold a bill of goods about our lives.'

'I disagree, Sailor.' He didn't look at me. 'We Americans have always coveted more; we've always hated those with different colour skin, with different values, with more money, less money; we mistrust those who are different from us. *That's* American history. *That's* American culture, not the flag-waving, anthem-singing that goes on when we win a speed-skating medal at the Winter Games. Who can blame others for hating us when we send twenty slobs from the suburbs to playact-starve in a country where people *are* actually fucking starving and call it entertainment!'

'What are you saying, Moses? Because this is all very interesting, but I'm still not getting it: why fat people go to Walt Disney World or Stallone movies doesn't interest me. I think America is about Joe and Grace Everyman trying to feel good about being Joe and Grace Everyman. You're looking through a telescope when you ought to be using a microscope.'

'You're wrong, Sailor.'

'It's America; that's okay,' I said. 'But I am going to break both your legs if you don't get to the point. The sun's coming up and my family's waiting for me. What does this possibly have to do with your injured arm?'

He closed his eyes and quietly said, 'I took money. I told you that I needed money, and I did. I needed money to be the husband I wanted – I *needed* – to be. I think you can understand that. Kate was *infatuated* with Charles Dunning. He was smart and impressive and a frigging adventurer, like a guy from a movie, and she got herself pretty caught up in that larger-than-life aura that preceded him into the room.'

When he didn't go on I said, 'But the way you described your life together, your time in Asbury Park back in 1975—'

And I saw you, Moses, the other night, I looked back in time and I saw how much she loved you.

'Who knows?' he said. 'My anger's faded over thirty years; I have a different perspective. But at that time I *needed* that money.'

'Okay,' I said, 'big deal. So you took some cash to ensure that a bunch of birds would have a nice place to roost for the next ninety-nine years. Personally, I sleep better knowing we still have some hot missile silos around the world. Having a few in remote locations is even better; they've got to be harder to take out. Right?'

'You're still missing the point,' Moses said. 'Kate, Dunning, her father, the MPs they won to their cause, they were paid handsomely by the US Department of Defense – the CIA, really. Kate's share was nearly a million dollars; I shudder to think what her father got.'

'So what?' I didn't understand. 'What'd you get? Less? Big deal.'

'Not less. *Different.*'

'Different how?' And then I paused.

Moses didn't look at me. 'I took money from the Chinese, Sailor. I sold information to China in exchange for a small fortune. People *died* thanks to my words – just worthless shit I heard on the golf course, or over drinks with Kate's father.' He wiped his eyes. I hadn't seen him start crying, but his voice remained steady even as tears welled up, clouding his vision of the rising sun. 'My arm was injured in a bar-room in Tempe, Arizona. Three CIA thugs made it look like a fight. I lied to Kate, told her I did it during practice, but the truth was, I'd been set up. Those spook-fuckers wanted information on Dunning and they wanted me to get it for them. They were paying someone else to get information on Kate, and her father. When I told them to bugger off, that I wouldn't spy on my own wife, they ended my career.'

'Holy shit,' I whispered.

'And when the Chinese came calling – *heh*, it's not like you read in the paperbacks, you know, with dark sedans beneath a highway overpass, not at all. I shared this condo with three other players, just for the winter, right there in goddamned downtown Tempe. One night I'd just hung up with Kate, after I'd listened to Lauren on the line, whatever eighteen-month-olds babble about, hippos and giraffes; you know. Anyway, I'd just cracked a beer and put my feet up when the doorbell rang. A couple of the other guys used Winter League time to hit pretty hard on the college girls and local honeys and I figured it was one of them stopping by for a quickie, so I didn't even get up first time.

'It was a kid,' he snorted, 'when I got to the door: not William Holden or James Bond, just some frigging kid a couple of years younger than I was. He had that perma-pressed look of an Ivy Leaguer about him: all clean-cut, short hair, nice suit. Anyway, we took a walk and the next thing I knew I was signing on as a dummy broker for a gazillion shares of a Brazilian farm equipment company, all legit. Ten minutes after that, I signed brokerage rights over to a futures trader who bought me the opportunity to speculate on several hundred thousand barrels of oil.'

'I don't get it,' I said. 'Of course, Jenny only lets me have twenty dollars a week. Did this launder the money for you?'

'Sort of,' Moses explained. 'You see, I had insider information into a Canadian parliamentary vote against prospecting rights for a massive British multinational. Investing in the futures market gave me the chance, thanks to my new Asian friends, to use their pay-off and that knowledge to really break the bank. The Chinese funnelled money into the Brazilian equipment exporter; young Harvard coached me through the process, and I hit the mega-jackpot when the Brits got kicked out of Canada. You see, the prospecting legislation had looked like a slam-dunk. The price of oil jumped for about six months and I sold everything for a couple of dollars under the going rate, but still significantly more than I'd paid for it. Ka-Blam: instant multi-millionaire. Actually, looking back now, I don't know if the Chinese agents who arranged for me to pass on information ever knew that young Harvard and I had turned my insider knowledge into hard cash. And what could the SEC do? Some brass-balls broker from Harvard gets a Brazilian coffee millionaire to roll the dice on oil; the price jumps, and he makes a killing. It's just another day in energy speculation.'

'Did the Ivy League kid know he was helping an American citizen sell information to a hostile nation?'

Moses shook his head. 'No idea – but what better cover for a pay-off?'

'And this was before or after the CIA contacted you?'

'After,' he said. 'They paid me to spy on Kate's father and at first I told them to get lost, but they came back.'

'To *persuade* you.'

'At first, yeah, with more money, then with pain, but by that time I had already agreed to funnel information to the Chinese. I was scared shitless. I never knew when I made a drop if I was really leaving information for a CIA agent and further implicating myself in some spy deal that would topple the whole Canadian government, or at the very least the senior staff.'

'Risky,' I said. 'Even now, you might not truly know where the information went. Could the American government have owned the Brazilian company and sent Harvard to dupe you?'

'Probably,' Moses said. 'I was a kid, Sailor, younger than you are now, and I was neck-deep in hardening concrete before I realised that any number of agencies might send some bruiser up behind me with a silenced .22: one quick POP, and that'd be lights out.'

'At least now all that nonsense about your arm injury makes twisted sense,' I said. 'You were angry with the CIA for dildoing your curve-ball and decided to put the entire nation at risk by selling information about a secret American defence plan in the Canadian Arctic – and all because you were a poor kid from Jersey, a second-rate pitcher, who thought his wife might be falling for her boss. Forgive me, Moses, but that's pretty selfish on your part.'

'Not selfish.' He dabbed at his eyes again. 'I was *disillusioned* – it's what I was trying to say earlier: that's where spies come from, hope-lessness and disillusionment. All my childhood dreams came to an end in that bar-room with just a twist of that fucking gorilla's wrist. And yes, I hated everything about the American government and its culture – living outside the US will do that for you.'

'You married the Assistant Principal Secretary's daughter, shithead: of course you're going to be immersed in a one-sided perspective on America. Where's your head, Moses?'

'I was young.'

'Yeah.' Disgusted, I paced back and forth beside the table. Part of me felt sorry for him – he was as tragic a person as I'd ever known. But another part of me wanted to walk away, forget I'd ever known him, and leave him trapped between Lauren and Kate, between Sea Girt and Asbury Park, a lonely, rich dinosaur with no hope and a standing order for the Insomniac's Breakfast Special.

With sunlight colouring the wide verandah, I lifted the hurricane glass from Moses' candle and let the wind extinguish it. I had one more question for him. I could probably have figured it out on my own, but at this point I was too tired to think any more. I wanted a handful of pills and a long nap tucked safely between Jenny's thighs. Still pacing, I asked, 'So who killed Lauren?'

'Mikey Bartollo did.' The threat behind this simple response rang crystal-clear: *Back off, Sailor.*

'Who killed her?'

He crossed to me and I backed away a step. Through clenched teeth, he said, 'Anthony Michael "Mikey" Bartollo killed my daughter, Detective Doyle. And we're done here.'

'Kate found out, didn't she?' I backed off another step, moving towards the Persian welcome mat. 'Did Dunning tell her? Did he find something on King James Island? An empty missile silo, now that time and money and starvation and the fucking Internet have done away with Soviet Russia? Yeah, I bet that was it: I bet Dunning was up there to see thousands of his curlews flying in for spring and he stumbled across something he wasn't supposed to see, some evidence of missiles pointed at China. They couldn't kill him, not twenty years later, but he told Kate, right? And Kate got to feeling guilty, or maybe angry – you told me she could be difficult when she got mad – and she decided to spill the whole works. And one of those very agencies that you worried might put a bullet in your head jabbed a needle full of smack into Lauren's arm. Holy shit! That's it – holy frigging shit! J. M. McMichael – bullshit!'

Moses leapt forward and shoved me hard in the chest with both hands. I landed flat on my back, winded, which was a blessing because bright, jagged pain thundered through my side. At least I couldn't embarrass myself by screaming. Instead, I curled into a gasping ball, hoping desperately that Moses wouldn't kick me in the ribs – that'd be the end of me. It'd be six months before I breathed again.

He bent over, anger still contorting his leathery face. 'You clear out of here, Doyle, and leave me in peace, you hear? I don't want to see you again, to even hear you've passed by on the boardwalk, you understand? I'm an old man, but I will beat you to death if you so much as *think* about my daughter again!' He grabbed a handful of hair and punctuated his words by bouncing my head hard against the planks.

I saw stars and as I blinked to clear my vision Moses hovered over me, as if daring me to mention Lauren again. I knew it would sting, but I couldn't help it. I took a stabilising breath, then whispered, 'Dunning and Kate took the Americans' money, but they thought it was from the environmental lobby … oh, that's rich: even Kate's own father wouldn't tell her. The perfect patsy.' I tried to laugh, but I couldn't get enough wind. 'She tortured Bartollo, but he *couldn't* confess, because he didn't know. I bet Dunning's death pushed her over the edge. Or—' I coughed up phlegm.

'Or *what?*' Moses checked the patio. Tony from Bergen County suddenly appearing while he was beating me senseless wouldn't help his play for respectful empathy from the staff. 'What do you think you know, Sailor?'

'I think,' I wheezed, 'I think that Dunning found out about you and went to King James Island. He saw empty silos, biological weapons, a platoon of half-frozen guards – or maybe the whole project had been scrapped, leaving nothing but a bunch of deep holes and rusty Quonset huts, especially if the right people'd found out the Chinese were wise to their plan. But Dunning saw something.' I coughed again; the pain made my eyes water, but afterwards I breathed a bit easier. 'They killed him. NATO didn't need the fallout so they offed him – but not before Kate learned about your part in this sorry mess. She blamed you for Lauren's death, then killed herself – and who can blame her? Jesus Highdiving Christ, imagine finding out that her *husband* – Lauren's own *father* – had spied on the US *and* Canada, and then sold the Chinese the very information that got his daughter killed.' I tried to roll onto my injured side to keep him from driving bone shards into my lungs with his six-hundred-dollar shoes. 'You think this place protects you as you stand with your toes dangling off the bottom step, scared shitless even to step into the grass. Your history here doesn't protect you, Moses. Nothing does.'

He knelt down, brought his face close to mine, and whispered, 'If I see you again, Detective Doyle, I'll kill you. What I told you before is true: I admire what you did this summer. I wish I had that kind of honour in me. I don't. So if I ever see you again, I'll kill you.'

He rose without another word and started towards the hotel's grand entrance.

'She's here,' I said, a whimper behind the breakers' yammering.

Moses heard me, though. 'Who's here?'

'Your wife – we met long ago, on the beach in Asbury Park. I know it sounds impossible but she's found me again, and now I understand why she called me.'

'*Called* you?'

'With Hardass Hanley, my history teacher the year I first met your wife. It was coarse, but effective.'

'My wife's *dead*, Sailor.'

'I know: I read it in Mark, Chapter 4, Verse 37, *Martin* Heston.'

He stopped short, his silky affability trying to rebound, but he was too angry with me and just managed to look confused. 'I woke at 4:37 that morning, the morning Kate passed away. She'd come down here' – he pointed east towards the beach – 'right here, actually, to end her life in the shadow of this old hotel. Someone saw her, the overnight concierge on a smoke-break, she said it was "about 4:37" when Kate walked into the water. You know, I've never understood that. You don't say "about 4:37". You say "about 4:30" or "about 4:45", but you don't say "about 4:37". That's *exact*, 4:37, spot on, not *about*.' He wiped his eyes with his handkerchief. 'I found the bit about the furious squall a few years later, changed my name to Mark, and— Well, I have been up at 4:37 ever since. I don't know why.'

'Ask Kate.' I hadn't tried to get up.

'My wife is *dead*, Sailor. Stay away from me.' Moses strode across the Persian carpet and through the heavy oak doors, looking confident and self-assured, still strong after seventy years. But Moses Heston had failed to hide the nervous tremor in his voice. Like me, he understood that the epilogue for a thirty-six-year-old story was being written around us.

I sucked breath like a pearl diver and squinted against the sunlight. 'I caught you, Moses, you secret-selling, second-rate Little Leaguer. I may be broken, but I still caught you.' I laughed, a damp rattle from deep in my chest. 'It's three decades late, asshole, but I caught you.'

Wincing the pain away, I watched the sun rise over Spring Lake. Two joggers ran north on the sidewalk and both saw me, but made no move to help, to dial up paramedics on their Bluetooth headsets or even to check if I was still alive.

After a while, I caught my breath, found my feet and headed home, fresh lies already taking shape in my head.

A scalding-hot bath; helps quell the cravings. Six hundred milligrams of Ibuprofen and a bowl of soup. Funny, eating soup at 7:30 in the morning, but I need comfort food. I'm broken up pretty bad: I feel like I've been thrown down a flight of stairs. Jenny believes the North Side Playaz story – thank Christ for that. It'd be worse if Ben seemed at all traumatised, but he buys Jenny's Poseidon lie without a hitch. The twenty bucks helps. My lie about arresting Big G and Blade will hold for a few days. I just hope that's long enough. I worry that Jenny'll read the paper and learn that Blade is already dead, his head crushed like a Pepsi can, and Big G's sole hand is cuffed to the bed at Jersey Shore Medical Center.

Jenny sits with me, kneeling by the side of the tub, asking questions, pressing me for more and more information. And I lie to her again. Moses is wrong: there is nothing honourable about me. I hope Ben and Anna will be better than me when they grow up. I'm sure they will. Jenny'll make sure of it.

When she leaves, I try to sleep.

I'm supposed to see the orthopaedic surgeon today about my shoulder but I'll cancel, go tomorrow, or Wednesday. He wants me to lie around the house swilling Ibuprofen to stop the damaged tissue swelling. I'll tell him I chased a monster—

That's what it was: a monster. You've met several this week.

—through an abandoned hotel and down a deserted beach, just before I lost a fight with a former baseball player over his role selling Canadian political information to Chinese spies.

Yeah. He'll probably put the surgery off for a day or two.

It's Kate Stillman; you know it is. Not that it's possible she's here, but it's her, or the memory of her, or the ghost of her, or the acrobatic ocean-borne changeling creature that embodies her anger and vengeful spirit. But it's her.

It can't be Gabriel Lebow; I was wrong. The attack on Auntie Carla happened three days before the shooting at Robert Morris Middle School. Lebow didn't scratch up that pigpen; he didn't scratch up that lobster tank.

Auntie Carla was meat.

The lobsters at Seibert's were meat.

Jeremy Landon was – God save us all – meat.

Lebow was revenge. That'll show you, Grandpa.

Blade was – what? Exercise. Protection. Protection for what – for whom? For Blake Street? The old homestead? For me, the detective hunting around in Kate's old house? Meat for me? No, not meat, protection. Why?

She needs me. She called me.

Hanley – Harold Hardass Hanley was just to get my attention, to hire me.

I've got to see Hodges today, just to clear my head. Jenny'll believe me. I'll tell her I've got to give another statement; it won't take long. I'll just run over to the Prosecutor's Office.

I'll lie to my wife. Again.

Jenny and Ben insisted on coming with me to the Monmouth County Courthouse, but on the run up to Freehold I convinced them to drop me off, and go and visit my mother for lunch. She'd be home, and happy to see the kids for a couple of hours. Marta Hodges wasn't expecting me – I had no idea if she'd even be in her office, but screw it; I'd lied myself into this little excursion, so if Hodges wasn't around I'd sneak down the street to a coffee shop, kill a couple of hours, and then call Jenny to come and pick me up again: no blood; no foul.

Running up Route 18, Jenny reached for the radio, but I grabbed her wrist before she could press the POWER button.

'What?' she asked.

'Nothing,' I said, 'I just figured Ben might want to hear some of his music. Whaddya think, monkey-man? You wanna hear some of your tunes?'

From the back seat, Ben squealed, 'Yes! Daddy, can I have the fish names?'

'Fish names?' I looked to Jenny, who handed me a red disc with a bug-eyed fish wearing a bow tie and a top hat.

'Looks like a winner.' I slid it into the dashboard and the minivan swallowed it whole.

'Turn it up, Mommy!' Ben yelled, ready to sing along, but when Jenny turned up the volume, what came out of the speakers wasn't the happy, bouncing music of cartoon fish at play. Instead the confined space filled with a squealing, high-pitched wail. Ben started shouting for us to turn it down as Anna cried from her car seat.

'What was that?' he asked, holding his ears.

Okay, I get it: it's backwards – backwards through time. I get the point.

'I think it was playing backwards, buddy.' I pushed the EJECT button and the fish disc was vomited out again.

'That's strange,' Jenny said. 'It was working the other day.'

My mind raced, searching for something to distract them – I didn't want to try another disc and have it play backwards as well – then I saw Ben's favourite book, about the bicycle-riding bear, tucked under his seat. 'Hey, monkey-man.' I reached back painfully and extricated the book. 'How about if we read instead? I think you should read it out loud to me. Can you do that?'

'Sure.' Ben took the book from me. 'I know *all* the words.'

'Excellent.' I adjusted the seat, closed my eyes.

Ben said, 'Don't go to sleep, Daddy, you have to listen.'

'I'll hear every word, buddy.' I listened in silence as Ben read from memory. He might have recognised a few of the words, but he didn't hold the book still long enough to see any of them. I could hear him hoisting the pages up to show Anna pictures of the bicycle-riding bear he loved so much.

Jenny complimented Ben's storytelling, encouraging him to read more books so his acceptance to Columbia might be wrapped up before he finished first grade, and in a turn of events as familiar in our house as a Diet Coke commercial, Ben retold the story of the cycling bear. After seeing the world with the circus, the bear finds himself near his former home. Naturally, while he's there, his old buddies come knocking, looking for a cyclist to haul their berries and shit around.

Ben read, 'Come back to us, Bear. We've all missed you so. And with your bicycling talents, o'er the great hills you'll go. You'll carry our harvest, our honey, our roots, up and down steep passes in your bright circus suits.'

Bear's circus friends convince him to strike out for uncharted lands over the mountains. He thumbs his nose to his former clan, herd, pack, whatever, climbs on his trusty bike and starts pedalling.

Ben's voice rose in anticipation of the happy ending, when Bear leads the circus caravan into the sunset. He read, 'When Otis the cowpoke joined them on their ride, he told the bear's friends Hanley was no— Mommy, what's S-U-I-C-I-D-E?'

Jenny drove with one hand. 'That spells suicide, buddy. It means to kill yourself. Plenty of people do it when they get really angry or sad.'

Ben found this riotously funny. 'Thanks, Mommy!' he shouted, then returned to his story. 'Hanley was no suicide!'

I snapped awake.

Anna slept in her car seat. Ben had finished the bear book and let it fall to the floor. Jenny ran a hand up my thigh. 'Hey, sleepyhead.'

I yawned. I wanted to stretch, but I feared the burst of pain I knew would accompany any such movement. 'Where are we?'

'Freehold.' She wound her way through a residential part of town. 'We're almost at the county building now. You ready? Or do you want to stop at your mom's for a while, take a longer nap, maybe get something to drink?'

'No, no, I'm fine,' I pulled down the sun visor, checked my tousled hair and bleary eyes. 'Oh, yeah, sure: I look like seventeen dollars worth of mouldy cheese.'

'Hodges won't mind,' Jenny pulled into the fire lane in front of the Monmouth County Court House. She leaned over to kiss me. 'How long?'

'Longer than most men, but not porn material.'

'Jackass.'

'Two hours?'

She kissed me again.

I kissed her back, just a peck, but an important peck, because it said: *See? We're falling right back into that comfortable married groove where ten thousand kisses occur without anyone even noticing.*

'Yeah, two hours.' I climbed out, said goodbye to Ben and blew a kiss to Anna. Ben liked that move as well. To Jenny, I said, 'You can hang out at Mom's as long as you like. I'll call when we're done here.'

'Okay, see you later.' Oblivious to my lies and misdirection, Jenny drove off towards my mother's house not half a mile away.

I got lucky. Not only was Hodges in, but the executive secretary, the one at the main desk in the Prosecutor's Office, was out for the day. I could tell, because the nine-hundred-year-old temp who showed me where to find Marta Hodges was actually pleasant, not the normal stressed-out miserable bitch most Prosecutor's Offices have guarding the front door, like Cerberus, only meaner. The kindly woman, who introduced herself as Beatrice Hartwell, wore a pleated skirt and a floral print blouse that might have matched something I'd seen Travolta wear in *Saturday Night Fever*. She offered me a cold drink and tottered with me down the hallway. Together we looked like two drunks stumbling home from a bender.

The executive secretary at the Commonwealth Attorney's Office in Richmond, Helga von Wiener Schnitzel (I couldn't remember her name), was also old enough to have worked with the Nazis back in the thirties, but unlike nice Mrs Hartwell, Helga didn't have a kind bone in her entire body. Huck and I were sure she'd have found the Nazis overly mild-mannered. I immediately wanted to box Beatrice up and take her back to Virginia with me.

'You can go ahead in. Detective Hodges is just about done with Mr Porter.'

That little move would have got her kindly ass canned at the Commonwealth Attorney's Office, too: never never *never* interrupt the lead investigator during a meeting, because all meetings are interviews, and all interviews end up documented in the murder book, and everything in the murder book can come back to bugger you regally when you go to the Commonwealth Attorney for an indictment. Around here, the County Prosecutor was God.

I hung around outside Hodges' office until she saw me through the window.

She raised both hands to me in a *What are you doing here?* gesture.

I waved, trying to communicate one-handed that I was okay waiting until she was done. *No rush.*

It didn't work; Hodges motioned me in and I recognised the assistant principal from Robert Morris Middle School, Whatshisname C. Porter, the one with the golfing Mickey Mouses on his tie.

He stood when I came in. 'Hello, Detective Doyle.' He'd ditched Mickey for a dressier tie to go with his suit. I guessed trips to the Prosecutor's Office weren't on the normal rounds for a middle-school assistant principal.

'How are you?' I shook his hand, lefty.

'What's going on, Doyle?' Hodges didn't get up.

'Nothing much,' I said. 'I was in the neighbourhood and wanted to check in with you on a couple of things. I can wait, though. Please don't let me interrupt.'

'No problem.' Hodges gestured towards a seat beside Porter. 'Take a load off. You look like a warm corpse. You all right?'

I lied for Porter's benefit. 'I tripped down some steps in Spring Lake, reinjured my shoulder and banged up my ribs. I'll be fine, though.' The chair, a Wal-Mart special, squealed on the chequerboard tiles when I slid it back.

Hodges raised her eyebrows. *Nice job, shithead. You're getting good at that little fabrication.*

Using my arrival as an excuse, Porter shuffled a stack of pages into a manila folder. He looked anxious to get out of there.

'You okay for tonight?' Hodges asked him.

'Yeah,' he said without any confidence, 'the superintendent's coming. It's funny; I've been at Morris for four years and every month I break my back to get parents to come to the PTA meetings. Most

437

meetings, I have two or three die-hards complaining that no one else gets involved or helps out.'

'Not tonight,' Hodges said.

'Tompkins, our SRO, has three officers coming, and Neptune City PD are on call too, just in case all Hell breaks out.' He stuffed the folder into a nylon backpack that clashed with his suit—

Teachers. Jesus, buy a briefcase.

—and stood to leave. 'We may have a thousand people trying to cram into the gym tonight; there's no way it'll go well, just no way.'

'You bringing everyone back tomorrow?' I asked.

'Yeah,' he said, 'the CSI guy is done. They released the school to us on Friday afternoon. We've been there most of the weekend putting things back in order.' The SWAT guys would have torn the place to shreds.

'You're ready though?' I asked.

'Yeah,' he said. 'Superintendent Mihalko and the School Board Chair are addressing the community tonight. I imagine it's going to be a nightmare. We've converted the library for the week, we've got grief and anxiety counsellors available, and the city cops will keep the media out. They'll cordon off a space in the parking lot of that DOT building where the buses picked up the kids last week. So far this weekend, I've heard that CNN, FOX, Jersey Channel 12, NBC, CBS, ABC, WNYW and just about every Internet blogger and on-line Scream Site will be over there. So assuming that parents come directly to Morris and find parking in our lot – we have exactly two hundred and eight spaces for the twelve hundred attendees I expect to show up – and no one walks across Steiner Avenue to voluntarily give a statement to the media, and we don't have any race or religious riots break out in the gym after we've stuffed over a thousand furious citizens in there, everything should be business as usual tomorrow morning when the buses run.'

'Just kids doing school at school,' Hodges tried not to laugh.

'Right.' Porter pinched the bridge of his nose. 'Students solving for X and teachers touching the future!'

'My teachers could only ever reach to about next Thursday,' I said.

Porter shook my hand. 'Take care of yourself, Detective. I know I'm not allowed to use your name, but I'd love to tell this community that you were the one who saved their kids.'

'I didn't do anything of the sort, and you know it, Mr Porter. But by keeping my name out of it, we've kept legions of thugs from descending on my house, killing me and enslaving my family. That, in my opinion, has been a good thing.'

'I get it.' He thanked Hodges, promised to call tomorrow, and left us alone.

Hodges said, 'Holy shit, huh? Let's add that to the list of jobs I don't want.'

'Middle School administrator? Oh yeah, I bet that ranks right up there with bovine inseminator or sump pump technician.'

Her forehead creased. 'So what *are* you doing here, Doyle? I have to tell you: if your little stunt the other night hadn't led to another ice kitchen *and* Big G's arrest, I'd have you in leg-irons by now. I'm not going to ask the question, because I'd have to document your answer and keep you in Monmouth County for the next eighteen months.'

'Can you phrase it as a statement?' I played along.

'Sure: Stay the fuck out of Asbury Park, New Jersey, or I'll arrest you myself.' She considered this for a moment, then said, 'There. How's that?'

'Pretty clear,' I said. 'I take it the Street Crimes Unit knew about the lab at 1720 Blake?'

'You're a quick study, Doyle, for a dumbass.' Her BlackBerry buzzed; she ignored it. 'They'd been staking the place out since we arrested RJ, hoping Big G and or Blade would show up.'

'They weren't there the other night,' I pointed out. 'I could've used the help.'

'Night off,' she said. 'I had their LT pull them when I heard you were on your way. I told him Ed and I needed to be on Blake for a couple of hours with some CSI techs. There wasn't any reason to have anyone staking out 1720. The two narcs on duty probably toasted me all night over at the Stone Pony.'

'Nice. I have to admit, Lieutenant, you're creative and resourceful.'

She gestured around her modestly appointed office. 'I didn't get all this being stupid.'

'I guess not,' I said.

Hodges had one of those stress-busting executive toys on her desk, the one where you let a little metal ball strike another little ball in a row of little balls and the energy is somehow transferred to the little metal ball at the other end, proving something Isaac Newton probably discovered while my ancestors were starving on a Donegal potato farm. I'd never owned one, but I couldn't understand how that clickety-clacking could possibly reduce anyone's stress – I'd have listened to it for five minutes and shot someone in the next office. Hodges fidgeted with the thing now, watching it pendulum back and forth for a second, then asked again, 'What do you need, Doyle?'

'Um,' I said finally, 'well, I hadn't heard from you so I thought I'd see how things were going. Things seem pretty shitty, judging by the news and the sound of Porter's weekend at Morris Middle.'

'Take you all week to figure that one out?' She grabbed the clickety-clacker, silencing it. 'And thanks to Ed Hess' and your antics, I've also got two Asbury Park detectives calling every fifteen minutes trying to figure out how it's possible that Richard B. "Big G" Harris managed to get his hand blown off while Tejon G. "Blade" Butler ended up awfully dead in some old woman's back yard, his head neatly caved in as if crushed by a grizzly bear, when, for their very lives, neither of these fine detectives can find any sign of a fucking grizzly bear in Asbury Park. And all this happened while I was apparently poking around in a house across the street with Ed Hess and some CSI techs. My boss found that oversight hysterical.'

'Teach you to lie.' I wagged a finger at her.

'About grizzly bears? Eat shit, Doyle. I need trust and communication problems with Asbury Park PD like I need an unscheduled pap smear.'

'Maybe they should try Long Branch,' I teased. 'There're a few pretty rural spots there, plenty of room for a bear to hide.'

'Not funny.' Her phone buzzed again. She peeked at it quickly, then slipped it into her bag. 'I've got a baby detective working the Hanley suicide, which is nothing but that, a suicide, but because he's never been through the paperwork before, I might as well be handling the whole frigging thing myself anyway.'

'Buy a man a fish; teach a man to fish,' I said, 'in the end, it all smells like tuna.'

Hodges wasn't amused, which was sad as I was trying to be amusing. She said, 'RJ's getting arraigned for murder today. We held him on drug pinches. I've asked that the courtroom be closed, but the judge we pulled for the hearing, she's not a bad egg, but she believes in a free press, as long as they behave themselves.'

This got my attention. 'You can't keep them out?'

'I've asked,' she said, 'but it doesn't look good.'

'Shit. That's an unpleasant surprise.'

'I don't think you've got much to worry about from the North Side Assholes,' Hodges said. 'They've had their head cut off and their kitchens closed down. The Street Crimes Unit loves me because I let them come along when we snagged RJ. They might not know what the hell happened, but no one is shedding too many tears for Blade, and Big G's so heavily medicated he isn't giving orders for chicken chow mein, never mind orders to have your family greased.'

'Yeah, but still, you can't arraign RJ for murder without disclosing my identity, and even if you do get the judge to close the courtroom, you can't keep the media out of the lobby, or from working the benches if the early docket runs long. And to top it off, Ed says RJ's lawyer's a tree-hugging pinko or some damned thing, wants to empower the poor, disenfranchised drug dealer and gangbanger.'

What had started as a pleasant distraction from the stark reality that Moses Heston's late wife might want me dead had just turned into a potential nightmare for Jenny and me. Even if the beach house wasn't overrun with gangbangers by dinnertime, we'd have fifteen news vans parked along the street, each of them trying to get a look at me through the windows. And for seven bucks, any of them could come down to the beach, right onto the sand with me and Curt the Blurry Lifeguard. And the boardwalks were free; I wouldn't be able to take five steps the rest of the month without a camera in my face. To make things worse, Jenny and I would probably have to stick around New Jersey until RJ's lawyer deposed me and even without meeting him, I had a feeling that sonofabitch would sing my name to everyone: Fox, CNN, YouTube, Facebook, TacoBell.com, *everyone*.

Hodges dug in a drawer, found a pen and made a quick note. 'I've got an idea.' She punched two numbers on her desk phone. 'Mrs Hartwell, can you come down here please? Thank you.' She hung up. 'Where's your mother live, Doyle?'

'About five blocks from here. Why?'

'Can she hit the beach with you for a couple of days?'

'I don't see why not,' I said. 'But I don't know how—? Oh, wait. I get it.'

'Let's give them that: you bring your mother down to the beach and in three days the world has moved on.'

Mrs Hartwell, the ancient temp in Travolta's blouse, knocked quietly and poked her head inside the office. 'Yes, ma'am?'

Hodges looked up. 'Would you log onto the file database and see if lead counsel on the Mercer case has uploaded the documents for the arraignment today? They'll either be under Weston or Hilton, the two attorneys I saw this morning.'

'Yes, ma'am. With Ms Jeppesen's login?'

'You've got it?'

'I do.' Her voice barely rose above a whisper. She struck me as someone who might find the prospect of making toast exhausting.

'Thank you.' Hodges dismissed her with a wave, but before the door closed she called, 'You can print the whole thing for me, but for now I just need the pages on the attack on Robert Morris Middle School playground and the witness list we submitted for the warrant on Mercer.'

'Yes, ma'am.' Mrs Hartwell left without a sound. At one time, there must've been one overbearing bastard of a husband.

When the door clicked shut, Hodges said, 'There. I'll check what we're bringing forward today.'

'I get it, Lieutenant; I do, but Jesus, I hate giving up my mother's address.'

'They're going to find it anyway,' she said logically. 'The beach place is the one that's below the radar. I guarantee every major and minor network and newspaper remembers where you live, given all the press you had last month, so this way it'll look like you were in town visiting your parents – easy. And to top it off, I'll call the prosecutor, have him add some first-year associate to the trial team, some pretty blonde tan babe in a tight skirt, just out of law school. She can show her face in the courtroom and when she leaves, shaking that pert little booty, she'll be trawling a veritable net for reporters and cameramen in her wake. I'll have her pass the benches and take the stairs down to the lobby before saying anything, then she can confirm that she has no idea about anything related to Roland James Mercer, *except* that she believes the Samaritan came from somewhere up in Allenhurst, just a jogger out training for the New York Marathon. She won't be able to answer any questions, but we can have her "slip up" and drop the news that Superintendent Mihalko has asked the Samaritan to appear at the school tonight to receive a Community Hero Award for his actions – that'll get half the media hightailing it for Cameron Drive while the other half head over to stake out your mother's place. You collect your mother this afternoon, head back to the beach and wait for me to call if I hear that anyone's got wind of where you are – to do that, they'd have to connect your mother to the beach place, and I bet you a martini that the cottage in Belmar is still in your father's name.'

I flushed; I didn't enjoy looking like a loser son in front of Marta Hodges. 'We never got around to the paperwork,' I admitted. 'It's been years since Dad died, and it's still in my mother's desk.'

'Well, today be glad you overlooked it,' she said.

I was truly impressed. 'Damn, lady, but you're like the Vince Lombardi of misdirection.'

'Comes with the territory, Doyle,' she said. 'You forget where you are.'

I stretched my aching back, then changed the subject. 'You mentioned Hanley. Anything strange there at the Warren & Monmouth?'

'Nah – why? Because you knew him?

'My sister liked him,' I explained. 'She used to think about teaching at Freehold Catholic, swilling down coffee in the teachers' lounge with old Hardass.'

'Sorry,' she said, 'he must've got depressed.' She scratched another note on her pad. 'I'll check with the kid working the case, but I doubt there's any smoke, let alone fire – we both saw Ed Hess this weekend, and he didn't say anything, right?'

'Yeah. I know.' I'd reached the moment of truth. I could either tell Hodges what I knew about Moses and Kate and risk having her dial up a loony wagon to haul me away, or I could keep my mouth shut and deal with Moses' past on my own.

Hodges watched me considering my options, then said, 'Doyle? You got something you haven't told me?'

'Nope.' I gave up. 'I was just wondering if anything had emerged on that.'

She lifted the phone again, dialled another number, covered the mouthpiece with her hand. 'I'll check in with you later. Go and get your mother and lay low. I'll do what I can, but in exchange you're going to be the best, most compliant prosecution witness Monmouth County has seen since the Hindenburg went down.'

'You know it.'

'You've got my cell number.'

I let myself out while she made plans with the attorney assigned to the RJ Mercer case. At the end of the hallway, I passed Beatrice Hartwell's desk. She sat unmoving, hands folded in her lap, staring stone-faced at a laser printer. The green light blinked, but none of Marta Hodges' reports were running.

'Can I help you?' I asked.

Beatrice jumped. 'Oh— Oh my, yes. I— I don't understand these new printers.' She looked afraid to touch it. 'Back when I started, we had typewriters – Thomas Watson from IBM, he said they were all we'd ever need.'

'Yeah,' I leaned over her keyboard, 'but look where it got him.'

Beatrice didn't get the joke – or maybe she couldn't hear me; she didn't look to be more than a day or two ahead of the Grim Reaper. I opened the computer's control panel, found the print queue, resent the document, then waited for the printer to hum to life. 'There you go,' I said, 'that ought to do it.'

'Arnold and I never had a printer,' she said. 'My grandson prints everything I need in his dormitory room. He can send documents from his phone to his room, where they print automatically. Can you believe that?'

'Next thing you know, they'll put a man on the moon!'

Now Beatrice did laugh, a terrible, wheezing sound that left me poised to dial 911, and I silently swore never to get that old. As the final pages printed I said, 'Can I take these down the hall for you?'

'Oh, no,' she said, 'I'll put them in a folder and run them in to her.'

'*Walk* them,' I said, 'Detective Hodges can wait.'

Beatrice laughed again and I left her there, sitting as still as a column of weathered granite.

Punching numbers on my phone, I took the stairs instead of the elevator. Over background noise of my kids whooping it up with Grandma, I told Jenny where to find me.

'You done already?' she asked. 'I feel like we just got here.'

'Well, we've got to go,' I said. 'Will you tell my mother to pack for a few days at the beach.'

'What? Why?' Jenny started.

'Too much to explain now,' I said. 'I'll tell you as we go, but the short version is that the Prosecutor's Office is arraigning RJ Mercer for Lebow's murder today and my statement is included in the documents going to the judge and the defence team. I listed our address in Fredericksburg, but Hodges has to let them know where to find me for a deposition.'

'So? We knew that, didn't we?'

'It's not them, Jenny,' I explained. 'With all the press this story has got in the past week, she's expecting a media circus, here and at Morris Middle tonight when the superintendent speaks to the Neptune City parents and students.'

Jenny still didn't get it. 'Sailor, look, it's noisy as hell here and I've OD'd on your mother's sugar cookies, so why don't you just spell it out for me?'

'The defence attorney is going to have our address today, and that in turn means the media will have it, and it'll take them less than five minutes to connect me, this summer's plague carrier, with me, at my mother's place in Freehold.'

'Shit.'

'Exactly.'

'But won't that lead to the beach house?'

My face reddened again. 'I never switched it from my father's name.

It may not stop them completely, but it ought to slow them down.'

'I'll never tease you for procrastinating again,' she said.

'Sure you will – but for now, how about if you just come and get me?'

'On my way.'

'I'll be on that concrete porch out front, the one with the old stone banister—'

—like weathered granite . . . a gargoyle—

'Thanks, Jenny.' I hung up, then called up the photos on my BlackBerry and scrolled through the shots until I found one of the stone gargoyle on the slate roof above Harold Hanley's room at the Warren & Monmouth Hotel. Around me the Monmouth County Courthouse bustled its way through another Monday afternoon.

I couldn't think, couldn't *remember—*

Outside, I sought a quiet corner under the wide stone portico, closed my eyes and cast my thoughts back to Tuesday night, with Tony, Chef Sam and Moses. Had it rained all day? No, by the time Jenny and I had left the library with the kids the storm had moved out over the ocean. So plenty of time for the slate roof to dry.

And the concrete, Sailor: the gargoyles should have been dry as well, certainly by the time you took this picture.

I rechecked the photo. 'But it's wet, no doubt about it; that gargoyle is *wet.*'

My BlackBerry's images were never going to rival Ansel Adams. The shot of the Warren & Monmouth's gargoyle was blurry, with shitty colour definition; the stone creature looked as much like – like a pile of weathered granite – as an actual sculpture. I tried the ZOOM feature, but that made things worse. But . . .

It should have been dry. The weather had changed early that afternoon, before we took the kids to Nagle's for lunch, before . . .

I checked the photo of the gargoyle on top of the carved cornice alongside the Ocean Grove firehouse: it was wet too, but it had been exposed to the deluge all morning, so not really surprising. 'But the weather . . .' I racked my memory. 'The weather had cleared – the *weather.*' I clicked the CLOSE button, distracted again by some vestigial memory tickling the OxyContin-beaten edges of my brain. 'The weather,' I murmured, watching for Jenny's minivan, then, 'That's *it*! The goddamned weather! *Merri*weather: Rawlings Merriweather!'

My mother watched the kids for us – I felt bad asking her to do it; she'd only just arrived and already I was playing the Grandmother card. But actually, she was happy to shoo Jenny and me out the door; us living in Virginia meant time alone with the kids was always welcome. Of course, she made me promise that I'd take Jenny to dinner in Spring Lake or Bradley Beach, *not* Neptune City or Asbury Park. I didn't intend going anywhere near Neptune City until a judge subpoena'd me. As for Asbury Park, I'd have been happy to avoid it for the rest of my life ... but who knew what the evening might hold?

While I was getting cleaned up, I started to worry that we shouldn't be leaving the kids alone – we'd not told Mom that there'd been a break-in; we didn't want to worry her. But Jenny believed the thugs had been corralled already and I knew that Kate Stillman wouldn't come back until I was home. So I shaved, changed, and tried to purge the insecurity from my mind.

We ended up at Seibert's Seafood. I griped about wanting to try someplace new, but quietly celebrated a chance to go back to a restaurant I'd loved as a kid.

Except for the groovy new lobster tank under the forest-green awning, Seibert's hadn't changed in twenty-five years. Though quiet this late in the season, it was still easy to imagine crowds of beachgoers, sarongs and towel wraps pulled over damp swimsuits, juxtaposed with the white linen and crystal glassware dressing each of Mrs Seibert's tables.

I ordered the same fish stew my sister had got me addicted to twenty years earlier; every bite tasted like a trip through time. Jenny's lobster cost something like our combined salary for a month, but I didn't care: watching a woman rip a lobster into edible bits with her bare hands is something every guy should enjoy at least once in his life. Jenny, in a long cotton skirt and a sleeveless ivory blouse, shivered in the air-conditioning. She'd wanted to look nice, and hadn't brought along a sweater.

For me, I wondered, *or for everyone else, maybe just proving she doesn't have to wear barf-stained sweats every day?*

Jenny drank white wine. I had a Diet Coke, but I would have invaded Macedonia for a Scotch.

Halfway through the main course, I screwed everything up by checking my watch for the third or fourth time.

'What's up?' Jenny finally asked. 'You got a hot date I don't know about?'

'Nah,' I toyed absently with the pepper grinder, 'I just want to make it to the library before it closes at nine.'

'The *library?*' This she hadn't been expecting. 'I thought perhaps we could see a movie, or go to an art gallery, or do something adults do when they're not hauling around two children and bags full of bottles and half-eaten sandwiches.'

'I need two minutes in there, Jenny, that's it: I've just got to get a look at one book I noticed there the other day. I don't even need to read it, just peek at the cover.'

'Why?' she asked, the gooseflesh tight on her forearms. 'I've got two weeks of backlogged work to get done, so if we're not doing something fun, I ought to head home and get cracking. I'm still a lawyer on some planet somewhere, aren't I?'

'You are.' I tore off a piece of bread and sopped up the last juice. 'I saw a then-and-now book about Spring Lake the other day. I wanted to check out a couple of images of the Warren & Monmouth Hotel.'

'You've been down there a lot this week. That baseball player, right?'

'Yeah, and I noticed a few things the other day, when Harold Hanley jumped, that struck me as odd. I wanted to see if they were the same as way back when. No big deal, but the library closes at nine, and I don't want to miss it.'

'Whatever.' She finished her wine and gestured for a refill. 'Weirdo.'

'That's Officer Weirdo to you, missy. That hotel's a crime scene.'

'Exactly two hundred and fifty miles outside your jurisdiction, Officer Weirdo.'

'True,' I said, 'but there's a great dessert place on Third, a French

448

café with Napoleons as big as your sister's thighs. I'll take you there afterwards.'

'Deal.' She cracked a lobster claw. 'But *never* mention Kelly's thighs and dessert in the same breath again. Ever.'

'Deal,' I echoed.

We finished dinner, talking a bit about the timeline for RJ's trial and my return to the VASP. Jenny had two more glasses of wine to my half a gallon of Diet Coke. If I planned to sleep later, I'd need a convenient truck to run me over outside the bedroom. Though I was revved on caffeine and needing to pee, I tried to pace the evening to Jenny's mellow white-wine buzz, but it was hard not to check my watch every ten minutes.

Rawlings Merriweather's honking tome, *Spring Lake: A Photographic History*, had been shelved and I had no clue where to find local history stuff so I asked at the main desk. Old Quadrafocals was off-duty, and her replacement, an elderly gentleman anxious to lock up and go home, wasn't best pleased to be answering reference questions at 8:50 p.m. He had a mole on his cheek that might have had its own zip code. I tried, and failed, to avert my eyes and eventually I managed to focus on his ratty cardigan with its faded leather patches on the elbows. Grumbling at me, Moley punched keys on a laptop, then gestured upstairs. My chances of talking Jenny into a bit of sex later were good, and I felt sorry for the old bastard – in that sweater he couldn't possibly have got laid in the new millennium.

Jenny slumped in an easy chair beside Bruce Wayne's empty fireplace, flipping through a news magazine, while I trudged slowly up the spiral staircase and navigated the narrow balcony, which creaked and complained with every step. I eventually found the Merriweather book stashed in an upstairs alcove; I needed only a glance at the cover. 'Sonofabitch,' I whispered, scrolling through the photos on my BlackBerry again.

There were no gargoyles, not now, and not a hundred years ago.

'Sonofabitch!' I slapped the book down on a nearby table.

'Honey,' Jenny called from down below, 'there's quite an echo in here. You might want to clean it up.'

'Yeah, yeah, sorry,' I said, without meaning it.

'You find what you need?' She spoke without raising her voice; I heard her clearly thanks to the strange acoustics of the two-level great room.

'Um, yeah, I think so,' I said, and snapped a picture of Rawlings Merriweather's cover. 'I'll be right down.'

We strolled along, my arm around Jenny's waist, her head resting on my arm. I smelled her shampoo, fake lilac blossom, but it did the trick and my mind left Moses and Kate Stillman and meandered over to thoughts of my wife.

'You find your book?' she asked. 'You were only up there for two minutes.'

'Yeah,' I said, 'speed reading. You want dessert or coffee?'

'That depends,' she said, 'on whether you want to go to bed with a chunky woman or a thin woman.'

'Who is she?' I teased. 'It depends on the size of her boobs, honestly.'

Jenny broke away long enough to slug me in the chest. 'Jackass.'

'Chubby.'

'Okay, then, so no dessert.' She baited the hook. It was just a matter of time before I bit.

Naturally, I didn't disappoint, 'Hey, now, hold on: you're not chunky or chunky or fat or even full-looking – you can have dessert if you want it.'

And she reeled me in: 'Uh huh, sure! Don't bullshit me, Sailor; I had a whole lobster, potatoes, that green stuff, whatever it was, and four glasses of wine. If I eat dessert, you have to promise the lights'll be off. I don't want you to see my paunch.'

Laughing, I ticked points off on my fingertips. 'Okay: A. You look fine, downright edible. I've been horny since the moment my mother agreed to babysit. B. If you want to keep the lights off, that's fine with me, I'll practise my Braille. C. You can have dessert, and I will still love you, even if you look well fed. And D. Wait, is there a D? Oh, yeah, D. I have no idea what a paunch is.'

'A little belly.' She snuggled back beneath my arm.

'A little belly? Really? Gross. *Ick*. No, we'll have to call the whole thing off: I couldn't possibly achieve orgasm with a woman with a little belly.'

'"Achieve orgasm"? You going for a medal or something?'

'Sounded pretty good, doncha think?' I looked both ways before we crossed. 'And I've got to be honest with you here: all the best orgasms are with women with really big bellies. So I suggest you double up on that Napoleon order.'

'Have I mentioned that you're a jackass? Because if not, I can reiter—'

Jenny jumped as an explosion of breaking glass followed by an alarm claxon shattered the peace in Spring Lake. 'Jesus. What's that? A fire?'

I knew already. My guts wrenched into a knot. The world around us, which had been moving at a leisurely, white-wine pace, sped up. 'Shit.'

'What?' Jenny looked at me, worry evident in every line on her face. 'You know something? Call your mother, Sailor. Damn it, we should have stayed home, should have stayed with the kids—'

I cut her off. 'They're fine, honey, believe me.'

The only dangerous place is right here, with me.

'What is it? Should we call someone?'

'It's the jewellery store—'

'You think it's another attack? Are the owners Jewish? I know that's a cheap stereotype, but why else?'

'No.' I kept us moving down Third Avenue, towards O'Malley's Fine Jewellery. 'They're Irish, like most of the old-timer businesses around here. Let's— Um, let's go; the Spring Lake cops can handle it.' I peeked up, knowing I shouldn't, and there, glaring down at me from the top of the two-storey roof, was Kate Stillman, framed by the darkness: a damp, obsidian figure. Her cadaverous face peered from the same tattered cowl and she hissed a warning, drowned out by the piercing shriek of the store alarm. She leapt across Morris Avenue, bounded over the rooftop above O'Malley's and disappeared into the trees along Devine Park. In three frantic leaps, she was gone, south towards the Warren & Monmouth and her protective perch above Moses' breakfast table.

Sirens wailed in response to the alarm as shoppers, tourists and well-dressed diners all spilled into Third Avenue, some looking to help, others hoping to catch a bit of mayhem on their camera phones. A crowd quickly formed on the sidewalk in front of O'Malley's and within minutes two police cruisers had pulled up out front.

'C'mon,' Jenny said, 'let's get the car. We don't need to hang around here.'

We'd parked near the library, just a couple of blocks away. As I buckled my seatbelt I said, 'I'm going to drive down there, real quick. I think I saw that one cop, Ed Hess, the one who took me to the hospital when I fell the other day.'

'All right, but just for a second, okay, Sailor? I'm scared to be away from the kids – every time we leave the damned house the shit hits the fan around here.' Jenny's voice was shaking a little, but clearly any would-be felons would have fled the neighbourhood two seconds after hearing that alarm go off.

'Just for a minute,' I said, and parked outside the waning throng. With no shots fired, no burglars in cuffs, no Cary Grant dangling from the weathervane, onlookers were quickly losing interest. I spotted Ed Hess, dressed casually in khakis and a light sweater, training his flashlight through a ragged wound in the store's plate-glass window. I called, 'Ed!' through cupped hands, 'Ed Hess!'

He shielded his eyes against the high-beam headlights of the police cruisers. 'Who's that? Doyle?' He said something to a thin, pasty-faced cop in uniform. I recognised him, Kyle Cheese-grater, Ed's partner on the Hanley case last weekend.

Kyle nodded to Ed, then tipped his hat to me.

'Nice police work,' Jenny said wryly. 'Maybe he'll run out and get us lattes.'

'It's a nice town,' I defended, 'and not much crime. These guys're friendly.'

But when Ed reached the minivan, he was anything but friendly. 'Why am I not surprised?'

452

'Whaddya mean?' I said. 'We were just looking for a place to have dessert when somebody smashed the window—'

'Doyle,' he warned, 'look me in the face and tell me you know nothing about this. My wife made pot roast – you know how often she makes pot roast? Twice a year. So if you know anything that will get me home before it gets cold, I'll speak well of you at your wake.' He looked past me to Jenny. 'Good evening, ma'am.'

'Ed Hess, my wife, Jenny Doyle. Jenny, this is Officer Edward Hess, Spring Lake PD.'

'Edgar,' he corrected.

'Sorry!'

'Just Ed is fine.'

'How are you, Ed?' Jenny reached across me to shake his hand.

'Nice to meet you, ma'am,' he said.

'I understand I have you to thank for getting Clutzy here to the hospital the other day?'

Ed's face brightened. 'That's right, ma'am. He took a nasty fall over there. I'd have been too embarrassed to show my face in public again, but there's no accounting for stupidity with this one, huh?'

'You said it.' Jenny smiled, and all but owned Ed Hess. 'But I've got to side with Clutzy on this break-in. We were just taking a walk when that alarm started.'

Looking grumpy again, Hess turned to me. 'C'mon Doyle, don't jerk me off, excuse me, ma'am. I'm hungry and tired and off-duty tonight, so how about you help me get home, huh?'

'The Warren & Monmouth,' I whispered.

'What's that?' Jenny asked. 'What did you say? Are you—? Did—? Do you know who did this, Sailor?'

I unbuckled and opened the door. 'One second, sweetie.'

Jenny's face contorted in a mix of confusion and don't-you-call-me-sweetie-asshole as I stepped out and walked Ed Hess across the road.

'So what's going on, Doyle?'

'Let me borrow your light.' I shone it across the empty terraces of black velvet and the locked display cases, some still sporting less expensive watches and faux gemstones. I found the rosewood case on the wall behind the counter. The single hanging penlight that had been illuminating the strand of Tahitian pearls had been torn out and the case lay in darkness.

'What're you looking for?' Ed asked, his gaze following the circle of light.

'That,' I said. 'You see that case, there on the wall? It's empty. That's what you're looking for: a strand of black pearls. The centrepiece is a whopper, worth more than you and I will make this decade, combined. The locals think that the strand hanging here was a fake, with the real deal locked in a safe downstairs, but I don't buy it. These were the real thing.'

'Holy Christ,' he said, 'how'd you know?'

'The Warren & Monmouth,' I said. 'You want to check out Moses Stillman – his real name is Martin Heston. He's been living in a suite there for years—'

'The old guy? The one you had breakfast with last weekend? *He* did this?'

'You want the pearls? That's where I'd start looking,' I said. 'Now, walk me back to my car and tell my wife what a grand job I've done helping you, and how you'd forgive me if you and I were married.'

Hess frowned. 'Jackass.'

'Ha! That's just what she'd say!'

As we drove I tried to explain without lying myself into a corner. 'There may be a connection between Moses Stillman and a strand of pearls missing from O'Malley's – he mentioned it a couple of times this week, he even brought me here to check it out one morning. Hess is just going to look in on him. It may be nothing.'

'Someone stole pearls out of a display case in the three seconds between that glass shattering and the whole street filling up with people?'

'It looks like they broke out a back window, maybe to run down here through the park by the lake. Ed's got it under control. Don't worry.'

Jenny seemed to believe me, so far at least. 'So why are *we* going? Can't he take care of this alone?'

'He's just one guy, Jenny, and he's got to leave Kyle, his partner, there at the scene – if he waits around for someone from Belmar or Sea Girt he might miss something at the hotel. You can wait in the car; call Mom if you want to check on the kids. I'll go in with him and be out in ten minutes.'

'Okay, fine,' she said, 'I get it – but let's not be a hero tonight, okay, my plague-carrying, school-saving, gang-busting suspended trooper? You owe me dessert and then my chubby ass is going to bed, with or without you.'

I leaned over far enough to convince her to kiss me quickly on the lips. She sneaked another on my cheek; I whispered, 'Your ass isn't chubby, it's perfect. Trust me; I'll be more than happy to point out the finer contours later.'

I drove past the hotel entrance and parked beneath one of the sodium lights on Ocean Avenue. A few cars passed us going north towards Belmar, but apart from that the wide boulevard lay silent, the off-season taking hold with a chilly talon.

'Come to think of it, why don't you wait in the lobby? I don't like the idea of you out here with some felon running around.'

'Are you going to walk me to the school bus stop tomorrow?' Jenny reclined in her seat. 'If I'm in imminent danger here maybe you'll hustle to get back.'

'C'mon, please.' I took her hand. 'The lobby's like a movie set. You can hang out in the bar, have a martini or a bowl of cornflakes, whatever. Jay Gatsby will be there. I hear he's nice.'

'All right,' she said, giving in grudgingly, 'but only because I'm kind of happy with my hair tonight.'

'Men will be lining up around the block just to catch a whiff of it. What is it? *Eau de Something Deep-Fat-Fried?*'

'Jackass.'

'Quite an echo around here tonight.' I reached for my bag and Uncle Paul's .357. 'Let's go.'

Jenny stopped short, three steps into the hotel's opulent lobby. 'God damn, will you look at this place?' The lobby of the hundred-year-old seaside hotel looked to have been dropped here by some wayward Hapsburg architect. Stalwart marble columns rose two storeys from the marble floor to the elaborate cornices supporting an upstairs lounge where an invisible cellist played. Twin staircases curled lazily from either side of a huge fireplace with a carved marble mantelpiece. Framed portraits of dead white men hung between sundry landscape paintings and tapestries stitched with various dusty crests; I guessed they'd come from Ireland, a bit north for the Hapsburgs. The room made me feel insignificant, poor and dirty. I'd been in hospital operating rooms that hadn't been this clean.

Jenny turned abruptly to a framed mirror beside a painting of sunrise over the boardwalk. She fussed with her hair and checked her make-up. 'Sailor, you've got to tell me when we're coming someplace like this. I look like a mother of two.'

'My mother had two of us,' Ed said, 'and she *never* looked like you, Mrs Doyle.'

'Oh, Officer Hess, please don't call me "Mrs Doyle". I don't want to pass out and hit my head on the marble!'

'Look there.' I pointed across the lobby. 'They've got a fire going in the fireplace. Order a drink, something nice. We won't be long.'

'All right.' She gave me a quick peck on the cheek. 'I'll check on the kids.'

As Ed and I watched her go, neither of us noticed Thomas the Fop behind the concierge desk until he stood and asked, 'May I help you gentlemen?' I don't know how he'd managed it in only a week, but somehow Thomas had sprouted a narrow, closely cropped moustache. Every cell in my body wanted to knock him senseless.

'Ah, shit,' I groaned under my breath, 'this guy hates me.'

'I'm the only one here who gets to hate you, Doyle,' Ed whispered. He pulled a badge from his pocket, flashed it at Thomas and said, 'Spring Lake PD, sir. I need a master key or a security staff member with a key, and access to Mark Stillman's suite. Right away.'

Thomas looked as though he'd caught a whiff of something foul. 'I'm sorry, officer, however, that won't—'

'Now,' Ed interrupted, 'not another word, milquetoast. Find the fucking key, or I'll find it for you.'

456

Thomas huffed, 'I will remind you, sir, that without a warrant—'

Moving incredibly quickly for an older guy, Ed grabbed a handful of Thomas' suit and heaved the wiry concierge onto his toes. His forearms rippled with muscle, turning his fading Coast Guard tattoo into a blur of patriotic colour. 'We are in pursuit of a felon and thus I do not need a warrant. Where's the key, or do I kick the fucking door in and arrest you later, *Milky*? Make up your mind, *now*.'

'Where's Mitch?' I asked, remembering the security guard's name.

'Yeah, Mitch,' Ed said, then, 'who's Mitch?'

'Security.'

'Perfect.'

'Not on until eleven,' Thomas choked, still on his tippy toes.

Upstairs, the cellist rocked and rolled, but in the lobby, the few guests and staff members had stopped whatever they were doing to watch Thomas get his ass whipped. From the corner of my eye, I saw an off-duty bartender raising a camera phone, immortalising Ed's assault for YouTube. Jenny sat near the fire; no one had brought her a drink yet, or a bowl of cornflakes. She looked at me and shook her head disapprovingly.

Sorry, honey.

'Detective Doyle! Officer Hess!' This from behind me, down an adjacent hallway: Tony from Bergen County.

I put a hand on Ed's shoulder. 'Tony! Come and save us. Chop, chop!'

The burly Italian kid jogged through the lobby, his shirt open at the collar, his bow tie dangling. 'Hey guys,' he said amiably, maybe five drinks into the evening. 'Can I help you?'

'Yes,' Thomas managed, 'you can.'

'Whaddya need, Detective?'

'You got a master key, Tony?' I asked.

'Yeah, sure.' He produced a ring of tarnished brass keys from his vest pocket. 'Where're we goin'?'

To Ed, I said, 'Let him go.'

'Right.' Hess dropped Thomas the Fop, who gasped for breath while straightening the wrinkles in his jacket. 'Stillman's suite.'

Tony looked confused, but he said, 'Sure, I guess. This way.'

Once out of sight of the lobby, I unzipped my backpack and dug around for the .357. Without bringing it into view, I opened the cylinder and checked the load: six silver bullets.

Perfect for monsters, right? Shit, who knows?

Ed knocked with a fist. 'Mark Stillman! This is Officer Ed Hess of the Spring Lake Police Department. I need you to open the door right now, sir!'

Nothing. As we waited I traced a shit-brown *fleur de lis* on the beige wallpaper, hoping to hear Moses' footsteps through the drywall.

Ed pounded again. 'Mr Stillman, open up, please. This is the Spring Lake Police.' He drew a deep breath, held it a few seconds, then turned to Tony. 'The key?'

'Um, sure.' Tony found the master on his keyring and handed it over.

Ed drew his gun, a Beretta 9 mm. As I pulled Uncle Paul's cannon from my backpack he said, 'Thought I told you not to carry that thing around.'

'Yeah, well, I sometimes disapprove of my own behaviour,' I replied, elbowing Tony away from the door. 'Go ahead.'

Ed turned the key. The door opened inwards and I knelt, aiming the .357 inside, while Ed burst through, gun drawn, shouting, 'Spring Lake PD! On the floor! On the goddamned floor!'

Two steps in, Ed froze, then backed out. 'Holy fuck, Sailor: look at this.'

'What?' I stood and looked past him into Moses' small dining area. 'Don't go in. Don't walk on the carpet. You got a radio?'

'In the car.'

'Use my phone.' I handed him the BlackBerry.

Martin Mark Moses Stillman Heston, whoever he was, sat upright at the head of his small mahogany dining table, the very place where Tony, Chef Sam and I had joined him for a bottle of expensive Scotch. He was clearly dead. His face and neck were drained of all colour, now that ashen greyish-white that God reserves for the dead. His mouth hung crookedly open, his tongue lolling, a sticky tail of thick slobber still dangling from his bewhiskered chin. His eyes stared in mute disbelief at his spotted hands, flat against the polished wood, nailed there with rusty spikes, like rail spikes or weathered nails from the hull of a shipwreck. In the space of twenty-four hours his greying Clint Eastwood hair had gone all-over white, as if terror alone had sent his soul to Hell; this healthy, athletic man had been reduced to an emaciated ghoul, his face hollowed by shadows, like black grease-paint on a white foundation.

Moses' dining table was covered with framed photographs, too waterlogged and blurry to make out from the door. The frames had all rusted or faded as well, and there were clusters of white barnacles on some, as if they'd spent the past decade beneath the ocean.

Half a dozen candles were burning, colouring the indecipherable pictures a flickering yellow and orange. Two candles, close together, brought tentative light to a large frame, and as I peered at it, trying to make out the subject, I thought it might be a man in a baseball uniform. Even from the door we could see what had been written across the glass – most likely in Moses' blood: GUILTY.

And over everything was a thin film of clear fluid, as if from an overturned glass of water.

'Christ almighty!' Tony tried to push his way into the room, but I held him back. 'C'mon, Sailor,' he cried, 'he could be alive—'

'He's dead,' Ed said, with the same certainty he'd shown upon see-ing Harold Hanley upside down in the wrought-iron table struts.

'God.' Tony crossed himself. 'Oh, my dear God – what *happened*? What is that?'

'My best guess,' I said, 'is that it's seawater.'

'How do you know?' Tony asked.

I inhaled deeply. 'It smells like low tide in there.'

Behind Moses, I could see the dining room window stood open, the curtains wafting gently in the onshore breeze.

'Think they're gone?' Ed said. 'I mean, they could be hiding down the hall.'

'They're gone,' I said. *She's gone, anyway*.

'We should go in,' Ed said finally. 'We should call for help and then clear the place. Jesus Christ, Sailor, they could be in a back bedroom.'

'All right,' I agreed, 'we'll go, but they're gone, Ed. I know it.'

He passed my BlackBerry to Tony. 'Call Spring Lake and Belmar PD. Get us some help here, pronto. Go out to the lobby, meet them and show them where we are; got it?'

Tony disappeared towards the centre of the hotel, already dialling, as Ed and I, covering one another, checked each of Moses' rooms, and found no one. There was seawater soaked into the carpet and more on the windowsill. 'This is righteously fucked up, Sailor,' he said. 'It's like this sonofabitch came in here after a swim – and what's with those photos? They look like they've been dunked in the ocean.'

'They have,' I said. 'They're family shots: mother, father, daughter, whatever. And I bet you a round at the bar they've been under water for about seventeen years.'

'What're you talking about?' He leaned out of the window, careful not to touch anything.

I crossed to the photos hanging on Moses' sitting room wall and found the image of Lauren and Kate in the canoe. Carefully I checked the top edge of the picture with a fingertip. It was wet. I touched my finger to my tongue: salt water.

No wonder you had the goddamned things bolted to the wall, Moses.

The screws holding the picture in Moses' bedroom, of Kate and Lauren with the melted ice cream and the macramé bag, had been yanked halfway out of the studs. The picture dangled from one resilient screw, leaving Kate and Lauren on their sides, precariously close to dripping ice cream all over Kate's lavender dress. Five or six drops of water had run down the panelling, leaving streaks like tears. I tasted one, but didn't need to.

Covet and regret.

A siren wailed in the distance. Ed said, 'Cavalry's coming.'

I joined him in the dining room, trying hard not to look down at Moses' body. 'I'm going to run out to the lobby. I ought to let Jenny know we'll be here a bit longer.'

'Send her home, Doyle,' Ed said. 'Hodges will get this soon enough and she's going to want to know what the hell is going on – shit, *I* want to know what the hell's going on, and I'm not even supposed to be here tonight. You and Stillman happen to have a body fall into your omelettes last weekend, and now he turns up awfully frigging dead. It's not looking good, buddy. You're becoming a maelstrom of bad news this week.'

'That's all bullshit, and you know it. I was on Third Avenue when you arrived, and at the library before that. So don't waste your time chasing me.'

'Well, you got any ideas about what happened here? Because this is royally frigged up.'

'Yeah, I do,' I said, 'and I'll tell you when I get back. Let me deal with my wife real quick.' And I hurried down the hall, my ribs, shoulder and leg aching ardently. I didn't have a clue how I might explain to Ed what I believed was happening in Spring Lake at that moment.

By the time I saw him again, it didn't matter.

In the lobby, I grabbed Tony. 'Hey, can you tell me if anyone is staying in the room just below Harold Hanley's, on the fifth floor? Room 5103?'

'Sure, Detective.' Tony headed for the check-in desk.

Thomas the Fop, as irritating as ever, overheard us and slid quickly behind the computer terminal. 'He most certainly cannot. I don't know what the Spring Lake Police are doing taking over this estab-lishment this evening, but you, Detective Doyle, have no jurisdiction here whatsoever.'

Tony sighed. 'Jesus Christ.'

To Thomas, I said, 'Fine, but I ought to tell you that you've got a dead body in a suite at the end of the hallway. I believe I might be able to find critical evidence in Room 5103. If you're unwilling to give me access to Room 5103, I'll have one of the detectives from the Monmouth County Prosecutor's Office talk with you when they arrive.'

Until then, why don't you put a sock in it, douche-bag. If Thomas had been in swiping distance I would have clobbered him this time, but I was too tired and too goddamned lazy to walk the three steps to slap some cooperation into him.

'C'mon, Detective,' Tony said, 'let's just go up. We'll knock politely.'

'You'll be summarily dismissed in the morning,' Thomas warned.

Tony gave Thomas a dangerous look, one I'm certain he practised in the mirror after watching the *Godfather* movies, then he leaned over the desk and said, 'I'm not asking, Thomas. And if you do try to have me fired in the morning, then it's a trip out back for both of us and I'll enjoy it a great deal more than you will.'

'I must say, Tony, that I would not have expected such—'

Tony ignored him and stalked towards the elevators; I followed. Pressing the UP button, he turned back to the desk, pointed a meaty finger at Thomas and said, 'Out back. Tomorrow. I'm whipping your ass – *Milky*.' He slugged me in the good shoulder – it hurt – and laughed. 'Milky! I like that one!'

As the elevator doors closed, Tony shouted to Thomas, 'And when the police get here, make sure they know where to go.'

We were passing the third floor before I realised that I hadn't seen Jenny.

Room 5103 was empty. When no one answered Tony's knock he opened the door for me. I flipped on the lights, crossed to the balcony, grabbed a chair and said, 'Hold this steady, will you?'

'Sure, whatever you need.' Tony braced the chair while I climbed up, supporting myself with my good arm against the edge of the white-washed bricks.

I couldn't see anything. 'Hit the light out here, will you?' As he let go of the chair just long enough to reach inside and turn on the balcony light my stomach roiled at the thought of being balanced five storeys up on yet another chair.

I suppose I had always known they'd be there: claw marks scratched into the concrete base of the overhead balcony, *Hanley's* balcony. 'Look at that,' I said.

'Whaddya got, Detective?' Tony gripped the chair again.

'See these?' I dragged my fingers over the pattern.

'God *damn*. You saying Mr Hanley was thrown off? That someone climbed up from here to toss him down on top of you and Mr Stillman?'

The bricks on the south wall showed a similar pattern. 'That's exactly what I'm saying, Tony – and look there: you can see where

462

she gripped the stones on her way up. I had it wrong: she didn't come from the roof; she came from below.'

'*She?*' Tony helped me down. 'Who are you talking about, Detective? Do you know who did this?'

'Yeah.' I started past him, leaving the chair on the balcony. 'I do.'

'Not much of a locked-door mystery now!' Tony beamed at our discovery.

I led the way back to the elevators. 'No, Tony, not any more.'

In the lobby guests and staff members watched as police and paramedics rushed down the hallway to Moses' suite. Rumours were already circulating, barely audible whispers that a dead body had been discovered in one of the rooms.

—two dead in one week—

—more excitement than this place has seen in a hundred years—

—drug dealers—

—another attack on a Jew? Was it a Jew? We should call someone—

—probably an old geezer with a heart condition. You know—

I checked the lounge by the fireplace: no Jenny.

Tony left me and hurried to the front desk where he punched in three numbers on the house phone, turned his back to the lobby and covered the mouthpiece with his hand.

Chef Sam, tucked in somewhere upstairs, I bet.

I didn't see Thomas the Fop either.

I dragged myself up the grand staircase to the cocktail lounge. The cellist had stopped playing. An elderly couple sat at the bar, sharing a bottle of white wine and eating salads. They looked familiar.

I asked the *maître d'hôtel* if anyone had seen Jenny come up, but the hostess and a distracted waiter shook me off, claiming they hadn't noticed anyone. Both went back to leaning over the polished railing, watching the drama unfold in the lobby.

'Thanks,' I said and started down again, icy dread solidifying in my chest. The cellist, reading my mind, started up again, sawing an unhurried melody, rich with vibrato, she played the song I'd heard in my nightmares.

East Side, West Side, all around the town . . .

The old man, the salad eater, laughed at something the woman said and now I remembered them; his wheezy, cigar-smoking laugh gave him away. *The geriatric lovers from the hotel in Manhattan. Of course they're here.*

I ran for the front door, nearly falling on the slippery marble, yelling, 'Jenny! *Jenny!*' but police, paramedics, hotel staff and guests, everyone ignored me, even Tony from Bergen County.

Thomas' body was lying in the grass, about fifteen feet from Jenny's minivan. A Sea Girt paramedic worked on chest compressions while another fastened an oxygen bag over his bloody face. Roiling red and blue emergency lights lit the macabre scene. I really hoped my eyes were playing tricks on me, but from this distance, in this light, it looked horribly like Thomas had been hit on the head.

Like Blade. He'd been hit with something sharp – a garden rake, a ball-peen hammer, something with points.

'Those fucking claws—' I dug in my pockets for the car keys; I didn't have them. 'Jenny!' I shouted across the manicured lawn, 'Jenny Doyle!'

I'm going to check on the kids.

'Did she have her keys? Her phone? Or did she leave them in the car? *Fuck!*'

Now I ran, and pain crescendoed through my sprains, fractures and tears. Beside the van I felt the first shards of tempered glass crackle beneath my feet; the driver's-side window had been shattered. A splash of blood trickled down the silver door and a few strands of dirty-blonde hair were stuck to a jagged finger of windowpane that hadn't broken off.

The paramedics working on Thomas didn't notice me at all. The Sea Girt lighthouse flashed the hotel with its searchlight, just for *auld lang syne*. I brushed shards of glass from the driver's seat, got in and rested the .357 in my lap. 'Kate Stillman yanked your wife head-first out of the fucking window, Sailor.'

In a rare stroke of capricious luck, Jenny'd left the keys in the ignition. The night had grown cool, and she'd probably wanted the heat on while she talked to my mother. *She hadn't worn a sweater because she wanted to look nice for you, shithead. She was just wearing that ivory silk blouse. She'll be cold.*

I turned cautiously around on Ocean Avenue, careful to avoid the mass of emergency vehicles parked outside the hotel, but a block north I stood on the gas and roared through Spring Lake towards Belmar.

'Check the kids first,' I shouted over the breezy howl through the broken window. 'She'd want you to check the kids first. Then go and get her.'

I didn't go in – I didn't have the time or the energy to lie to my mother. Instead, I parked in the O'Mearas' driveway, snuck in beneath the old pear tree and peeked into Ben's room. Kate Stillman hadn't striped his window with fresh greasepaint. She'd made her point and knew I understood; there was no need to call me out again.

Ben lay curled in a foetal ball, his Spider-Man blanket wrapped around him like a hungry python. 'Sleep well, monkey-man,' I whispered, then moved to Anna's window. The light from the hallway made it hard to see her. When I cupped my hands against the window and peered through I found myself face to face with Eeyore, propped up in Anna's crib and looking like one of those dog carvings old-time Catholics always mounted outside the pulpit. Nothing better to keep evil spirits away.

'Stay with her, Eeyore,' I said, feeling stupid. 'You're on guard duty.'

Back out front I ducked beneath the rectangle of soft light spilling from the living room window and peeked over the sill, just long enough to see my mother, fast asleep in my father's old lounge chair, her legs wrapped in a crocheted blanket. Save for the hallway and living room lights, half blocked by the curtains, the beach house lay in darkness, a hulking tableau awaiting sunrise. I watched the line of the roof, black against the moonlit sky.

Nothing moved.

I closed my eyes and listened to Twelfth Avenue and D Street; training my ears for that telltale scratch or shriek I'd heard from Kate

Stillman's demon, whatever she'd become in the years since I'd found her washed up on the beach north of Asbury Park, but again, there was nothing.

That's where they are. I stuffed the .357 into my waistband and hurried to the minivan. *North of Convention Hall, but just south of the jetty.*

I drove to Asbury Park, bombing up Ocean as fast as the minivan could go – I didn't know if I'd be too late, if Kate had already taken her into deep water, but I knew that Jenny would never forgive me if I hadn't checked on the children first.

I remembered the unnerving sound of Kate's scream when I'd shot her the other night. 'If she screams in pain, you can kill her.'

But they're not real silver bullets.

You gotta have faith, shithead.

Fuck it, shoot her, choke her, rip her heart out with your hands – hand. One good hand.

Beyond Convention Hall, north of the Berkeley-Carteret Hotel, Asbury Park's boardwalk petered off until it was little more than a few abandoned planks, the only beach access down rickety old stairs. I hit Seventh Avenue at nearly a hundred miles an hour and demolished three trashcans as I turned towards the dark stretch of empty sand. I pulled right onto the patchy grass running the length of the boardwalk and left the headlights on, bringing an eerie triangle of white to the cordgrass prickling above the dunes like the whiskers on Moses Heston's chin. Ignoring the laws of physics, the rest of the boardwalk and the beach refused to brighten.

I left the car running; Jenny would need it if – *when* – I broke her free. Whether we would leave together remained to be seen. I unwrapped my sling and tossed it away, then grasped Uncle Paul's cannon in my bad hand.

'Katherine Stillman!' I shouted, breathing deeply enough to send fiery shards of pain lancing through my ribs. 'I'm here, Katherine!'

Someone shouted from a dilapidated tenement on Ocean, 'Shut the fuck up!' and for a moment I thought about lobbing a round towards the sound, maybe ridding the world of another asshole, but I decided against it. I might need all six shots if I got close enough to Kate to try and kill her once and for all. And the last thing I needed was to have the Asbury Park PD ask why I'd left two dead bodies at the Warren & Monmouth only to come up here and start shooting at homeless people.

'Kate!' I screamed again, and sweat broke out on my body despite the chill. I moved up the abandoned boardwalk towards the jetty where I'd stumbled onto Kate Stillman's corpse seventeen years earlier and found that I could hustle if I bent at the waist, alleviating some of the weight on my ribs. Stumbling like a latter-day Quasimodo, I shuffled towards a set of broken stairs. I managed the first, but missed the second; my foot slipped off a fractured tread, and I tumbled into the sand, cursing volubly as my body threatened to shut down entirely.

I sucked in desperate breaths, sobbing, 'Oh God – God *damn* this.' Except for a deep, resonant thrum, I'd lost all feeling in my shoulder. If there was any mercy in the universe, my entire arm would just get ripped off before morning: that'd be easier. As I lay there for a minute or two, catching my breath and waiting for the pain to subside, I heard them arrive. Behind the waves, the light breeze and the soft hum of the minivan's engine I caught a brief whisper, like a hiss, then a cry: Jenny's voice, but no words I could actually make out.

Above and behind me through the darkness I heard another shriek, another sibilant hiss, and I realised where they were. I rolled onto my left arm, far enough to lever myself up; the splintered steps provided handholds as I clawed my way upright, a truly Herculean task.

South of me, above the moonlit ribbon of sand, the Asbury Park Convention Hall sat, slowly disintegrating, like a forgotten train on a siding. Kate Stillman howled from the roof of the once-grand edifice, summoning me to watch as she disembowelled my wife. The shockwave of her cry reverberated through my head. I held my ears until it passed.

'I'm coming!' I shouted. 'Give me a second, will you?'

The asshole in the tenement yelled down again, telling me to shut up, and this time I did shoot, just one round, into the wall. Hopefully, it would scare him off. For good measure I shouted, 'Dumbass! You're going to get killed. Stay inside!'

I hobbled down the boardwalk. 'Kate! Come down here; leave her alone. I'm here – I'm ready.' Try as I might, I couldn't evict images of Auntie Carla from my imagination. If I had to stand by and watch as Kate tore Jenny to ribbons, I'd shoot myself. It was more than God could ask of me. The kids were with my mother; they'd be all right together. I'd lob four rounds at Kate, hoping to get lucky, and then send the last one through my own head.

In the shadow of Convention Hall, I braced myself, the .357 ready, my good hand, my good arm also ready, waiting for Kate to drop down on me, fangs bared, webbed claws ripping. When she didn't appear, I called again, 'I did what you wanted, Kate: I proved him guilty – I did it. And I understand now, I do: you *hired* me – Hanley was my invitation. And in the end, Moses was guilty; you were right. I collected the evidence, unravelled Dunning's mystery and built the case against Moses while you watched from your perch above his breakfast table. I figured it all out: Mark 4:37, the lies, the money, and I got my confession! I found him guilty, Kate, and you punished him. *We should be done,*' I cried.

I wiped my eyes and nose on my sleeve, then shouted, 'Why *aren't* we done? Because I haven't suffered enough? I haven't apologised enough, repented enough? I don't underst—'

Kate Stillman, dragging Jenny in one arm, dropped from the Convention Hall roof to land nimbly on a concrete bench sporting a torn advertisement for an *Asbury Jukes* concert. I covered my ears and closed my eyes as she wailed at me – I knew I wouldn't have many opportunities to get a decent shot at her, she jumped around like a gymnast crack addict – but her voice made me sick; I had to hold my ears.

Jenny moaned. I couldn't be sure, not from this far away, but she looked relatively intact: no broken bones, just a nasty gash above her left eye which was bleeding like a frigging river. Her ivory blouse looked like it had been dipped in blood. Jenny's hands moved a bit, but she did nothing to defend herself, to fight back or break loose. I guessed she'd come head-first through the window, cut her eye pretty badly and got herself knocked halfway to senseless. Having seen Kate cover several miles in just a few seconds the other night, part of me was glad that Jenny hadn't been entirely lucid for the trip.

'Put her down, Kate. We're done,' I said. 'You can go back, go—Go home, wherever you came from.' I looked at the water. 'Lebow's grandson is dead, so you've ruined Isaac's life. Moses is dead. It's time for you to go.'

She hissed again, leaning into it to be sure I understood how utterly reprehensible she found me.

'I get it,' I said, waiting for a chance to shoot. I couldn't risk it left-handed, not while she held Jenny so close. This close I could see her face had either rotted off or been picked away by bluefish and striped bass. Clumps of waist-length hair, salt-and-pepper grey, held fast to islands of flesh still affixed to her narrow skull. Her hands, wrists and forearms were all the colour of mouldy cheddar, decomposed enough that I could see the inner workings of muscle, tendon and ligament, tautening and loosening as she carted my wife around like a sack of stolen lobsters. Kate – what was left of Kate – wore a tattered cowl of threadbare sailcloth, something she'd doubtless torn from one of hundreds of shipwrecks off the Jersey coast – why she felt she needed clothing escaped me, but I was glad; I didn't think I wouldn't have been able to stomach seeing what remained of her disrobed.

The spaces between Kate's fingers, her toes, even the hollows beneath her arms had become webbed. One of her ears had long since been torn away; the other hung, useless, from a pencil-thin length of puckered flesh. She moved with the inherent wariness of a creature who's hunted and being hunted, glancing left and right like a nervous bird, moving constantly as she gripped the edge of the park bench with her taloned feet. Her eyes were as black and insidious as a shark's. I remembered seeing her outside Dunkin' Donuts late Tuesday night; they'd been sexy then. Now her eyes frightened me. Kate lived where no light penetrated. When she hissed at me, even ten feet away, I caught the scent of rotten fish on her breath and I gagged. Still holding the .357 I wiped my face clear and said simply, 'Please, let her go.'

Jenny moved, tried to lift her head. She mumbled something, and actually took hold of Kate's hideous wrist.

Hunkering down for just a second, Kate's sailcloth fell about her body, making her look like a crouching gargoyle.

'Jesus,' I whispered. 'It *was* you.'

Rising to her full height, an intimidating predator, she glared at me, raised her free hand and clubbed Jenny unconscious, striking her hard behind one ear.

The sound, that thud, woke me from my stupor and invigorating rage poisoned my blood. I raised the .357. 'I asked you to let her go!' Aiming high, I squeezed off a round. The old revolver belched a tongue of orange flame that lit up the night and illuminated the horror that was Kate Stillman, blinding me in the process. I felt Jenny's body hit the boardwalk, then, with a gust of musty air, Kate launched herself high into the night sky. Willing my eyes to adjust, I hurried over to Jenny and knelt beside her, but I couldn't do more than confirm that she was still alive.

From the roof of Convention Hall Kate bellowed the same vicious curse she'd howled at me in the Bentley Hotel; I'd hit her. Still shrieking, she leaped across Ocean Avenue to the shoddy tenement, then to the roof of the old Berkeley-Carteret – and then she fell silent.

She was hunting me.

I pulled my T-shirt off and pressed it hard against Jenny's forehead. 'Come on, baby,' I murmured, 'we've got to get you out of here. I hit her, but that crazy bitch is coming back.' I tried to get an arm under her, but couldn't manage it; I had nothing left, no strength in that arm and only bright, sharpened agony in my ribs. 'You'll have to help me, honey,' I begged. 'I can't pick you up, and I've got to hold on to the gun.'

Jenny moaned between shallow breaths.

'That's it.' I swallowed a sob. 'You can do it, sweetie. I need you to help me, just a little.' All the time I was pressing hard on the gash above her eye, I kept my head swivelling, searching the darkness for any sign of Kate.

Maybe it worked, Sailor; maybe you scared her off.

The lightest thump, little more than a child's footstep on the ancient planks, told me I was wrong. The tiniest of vibrations tickled the skin on my knee and I understood then that Kate had returned, silently, to finish me or Jenny or both of us.

I faked it to buy myself a few seconds more, time enough for my eyes to fully recover. I said, 'You'll be okay, honey. You're going to be just—'

I threw myself backwards, landing hard and driving splinters deep beneath the skin on my shoulder blades. Screaming with the effort, I found Kate, a mere five feet away, took aim, closed my eyes and fired twice, as quickly as I could pull the trigger.

There was no howl this time, no demon scream letting me know I'd hit her, no maddening hiss as Kate decided what part of me to rip from the bone.

Instead, Kate Stillman landed lightly astride my paralysed, helpless form and pain flooded every crevice of my tired soul. I raised the .357, not really sure whether I should try to kill her one last time, or just find my own head and kill myself – but Kate didn't give me a chance to do either. She slapped the gun away, dug her talons in and lifted me as easily as if I'd been one of Lauren's stuffed animals.

'No,' I murmured, '*no*.' I tried to get a hand around her putrefied throat. Cradling me in cruel imitation of a mother holding her child, she leaped to the roof of Convention Hall, and sprang high into the night, across the beach, past the jetty, and over the inky water.

We seemed to hang for a few seconds, a hundred feet over the ocean and a quarter of a mile beyond the breakers. Beneath me I could see the rolling red and blue lights as the Asbury Park Police raced to the boardwalk. They might have been the toy cars Ben would push up and down the driveway, playing at cops and robbers. I'd fired four or five shots, so the road guys would be expecting a gang shooting – instead, they'd find my wife, and in that fraction of a second before Kate Stillman and I plummeted towards the water, I was glad: Jenny would be okay. She'd get home, eventually, to Ben and Anna, and Ben would want to count the stitches in Jenny's face, to touch them and worry over them. She'd have to tell him again and again how she'd been in a car crash, how her head had hit the window—

I'd be sorry to miss that.

Kate used her body to shield mine when we hit the water, but either way, it felt like being in a car wreck.

471

Finally, thank Christ! That fucking arm is gone – ripped from the shoulder or just numb?

I held my breath as Kate dragged me towards the bottom. My ears popped at what I guessed to be twelve or fifteen feet, and then again at what might have been thirty, but we were descending too fast for me to judge anything accurately. The water which on the surface had been still warm from summer grew shockingly cold as we fell into Egyptian-tomb darkness.

Improbable darkness.

I didn't know we'd reached the bottom until my head and shoulders slammed into the sand and finally Kate let go of me. I drifted a few feet until a clump of smooth seaweed brushed over my face and I almost cried out in fear. As a heavy smoker, I figured I could hold my breath for thirty seconds, maybe a minute at best – and here I was, forty feet down and fifteen seconds already gone. It'd take every ounce of breath I had left to make it back to the surface.

But Kate had other plans. Gripping my arm, her talons digging half an inch into my flesh, she swam hard along the bottom, pulling me with her. I careened about blindly as she followed the contours of the ocean floor. I had only ten or fifteen seconds left when she tugged me down even deeper, plunging off an undersea ledge into another twenty or thirty feet of briny oblivion.

I wrestled with her, trying vainly to yank my arm free, then panic took hold and I screamed, flailing blindly, ignoring the pain in my limbs as the pressure in my chest drove me mad, and all the while Kate dragged me deeper towards a death too agonising to imagine.

And I breathed.

Freezing, life-affirming air filled my lungs, first one glorious breath then another as I hit my head, my elbows, my knees inside the confined space. Irregular shapes wedged themselves around me and I lashed out, but didn't find Kate. I screamed, revelling in the hoarse sound of my own voice, and reached up to wipe my eyes clear.

Somehow my head and torso were out of the water and bathed in wintry air. I breathed again, deeply, cleared my head, and felt around: smooth surfaces, toggles, torn leather, sodden stuffing, and finally half a circle, padded, on a raised, metal stick.

A plane. Holy shit! I'm in the cockpit and there's air – how much? Five minutes, ten? Slow down, Sailor: slow down, breathe easy. You're maybe sixty feet down. You can make this as long as she's not . . .

Gasping, trying not to use too much precious air, I felt around the cockpit, even held my breath to search on the floor. I didn't know where Kate had gone, but I needed a weapon for when she came back. Panic would kill me, so though my heart was thudding along madly, I clenched my fists tight and forced myself to breathe as slowly as possible.

I cried out when I finally remembered my new watch, and pressing the LIGHT button, I held the readout up to my face, read those welcome blue numbers. My breathing slowed as the seconds ticked off.

After two minutes of listening to myself breathe, I found the aluminium canister on the floor near my right foot: *a SCUBA tank – she filled this space for you. Why? Where'd she—?*

I could see. I wiped my eyes again, and when I held my fingers three inches in front of my face I could see them moving. I looked around, straining to make out details. Slowly, as if dawn were breaking, I started to make out the control panel.

Drug plane, gotta be – otherwise someone would have come out and got it. Must've crashed at night. Probably full of soggy coke destined for Manhattan.

No weapon, so I decided to take my chances outside. Sucking in a deep breath, I moved backwards through the plane to the open hatchway behind a row of empty seats, but forward of the storage area and whatever ruined crates might be lashed back there. A greenish-blue glow lit the sea floor with eerie light and I realised Kate was out there, stirring up luminescent plants – to help me to see?

But why?

I retreated to the cockpit and took three deep breaths before heading for the hatchway and freedom – unholy panic waited for me in every shadow, but if I didn't try to reach the surface I would slowly succumb as carbon dioxide built up inside my unnatural prison.

Kate met me in the hatchway, appearing suddenly like a monster in a slasher movie, and I swiped wildly at her, then lunged, hoping to knock her backwards far enough to make a go for the surface. She shrieked, and my ears felt as though they might rupture. I gripped the sides of my head, retreated to the cockpit and dared her to come in after me.

Instead, she moved in front of the window and gestured unmistakably for me to join her. Enough hazy light glowed that I could see where those silver bullets had found their mark; clouds of black blood billowed from three places on her torso. I prayed that enough oxygen might remain inside the cockpit for me to have a front row seat when some big-assed shark swam by to eat her rotting, nightmarish head.

She gestured again, trying to make me understand something. 'What?' I shouted. 'What do you—?'

Gabriel Lebow stared at me through the cockpit window, his face – Kate's face – that same greasy smear I'd seen in the Cape Cod house on D Street. He tapped the window with a gnarled talon and beckoned me outside.

'No,' I said. 'I can't – I'm not ...' I watched, paralysed, as Gabriel's deathmask blurred and morphed back into Kate's haggard face. I bit my lower lip hard, but didn't feel anything. *It's too cold down here.* I didn't have enough air to stay much longer, and I found myself wondering briefly if I'd have a seizure before dying, or just slip quietly to sleep.

Kate disappeared for a few seconds. The pallid glow outside the plane brightened and when she returned, it was clear she'd stirred up more plants – she'd turned up the lights for me, and now she wanted me outside with her.

'Fuck. Fuck. *Fuck!*' I wagged a finger at the window. 'Okay, okay, you crazy bitch. I'm coming. Let's get it over with.' I took my last three breaths of blissful air, held the third and kicked towards the glow of Kate Stillman's luminescent garden.

Not two feet outside the plane's hatchway she gripped me hard by the shoulder, tearing my skin again, and dragged me quickly over a hundred feet of greenish-glowing plants. I might as well have been on another planet, trying to escape an alien while holding my breath. Finally she pulled me over another ledge and down into a circular chamber, maybe twenty-five feet across and twelve feet deep. Its walls, mostly rock, grew thick with fiery glowing algae and microscopic undersea lightning bugs, whatever they were – I was a little sad that I didn't have time to appreciate this strange place because I had maybe thirty seconds before I had to get back to the plane or above the surface.

Kate drew me to the centre of the depression where dozens of framed photos lay scattered about; some rested flat on the sand, but most had been propped against rocks or bits of broken spar, or ballast stones stolen from nearby shipwrecks. With salt water burning my eyes, I couldn't tell if any of the photos still bore clear images of Lauren Stillman, but as a father who would love my children until the end of time, I knew what Kate saw when she looked at them, even this Kate, the monster who'd been spawned over two agonising months torturing a piece-of-shit mob enforcer and seaside drug dealer.

I nodded to her: *I understand. Yes.*

But she shook her head and gave a quick shriek as a means of explanation.

I tried to break away, needing to get clear of her and her glow-in-the-dark underwater shrine; I believed that she meant for me to live, but I had to impress upon her that I couldn't stay any longer.

Kate tugged me once more, through a billowy curtain of her own blood, and now I saw him, sitting upright in an old captain's chair, probably ripped from the very plane that had saved my life. Still duct-taped to three concrete blocks, Mikey Bartollo had been all but picked clean by passing fish. Only a few bits of connective tissue held his skeletal frame together. Burning pressure was building up again in my lungs and I pulled feebly at Kate's wrist, gesturing for her that I had to go. She seemed to understand because she renewed her grip on my shoulder and started us back towards the airplane wreckage.

My lungs burning, I tried kicking, wanting to help her get me back for another breath, but I couldn't. In the moment before she hauled me away, I watched in mute stupefaction as Mikey Bartollo turned and tried to speak. Wriggling a hand free from his bonds, he reached for me with non-existent muscles, pleading silently for help.

My mind clicked off and instinct alone kept me holding my breath until Kate jammed me unceremoniously inside the cockpit. I stayed there, shivering and breathing deeply until I felt my vision blur: my clean air supply was dwindling dangerously low.

Through the plane's window, I watched Kate bleed, and I hoped she'd die. She didn't.

Finally, with my thoughts addled and my memory permanently scarred by the image of Mikey Bartollo, imprisoned here for seventeen years, I sucked in the very last of the SCUBA tank's air, climbed through the hatchway and started towards the surface, the ocean floor aglow beneath me.

Twenty feet up, Kate caught me by the ankle. I kicked her hard in the face, but her grip was an iron band; I was going nowhere until she freed me. I tried not to panic, instead concentrating on holding my breath. The bitter chill had found its way into my bone marrow and I worried that I wouldn't be able to swim to shore.

She held fast and looked long into my face, the tendons in her jaw contracting grotesquely. Kate squeezed my arm until it bled again, and then, finally, she let me go.

I kicked for the surface, all the while watching her grim outline as it fell slowly into the ghoulish light below. Blood bloomed from her gunshot wounds in serpentine spurts. She didn't swim, didn't gesture to me, just fell away.

I broke the surface with a cry. The water here was much warmer than sixty feet down, but the cold, my injuries and the prolonged stretches holding my breath had sapped my strength. The bright lights of the police and ambulance beside Convention Hall were maybe a quarter of a mile away – four hundred yards, twelve hundred feet. It was too far to swim tonight.

'Where are you now, Curt, you dipshit, when I really need you? Sleeping, I bet.'

My sister Marie had nicknamed me Sailor one windy afternoon three miles off the coast of Belmar. Trying to impress the girl I'd been in love with for more than a year I borrowed a friend's sailboat, convinced the girl that I knew what I was doing, then headed out to the deep blue sea for some beer, some sun, some serious necking, and hopefully even a quickie if I tied off the tiller and talked her out of her bikini.

Naturally, the winds offshore changed with the tide. I didn't know they did that. However, rather than signal for help, I came about, lost the wind, couldn't figure a tack that looked even remotely like the right direction and eventually turned so sharply into the breeze that the mainline tore from my hand, I dropped the tiller and the boat capsized, dunking me, whatshername, and any hope of afternoon sex. Neither of us had been wearing lifebelts, what with the promise of nudity on the horizon, so we paddled after the boat, clung to the overturned hull and waited for my sister and Uncle Paul to pick us up in my father's old Grady White, a seventeen-foot fishing boat that most certainly did *not* impress women.

Hauling me out of the water, Marie had said, 'Nice work, Sailor.'

And the name stuck.

The girl, whatshername, she never spoke to me again – who could blame her? And while I told everyone she hated me because I'd lied to her about knowing how to sail, the truth was that she'd kind of lost her cool while we clung on to the barnacled hull of that old catboat. Imagining monsters, sharks, hungry schools of nasty bluefish, she'd wigged out, screamed herself hoarse and developed an unhealthy terror of the vast emptiness beneath our dangling feet.

I'd never thought much about it, but after that day I too sometimes panicked when I considered the array of disagreeable creatures that might be swimming along beneath the water. Having just met two of them face to face, I wasn't sure I'd ever get back in the ocean again.

It was eleven o'clock at night and I was foundering a quarter of a mile off the beach. I found myself fighting to keep my composure, certain some twelve-foot-long night hunter was about to swim up and take my leg off. I was scared shitless, waves of dangerous panic washing through my body, and so tired, so bloody, so worn to the nub as I floated in what I imagined were clouds of my own blood – shark magnets – alternatively paddling one-arm and treading water, hoping for a rising tide and an inbound current.

The ocean at night is as terrifying a place as anywhere on Earth; just ask anyone who's ever spent a night treading water and praying to be rescued. To pass the time I practised all the things I wanted to say to Jenny, to Ben and Anna, even to Huck and Lieutenant Harper if I ever got back to Virginia. I figured Marta Hodges would arrest me for Moses' death, for Thomas' death and for firing an illegal handgun up and down the boardwalk in the middle of the night. The very real fear that I might actually have to spend time in prison, *in New Jersey*, frightened some warmth back into my bones and I moved with renewed vigour towards the distant sound of breakers on the beach.

When my foot came down in sand, maybe three hundred feet offshore, I squealed like a third-grade girl and started to drag myself up the beach, where I grabbed the first Asbury Park cop I could find among the cruisers, paramedics and nosy bystanders.

A young Italian kid, muscular in his uniform, told me that an ambulance had taken Jenny to Jersey Shore Medical.

'Okay, thanks,' I said, and staggered dumbly in that direction.

'Whoa, whoa!' He grabbed my arm. 'You're Doyle, right? Her husband? The cop from Virginia?'

'Yeah,' I said, 'I gotta get over there, unless you want to give me a ride.'

'Sure, Detective,' he said, 'I'll run you over, but I gotta put you in cuffs first. Sorry.'

'I figured that,' I said, and let him put the bracelets on me. He didn't ask why I'd been in the water.

In the back of his cruiser I let my head loll against the window. I'd not been this exhausted since Molly Bruckner and I had fallen from that rusty bridge last July fourth.

'You all right back there, Detective?' the young cop asked me.

'Just tired and cold and broken and punctured and maybe infected with who knows what, but otherwise, yeah, I'm good.'

He keyed his radio, sent word ahead that we were en route. 'That your gun, back there on the boardwalk?'

'You know Marta Hodges, Detective Hodges, from the Prosecutor's Office?'

'Yes, sir. You want me to call her?'

'Before I answer any questions, yup, I'd appreciate it.'

'Got it,' he said, then, 'Who were you shooting at?'

'Hodges, please.'

'Right. Sorry.'

'What's your name, kid?' I asked, just to make conversation.

'Bartollo, sir. Eddie Bartollo.'

My heart seized; I had to close my eyes and will it to keep beating.

'You all right, Detective? You need me to pull over? Gotta puke or anything?' His accent, while faint, was New Jersey Italian; I could hear it now. I couldn't bear to ask if he'd misspoken. Was his name really Bartollo? I considered asking if he might be related to the Michael Bartollo I'd just met and failed to free from an eternity staring at photos of the teenage girl he'd raped and murdered just down the beach.

'I'm fine, Eddie,' I said at last. 'Just take me to my wife, please.'

'Sure thing.' He kicked his cruiser in the ass and made up the time blowing through red lights while I concentrated on breathing. It seemed like a worthwhile place to start. I'd met several monsters this week, all in different guises, all motivated by different—

My hands, cuffed behind my back, touched on something unexpected, something I hadn't noticed before. I shifted my weight and dug in my pocket with two fingers.

'Holy shit,' I whispered. Eddie didn't hear me.

It's payment, Sailor. She hired you; you finished the investigation and caught the bad guy. So she paid you.

I dug down a bit deeper, confirming for myself that I'd been given Kate Stillman's strand of Tahitian black pearls.

At Jersey Shore Medical, Eddie Bartollo took the cuffs off long enough for me to hug Jenny. She lay awake on an emergency room gurney, eighteen fresh stitches in her forehead and an icepack fixed over her ear. They'd given her something for the pain and she wasn't making much sense, but I gathered that she'd called my mother, told her we'd been in a car crash and that we'd be back either late tonight or early tomorrow.

I kissed her forehead. 'That's perfect, sweetie. Nice work.'

'What— Where did you go?'

'I'll explain in the morning,' I said. 'Please don't worry. Everything's fine now.'

'Okay.' She closed her eyes. 'I'm going to nap for a few minutes.'

'That's great,' I said. 'I'll stay here with you until they come to patch me up.' From the corner of my eye, I watched Officer Eddie Bartollo sidle over to the nurses' station.

Cops and nurses, perfect together.

I circled around behind Jenny's gurney and silently slipped the pearls into her bag, burying them beneath a plastic case of diaper wipes, a spare diaper, two pacifiers, a half-eaten pack of cookies and a worn paperback copy of *Mr Mullen's Favourite Farm Animals*. They'd search me before the night was over; the only reason Eddie hadn't already was because I was a fellow cop and merited a measure of professional respect.

I pulled up a plastic chair, rested my head next to Jenny's hip and waited for a doctor. Counting her breaths, I drifted off until a nurse arrived to escort me up to surgery.

EPILOGUE

Belmar Beach

October

Yellow: *Okay, I can almost do this.*

The autumn breeze tug-o-warred with summer sunshine as the New Jersey coast straddled the ephemeral seam between seasons. Cyclists, joggers and a smattering of sightseers took advantage of the nearly empty boardwalk. An ice cream stand queued up half-price cones and Neapolitan sandwiches. A pizza delivery driver parked a rusty Camry outside a barn-red hut, collected two pies through a side window and drove west on Twelfth, towards my mother's place. I hadn't been hungry for a few days, but I silently promised myself at least a slice of Jersey pizza and maybe one of those ice cream cones before bed. Other than the ice cream shack and the delivery kid, the Jersey shore had about closed for winter.

An auto parts delivery truck passed, headed south on Ocean Avenue. Through the open window I heard The Dropkick Murphys. No Pink Floyd. No farting calliope.

I was taped, bandaged and stitched beneath both arms, across my upper back, around my shoulder and ribs and behind my right ear. I sat on a beachside bench, feeling like Boris Karloff in my gauze. I didn't read, or listen to Jenny's iPod; it felt good to be up and around and I was content to chat to my daughter.

On the sand, Jenny and Ben tossed the Giants football, and for every pass Ben dropped, Jenny asked him a maths problem, something simple he could calculate in his head. For every catch Ben made,

Jenny had to answer whatever Ben dreamed up: questions about dogs, Ferris wheels, goldfish food, snowmen, the recipe for chocolate – just about anything was fair game. Ben wore a bathing suit – he planned to get in the water, the madman – and a T-shirt Jenny had negotiated over breakfast. Jenny wore her Army Surplus cargo shorts and that old Rutgers sweatshirt I planned to wear into my coffin some day. Jenny also sported a strip of surgical tape above one eye, protection for the row of tiny stitches she'd collected last weekend.

We'd talked about it. Twice.

Jenny didn't remember much after Katherine Stillman dragged her head-first through the window of our minivan and that was fine with me; it bothered me to tell her that she'd been abducted by North Side Playaz bent on revenge. It'd be months, years possibly, before she visited a city again, and maybe longer before she was able to walk through a parking lot or down an unfamiliar street without looking over her shoulder. While I'd be glad for her heightened vigilance, it broke my heart to have her believe she'd been attacked by gangbangers.

But Jenny hadn't been to Kate's underwater gallery.

That nightmare belonged only to me, thank Christ.

Anna, sitting beside me in her stroller, slobbered over a colourful set of plastic keys. Across her legs, a bedraggled Eeyore stood his post, nose to the breeze, enjoying the sunshine. I couldn't smell him from my end of the bench, but he looked in desperate need of a bath. I checked my watch – I didn't need the LIGHT button this time. 11:38 a.m. I wasn't sure I'd ever take it off again.

It's still early. We can stay all day, right here.

Two herring gulls soared overhead, checking to see if Jenny or Ben had left a bag of popcorn unattended. One cawed musically, then both turned south towards Spring Lake.

Yup. All day would be fine. Maybe the day I die I'll come down here and just sit on this bench.

The breakers rolled in, some of the same water that slammed the headlands on King James Island, redolent of cleanly scrubbed autumn. Blue-collar Belmar might have been an oceanfront paradise in an F. Scott Fitzgerald story.

Anna chattered in five-month-old and I tickled her toes and turned her stroller away from the midday sun. I'd weathered a bitch of an OxyContin craving before dawn, puking up two handfuls of Ibuprofen and a three-egg omelette, but I didn't shit my pants, which was a step in the right direction. Maybe Huck had been right: I *could* beat this. I pulled my BlackBerry from inside my sling and pressed his speed-dial number. I clicked off before it connected, though.

Call him later. Just sit here for now.

Ben ran full throttle for the surf, but despite outstretched fingers he missed the pass and tumbled in the sand. He rolled to his feet, laughing and spluttering and I clapped as well as I could with one arm taped down and the other stitched in six places. 'Way to go, buddy!' I called. 'Good try!'

'You starting him early, Doyle?'

I jumped and turned awkwardly. 'Detective Hodges! Nice to see you.' I slid closer to Anna's stroller. 'Have a seat.'

She did. 'You thinking NCAA Division 1?'

'For Ben? Oh yeah. We figure it'll take the pressure off when he comes to sit for the SATs.'

Hodges waved to Jenny and Ben. She wore a tailored suit with a knee-length skirt and actual stockings. I couldn't remember the last time I'd seen Jenny in stockings. 'How're you feeling, Sailor?'

'Like a chilled barrel of squirrel snot.'

'So. Better?'

'Some, yeah.'

She tucked a frayed end of bandage inside my sling. 'Who did your shoulder?'

'Some ortho-guy up in Freehold – Southcott, tall, looks like a former basketball player.'

'Centra State? I had two kids and a tubal ligation there.'

I tried to sit up straighter, braced a foot against the boardwalk to keep myself upright. 'You're all dressed up today. Big meeting?'

'Yeah: the State Police detectives handling the Thomas Smalls and Tejon Butler murders. The Attorney General called Tuesday afternoon, her panties all in a frigging twist, and suggested I needed help down here.'

'And your boss?'

'Called the Major Crimes lieutenant at CID in Trenton. They worked it out. I'll keep the Blake Street investigation, the ice labs, the North Side jackasses and the Lebow shooting.'

'But Smalls and Butler—'

'Are going to the State Police.'

I watched Ben chase a seagull. He didn't get within fifty feet of it. 'That'll be a confusing jurisdictional mess, huh? Just the overlap of evidence could give you a headache.'

'Damn straight. And I don't think these Major Crimes guys attended preschool the day they taught sharing – they're used to dealing with the county prosecutor and, basically, telling pukes like me where to stand, what to say, when to pay the bar tab, when to give a blowjob. You get the idea.'

'But they'll catch the bad guys,' I said.

'We'll see,' she said. 'That's where you come in.'

I dodged the invitation. 'What are they working now?'

'Jurisdictional shit. That's today's meeting.' She kicked her shoes off, nice pumps, and let her stockinged feet soak the residual heat from the boardwalk. 'Tejon Butler—'

'Blade, please,' I joked.

'Sorry, *Blade* was killed on Blake Street in Asbury Park, dead, smack between two meth labs and a gang flophouse, all of them *mine* under the auspices of the Asbury Park Street Crimes Unit. But then, Thomas Smalls—'

'Thomas the Fop,' I interrupted again.

'Knock it off, Doyle.'

'Sorry.'

'Thomas Smalls was killed on the lawn at the Warren & Monmouth while you and Ed Hess were inside clearing Martin Heston's suite. The apparent connection between Thomas the Fop and Blade – not to mention the likelihood that Heston's hands were nailed to the table with the same weapon – are what pushed the Attorney General over the edge, despite the fact that all three murders ought to be mine. And with Spring Lake cops chasing down evidence in the Smalls killing, while Asbury Park is just about frigging clueless in the Blade homicide—'

'—*and* with you neck-deep in concrete on the Lebow shooting and the RJ Mercer pinch, they decided to send in the cavalry. That's fine, Hodges, really. There's no shame. You've had a bitch of a week. Let the troops handle the murders.'

'I can handle them, Doyle. We both know it's gang-shit, retaliation between the Neptune Bloods and the North Side Playaz.'

'I don't doubt it, truly,' I said, 'but as a state cop who's been on the other side of the desk on my share of these shitstorms, I'm telling you: play nice, make your pinches, share the spotlight, and your star will be on the rise in places you've never even seen.'

'I'm no climber,' she defended herself.

'Bullshit,' I laughed. 'You said so yourself about two seconds before you busted RJ's nose with that flashlight: *Do you have any idea how hard I've had to work? How much shit I've had to shovel as a black woman?* I was there, Hodges, and you're right. Fuck it: you're doing a nice job, so climb a few rungs. No cop I've ever known would blame you, not with the hours you're putting in these days.'

Hodges looked about two seconds from supremely pissed off. I didn't care. I'd done my job: I'd collected the evidence against Moses, found him guilty, then got the hell out of the way as his wife exacted punishment. The rest of this rodeo belonged to someone else: Hodges, the State Police, the Monmouth County Prosecutor; it wasn't my headache any more. I'd have a hard enough time ever going to sleep with the windows open, walking on the beach after dark or watching my kids play in the ocean from now on. Marta Hodges' jurisdictional woes didn't interest me at all.

She said, 'You know I ought to arrest you, put an end to this whole show.'

I played along. 'Arrest me for what?'

'I know that silver cannon was yours.'

I didn't flinch. 'Bullshit. Run the numbers.'

'Ed Hess—'

'—didn't say shit about that .357, did he?'

She hesitated, then asked, 'Come on, Doyle. What happened? Who were you shooting at?'

'I never fired a shot, Detective. As a matter of fact' – I decided it was worth the risk, and went on – 'the first shot they fired at me is probably embedded in the wall of that shitty tenement place across the street up there near Seventh Avenue.'

She stared across the water, then nodded slightly. 'It was. Prick. And you know what else? They matched that slug to a pair Asbury PD pulled from a rooftop down on Cookman, across from the old Bentley Hotel. You wouldn't know anything about those either, though, would you, Doyle? How many trips to Asbury did you make this week?'

'Run the numbers on the gun.'

She said, 'Cut the shit. There were no numbers on that .357, which, and I'm sure you're aware of this, adds a complicated arms piece to this frigging puzzle. And I have about ten minutes' patience for—'

'Come on, you really don't need an arms conviction. You've got the North Side Playaz on about thirty-nine far more interesting, costly, colourful and tasty felonies; one bullshit .357 isn't going to make any difference, and if you lean on Ed Hess to admit that he saw that gun in my possession then you are just a mean old fart, and I hope you don't get anything nice for Christmas this year.'

'Your prints were all over it.'

'Of course they were,' I said, 'I picked it up when the thugs took off.'

She sighed, realising I wasn't about to cave, cuffs or no cuffs. 'How'd you end up in the water?'

'I chased one.'

'One of your wife's kidnappers fled into the ocean.' It wasn't a question, just disbelief.

'Up the beach, yes,' I said. 'I chased him and he turned on me. We wrestled around for a few seconds and I fell into the water. I didn't have any strength in my arm and my ribs were cracked. I didn't stand a chance against him; I just wanted to keep him down until the Asbury Park guys got there. I figured they must have heard the shots.'

'Can you describe him?'

'Hell yes,' I lied.

'You're probably going to need to do better than that when you meet with the lawyers working the RJ Mercer case.'

'Why? You need more to put him away for the rest of his miserable little life? The stupid bastard was so pissed at you for being black and in charge that he all but confessed to me, and I don't know a prosecutor on Earth who can't make that sting with a jury. Christ, you've got it on a plate. Actually, I bet the fucker pleads, even with his show-off public defender. This ain't the Chicago Seven, Hodges.'

Anna tossed her blimp keys and started whining; she either needed sleep or food. Jenny'd pumped some earlier, but I tried the pacifier first. Anna sucked on it, quieted, and drifted towards sleep, her eyes narrowing to slits. 'Good girl,' I whispered. 'Take a nap. We'll eat later.'

Hodges waited until the baby passed out. 'Who were you shooting at, Doyle? Be straight with me – you know as well as I do that this is the only piece missing from the Smalls and Butler killings. How many were there? Did you wing any of 'em? Kill any? Is that it? Did they drag someone off? There was no blood besides Jenny's, so I figure you're as bad a shot as you are a liar. And what was that slimy shit all over the park bench? I'm waiting on the lab reports, but what exactly went on up there?'

'Slimy shit?'

'Yeah, greasy, like oily fishy slime. The CSI techs found more of it upstairs in the Bentley, where a picture window had been broken out, and even more of it on the rooftop where they retrieved those other .357 slugs. You have any idea what that might be?'

'Maybe something having to do with cooking meth? Some new solvent? Something organic?'

Hodges frowned. In her mind I was probably choking to death on a bologna sandwich. 'Do I look like a mule-kicked idiot to you, Doyle?'

I ignored this, tried to redirect her. 'Hey, what do you mean, Smalls and Butler can be tied up with one missing piece? I don't get it. How can a faggy hotel concierge in Spring Lake be connected to a dead gang leader from— Where was it? Newark? That doesn't make sense. Why not start there rather than with some untraceable gun?'

'Thomas Smalls – Thomas the Fop, if you prefer – had a brother he didn't mention at cocktail parties. Malcolm is a smack junkie who recently developed a taste for crystal meth. You almost met him two weeks ago; he lives in an abandoned cottage out on Steiner, near Cameron Drive in Neptune.'

'Tubby! Holy shit! That – *thing* – was Thomas' brother? No wonder he was such a pretentious dick. Imagine how hard he had to work to get clear of that neighbourhood, all the uptight lessons he figured he had to learn from snooty New York zillionaires. I bet he held his breath every time he looked out of the door in case his brother was waiting on the front lawn, jimjams soiled, looking for a handout. But wait— Why would North Side go down there—?' I didn't know what I wanted to ask. Thomas the Fop's connection to Tubby Smalls hadn't gelled for me yet.

Hodges filled in the blanks. 'Neptune Township has a strong contingent of Bloods, big-time bad-asses with national connections. Apparently, for a cut of the ice market, they allow thugs from Blake Street to deal meth south of Asbury Park. No fuss, no mess, no exploding apartments, just cash. Well, when RJ, a North Side fuckhead, killed a white boy on a school playground and attracted state and national media, things got hot for the Neptune City Bloods, riots broke out and Bloods got arrested. Small shipments were seized – all of it a pain in the stones for the Neptune City boys. Drug traffic and gang recruitment slowed or moved west and south, irritating the bosses. When RJ's ugly mug and even uglier rap sheet made the papers, someone had to pay. Malcolm, a wannabe Blood, rolled over on RJ when it looked like he'd do a stretch in the county lock-up, where we don't serve meth with breakfast.

'Blade and Big G came to Asbury on clean-up duty. The rumour is that Big G was shot by Blood enforcers, while Blade had his head caved in with a ball-peen hammer; Street Crimes detectives figure it's Neptune City taking over Asbury's ice market for themselves, so half vengeance and half business.'

'But you think you know better?' I prompted.

'Don't I?' she asked. 'I know it wasn't Blood enforcers who blasted Big G's hand off.'

'Now there's a moral dilemma for you, Detective,' I teased again. 'But I can't imagine you'd indict your Spring Lake buddy, particularly given the years you spent in the Coast Guard together. Right?'

'Don't play with me, Doyle,' she said. 'I'm willing to be open-minded about a lot of this, but you're seriously trying my patience.'

I chuckled. 'Listen, this is all very interesting, but I still don't see a reason to kill Thomas the Fop. He was harmless, a varsity-level asshole, but harmless, nevertheless. Did Bloods kill him, too? That doesn't make sense, not if Malcolm was a Blood wannabe and daily customer.'

'You tell me: you were there. You've said that the North Side Playaz snatched your pretty wife through the window of her minivan because RJ's lawyer let slip your name, address and underwear colour – is that the case? Did the Playaz copycat Thomas with a ball-peen hammer because they couldn't get to Malcolm in the county tank? Huh? Sounds pretty tight, don't you think?'

I nodded. 'Actually, it does: there's motive and opportunity for both, but no murder weapon, I'd wager. No assortment of bloody hammers turning up?'

And they won't, because it was claws, not hammers – but with my back all wrapped up you can't check the wounds on Thomas or Blade against mine. Good thing, too.

Hodges didn't press me, figuring she already knew I had an alibi – Ed Hess – for each killing. 'But then again, this isn't really my problem any more.'

'The Major Crimes Unit,' I said. 'Sounds ominous, doesn't it?'

'Ass-wipe,' she said.

'That's Officer Ass-Wipe, to you, Detective Hodges.'

'Hey, Doyle, come on, really. How about you—'

'Hodges,' I interrupted, 'look, I gave already at the office, okay? I helped out on the Hanley suicide when I could have taken off for home. I tackled Lebow, kept him from shooting up that school. Granted, he didn't have any shells, but I didn't know that at the time. I drew tattoos and ID'd RJ Mercer for you, went along for the pinch and even stood witness while he essentially confessed to killing Gabriel Lebow. I've provided statements stating as much, and I'll be happy to come back here to testify against RJ and help you send his bandy ass to prison for the next millennium. I helped Ed Hess track a jewel thief to the Warren & Monmouth, where we discovered a body. While I was assisting the Spring Lake PD, a hotel concierge and brother to a gangland loser was assassinated on the lawn. What he was doing out there, I have no idea …'

He heard Kate Stillman outside, probably a shriek, something worse than a sour note on that cello upstairs. He went out to check on it. Jenny'd gone to the car to get her phone; she wanted to call the kids – easy pickings for Kate. Thomas was just in the wrong place at the wrong time.

'… but he was killed, probably by the same assholes who snatched my wife and brought her up to Asbury Park. Does that lead me to believe it was the North Side Playaz? Yup, and I think it does for you, too. Instead of sitting on my hands, I drove to Asbury, got wildly lucky and found the shitheads who'd taken her. I managed to get them to let her go. So from my perspective, Detective Hodges, I don't need to help any more. I'm broken and scarred and stitched and torn, and I just want to sit here and watch my son play in the sand. If you want to arrest me, that's fine. If you want to subpoena testimony from me, that's fine too. But I'm done helping.'

'You're full of shit, Sailor,' she said. 'You mind telling me how you managed to get – how many?'

'Three. I told you that already. You're not going to catch me lying.'

She ploughed over that. 'How you managed to get three gang-bangers to let your wife go without a hitch?'

'Without a hitch? Have you seen her head? I think we were frigging lucky to come away with our asses intact.'

'How?'

'I don't know,' I lied again. 'There were some people in the tene-ment shouting once they heard the screaming, the shots; maybe they called the police. Maybe it was sirens, but I honestly don't know – I wasn't keeping notes. My wife was bleeding and incoherent and I just wanted her back. I swear I can't remember when I heard sirens or how many people from across the street had been shouting at us.'

'Uh huh.' She stretched her legs out, rested her ankles on an alu-minium bike rack that looked like the skeleton of a sea monster. Some thug had tagged it with a Sharpie. Hodges unbuttoned her jacket and let the sun colour the smooth skin of her face. 'So I get nothing.'

'Nonsense,' I said. 'You're getting the RJ conviction. Slam-dunk.

You're getting national coverage on Robert Morris Middle School and the Blake Street bust. You're a goddamned hero.'

She wouldn't be swayed. 'This whole thing stinks.'

I tried again. 'Hell, you lean on enough North Side Playaz and you might even get a confession on Jenny's kidnapping before the State Police even get around to asking the right questions. That's a frigging Christmas list of felony convictions, Hodges. You keep wearing those snazzy suits and you'll be on the Governor's staff in about two weeks.'

'Bullshit, Doyle.'

'You wait and see,' I said. 'You'll be turning down offers left and right.'

'Martin Heston.' She shaded her eyes, wanting to see my reaction.

I looked away, pretending to fuss with something in Anna's stroller. 'What about him?'

'What happened?'

'I don't know,' I said. 'I was with Hess.'

'Uh huh.' She waggled her toes at me. 'Next time, pull this leg, Doyle. The other one's getting tired.'

'So what?' I asked. 'What do you think I know?'

She considered this a moment. 'I don't know – I guess nothing. It's just that you seem to have been at the epicentre of every open-sore nightmare that's blown down this boardwalk in the past two weeks.'

I played dumb. 'You think Heston has something to do with the heist at O'Malley's jewellery place?'

'You're the one who sent Hess down there; you tell me.'

'He really did have a thing for those pearls. He mentioned them a couple of times, even took me there to show them to me.'

'Whatever, Doyle,' she said, 'but to be honest, I haven't had five minutes to look into it. Spring Lake's handling the robbery, and getting nowhere, I might add.'

'Why not?'

'O'Malley clammed up on the necklace. He's claiming the pearls were fakes, and he's got no paperwork, no certifications on them, nothing to show that they were ever acquired legally, so the insurance company won't come within a mile of him. So he gets a new window and a hearty heigh-ho piss-off on his claim.'

Of course he does. They were an under-the-table kickback from Prime Minister Baldwin to his Assistant Principal Secretary's daughter. Oops.

'The stones on some people,' I said. 'I bet he had them appraised by a cousin from the Jewellery Exchange in Newark, right?'

'Something like that.' Hodges reached over to tweak one of Anna's toes. 'That's not my problem, but the insurance company's refusing to budge. We'll know better if O'Malley ends up swinging from a rope in his basement.'

'Hard to get paid for stolen goods.'

'Yeah,' Hodges said, 'woe is me.'

'So what's the link to Heston? Old money? Someone checking on how he paid the bills? That hotel doesn't come cheap.'

'Stockmarket money,' Hodges said, 'oil or something. I spoke briefly with Ed this morning. But there's only so much we can get from his lawyer. Heston's the victim; he's not suspected of any crime, not yet, at least, so all we can do is ask nicely and hope for cooperation.'

'Any sign of the pearls?'

'Nope,' she said, 'whoever did Heston got away – that is, assuming the thief killed Heston before hitting O'Malley's.'

'Makes sense if they're connected. It could have been a team – I bet if you dig deep enough into Heston's background you'll find something. Those rusty crucifixion nails and waterlogged pictures have got to mean something – organised crime? Jersey mob?'

'Someone's on it – I'm sure you'll be hearing from him now that you're up and around. As for me, I'm dealing with gangbangers, ice dealers, actual murder suspects, and – oh Happy Holidays – a kidnapping with only one material witness, an out-of-state cop who's lying to me. I don't have the time or the energy for a dead baseball player who got himself caught up in a jewellery heist.'

'If that's truly what happened.' I muddied the waters further. What the hell.

'Yeah, whatever.' She helped me get a cigarette out of my pack, even lit it for me. 'You hear from your captain back home?'

'A couple of days ago,' I said. 'He hopes to have the IA case against me wrapped up in the next two weeks. At this point, it doesn't matter if it drags on a bit – I might be up and around, but I'm not moving any too quickly just yet.'

Hodges said, 'I spoke with him yesterday, filled him in on your participation in our investigations – from my perspective.'

'Really? How'd I do?'

'Just fine, shithead.'

'Thanks, Hodges, truly.'

'I honestly don't think my opinion made a bit of difference with him,' she explained; 'he sounds determined to get you pardoned and back to work.'

'He's a forgiving soul, what can I say?'

'Yeah, well, it's funny what some people will do when the shadows get long.'

'What—? What's that?' I sat up, felt my stitches pulling beneath my arms.

'Captain Fezzamo: he sounded older. Maybe he's getting soft. You know: when the shadows get long—'

'—it's funny what people will do.'

'Exactly,' she said.

'Huh.'

'What?'

'Nothing.' I finished my cigarette, crushed the butt.

'How long are you in town, Doyle?'

'Until you tell me I can leave, I guess. Tonight we're headed to the Monmouth County Fair – Ben keeps seeing the commercials on Channel 12 – he's determined to ride that bad-ass octopus-looking thing. Me, I'd rather take my chances in a Uruguayan aeroplane.'

She laughed. 'I don't trust those rides. Make sure your tetanus shots are up to date.'

'We'll try to distract him with the farm animals. He still gets pretty fired up by the sight of an actual cow.'

'Well, enjoy it.' She stood. 'I'll be in touch as we start pulling evidence and witness lists together.'

'You hear from Lebow's parents? Or Isaac? Anything?' There was no reason to believe that Hodges would know if the Lebows planned to file suit against me in civil court, but I asked just in case she'd heard any rumours.

'Nothing on my end, but I'll keep my ear to the ground.'

'That's all I need.'

'Isaac's pretty broken up about it,' she said. 'When the smoke clears, he's gotta know it would mean a lot of painful testimony to no avail. There's no way you could possibly know that shotgun was empty in the two seconds you had to make a decision.'

'Let's hope.' I pulled Anna's stroller shade down a few inches and watched her sleep. I couldn't begin to guess how distraught Gabriel's parents must be, and I wondered if his mother would keep me locked in her basement for two months and torture me, maybe cut off my earlobes or wear my pinkie as a pendant. Probably. I winced, recalling Mikey Bartollo's remains, somehow alive seventeen years later, thanks to the incomprehensible force of Kate Stillman's anguish.

'You all right, Doyle?' Hodges asked.

'Yeah,' I said. 'Anything from the Public Defenders' Office?'

'They don't talk much with me, not polite conversation, anyway.'

'I guess not.' I stood, wanted to look her in the face. 'Thank you, Detective.'

'For what?'

'You know for what.'

'You have anything you want to tell me?'

'Nope,' I said, 'but that won't keep you from getting your convictions.'

'Asshole.'

'Sadly, yes.' I shook her hand, awkwardly, with my left. 'Call if I can help.'

'Will do. Take care, Sailor.' She started across the boardwalk towards her county cruiser.

'Hey, Hodges,' I called, 'you go to church?'

She looked at me disapprovingly again, then gave me a grudging smile. 'Just about every Sunday for the past forty-one years. Why?'

'You know *Psalm 88*?'

This threw her, but just for a moment. She let her gaze wander over the ocean, as if remembering, then said, '*Do you show your wonders to*

*the dead? Do their spirits rise up and praise you? Is your love declared in
the grave, your faithfulness in destruction? Are your wonders known in the
place of darkness, or your righteous deeds in the land of oblivion?'*

'What's it mean?' I asked.

'Hopelessness, I guess. The worst of all sins.'

'Okay – and—?'

'And don't turn your back on God, because for those sinners, there
is nothing but darkness for a long, long, long time.'

I thought of Mikey Bartollo again and shuddered. I'd never been
the best of Sunday School students; I tended to take Doc Lefkowitz's
opinions on most things, religion in particular, as damned-near gospel.
But considering Marta Hodges' interpretation of *Psalm* 88, I hoped
Doc had been wrong, or maybe that God had called Gabriel Lebow
home before tallying him as a suicide.

Hodges watched me mull this over. 'I take it you're not much of a
church-goer?'

'Catholic,' I said, as if that explained everything. 'We don't really
read the Bible all that much.'

'Ah, yes.'

I watched her turn away, then called, 'Check out Lebow's house,
maybe the wall or the windowsill outside his bedroom. If it's all
scratched up, as if someone climbed up there, maybe lots of times –
well, let me know.'

'So you *do* have something you need to tell me after all.' Hodges
had a way of asking a question as a statement; she'd been a cop for a
long time. 'Sailor?'

'Maybe,' I conceded.

'Scratches?'

'Yeah, like hook-marks or claw-marks.'

'Claws?'

I tried, again, to shrug. 'Let me know.'

Now she laughed, unexpectedly.

'What's funny?'

'I may get to arrest you yet!'

'Oh, that. Yeah, hilarious.'

'See you.'

I waved goodbye, then dropped myself onto the bench, once again facing the beach where Jenny watched Ben dash into the waves. He collected the football, then hurried up the beach, tugging futilely at the waistband of his bathing suit. Jenny took his hand and half-dragged him towards me. Clearly Ben would have been content to play ball until the moon rose over the Atlantic. Together, they climbed the weathered stairs. Jenny slipped into a pair of flip-flops; Ben hadn't worn shoes in two weeks. He pulled two handfuls of shells from the front pocket of Jenny's sweatshirt, sat cross-legged on the warm planks and started picking through them like a jeweller, discarding chipped or broken ones absently over his shoulder.

'You okay?' I asked Jenny.

'A bit of a headache.' She fingered the tape above her eye. 'I'm hungry, though. You wanna eat?'

'Nah,' I said, 'not sure I'm ready yet.'

'Baby okay?'

'Still sleeping.'

'What did Hodges want?'

'Just an update.'

'Everything good?'

'Yeah.'

'You tell her about the pearls?' Jenny sat beside me, rested her head on my bandaged arm.

'Slipped my mind,' I said.

'You have to turn them over, Sailor.' Jenny hadn't asked how I'd come by them; she had only the foggiest memory of her journey north from Spring Lake to Asbury Park and didn't want to know, not yet, anyway. I wasn't sure what I'd say when she eventually asked me. I'd been lying to her for two weeks; perhaps I'd try the truth. She said, 'You're going to get arrested if you keep them. Why not just take them to the police?'

'And complicate matters to an impossible degree? Sure; I'll call you from jail and let you know how that worked out.'

'We can't do anything with them,' Jenny said. 'They're stolen property – maybe three times over!'

'We'll put them away someplace safe. Maybe our grandchildren—'

'Great-*great*-grandchildren.'

'Fine. Our great-great-grandchildren can fence them and buy a yacht or an island.'

'I think you should wrap them up and send them to Ottawa,' Jenny said. 'Ship them back where they belong.'

I thought this over as the incoming tide drowned out all the ambient sound. 'That's not a bad idea, actually.'

'Good,' she said. 'I'll cut letters out of magazines for a cryptic note. We can even do it all mysteriously, with rubber gloves and plain brown paper.'

'Groovy,' I said, 'I've been wanting to do it with rubber gloves for a while.'

'Dumbass.'

Anna lost her pacifier, stirred, then let go with a wail to wake the dead.

Ben looked up from his work. 'Uh oh, Annie's awake.'

Jenny fetched her from the stroller. 'She sure is, monkey-man. Why don't you come over here and talk to her while I get her bottle ready.'

'Okay, Mommy.' Leaning on my knee, Ben told his sister all about the friendly shark that haunted the pear tree outside his window and his elaborate plans to capture it; he promised to share it with Anna as long as she helped take care of it.

'Shouldn't the shark go back in the ocean?' Jenny asked. 'With the other sharks?'

'Nah,' Ben explained, 'it'll be like the bear with the bicycle. We'll keep the shark with us as we travel around to different places—'

He went on, regaling his sister with his ornate dreams for joint shark ownership as Jenny sat beside me, leaning on my shoulder as she fed the baby. The midday sun coloured the Jersey coast brilliant summer gold, while the first tendrils of autumn blew in from Canada. I'd found a measure of welcome contentment on that bench; now, if Jenny and I were to find each other again, to have another go at *happily ever after*, that moment was as good a starting point as any.

As the rolling breakers hypnotically marked time, I managed briefly to forget Kate Stillman and Mikey Bartollo, hopeless and lost somewhere off Asbury Park.

Acknowledgements

Sea Girt, New Jersey, has a lighthouse just off the beach. It's a couple of dormers larger than the average suburban McMansion, but not nearly tall enough to illuminate the upper floors of Spring Lake's old Essex and Sussex Hotel, now a high-end retirement home that's lost its charm. To paint a prison stripe across the façade of the hotel a mile away, Sea Girt's light would have to rival the Lighthouse of Alexandria for sheer size and brilliance. It doesn't; I lied.

I've taken a few other liberties with New Jersey shore towns from Point Pleasant up to Asbury Park, hopefully nothing too egregious. While I probably should have set this story someplace fictional, I couldn't resist that collection of oceanfront towns and hope the people of New Jersey will forgive me for misrepresenting – all right, *lying* – about their neighbourhoods. I don't know of a better place along the Jersey coast to set a story about unrealised hopes and grudge-holding ghosts than Asbury Park. For an honest look at the city over the last century, I recommend Helen-Chantal Pike's book, *Asbury Park's Glory Days* or the archives of the *Asbury Park Press*. Similarly, my apologies to members of the Ottawa Linx and Rapidz baseball organisations, who have no affiliation with my fictional Ottawa Pioneers. I understand the Linx and Rapidz players and staff are a decent group of folks and not in the habit of hiring spies, murderers or jewel thieves to pitch middle relief out of the bullpen.

Writing about 1970s Canadian politics, Arctic geology, rare Polynesian pearls and counter-espionage pay-offs, I was soon in water well over my head. I owe a debt of gratitude to many readers, experts and teachers and would need several pages to note them all here, but special thanks to John Fennell and Neta Lowe, who probably already *have* discovered oil above the Arctic Circle. If they haven't, I'm convinced they could with just some duct tape and a few cardboard toilet paper rolls. Thanks as well to Brian Taylor, who has enough esoteric political and historic information in his head to overthrow Paraguay. Thankfully, he's a good-hearted guy and doesn't lean towards aggressive imperialism.

Thanks to Steve Walts, the faculty and staff at Brentsville – who were patient with me every day – and to Dad & Mom, John Lavely, Michelle Nemerow, Mike, Artise and Jen for reading early drafts or for slapping me when I had something wrong. Thanks to Jo Fletcher, Beloved Editor, and Ian Drury, Agent 0098.6, for taking a risk with Sailor Doyle, despite his bad behaviour outside Richmond. And thanks to Marcus Gipps for making my transition across the hall a smooth journey. I owe a debt of gratitude to Kat and Jan for taking on too much so that I could downshift, and thanks, as ever, to Kage, Sam, and Hadley.

Thanks Neil.

And finally, special thanks to Mickey Mulgrew and Roger Waters.

Rob Scott
Virginia, 2011